LOST IN MECCA

Bothayna Al-Essa

Lost In Mecca (Novel)
Originally published as *'Karaet Alteeh'*

Translated by: Nada Faris

© 2024 Dar Arab For Publishing and Translation LTD.

United Kingdom
60 Blakes Quay
Gas Works Road
RG1 3EN
Reading
United Kingdom
info@dararab.co.uk
www.dararab.co.uk

First Edition 2024
ISBN 978-1-78871-093-0

Copyrights © dararab 2024

دار عرب للنشر والترجمة
DAR ARAB FOR PUBLISHING & TRANSLATION

Text Edited: Marcia Lynx Qualey
Text Design: Nasser Al Badri
Cover Design: Hassan Almohtasib

BOTHAYNA AL-ESSA

LOST
IN
MECCA

A NOVEL

TRANSLATED BY NADA FARIS

CHAPTER ONE

NAFEER

exclusive group of people; a horn or trumpet; departure into battle

Day 1

Mecca. The Sacred Mosque

7 Dhu Al-Hijja, 1431

13 November, 2010

12:16 P.M.

Before that moment, everything had been fine.

Sumaya had been completing her fourth circumambulation among a multitude of weary pilgrims spinning in a massive chain around the Kaaba, the pilgrims chanting: Labbaik, labbaik; Sumaya's lips whispering the supplication: I'm here.

Captivated by the holiness of the moment and soaked in sweat, her eyes had been erratically skimming the heads of worshippers crammed in the central courtyard of the Sacred Mosque. Glancing to the right, she'd catch a glimpse of Faisal's back—for though he was marching a few steps ahead, Sumaya could still distinguish her husband from the bald, the sweaty, the black, the white, the shaved, the grey, and the veiled. The Kaaba had been to her left, cloistered in fabric, wearing an ihram of her own: her red bricks stacked on the ground, her white cloth wrapped around the middle. The rest of the cuboid edifice was swathed in black with two belts of golden thread weaving calligraphic motifs.

Sumaya had felt the little one's hand growing damp in her grip, and because she had noticed his legs hurrying to match her pace, she'd asked him, Ha Mishari... Tired?

But he had shaken his head.

They had both slowed down near the believers crowded at the southwestern corner, where Sumaya had raised her right arm toward the Kaaba—the beating heart of the Muslim world—and declared: Allahu akbar!

With her left, she'd been holding Mishari's hand when a caravan of Asian pilgrims, walking in a single file, their arms interlocking, rammed between her and her son. Although the collision had flung Sumaya's body only two steps forward, she thought her shoulder might dislocate from the pain, and stumbled briefly on the hem of her abaya until she regained her composure. But once she stood upright, she couldn't find Mishari anywhere—no matter where she turned.

He was gone.

She swivelled around to look for him as the tidal wave of believers surged on all sides, and she cried, Mishari! Don't move! Stay where you are! But once she remembered he could be trampled to death, she howled, Mishari! Move! Move! Move!

While scanning gaps between bodies, Sumaya thought, *A slender boy like him could be anywhere!* Her legs stiffened and her heart pounded desperately. A naked shoulder, bumping into her face, left a wet smudge on her cheek, and a wheelchair trundled over her foot before a pedestrian jam of pilgrims, swaddled in white garb and black robes, swallowed her whole. At that moment, she began to call out to her husband, whom she could still identify among the throng, Faisal!

And at that moment—Faisal turned. He saw Sumaya screaming, her face pale, her eyes red, so he rushed toward her, tearing his way between bodies like someone swimming against the tide, withstanding scores of blows and knocks to his face and shoulders.

When they were near each other, Sumaya reached out and pulled on Faisal's ihram, the white cloth wrapped around his shoulder and waist signifying purity and readiness to surrender to the will of God. Sumaya's bewildered eyes, gaping at her husband, conveyed all her horror—and without uttering a single coherent sentence, Faisal understood: Mishari had vanished.

A cluster of African pilgrims, jostling between Faisal and Sumaya, forced the couple apart, leading Sumaya to deviate, through no fault of her own, from the ring of worshippers, while Faisal, who stood rooted in place, stretched his arm in the air like a mast and cried at the top of his lungs, Sumaya!

They tried to reunite, like two boats rowing in opposite directions. When their fingers finally touched, Faisal grabbed Sumaya's thumb, drew her close to his body, then left the ring.

Don't worry, we'll find him, Faisal told his wife. Sweep the central courtyard, and I'll look outside. Faisal thought he had to follow the current. No doubt it carried his son. *Mishari, the frail, the slim, the delicate—he'd be subsumed by a human stream, let alone a flood.*

And so, Faisal began to search among the masses. Search and scream. Sumaya, like him, began to search and scream. They bounded frenetically despite colliding with dozens of arms and backs, amassing blows and knocks to their faces, their tormented shrieks echoing as if they were tumbling into hell.

Mecca. The Sacred Mosque

7 Dhu Al-Hijja, 1431

1:36 P.M.

An hour later, Faisal thought he needed to do something other than frantic running. In the midst of the undulating bodies covered in white and black fabric, moving in an endless circle around the Kaaba like a human eddy dancing around itself, Faisal's own fear pushed him to the edge.

Can everyone stand still for five minutes?

No, this vortex won't stop, and neither will you. Terror will continue to sweep you to the farthest concentric circle.

While surveying his surroundings, Faisal thought, *Maybe the little guy is nearby but can't see me searching for him?* So, he curved his fingers around his mouth and yelled, Mishari! But as he dashed toward the human congestion near Maqam Ibrahim, the small square stone associated with Ibrahim's and Ismael's construction of the Kaaba, Faisal thought, *What if Mishari has fallen? What if the great mass has trodden on my son and broken his bones? Why hasn't he called yet, even though he knows our numbers?*

Faisal turned his back to the Kaaba and, as fast as one could sprint in a dense crowd, made his way toward the nearest gate, where officers in military uniforms stood guard. The badges on their chests read: Saudi Emergency Forces.

Faisal blurted out as soon as he reached them, We lost Mishari! We lost him! He was panting, his forehead dripping sweat, his eyes bulging—full of fright.

The officers, frowning at Faisal, couldn't understand a single word.

What exactly happened? one of them asked.

After producing his iPhone from a leather holster on the belt that kept his ihram secured around his waist, Faisal showed each officer a picture of his son, then repeated the word as if he were explaining the tragedy to himself so he could come to grips with the awful truth. Lost! He held his phone high, standing in a pool of slippers as believers knocked into him left and right. The rectangular screen showed a picture of Mishari in black pyjamas, a Batman logo on his chest. Still, Faisal described his son to the officers as though the picture wasn't enough: He's got thick black hair that's denser in the front, a brown beauty spot on his neck, and a gap between his front teeth. Light-skinned and skinny, looks five instead of seven, and he was wearing an orange T-shirt and beige pants when he went missing.

When did that happen?

An hour ago.

Where was he?

In the central courtyard.

Kuwaiti?

Yes.

When the officer reported the news of Mishari's disappearance into his transceiver, the announcement echoed like the endless pounding in Faisal's chest: A seven-year-old Kuwaiti boy with a beauty mark on his neck, wearing an orange T-shirt.

He didn't mention the dimple, or the colour of the pants, or the missing tooth that made a noticeable gap in Mishari's smile. More importantly, the officer didn't describe Mishari's height, which made him look younger than he was—the officer thus ignored the details that distinguished Mishari from other kids.

The pants are beige! Faisal insisted on adding.

Inshalla khair, the officer said.

May it be a blessing? Faisal repeated incredulously.

Listen. Our men are stationed at every exit. With God's help, we'll find him. Just give me your number and go back to where you lost him. Don't waste your time here. Keep looking.

Faisal hesitated before asking, Will you organise search parties?

The officer suppressed a smile. Search parties?

My son is missing!

Ya hajj, we've got three million pilgrims... He shrugged and didn't continue his point.

How could you ask the ocean about a single drop? Three million pilgrims: one child lost. People go missing all the time, including seniors, women, and infants. What makes Mishari any different? And what do you want exactly? To stop the rotational ritual?

Faisal stood in place—his eyes wide, barely able to digest the words he'd just heard. What about my son?

Search for him. Don't waste your time here. We'll contact you when we find him, the officer said apologetically.

Faisal gave the officer his phone number, swerved, then ran away, unable to fathom how he could face this hell alone.

Mecca. The Sacred Mosque

7 Dhu Al-Hijja, 1431

5:02 P.M.

In his frenzy, the shoulder part of Faisal's ihram dropped in a flutter. He left it crumpled on the floor and carried onward, chest exposed, thighs chafing with each step, sweat drenching his palms and temples, his iPhone held in his hand, Mishari's picture in a Batman T-shirt plastered on the screen. Faisal kept stepping in front of worshippers, pleading, Have you seen my boy? He's missing!

Meanwhile, instead of completing seven circumambulations, as was expected of pilgrims, Sumaya had by now completed seventeen, and was beginning to feel that her legs might disconnect from her body to forever continue the rites on their own, meandering in this never-ending circle in search of the boy who had melted into the crowd. Sumaya was aching to find him where she had lost him, diligently continuing his rites in the same spot.

She raised her arms in the air and cried, Ya Rab! Forget my other desires! Just give me back my child! Though her face was wet with tears and sweat, she went on, My health! My wealth! The promotion I'd prayed Faisal would get! The second baby I had begged for after my four miscarriages! I no longer want any of it!

She was checking her phone between one moment and the next, hoping it would ring, hoping she would hear her son's voice on the other end whispering, Mama? She wanted Mishari to lead her to his location and for all this horror to come to an end.

At the five-hour mark, however, her dread became vicious. *Why hadn't he called yet? Mishari knows our numbers! What happened to my boy?* Her knees buckled—and when she collapsed on the ground, she was almost trampled by the multitudes, those hundreds of thousands of rapturous travellers wading through the shadow of divine glory. Crouching on the ground and using her arms to shield the back of her head, Sumaya pressed her forehead on the cold marble and mumbled a prayer: Anekhna matayana bibabik—Lord, our livestock is at your gate and we are ready to serve.

A hefty foot stomped on her thigh. Another kicked her right shoulder. She shut her tearful eyes and cried, Ya Rab!

Then, two hands reached under her armpits and dragged her out of the crowd.

When Sumaya found herself kneeling on white marble steps, and that a heavyset Egyptian woman was rattling her shoulders and patting her cheeks, she bawled, He didn't call! What could've happened to prevent him from calling?

Hey! Hajja! Answer me! the Egyptian woman raised her voice.

But Sumaya, who was hyperventilating, uttered a sorrowful moan, Mishari! Oh God! My son!

The Egyptian woman kept shaking Sumaya's shoulders.

And Sumaya continued to experience successive mental breakdowns.

However, she did hear the stranger ask at some point, Are you here with anyone?

And though Sumaya had answered, My husband, she couldn't add—And my son—so she bit her lower lip, and her face contorted with tears.

Where's your husband?

Sumaya didn't answer.

The Egyptian, raising her voice even louder, asked again, Where is your husband?

Resting her forehead on the marble steps, Sumaya began to sob. Allah! Will my son be lost in your house? Then she moved her head and buried her face in her purse.

The stranger panicked when she realised that the woman she was trying to help was swimming in delirium, unable to register anything that was shown or said to her. So, the stranger jogged to the nearest Zamzam fountain and returned carrying holy water in a plastic cup. She splashed some on her palm before washing Sumaya's face with it and reciting protective invocations.

But Sumaya's sobbing only metamorphosed into louder and more desperate howls.

By the time Faisal spotted his wife, several men had already formed a circle around her. One in particular, a red-bearded man leaning on a crutch, was hissing. Allah deplores the wailing woman!

Sumaya, who was kicking on the floor like a slaughtered lamb—a Hajj sacrifice—recognised Faisal's face among the cluster of gawking men, but when she interpreted his expression to mean that he hadn't found Mishari in the five hours since the boy's disappearance, she began to hit her face, bite into her hands, and slap her thighs, shrieking loudly, Mishari's gone! Gone!

Faisal penetrated the wall of bodies separating him from his wife, yanked her forearm, and lifted her off the ground. Enough, Sumaya! I said stop! It's not the time for you to cry!

Yet her tears continued to cascade down her sweaty and swollen cheeks, and as she raised two wide, reddened eyes to her husband, she asked him, Faisal! Why hadn't he called us? Mishari knows our numbers!

More to reassure himself than to answer her question, Faisal suggested, Maybe he forgot.

Forgot to call us? That's not like him!

Maybe he returned to the hotel.

Impossible.

Maybe he fainted and someone called an ambulance!

Wiping her tears with the heel of her hand, Sumaya nodded and thought, *That's plausible!* Since her heart began to stir with a glimmer of hope, she got up immediately to resume her search. It shocked her that she hadn't considered the option herself before: *The little one must be lying unconscious in an emergency room. He couldn't still be in The Sacred Mosque or he would've borrowed a phone and called us. Of course he fainted, and he's now resting in a hospital bed. As soon as he wakes up, he'll ask for a phone to call his mom and dad.*

Mishari knows our numbers by heart.

Mishari knows exactly what to do next.

Mecca. The Sacred Mosque

7 Dhu Al-Hijja, 1431

6:11 P.M.

May he welcome you into paradise. May he welcome you through the gates.

A young Black girl, extending her only arm toward Sumaya, shook a white plastic cup in her hand. It looked as though the other arm had been amputated.

Faisal's heart clenched when he noticed the stub: a tapering, dark, and emaciated part-limb that pierced his heart like a blade.

The girl, who appeared to be six years old, was wearing blue rubber slippers and a dull pink blouse. Dozens of small braids jutted out of her head, and her large black eyes, lined with kohl, were goggling at Faisal when she opened her mouth to chant once more, May he welcome you through the gates. Her voice was frail. Her persistence wounded him. Peering at Sumaya's wide shoulder purse, she pleaded, Auntie, give me a Riyal.

After unzipping her spacious bag, Sumaya produced a green prayer mat, a Quran wrapped in purple velvet, and a nylon bag containing her spare pair of shoes and Mishari's slippers: black Crocs with a yellow Batman logo. Sumaya's chin trembled and her lips pursed as she dug into her cavernous purse again, scraping the bottom until she found the crease of the ten Riyal bill she'd been searching for, pulled it out, and dropped the donation into the cup, her fingers trembling.

Faisal clutched Sumaya's arm and dragged his wife away from

the reach of the Black girl—as if he were rescuing Sumaya from the nightmarish scenarios that had come to life in his mind once he saw the ten Riyals settle in the cup. Together, they walked in silence toward King Fahad Gate, where the sky had cast a dark shadow. Lifting his head to watch the last rays of light retreat into the void, Faisal thought, *The sun has set. And my son has disappeared.* Pausing in front of a squad of officers, he took out his phone from his leather belt, showed off Mishari's photograph, and said, May God be pleased with you. Are there any updates on my kid?

Haven't you found him yet? the officer asked, seeming puzzled.

Power drained out of Faisal, and he replied as if suffocating, No. We haven't found him.

Turning his back to Faisal, the officer spoke into his transceiver and returned with a blank expression. Nothing new, Bu Mishari.

Faisal's vision blurred. Faces became hazy. The world began to slip into an oppressive gloom. And though his weak knees could barely hold him up, Faisal still managed to level his eyes at the officer and ask, So what now?

Organise search parties. Spread his picture all over the internet. Check with hospital staff. Inform your embassy... The officer went momentarily quiet, then added, Did you come here with a caravan?

We're registered with a Hajj caravan. But we didn't join them. We booked the flights and hotels ourselves.

Bu Mishari, you'll need help. The officer knitted his brows, pity visible on his face.

Sumaya had been looking back and forth between the two men.

Faisal faced his wife, swallowed, then said, I'll call our family in Kuwait.

Eyes glistening, she replied, Faisal... I'm afraid.

Me too.

They realised, as they gazed into each other's eyes, that what had happened to them—what was still happening—was far greater than either one of them could handle alone. They were both drowning in Mecca's human flood and needed rescue.

So, Faisal pulled out his phone again to dial the first person who came to mind, the only one he could count on. But as soon as he heard his younger brother's voice, Faisal lost the remnants of his strength, fell to his knees, and wept.

Saud! Please hurry! Your brother needs your help!

Mecca. Ajyad Hospital for Emergency Cases

7 Dhu Al-Hijja, 1431

6:50 P.M.

Faisal and Sumaya plodded through the human ocean on their way to one of the exits, but their movement was impeded by believers standing still near the sinks in the men's washing area.

Sumaya implored the pilgrims to move aside, God be pleased with you! We're in a hurry! Please let us pass.

Her request flabbergasted those who heard it.

Cross what? And where to?

Because people had crammed every nook, no one could move an inch in any direction.

Thus, Faisal held his wife by the arm and shoved people to his right and to his left. As dozens fell, their ire began to escalate. Some shrieked. Others hurled profanities. A pilgrim even roared behind them. Woe to you from God almighty!

Faisal continued, dragging his wife behind him, stubbornly forging forward through the stationary crowd. He didn't even turn around to assess the chaos he'd caused, but trudged alongside the towers, where the digital clock showed the time in green: 6:50 p.m.

Veering to the right, Faisal and Sumaya found a stooping hallway, which took them to the lower marketplace, where they came across a sign on the wall that read: Entrance to the Souks of Al-Safwa Towers

& Ajyad Hospital for Emergency Cases.

They stopped near the first clothing shop and Faisal said, as he pointed at the shirts dangling from the storefront, I need one of these and a pair of pants.

The vendor fixed Faisal with a scrutinising look. Which one?

Any will do! Faisal replied impatiently.

Although the vendor handed Faisal a white shirt and grey pants, he was nonetheless baffled when the bare-chested man parted his legs and slipped his new pants underneath the lower part of his ihram.

Faisal's inner thighs had chafed and were now stinging. Ignoring the pain, he unclasped the multiple clips securing the ihram around his waist, gathered the white cloth into a heap, then left it beside the nearest wall.

Gawking, the vendor cried, Ya hajj! You can't do that! You're breaking your ritual!

Faisal buttoned his new shirt without lifting his eyes, reattached the leather belt to his waist, and pulled out one hundred Riyals.

Before he could hand over the bill, however, the vendor waved his arms and yelled, God, protect me.

Don't you want your money?

Wagging an index finger at Faisal, the vendor recited holy doctrine: You ought to complete the rituals of Hajj and Umrah for God!

Faisal averted his eyes. I can't.

Moments later, all the minarets in the mosque began to sound the call for nightly prayer. Hayya ala assalat—the athan resounded across the sky, reminding Muslims to make haste and perform the rites. Therefore, merchants closed their stores, and people made their way in droves toward the countless prayer halls of The Sacred Mosque.

Faisal glanced at his watch. Ten past seven. Every passing moment amplified his fear.

We missed our prayers! Sumaya whispered anxiously.

What a pointless observation, Faisal thought before an ache in his guts forced him to drop to his knees and hurl over the floor, stomach contorting in pain, vomit coming out gooey and yellow.

What's wrong, Faisal? Are you sick?

No. He raised his head, wiped his mouth on the hem of his new shirt, and said, Let's go.

They walked, together, between two rows of shops offering similar merchandise: tables stacked with kohl pens, nail clippers, scissors, varicoloured prayer beads, wooden teeth-cleaning twigs known as miswaks, metal tweezers, silver rings, and metal baskets sporting green, glassy hearts. A gentle breeze that picked up the smell of henna diffused it in the wind.

Ajyad Hospital for Emergency Cases was printed on the sliding doors at the end of the souk.

The security guard, a slim Black man with bushy hair and a white face mask, stood in Faisal's path. Got an emergency?

Faisal knocked the guard's arm away and said, My son is missing.

The watchman stood aside, allowing Faisal and Sumaya to stride into the hospital, where three male receptionists sat at a circular desk in the centre of a marble plaza teeming with hundreds of patients: victims of sun strokes and stampede-related injuries, some of whom were crowding the metal chairs hammered into walls, others— hunched in ground vehicles—were being transported back and forth across hallways.

Faisal and Sumaya had to exert great effort to carve their way through the clot of human bodies blocking their path to the reception desk. Jostling men out of his way with one arm, Faisal raised the other high above his head, his iPhone again displaying Mishari's photo. Move guys! Move! My son is missing! By the time he reached the desk, sweat had soaked his forehead, and he was breathing heavily. May God be pleased with you. This is my son. We lost him in The Sacred Mosque. He could have fainted, and kind people could have brought him here.

One of the receptionists tapping on his switchboard shook his head. We've got an unknown three-year-old, and an ambulance on the way from the Sacred Mosque is carrying an unconscious kid. The report suggests he could be ten.

It can't be him, Faisal said, also shaking his head. My son looks like a five-year-old. Six—max. Gesturing to the middle of his thigh, he added, My son is short. He doesn't look his age. The diminutive stature of his son magnified Faisal's distress, who asked, after a beat, Are there other medical centres in the area?

Of course. There's King Abdulaziz Hospital, Noor Specialist Hospital, and many others. But we are the ones who receive the emergency cases from The Sacred Mosque.

Faisal's voice wavered. May God be pleased with you, brother. Surely there is a way for you to call these other hospitals and ask about him? Tears drenching his eyes, he swallowed, then said, Please help us, and may God help you in return.

The receptionist, who was looking into Faisal's red eyes, sighed before motioning for Faisal to wait. Give me a moment.

After thanking the man, Faisal left. He found space against a wall and slumped to the floor. His wife perched beside him. They both waited for the receptionist to call in his favours and to inquire about the seven-year-old Kuwaiti boy who had disappeared from The Sacred Mosque about seven hours earlier, a boy with a beauty spot on the neck and a missing tooth.

Faisal's phone hadn't stopped ringing and was now registering calls from the assistant undersecretary, general manager, and colleagues in his department; male cousins from his dad's side of the family; a female cousin from his mother's side; one of his aunts; his neighbour the lawyer; his friend the journalist; his son's American schoolteacher; and his mother, his mother, his mother. Faisal told Sumaya emphatically, I'm not picking up unless it's an unknown number! For he was anticipating a phone call from an unknown caller or a Saudi one. When Faisal answered at last, his son's voice would be on the other end, asking: Daddy? Only then would everything return to the way it was, and Faisal would be alright again. Until then, Faisal wasn't ready to communicate with anyone, including gossipmongers, sympathisers, or pessimists.

Nodding in agreement, Sumaya leaned back to rest her head on the wall, then began to recite: Allahumma ya jama' al nas—God Almighty, Gatherer of the People...

Faisal and Sumaya sat in silence amid the background clatter:

applicants yelling across the plaza; announcements by receptionists buzzing through speakers; ambulance wheels screeching; newborns shrieking and toddlers weeping; loud, dry coughs; and intermittent pings, Faisal's phone alerting him to new text messages and social media updates, communications from relatives, work colleagues, friends, and benevolent strangers on Facebook and Twitter, whose prayer wave had inundated the internet.

Meanwhile, the little one's image was spreading from one phone to the next, a picture Saud himself had taken that showed Mishari in a red Ferrari T-shirt, standing in the yard on artificial grass in front of a green metal gate, which crimson bougainvillea vines had climbed.

Oh, baby! Sumaya gasped.

Mishari's full name appeared under his photo, followed by a brief description and Saud's phone number: Mishari Faisal Al-Saffar. A seven-year-old Kuwaiti boy. Lost in the Sacred Mosque. If you find him, contact this number. Do not forget to share this message for blessings.

People were spreading Mishari's photo along with comments such as:

Pray louder!

Allah is listening!

May God help his parents.

May he provide the mother with patience.

The outpouring of support brought tears to Sumaya's eyes, and she suddenly whispered, Faisal, we have to pray.

Pray? Faisal raised his eyebrows.

Yes! We've got to be praying and pleading, not sitting around twiddling our thumbs. Maybe God will answer. After all, it's a holy month.

He looked away, and a cold voice came out of his mouth. Go on, then.

What about you?

What about me?

Won't you pray?

Faisal barely parted his lips once more before his stomach billowed. A viscous rush of fluid erupted and fell with a splatter on the floor. Leaping up mid-vomit, Faisal grabbed the nearest garbage pail to continue emptying his stomach. He stood there, leaning on the circular rim, until a janitor hurried over offering a napkin.

Sumaya asked her husband, who was wiping his lips and chin, What's wrong, Faisal? Are you sick?

No, he answered, sharpness tingeing his voice. Faisal cocked his head against the wall and wondered, *What's happening to me? It's the second time I've puked today.*

Are you sure you're OK?

He nodded.

Sumaya rested her palm on his shoulder, then pushed herself up, and left to search for the women's prayer room.

As he watched his wife disappear into the hallway, Faisal felt a strange wave of disgust.

Mecca. Ajyad Hospital for Emergency Cases

7 Dhu Al-Hijja, 1431

8:32 P.M.

Sumaya's knees were shaking, and her lips were softly reciting the holy names of God: Allah, The Most Loving, Who Owns the Mighty Throne, Who Carries Out His Will. She had just returned from the prayer room.

Faisal reached out to hold one of her knees, then said, Sumaya, please. She was driving him crazy with her trembling and those murmured supplications she was exchanging with the wind. *I ask in your great name, the one through which prayers are answered and questions are heard...* It was all so suffocating.

But I don't feel good, she grumbled. I'm worried he might still be at The Sacred Mosque.

If he were, he'd call.

Maybe the network's down because of the pressure. It's so crowded!

My phone hasn't stopped ringing, Sumaya. There's nothing wrong with our networks.

She thought for a moment, then said, Fine. I'll go back to The Sacred Mosque, and you can search for him here. Without waiting for a response, Sumaya got up and made her way toward the sliding doors.

Faisal felt instantly lighter as he watched her depart with her army of invocations. *Oh, Living One! Sustainer of All Things! By your mercy I seek guidance to rectify my affairs and to correct their consequences. Do not entrust me to myself even for a blink of an eye.* Faisal sought within him that thing he'd always taken for granted—that thing now driving Sumaya to press him about the importance of prayer and to persist in it herself. He couldn't find it. He couldn't find anything.

Faisal glanced at his watch: several minutes past eight-thirty.

A message from Saud read: Just landed in Riyadh.

Faisal wrote back, When's the flight to Jeddah?

In two hours.

This time, Faisal noticed his own knees quivering. The shudder crawled all the way up to his fingers. He didn't know why he thought of the black amputated arm piercing his chest like a blade.

When Faisal noticed the receptionist waving, he rushed to the circular desk and implored, Give me good news, brother. Please, console me.

The receptionist's face bore a sorrowful expression. After taking his time to deliver the much-awaited news, the receptionist finally said, Ya hajj, I called everyone, but nobody's seen a child with your son's description.

Faisal's heart dropped. His knees wobbled. He felt overwhelmed and alone, desperate for guidance, evidence, or anything to help him navigate this labyrinth of loss. He asked, What now?

The receptionist, contemplating whether to share more information, paused before uttering a single word: But...

Faisal urged him to continue. But what?

There is a corpse.

A corpse?

An unknown child. Seven or eight. Flattened to death in The Sacred Mosque.

Faisal repeated the question as though he hadn't understood what he'd just heard.

A corpse?

Mecca. Ajyad Hospital for Emergency Cases

7 Dhu Al-Hijja, 1431

9:10 P.M.

The receptionist explained: A janitor, sleeping on the job in The Sacred Mosque, had left his cleaning vehicle unattended. One of the kids who had decided to take advantage of the situation caused the injury of two women and the death of another boy standing alone, about seven or eight years old. We still haven't found his parents.

Faisal shook his head all the way to the morgue. *No way! My son is tiny.* Mishari's stature had won him a series of nicknames that now whirled in Faisal's head. The boy's grandmother, for example, called him The Button. His aunts preferred Snail on a Seashore. While Saud had dubbed him: Al-Nitfa—The Tidbit. *Mishari is short and slender. No way he'd be considered a seven-year-old, even if that was his real age. No way.*

As Faisal moved toward the giant metal freezer, the cold air penetrated his pores and seeped into his heart.

The doctor yanked on one of the many drawers, and the metal tongue stretched out, revealing a small body wrapped in white.

Faisal felt a pinch in his chest, then took one step closer to the freezer, his heart wildly palpitating, and noticed that the child on top of the drawer was taller than his son, perhaps by a single inch, so he took a deep breath, felt his migraine evaporate, and exhaled, thinking, *Not my kid!* He watched the morgue attendant move toward the corpse's head.

After unwrapping the white shroud swaddling the body, the doctor removed an additional layer, a white cotton gauze covering only half of the child's face. The removal of the gauze exposed a crushed and flattened skull, where flesh and skin had meshed into a single blue glob with black splotches.

That's where the wheels ran over, the morgue attendant explained.

Were it not for the difference in hair colour, even if the corpse had been his son, Faisal would not have recognised him. Mishari, after all, had thick, black hair, whereas the non-trampled part of the corpse still retained its brown mane with blond streaks. And there was no beauty mark on the neck. Not even half a mark.

Faisal let out a deep breath. It's not my son! Giving his back to the dead boy, he buried his face in the crook of his arm to fight back his tears, unsure whether he was lamenting the tragic loss of the young boy's life or celebrating the knowledge that his child might still be alive. This dual emotion of happiness and sadness sliced him in half.

The morgue attendant returned the cloth to the crushed part of the deceased child.

Faisal looked away, found a wall to lean on, and slid to the ground, stomach churning. As he rested his back against the wall, Faisal wiped his tears with the bottom of his shirt, then turned to watch the doctor cover the young body with a white shroud. *They'll wrap him in green tomorrow and urge everyone to pray for him. Pray for the child! May God have mercy on your souls! The four articulations of God's grandeur will be repeated by the lead cleric of The Sacred Mosque, while millions will echo: Allahumma do not deprive us of his reward or distract us after his death.*

The morgue attendant said, Although the young corpse has been lying in the freezer since the afternoon, nobody but you has come to see him. His family members are likely still searching the hallways and the courtyards. One must never leave their children unattended. Anything could happen at that moment a child wanders alone to bring a cup of Zamzam water. Anything! The morgue attendant seemed agitated, yet he shook his head apologetically and mumbled, The dead have a right to a swift burial. Turning to Faisal, he added, I hope you find your boy soon.

Faisal glanced at his watch. Nine hours had passed since Mishari's disappearance. The horror crawling over his body now gathered in his chest, and the words of the morgue attendant echoed in his ears: *Anything could happen!* And Faisal wondered, *What had Mishari experienced in the past nine hours?*

Faisal got up to leave, forcing his legs to move forward, suddenly eager to burst out of the building and into Mecca's alleyways to comb them inch by inch, and for the first time since Mishari went missing, he found himself asking: *Did we make a mistake bringing him along with us? Did we make a mistake? But it was Sumaya who wanted Mishari to see the Kaaba.*

And Faisal only wanted to make her happy.

So, is she happy now?

Mecca. The Centre for Lost Children

7 Dhu Al-Hijja, 1431

10:42 P.M.

Before Faisal left the hospital, the doctor asked if he'd already been to The Centre for Lost Children.

Faisal's eyebrows arched in surprise. Centre for Lost Children?

Nodding, the doctor said, It's where you should've gone first.

They were walking side-by-side in the hallway.

Faisal's heart filled with unexpected hope. *Why didn't anyone mention this centre to me before?*

More than a hundred children lose their way daily in The Sacred Mosque, the morgue attendant explained. The Centre is where people bring them in when they find them.

And where is it?

Not far from here. It overlooks the central courtyard of The Sacred Mosque.

Faisal left at a sprint and would've smiled had he not been beset by the following thought: *If Mishari had been waiting all this time in a centre specialising in missing kids, why hadn't he called?* The question convinced Faisal that he wasn't going to find his son. Yet, he went anyway.

At The Centre, he saw a twenty-something woman dressed like a scout handing out colourful plastic bracelets to an Asian family, whom she was instructing, You write your name and address here before putting these bracelets on your children.

His heart constricted. *What's the point? What of the paper in Mishari's pocket? The one with my name, number, address, and even the boy's blood type! Where was he, and why hadn't he called?*

Once the Asian family walked away, the young woman turned to Faisal.

He told her about his missing son.

She said, Follow me.

Faisal trailed behind her until they came upon a lobby crawling with kids.

Faisal's mournful eyes scanned the room. Dozens of children sat frozen in front of a large plasma screen on which a cartoon elephant was marching toward the Kaaba—to destroy it. Other children, who had forgotten their fears, hunkered among the toys, crayons, and small juice and laban cartons scattered in the foyer. After examining their faces, one by one, and noting their hollow sockets and bloodshot eyes, Faisal raised his voice and cried, Mishari Faisal Al-Saffar! Mishari!

But nobody turned.

The young woman walked Faisal out of the lobby into a hallway, where she explained that once children are brought to The Centre, a staff member documents their names, ages, and nationalities before informing the local agencies of each case. She then asked, What does your son look like?

And Faisal found himself opening his mouth to recite mechanically: A seven-year-old boy with black hair, thick bangs, a beauty spot on the neck, a gap in his front teeth, wearing an orange shirt and beige pants, looks like a five-year-old...

The young woman wrote the description on a sheet of paper before saying, If anyone shows up here with a boy who fits this description, we'll contact you immediately.

Faisal felt strangled.

She gave him a sympathetic look and added, I really hope you find him soon.

Faisal gave the woman his name and number and walked back to the gate. Outside The Centre for Lost Children, he turned around to goggle at the looming edifice. Night had fallen onto Mecca, and Faisal's burden was weighing heavily on his chest. He looked up at the gaping minarets that pierced both the black sky and its deafening silence.

Then he whispered, Where are you?

Mecca. Hajar Tower

7 Dhu Al-Hijja, 1431

11:45 P.M.

Faisal returned to Hagar Tower, dashing through the marble halls. The air indoors was saturated with coffee, cardamom, and frankincense. Faisal pierced through the smoke, pushing back the black arms offering sukkari dates, and slowed down near the shops, where he ducked into the elevator hallway, lunged into the nearest platform, and pounded on the button for the 14th floor. He emerged from the elevator, cursing technology, his dead phone, the charger he had forgotten in his room, and his humiliating dependency on all three during this crisis.

What if Mishari calls me now?

Can you even continue searching without your phone? Or must you surrender, even though your son is missing in this strange land somewhere among three million pilgrims?

Text messages from nephews, neighbours, uncles, work colleagues, friends, politicians, journalists, activists, bloggers, and Twitter celebrities flowed throughout the day. *You've only answered anonymous callers. Yet, even they have let you down in the end, for they keep asking the same question—Did you find him? The way they start their conversations doesn't matter: Our hearts are with you. My mom is praying for you. If you need anything...* But Faisal didn't need anything from them. *You don't want your phone to die! You don't want to brood within four walls while every minute and every hour increases the danger your boy might be facing.*

Faisal plugged the damn phone into a charger, then sat in front of it, waiting for electricity to trickle into his device and zap it alive. He rested his forehead on the wall for a minute, closed his eyes, then repeatedly smacked his head against the surface. It felt as if Mecca had gobbled him up, and now he was in the dragon's belly, wading up to his knees in burning slime, gradually roasting. The sacred capital, holy month, greatest days of the year, guests of the Merciful... Everything obstructed his movement.

The screen then turned bright as an incoming message from Saud asked, Any updates?

Faisal wrote back, No. Where are you?

Jeddah.

Help your brother, please! Saud's voice, when Faisal had asked for help, was still ringing in his ears, for as soon as he had learned that Mishari was involved, Saud had exclaimed: *I'm on my way!*

In Kuwait, Saud's friends were tracking potential leads and collating online witness testimonies. Others kept calling the Kuwaiti Embassy in Riyadh to intercede on Faisal and Sumaya's behalf. And then there were those who had voluntarily joined local and international campaigns to search for the boy who...

The tidal wave of unanswered calls continued to grow. Though Faisal recognised only some of the digits and callers on his list, he couldn't help but notice that Sumaya wasn't among them. He pictured her still circumambulating the Kaaba, melting in a rotational ritual, completing her fortieth lap, her fiftieth, her... The people around her would be supplicating—Labbaik, labbaik. Whereas she would be pleading—Mishari! Mishari!

A few minutes later, Faisal's screen lit again. This time, it was a Saudi number, so he picked up.

Is this Faisal Al-Saffar? a man with a Kuwaiti accent asked.

It is. Who am I speaking with?

I'm the first secretary of the Kuwaiti embassy in Riyadh. Are there any developments in your son's case?

No trace of him yet, Faisal said in a hoarse voice.

God permitting, you'll find him. Strengthen your heart.

How dare he...

Listen to me, Bu Mishari... The undersecretary fell silent for a moment, then carefully added, as though he were dictating each word, I want you to go to The Sacred Mosque's Operations Room.

Operations Room?

Yes. The Sacred Mosque's Security Operations Room. The agents are expecting you. We already informed them that you'd be on your way. The Sacred Mosque has over 700 surveillance cameras and more than 30 observation screens. I'm sure you'll be able to uncover what had happened to your son. The agents need to know where he was before he disappeared and the time, of course. The hour, and, if you know it, the precise minute you lost sight of him. I promise they won't let you down.

Faisal unplugged his phone and bolted out of the room.

Day 2

Mecca. The Sacred Mosque's Operations Room

8 Dhu Al-Hijja, 1431

12:52 A.M.

The surveillance monitor had captured Mishari's disappearance.

The two-hour process involved combing through recorded content as agents replayed scenes from various angles to no avail, for Faisal and the surveillants were struggling to locate a boy of Mishari's stature among the multitudes of bodies swirling in the courtyard. Thus, switching tactics, Faisal began to look for his wife—but Sumaya was a woman in a black abaya amid countless others dressed the same. After some time, therefore, Faisal's eyes began to dart across the screen in search of his own image.

He found the bottlenecking that had occurred near the southwestern corner of the Kaaba and thought, *That's where she supposedly lost him.* Marking the congestion with the tip of his finger, Faisal began to scan its surroundings for the group of African pilgrims Sumaya had mentioned earlier. The digital clock of the recording was flashing 12:17 p.m. *Here! Everything happened here!* Faisal swung his index finger toward the new area, yet no matter how many times he skimmed it, he found neither Sumaya nor his boy. *This doesn't make any sense. He must be right here!* Faisal, who was now breathing faster, wiped beads of sweat that had gathered on his forehead. By then, he'd spent an entire hour staring at the screen, looking for the boy who...

Here's a kid in orange! One of the agents, examining the footage on a different TV, glanced at Faisal, then added, Is this your son?

Faisal leaped in the direction of the other monitor displaying the image of a boy standing outside the crowd. Mishari! That's him! He couldn't believe how his son had crossed all that distance alone. Faisal's mouth went dry. Tears sprang from his eyes. Thank God! he cried and pointed at the boy on the screen who had his back to the pilgrims, hands cupped around his mouth, screaming for help. Turning to the agent, Faisal exclaimed, That's him! That's my boy Mishari. But he had no time to enjoy his elation, for he wondered, *Why didn't anybody help him?* His son was right there among countless people, shouting as loud as he could, and not a single pilgrim had even looked at him.

When the feed resumes, a thick-armed and dark-footed woman, wearing white gloves and a black niqab, approaches the child. She is followed by another woman who briefly communicates with the former before walking away.

Faisal kept his eyes fixed on the rotund woman who stayed behind.

She waves, then gently ruffles Mishari's hair.

Mishari opens his mouth to say something, dips his small hand into his pocket, then pulls out a folded piece of paper that he hands over to the stranger.

Mishari and the foreigner exit the courtyard hand in hand.

Faisal heard a buzzing in his ears, but he continued to follow the stranger strolling with his son, feeling sick to his stomach. He had felt his heart drop already, but now it sunk even deeper, as though making its own descent into hell. Faisal grabbed and squeezed his throbbing head and kept gawking at the monitor.

The stranger is now leading Mishari up a flight of steps away from the courtyard. She makes a swift detour before the gate, then yanks Mishari under a staircase.

The agent searching for a camera angle that had captured the scene under the staircase quickly flipped between numerous frames until he paused on the following one:

Mishari—pointing at the gate.

The woman—pointing at the stairs.

He pressed play.

A man wearing a grey kurta, cocooned in a prayer mat, is dozing off on the floor. He doesn't see the woman grab the little one's face with her gloved hand, and he doesn't witness the little one tremble, resist, kick, or sag into the stranger's arms.

The woman kneels beside the child, pulls up his socks to cover the colour of his ankles, then sweeps him under her loose, black cloak, where she picks him up, vaults him over her shoulder, and passes a squad of officers stationed at the gate, looking like any other mother carrying her sleeping child, before slipping out of The Sacred Mosque among scores of pilgrims as though she were invisible.

Before Faisal dropped to his knees, before his head banged against a metal pipe, and before he lost consciousness, a series of images flashed in his mind: *A flattened corpse. Black eyelids. White ihram. Black stone. Arms stretched out. Black stub. God almighty, we are here, ready to serve—Labbaik, labbaik. White gloves. Black feet. May he welcome you into paradise. White shroud. Green cloth. Pray for the child, may God have mercy on your souls. Do not deprive us of his reward or distract us after his death.*

Amen.

CHAPTER TWO

HAJEER

midday; scorching heat; forcible displacement

Mecca. Dogon Gida

7 Dhu Al-Hijja, 1431

1:32 P.M.

She was marching in the opposite direction of the multitudes, inconspicuously weaving in and out of alleyways, probing deeper and deeper into Meccan lanes brimming with mystery. The niqab-wearing woman had thick legs and a jiggling rump. The child she'd hauled over her shoulder lay slumped underneath her loose black cloak, as though she were shielding him from the sun.

Ruwaina arrived at Dogon Gida market at 1:30 p.m., but continued striding alongside idling cars and stores hastily built from wooden panels, rugs, and flimsy metal sheets. She passed other African women in coloured robes standing around big bowls filled with stolen merchandise, past men in ribbed tank tops, their biceps tanned and moist, squatting on big cans and plastic boxes, decorated skullcaps perching on their heads. She kept on meandering between various items: men's shirts and pyjamas dangling from rickety wooden beams and wagons selling pillows, chairs, television sets, carpets, phones, wallets, spices, Swiss army knives, perfume bottles, cans of peas and beans, watches, bracelets, dates, laban cartons, formula milk, and identity cards.

The spicy scent of Sula meat tingling in her nostrils mingled with the sour smells of urinals and dank armpits. She stopped only to ensure that the little one's socks still concealed his ankles, caught her breath, then powered on—another haggard woman carrying her kid beneath her abaya to protect him from the sun.

Ruwaina left Al-Mansour Street behind her and continued to navigate narrow avenues, penetrating further into Mecca's slim veins until the ground began to slope upward. Though her trail became more strenuous, she climbed higher up the mountain, carrying a child on one shoulder and a large purse on the other. The sweat streaming down her abaya had thoroughly wet her niqab until the breathy, sour smell wafting from the fabric blended with the stench already emanating from her skin.

Bristles on the ground had been sliding into her sandals, scraping her heels. When her calf muscle cramped and her thigh spasmed, Ruwaina stopped for a reprieve.

She'd been walking for about an hour and a half. Now she turned to the left then to the right to make sure the coast was clear. She plopped down to lay the little one's body on the earth and pulled out a green prayer mat from her purse to blanket the top half of the kid, taking extra care to cover his face and arms. Then, she tugged on his socks again, and as she lowered the hem of his pants she thought, *No one must see the colour of his skin.*

Ruwaina smiled as she pictured Jerjes's reaction once he found out she had fulfilled her promise to him. After loosening her niqab, she grabbed the Zamzam bottle from her oversized handbag, took several gulps, and washed her face with the rest, tasting saltiness on her lips. She pondered the boy beneath the mat and found herself reaching out to inspect his small hand, flipping it back and forth. She was thrilled to discover that his nails were clean, clipped, and filed. It meant that she had kidnapped an important child. *Look at that. His mother cares enough to file his fingernails. What a gem!* Ruwaina carefully placed his hand back under the green prayer mat and mused, *Befitting of a precious jewel.*

She raised her eyes to the summit where the others were waiting. Despite the vertical sun scorching her back, she felt joy when she recalled how, ten years ago, she'd snatch boys and girls from camps in northern Ethiopia to unleash them as beggars in Mecca, but the operation became more dangerous when Saudi anti-vagrancy forces adopted a policy of capturing the kids, briefly committing them to rehabilitation centres, then repatriating them to their countries. Ruwaina's smile widened, for she did the opposite now: abducting children in Mecca and smuggling them across the south.

She looked at the boy lying beneath the mat and thought who would've believed that one day she'd kidnap somebody like him? Light-skinned, dressed in spotless attire, his fingernails clean and filed. A sudden excitement surged through her body. She removed the green prayer mat, folded it twice, stuffed it in her bag, leaned over the boy, and picked him up. *Sleep, little one. Sleep, my darling.* Ruwaina reached out to touch the back of his head, and once her fingers plunged into the unusually soft texture of his hair, she felt deliciously euphoric.

Mecca. Al-Tariqi Mountain

7 Dhu Al-Hijja, 1431

3:03 P.M.

On Al-Tariqi mountaintop, a 1989 blue Caprice Classic idled behind a deserted house with wide, rickety wooden shutters and white, flaking walls.

Uthman was reclining in the driver's seat, an unlit cigarette in his mouth. The AC slots he had previously nudged in his direction were blasting warm air at his dark face and tilted skullcap, which concealed large eyes and a cone-shaped nose.

Adania and Bahati sat in the backseat, their niqabs dangling loosely under their chins, revealing hungry, hollowed faces. Because the intense heat outside the car had stained their backs and armpits, the air inside smelled like sweaty skin.

Ruwaina's late! Adania let out a petulant huff before leaning forward to pick up the tissue box lying between her feet and using it to fan her face. Beads of sweat had gathered on her forehead and the bridge of her nose.

She's always late! Pouting, Bahati agreed, then cracked a smile that showed the greenish tint in her teeth. Lowering her head closer to her friend, she whispered, It must be tough for the old hag... To climb the mountain with a child and all that ass!

Adania's lips were so thin they disappeared when she burst out laughing. High-fiving Bahati, she shook her head and giggled. That child. And that ass!

Bahati rested her head on the windowpane, yawned, and stretched her arms.

But when the sun began to aim its rays at the glass, Adania felt trapped in an oven, so she grumbled, This abaya is cooking my body. Her back ached from the prolonged sitting position, and she wished to stretch her legs outdoors, but Uthman would never permit an action that could endanger their lives. And though her tongue was already as dry as a log, she feared that filling her bladder might force her to stop and relieve herself several times during the seven-hour ride to their small lair. I'm so done! she sighed. Ruwaina does this every time, she added churlishly. I wish I had Saliha's responsibilities: cooking and cleaning and—

You don't get to decide what you do, Bahati interrupted her. Only Jerjes assigns our roles.

Adania pursed her lips. But Ruwaina... Then she leaned closer to Bahati and whispered, I swear she makes us wait on purpose. She could've been done hours ago. But no. She picks them like she's picking rice. You and I know it doesn't take this long to...

The unspoken word hung in the air.

Don't worry. Bahati patted her friend on the shoulder. It'll be over soon.

Uthman, jerking awake from his nap, turned to the two women in the back. Is she here?

No, they said simultaneously. Not yet.

But, at that moment, they all heard a series of raps on the roof of the car. Their faces swerved to the right in unison, where Ruwaina was standing beside the Blue Caprice, barely breathing, her forehead glistening with sweat, salty white spots smudging her black niqab.

Uthman asked, Where have you been?

Her eyes bulged. What kind of question is that? Where else?

He got out of the car, greeting Ruwaina in Amharic, Salam nish.

Just open the trunk! She banged on the lid and ordered the others, You too! Hurry! My back's killing me!

The two women climbed out of the blue Caprice, then flanked Uthman and Ruwaina to block the trunk.

Uthman looked left and right. Once he was sure they were still alone on the mountaintop, he unlocked the trunk he had previously punctured for air to slither in through the holes. Inside the trunk lay two black girls that had been unconscious for the past three hours. One of them had a stub instead of an arm.

After scanning the girls, Ruwaina noted the reddish hue tinging their sockets and the creamy crust that had formed over their lips. Make space for the boy, she commanded her subordinates.

Bahati and Adania dragged the girls to either side of the trunk, leaving ample space for another kid.

Ruwaina lowered the boy between them gently: a white boy wearing an orange T-shirt and beige pants sporting a thick head of hair and a beauty mark on his neck.

Wi ni! gasped the two women.

Uthman briskly shut the lid and turned around. Are you insane? What have you done? Is he Saudi?

No. He's Kuwaiti.

We don't kidnap those! You'll get us killed!

Don't be dramatic.

You know the local police! They'll eat us alive.

They'd be too late.

We have to leave him behind.

He's worth a fortune! What do you even know about our work, huh? Ruwaina glowered at Uthman.

Adania shook her head. You really lost it, Ruwaina. You think you can kidnap anyone?

Ruwaina told her to shut up in Amharic, Zem bul, then added, And butt out.

Bahati crossed her arms over her chest. Jerjes will kill you when he finds out. You know that, right?

Ruwaina let out a resounding laugh. Kill me? I assure you, he'll thank me.

But you're risking our lives! Adania cried.

If you're so worried, why don't you call Jerjes and tell him?

Uthman's eyes widened. You've lost it, Ruwaina. You've absolutely lost it.

I don't see you dialling. You're not frightened, are you?

Uthman whispered, Ruwaina… He'll kill you.

Ruwaina grinned under her niqab. Eyes shining with mischief, she shook her head and said in Amharic that he wouldn't, Ayy.

Uthman took a few steps backward, pulled his phone from his pocket, and dialled Jerjes. The call itself was short. Uthman had tossed Ruwaina a cursory glance from the corner of his eye before shifting his gaze to the trunk. Minutes later, he got off the phone, eyebrows knitted, and all the things he wanted to share remained buried in his chest. He stuffed the phone back in his pocket and hopped in the driver's seat, and when he shoved the key in the ignition, the engine roared and rumbled.

Now what? Bahati said.

Get in! he yelled.

And where are we going? Adania asked.

But it was Ruwaina who answered with a smile, To 'Asir.

On the Way to Wadi Rada

7 Dhu Al-Hijja, 1431

5:02 P.M.

The first time Mishari woke up from his narcoma, he found himself in a dark and narrow place. Stretching his arms to explore his surroundings, his fingers bumped against the metallic surface above his head, then scraped against the rough fabric underneath his back. He opened his mouth to gasp for air, but his breath was shallow.

The clangour first made him aware that he was trapped in the trunk of a car with two other girls whimpering and weeping. As thuds on the bumpy road rattled his insides, the stench of piss rushed to his nostrils.

Like stars punctuating the night sky, the perforated darkness allowed slivers of light to illuminate the trunk. A thin flow of air gently brushed his face, so he moved his nose closer to the hole, took a deep breath, and wracked his brain to recall how he got here. Nothing came to mind, so Mishari opened his mouth and cried, Mama! Even though it came out weak, unlike his actual voice, he still hoped his mother was near enough to hear him.

One of the girls kicked the metallic sheet overhead. Her foot accidentally landed on his stomach, causing a tear to stream down his cheek. Mishari, grimacing from the pain, whispered, Mama? He cupped his fingers around his mouth and yelled, Mama! That's when he remembered standing in The Sacred Mosque among the crowd, as he called for his mom, his hands curled the same way they were now. He didn't know how she let go of him or how she disappeared in the flood of people, but he heard her voice from afar ordering him to: Move! Move! Move! So, he moved among the men and women, looking around for her and his father.

Mishari couldn't remember how he ended up here. His eyes welled with tears, and he felt a lump in his throat.

Because his mother had taught him to call her or his dad immediately, he knew what to do if he was ever lost, but the Hajj had swept him far away, forcing him to leave the ring and scream Mama! Mama! However, nobody heard him.

Mishari frowned. A teardrop had sprang from his eye, and he would have sobbed had he not seen a woman wearing a black niqab, an abaya, and two white gloves head in his direction.

Are you lost?

Another woman who had approached him also asked if he was lost.

The former had told the latter, Don't worry. I'll connect him with his family.

The newcomer, praising the former, had said before leaving, May you be blessed!

It was then that Mishari remembered the folded piece of paper in his pocket, so he yanked it out and handed it to the one who stayed behind.

Are you Saudi? she had asked.

I'm Kuwaiti, he had answered, shaking his head.

Don't cry, darling, she had cooed, as she ran her fingers through his hair.

Even though he had smelled a strange odour on her gloves, Mishari still asked her to call his dad.

She had said, I don't have a phone myself, but I'll help you, don't worry, adding as she gave him her hand, We'll go to the gate together. Officers will help you call your father.

Mishari had held her hand and walked beside her, heading away from the Kaaba toward the exit. He couldn't remember anything else.

And once he opened his eyes again, fear hammering in his chest, he found it hard to breathe. Girls beside him were screaming. He peed his pants, and yelled as well.

All three kids were now shouting and slamming their palms and the balls of their feet on the lid. Mishari tried to break the metallic sheet, but he was barefoot, so when his heel caught on one of the jagged ends of a perforated hole, he recoiled from the pain, and recalled the Crocs he'd left in his mother's purse.

The three captives whined in unison—Mama! Imai Ai! Ahbai Ai!

The car's sudden break sent the three kids rolling to one side. Their arms and legs collided, and as the sole of a foot knocked into Mishari's cheek, the back of his hand landed on a wet nose and a rancid smell filled his nostrils. All three kids raised their heads when a fist pounded on the lid before opening it.

Fresh air washed into their lungs. The sky above them was purple, tinged with orange clouds. They saw the mountains first, followed by a dark man leaning into the car. His eyes were wide open, and his fist was clenched around a white towel that he shoved onto the face of the girl to Mishari's right.

Her eyelids drooped until she fell asleep.

Mishari flinched, then tried to resist, waving his arms and legs in the air, but when the wet towel smothered his face, he remembered what had taken place at The Sacred Mosque underneath the staircase, left of the exit, near a squad of officers—for this man's towel and the woman's glove smelled the same.

A sleeping man had been wrapped in a prayer mat, a skullcap covering his face. He didn't see what happened to Mishari or hear the foreign woman say, Shhhhhh.

She'd been holding Mishari tightly with one hand when she used the other to press her glove against his face.

Mishari breathed in the strange fragrance.

Then fell asleep.

On the Way to Wadi Rada

7 Dhu Al-Hijja, 1431

7:03 P.M.

Uthman wheeled the car off the main road into bumpy desert terrain to avoid an upcoming checkpoint. He only returned to the tarmac when he left an appropriate amount of space between his Blue Caprice and the police patrol.

He did this several times throughout the trip, always before an upcoming checkpoint or traffic jam. He'd disappear into Mecca's hidden pathways: the smuggling routes he knew like the back of his hand. These routes were now packed with Muslims who didn't have permits to enter Saudi Arabia or locals who weren't allowed to perform the Hajj ritual. Those undocumented believers would teem toward Mecca on dangerous roads Uthman knew so well, for he used to smuggle worshippers directly into The Sacred Mosque and pocket 2,000 Riyals for every pilgrim he dropped at the Eastern Gate.

Some of these believers would climb mountains or cross jagged wastelands, hiding in trucks and tankers. Their sleeping bags and colourful tents would stretch for miles when they disembarked at night. The journey would last several days, during which the smuggling routes would all be packed with vehicles loaded with undocumented Muslims sneaking into Mecca—while Uthman's car, heading in the opposite direction, would be loaded with kids.

He knew what to do, and the map in his head was clear, for he had memorised the various passageways criminals used for specific operations. For example, he was familiar with the road between

Jeddah and Taif on which non-Muslims were allowed to drive, but Al-Khawajja road wasn't the only alternative route he had memorised. He was also familiar with Al-Jumum, Hada, Al-Rayyan, and Al-Qawba'iyah. In other words, roads clear of security checkpoints, spreading across Mecca's lungs like arteries, pumping The Sacred Mosque with thousands of undocumented visitors.

From his rear-view mirror, Uthman watched Ruwaina softly snoring in the backseat, her forehead resting on the windowpane, her jaw loose. She'd been in that position since she had climbed in.

How can she sleep after what she did? She defied Jerjes. Only a maniac would do that. Ruwaina astounded him.

Uthman had never worried during their trafficking operations because he always had a backup plan, even if he had to go through a checkpoint. First, he'd leave abundant space between himself and the police officers. Then, when he parked, he'd move the kids from the trunk to the backseat for each woman to nestle on her lap as though she were the child's mother. In this part of the world, Black kids and Black women didn't provoke anyone's suspicions. And Uthman could always play the role of the noble brother driving his sisters, nieces, and nephews to visit their father in the south. But what good was that backup plan with this child?

Uthman had spent years coasting on his luck and memory of Mecca's alternative routes, but now he was worried. Any encounter with local forces could mean the end for him. His mouth went dry.

Scratching the back of his neck, Uthman wondered why Jerjes would jeopardise their lives for a commodity that wouldn't even sell in their market.

And why was Ruwaina so confident? She had even gone so far as to provoke him into calling Jerjes!

Uthman peered at Adania and Bahati's reflection, whispering in the backseat, both appearing as dumbfounded as him. And perhaps even more flustered since their wide eyes kept vigilant watch out of their window.

So, how can Ruwaina sleep at a time like this?

But her eyes suddenly popped open, and she caught Uthman peeking at her through the rear-view mirror. Ruwaina moved her eyes around as though trying to remember where she was, then started to bang on the door and shout, Stop! Stop right now!

What the hell's gotten into you?

They must drink some water!

On the Way to Wadi Rada

7 Dhu Al-Hijja, 1431

10:17 P.M.

Mishari woke up several times during the car ride. The male kidnapper stuffed a date in his mouth once and gave him water seven times.

Three hours of constant weeping had exhausted the children, who lay one on top of the other like used rags, sopping with piss and sweat. A bony protrusion poked Mishari in the waist whenever the car changed direction. He would later discover that what had prodded his body was the stub of an amputated arm.

During their final reprieve, the criminals opened the lid, unclothed the young captives, cast their filthy apparel in the desert, rinsed their faces, and returned all three naked to the trunk.

Mishari closed his eyes, and his body, hot as coal, touched the skin of the girls. He fell asleep, dreaming of a yellow Ferrari.

Mishari is sitting in the passenger seat. The man behind the wheel fiddles with the radio, searching for a suitable song. He picks one, but the one he chooses irritates Mishari, who loves the man in the driver's seat.

Mishari woke up, then fell asleep again, time after time, dreaming of a male arm reaching toward him.

He hears the man behind the wheel complain about the length of his hair—but that song blasting through the speakers... It was the song that grated on his nerves... *What did it say?* Mishari couldn't remember. Neither the song's melody nor its lyrics seeped into his dreams. Nevertheless, Mishari kept waking up, thinking about the way it frustrated him.

The engine rumbled and Mishari felt the car skid along the asphalt tongue before it came to an abrupt stop. He heard a fist pounding on the trunk. The sound resonated in his guts, snapping him out of his dream and plunging him into his nightmare.

When the man who had pressed the towel over his face, who had sent him to sleep, who had given him a single date and some water, opened the lid again, Mishari noticed that the sky had gone completely dark.

That man aimed his flashlight at the two girls before a dark-skinned, niqabless woman, uttering words in a language Mishari couldn't understand, peered at him. Her cold hands suddenly stretched out, dipped under his armpits, then lifted him out of the trunk. Mishari's body dangled limply over her shoulder as she carried him to a building nearby. He wanted to kick her, to slip out of her reach, to run away in the dark, but he felt exhausted, his stomach churned, and at that moment, what he truly craved was to go back to sleep, to enjoy the presence of the yellow Ferrari, the man behind the wheel, and the loving fingers raking his unruly bangs.

His mother had promised him that she would take him to the barbershop after completing the Hajj. Mishari couldn't understand how a simple haircut had become this complicated.

Thank God, none of them are dead, Ruwaina said as she inspected the three kids who had formed a knot of tangled arms and legs, and who were squished, one on top of the other, to the right side of the trunk.

With an anxious expression, Uthman watched as he aimed his flashlight at the kids' yellowed skin, chapped lips, and bloodshot eyes. White streams of saliva had dried on their cheeks.

Ruwaina extracted Mishari from the arms and legs of the young girls, tipped him over her shoulder, and headed toward a two-story house made of bricks resembling an incomplete pyramid: wide at the bottom and narrower on top. It jutted out of the void in the middle of a valley, shrouded in darkness. The house had small, high windows and a door overlaid with tar. The interior walls flaunted red, green, and black designs. Inside, a green-painted staircase led up to the children's room on the second floor, where Saliha was watching over yesterday's catch: One Indian girl and several African children, some of whom were missing limbs.

One of the boys had puked on the floor, and Saliha was disciplining him, pointing at the stain on her faded olive-green dress and yelling, Third time, you dog! After which she whacked the kid with a thin wooden stick.

When Ruwaina passed by the open door, Saliha gasped, unable

to believe her eyes, for the naked, semi-conscious child on Ruwaina's shoulder had soft hair and light skin. Sprinting into the hallway, she asked, Is he Saudi?

Ruwaina clicked her tongue. He's Kuwaiti.

Saliha's eyebrows arched, and her eyes popped open.

Adania and Bahati arrived shortly after, each of them carrying one of the other catatonic kids they had kidnapped in the morning.

How could you let her do this?

Don't ask me, Adania said petulantly, frowning all the way to the bathroom, where she laid the girl with the amputated arm on the floor beside the other two captives.

Ruwaina spread their legs before hosing down the residue of puke and piss. They curled like worms, hugging their bodies, their soft, intermittent moans barely audible. Ruwaina lathered their naked bodies with a bar of soap, then filled a plastic bucket with water, and dumped it over their heads.

They gasped in unison, shivering with cold.

Ruwaina picked up the Kuwaiti boy again. When she entered the children's room, the other captives crowded around the pale newcomer. Her free hand swatted them as she cried, Step back, animals! I said move out of my way!

They huddled in the corner of the room, watching the scene unfold in front of them, their eyes wide.

Some even dared to ask for a cookie.

'Asir. Wadi Rada

7 Dhu Al-Hijja, 1431

11:24 P.M.

Jerjes, who was sitting on floor cushions, leaned against a pale blue wall, mouth partly open, fresh qat leaves ballooning his right cheek. A nylon bag filled with shiny, reddish-green strips rested between his sprawled legs. And though the leafy smell had saturated the room, he could still taste the sourness of the leaves. Their magically calming effect hadn't yet kicked in.

Jerjes!

He turned to face the door, where Saliha stood, glaring at him with her smouldering, kohl-smeared eyes, before erupting furiously, She kidnapped a white boy! Then she pursed her thick lips.

Oh, pretty little Saliha. It was the first time Jerjes had paid attention to the way her eyes hid a delectable lack of experience. *Gorgeously naive*! And the olive-green dress she was now wearing allowed him to picture the smooth ebony curves beneath. The mere sight of her knitted brows delighted him. Even with the vomit stain on her dress, he nevertheless felt a thrill coursing through his body.

Did you hear what I just said?

His lips stretched into a lazy smile, exposing a shiny green slab of leaves between his teeth.

A Kuwaiti child!

I know.

He wondered why he hadn't considered getting closer to her before this moment. Saliha, who had joined their group a few months earlier, was a fast learner, fiery, attractive, and jealous—everything he loved in a woman. Her sultry youthful body made his blood burn with desire.

Are you going to let Ruwaina defy you?

At dawn, when he'd sent his women to Mecca to kidnap more children, he'd asked Saliha to stay behind, watch over their captives, and cook his meals. The truth, however, was that he simply wanted to watch her hips wiggle up and down the stairs, over and over. And he would've coaxed her into bed that morning were it not for his delight in the distance itself. Keeping her at arm's length allowed him to fantasise about her and imagine the way she yearned for him. He pictured her, for example, aching for his touch and suffering profusely because she couldn't satisfy her craving.

It became a habit. Ruwaina in his bed. Saliha in his head.

And he could sense her noticing the way his eyes devoured her body. He felt that the same hunger emanated from her eyes. Sometimes, he even heard the hidden calls of pleasure in the crescendo of her footsteps when he shot her a glance.

You're the one who explicitly warned us against approaching those kids!

Her tone, brimming with jealousy, turned him on.

Ruwaina is risking all our lives!

When Saliha set the table this afternoon, she couldn't hide her bitterness while asking, What do you actually see in that old hag? She explained that Ruwaina exploited his kindness and that, by acting like a boss herself, she was usurping his power and annoying everyone else in the process.

Jerjes had been shaking his head throughout it all, for he knew Ruwaina. He knew her well because she was the crutch on which he leaned his entire life. *But Saliha...*

We didn't agree to this!

How anger becomes her. Oh, Saliha. Those enchanting eyes!

Do you think anybody will respect you after what happened?

The damn girl finally managed to aggravate him. The qat leaves Jerjes spat out left a green smudge on the ceramic tiles.

Call Ruwaina, he muttered.

'Asir. Wadi Rada

7 Dhu Al-Hijja, 1431

11:20 P.M.

Ruwaina's deafening yells echoed throughout the valley as Jerjes battered her head with a wooden stick.

She glared at him, unable to fathom why he was raising his voice and hurling insults like he wanted everyone to witness his authority in action: Uthman, Adania, Bahati, a tribe of black children, one Indian girl, a white boy, and Saliha, who was standing at the top of the staircase, stealing glances at the melodrama below.

Ruwaina had seen this ritual play out countless times before. It often marked the moment Jerjes found a scapegoat, usually a female member of their group, whom he'd pummel in front of everyone as a reminder of his authority.

The first time he slapped her that day, Ruwaina's jaw dropped. Genuinely confused, she asked him, What has gotten into you?

You better not forget who's in charge here, he huffed in her ear after slamming her cheek against the wall and punching her collarbone.

Ruwaina lost her vision for a few seconds. Everything went dark until she regained her sight and noticed a red stain on the pale blue wall and realised that her mouth tasted like blood.

You dare disobey me?

Ruwaina weighed her options. Still fixing Jerjes with a dumbstruck expression, she asked, What did I do?

Looks like you need a lesson in obedience.

But I—

He kicked her in the stomach.

Ruwaina fell, astonishment flashing on her face. She pointed her index finger at him and said a little louder, But I... You...

If you ever disobey me again, I'll kill you and sell everything you have. He hit her stomach with the butt of his stick, then shoved it in. This—right here—is worth 40,000 dollars! Never forget that.

Jerjes let Ruwaina go, then he went back to lean against the pale blue wall below her bloodstain, tearing at the leaves in the nylon bag until he stuffed a fresh batch in his right cheek. Within minutes, a filmy glaze enveloped him and he appeared to have forgotten about Ruwaina entirely.

Even though she stood there, still transfixed.

Raising his chin and his loose jaw with the glistening green leaves, Jerjes asked, What do you need?

Wanting to explain herself, she said, But you told me to...

He rummaged in his nylon bag again, then said without lifting his eyes, Hungry for more?

Ruwaina finally understood that she was this season's scapegoat, the sacrifice through which Jerjes could reanimate the fear in the hearts of his followers and regain his iron grip, so she said nothing.

Feeling a heaviness in her chest, she left the room, lips pursed, dragging her bulky legs up the stairs. The sound of gossipy whispers and mocking laughter that trailed behind her died down only when she entered the children's room.

Mere seconds later, Saliha spat an adage:

The frog who wanted to become an elephant blew up!

'Asir. Wadi Rada

8 Dhu Al-Hijja, 1431

2:20 A.M.

She was staring at the wall, laying on her side, a pillow under her arm. Although the piercing ache in her chest was spreading to other parts of her body, she tried to sleep like the rest, to act as if Jerjes hadn't humiliated her in front of everyone, but she couldn't shake the dark stain of his public ritual.

Why didn't he order me to leave the kid behind if he didn't want him?

Her blood boiled when she concluded that Jerjes had simply betrayed her, that he wanted the boy and the millions the boy would yield all for himself. Jerjes was willing to pay the fine for the lucrative transaction—the fine that was Ruwaina herself, Ruwaina who had procured the kid in the first place and who was the cause of the increased reward. As the pain spread across her body, she began to think more lucidly. *He used me as bait and prey.*

She remained frozen in place, pretending to sleep, and didn't move a single muscle even when Jerjes ordered the others to bring the Indian girl to his bed, nor when she heard the child screaming as Bahati hauled the girl onto her shoulder, nor when the Indian child clung to the rusty metal door refusing to move, nor when the rest of the young captives plunged into a crying fit. Ruwaina remained still even as Bahati and Adania swung their wooden sticks to wallop the children into silence. She didn't move, as if those events were taking place far away, for in the grand scheme of things, they were insignificant compared to the tumour of betrayal growing in her heart.

Drifting off for a few seconds, Ruwaina saw herself as a young girl again, her head full of braids, her legs weaving across the camp, her hands gathering wooden planks and white pebbles and anything else with which she could play. Then she saw a wooden bat striking her head and woke up gasping.

A flurry of voices reached her ears simultaneously: children calling for their mothers in their sleep, women snoring, and the hapless cries of the ten-year-old that Jerjes had gorged on in bed. After a while, silence enveloped the lower level. Ruwaina concentrated and realised that the Indian girl's screaming had morphed into a whimper that grew more audible the closer Jerjes carried the girl up the steps toward the room where they kept their young captives.

Once she heard his footsteps enter, Ruwaina raised her head to show him the aftermath of his brutality: her bruised face and swollen eyelids. She yearned for an apologetic expression and was willing to forgive him as a mark of respect for their shared history and companionship, but she noticed his yellow eyes devouring Saliha's body. Jerjes scanned the parted lips, slowing at the spittle that drooped down Saliha's chin, and he revelled in the rope that was wrapped around her wrists and legs, connecting her to the ankles of their young captives. It was then that Ruwaina recognised the reason she'd been sacrificed.

Jerjes lowered the Indian girl with the bloodstain on her dress among the other children, then signalled with his head for Ruwaina to follow him to slake the thirst the ten-year-old had failed to quench.

'Asir. Wadi Rada

8 Dhu Al-Hijja, 1431

2:30 A.M.

Jerjes lay on his back waiting for Ruwaina the way he did every night. He heard her slog down the steps and pant toward his bed, then saw her frosty eyes glaring at him through the partly open door. *Ruwaina...* His old hag.

After taking two steps forward, she sprawled beside him, staring at the ceiling, lips pursed, face bruised, one eyelid engorged, her tubby fingers slowly fumbling with the buttons of her dress. She knew what she had to do and wanted to get it over with as fast as possible. Unbuttoning her dress revealed a sliver of black skin from her stomach to her throat.

Jerjes ordered Ruwaina to remove his pants.

Her body heaving to the side, Ruwaina dipped her lazy fingers behind the elastic band of Jerjes's sweatpants, pulled down swiftly, then resumed her position, lying on her back. We agreed together, she said in a breathy whisper.

He grunted, I never agreed to anything.

You said—

Enough! He smothered her face with a pillow with his right hand and lifted the hem of her dress with his left.

The previous night, Jerjes had watched Ruwaina's dexterous fingers roll him a cigarette after satiating his desire. She spread the sheet, unclasped the lid, and scooped some tobacco from the small metal box while discussing the Eritrean boy from Assab she'd kidnapped that evening.

While sprinkling a pinch of tobacco powder on the flat sheet, she had asked him, Do you ever wonder where we come from? After realising that she had perhaps scattered more powder than was needed, she returned some of the tobacco to the box before closing the lid.

Jerjes couldn't decipher the motivation underlying her question. They had both been born in the same refugee camp and raised as orphans. Ethnically, they could be from anywhere: Eritrea, Sudan, Ethiopia, Somalia, Djibouti...

He followed her ritual, drowsily taking in her plump fingers rolling the cigarette sheet, her thick white tongue poking out of her mouth before it ran along the edge, her fingers that gently squeezed the stick, and her lips that gripped the butt when she lit the tip. Curlicues of smoke wafted out of her nostrils as she passed him the cigarette, after which she claimed, You'd make a lot more money if you stopped trading in Black kids.

Jerjes took a deep drag, exhaled the smoke from his mouth, then said, Black kids are safer, Ruwaina. Nobody cares if they disappear.

Raising her right eyebrow, Ruwaina shot Jerjes a knowing glance, and said, Exactly!

With a puzzled expression on his face, Jerjes retorted, But why would I kidnap anyone who'd cause an uproar?

Because uproars are profitable.

They're also risky, he said, shaking his head. Her argument thoroughly baffled him. More than anyone, he thought Ruwaina understood their market's demands: Ethiopians, Eritreans, Somalis, and Nepalis—people whose disappearance caused no commotion, people who were invisible despite the prominent colour of their skin.

He had sat there, recalling their history. *Ruwaina... Sturdy and safe like a metal box.* He could still remember how she first examined their new captives' eyes. Because beautiful eyes were assets that aided beggars in making more money, Ruwaina spared the attractive ones. Rather than blinding the good-looking captives, she fastened their bodies to the bed. Later, she complained about the filth collecting under their fingernails before amputating one of their arms. If she didn't like the eyes of the child, she'd grip the kid's head between her thighs, part the eyelids with her fingers and pour melted plastic on the eyeballs.

Even back then, Jerjes and Ruwaina had targeted a specific demographic, for they only hunted disabled youngsters and orphans from Leitchuor and Nip Nip camps, children brought up as burdens in non-biological families—children just like them. Jerjes snatched these kids, knowing that no one would miss them because no one had missed him when he was kidnapped. In fact, Jerjes truly believed that he was doing the refugees a favour and that, by kidnapping their orphans and their disabled youth, he'd be freeing up more space and resources for the other family members who might live longer.

So why was she harping on capturing someone who might attract attention and jeopardise our lives?

You betrayed me.

Ruwaina's voice was frail under the pillow.

Jerjes, panting, sweat pouring down his forehead, climaxed, then collapsed beside her.

Ruwaina moved the pillow away from her wet, bloated face.

While pointing a reprimanding finger at her, Jerjes said, You're responsible for your actions.

I have taken care of you my whole life! she screamed.

He smacked her face with the pillow and pressed on it with his whole weight. Jerjes could no longer stand the thread of time and misery that bound them to one another, a thread weaving a tapestry full of hunger and displacement. *What a loathsome past!*

You betrayed me, she screamed again.

I won't lose their respect.

You mean her respect.

Jerjes smiled. So what? *Saliha is attractive and malleable. Ruwaina is now nothing but a wrinkly old hag.* He moved the pillow away from her face and told her to get out.

Teary-eyed and dishevelled, Ruwaina stood up, rapidly buttoned her dress, then hurried out of the room, wincing from the pain as she moved up the staircase.

Ruwaina the old hag... Jerjes felt better after exhaling, as though Ruwaina were no longer squatting on his chest.

Their relationship had soured in a single day, as if a million walls had suddenly been raised between them. Sleeping together had often been part of a pleasurable ritual: her fingers rolling him his cigarette afterward, or, on other occasions, the two of them sharing a joint and, if they were fortunate enough to score a bottle of arak, sipping it together.

Ruwaina's raspy breathing disappeared when she reached the upper level. Jerjes heard the door of the children's room creak open, then close, and it dawned on him that the only thing that had united them throughout those long and turbulent years—throughout his entire life—had finally ruptured.

Last night, he had asked her, Just imagine what would happen if the police intercepted a car carrying a white boy in the trunk?

And she had pulled the cigarette from his mouth, taken a drag, and blown smoky clouds through her nostrils. You don't need to worry about Uthman. He knows the area well and can always choose another path before stumbling on a checkpoint. After another deep inhale, she'd added, Just think about it. One boy. Perhaps a Saudi. You'd hide him in one of the countless caves, call his parents, then ask for a ransom. You share the boy's location when they give you the money. After that, you cross the border into Yemen through Wadi Al-Jiniyya or Daffa. It's simple.

Jerjes had shaken his head. What about the black kids we've already got? Do we bring twelve children to Yemen when their buyers are waiting for them in Sinai?

Ruwaina had mulled it over quietly, then said after a few seconds, Maybe we don't need to swap the money for the child here in Saudi Arabia. Maybe we call the parents only after we cross the ocean?

Jerjes's forehead had creased in thought.

Ruwaina had explained with a shrug, It's what we do anyway, right? You can negotiate with the parents from Sinai or sell the white kid directly to the Ra'aida.

Jerjes had recovered his cigarette and sucked its last breath.

A mysterious smile had stretched across Ruwaina's face. Tomorrow, I'll kidnap a white boy.

That madwoman. She meant it.

CHAPTER THREE

SA'EER

land of the dead; fire; madness

Mecca. Emergency Room

8 Dhu Al-Hijja, 1431

3:01 A.M.

When Faisal woke up, he thought for a split second that he had escaped his nightmare, and it had to be a nightmare, for what he had just witnessed had been far stranger than anything he could picture happening in real life: an unknown woman, wearing a black niqab and white gloves, carrying his comatose son in her arms, passing through the gate of The Sacred Mosque and disappearing into a crowd of pilgrims without rousing anyone's suspicion.

He gasped awake and, for a split second only, believed that he had survived. *It was just a nightmare. Everything's alright now.* Faisal turned, confident he'd find his aging mother in the kitchen, stirring a bowl of chicken livers for her grandson, that his wife would be sitting crossed-legged in front of the television watching a Turkish soap, and that his brother would be reclining on the farthest couch in the living room, flirting with a woman on the phone. Meanwhile, Mishari would be splayed on his stomach, rollicking with a Batman figurine, his legs swinging back and forth in the air, his long bangs spilling over his eyebrows, and at some point, Mishari would raise the Batman toy as high as his arm would reach, then lower it with a smash onto The Joker's abdomen, crying, Bam! It's over for you! Coward!

Because this scene was a staple in Faisal's household, he was positively certain that Mishari would be there in the living room when he opened his eyes.

But Mishari wasn't.

He wasn't in the living room. He wasn't even in Kuwait.

And instead of smelling the appetising aroma of cooked meat, Faisal was now inhaling the stinging scent of antiseptic solution and naphthalene. He didn't see the pistachio-coloured furniture, the Persian rugs embroidered with deer and birds, the crystal candlesticks standing straight on circular tables, or the manifold copies of Ayoub Hussein's paintings hanging on the walls. The room he found himself in was endlessly white, crawling with wires. Faisal became aware of the intravenous fluids burbling through tubes beside a softly beeping screen monitoring his heartbeats. He spotted the surveillance camera jutting from one corner, and on his hand—secured by a sticky bandage—he saw a wire slinking around his thumb, connecting the IV drip to his veins.

A male nurse was parting Faisal's eyelids with two fingers.

Faisal rolled his eyes to the side, where he saw the Kaaba draped in white and black in a framed photograph hanging on the wall next to a digital clock that read several minutes past 3 a.m.

Sumaya, to his right, was sitting crossed-legged on a metal chair, hugging a pair of Crocs, rocking back and forth and banging her head against the wall, wide-eyed, red-faced, and teary, repeatedly muttering, Oh, baby! Oh, Mishari!

Faisal called his wife.

She didn't turn around.

The male nurse said something Faisal couldn't understand, yet Faisal nodded anyway, his eyes still glued to his wife. *Why isn't she answering?* Sumaya! *She wasn't the kind of woman who'd ignore her husband.* Lifting his head from the pillow, Faisal exerted more effort when, for the second time, he ordered his wife, Sumaya, I said, call Mishari. After uttering those words, his head fell back into the padding.

But she didn't move this time either.

Faisal thought she couldn't hear him, so he thrust his index finger into the air and raised his voice, Sumaya! Call Mishari right now! Tell him his dad wants to talk to him. Faisal's arm then lost the remainder of its vigour and fell limply onto the bed. Muttering wistfully, he added, Tell him... But didn't finish the thought.

Sumaya peered at her husband, frowning, her sockets hollow, her eyes bloodshot, drowning in tears. As she raised the young one's slippers in the air, she asked him, Where's my son?

At that moment, Faisal realised that his nightmare had just begun.

Mecca. Emergency Room

8 Dhu Al-Hijja, 1431

3:32 A.M.

Because Saud had no time to return home and pick up his passport or change his clothes, he used his Kuwaiti Civil ID to pass through Saudi customs and arrived in Jeddah in the blue uniform Kuwaiti oil engineers wore to work. Empty-handed but full of desire to help, he rushed to the emergency room, where he found his older brother reclining in a hospital bed, staring at the wall, eyes aghast and dry, one arm draped over his chest. And because Faisal had ripped out the IV drip, the blood trickling down his shirt had formed a burgundy smudge near his heart.

On the other side of the room, Sumaya was a heap of darkness, rocking to and fro under layers of black fabric. She reminded Saud of the Western Parotia—a dancing bird of paradise.

No sooner had Saud stepped into the room than he retreated into the hallway. Brushing away his tears, he struggled to steady his breathing after the overwhelming scene he'd just witnessed.

One of the paramedics, strolling through the hallway, found Saud standing alone. He squeezed Saud's arm and said encouragingly, Hang in there. Your brother needs you now.

Saud had come all this way to support his older brother, so he pursed his quivering lips, regained his composure, nodded to the paramedic, then stepped back into the hospital room. Saud wanted to wrap his arms around Faisal in a loving embrace, but the older brother flinched as soon as Saud sat next to him, giving his younger brother the impression that Faisal didn't want to be touched, so Saud did the next best thing and told his older brother, Repeat after me, Bu Mishari. There is no God but Allah.

Faisal didn't budge. He lay there, an absentminded expression on his face, apathetically gazing into the void as if he were numb to the pain.

Saud laid a gentle palm over his brother's hand. I'm here, Faisal. Giving in to the tears streaking down his cheeks, he declared more passionately, Believe me, we'll find him! With God's help, we will!

Faisal turned to his younger brother and said, as if he had just noticed him, Saud... You're actually here? Faisal added in a hoarse whisper, They kidnapped Mishari.

Saud shook his head to fight back the tears and mumbled, I heard.

They kidnapped Al-Nitfa... Faisal turned to the wall to stare in disbelief.

The unspoken words grew heavy and coarse in Saud's mouth, sharp enough to cut his tongue, but Sumaya's wailing tore his stupor of sadness.

Saud got up to sit beside her, but when he held her hand, Sumaya screamed louder, burying her face in her black veil and crying, Oh baby!

There is no power except in Allah, Sumaya! Repeat after me.

Faisal scowled, then sobbed.

His weeping mingled with Sumaya's wailing and sent Saud sprinting into the hallway.

But Saud could still hear their cries pulsating in his chest, sapping his last breath of fresh air even after he'd left the room. His perturbation made him stumble and bump into patients. After a while, he stopped to lean his arms and forehead against a wall. Mishari's face came to mind with all its little details: the bright and sandy colour of his skin, the beauty mark on his neck, the thick bangs, his prominent ears, and his missing tooth.

Saud banged his fist against the concrete, anger boiling in his veins. *Who the hell has dared to kidnap Al-Nitfa?* Bawling uncontrollably, his fingers swiped away his tears as he solemnly vowed: *In God's holy name, I'll never cry again!*

After quieting down, Saud rambled through hallways between hospital staff and convalescents until he descended a small staircase, passed through a sea of scattered slippers, and plodded alongside decorated pillars and walls, where he came upon a foyer housing countless men who slumbered on the ground, using red prayer mats as blankets. Massive, sparkling chandeliers dangled from the marble ceiling. And air, drifting from the electric fans propped on the floor near multiple power outlets, carried the stench of sweat, feet, carpets, wet skull caps, and the woody scent of oud. Though all these odours merged in the air, they broke apart in Saud's nostrils, reverting to their individual fragrances, because although he inhaled Mecca's crowded smell in one fell swoop, Saud tried rather to parse the fantastic menagerie of perfumes for a single clue—just one that could help him identify the woman who had dared to kidnap his nephew.

Mecca. The Courtyard of the Sacred Mosque

8 Dhu Al-Hijja, 1431

12:42 P.M.

Time is not your ally. Time is the enemy.

How could you halt its endless flow when it was never within reach? That thing we call Time keeps slipping farther away, toward the possibility of a tragic ending, and every passing minute helps to further expand the gulf that separates you from your son.

It's day eight of Dhu Al-Hijja, Yawm al-Tarwiyah, the day of fetching water and of quenching thirst.

The Sacred Mosque has fewer pilgrims now that most have begun the trek toward Mina. Gaps between the bodies of those who remained in the courtyard have widened. Yet, despite all this open space, there's still no trace of your son.

You just got off the phone with your liaison from the Kuwaiti embassy in Riyadh, who showered you with empty reassurances in his feeble attempt to grasp the unknown. We're trying to follow a lead.

What lead, though?

She is a single, niqab-wearing woman hauling a child amid millions of other women dressed the same, carrying their children in the same way. Only two facts are known about her. The first is that she's biologically female. The second is that she's of African descent. But are these details bulletproof?

The Saudi police are relying on secret agents they had planted in the African community to mine for information.

That's all well and dandy, but which community are we talking about? Sudanese? Ghanaian? Eritrean? Chadian? Somalian? Ethiopian?

Your ignorance is absolute.

When you get off the phone, you lean your back against the wall, a newspaper bundled under your arm. You've been following the headlines all morning. Mishari's image appears on the front pages of all the Kuwaiti periodicals, including al-Watan, al-Qabas, al-Rai, al-Anba, al-Jareeda, *and* al-Nahar. *Even the Saudi dailies have published his photograph. And a video of the kidnapper snatching the child in broad daylight has spread on the Internet and has been replayed extensively on various news channels. Your son's face, with all its details from the beauty spot to the missing tooth, has been circulating everywhere for the past twenty hours.*

The crushing weight on your chest makes you feel hopeless. Your gut tells you that the smugglers don't come from a world of laws and technology, so what good will any of this documentation do? You're searching in the wrong place and you know it.

You are still standing in the courtyard of The Sacred Mosque in front of King Abdulaziz Gate. The white marble of the walls and floor stretch out before you like a milky hallucination. The sun is shining in the sky, and two steps away from you, a pigeon on the ground picks up a grain of barley in its beak. You breathe deeply. It has just dawned on you that all the veils of holiness have been torn to shreds. This rupture is only now exposing the other face of Mecca: impotent, lame—a face without hope in a city without movement. No one is coming to save you.

Although your son has been missing for twenty-four hours, it's nothing but a speck in the shadow of three million pilgrims during their season of worship and its promised reward.

Divine light for believers.

Hellish blight for you.

When the call for noon prayer reverberated across Mecca's skies, Sumaya faced the Kaaba and prayed. She prayed and prostrated, prostrated and sobbed, and turned to you as soon as she was done.

Aren't you going to pray?

You looked away and said, Not until I find him.

Every moment spent on anything other than your desperate search for your missing son is a waste of time. Prayer is a privilege for those who can while away the hours and those who can feel the beating of their hearts—and you can do neither. Everything is lost. Not only the boy. The beating heart as well. You've become disenchanted with this crowded place, its hustle and bustle, and tussling pilgrims. Absolutely everything! You exhale again and wonder, When will Mecca's population disperse?

But why do you want people to go away?

Do you believe your chances of finding him will increase with fewer people around?

What if the smugglers disappeared as well?

Or would you lay there hoping they'd return?

What if they come back with your son, now missing an arm, waving a plastic cup with the other, begging pilgrims for a few Saudi Riyals?

You say, So what?

If Mishari returns without a limb, no problem. You'll take him to the best hospital in Europe, where they can rip out your arm and stitch it onto him. They can transfer your heart as well, or any other organ. What's important is that you reunite.

You've been going around in circles. Yesterday, you called it circumambulation. So, what are you calling it now?

Torture.

Your phone keeps ringing, but you lack the energy to answer anyone. Your voice no longer belongs to you. It belongs to your weeping. Your mother is calling for the hundredth time. Go on, explain to your sexagenarian mom that her grandson is missing—kidnapped. Why don't you interpret your calamity for her and make a narrative out of it, or use your calamity to fashion a cautionary tale for generations to come?

You've been handing out fliers for the past four hours, fliers with his photograph and a headline: MISSING CHILD! FINANCIAL REWARD TO THE ONE WHO FINDS HIM!

ONE MILLION DOLLARS.

You wrote down a figure you didn't possess without hesitation, knowing that the money would manifest and potentially overflow. You did not doubt that your family would dash to your rescue. After all, your brother has already organised several search parties, and even though some of the volunteers offered to help only because they were motivated by the reward, the majority have mobilised out of sympathy for the parents of the child who...

You move closer to Sumaya as she busily hands out her fliers to a group of Indian pilgrims. When your eyes meet, she asks immediately, Are you done?

Yes.

Here.

She places another stack in your hands. Then she dumps another. And a third on top of that.

You watch as Mishari's face spreads across The Sacred Mosque like a lie or some kind of propaganda. Your eyes follow Sumaya as she darts after black-skinned children.

Hey! Have you seen this boy? Maybe you ran into him near your house? Where do you live? Is this where your parents work? How did you come to Mecca?

You look away, no longer able to stomach the sight of her face, because Mishari was with her. She'd been holding his hand when...

Faisal! She is calling you now, waving her arms. Come here!

You force your feet forward. Khair?

Sumaya points at a thin, bald Indian man with small eyes, round glasses, and a wife clinging tightly to the crook of his arm. Sumaya tells you, Their daughter has been missing for the past two days.

You give the man a consoling look.

He says, I lost my daughter, Mariam.

You think to yourself, Another child? Then ask, How?

The Indian man struggles before he explains, She was napping near one of the pillars while her mother performed the afternoon observance and was gone when her mother completed her prayer.

You peer deeply into his eyes, for they reflect your own horror. How old is your daughter? you ask, feeling affinity with this man.

Ten.

Have you informed the authorities?

All of a sudden, the Indian man looked tired. We did! Of course, we did! Every time we came across an officer, we told him, too. But they've done nothing because they can't do anything! They're barely able to organise this ritual. One of the officers told me, 'You want me to leave my spot to search for your daughter?' And he's right! He can't leave his spot. And I can't find my child.

The Indian man pursed his lips as though fighting a massive wave of tears, but he couldn't restrain himself any longer, so he crumbled under the weight and wept from the pain.

Summoning up her courage, his wife took a step forward, stretched her open palms toward Sumaya as though begging for mercy, and pleaded, Help us, please. We don't have a million dollars like you.

Mecca

8 Dhu Al-Hijja, 1431

4:09 P.M.

Faisal returned to the vortex once more, this time dragging Muhammad Akbar along to comb hospitals, security checkpoints, mortuary services, and centres for lost children, yet Faisal thought, *My son isn't lost! He's kid...napped.* The word began to break in his mouth.

I'm the one who's lost.

At every juncture, Faisal and Muhammad reiterated the same statement with slight variations: a ten-year-old girl with kohl-lined eyes, arched eyebrows, thin lips, and dark brown skin; wearing a blue kurti with yellow hems.

Muhammad Akbar swiped to the most recent photograph of his daughter, which he had taken on his Samsung phone six hours before her disappearance. The image showed Mariam standing next to her mother, smiling in the central courtyard. Muhammad Akbar pointed at the golden hoops dangling from his daughter's earlobes and said, his face twisting in pain, Maybe she shouldn't have been wearing these. Then, he buried his face in his palms.

A receptionist at King Abdulaziz Hospital told them with nonchalance, Doesn't look like she left a trace.

And, this time, the employee at Ajyad Hospital was too busy to call other centres to inquire on Faisal's behalf, so Faisal and Muhammad Akbar had to go to different hospitals on foot, but there was no sign of Mariam anywhere—not at hospitals, morgues, centres for lost children, or at any mortuary service.

As Faisal was leaving Ajyad Hospital, Saud called his phone.

Bu Mishari! Where are you?

With the Indian man. Muhammad Akbar.

Any updates?

No. Where are you?

With Mazen. Handing out fliers.

Mazen?

My friend from college. We first met in America at college. He lives in Jeddah now, but he came to lend a helping hand.

God bless him.

Where can we find you?

We're on our way to the Security Operations Room.

We'll be there soon.

Faisal picked up the pace. Muhammad Akbar followed suit. Saud and Mazen were already waiting for them when Faisal and Muhammad Akbar reached the Sacred Mosque's Security Operations Room.

Mazen shook Faisal's hand, stood on tiptoe, then kissed Faisal's forehead.

Faisal felt as though his soul had aged a thousand years during this catastrophe. He struggled for air despite gently squeezing Mazen's forearm as a thank you, and then he walked up to the officers sitting at the front desk and said, while gesturing toward Muhammad Akbar, This man has lost his kid as well.

As well?

I was here a day ago. My son is missing. He's kid...napped.

Even with all the repetitions, it was becoming increasingly difficult for him to utter this word. When it came out, it shattered his heart the same way it broke apart in his mouth. Tears welled up in his eyes.

The officer spoke into his phone: The daughter of an Indian man went missing two days ago at The Sacred Mosque. He pointed at the waiting chairs, then whispered, Have a seat. And returned to his phone call.

Silence enveloped the four men as soon as they sat down. One of their phones beeped every once in a while, indicating a new text message or a call from friends and family that Saud and Faisal deliberately ignored.

But twenty minutes later, Saud got up to make a quick phone call and returned to ask Mazen if he could come with him on an errand.

Khair? Faisal asked.

All good, don't worry. We've raised a million dollars. The money is in Mazen's account now. We need to withdraw it in full, so we can be ready when Mishari is found.

Although Faisal nodded, he couldn't help but think, *There! They've already raised a million dollars! So, where the hell is my kid?*

When Saud and Mazen left The Centre for Security Operations, Faisal rested his head on the wall behind him and closed his eyes. Although the real ocean was far away, he felt the whirlpool in his head becoming more turbulent, so he opened his eyes and turned to Muhammad Akbar, who was sitting beside him—knees shaking and teeth clattering. Laying an open palm on Akbar's leg, Faisal said, Please stop moving.

Akbar started to squeeze his head.

Hang in there, Faisal drawled.

But she's only a girl, Mister Faisal. A young girl!

Does she know your phone number?

Mariam is smart. She has memorised my number, her mom's number, and her aunts' number in Delhi.

Does she speak Arabic?

She knows English very well and some Arabic. But she's a bright girl.

Faisal, closing his eyes once more, tried to recall his son's features. Mishari's face flashed into view momentarily before dissolving into Mariam's face. When he swayed on his chair, the sensation of floating in a whirlpool returned, and everything seemed to swirl—his thoughts, his body, and even his delirium tumbled violently on raging waves.

But he wasn't near the ocean. The real ocean was still far away.

Faisal slept without meaning to and woke up as if bitten by a snake.

How long has it been?

An hour.

Muhammad Akbar was neither shaking nor crying now. He sat rather stiffly and dry-eyed.

It worried Faisal, who got up to remind the officer at the front desk that they still needed to enter the surveillance room.

The officer assured Faisal that he hadn't forgotten them. There was just nothing new to report.

When can we go in?

An hour or two, perhaps. It's a hectic period. Every location is teeming with people. We need every screen to keep them safe.

Faisal returned to his seat, his thoughts steely, his body tense. He had forgotten all about the sacred rites. Did he really come to Mecca to perform the Hajj only two days ago? He called his brother. We haven't gone in yet. We've just been waiting all this time.

Saud exchanged a few words with his friend before returning to the call. Don't worry, he told Faisal. Mazen will handle the officers.

Half an hour later, Saud called back to say that Mazen had contacted his friends and colleagues. Some of the ones who lived in Mecca had direct contact with the officers stationed at The Sacred Mosque.

This is how things work around here.

Before you get off the phone, you ask your brother to share Mariam's photograph on the Internet. Although Saud uses his same network, only a few people engage with the post and even fewer share her image.

What changed?

Now you look at Muhammad Akbar and wonder if your son hadn't been kidnapped, would you have shown him compassion? Would you have even stopped to look at him? Would you have cared about Mariam? Or are you helping this man because it might lead you to your son?

The surveillance officers have all responded to Mazen's appeal. They usher you into the Security Operations Room once more.

Muhammad Akbar trails behind.

You enter the vast hall with thirty monitoring screens attached to thick, cylindrical metal pillars spread evenly along the walls.

Welcome, Bu Mishari! one of the officers calls. Over here, please.

The surveillants keep addressing you even though they're searching for Mariam and not your son.

The agent asks you to confirm: You said that you lost the girl two days ago during the afternoon prayer, and that she was sleeping near King Fahad Gate beside one of the columns. Correct?

Muhammad Akbar nods.

You nod.

Follow me, the officer says.

You step behind him.

Muhammad Akbar follows you.

The image on one surveillance screen shows a child sleeping next to a column. The officer resumes the feed.

A woman wearing a black niqab, white gloves, and a black abaya is caught on camera looking around, kneeling over Mariam, then sneaking the young girl underneath her loose, black cloak.

The little one can be seen kicking beneath the black fabric. But after a few moments, she stops.

The unknown woman hauls the limp kid over her shoulders, covers the child with her black robe, and hurries out of The Sacred Mosque.

Muhammad Akbar falls to his knees.

Muhammad Akbar falls into the abyss.

Mecca. Courtyard of the Sacred Mosque

8 Dhu Al-Hijja, 1431

6:30 P.M.

He barely recognised her.

Sumaya appeared almost ghostly: thin and frail—sitting in front of King Fahad Gate amid a flurry of sheets scattered haphazardly on the floor, each bearing Mishari's photo. But she was also holding a stack of monochromatic sheets in her hand, confusion visible in her eyes, and as she gave Saud one of them, she muttered, I don't get it.

What don't you get, Sumaya? Saud was equally baffled when he realised that the flier in his hand described the commandment against adultery and the guidelines for repentance. Someone had pasted a cartoon image of a grave on the bottom and a red rose with a fat dewdrop on the top. The dew resembled a teardrop blooming out of the red rose's pistil. Saud stood quietly, hoping for an explanation, peering back at Sumaya.

After Asr prayer, Sumaya began, a woman gave me these sheets and told me that Allah accepts my tawba. Sumaya's head dropped. A tear rolled down her cheek.

Saud, who was still gazing at Sumaya's red eyes and dry lips, asked, Who was she? And why did she say that to you?

It was hard for Sumaya to open her mouth and answer, I was in the mosque, kneeling on a prayer mat, crying my heart out. Maybe she assumed I was a—

A what? Say it!

Assumed I was...

An adulteress? Who regrets her sinful transgression?

Sumaya's eyes welled.

Saud felt disgust rumbling in his stomach. *How can a stranger assume that about another person?* Why didn't you throw the stack back at her face?

Sumaya wiped her tears with the edge of her sleeve. That woman gave me her fliers, and I gave her mine. Sumaya waved at the scattered sheets bearing Mishari's face, his bangs, and his gap-toothed smile.

Saud exhaled before scanning his surroundings. The sun had already set, and since most male pilgrims were on their way to Mina, the courtyard was nearly empty of men, though numerous women wearing black abayas strolled around.

I don't know, Sumaya mumbled.

What don't you know?

I don't know what I need to do, she said, her eyes bedevilled with pain and confusion, I performed all of my obligatory prayers and the optional ones, too. I gave the rest of my money to charity, all 500 dinars that remained from my salary this month. I donated every last fils. And I apologised to God. I spent all day begging him to pardon me. My sisters and friends back in Kuwait keep reminding me how important it is to seek God's forgiveness, and they told me that apologising earnestly to Allah wards off misfortunes, so I've been doing that all day. And I've been atoning... Believe me, Saud, I want to repent, but I don't yet know what sin I have committed.

Saud found himself sitting crossed-legged in front of her, asking softly, You think what happened to Mishari is divine punishment?

Her head drooped.

He held her hand and cried, Sumaya!

She let go of him, hiding her palms and fingers inside her long sleeves.

Her reaction made him flinch, since she had never jerked away from his touch before.

Sumaya muttered, God works in mysterious ways.

Saud's heartbeats raced as he wondered if he would ever discover the divine purpose behind Mishari's disappearance. *Was there a hidden meaning behind this hell?*

Saud, I want to atone for my sins! God wants me to repent!

Saud could only gape at her as she levelled her wet and bloodshot eyes at him as though it had just occurred to her to ask about her husband.

Where's Faisal?

Sumaya! Saud cried, holding her gaze. Look, it's already crazy that a stranger would approach someone crying and accuse them of infidelity out of the blue. But it's even crazier if you believe the accusation yourself!

She quietly pointed her index finger at the sky.

Saud's pupils dilated in anger. Have you lost your mind?

But Sumaya changed the subject again. Faisal... Do you know what's happening to him? He hasn't prayed since yesterday. She pulled on Saud's shirt and tearfully urged, Faisal needs to pray! He must!

Saud let out a deep breath. Steeling his nerves, he said, God alone is mighty, Sumaya.

But Sumaya pointed an accusatory finger at Saud's face. We won't find Mishari if we don't pray! How can we desert our moral obligations at a time like this? We are in desperate need of God's assistance, yet Faisal... There was a slight pause before she continued, Faisal has not performed a single prayer since yesterday—

Saud interjected, Sumaya! Don't you think you're worrying about the wrong things?

No! she screamed. Prayer is all we've got left!

Saud inhaled, then exhaled. Can't you see that Faisal is only thinking about his son? And don't you think God knows that?

She glowered at him with horrified eyes, lips arching in a frown, But I am Mishari's mother! And even though I always think about him, I still pray. My heart is breaking into shreds! I am dying, Saud. I am dying... Sumaya sobbed, burying her face in her black veil, her body shaking uncontrollably.

Relax, Sumaya, please.

But nothing could calm her in that state, so Saud got up, left her weeping on the floor, and went to search for holy water and some dates. He returned twenty minutes later to find her crying in the same place, her forehead plastered to the ground in the Kaaba's direction. Saud perched quietly beside her and waited for her to complete her sujood. Then, when she raised her head, he gave her a Zamzam bottle and said, Here. Drink this.

Sumaya accepted, her fingers trembling, her lips dry and cracked.

When was the last time you ate something? he asked.

She didn't answer. Instead, she thought, *What an absurd question...*

Saud calculated the hours in his head. *She hasn't eaten anything since Mishari disappeared thirty hours ago.* He opened the white plastic box and gave her a date. Go on, eat this.

She grabbed the box, then got up to share the traditional snack with other pilgrims.

Saud lunged forward to stop her. No, no! These are for you! You should eat them.

She retorted with a pout, But we have to be charitable.

Eat something, Sumaya. For Mishari's sake.

She shook her head. I'm not hungry.

But you'll faint if you go on like this, and if you faint, you won't be able to keep looking for him.

Still shaking her head, she said, I'm fine, then plopped down to collect her fliers.

But before she could hand them out again, Saud tried one last time to stop her. Sumaya, at least eat one.

Directing her pain-stricken eyes at him, she said, Tell your brother to pray, or else we'll never find him.

Mecca. The Sacred Mosque

8 Dhu Al-Hijja, 1431

7:37 P.M.

Faisal left the Security Operations Room, towing Muhammad Akbar along by the arm. By now, the hallways in The Sacred Mosque were nearly empty of male pilgrims and were filled instead with women.

Muhammad Akbar resisted like a child, repeatedly asking Faisal to leave him alone so he could drop to the ground and bang his head against the marble floor. Ya Allah! he cried.

But Faisal wouldn't let him go. He held on tighter and pulled him up, ordering the Indian man to come along: I'm only helping you return to your wife. She must be worried sick!

Muhammad Akbar continued his caterwauling.

There's no reason to scream, Faisal said, nobody's listening! You're alone now. Completely! Faisal didn't know if he was addressing these words to the man who couldn't understand a word of Arabic or if he was speaking to himself. As he loosened his grip on the foreigner's arm, Faisal suddenly felt an overwhelming vulnerability bursting out of him, forcing him to face his solitude—its inevitability and its endlessness. You are alone! He bellowed once more. Do you understand what I'm saying? It's every man for himself! It always has been! You need to handle your affairs from this point onward. His voice cracked before adding, You better not be sitting around hoping to be rescued because no one's coming. Tears streamed down his cheeks and his chest heaved. The ones you're especially relying on for help…? He added, They won't be coming.

The silence in the sky weighed heavily on his chest. For an instant, it seemed that even though he was speaking in Arabic, this bald and skinny Indian man in his forties, with round-rimmed glasses and wet eyes, feverishly mumbling in Urdu, might be the only person in the world who understood him. And because the English language they had both mastered professionally was now unreachable, as incomprehensible as a talisman, both men found themselves reverting to their mother tongue the way terrified children scamper back to their parents. Yet, despite their linguistic disparity, they understood, perfectly well, each word they uttered to one another.

Akbar's expression of fear morphed into indignation, and he screamed at Faisal in Urdu, Jili jao!

Saud then called to ask about their updates.

Faisal shared the same story: a woman wearing a niqab and white gloves carrying a sleeping child outside the mosque…

The same woman?

No. Slimmer.

Then there must be others.

Faisal turned to the Indian man. Will you stop trying to push me away?

Saud exhaled. Why don't you just leave him alone?

Muhammad Akbar still sobbed and begged, Mister Faisal! Please, let me go!

Stop acting like this! Come with me!

Saud spoke into the phone again, We have to search for them.

Who?

Can you please let the man go so you can focus on me for one second?

Faisal, who stopped moving, glanced at the man on the floor, beating his head with his hands. I can't leave him, he said into the phone. Something told Faisal that he had to hold on to this grieving Indian as if he were the last straw that would break the camel's back.

I said we should search for the rest of the children.

Faisal finally let go of Muhammad Akbar, stood in place, and wondered whether he could return to the vortex once more to watch another child kick under the black fabric then suddenly stop. And that's when he figured it out, and mumbled, They use their gloves to drug them.

In the corner, Akbar curled into a ball, snuck his head between his knees, and began to ramble in Urdu.

Faisal understood only one word: Allah.

Bu Mishari? Saud's voice called through the speaker. You there?

Faisal swallowed, then said, I'm here.

Could he re-enter the labyrinth again for other missing children?

Muhammad Akbar's face was now shining with devotion, and he was raising his arms high.

I'm also positive that there are others, Faisal said. But why should we look for them? Why not focus our efforts on our kid?

Saud replied, Because one child will lead us to another.

Faisal felt his chest constrict. *How many have already fallen victim to female criminals slithering between believers in The Sacred Mosque, drugging children before kidnapping them?* He ignored his thirst, swallowed with difficulty, then asked another question: How can we even begin to track the others?

We'll look at all the reports of missing children over the past few days. Mazen can help.

Faisal turned to Muhammad Akbar, who had now prostrated in the direction of the Kaaba, plastering his forehead to the floor, his wails escalating.

Fine. Let's look for the others.

Faisal got off the phone, marched toward his companion, and urged him to get up.

Mecca. Rooftop of The Sacred Mosque

8 Dhu Al-Hijja, 1431

11:47 P.M.

Pigeons were flocking in circles above the Kaaba in a parallel circuit, but now that male pilgrims had moved on to Mina, only women, guards, and janitors wandered through sacred squares and hallways. While the sky above was dark, the city of Mecca was vibrantly lit, anticipating the holy season's promise of endless blessings.

The two brothers had gone up to the roof in search of a quiet place, and they sat with four documents in their hands, looking down at the Kaaba.

Mazen had gathered every missing person report from The Centre of Lost Children and the Security Operations Room, which they realised included children from Chad, Eritrea, Ethiopia, and India.

Faisal's voice wavered before adding, And one boy from Kuwait. He closed his eyes to conjure Mishari's face: The beauty spot on the neck, the gap in the teeth—these consecutive details trickled out from a deep corporeal place, as if they were blood cells instead of memories. The sheer flood of piercing data pounding through his arteries made him smart from the pain. That's how he thought about the son he had sired. Flipping the four pages back and forth, Faisal asked, So, four more kids?

Saud, who seemed angry as he studied the sheets clenched in his fist, disagreed with a shake of his head. There must be others, he said, his eyebrows knitted.

What do you mean?

I mean children other than the ones mentioned here.

What makes you so sure?

He tossed the sheets away and ventured an explanation, These are the cases of the families who contacted the police. There must be others who didn't reach out to local authorities.

Why would anyone who's lost a child not file a report?

Saud scanned the cleaning crew below them, in their green uniforms, sweeping one of the hallways in a single line, then asked his brother a rhetorical question: If you were convicted of a crime, or if you were homeless, or an illegal resident, or an undocumented migrant who had managed to enter the country to perform the sacred rites—would you ask the authorities to help you find your child?

They sat in silence for some time until Faisal peered into his brother's face. Noticing the pursed lips and furrowed brows, he thought Saud must be mulling over the facts that they had accumulated thus far, so he turned to the pages in his hand and wondered aloud, Other than their youth, what do boys and girls from India, Eritrea, Chad, and Kuwait have in common?

They're all poor.

Mishari isn't.

It's true that the others are poor and desperate, but what good is that to the kidnappers? The children's parents won't offer a million-dollar ransom like you. Your son is different from the rest, and you know it. The criminals could now call you demanding millions, but what do they want with Mariam and the rest?

What are they after?

As though listening to your thoughts, Saud mutters, They're not in it for the money.

Your heart sinks, and you start to tremble. Your desperation has never been more pronounced. Those criminals don't care about the price tag printed on your fliers. They want your son—flesh, and bones.

Your voice trembles when you ask your brother, If they don't care about the money, then what do they care about?

I don't know.

Was Saud oblivious to the grim possibilities awaiting those young children? Or was he merely feigning ignorance to allay your fears? Your mind wanders to Mariam, her blue kurti, and her golden hoops. What connects her to Mishari? Nothing but their youth. Childhood is the only thing they share. It's futile to claim anything different. The world has been reeling over Mishari's disappearance for hours and hasn't shown any interest in Mariam's. You are privileged. And you are grateful to be privileged. But Mariam's face and her earrings aren't leaving you alone.

And now you feel like everybody else, standing on the same level of humanity—below the starting line. Your son has been kidnapped with others from India, Eritrea, Ethiopia, and Chad. Neither your wealth nor oceans of oil underneath your feet, nor your brother, who came to rescue you in his engineering uniform, can redeem your son.

Welcome to hell, where everyone is equal.

Welcome to the world of crime.

Day 3

Sumaya knew she wouldn't fall asleep but kept trying anyway. Drunk on hypervigilance, she had spent the entire day chasing children from India, Afghanistan, Pakistan, and various parts of Africa. She would open the Galaxy Jewels box that she had purchased from Bin Dawood's Markets and use the chocolate to entice children to stop and talk to her, and she would ask, as soon as one of them moved closer, to pick a flavour. Then: What's your name?

Abdulfatheel.

Where are you from?

Khartoum.

How old are you?

Seven.

Wow! You're big and powerful like my son. Let me show you his picture. Look! Mishari is your age. Do you like Batman? Because he does. Have you seen him anywhere? No? Listen. A poor woman confused him for her son and accidentally took him with her. Can you tell her I'm not mad at her if you see her? I swear! All I want is my son because he's mine and wants me to be his mother. Me. Not her. OK?

The kid would giggle at the madwoman and dart away.

And Sumaya would search for another and another.

She had been running all day. Her wide purse, hanging from her shoulder, included a green prayer mat, a Quran wrapped in purple velvet, and a pair of black Crocs stuffed in a blue nylon bag. She had come off as a nutcase, carrying the whole world in her massive purse, sprinting all over the place.

Her heart has been beating irregularly since her son's disappearance. A sheet of sleeping pills lay on her bedside table. She couldn't recall the number of pills she'd swallowed already, but she knew it was more than four because Saud had convinced her that sleeping would improve her ability to search for her son.

He had said, You'll faint if you continue like this, and you won't be able to find him.

And because she needed to find him, she needed the energy to keep on searching with all her heart.

However, despite ingesting one sedative after another, she found herself more alert than ever until half an hour later, when the room's inanimate objects began to speak and move and children, popping out of nowhere, began to populate the room.

Sumaya lunges after them.

Tell her I'm not mad! she screams. Do you want some chocolate? Come here, let me buy you some candy or a Happy Meal from McDonald's. Do you prefer a chicken meal from Al Tazaj? Or how about I take you to

Colour Me Mine instead, so we can etch your name on a ceramic mug? Or we can create a medallion out of crushed crayons! Just tell me what you want, and I'll buy it! Come here! Kids! I'll buy you anything you want!

That's when she spots him among the crowd. Sumaya can't believe her eyes. He is looking back at her and laughing.

Mishari? she says softly. Is that you? Honey?

He runs across the sandy plains near a golden hillock, the way he did in Kuwait last winter near Subiyah's desert, when the family went sliding over the dunes.

He is right here now, chortling.

Sumaya bounds after him. You're here? You're really here?

Hair full of sand, Mishari's thick bangs spill over his eyes.

I should've known you'd be here! she cries. You love sandboarding!

But Mishari keeps evading her.

Where are you, baby?

Mama! he calls to her before hiding behind a hillock and yelling, Come find me!

Honey? Where did you go?

Sumaya, who thought she was running, was stretched out on the ground, dreaming with her eyes open, her legs kicking in the air.

And when Faisal returned to the room, he found Sumaya in the sujood position, prostrating on bent knees, her face pressed to the floor—the Kaaba behind her—yowling with all her heart.

Mecca. Hajar Tower

9 Dhu Al-Hijja, 1431

8:06 A.M.

Faisal was buttoning his dishdasha.

Sumaya was staring at the ceiling.

He had a lot to share about last night, but the words remained dry and hard like stones in his mouth. He feared these words' endless potential to inflict damage and sought to escape the room as fast as he could—before Sumaya could pollute the silence—but she asked him a question as soon as he touched the doorknob.

Did you sleep?

No.

He wanted to leave. However, she parted her lips once more, and her voice came out hoarse, weak after hours of constant weeping. What about me? Did I sleep at all?

No. He found himself automatically clarifying, Let's just say that you spent the whole night wailing, that you vomited—twice—and that I had to clean the room after each time.

She peered at him, her eyes full of naïveté, full of that unbearable innocence that goes hand in hand with ignorance.

I don't remember anything.

Good for you. Get some rest.

I'm going down to The Sacred Mosque.

Suit yourself.

Although Faisal twisted the doorknob, his feet remained rooted in place, so he closed the door and asked, Sumaya, what pills did you take yesterday?

She turned to her bedside table, grabbed the pill strip, moved it closer to her eyes, and answered after reading the label, Stilnox.

Where did you get it from?

I found it in my medicine pile. They're just sleeping pills.

Faisal exhaled. Please, Sumaya, I don't need this right now.

Because she couldn't comprehend his statement, Sumaya asked, What is it that you don't need?

I can't be worrying about what you're up to, what you might do, and the impending chaos it would cause—all of this while I'm busy searching for my son. You could've died last night. I don't need this on top of everything else.

Sumaya couldn't believe what she was hearing, so she said while gaping at her husband, Faisal... I was only trying to sleep.

Maybe you should stop trying. He looked away.

What's that supposed to mean?

How could you be thinking of rest at a time like this?

She gasped.

You're thinking of rest and prayer while your son—

Sumaya's voice came out shaky, Why do you think I tried to sleep last night? Hm? I did it for him!

Grimacing, Faisal let out a sarcastic huff.

Sumaya's eyes filled with tears and her arms wildly gesticulated as she said, I couldn't see straight! I couldn't hear anything! I fell down the stairs twice! And people kept laughing at me whenever I talked. That's when I realised that nothing I said made sense! So, it occurred to me that... It occurred... If I slept, maybe for two hours... Maybe I'd be able to search for him again.

Her tears, her weakness, and her flailing arms were too much for Faisal to bear. Although it became harder for him to breathe, Faisal still told her, Don't cry, Sumaya. I don't need this right now.

You blame me!

For the first time since Mishari's disappearance, he yelled at his wife, Blame you? Me? Have I ever opened my mouth and accused you of anything? Have I ever mentioned who let go of Mishari's hand? Have I done that?

Peering deeply at her husband, Sumaya said, Then look me in the eyes and tell me you don't blame me for what happened! Do it! Right now!

Faisal averted his gaze.

Tears welled in Sumaya's eyes.

When Faisal next spoke, his voice came out harsh and cold, But it was your idea, wasn't it? You're the one who wanted him to come here.

Sumaya buried her face in her palms. Eyes still brimming with tears, she wailed, I couldn't leave a boy his age with his grandmother! He'd drive her crazy!

This time, Faisal's voice adopted a veneer of eerie calm. Sumaya, you don't need to lie to me. We could've left him with Saud or one of your sisters, but you're the one who wanted him to come and gaze at the Kaaba! And I...? I'm the son of a bitch who tried to make you happy! So, tell me. Are you happy now?

Lifting her head, Sumaya watched her husband through wet eyes, then pointed an accusatory finger at his face. If you care so much about your son, then why did you circumambulate alone? Why didn't you walk beside me and hold my hand? Why didn't you hold his?

Shut up! he cried, his face turning red, his own eyes watering as he felt the weight of a million fingers clasping his throat.

You preceded us by a whole turn! You were that far ahead! Sumaya wept again.

Faisal wracked his memory for yesterday's events. *When did all this space come between us? Sumaya's footsteps are smaller. So are Mishari's...* Faisal didn't mean to leave them behind. *It just happened.* First, he found himself ahead by a few steps, then he walked and walked until it became a whole turn. But he kept looking back! He did! Now and then, he turned to check on his wife and son...

Sumaya said, Faisal, nobody's to blame. She'd had an epiphany while wiping the tears from her eyes and nose, so after taking a deep breath, she added, We cannot circumvent God's will.

Faisal grimaced again. Who are you lying to? A disparaging snort escaped his nostrils. What the hell were we thinking, Sumaya? We brought a seven-year-old child to a city already choking on its countless visitors. Just what were we thinking? Then, lowering his voice to a piercing whisper, he spat, And what were you thinking when you wanted your son to marvel at the House of God? Well, he's seen it now. What happens next? Do you get your one-way ticket to paradise? Do you get showered with heavenly merits? Just tell me, Sumaya, are you happy now?

Gawking at her husband, she asked, How can you say all that to me?

Faisal let out a deep breath. It might be best if we avoided each other for a while. Sumaya, I can't stand the sight of you anymore.

This time, his fingers did not hesitate. He turned the doorknob and stormed out.

Mecca. Between The Towers and Mecca Centre

9 Dhu Al-Hijja, 1431

8:47 A.M.

Faisal, Saud, and Mazen stopped on the path between Mecca Centre and The Towers.

They had been walking beside the old shops that sold an assortment of items: miswaks, prayer mats and prayer beads in different colours, watches that sounded the call to prayer, nail polish, and kohl pens.

In the top corner of the nearest shop, a small television was broadcasting the loud voice of a cleric who was preaching into a microphone, Dear pilgrim! You cannot even imagine the grandeur of the blessings God will lavish upon you if he deems your Hajj ritual valid and if you manage to stand obediently on Mount Arafa!

Is it Arafa already? Faisal muttered, then turned around to take in his surroundings. Every inch of the courtyard in The Sacred Mosque was overflowing with female pilgrims strolling in their black abayas.

What's going on here? he asked.

Mazen explained, It's a Meccan tradition. On Arafa, male pilgrims continue their ritual. Those who haven't participated in the Hajj resume their daily work. And women usually come here.

Faisal surveyed the legions in black, hoping to locate the one who...

Suddenly, the cleric exclaimed, You cannot even comprehend how merits are aggregated on this day. It is said that pilgrims will receive a 700-fold increase in blessings. This does not mean a multiplication of 700! The cleric held a sheet of paper high above his head, which included increments of 21, and then he said, Look at this! When it comes to spiritual merit, 21-fold equates to 1,048,576 hasana! So just imagine what a 700-fold increase means, spiritually! It is a number that cannot be grasped, and we can neither write it down nor read it out! But this is your gift, dear pilgrim, 700-fold for every good deed you perform today!

Faisal's mouth went dry as he watched the integers spread across the page. He saw them roll over to the following line, the one below, and the one after until they hit the bottom of the sheet, and he still couldn't believe that it was Arafa, and that Time had carried on despite his son's kidnapping, and that millions of pilgrims would now trek to the sacred mountain as though Faisal's world had not experienced a complete and utter demolition.

He felt exiled under the silent sky.

Then, returning his absentminded gaze to the row of integers on the cleric's sheet of paper and the pudgy finger still moving across the document, Faisal noticed a confident smile on the cleric's face as he calculated the profits in this business without losses.

But then he thought of Sumaya, and his blood boiled. Taking a confrontational step toward the store, Faisal glared at the TV in the top corner, yet when he heard Mazen's voice behind him speaking on the phone, Faisal turned to reflect on the local man who had come to lend a helping hand.

Faisal recalled their first meeting.

Mazen, who wasn't wearing any headgear, had been handing out fliers in a white dishdasha, his sleeves rolled up, his fingers stained with black from the fliers' photocopying ink.

He was now sporting a white T-shirt and grey sweatpants and speaking to his wife on the other line, saying, I can't return to Jeddah and leave my friends at a time like this.

An involuntary smile spread across Faisal's lips. *What's the point of offering to help? Does Mazen think he can respond to a crime in a city as holy and as crowded as this one? Nobody can.*

Faisal looked up. The clock on the Tower, which penetrated the vast blue sky like a mast, flashed 8:47 a.m., confirming Faisal's hypothesis that Time was on the side of the criminals.

Then, a small, open palm stretching below Faisal's nose interrupted his thoughts.

Hey, haj! Give me some of what Allah has given you.

I'm not a pilgrim.

The cleric on the screen was now accepting phone calls from his viewers. A woman called to inquire about the heavenly reward for children who perform the Hajj.

Faisal felt his stomach lurch.

Would I get any merits for bringing my five-year-old son with me? the woman asked.

Nodding slowly before responding, the cleric said with the confident smile that never wavered, My dear sister, your son doesn't need to go on this trip because only adults are obligated to perform the Hajj. Having said that, if the kid undertakes this sacred rite with his parents, God will certainly accept his Hajj ritual. This boy will receive the full merits of completing the rites, and all those who helped him will receive their shares on top of an additional batch equivalent to the child's blessings!

Faisal's stomach rumbled, so he bent over, squeezed his waist, and tried to resist the vomit threatening to surge out of his mouth. *Those who help the child complete the Hajj ritual receive an extra batch of blessings? What about the cost of his kidnapping? Who pays that price?*

Saud hurried over. You OK?

Attempting to stand upright, yet feeling all his weight on his knees, Faisal shook his head and told his brother, It's nothing.

His phone rang, so he looked down at the name flashing on the screen, and exhaled before saying, She keeps calling.

Who?

Mom. I don't want to hear her voice. I can't.

Let me talk to her.

Faisal lobbed the phone to his brother. *Why not? Let him be the one to recount the disaster.*

Hi mom. Thank God. No. Not at all. I hope we find him today. Please pray for us. Faisal is busy. He'll call you later. God bless you too.

Faisal gave his brother an appreciative nod, feeling as though Saud had just martyred himself for his older brother's sake.

Saud got off the phone. But before he could return the phone to Faisal, the phone rang again. This time, an unknown Saudi number was blinking.

The two brothers locked eyes.

Give it to me, Faisal demanded, stretching his arm toward his brother.

Saud didn't budge.

I said give me the phone.

The younger brother took a step backward, turned around, then answered the call himself. Hello?

I have your son.

CHAPTER FOUR

'ASEER

arduous; composed of numerous parts; a mountainous district in
southwestern Arabia between Hejaz and Yemen

A long, jagged crack in the mirror cleaved Ruwaina's face in two.

Standing in a stark restroom next to a broken squatting toilet and a plastic bucket, she carefully studied the bruise on the corner of her mouth and her turgid eyelid. As she leaned across the sink for a closer look at her reflection, Ruwaina noticed a cluster of red spots festering on both cheeks.

A long time had passed since she'd last seen rashes like these. It was twenty-five years ago, at Leitchuor Camp, after her aunt had toppled over from the pain of scraping off her own black skin just to become lighter. Ruwaina saw the blood gushing out of her aunt's mouth turn black. She then started to groan like someone spewing their intestines. As her aunt lifted her head for the last time, blood streamed down the sides of her mouth, and the whites of her eyes turned completely yellow.

The rashes first appeared on Ruwaina's face while she was bolting out and screaming for help. By the time she had returned to their tent, men from a UN refugee agency were already carrying her aunt's white-shrouded corpse on a stretcher.

And now, standing in front of the broken mirror, Ruwaina tried to recall the features of that same woman who had raised her, with whom she had shared a home—the woman she had called aunty.

She couldn't.

It was as if a massive brick wall now stood between her current life and her previous one.

Ruwaina stooped to lift the hem of her dress, tied it around her waist, filled the bucket with water, then washed between her legs. For the second night in a row, Jerjes had buried her face in a pillow with one hand and reached up her leg with the other. He had even asked her to roll him a cigarette when he was done, but she had buttoned up quietly and left, followed by his mocking laughter. *It's over,* she thought, and yet she couldn't help but contemplate another incomprehensible fact. Despite pummelling her in front of everyone during yesterday's lunch and pursuing Saliha with his eyes all day—it was Ruwaina whom Jerjes had called to his bed at night.

Again and again, she let the water rush out of the plastic bucket and stream down her crotch, thighs, calves, and shins. Ruwaina scrubbed her body with a bar of soap, washed then dried her skin, untied the hem of her dress, which was knotted around her waist, and let it drop around her ankles before closing up her buttons. When she removed her silk headdress to drape it around her shoulders, her curly hair with numerous braids popped out, then hung loose—red at the edges, white at the roots. Ruwaina leaned over the sink again to reinspect the tumescent bruises on her dark face, her distress at their familiarity mounting.

She wasn't sure why she remembered her old life or her aunt's torn skin and bloody guts. Ruwaina had never been a stranger to gore, for she had witnessed bucketfuls of blood throughout her life—enough to flood a whole desert. But the sight of her bloodstain today, her swollen eyelid, her frizzy braids, and the memory of Jerjes dragging her by the hair the day before...

For the first time, she felt truly exhausted. Quickly splashing water on her face, she tried to conceal the tears that filled her eyes. Ruwaina didn't know why she was now recalling all these incandescent memories she assumed she had forgotten. Yet, they pulsated out of that revolting period of her life as if they'd always been buried deep inside her.

The night before, while Jerjes's elbow kneaded the pillow smothering her face, Ruwaina was bombarded by a flurry of thoughts, beginning with their first meeting.

Jerjes was only five years old, standing amid a sea of corpses: refugees in the camp who had lost their lives to the fever that had claimed her aunt's life a few weeks earlier. Tears had streamed down Jerjes's cheeks and snot had dripped from his nostrils. Because he'd been left alone in the world, Ruwaina scooped him under her wing and into her tent. Shortly afterward, everyone treated them as if they had always been siblings.

Ruwaina, who was fifteen at the time, had often carried him on her shoulder among thousands of refugees, whenever she sought their share of malt and milk. On days when journalists and photographers visited the camp, Ruwaina would dart toward them, Jerjes latching tightly onto her back, so that he could be photographed and appear on the news. It was one of the few joys they'd shared.

Among the flurry of memories, Ruwaina also recalled the hours she'd spent waiting in front of the tent of the United Nations' High Commissioner for Human Rights, her bare feet aching from standing on the jagged white pebbles that paved the path toward the tent until the Commissioner came out to offer Ruwaina a new set of clothes.

She also remembered the group of unknown men who had shoved her into an empty tent, where some of them had clasped her mouth, and others had let their hands crawl under her skirt. Young Jerjes, her supposed brother, bawled outside until the men were done.

The rainy seasons then crossed her mind. It was a time when their camp would drown and their toilets break down. Jerjes would be plunked on her shoulders as Ruwaina sloshed through knee-high muddy water in search of a dry spot. She would sometimes seek a steep rock face to shield them from the rain, sit beside Jerjes on the dirt, and gaze at the men below trying to direct wastewater back toward the riverbed, and she would wonder, as she peered into Jerjes's face, if they both came from the same place. Jerjes. Ruwaina. These were common names of the indigenous, which had been assigned to them, like all the other orphans, by the camp administration, and just like everybody else, they had learned to speak Amharic.

Ruwaina often wondered how she ended up at Leitchuor camp. Her aunt had only said she'd found Ruwaina as a newborn baby soaked in blood and vernix, waxy and white, her umbilical cord still attached to her abdomen. Like other children in the camp, she was probably the fruit of an illicit affair.

Ruwaina also tried to find out Jerjes's background from him, but he didn't know what she was talking about, and though she had asked around, no one at the camp could tell her anything about him. Why would anyone waste time on such trivial details in an overcrowded oasis, where resources were scarce and need aplenty? Why indeed would anyone waste time on such insignificant details? She wondered whether armed conflict, famine, plague, or something else had caused Jerjes's family to leave their homeland, since one could generally surmise people's places of origin based on the reason for their family's displacement. There had never been much difference between her facial features and his—but now, as she pondered her reflection in the mirror, she realised that she couldn't even recognise herself.

Last night, she had angered Jerjes by reminding him that she had cared for him her whole life. But it had become clear to her that he now sought to renounce their old ties, forged in their shared histories of hunger, orphanhood, and disease—their old ties that kept forcing him back to her. Jerjes thought he was capable of escaping the inescapable fact that it was Ruwaina, and nobody else in the world, who knew him inside out.

But what made her think of Leitchuor now?

She left the camp thirty years ago. It happened at night, when an armed militia member used a black cloth to blindfold her before ushering her and Jerjes into a Jeep that transported them to their new life—a starkly different life—one of clean clothes, abundant food, medicine, and vaccines. The militia, which needed recruits, had kidnapped ten children from Leitchuor, all orphans. In the beginning, Ruwaina couldn't refuse the militia's orders because one of them would put a gun to her head as he ordered her to pour melted plastic over the eyes of their new young captives. Months later, however, the militia no longer needed to intimidate Ruwaina, for she had started to perform her tasks without hesitation.

Jerjes had grown up among the smugglers, carrying a gun and dealing in food, money, and women.

In sync and intimate, they worked together: Jerjes kidnapping the children and Ruwaina inflicting them with disabilities. Despite all the other women who'd previously shared his bed, it was Ruwaina to whom he always returned—for she was a mixture of older sister and experienced mistress.

Ruwaina opened the bathroom door and shuffled out, struggling with each step from the residual pain of Jerjes's aggressive penetration over the past couple of days, the pain of her head repeatedly smacking against the concrete floor, and the pain of the stinging in her eyes from the dust that had scattered once her head slammed against the wall. Even the mere sight of her wrinkled dress aggravated her emotional distress. Everything, it seemed, was clashing. Yet, this emotional turmoil strangely afforded her a newfound clarity—a broader, calmer perspective, as though she had managed to dissociate and float outside her body.

Ruwaina unlocked the door to the house and left to sit on the stoop and contemplate the sunrise, her heart twisting in agony, her eyes scanning the wilderness: 'Asir's towering mountains and the grove formed by juniper, acacia and cypress trees. Looking up, she saw the sparrows and goldfinches swirling in the sky, then she closed her eyes.

Details from varied memories weighed heavily on her chest: the path paved in white pebbles that meandered between the tents, the tents themselves filled with famished Black bodies, and Black bodies with hollow cheeks and protruding cheekbones.

And for the first time, she found herself yearning for her little tent at Lietchuor camp and the innocence she'd lost.

'Asir. Wadi Rada

9 Dhu Al-Hijja, 1431

6:03 A.M.

When Uthman parked the blue Caprice in front of the house and killed the motor, a cloud of dust huffed out of the exhaust pipe. Turning to the passenger seat, he quickly grabbed a roll of fliers with his right hand and tucked a folded newspaper under his left arm.

As he got out of the car, he found Ruwaina sitting on the stoop, her face bruised, her eyelid swollen. She seemed unhinged; a filmy glaze had coated her eyes, and she was muttering and chuckling to herself while drawing in the sand with a scrawny twig: stars, hearts, and Amharic letters.

Uthman slammed the car door shut.

Ruwaina raised her head, and when her eyes met Uthman's, she smiled.

It was a smile that made his skin crawl. *Damn the old hag when she smiles!* Uthman couldn't tell whether Ruwaina was happy or upset. *What does that strange expression even mean?*

Upon returning from lunch the previous day, he'd found Jerjes choking Ruwaina before punching her neck, slamming her head against the wall, and reprimanding her for squandering a full day's work. In his rage, Jerjes had said that because of her they could no longer return to The Sacred Mosque to abduct more kids.

The whole world is turned upside down over that Kuwaiti son of a bitch! Jerjes had howled.

Ruwaina had tried to communicate something to Jerjes with her large, bewildered eyes, but she...

You cost me a fortune! Still fuming, he had flung her rotund body at the wall.

Ruwaina had gotten up while rubbing her head.

Saliha, who'd let out a squeaky laugh, had swiftly covered her mouth with the palm of her hand.

After glaring at Saliha from the corners of her eyes, Ruwaina had turned her attention back to Jerjes to gibe: A traitor can only betray another traitor.

He'd peeled off one of his slippers to hurl straight at her.

But Ruwaina had dodged, swerved, and bolted away—her wide backside wobbling left and right.

What are we going to do now? Adania had asked.

By then, Jerjes was heaving, so he plopped down while leaning against the wall, and Saliha went to bring him a glass of water after which he'd said, Let's wait until tomorrow. We can kidnap five more children during Arafa. It's the only day pilgrims gather in one place, so even if the world had a single police force, it wouldn't stand a chance against us—and those pilgrims won't ruin their prayers for a few missing kids.

Uthman, who was now standing in front of the house, began to wonder what Jerjes would do once he'd found out about the flier that had recently spread, the flier Uthman currently held in his fist.

With suspicious cordiality, Ruwaina greeted Uthman in Amharic, Salam no!

Shut up! he said.

You too, Uthman? She chuckled. Since Jerjes started battering her in public, all the other members had become more emboldened, *Even this skinny, ignorant youth.* She noticed the roll and the folded newspaper and asked, What do you have there?

None of your business!

Uthman tried to walk past her, but she wouldn't budge. Jerjes is asleep, she spat.

Get out of my way! Uthman stretched his lanky leg over her but couldn't curl it around her massive, flabby body. Her corpulence made him panic.

Ruwaina was laughing at his gangly body and the way it struggled to step over her wide backside, which was blocking the entrance to the door. Show me what you got.

Uthman lifted his leg and stepped on her thigh. His blood was boiling. I said move!

Seizing upon their proximity to each other, Ruwaina snatched the newspaper, spread it open, and gasped when she saw Mishari's photo above the astronomical figure, so she cried, Wi ni! Her face was beaming with pleasure

Give that back, he said, grasping the sheet and holding on.

Ruwaina chortled as she let go. I told you! I told you guys he was worth millions! When Uthman kicked her waist, she stumbled sideways, clutching her stomach, a joyful expression on her face despite the pain.

That demented smile seemed like an organic feature of her face—like a nose or an eyebrow. Damn it! I said move!

Scooting an inch to the side, just enough to let Uthman squeeze through the doorway, she muttered before he left: Too bad, he'll hog it all himself.

Like electricity shooting up his spine there was a piercing effect to her words that made him anxious.

Uthman looked down and saw her whispering to herself: A million dollars.

Who? he asked. Who are you talking about?

A fool swimming in the river would still die of thirst.

She spoke only in idioms: The frog who wanted to become an elephant blew up, a traitor can only betray another traitor, the devil enters like a needle and spreads like an oak tree, a fool swimming in the river would still die of thirst—her idioms were endless, and nobody knew why she said them.

What do you mean? Tell me!

You're useless.

Tell me!

But Ruwaina went back to her previous position. Chanting softly to herself, she grabbed the twig and drew more stars, hearts, and Amharic letters in the dirt.

'Asir. Wadi Rada.

9 Dhu Al-Hijja, 1431

8:07 A.M.

His uncle taps his fingers on the wheel to the beat of the song blasting through the speakers, joyfully swaying his head to the melody, sighing and crying every once in a while, Allah! Allah! Just listen to his talent!

Muhammad Al-Misbah's voice, crooning through the radio, seeps into Mishari's skin.

> *Time has betrayed our reunion,*
>
> *separating me from you...*

The song twisting Mishari's heart was a song he didn't like.

His uncle turns to him and asks, Have you fastened your seatbelt?

Mishari checks first, then comfortably sits, happy to be surrounded by some of his favourite things: his red T-shirt with the galloping horse above his heart; the yellow colour of his uncle's car, its black leather seats, and its convertible top. He also adores his glossy Crocs with the Batman logo and their new, rubber smell.

His uncle sings along to the chorus: When brittle hearts disintegrate, their ashes burn...

Mishari's heart constricts, though he watches his uncle's sheer delight in al-Misbah's voice, turning up the volume during the parts he enjoys most and lowering it again to resume their conversation.

Hey, tiny pilgrim, ready for your first pilgrimage?

Mishari nods.

Saud continues goading his nephew, I'm expecting the most expensive souvenirs.

Mishari asks his uncle what sorts of gifts he hopes to get.

A miswak bundle, rare prayer beads, and a bottle of cologne from Junaid. Then he lowers his voice and says cheekily, I want you to spend all your father's money.

Mishari wonders if Mecca has any shops. His uncle's laughter makes him turn his head to the side.

Al-Nitfa's going to Mecca!

I'm not little anymore! Mishari complains, since he is now seven years and three months: a perfectly suitable age to perform the Hajj ritual.

The pilgrims better not mistake you for a pebble during the Stoning. I don't want them to cast you at the Devil!

Uncle!

But his uncle goes back to singing: If now's the time for us to part, when will we reunite?

They both get out after the car stops near a juice bar. Saud holds Mishari's hand so they can cross the street together. Mishari glances at his uncle's hand, which suddenly transforms into a smaller, darker fist marred by scars.

Mishari looks up and sees a massive woman wearing a niqab, who tightens her grip on his hand and asks: Are you lost? They walk side by side, cross the pavement, then stop on the sidewalk.

Mishari looks up again.

Now his uncle is standing still in her place. Only after a beautiful woman passes by does his uncle's facial expression change. He knits his eyebrows and purses his lips, then whispers unintelligible words.

Slice!

When his uncle describes feminine beauty, he uses different terms: slice, cake, demolition, bomb, and rocket.

Mishari examines the features of the woman his uncle has just called Slice. She has light brown skin, long black hair, wide Arabian eyes, and a celestial nose.

Patting him on the shoulder, his uncle says, Ready to pull off Operation Prophet of Love No. 34?

Mishari nods.

Yes, Beast! exclaims his uncle softly. That's what I'm talking about!

Beast is what his uncle calls the little one when praising his gargantuan   feats.

His uncle drops to his knees and rakes his fingers through Mishari's hair, combs the bangs away from the eyes, then straightens his nephew's shirt. Smile, little guy, and give her your puppy eyes.

When Mishari blinks, an ailing Indian girl flashes into view. Two

African women speaking in a low voice lift the young girl's bloodstained dress. Mishari glimpses the torn flesh between her skinny thighs.

He thinks he must be dreaming, so he closes his eyes.

The yellow Ferrari parked beside the juice store pops into view once more, but when his uncle presses the folded piece of paper on which he'd written his phone number into Mishari's palm, his uncle's hand shrinks and darkens.

The stranger wearing the niqab asks, Is this your father's number? Come with me. The guards will help you call your dad.

Mishari closes his eyes. When he opens them again, he sees a pretty woman with light brown skin and long black hair. She pinches his cheeks and asks: What's your name?

He answers the young woman.

He answers the older one.

Mishari Faisal Al-Saffar.

He gives the piece of paper to the young woman.

He gives the piece of paper to the older one.

This is my uncle's number.

Is this your father's number?

Mishari turns around and finds his uncle inside the juice bar, holding two cups of avocado smoothies.

Mishari runs back to give him his hand so they can cross the street together. Once they reach the Ferrari, his uncle ruffles his hair and warns him against divulging their secret to Mishari's mother.

Mishari blinks.

His uncle's hand shrinks and darkens.

Then a woman with a puffy eyelid and a bruised cheek appears and her fat fingers brush his thick bangs.

Blinking once more, Mishari sees his uncle's fingers turning the dial in search of another song, but the same one he doesn't like blasts through the speakers:

Eyes are gushing from the pain of separation...

If now's the time for us to part,

when will we reunite?

I hate this song, Uncle Saud. Please choose another one.

Ruwaina made her way up the stairs to the children's room, then sat near the little one's head, dipped her fingers into his hair, and eavesdropped on the conversation taking place in the lower level between Jerjes and Uthman.

Mishari was mumbling deliriously.

Gently, Ruwaina tapped him on the cheek. Kid, wake up and drink some milk.

He opened his eyes and rambled in Arabic.

Squeezing his cheeks with one hand, she forced his mouth open to pour in a spoonful of milk with her other hand.

Mishari coughed before his glazed eyes moved around him searchingly without registering his surroundings. His eyelids then drooped again.

Ruwaina stuck her fingers in his mouth to pry his jaw open. With her other hand, she dropped in a seedless date for him to chew on. Eat, boy. Eat, she cooed. Because the little one remained motionless, she called him by name. Mishari! My sweet boy Mishari.

Adania, Saliha, and Bahati exchanged sidelong glances. Ruwaina was breaking protocol again, using the child's real name instead of the usual: boy, girl, demon, gremlin, dog, or animal.

The little one woke up, and this time, when he looked around, he saw children huddling in the corner and an Indian girl moaning, her legs spread apart. Mishari realised that a rope was tied around his ankles, scraping his skin. He frowned.

There he goes again, the crybaby, Ruwaina thought with a smile. Stroking his hair and brushing his cheeks, she told him, Kuwaitis don't cry.

The other women exchanged stunned and disapproving looks.

And Bahati said, The old hag has lost her mind.

The tenderness that Ruwaina lavished on Mishari inspired one of the young captives to scurry toward her for affection. Shoving him away, she cried censoriously, Get back, filth! The kid stumbled backward, frightened and confused, and went to snuggle with the other children who were standing in the corner.

Adania gawked at Ruwaina. What do you think you're doing?

Ignoring Adania, Ruwaina leaned in until she was a hairbreadth from Mishari's earlobe and began to lull him with a soft melody.

Mishari wriggled in her lap and tried to crawl away.

But she held on to him and mumbled, You stay with me.

Mishari's weeping affected the others. Soon, all the children in the room began to sob in unison.

Saliha yowled, Look what you've done! They had just quieted down!

Zem bul, said Ruwaina coldly, still twiddling her fingers through the little one's hair—who was now crying as loud as the others.

Saliha, Bahati, and Adania got up to silence the kids once more, each waving a wooden stick and screaming, Shut up! Be quiet! Enough! Their sticks, swooshing through the air, landed on tiny backsides, exacerbating the children's pain and increasing the volume of their wailing.

However, amid all this commotion, Mishari went abruptly quiet. He loosened up as tension left his body, and he found a more comfortable position on the lap of the foreigner who was still whispering in his ears.

A few minutes later, Uthman entered the room, and all the children fell into a unanimous hush. All of them, apart from the Indian girl, who was still faintly moaning, Paani, paani.

What the hell is going on here?

Ask her! Adania waved an accusatory finger at Ruwaina.

Uthman heard the young girl moaning and growled, Just give her some water already!

Ruwaina chuckled. What's the point? She'll be dead soon.

Mishari tried to crawl toward the other children, but Ruwaina pulled him back, wrapping her arms around his tiny figure. Come back, little treasure. Come back, habibi, she whispered in his ears.

What are you doing? Uthman asked. Let him go!

Ruwaina squeezed the child on her flabby lap and continued to sing.

When are we leaving? Bahati asked.

We're not going, Uthman said, pursing his lips.

What do you mean?

Change of plans, Jerjes said, now standing in the doorway, his eyes fixed on Ruwaina.

Ruwaina grimaced, which allowed Mishari to slip out of her loosened embrace, then sneak across the floor to join the other children huddled in the corner, where he looked as out of place as a white hair in a dark plait.

For a few moments, everyone was quiet, everyone except the Indian girl who was still whimpering for water.

Adania finally brought her something to drink.

And Bahati asked again, So, what now?

A knowing smile crept over Ruwaina's face, and she looked at Jerjes before she said, Now, we cross the sea.

'Asir. Wadi Rada

9 Dhu Al-Hijja, 1431

10:05 A.M.

He knew 'Asir's mountains intimately—the way he knew his own body.

Sometimes, Uthman even confused this familiarity with fondness, for he knew where to find a running stream, where to seek shelter from the sun—under the cypress, juniper, or sidr trees—where to turn to for natural honey, and where each dam stood. He knew the pathways to the banana farms and those that detoured into dens, where men living in a clutter of tin and wooden shantytowns manufactured arak and opioids. And he was aware that if he climbed up to the peak, he'd find armed groups selling mobile phones, inflatable Suzuki boats, and Land Cruisers spacious enough to fit a few plastic boxes containing several days' worth of meals, a burlap sack in which everyday clothes were heaped, honey jars stacked on top of one another, a first aid kit, four adults, and seven kids—if you lay them next to each other and bind their feet.

Uthman escaped the geography of Black hunger five years earlier by trekking across the Yemeni border on foot, accompanied by seven different men from Ethiopia, Eritrea, and Yemen, thirsty the whole time he made his way toward Harad, for he had heard others refer to it as a centre for Yemeni criminals. Then, at Mubkhara village, he paid a smuggler five hundred US dollars to help him sneak into Saudi Arabia. Uthman preferred to work with a smuggler over attempting to break through the fenced borders in Abi Al-Dhabra on his own, despite it being well-known that countless migrants infiltrate Saudi

Arabia daily.

After crossing the border, the smuggler told Uthman to make his way to The Valley of the Devil, where he would find Saudi residents willing to transport unauthorised immigrants to Jazan, and from there to 'Asir, for the price of two hundred Saudi riyals. Like many before him, Uthman thereafter could disappear into one of the farms at Al Batila, Haswa, Ruqaa, Al-Ayna, Showqab, or Dalij.

But he ended up settling in Rijal Almaa, working as a farmer until he learned that it was rather more profitable to deal in opioids, bottles of arak, and Captagon pills. That's when he met Jerjes, who tended to operate during seasons of worship and was most active throughout the six days of Hajj and the thirty days of Ramadan. As business dwindled with Jerjes the rest of the year, Uthman managed on his own through smaller jobs: farming, petty thievery, and distilling arak. He would stand, concealed in the dark, in a small farm near Rijal Almaa Bridge, waiting for customers. Then he'd whisper: I got ten kilos of hashish. Boxes of bootlegged whisky. And Captagon pills.

He would sneak through empty storm drains until he found fields and sheds known among criminals as centres of illegal activity. During raids, he'd run up the mountains confidently, knowing that his stealthy friends who were concealed in ditches and behind rocks were watching over him, and that they would send a warning signal whenever danger was afoot. Uthman would change the site of his operation depending on the risk level of each location where he chose to lurk in and on the trending product at the time—for Uthman was aware that the language of the market was namely: supply and demand. An increased number of trucks meant an uptick in a desire for Captagon pills, which likewise meant standing on the outskirts of Hamama, near the triangular sign on the road. How much do you want? A thousand? Two thousand? Three? Uthman would rely on his partners to turn on flashlights and show customers where to go.

He lived like this for three years until he met Jerjes through an acquaintance. Jerjes, a man who appeared to be his opposite, was a towering figure, yellow-eyed and thick-lipped. Wherever Jerjes went, rumours followed, some true and some false, and others still fantastic enough to rival myths and legends. Some thought of him as a God among men. Others viewed him as the Devil. It was also said of him that he abducted children for an international mafia and that no one would dare provoke him. Jerjes was connected to numerous smuggling networks. In addition to his contacts in the Middle East, it was said that he communicated with criminal groups that operated within refugee camps in Ethiopia, Somalia, and Sudan. Uthman himself had heard that Jerjes could strike deals worth thousands of dollars and that he tended to avoid smaller gigs.

It's child's play to sell weed and arak to customers. One or two massive operations could lavish you with enough comfort to last the rest of the year. That's how you live a good life!

Uthman salivated. He wanted to dabble in that world, too, so he joined the group and began to move back and forth between Mecca and Wadi Rada, transferring their commodities: catatonic black kids that nobody wanted, children who wouldn't elicit a single ounce of concern from the world—just like him.

Uthman wanted to emulate Jerjes, to become a wealthy boss, feared and talked about, someone around whom falsehood and gossip swirled, to whom youthful men flocked for work and women competed for his bed—women even more beautiful than Saliha.

At the crack of dawn this morning, Uthman had contemplated

the astronomical figure printed on the boy's flier and had determined that it was time for him to become such a man. He had snatched the flier from a stranger's hand during his reconnaissance tour of Mecca and could barely stand there ogling the number offered in a massive font: ONE MILLION DOLLARS — To be instantly awarded to the person who discovers the whereabouts of the Kuwaiti boy photographed above.

On the drive back to 'Asir, Uthman had lost himself in a seven-hour daydream in which he explored the manifold ways he would spend his share of the treasure. *A million dollars, ya Uthman! Your mother had prayed for you! A goddam million!* Uthman's share from their current operation paled in comparison: a mere ten thousand Saudi riyals. What might his new share become if the group agreed to split the ransom among them? *A hundred thousand dollars?*

Did you just ask for a hundred thousand, you fool? Ask for a quarter million! How much longer will you wade in the river only to die of thirst?

Uthman considered negotiating with the young captives' family, confessing to the kidnapping, and demanding an even higher ransom. Or, he thought, he'd take the simpler and safer route by pretending to be the child's saviour. *A hero!* He'd collect the full ransom himself and revel in the good life. Uthman kept oscillating between the two options: the safe million or the unsafe millions, wondering, *What would Jerjes do? No doubt he'd pick the dangerous option! Instead of one meagre million, Jerjes would demand ten or twenty! Those Kuwaitis are mocking us with this number. Do they really think we were born yesterday? They must think of us as bums who'd settle for scraps!*

He drifted for hours, lost in calculations and every possible outcome. *How much would I get?* The six zeros made him dizzy, and he pictured himself crossing the sea, his bags full of cash. He saw himself immigrating, perhaps, to Addis Ababa or Asmara. Hell, he could even move to Europe as a new millionaire. Instead of selling weed, he'd buy it. And instead of manufacturing arak, he'd own a whisky distillery. And instead of squatting in uninhabited homes or finding shelter in slums, storm drains, millet farms, or distant caves, he'd own a castle. Who knows? He might even donate his money to charity, build a hospital, and be born again as a righteous man. It's not that he refused to live such a moral life. It's that he couldn't currently afford it. A moral compass for people like him pointed to unbounded hunger. Who'd be able to survive such a life?

And because of this daydreaming, Uthman couldn't believe his eyes when Jerjes took one look at the flier before his lips twisted into an indifferent smile, qat leaves swelling his right cheek. Jerjes seemed calm in a worrisome way, considering the situation they were in, and while contemplating the six zeros briefly, his disturbing smile stretched into an incomprehensible grin, We need to leave. Now, he muttered.

Are we leaving behind the million dollars? Uthman couldn't understand the order, so he asked after taking a deep breath, Leave? Now? Where are we going?

We'll cross the Red Sea.

What about the ransom?

We don't mess around with them.

Uthman's mouth went dry. He could only stare in shock as he tried to make sense of Jerjes's intentions. *How could he gaze at that enormous figure and not tremble? How could he leave behind a million dollars?* Uthman tried to reason with his boss again, But Jerjes, it's a million dollars!

Jerjes levelled two large, yellow eyes at his subordinate, then spat the qat leaves on the floor. His thick and veiny fingers hurriedly untied the knot on the nylon bag. As he raked through the content, his fingers picked out fresh leaves that he shredded then stuffed in his pipe. They're mocking us with this silly number, he said at last.

We can negotiate. Or simply double it. They'll pay! Uthman swallowed. The flier quivered in his fist. Jerjes, he whispered, the price of all our captives doesn't even come close.

Jerjes, who was beaming, waved the pipe, where the green leaves now burned, permeating the room with their smell. One million. Ten million. Or a hundred million dollars. They are nothing but numbers. At the end of the day, no matter what you do, you'll end up at Qasas Square, your corpse dangling from a crane. Don't tell me you don't know how this story ends? Because I've seen this once with my very eyes, and I didn't like the scene.

Uthman's body stiffened. A cold chill trickled up his back. Although he didn't want to end up at Qasas Square, he was still attached to the ransom, so he asked, What about the Ra'aida?

What about them?

What if they ask for the ransom themselves?

That's their business.

Uthman thought about their overlords. *The Ra'aida will ask for the money, but it's easier for them to do it because they're in Sinai. An armed militia in a demilitarised zone—the Ra'aida can raise the price and still survive the consequences. But here? What can you do when local authorities have tightened the noose around undocumented immigrants and, every once in a while, you hear of another execution?* Uthman didn't want to die. *But the flier...! And those wretched zeros!*

Now go, Jerjes said, and bring the other car.

Because Uthman heard screaming on the upper floor as soon as he opened the door, instead of retrieving the car, he rushed up the staircase, skipping steps, then found the female members smacking the children with their wooden sticks. The children were weeping from the pain, while Ruwaina was sitting crossed-legged on the floor, hugging the Kuwaiti boy, kissing his face, brushing her fingers through his hair, and calling him: My treasure. Immediately after, she managed to divine Jerjes's decision to sail across the sea.

How does she know everything? If Jerjes wanted the money for himself, why cross the Red Sea with us? The boy's parents are still in Mecca, so what good will leaving do? Uthman felt the deep ache for the million dollars and craved it all. But Ruwaina, referring to Jerjes, had said, *Too bad, he'll hog it all himself. What exactly did she mean by that?*

The blue Caprice set off, probing the valley between juniper and cypress trees and white boulders on either side. *What if Ruwaina was right? What if Jerjes had gotten rid of her to secure a larger portion of the ransom for himself? What if he'd already agreed to share half of it with the Ra'aida? What if that's where our meagre shares are coming from? Ten thousand Saudi riyals to each member... We are damn fools to have agreed to that lousy currency. We even broke into joyful dancing when we heard the price!*

Jerjes won't carry out the swap in Saudi Arabia. I bet he decided to abandon the whole operation as soon as he saw that number. Although we're still expected to kidnap five more children, it seems that Jerjes has lost interest in the original bargain. He must've been waiting for this signal to make a move. Uthman mulled over his boss's motive furiously. *Why did he ask us to bring the boy to 'Asir if he didn't want him? Why didn't he tell us to leave the Kuwaiti behind in Mecca? Why has he risked all our lives? And what of the girl he took to bed? What happens if she haemorrhages to death? By endangering her life, he has risked an even greater financial loss. We were supposed to kidnap twelve children! But we've only managed seven, one of whom is dying—because of him!*

I think Ruwaina is telling the truth. She always does. The Ra'aida will pocket the ransom, and they'll give Jerjes his cut. But what about us?

Like fools in the river, we may all die of thirst.

Jazan. On the way to the Coast

9 Dhu Al-Hijja, 1431

7:00 P.M.

When Uthman returned in a decrepit Land Cruiser, the children's arms and legs were bound, their mouths gagged, and their bodies limp. Ruwaina, who'd already pressed her soggy towel against their faces, had sent them to sleep one by one.

After unlocking the tailgate, Uthman began to lay the children in the Land Cruiser's boot, face to feet, one beside the other, like sardines in a can. He then fetched a wooden shelf with hooks on the sides that resembled a wide dining table and attached it several inches above the slumbering bodies. Once he'd laid a white sheet on top, he stacked four boxes containing an assortment of mason jars, some filled with beeswax, honey, royal jelly, and bee pollen. The rest were left empty.

In the unlikely event that policemen would intercept their Land Cruiser, Uthman and his female counterparts would assume the roles of honey traders: humble African workers trying to gather resources for their Saudi employer, natural resources from the mountains such as white honey, willow, and sidr, every one of them esteemed for its healing properties, proving to the police officers that nothing sinister was going on.

Jerjes waited until the sky had turned dark. Only then did he get in the passenger seat. Saliha and Ruwaina were already sitting in the back, and Uthman was waiting behind the wheel.

They had decided to leave Adania and Bahati in the house, having already received their shares in advance—five thousand Riyals each—along with clear instructions.

Soon after we leave, Jerjes had said, a car will pick you up and drive you to a shantytown, where you'll both work as arak distillers. Stay out of sight until I call on you for our next job.

After that, the Land Cruiser set off along the rocky ridges. Imam Al-Shuraim's voice emerged from the radio: This book includes guidance to the pious, about which there is no doubt. All four adults held on to their silence as the holy verses poured out.

Although his eyes were fixed on the road, Uthman thought, *What if I run away with the Kuwaiti before the boat leaves the shore? It would be difficult for Jerjes to follow because he's big and bulky, while I'm lithe and quick.* Uthman considered calling the number on the flier to tell them that he was undocumented and a petty criminal, who sold qat and smuggled unauthorised immigrants in and out of Saudi Arabia. *Nothing major.* He would say he was selling qat leaves to one of his friends in a shantytown in the foothills when he first came across the kid. He'd add that he tried to distract his friend, grab the boy, and dart away. He'll also assure the parents that the kid is in good health, soundly waiting at a place nobody knows its whereabouts but him, and that he's willing to disclose this location only after he receives the full reward, along with a full pardon, and safe transport to Yemen.

Have you lost your mind, Uthman? Yemen? You'd be robbed and kidnapped by armed groups, who'd stuff you in one of those Ghost Houses and demand ransom from your parents, but no one would pay because you're an orphan. In the end, you'd experience the full force of torture by nitric acid, and your corpse would be cast into the desert to decompose under the sun—a burial worthy of gerbils. No. I won't go to

Yemen. I'll go to Asmara on a safe boat, not on some dilapidated Cobia as planned. In fact, The Coast Guard themselves will protect me and make sure that my bags of overflowing cash and I will arrive at our destination unharmed. Only then will I inform the parents of the kid's location. Uthman thought about stuffing the boy somewhere no one else would think of, a cave, for example, or in one of the abandoned houses in the valleys of 'Asir. In Wadi Shawqab, perhaps, or Wadi Fo.

Uthman, who wandered far and wide in his thoughts, was inadvertently smiling. But when he glanced in the rearview mirror, he wondered whether he was imagining it.

Or was Ruwaina smiling like him?

Jazan. Red Sea Coast

9 Dhu Al-Hijja, 1431

8:40 P.M.

When the Land Cruiser arrived at the coast, the inflatable dinghy was already pumped and anchored on the shore. A Jeep with tinted windows, parked nearby, was enveloped in the dark. Night had fallen, silent and still, on all the water and all the land. Only the patches of sand illuminated by Uthman's and the stranger's headlights were visible.

Uthman killed the motor and got out. He then approached the man in the other car to pay for the Suzuki boat.

The Jeep's engine rumbled, then, as soon as the stranger received the cash, it skidded away.

Uthman hurried to join the others, who had all briskly fallen into their prescribed roles. Saliha and Ruwaina removed jars and boxes from the shelf in the boot, while Uthman joined Jerjes in pushing the inflatable boat with its 15-horsepower engine into the ocean. It could fit eight passengers.

Uthman, Ruwaina, and Saliha stood in a line, transferring one child after another, from one person to the next, from Land Cruiser to Suzuki.

Jerjes, who was standing to the side, aiming his flashlight at the children, watched the whole operation silently.

The Kuwaiti boy was the last to be transported from the four-wheeler to the dinghy.

As Uthman leaned over the boot of the four-wheeler, he found Mishari gaping in the dark. You're awake? Uthman cried.

Jerjes dashed over. He aimed his flashlight at the boy to check, then tossed an accusatory glance at Ruwaina, who was walking toward them.

What's going on?

He's awake, Jerjes answered.

Oh. Weird.

Didn't you drug him like the rest?

I did. She shrugged and added with a pout, Some of them wake up early.

Glaring at her from the corner of his eye, he shoved her away, then bent over the boot to carry the boy himself.

Only Uthman beat him to it, swiftly hauling the kid over his shoulder and taking quick, long steps toward their inflatable boat.

Ruwaina stretched her arms in his direction, letting him know she wanted to carry the child herself.

Uthman shook his head. Get the rest of our stuff, he suggested, nodding his chin in the direction of the burlap sack, which contained their clothes and their first-aid kit, and continued.

Ruwaina picked up the bundle and the box and wondered as she cast furtive glances at Uthman and Jerjes, *Did we all decide to betray each other?*

They moved side-by-side toward the boat: Jerjes to Uthman's right, Ruwaina to his left. Saliha stood in the middle of the dinghy, aiming her flashlight at all three, her shaky voice urging them to Come on! and Hurry!

Ruwaina, who mounted first, was still calculating her next move. She could snatch the boy and hop into the water when Uthman started the engine. She and Mishari were bound to reach the shore before Uthman could turn the inflatable around, and by the time Jerjes decided to follow on foot, it would be too late. The protective belly of Darkness would've already swallowed her and the kid.

Ruwaina could feel her heart beating louder the more she mulled over her options. Ultimately, she decided to rely on the simplest plan—and perhaps on a sprinkle of luck. *But what if Jerjes grabs hold of the child from the start?* Ruwaina would lose a physical fight with the towering man. *What if the tide increases the boat's speed? When the boy and I jump into the water, we might find ourselves far from solid ground.* Her heart raced erratically as she weighed her choices. *If I don't get him, no one will. I'm the one who kidnapped him in the first place, and I'll be the only one who returns him to his parents.* She traced the shape of the Gyuto blade hidden in a pocket she had sewn into her underwear. *Otherwise, I'll slit the boy's throat and drop him in the ocean. Let the sharks devour him! And after...* Ruwaina swallowed and felt once more that strange yearning for Lietchuor. *I'll jump after him. Yes. I will. I'd rather be gobbled up by sharks than shot by Jerjes!*

Ruwaina kept a vigilant eye on Jerjes as he clambered onto the rubber dinghy. She even offered him her arm for support.

As soon as he got in, Jerjes stood up, then, turning around to face Uthman, who was still in the water, and as Ruwaina had done to him earlier, Jerjes gave the young man his arm while staring down his subordinate, and whispering, Hop on, Uthman. Quick.

Uthman slowed down instead.

In a cold and steady voice, Jerjes said, Give me the boy, Uthman. Come on. Give me your hand.

But Uthman was now retreating, his eyes fixed on Jerjes who was hissing, Get on the boat! I said give me the boy! You better not dare! Uthman!

Saliha was also whispering. Hurry! Come on!

But Uthman kept moving backward until the water reached his thighs.

Uthman! Ruwaina gaped at the young man. She was so shocked by his behaviour she thought she was hallucinating. Suddenly, she turned around and snickered.

What's so funny? Jerjes growled.

But Ruwaina was chuckling now, her mouth wide open, her eyes still following the young man who was retreating to the shore as the boy dangled from his shoulder. In all the scenarios she had visualised, she hadn't seen little, lanky Uthman as the one who'd double-cross them.

Uthman was holding a rescue knife in his hand.

Ruwaina only noticed because he used it to slice the paracord around the boy's ankles. When Uthman dropped the boy into the water feet first, Ruwaina couldn't hold it in any longer. She began cackling.

Lower your voice, Saliha urged, frustration audible in her tone.

Jerjes aimed the flashlight at the face of the young captive. Catch him! Don't let him go! he ordered.

Mishari's eyes were moving all around as though searching for something.

Ruwaina waved her arms and bellowed, I'm here! I'm here! She jumped in the ocean, screaming, Run, boy! Run away!

Mishari coursed through the water as fast as his legs could carry him until he finally reached the shore and vanished in the dark.

Ruwaina couldn't remember who got shot first. Was it her? Or Uthman? She recalled the sound of the gunshot and Uthman's dead body floating on black water. She remembered the smell of saline, fuel, and blood. She also remembered that Jerjes had jumped off the boat to grab the boy, that she had followed, and that they'd wrestled in the sea. To delay his pursuit of the child, Ruwaina had clung to Jerjes's colossal body, yet he had managed to grab her head and shove it deep underwater.

By then, Saliha was screaming, Just let her go! We don't have time! Come on!

But Jerjes refused to let go of the submerged head, forcing Ruwaina to take a bubbling breath that flooded saltwater into her lungs.

And once Ruwaina popped out of the water, she continued to

cry as loud as she could, Run, kid, run! The gyuto knife she'd been gripping a second earlier was now jammed in her guts. She did not feel the blood rushing out of her wound. And she felt no pain. What she did feel was the cool, soft crashing of the waves, ferrying her along. She also heard the roar of the engine when Jerjes hopped on the boat to flee the scene of the crime.

CHAPTER FIVE

MASEER

travelling route; deprived of free will; propulsion

On the Way to Rijal Almaa Province

9 Dhu Al-Hijja, 1431

9:30 A.M.

A black Tahoe heading south swiftly coasted along the asphalt tongue stretching across the mountains toward 'Asir.

Faisal pressed his forehead against the tinted windowpane, then exhaled. *There is no God but Allah.* His forehead left an oily imprint on the glass when he reclined on his seat. His knees and fingertips had been quivering since morning, and his body felt both hot and cold—as though on the verge of a fever. While wiping his face with the heel of his hand, Faisal told himself, *I can't get sick!* Then he went back to peering out the window, gazing at Mecca's rocky landscape and the majestic mountains flanking a seemingly endless road.

Saud said reassuringly, We'll find him soon, Bu Mishari.

Faisal sighed and a tear glistened in his eye. Ya Rab!

He had felt relief upon leaving Mecca, like a man who is pulled out of the water in the final moment before drowning. *Free at last of that mosque with its ceaseless cataclysms and its senseless circumambulations; and free of that sky that has enveloped the whole world in utter speechlessness...!* At least, now, Faisal believed he could sense a glimmer of hope. Ya Rab! he uttered once more.

A gentle touch on his shoulder made Faisal turn around. He found Saud's outstretched arm offering a white box containing two types of maamoul: date and pistachio.

Saud said, Have one.

Faisal shook his head. He didn't think he could eat.

Saud persisted, Come on. For me.

Later, Saud. Please.

Saud continued to peer stubbornly at his older brother through the rearview mirror.

Because Faisal realised that his brother would stop asking only once he'd eaten something, his trembling fingers grabbed a piece, then dropped it on his tongue. The maamoul's slightly sweet and earthy texture melted in his mouth immediately, reminding him that he hadn't eaten anything for two whole days—fifty hours straight. It made him wonder whether his son had eaten anything either. So, for the third time since their departure, he asked Mazen, How much longer until Rijal Almaa?

And for the third time, without a hint of frustration, Mazen answered, Six more hours, maybe seven. Get a little shuteye, Bu Mishari. Rest a little.

Saud agreed with his friend. Clasping his brother's shoulder and gently kneading it, he urged, Yes, rest a bit, for everyone's sake, especially mine.

Faisal, whose eyes were now filled with tears, inadvertently thought of Sumaya: their argument in the morning, and her panic attacks at night. She had slept, kicking and screaming, her eyes wide open. Faisal had tried to calm her, grab her by the arm, and shake her awake. Get up, Sumaya! He'd even shouted at her face. She couldn't see him standing right in front of her even though her eyes were bulging, and she merely mumbled unintelligible words until she puked all over his shirt.

All she wanted to do was rest.

And Faisal couldn't forgive her for it.

Saud had asked before leaving Mecca, What about Sumaya?

Faisal's eyebrows had furrowed like someone trying to figure out who the name belonged to, and, after a while, asked in a puzzled tone, Sumaya?

Om Mishari! Saud had replied, startled.

Faisal had indeed forgotten his wife. Yet, her name was both strange and familiar, referring to a woman from another lifetime: a topsy-turvy version of their current events, or a lifetime that was unravelling in a parallel universe—either way, her name reminded him of something imaginary, persisting only in a world of dreams, a world at odds with his corporeal experiences.

Saud had asked, Shouldn't you let her know?

And Faisal had tried to reconstruct Sumaya's features in his mind, but the only image he conjured up was a sponge drenched in tears beside a comically broken heart. Sumaya—his wife, his life partner, the mother of his child—was the last person he wanted to see. And her voice was the last sound he desired to hear. He had promised his younger brother with a shake of his head, I'll call her on the way.

Yet, a whole hour had passed and Faisal still hadn't called his wife. He simply couldn't, not after everything he'd said, for he had hurled rusty words with cruel edges. The problem wasn't the ferocity of his delivery or the harshness of his accusation. The kernel of truth embedded within each tainted word made them especially lethal. He closed his eyes again, and this time he imagined Sumaya the way Hagar, the bereaved, was driven to manic pacing over her son's impending demise, passionately yearning for the miracle of water to save Ismail's life.

Faisal thought that if Mishari was rescued in five or six hours, if things went back to the way they were, if everything became alright again, and if he could go back to his simple life, his normal life, his peaceful life, then maybe he'd be able to return to his wife, look her in the eyes, brush her black hair with his tender fingers and whisper, Don't worry my love, everything has gone back to normal now that Mishari has come back to us.

Everything's alright now.

Faisal felt a stirring in his heart. *If I find my child, I'll sacrifice a hundred lambs, feed ten thousand people, and run back to The Sacred Mosque, to the southwestern corner where I abandoned my ritual. I will drop to the floor and kneel for a long time. Then everything will go back to the way it was. I can even pray again without throwing up a fountain of fire whenever I try.*

Faisal exhaled and closed his eyes, feeling calm and refreshed, and for the first time in the past three days, he thought if he could seize the opportunity to get some shuteye, he wouldn't be betraying his son, but showing him, rather, more devotion. Faisal's body responded to this thought, and, as he slumped into a soft slumber, he finally got some rest.

Mecca

9 Dhu Al-Hijja, 1431

10:30 A.M.

In the beginning, she was chasing a child.

Sumaya believed that the small back resembled Mishari's even though the child she'd been pursuing had brown hair and blond streaks, as well as a reddish birthmark on his neck. She still thought, *Maybe I just hadn't noticed the birthmark, or maybe I didn't realise that my son's hair colour had changed right in front of me.* The boy Sumaya was following wore a tiny ihram, and he was holding his mother's hand. Upon further inspection, he seemed taller than Mishari, perhaps by several inches. Nevertheless, Sumaya still believed it was her son, despite all these differences. *Maybe he changed his clothes. Maybe he grew taller.* Because she wanted to look at the child's face, she advanced quickly, then turned around to examine his features, but couldn't believe her eyes, for she'd been nearly certain that she was following her son.

However, the kid looked nothing like Mishari.

Her legs suddenly stopped moving. *How could it not be him?* She tried to understand how she had mistaken a stranger for her son. After swerving around again to ensure that she hadn't missed Mishari, who could've been standing among the pilgrims, Sumaya looked up at the sky and thought, *I'll go back to The Sacred Mosque.*

But she couldn't move, because the worshipful crowds pouring all around her began shoving her forward, first one step, then another.

How did I get here? Pilgrims moved her hundreds of miles by the sheer force of their will to proceed in their Hajj ritual toward Mount Arafa. Despite trying to resist, Sumaya was buoyed like a log on a human river. No! Stop! I need to search for my son!

She tried her best to extricate herself from the tide. Yet, whenever she managed to slip through an opening in the human wall, she came across more people blocking her path. Ya Rab! she pleaded to the sky. Thoroughly subsumed now by the spiritual wave, Sumaya stood on tiptoe and watched herself merge with the multitude, then she disappear among the millions walking and talking in absolute devotion: Labbaik Allahumma labbaik! Sumaya raised her chin again to exclaim, I can't do it!

Tears streamed heavily down her cheeks. *Why are you pulling me in that direction as though I cannot find you here? I lost him in your house!*

A cleric blurted to her right, Oh pilgrims, surrender to the Most Merciful, for you are guests in his abode!

Sumaya gaped at the cleric, whose bones were protruding and whose beard was long and white.

He shouted at the ambulating masses, There isn't a day that is more favourable to Allah than today! He will descend to our earthly skies, and the People of Heaven will bless the People of Earth, who surrender and praise on this day.

Sumaya was still gawking, but her jaw now dropped. *Does God himself descend?*

Her watery eyes, surveying the cleric, focused on the wrinkles around his still-speaking mouth: And he will say, look at my worshippers! Look how dusty, how dishevelled, how full of lack! They have sought me out from every cranny, imploring for mercy! The cleric turned around, urging pilgrims to heed the call and obey. When his eyes fell upon Sumaya, he yelled, You too, hajja! Let go!

She was surprised to find her legs still moving—as if they'd found a will of their own. Her whole body then surrendered to the beat of the plodding masses thrusting in one direction. Raising her bright, astonished eyes above her, she mumbled softly. Labbaik Allahumma labbaik. Afterward, she began to praise like the rest, her lips parting on their own, words coming out of her mouth unknowingly: Mishari. Labbaik. Allah. Mishari. Labbaik. Allah, Allah, Allah. Still gazing at the sky, she raised her voice: Are you telling me something?

Sumaya was sandwiched between two female pilgrims when she thought of herself and all the other worshippers as isolated parts of a unified whole: a single entity that was ultimately solid, sturdy, and stone-deaf. She began to flow effortlessly, as though obeying a hidden force—as if that unseen power was dragging her toward Mount Arafa. Her lips kept moving on their own. Sweat sluiced out of her temples, a filmy glaze coated her eyes, and devotional phrases clattered in her head.

The Hajj itself is Arafa, and God will boast to his angels about the People of Arafa, and he will say, Look at my believers! They have sought my presence, dusty and dishevelled!

Sumaya looked down at her dust-covered abaya, then raised her eyes to the sky and thought, *Maybe I'll find him there. Maybe I'll find him.*

On the Way to Rijal Almaa Province

9 Dhu Al-Hijja, 1431

11:00 A.M.

Faisal slept in the passenger seat, neck bent, jaw relaxed. A trail of saliva that had slid down the right corner of his mouth left a spit stain on his shoulder. He was snoring the way someone might gurgle with his soul.

Saud leaned over Faisal to make sure he wasn't in pain, then whispered to his friend, That's weird. I've never heard Faisal snore.

Mazen shook his head and said, I'm not surprised. Don't forget, it's the first time he's gotten any rest since he lost his son.

Poor guy.

At least he's resting.

Why didn't we suggest he lay in the backseat? He'd have more space here.

It's too late now. And, as I said, at least he's resting.

Saud scooted to the middle, reached behind his brother's chair, and pulled the lever.

Faisal's chair began to recline until he could roll on his side, cushion his cheek with his palm, and sink into a deep slumber, snorting, grunting, and gulping as though no power in this world could rouse him. Occasionally, the other men heard him whispering

Mishari's name. And once, he even said: Sumaya.

Saud's thoughts wandered to his brother's wife distributing her fliers, darting around The Sacred Mosque like a woman in the throes of psychosis, chasing children and beggars alike. She didn't know about the phone call they had received from the female criminal because Faisal worried about her when asleep and avoided her when awake.

Why didn't he tell his wife?

The last time Saud had seen Sumaya, she'd been rambling about repentance and forgiveness. He had asked her when she had eaten last, and she had peered back at him with a vacant expression, as if she couldn't understand his question. It seemed as if Sumaya had forgotten her physical needs, for she was acting like someone who'd successfully liberated her soul from her body, and who was relying entirely on her pain as fuel. Her image—sobbing during sujood— was still etched in his memory.

Saud had given her a bottle of Zamzam water and a box of dates before leaving for an hour. When he returned, she was still circling the same spot. The package he'd given her was almost empty. He knew she hadn't tasted a morsel, so he had snatched the fliers from her hands and said, I won't return these until you eat!

Sumaya had picked out two dates and dropped them in her mouth.

Saud couldn't help but wonder what made her stand before him on the brink of a blackout. Sumaya, he had said, you've got to rest.

Rest? How can I rest when my son is still missing?

But you need to sleep, Sumaya, because you won't be able to find him in your state. Please, sleep for Mishari's sake.

He hadn't seen her since this exchange. *Did she sleep?* He looked into the rearview mirror and asked Mazen, Do you think I should contact Um Mishari? To let her know about the call?

Let's find the boy first.

Poor thing. I bet she's still at The Sacred Mosque, handing out her fliers.

It might be better for her to keep doing that than risk hope and have it crumble afterward under the crushing weight of disappointment. God forbid anything like that happens. We're men, you know, we can respond to this disaster. But she's a mother...

Are you saying Faisal is handling it well?

Still. He's a man.

Saud wondered whether Faisal or Sumaya was better equipped to respond to challenges. Faisal's broad chest, towering height, and rock-solid biceps could never fool Saud. Faisal's exterior masked a fragile ego and a moral compass made of glass.

Ever since Faisal got married nine years ago, Saud had been rising to every occasion, showing up at difficult periods, always ready to take the reins from his older brother. Saud was there when Mishari needed a root canal, when he was bullied by a student two years his senior, when he fell and hurt his head, and when he suffered from a stomach virus that sent him to Al-Amiri hospital.

Faisal, on the other hand, quickly fell apart. He could often be seen rocking back and forth on a hospital chair, squeezing his stomach. For example, when the pain of labour made Sumaya scream in agony, Faisal could only wait for her pain to subside, and kept frequenting the diwaniyya's bathroom until she was ready to receive him.

Saud felt heaviness clamping on his chest. Faisal and Sumaya were like the shanks in a pair of scissors, slicing him in two. He let out a deep breath.

God is one, Mazen said. Repeat after me.

I can't breathe.

Try to rest.

I can't.

You have to. We've got five more hours to go. No need to keep stressing.

Saud looked out of the window. He closed his eyes. Sighed. Then wondered, *How am I going to survive the next five hours?*

Saud?

Yeah?

We need to discuss something.

Khair?

Mazen searched for the right words in silence until he finally said, We need to know what each of us will do during the exchange. He drew a hoop in the air with his index finger, then delved back into his explanation, I suggest we move in a circle. Picture Mishari at the bottom and the ransom at the top. We'll slowly move away from the ransom toward the boy, while the criminals move away from the kid toward the cash. We don't move an inch unless they do. One of us must remain in the car. God forbid anything goes wrong, but if it does, that person will need to call the police. No doubt the criminals will be armed. And I'm sure Faisal would want to be involved in the action, maybe even take centre stage, but I genuinely believe it's best if he's the one who stays behind. He's mentally exhausted, and I don't think I can count on him to act rationally.

But there's something even more important I need to share. We better be prepared for anything and everything, including a tragedy. Faisal won't be ready. But you? You've got to be. And remember that we could find the boy in a state... Let's just say it might be painful for all of us, God forbid. We don't really know what his kidnappers have done to him over the past three days. I understand that I'm dwelling on terrible ideas, but it's better to voice them now than be paralyzed by shock later. Mishari could've been hurt. Do you understand what I'm saying? I'm talking about the gangs in Mecca that amputate children's limbs. And, as you know, Saudi authorities have recently stumbled on small, severed body parts dumped in the desert or stuffed in garbage pails.

What are you saying? Saud asked. He felt his head go numb and his ears start ringing.

Saud, listen to me. We don't know these people. But who other than a psychopath would kidnap a child from the Sacred Mosque during the Hajj ritual? Mishari could have been raped, or tortured, or—

God forbid! Saud cried.

Pressing his index finger to his mouth, Mazen said, Shhhh! Your brother's sleeping.

Saud buried his head in his palms and squeezed as hard as he could.

Calm down, Saud. Relax. You are the one who needs to be strong now.

Saud could no longer listen to his friend. A picture of Mishari's bruised face and amputated arm flashed in his mind. He saw the boy limping in the desert, crying for help. Saud trembled. Whatever nightmarish image he had conjured up in his head might not even compare to what had actually happened to the kid, but he said with a shake of his head, They couldn't have tortured him because they still want the money.

Mazen nodded. That is true, but what would you do if they'd mangled him or if he returned with a missing arm? Would you send him back like a faulty appliance? The truth is they've got the cards, so they make the rules, and they know it.

Saud had never considered Mishari returning in a form other than the one in which he'd vanished, but now the possibility dangled before him like a rope from the gallows. *How would Mishari show up?* A tear slid down his cheek. Saud wiped it with the back of his hand and acted as though he hadn't cried. A flurry of images flashed in his mind, one after the other: Mishari running in his underwear through sprinklers in the yard; Mishari lying on his stomach watching a Batman movie; Mishari on the beach in red swimming trunks, arms raised in the air like a wrestler, a large slice of watermelon balanced on his head. Consecutive images of the boy who...

Will we find him?

Mazen said, Hang in there and stay strong.

Frowning, Saud shook his head and wondered, *What kind of monster will I become, Mishari, when I lay my hands on your captors?*

On the Way to Rijal Almaa Province

9 Dhu Al-Hijja, 1431

1:04 P.M.

Faisal woke up screaming, like someone fleeing a disturbing dream, his arms flailing, his red eyes wide open.

The mountains cascading to his right flashed into view. He turned left and found Mazen and Saud repeating the prayer to ward off the devil. Faisal peered into their worried faces for some time. Only then did his body relax. Resting the back of his head against the car seat, he took a deep breath and recited the prayer: I seek refuge in Allah from you, Satan.

Saud twisted the lid on a water bottle before giving the bottle to his brother.

Faisal chugged it all in moments, tossed the empty plastic between his feet, then went back to gazing outside the window and recalling details from the nightmare he'd barely escaped.

In the dream, Faisal was wearing an ihram and circumambulating, though he couldn't see the Kaaba. When a cleric sounded the call for prayer, men began to stand in rows. Faisal searched between them for space in which to pray, darting from one row to the next, but whoever he stepped in front of shoved him backward, yelling: You're the devil! Faisal ran on and on, as though he'd never stop, until he finally found a gap between two believers, slipped between them, stood upright, and raised his hands to his ears—but before he could utter Allahu akbar and begin the prayer, he felt the force of something heavy knock into his back, dismantling his concentration. Although he turned around, he found nothing, so he started to pray again. After raising his arms and cupping his hands behind his ears, he felt that heavy force pound into his back once more, so he swerved, and, this time, not only was there nothing behind him, but all the believers standing in rows, the voice of the cleric leading the congregation, and Faisal's ihram had also vanished. Moreover, Faisal found himself stark naked on the prayer mat. It was then that he noticed a sprite standing beside him. The diminutive man with skinny legs and sharp fangs flew into the air, wrapped both arms and legs around Faisal's torso, and hissed: Indeed, you are the devil!

Faisal didn't share this nightmare with either Mazen or Saud, for he had been taught that Muslims should neither disclose nor interpret their dreams. But he also tried to convince himself that if he acted as though he hadn't had that nightmare in the first place then maybe he'd be able to escape its significance—maybe he could rest assured that he wasn't, in fact, the devil he'd been trying to fend off his entire life.

Turn on the radio, Saud said to Mazen.

Sure.

Once Mazen pressed the dial, Imam Al-Shuraim's voice, reciting a holy verse from the Quran, blasted through the speakers: Oh Prophet, we see you turning your face toward the sky.

Faisal's heart sank, and he exhaled before turning to Mazen to ask, How much longer until Rijal Almaa?

Still four hours.

Faisal held his tongue.

Saud reached out from the back and squeezed his brother's shoulders. Relax, Faisal, relax.

Faisal patted his younger brother's arm and said, I'm good. Don't worry about me.

Don't you want to nap some more?

Faisal answered emphatically, No! I'm not going to sleep.

He didn't want to return to that dreadful place where his pain adopted its truest form. His heart was palpitating, his temples burned, and he began to hyperventilate. *No.* He wasn't going to sleep, no matter what happened to him.

Saud, who was still massaging Faisal's back, acquiesced. Whatever you say, brother. Whatever you say.

Mecca. Mount Arafa

9 Dhu Al-Hijja, 1431

1:05 P.M.

The earth is elevating.

Sumaya thought this when she looked down at the ground on Mount Arafa and found it sloping upward all the way to the peak.

I too will elevate!

She reasoned that if she only climbed higher up Mercy Mountain, she'd have a better view and would thus find him. Sumaya wiped away the beads of sweat on her forehead using the sleeve of her abaya before steadily carving her way among the millions of other shaggy pilgrims, some draped in white, others carrying multicoloured umbrellas to protect them from the sun. They appeared like a palpitation from above or a succession of waves rolling toward the summit.

A thin, bald cleric holding a green umbrella was fervently extolling with his two chapped lips, Those who raise their voice in praise will themselves be raised!

As he trudged past Sumaya, she merely gazed at him, so he urged her, Shout the praise, my girl! Shout it loud!

Sumaya got chills, even though she gave him a nod of resolve and started to praise like the rest—Labbaik! Labbaik!—but Mishari's name kept slipping into her devotional phrases. Once she reached the gravelly part of the mountain, she leaned on a massive rock, pressed her palms to the solid wall behind her, and raised her eyes high.

Somewhere in the distance, she heard a man exclaim, You can stand anywhere on Mount Arafa, but you must stay clear of Wadi Uranah.

Sumaya pushed against the rock behind her to thrust her body forward. Although drenched in sweat, struggling to breathe, her body shaking, and her legs wobbling on the ground, Sumaya staggered onward, and when she stumbled and fell, she got up to recite—Labbaik, labbaik! Mishari! Allah! She relied on the earthy wall beside her for support, her bloodied fingers stabbing the wall consistently to propel her body forward.

But when she reached the summit, a male pilgrim intercepted her path. He hollered, because women are not expected to continue beyond this point, What makes you think you can climb up the mountain? You can stand anywhere on Mount Arafa! Go back down and wait with the other women!

Sumaya ignored him and continued her ascent, her heart beating erratically, her fingers quivering, her sweat dripping down the side of her face, stinging her eyes, sliding down her nose. She could taste the saltiness in her mouth. *I'm climbing my pain. This is the terrain of my wound! I am crossing it to get to you because I have nobody else. Shower me with your mercy. Labbaik! Labbaik!* She repeated the phrase until the world's noises dissipated into silence, and a great serenity prevailed. The only sound that was left for her ears to dwell on was her beating heart.

Sumaya continued her upward trajectory for four hours. When she reached the peak, she turned around to sweep her surroundings. The sun was setting, and the erect multitudes were waiting for the blessings of the final moments of the year's holiest day, unanimously raising and shaking their palms in the air. The pilgrims below Sumaya, standing close to one another, had filled the entire ground. Like grains of sand, they stretched as far as Sumaya's eyes could see. Tears streamed down her face, and she gasped as she stretched her arms like two masts and cried, I got it! God! I got it! The angel Gabriel had asked Ibrahim, The Friend of God, Did you get it? And Ibrahim had answered, I got it! And now I got it too, God! I'm a grain of sand in a wasteland. A drop of water in an ocean. A single hair on a bull's back. That's all! Everything that was. Everything that will be. Everything I need to know in my life.

She trembled as she moved her watery eyes around in search of an opening, a single inch of space between one worshiper and the next, one uninhabitable inch that might've escaped the gathering of heads, arms, legs, backs, and bellies—otherwise known as the Quranic resurrection—but there wasn't any. Believers had wholly blanketed the earth, and Sumaya thought, *They have all managed to carve a way to you by any means necessary, and I finally got it! You. Me. We. You...*

What I had struggled to comprehend had been quite simple, in fact, and the pain piercing through me is nothing but a mere atom in a cosmic desert, buried among the buried, living among the living. And you are God: The Merciful. You. Me. Each of them. Us. We. Every one of these pilgrims has crawled to you, scraping knees, eyelashes, fingertips, livers, and hearts: as obedient servants—subservient to you. I got it!

Standing as straight as an arrow, meditating on the sky and the setting sun, Sumaya kept saying, I got it, God! I got it! A weird sensation coursed through her body as she scanned the vastness ahead. Now that she was on the highest peak of Mercy Mountain, Sumaya felt strange, as though she could see him and he could see her the way he watched over the entire world. The force that manifested in splendour was now recognizable to her in the smallest grain of sand and the farthest cloud, and for a second, a single second, she forgot everything: the husband, the son, and the throbbing pain. She felt herself fade away like dust particles dissipating in space. Then, she felt her presence everywhere, simultaneously—in the earth, in the mountains, and in the setting sun—and she understood that if a person disintegrated, their pain would likewise shatter into smithereens, and if a person tried to rebuild themselves into a solid entity once more, their hurt would similarly reemerge.

Sumaya lost herself in thought until the topography of suffering that she had ascended with bloody fingers disappeared—and nothing remained anywhere but him.

On the Way to Rijal Almaa Province

9 Dhu Al-Hijja, 1431

1:16 P.M.

His left hand is gripping the wheel. His right is holding up the victory sign.

Mishari, in a red T-shirt, is sitting beside him, legs raised above his uncle's leather seat to show off his new Crocs to the camera.

Mishari and Saud are both smiling.

Sumaya—who recorded the video on her phone—can be heard cautioning her brother-in-law, Take care of him, Saud. And he better not cross the street on his own!

Frustration is audible in Saud's reply, Enough, Sumaya! You're killing me with all this nagging. You're acting like you're the only mother in the world.

Don't buy him candy!

Fine!

And don't eat hamburgers for dinner, either! Find a clean restaurant with healthy options!

Saud taps his nose with the tip of his index finger. I promise. Are you happy now?

Mom, you can leave now! Mishari waves his tiny arms.

Laughing, Saud dips his fingers into Mishari's locks and lightly admonishes his nephew, Behave, little guy.

Uncle Saud, stop! You're messing up my hair!

Saud pushes Mishari's forehead backward. You got a big mouth, huh? Then he turns to Sumaya and asks, When were you planning on giving him a haircut? He looks like a girl!

Faisal wants to shave it all off in Mecca after the ritual, Sumaya answers.

I've seen it all for sure when even this tidbit becomes a pilgrim!

Uncle!

The recording ends.

Saud sat there in the black Tahoe, remembering how Sumaya had stood behind the crimson bougainvillea, her neck wrapped in a cashmere scarf, her long black hair cascading down her back. Be careful! she had cautioned them again before making her way across the yard and back to the house. The little one had waved goodbye, and Saud had pressed on the gas. The car had pelted toward the juice bar and the mellow voice of Al-Misbah had spilled out of the radio, chanting: Time has betrayed our reunion.

Mishari had exhaled. Uncle, I don't like this song. Please change it.

Saud's head pounded with details from this memory, echoing his loudly beating heart. He recalled: the smell of the cigarette smoke in his car, the aftershave on his chin, and the Dunhill cologne on his red and white headgear. He also remembered the texture of Al-Misbah's voice, Mishari's crankiness, and Sumaya's hand as she gestured for them to smile for the camera.

Her text, moments after Saud and Mishari had driven away, had said: You better not flirt in front of my son!

How he'd laughed afterward and responded, Flirting? Me? I don't do that sort of thing. I'm a straight-and-narrow kind of man.

How Sumaya had typed the prayer to ward off the devil, then added. You've been warned.

Ohhh. Spooky.

Small details—like memory crumbs. Saud had never imagined for a moment that the vibrant minutiae he had taken for granted would flood his mind: the redness of the bougainvillea vines, the green metal gate, the fragrance of his cologne permeating the air, the texture of Mishari's hair on his fingertips, Al-Misbah's soothing voice pouring out of the speakers, and all the words he had shared with the kid.

He remembered filling Mishari's head with talk of adventure throughout the ride to the juice bar.

Little guy, listen up! You can be the superhero. And I can be the anti-hero. But we are both apex predators, trampling the ground like lions! This, right here, is our indestructible car, which we use on our secret missions to save the world, and by that, I mean, as you well know by now, rescuing pretty girls. That's the fate of any hero. A superhero like you or an anti-hero like me. Every legend needs a legendary car, and there isn't a vehicle in the whole wide world that can compare to this one. She's your uncle's beloved. Saud had tenderly caressed the back of Mishari's leather seat, then whispered, his lips inches away from his steering wheel, La mia bella signora!

How do you know that her ear is in the wheel? Mishari had asked. Maybe it's in the speakers?

Saud had responded with a shake of his head, Can't be. 'Cause that's where her mouth is.

Where are you now, Mishari? What has happened to you?

Saud's index finger began to trace the bangs spilling over the laughing face on his iPhone screen. When he swiped left, a photograph appeared of Mishari lying on his stomach on Saud's bed, cupping a box of popcorn between his palms. It was Thursday, and Mishari had come over to spend the night at his uncle's place to watch movies as usual.

That day, Saud and Mishari had both enjoyed Christian Bale's performance as Batman. Saud had launched into a playful explanation, Batman is an apex predator like us. Another member of the League of Heroes who protects the world in general, and pretty women in particular. Like all heroes worthy of respect, Batman rides in a phenomenal car. Of course, it pales in comparison to your uncle's, but that doesn't mean we deny our good friend his exquisite taste. Just marvel at this fine specimen! Gaze upon those fins around the wheels and its pointed nose. Check out how it shoots grenades from the sides and how it fires from this machine gun in the front! And don't forget those hooks that prevent the car from sliding out of control. What a truly magnificent ride!

Mishari's eyes were shimmering as he sat transfixed in front of the TV, almost tearing up from the excitement. When I grow up, I'll buy one just like it!

Saud had chuckled at that announcement, grabbed a handful of popcorn, tossed one in the air, and caught it in his mouth, delighting the boy with his talent.

The way Mishari was beaming at his uncle had made Saud feel heroic, as though he were Batman himself, an extraordinary creature, mighty and monumental, someone always brave enough to intervene on behalf of the vulnerable.

Where is he?

A while back, Saud had asked Mishari: What's your favourite part of the Batman movie?

I love how the bats fly out of their cave to save him! They swoosh out and rush to his rescue!

Saud had nodded appreciatively, admiring the little one's logic. But he had said, As for me... Then pursed his lips, choosing his words carefully, knowing that the boy was holding his breath in anticipation. I love the movie for a different reason.

Mishari's eyes had bulged with excitement, eagerly waiting for his uncle to open his mouth again and share his unbounded wisdom.

Saud had milked the moment, lingering until the delicious tension reached its peak. I love those movies because of Christian Bale himself, the actor, not the character of Batman.

Mishari had craned his neck to study the man playing the role of Bruce Wayne on the screen. He didn't understand what his uncle was alluding to, so he turned back once more, confusion visible on his face.

Saud had ventured an explanation, He's not handsome, at least not by Hollywood standards. Christian Bale is like any average man you'd encounter on the street. And this, little guy, is actually profound.

Why? Mishari had asked. What's so great about an average-looking superhero?

It means that anyone can become one! Become a superhero, win the affection of a gorgeous girl, and drive an exceptional car! Saud saluted the television, where the actor, contemplating the weight of his responsibility, stood in a suit and tie in front of his superhero outfit.

Mishari, who was still pretty lost, had mimicked his uncle anyway. He'd raised his right arm in the air and, visibly revering his uncle's perceived omniscience, saluted the colossal figure on the screen: Batman, played by Bruce Wayne, played by Christian Bale.

Saud continued to flip between photographs and short videos and landed on an image of Mishari standing in front of a juice bar, his arms raised in the air, his fists balled like a victorious boxer. That picture had been taken after Mishari had completed Operation Prophet of Love No. 34—in other words, after helping his uncle flirt with another woman. This was the most exciting part of the adventures they'd often shared.

Saud would slip a piece of paper in his nephew's hand, call his name, and order Mishari to run up to the prettiest young woman, then flash his puppy eyes.

Hold on! Not before I fix your hair! Saud would comb his fingers through Mishari's locks, grab the kid by the back of the neck, and shove him forward. Alright, you can go now!

Saud remembered that time Mishari didn't move. After looking at the young woman, he'd turned back to whisper, But Uncle Saud, she's not pretty.

Hey little guy, why don't you just do your job? Saud had replied, snickering and tugging on Mishari's ear.

His nephew, who did as he was told, scored the young woman's number, then returned with a strut and a grin like a champion.

At midnight that evening, Saud's phone would ring, and the woman he had picked up via his nephew would be on the line, ready to fall in love.

Flipping through his phone's gallery albums, Saud landed on the last video Sumaya had recorded.

Saud is lying face down on a Persian rug in the living room, arms spread. Hey, little guy! he calls his nephew. Walk on my back!

It was a remedy to heal his back pain, which he frequently sought. At first, Mishari would take hesitant steps over his uncle's back, but once the little one gained confidence, he'd jump and dance, buoyed by his parents' laughter.

In this video, Mishari steps on his uncle's neck, Saud's body begins to shake, and the boy quickly runs away. The uncle roars like a lion and chases his nephew until he grabs hold of him, peels off Mishari's T-shirt, and lays a succession of quick and soft nibbles over the little boy's neck and shoulders. You can't escape the Dark Knight! he warns.

Mishari, who's laughing throughout the video, manages to slip out of his uncle's grip, darts away, and nips behind his mother, who is capturing the entire scene on her phone.

You can't escape me, little guy! I'll find you wherever you are!

The footage shakes.

The recording ends.

Mecca. Mount Arafa.

9 Dhu Al-Hijja, 1431

6:16 P.M.

Sumaya didn't know what happened to her on the mountain, but she realised when she came down that she would never be the same again.

Back on ground level, the stench of diesel fumes and piss saturated the atmosphere, and garbage littered the earth: orange peels, laban cartons, plastic cups, used napkins, rice, boxes of half-eaten dates, and diapers full of excrement. Sumaya ambled between two rows of buses preparing to head to Muzdalifa. She seemed intoxicated, gazing at the sky, a hint of a smile on her face, her body awash in a cool serenity. *I know that you're with me.* She took a deep breath before wrapping her arms around herself. *You are always with me.*

To her side, a family was rushing to a bus that had started its engine. Sumaya could tell from their demeanours that they were Kuwaiti.

One of them, a young woman who noticed Sumaya staring, smiled back as she boarded the bus, then turned around on the steps and asked as she held the railing, Are you coming with us?

Sumaya shook her head. *I'll walk to him.*

Suddenly, the woman's eyes widened, and her eyebrows arched in shock. Wait! I know you! Aren't you Um Mishari?

Sumaya nodded.

Did you find your son?

Soon, Sumaya answered, her voice painless, brimming with certainty.

The bus driver yelled at the woman to stop blocking the path of the other pilgrims trying to get in, and find her seat.

Ignoring him, she said to Sumaya, May God reunite you with your child, Um Mishari! I've been praying for you day and night since I found out. Oh, Allah, Gatherer of the People, on a day lacking all doubt... Um Mishari, Don't forget to keep reciting the prayer to help reclaim what was lost!

The woman finally went inside to find her seat, thereby allowing the group of pilgrims who'd huddled near the door to board as well.

The woman's words reverberated in Sumaya's head as she went on her way: *Oh Allah, Gatherer of the People, on a day lacking all doubt...* She repeated the phrase throughout her trek toward Muzdalifa. *Help me reclaim what I have lost.* Sumaya felt, for the first time, that she wasn't alone and that she wasn't walking under a taciturn sky.

For hours, she travelled among the spates of pedestrian pilgrims trudging toward Muzdalifa. When she saw a one-legged man beside her, leaning on a crutch, heading in the same direction, she felt that she was in the right place, performing actions God had prescribed to her directly. Then she heard his voice—a voice she could never mistake—crying and calling out to her.

Hope flooded her heart as she followed the faint aural thread, crying, Mishari! Mishari! Where are you? She found him standing between two lines of buses, facing away from her.

The neck. The head. The hair. It's him! Mishari! She screamed as loud as she could! Mishari! Baby!

When the boy turned around, she was stunned.

It was somebody else: a child with Asian features. Perhaps six years old. He had a round face and chubby cheeks, and he was weeping uncontrollably.

Her legs stopped moving. Sumaya had been sure it was him. How could she make this mistake again? The sound of the boy's persistent crying twisted her stomach in knots. Slowly, she approached him, bent down, then asked, Are you lost?

He burst into tears again, this time spewing Asian words.

Do you speak English?

He reached out to grab her abaya.

Sumaya took a deep breath and addressed her thought to the sky, *It's not my son.* She then tried to comfort the kid tugging on her abaya. Relax, relax, she said, parting his soft black hair with her fingers before searching his pockets for information, but he didn't have a single card. *What am I going to do now?* She asked, Mama?

And he burst into tears again, repeating the word after her.

She felt a pain in her heart as if a serrated knife had carved her chest in two. Mama: a word that transcends international borders—a word that pierces the heart like a blade.

Surveying the features on the boy's face, which seemed foreign to her, she began to consider that perhaps they weren't quite dissimilar from Mishari's.

Sumaya stretched her arm toward the boy and smiled when his fingers coiled around her hand. Let's look for your mom together, she said before asking, Are you from the Philippines? He didn't seem to understand her question. China? she suggested. Still nothing. When she tried, Indonesia?—his face lit up. Oh! So, you're Indonesian? I'm a social studies teacher. Geography is my favourite subject. You know, I teach children your age! You look to be about six. When Mishari was six, he could already speak in complete English sentences. How come you can't? Perhaps it never occurred to you that you'd need it in Mecca? So tell me, are you from Jakarta?

There was a glint in his eye as he repeated after her. Jakarta!

My name is Sumaya, she said, smiling, pressing her palm on her heart. Then, she said her name three more times.

The kid sniffed twice before wiping his nose on his sleeve.

Sumaya touched his chest and asked, What's your name?

This time, it seemed that he understood her question. Like her, he said it thrice: Kali, Kali, Kali.

Sumaya held his hand and walked beside him. Alright, Kali, we'll search for your mother together. And raising her puzzled eyes to the sky, she asked, *Is this why you brought me here?*

On the Way to Rijal Almaa Province

9 Dhu Al-Hijja, 1431

2:11 P.M.

He exhaled.

Saud could no longer scroll through his media gallery since the vibrant minutiae of his memories, flashing in succession and lashing at his heartstrings, kept crashing into one another—like the fated clash at the end of days. Mishari's red shirt. The Batman Crocs. Bougainvillea vines. The gate in the yard. The grey sidewalk. The gap in Mishari's smile. One detail after the other—bearing love and bearing pain. Although he had frequently heard the phrase: God is in the details, he only understood what it meant today.

Stuffing his phone back in his pocket, Saud looked out the window. He did not absorb the scenery despite skimming the road ahead, the sky and clouds above, and the mountains to the side. Instead, he paid attention to his thoughts where Mazen's warning echoed: *We need to be ready.*

Saud understood that, but...

How can you prepare for a moment with infinite possibilities for pain? What if the end is tragic? What if there was no closure? And where do you begin, you self-proclaimed Dark Knight, you fleeting illusion? You've been filling the little one's head with superhero stories, so why haven't you swooped in to save the day? I'm on my way! Isn't that what you promised? And didn't Mishari answer the phone? Didn't he say, Uncle? in that raspy voice that carried the strain of constant weeping.

Now, it's your eyes that are stinging from tears.

Look, your brother in the passenger seat has turned around to face you. His eyes drill into you as though he can discern every damn thought ebbing and flowing in your head. You pretend to be focused on the road because you don't want your brother to notice your fear. You're the Dark Knight that has come to save the day! I'm on my way, Faisal! You're always on your way. When will you reach your destination? And what exactly can you do when you finally show up?

Nothing.

Saud?

Your brother's voice attempts to summon you from your self-imposed reverie.

Yeah?

He asks you the question he's been avoiding for the past three hours.

What exactly did she tell you?

You knew he would ask, so you open your mouth mechanically and select a neutral tone to say, That we have to go to Rijal Almaa, then wait for her next call.

Where does she want us to wait?

It sounded like Kharar Bridge. Just under it.

Faisal hesitates before asking, Is that all? Didn't she tell you anything else?

Your eyes dart sideways. Heat permeates your skin, and you flush when you confirm, Yeah. That's all. You've always been masterful at bending the truth. After all, you're The Fibbing Flirt: someone who has never found it difficult to tell a lie. So, what's wrong with you today?

The sorrow visible in your brother's eyes amplifies your pain.

When he asks, And Mishari?

You fake a smile. He's fine. After wetting your lips, you add, Don't worry. The boy immediately recognised my voice. He sounded calm.

Faisal let out a deep breath. Thank God!

A few moments of silence pass before Faisal bursts into tears.

You okay, Faisal?

I should have spoken to him myself! He sobs.

A gentle smile spreads across Mazen's face, and he says with a shake of his head, You want the truth, Bu Mishari? I'm glad that Saud answered the call instead of you. I don't think you could've handled it.

To your surprise, Faisal nods.

If he had heard her voice, he would've showered her with obscenities.

If he had heard her voice, he would have fallen to his knees.

You're cornered.

How can you escape your brother's searching eyes? Those eyes submerged in tragedy? All your assurances are fake. You fraudster par excellence! In fact, the criminal made countless claims that frightened you. She said things so strange; you couldn't even tell what context you'd have to put them in to comprehend them.

The moment the phone rang in your hand, and the unknown number started blinking on the screen, you heard a small voice inside you saying it was her and that you should answer. A twinge in the left side of your chest told you that you were in the right place at the right time, doing the right thing: Answering the call—as though you had flown to Mecca to perform that very task at that very moment. You didn't know why you heard that inner voice or felt that twinge, yet you raised the phone to your ear, and every part of you keenly listened.

Damn her! She had spoken like Pharaoh.

I took him from you.

And I can return him.

If you want your son back, you'll follow my orders. Listen closely, now. I got the kid. You got the cash. We'll swap the two, but you've got to do what I tell you first. If you don't, you can kiss your son goodbye, 'cause I can sell him to someone else. Now pay attention. Memorise these terms like holy verses.

You never call me. I'm the one who calls. And you don't contact the police, either. If they get involved, I'll chop the boy up and sell him piece by piece! Eyes! Heart! Livers!

Bring the million dollars to Rijal Almaa. Park your car under Kharar Bridge at 10 p.m., then wait until I call you again to tell you where the trade will take place. Clear?

You don't know how you found the strength to reply, Let me hear my son first.

Faisal's eyes had bulged when he heard you speak those words. He had even tried to reach for his phone—but Mazen had lunged between you both, and as he grabbed Faisal tightly by the forearms, Mazen whispered gently in his ears, Let your brother handle this!

Mishari's voice then billowed toward you from the depths of fear itself. Dad? It was hoarse, as though he hadn't stopped crying.

You had burst into tears and, feeling strangled, had thrice tried and failed to open your mouth and utter a word.

Dad? The little one had asked a second time.

Mishari? You had said, at last, struggling to keep your voice steady.

Uncle?

I'm on my way!

CHAPTER SIX

NATHEER

a messenger bringing news; vow; omen

The Red Sea

9 Dhu Al-Hijja, 1431

10:20 P.M.

The inflatable dinghy was floating in the night; in the ocean; in the silence.

The boat, which was carrying six unconscious kids, their wrists and ankles bound, their mouths taped shut, stopped navigating away from the coast when Jerjes killed the engine and dropped the anchor. He then proceeded to burrow in a burlap bag.

Saliha was dripping sweat, and she was squatting on her heels on the polymer floor, near the inflatable siding, when she realised that she was far away from solid ground for the first time in her life, so she wrapped an arm around the rubber edge to hold on tight. The engine's burning oil had mixed with the ocean's briny smell, and the waves crashing against the plastic flooring echoed the rumbling in her stomach. She thus turned her attention to Jerjes, who was ferreting around scattered items, waving his flashlight back and forth.

Jerjes pulled a transponder from the pocket of one of his vests, then mumbled, Where are my cigarettes? Where are they? When he found the nylon bag with the box of tobacco and cigarette rolls, he suddenly laughed, unclasped the lid, extracted a roll, and slipped it between his lips. Checking the device in his hand, he muttered, Good. The Coast Guard hadn't been informed. We're still safe, for now. Jerjes appeared to be talking to himself. He turned off the flashlight and sat on the port side of the bow.

A dense ribbon of clouds hovered in front of the moon, blocking its refracted light and filling the world with absolute darkness. Apart from Jerjes's mouth and chin, illuminated by embers of the cigarette dangling from his lips, Saliha couldn't see anything. She stared absentmindedly at the hairy stubble around his lustful mouth. Feeling her nausea swell, she asked him, What are we waiting for?

The skiff, he answered.

They were then enveloped by a doleful quiet the way night itself had spread. Saliha felt Jerjes's eyes attempting to pierce through disparate layers of darkness. *What is he thinking? A bullet in Uthman's head. A blade in Ruwaina's belly. The Kuwaiti who escaped and the Indian who's dying. Jerjes lost control of everything in one fell swoop.* Saliha sensed him unveiling her physical details despite the surrounding gloom. Was he looking at her, or was she imagining it? She felt fear for the first time, as though she had finally understood that anybody who worked for Jerjes became a slave, and if they ever dared to leave or deceive him, they'd end up—just like Uthman and Ruwaina— with a bullet in the head or a blade in the gut. Meanwhile, he'd leave in a rush to watch as their dead bodies glided on black waves.

Jerjes's chin was visible in the nimbus of light cast by the cigarette. Focusing on his lower lip, Saliha wondered if he'd kill her, too. She trembled. A cold bead of sweat that ran down the back of her neck slid down to her lower back. Suddenly, waves crashed under the polymer floor. She shut her eyes and held on to the inflatable edge.

It's the sharks, he whispered.

Her face paled and she shivered.

Are you scared?

Did she imagine the sadistic joy in his voice? It seemed to her that he was enjoying himself, uttering her name in the dark, Oh Saliha, Saliha, Saliha... She felt like a mouse in a lion's den. Something else banged against the bottom of the boat, and she screamed.

Jerjes laughed and told her not to worry. Just relax.

But Saliha panted anxiously.

It's just a hungry shark trying to tip over the raft and devour everyone aboard.

Saliha continued to hold on with all her might.

Ruwaina was never afraid of sharks. She spent her time rolling cigarettes, Jerjes said sardonically, then softly chanted: Ruwaina, Ruwaina, my old hag Ruwaina...

It dawned on Saliha that she was being mocked by Jerjes, who must've known all along that she had been angling to usurp Ruwaina's position as his confidant. Saliha had dreamed of being chosen by the man deemed a god by some and a demon by others. She had coveted Ruwaina's position, however... *Ruwaina, the old hag, is incomparable.* Saliha, who was struggling to lift her head, tried to see beyond the gloom, to penetrate the thick layer of darkness, beyond the ocean, beyond the sharks, and beyond Jerjes himself. Her breathing escalated and sweat dampened her forehead.

The children, who began to stir awake, broke into tears. Their sobs came out of their muffled mouths in a faint crescendo.

Jerjes said forcefully, Shut them up now, or they'll get us killed.

Exerting great courage, Saliha forced her fingers to let go of the rubber edge. Then, crawling on all fours toward the weeping captives, her quivering fingers extracted the towel soaked in chloroform from the first aid kit. One by one, she pressed the drenched cotton to each young face. A few minutes later, silence reigned again: a sound devoid of human speech yet loud, encompassing the waves rumbling and crashing against the boat, and her own frenzied heart beating out of control. When she spoke next, distress was noticeable in her voice, They better hurry. I don't feel safe here.

Wait till you lay your eyes on the Cobia boats, Jerjes said wryly.

Cobia boats?

You don't know what that means?

Since he was clearly ridiculing her ignorance, Saliha decided to err on the side of strength instead of exposing her fear and thus fired back, her tone as strong as she could muster, And how the hell would I know? It's my first time on a damn boat!

That's right, he said, a mysterious smile stretching across his lips. Jerjes blew the smoke out of his nostrils, then took another deep puff before explaining, Cobias are immigration boats. After a pause for dramatic effects, he added, Cobias are synonymous with risking one's life.

The boat rocked again, leading Saliha to scooch toward the inflatable edge once more.

He simply went on, If you'd ever been to Sawakin on the West Coast of the Red Sea, you'd be familiar with this word. It's a word smugglers use. Flicking his cigarette butt into the water and lighting another, Jerjes slowed down the pace of his speech and said, Cobias are small fishing boats. Although they're unsafe for sailing across long distances, they're frequently used to smuggle people into Saudi Arabia or Yemen. Each person costs ten thousand dollars.

Saliha felt her headache swirl with nausea, then quickly snapped her palm across her mouth to stop herself from hurling.

Can you roll?

Saliha raised her chin with difficulty to look up at the darkness stretching across the sky. Everywhere she turned was dark, except for the tiny glow of Jerjes's cigarette, illuminating the sneer on his thick lips—despite the lethal ocean and the hungry sharks beneath.

His smug grin widened. Here. Have one.

A blustery wave knocked against the inflatable dinghy, causing Saliha to scream.

Hushhh. Relax! Jerjes turned behind him to survey the ocean. The sharks are starving, he added snidely.

She thought about those aquatic monsters chasing a dilapidated skiff, slamming their tails into it, their sharp teeth snapping its boards to pieces. Saliha imagined the water leaking into the boat and how they'd all topple over. She saw herself screaming and thrashing about, then sinking into the deep black sea. The sharks, devouring her body, would tear it limb by limb. She swallowed before asking in a shaky voice, Why board the Cobia if the inflatable is safer?

Specialization.

What?

Jerjes sighed in contempt, and though he deigned to explicate, it seemed he was getting fed up with her trepidation and her dull-witted questions. Do you think anybody can wander into our turf and compete with us for profit? It's not that simple. He took another drag on his cigarette, blew the smoke out of his nostrils, then added, The truth is we're all obeying the same master at the end of the day.

He was no longer smiling as he tried to picture the man in charge, the man who plots and plans these operations, the man who orchestrates the boats, who receives the children, and who gets paid millions of dollars: the man behind the curtain.

Jerjes wondered in silence what he would tell that man.

Day 4

He could still hear the woman screaming in his head. Although she had promised to return him to his mother, she had stayed behind, in the ocean, ordering him to run—alone. Her command was followed by the sound of a gunshot that penetrated the night with a bang. When he came out of the water, Mishari sprinted on foot, despite the thistles on the ground pricking his soles. He carried on because the woman had told him that she would hide him in a cave until his father arrived. After all, she was the one who took him from his parents, and she was the one who'd return him...

But she didn't.

When Mishari tripped on a log, he stretched out his arms to cushion his fall and latched onto the thick stem of a cactus. The sharp spines pierced his palms, so he let go and fell face-down to the ground, his body tingling with pain. He was terrified, however, of screaming in case it helped the kidnappers find him. He therefore swallowed his tears and snot and pushed himself up to resume his sprint.

And though the bristly ground below his feet continued to sting, the sprint became a canter, the canter a walk, the walk a stumble; from then onward, the cycle reset, from bolt to jog to slog to stagger—for hours on end. Mishari crossed the boundaries of thirst and hunger in pitch darkness and grave silence, tongue rough like a log, vision blurry and glazed, his physical grasp of reality rapidly fading. Weakly, he whispered, I'm sick! He wanted to shout, Mama!—but he feared that it might lead the thugs right to him, so he carried on moving, his palms still twinging, he was faintly uttering, I'm sick, dragging his heavy legs across the gloomy void, scarcely breathing the brackish air hanging densely all around him. His soles, already bare and bruised, once even landed on a jagged rock, and blood gushed out of one of his heels. Collapsing to his knees and sobbing, he imagined the Crocs in his mother's purse and feverishly mumbled until he finally collected himself. Mishari was all cried out when he noticed a dilapidated wall and decided it was time for him to lie on his side. Mama, I'm going to sleep now, he said out loud. Once he closed his eyes, he began to dream that he was dreaming.

Five children are trembling in the corner of a sparse room. Mishari crawls on all fours to join them, tears streaming down his cheeks—but the foreign woman grabs his heels and pulls him back onto her lap, her dank sweat filling his nostrils.

Wriggling on her lap and trying to get away, Mishari screams and stretches his arm to one of the dark-skinned children, whose green snot had coagulated on his upper lip. From the corner of his eyes, Mishari spots a young girl lying on her back, legs apart. He looks at the damaged flesh between her slim thighs and panics when he sees the bloodstain on her dress begin to spread. Mishari waves his arms and desperately kicks as the dark-skinned boy approaches the foreign woman, but she spits out, Get back, filth! Then she says to the child on her lap, You on the other hand stay with me.

At first, Mishari doesn't comprehend her instructions, but then something clicks and he pays attention, parsing out her words, making sense of her whispers: If you behave, I'll return you to your mother. Mishari shakes his head in disbelief. The woman cups his head, then asks, Do you want to speak to your mother now? If you calm down, we will call her.

So Mishari quiets down. Tension leaves his body as he wipes his tears, curls into a ball, and wraps his arms around his knees in the woman's lap. She goes back to her singing, but every once in a while, she leans down and whispers something in his ear. Mishari is only able to understand some of the things she tells him.

Sitting amid the weeping children and the other female thugs, the foreign woman continues to dictate her escape plan. Nobody notices because she shares all her details while pretending to sing.

She tells Mishari about the ocean and the cave. I won't drug you like the others. They'll all die. She says, chantlike. But you won't die if you listen to me.

Mishari's horror-stricken eyes glance at the others, his body stiffening.

You must run away on the beach when I untie your rope.

She peppers her instructions with songs in a different language.

Mishari tries his best to comprehend her words.

I will hide you in a cave, she says, then delves into her sorrowful song. After some time, she adds, In that area, there are wolves...

The cycle goes on: she croons, kisses him all over his face, squeezes his forearms, then threatens his life.

Mishari keeps flinching between her thighs until his eyes dart across the room to the young brown girl moaning in the corner, begging for water.

But the foreign woman gives the bottle to him and a bit of bread. Mishari eats and drinks as the other children resentfully watch from a distance.

And this time, the woman doesn't even whisper. She asks aloud, Do you need to pee?

Mishari shakes his head before realising that she expected him to say, Yes.

One of the other women mentions something, but the woman holding Mishari waves dismissively and says in Arabic, The boy needs the restroom.

She grabs Mishari's hand and leads him to a stark lavatory, where she peels off his underwear, then turns around to inspect herself in the bifurcated mirror and give Mishari some privacy to relieve himself. When the smell of urine saturates the air, she turns and presses an index finger to her lips. With her other hand, she pulls out a phone and the folded piece of paper that Mishari had handed over when they'd first met. After dialling the number on the white slip, she moves the phone a hairbreadth away from her lips, curls her fingers around the speaker to prevent the sound from spilling out, and says—I have your son.

She then passes Mishari the phone.

He's expecting to hear his father's voice, but... Uncle?

Suddenly, someone starts rapping their knuckles on the wooden door, and she snatches the phone from his hand.

What are you doing in there? Open the door! Open it right now!

The woman hangs up. She clutches Mishari's hand once more and turns the key with the other. What's all this about? she asks while swinging the door open. He needed to pee!

The man's yellow eyes glare at both woman and child before saying something in a language Mishari could not understand. The woman responds in the same language, her arms wildly gesticulating. But the man shoves her away from him. Her head bangs against the wall as the man's voice rises angrily. She pushes herself back up, but the man points at the door. The woman grabs Mishari's hand again and makes her way toward the children's room, then sits Mishari down in the corner, all alone.

He stands there, gazing at the children huddled across from him, the children who will die—every one of them...

The Indian girl keeps moaning: Paani! Paani!

Mishari crawls on all fours to press the lip of his water bottle on the lips of the young girl.

The Red Sea

10 Dhu Al-Hijja 1431

12:21 A.M.

Saliha began to crawl toward Jerjes, meandering between the young unconscious bodies, crumpled trousers, and balled-up T-shirts. She hunkered down when she reached him and wrapped one arm around the inflatable siding before stretching the other to snatch the cigarette from his mouth and suck on it herself. She took consecutive drags until she calmed down, leaned back against the edge of the dinghy, and asked, Who is he?

Jerjes grimaced, but instead of answering her question, he simply ogled her body, wondering how things would pan out between them. Can you roll a cigarette?

Who is he? Tell me, she asked again with a frown.

You're useless, he said, taking his roll back.

Won't you tell me?

No. *That brat wants to know who she's working for.* Jerjes thought that Saliha's curiosity might've bested her fear for the moment, so he pursed his lips, then added, You have to learn.

After all, he did enjoy his post-sex ritual: Watching the small, brown fingers of a woman handle his tobacco, sprinkle it on a sheet, and press her tongue along the narrow strip. Suddenly, Jerjes felt the gaping hole Ruwaina had left behind when he'd swivelled the boat around to leave her floating in the ocean with a blade in her gut. He attempted to erase the memory of her face with a shake of his head, to forget the swollen eyelid, the bruise in the corner of her mouth, and her numerous braids, their ashen roots, and their ruddy edges. He had repeatedly invited her to his bed, and she had welcomed him deep inside her without naively asking about his business. Ruwaina would figure it out herself. *This brat, on the other hand, keeps on whining.*

Have you ever met him? Where is he from? Is he one of the elites?

Jerjes dumped the cigarette butt in the water and muttered, The boat's late. *What a moron,* he thought. *Her naïveté is unforgivable.* How else would he have successfully run the types of operations he'd been relying on to survive without the backing of a very important person? Jerjes had never interacted with his patron in the flesh; they had communicated only through intermediaries. One in particular: a man from the desert, known as The Sultan. He was the one who received the children and who paid Jerjes for his services.

Jerjes began to search for his flashlight among the objects he'd scattered across the floor. When he found it, he turned it on, then aimed it carefully at each captive to examine their faces. They were all unconscious, one Indian girl and five African boys, all of them naked, two of them missing limbs. *The perfect merchandise,* he thought, before starting to plot an even bigger operation to cover his losses.

He was supposed to deliver twelve prepubescent boys and girls to his superior, but he had managed to accumulate only six—one of whom was dying. It was upon taking one look at the Kuwaiti boy's flier that he had decided to forgo his original plan and pursue a bigger fish: to cross the ocean, to reach Sinai with the Kuwaiti kid, and to negotiate a higher selling price for him. *But now he's gone.* So, Jerjes decided to return to the camps he knew so well, the ones in which he had spent a good deal of his life, the ones from which he had previously kidnapped dozens of boys and girls. He was now sick of pennies and craved a cushier job. *Damn you, Uthman!*

Jerjes had recently heard about a gang that kidnapped a hundred children, a group of Europeans who had entered under the guise of missionary work. They paid the parents a thousand dollars per child on the pretext of enrolling those children in a Christian school. Because the group's name and the school's name were both made up, nobody was able to determine the fate of the children. *Damn those white folk.* If Jerjes had gone to the camp and introduced himself as a preacher or a missionary, nobody would've believed him—the colour of his skin needed to be different, like the colour of the modern world: the colour of those who committed crimes with a silk tie and clean gloves.

Jerjes aimed the flashlight at Saliha's face.

Her big and curious eyes were now studying him.

Lowering the beam down to her throat, he paused on one breast, then the other, lingered on her midriff, dropped to her thighs, and returned to her crotch—all the while wondering how he could climb higher into the network, to become like The Sultan, the boss's right hand. Except his current patron didn't know who he was, and why would he? After all, Jerjes was only another cog in the global machine.

The patron didn't know Jerjes, however—Jerjes knew him, for he had seen his overlord's picture in newspapers and on television screens, always appearing in a slick suit and a red silk tie. In fact, Jerjes even knew his partners: the whole lot who scrubbed their hands with French soap and rinsed the scum with perfumed water. The boss's partners never left their air-conditioned offices, where massive income streams directly spilled into their pockets.

The Sultan had divulged the identity of every one of their boss's associates: generals, ministers from different countries, and the rabbi they all obeyed. So, even though none of them knew him, Jerjes knew those demigods by name.

What are you doing? Because the flashlight was aimed straight at Saliha's face, she shielded her eyes with her thin, brown forearm. What's with you today? she asked, a look of disdain on her face. What the hell happened to you?

Jerjes, who was deeply immersed in both his thoughts and her physical details, mumbled, You better learn how to roll a cigarette or else.

What's the big deal? You're obsessed with rolling cigarettes!

He said, I don't like idle hands, and aimed the flashlight at her fingers. Get it?

Saliha swallowed. I never...

Placing a hand on her thigh, he added, You better learn. It's not that difficult.

A moan, doleful and frail, asking for some water, dissipated the tension.

What now? he grumbled.

Paani... Paani...

Jerjes moved closer to the Indian girl to inspect her face. Her breathing had slowed down, and the colour of her skin had become concerning. She's very pale, he said.

Saliha lifted the hem of the young girl's dress to expose the torn flesh, then said, She's lost a lot of blood.

Give her some water.

How will she drink it? She's unconscious!

Just do it.

The girl's condition bothered him, because he finally realised that she could die before the swap. *Another terrible loss to add to all the others!* It reminded him of Ruwaina, who had already predicted the girl's demise. Jerjes had been willing to risk it, for he'd been betting it all on the Kuwaiti boy, but now... He'll need to keep the Indian girl alive another week.

We barely have enough water for us. Plus, she's already going to die.

Shut up and do as you're told.

Pouting, Saliha brought the water thermos closer to the girl's lips.

Jerjes ignored her petulance. He returned to his spot, where he aimed the flashlight at the girl and his subordinate, then smoked another cigarette. Just as he was about to tell Saliha to obey his order, the transponder near him began to buzz, so he said with a grin, The Cobia's here.

Jazan

10 Dhu Al-Hijja, 1431

7:02 P.M.

When he opened his eyes, he saw a long black silhouette surrounded by white mist. That dark, vertical mass was approaching.

Mishari heard someone say, Paani! Paani! And tried to move his lips but couldn't.

The voice kept repeating the word. Paani, larka. Paani.

Body burning from fever, Mishari felt a hand cup the back of his neck, forcing his head upward. A cool, hard object touched his dry lips before water began to spout out, trickling into his mouth and down his neck. Mishari craved more, but his lips wouldn't move, so he closed his eyes. When he opened them again, the white mist receded, and colours regained their vibrancy: grey, black, and blue.

The face of a brown man came into view, followed by a white plaster ceiling and a static fan hanging from its centre. Mishari turned his gaze elsewhere, landing first on a television set, then on a metal door. He returned to peer into the stranger's face and focused on its clean-shaven chin, thick moustache, hollow sockets, bushy eyebrows, and the four squiggly lines on its forehead.

When he zoomed out, Mishari realised that the man was wearing a kurta, a white cap was perching on his head, his left hand was tucked under his chin, and his right hand was holding a glass of water. Mishari turned around again, but he found a wall covered in photos of naked women, so he quickly closed his eyes.

After splashing water on Mishari's face, the foreign man poured some of it into his palm for Mishari to drink.

Mishari endeavoured to move his chapped lips. He drank from the foreigner's hand and softly asked for more water in Arabic: Mai.

Paani, replied the stranger who, upon pressing his palm to Mishari's chest, began to whisper protective invocations.

Mishari understood that if he said paani, the man would give him water, so he said the word and was finally able to quench his thirst before closing his eyes. He dreamed of himself as a pebble cast against a wall, then gasped awake. This time, Mishari could see the man speaking in a strange language more clearly. He noted the white cap and the thick moustache, then heard the cooler humming in the corner of the room.

Jarna? the man asked, bringing his fingers near his mouth.

Mishari did feel hungry, so he nodded.

The man got up to leave and returned carrying a copper pot full of rice. He dipped his fingers into the pot, scooped out some rice, and fed Mishari with his own fingers.

Mishari closed his eyes the instant the cold dry morsels touched his teeth and tongue, and this time he saw their faces.

All of them are laughing.

Stretching his arm toward Mishari, his uncle says, Come on, little guy, crack my fingers for me.

Mishari tries his best. First, he grabs his uncle's index finger with both hands. Then, he pulls and hears a: Pop! The sound of victory.

After lunging, his uncle envelopes Mishari in a warm embrace, squeezes tightly, and taunts, Go on! Try to escape me if you can.

Mishari squirms while laughing.

His uncle peels off Mishari's shirt, lifts him high, tosses him in the air, then catches him and proceeds, once more, to tickle his giggling nephew underneath the armpits.

The sound of rising gibberish, however, caused Mishari to part his heavy eyelids.

The tanned man with the white cap came into view again. He was mimicking Mishari and chuckling. Kiyoon bansa, larka?

This is the second time Mishari noticed the word, larka, so he assumed it was his new nickname. Yet, the dizziness he felt jumbled everything in his head. Raising his arm weakly, he pointed at himself, opened his mouth with some effort, then said in Arabic: Ismi Mishari.

The man peered at him inquisitively.

Mishari coughed and jabbed his chest with his index finger. This time his voice came out more clearly when he said his name, Mishari Faisal, before repeating the entire sentence in English: My name is Mishari Faisal.

Misaari, larka? the man asked, mispronouncing the name.

The boy corrected the man with a shake of his head, Mishari.

The second time the stranger tried, he nailed the pronounciation.

Thus, Mishari asked in English, What's your name?

The adult first touched his own chest and said, Nitham. After a beat, he provided his full name, Nitham Shuja a-Din.

The little one repeated after him, Nitham Shuja a-Din.

The man said with a chuckle, Smart, larka... Mishari.

The Red Sea

10 Dhu Al-Hijja, 1431

3:14 A.M.

The wooden skiff, a ramshackle Sanbuk with a single engine, carrying Saliha, Jerjes, its captain, and six sleeping children, was zipping across the Red Sea toward Sinai.

It had been sailing for three hours before the captain killed the engine.

In no time at all, Saliha became aware of the presence of others: dozens of African men, women, and children cramped in boats that would be undetectable, were it not for the burning embers on the passengers' cigarettes, glimmering in the heart of darkness.

As the clouds above receded, they revealed a gibbous moon refracting its light upon a star-studded sky.

Despite its smaller size and shabbier conditions, Saliha found the skiff sturdier than the inflatable dinghy they had already abandoned in the middle of the ocean. And because the Sanbuk was more resistant to the volatile waves, it made Saliha believe that they had escaped the risk of being devoured by sharks. With this newfound confidence, she got up to explore, but her legs began to shake almost instantly, so she leaned on the paddle for support and counted with her index finger the number of boats in their vicinity, then asked, Are all of them Cobia boats?

Jerjes nodded. Those passengers are being smuggled into Sinai. And from there to Israel.

To the promised land, she muttered with a confident nod of her head.

After all, Saliha was familiar with the campaign from twenty years ago—that launched in 1990—a campaign called Operation Solomon. It involved ten thousand Ethiopian migrants who bought into the assurances for housing, work, and governmental stipends various media outlets were circulating at the time. Hence, thousands of African Jews gave up their hometowns in Addis Ababa and journeyed to Tel Aviv. Peasants and farmers, in multitudinous packs, began to turn their backs on villages and rivers—often wracked by starvation, epidemics, and droughts—to claim their Right of Return. But what were they returning to? A place they'd never even left?

Still, when the thousands of undocumented Africans arrived in Israel, they were challenged to prove their Jewishness, and those who failed their tests were forced to re-confront their Black hunger. Among those who were denied entry to Israel was Saliha's own family. She was only three at the time.

Fools, she said at last.

The captain concurred with a slight nod. As he lit a cigarette, he added, Most of them perish on the way. Curlicues of smoke wiggled out of his nostrils before he said, They drown here in the water, but their corpses are buried afterward in the desert.

Jerjes grinned. The road to the Promise Land is paved with fire and brimstone.

Saliha remembered her father's words. Back then, most Africans would be yearning to join the Falash Mura Jews' community, since their Muslim heritage could do nothing to alleviate their hunger.

Her eyes darted across the black void, where dozens of orange sparks flickered. Falash means exiled, she said. It means—Other. Then, she wondered what kind of life she'd be living today had her family succeeded in their endeavour, what sort of bed she'd be sleeping in, what type of utensils she'd be using to eat her meals, and which outfits she'd wear for work?

Jerjes said, I can make it happen.

Saliha's jaw dropped. Make what happen?

A life in Israel.

If you could do that, why haven't you gone there yourself?

He didn't answer.

Waves, ebbing and flowing, murmured all around. A baby on one of the boats suddenly began to weep, the faint cries audible from a distance.

Saliha asked Jerjes, Is it really possible to live a life—a normal life—away from the world we currently inhabit?

As the moon ducked behind one of the dense clouds, the newborn began to wail.

Jerjes muttered, He's going to get us killed.

The captain nodded. Either the mother throws her baby in the ocean, or the others will drown both mother and child.

After a few seconds of silence, Saliha said, Seems like the baby calmed down. She grabbed the flashlight and aimed it at the faces of the sleeping children on their boat. The pallid Indian girl had stopped moaning. She's dying.

Jerjes said, She better not.

She will though.

Have you heard the story of the boat that recently sank? the captain interjected.

No, she answered.

About a hundred and fifty migrants, jam-packed in a fishing boat, were trying to sneak into Saudi Arabia. All but three of them drowned. Those who were rescued were discovered three days later.

Jerjes, staring absentmindedly at the dying girl, appeared uninterested in the conversation.

The captain continued anyway, The rescue boats recovered at least ten swollen and decomposing corpses of those migrants. They had washed up on the Sudanese coast. Not to mention, authorities had found dozens of mangled bodies floating around in the ocean, just bits and pieces of flesh among the flotsam. I swear, only last night I watched with my own eyes a torso floating unattached to a head, a pair of legs, or anything else.

Jerjes flashed Saliha a smile. That's why it's better to work with kids.

Is that the only reason?

What are you getting at?

Come, she told him, take a look at this.

As the gibbous moon emerged again, it illuminated the girl's corpse.

Jerjes asked, What now?

She's dead.

Are you sure?

Of course. Here, see for yourself.

He crawled over. The girl's skin had turned yellow. Her jaw was loose and her eyes were gaping at the sky as though awaiting an answer.

The captain glanced at the girl, then asked, What happened?

She died, Saliha answered.

How?

Saliha looked at Jerjes from the corner of her eye and said, She bled to death.

That's pretty common, the captain remarked with a satisfied nod.

So what now? Saliha asked Jerjes.

He blew smoke from his nostrils, then said, Throw her overboard.

The captain picked up the dead girl, then tossed her into the water. The bloody wound between her legs attracted the sharks, who devoured her in minutes.

All three watched the girl become a feast for aquatic beasts, whose fins appeared and disappeared beneath the water, while the waves rumbled all around.

Once the moon vanished, the three adults began to ponder in absolute darkness. The heavy silence that permeated the scene for some time was like a covert cover, erasing the crime.

Right before the captain restarted the engine, however, Saliha mumbled, I think her name was Mariam.

Day 5

The Red Sea

11 Dhu Al-Hijja, 1431

3:56 AM

The latest Land Cruiser model was already parked on the western shore of the Suez Canal beside the tunnel of Ahmad Hamdi the martyr. The four-wheeler was equipped with weapons, tents, and canned food. Three men in white robes and red-chequered headdresses that concealed their faces were standing nearby, each carrying a Kalashnikov on one shoulder, each expecting a boat to deliver their merchandise: five new kids and a woman.

Once the rickety Sanbuk moored near the coast, Jerjes and Saliha began transporting their young captives to the shore.

They hadn't yet decided on a price for Saliha's venture to Israel. While Jerjes waded through the water on his way back to the boat, and Saliha made her way to the shore after having left the skiff, one of the children missing an arm dangling on her shoulder, she whispered: Who are these guys?

The Ra'aida, Jerjes replied.

After the sharks had gobbled up Mariam in the water, Saliha agreed to the offer of being smuggled into Israel. She had answered softly, sweat dampening her palms and temples.

Jerjes had responded with a silent nod.

And she had leaned against the gunwale to gawp at the ocean with her fear-stricken eyes, quietly standing there until she'd spotted land looming on the horizon. She had decided, then and there, to never return to these boats again.

How much do you want? she now asked Jerjes breathlessly.

Half your share.

That's a lot.

That's the price.

What's my guarantee that I'll get there safely?

Nothing.

As they went back and forth from boat to shore, Saliha ruminated on the ocean, the night, the young girl's body that had been eviscerated by sharks, and she knew that she'd never want to find herself in a similar situation. And Israel? That other place where ordinary life could be experienced was only miles away. Was she crazy enough to waste an opportunity like this one?

So, she said: OK.

The skiff vanished half an hour later, and the children, awake and exhausted, were too dizzy and weak to cry. Instead, their low, intermittent groans spurted out from the back of the Land Cruiser as it tore through the desert.

Jerjes was sitting in the passenger seat.

Saliha who, on the other hand, was sandwiched between two

armed thugs, tried to follow the conversation that was happening in the front between Jerjes and the man in the driver's seat, wondering all the while, *Is that The Sultan?*

Although they were softly mumbling, she managed to catch most of their dialogue.

We said twelve kids. You brought five. You think this is a game?

Saliha was surprised to see Jerjes's head drop between his shoulders. His hands waved anxiously in the air as he explained himself.

The man behind the wheel raised his hand to cut him off. Save your excuses.

He seems small. Half-god, half-devil? More like the frog who wanted to become an elephant.

She heard him whisper, You know what happened.

The driver surprised her when he suddenly shouted, But why did you leave before completing the job?

Jerjes muttered, The Kuwaiti... I thought his ransom would cover the losses and then some.

You were supposed to deliver twelve in addition to the Kuwaiti. We had an agreement.

Nodding submissively, his expression full of shame, Jerjes protested, I understand that, but his disappearance caused a commotion, and everyone started to look for him. His photograph is plastered on every front page and is still spreading on the Internet. We had to leave sooner than expected.

And how did he escape?

One of my men betrayed me.

Admitting your incompetence?

There was nothing I could do about it.

What about the girl? How did she die, hm?

Ears turning red, Jerjes sheepishly answered, Fever.

You've let me down.

I'll make it up to you. I swear. I'll head straight to a camp.

Save your breath.

Jerjes bowed his head.

The man behind the wheel drove in silence, barrelling down golden stretches and rattling through valleys. For some time, only the sound of the young captives' intermittent cries could be heard.

Saliha, who was still wedged stiffly between two armed men, dripping sweat, her eyes shining with fear, noticed Jerjes peeking at her every once in a while through the rearview mirror.

After seven sombre hours, the Land Cruiser finally parked in front of a metal building surrounded by a barbed wire fence. An armed man was guarding the door, his red-chequered headdress masking his face.

Jerjes turned around. This is your stop, he told Saliha.

Where's my money?

Half your share belongs to me—the other half belongs to the

smugglers, who'll help you sneak into Israel.

Saliha studied the building's drab metal walls, the barbed wire fence, the savage wasteland surrounding it, the Kalashnikov hanging from the guard's shoulder, and the greyhound beside him. The panic that flooded her heart was now reflected on her face. She shook her head and said, I changed my mind. I'm not going.

Jerjes smiled, said nothing, and turned back to face the front as one of the armed men flanking Saliha grabbed her forearm. The thug began to drag her out of the car, but she screamed and resisted. Jerjes! No! Saliha sunk her nails into the warm flesh of the criminal, who smacked her nose, and blood dripped down from one of her nostrils. The thug then tried to follow the smack with a chokehold, but before he could wrap his arm around her neck, Saliha bit into his forearm, so he let go, and she used this opening to stumble out of the vehicle and bolt, but she tripped and fell, then got up to continue running as fast as she could, screaming at the top of her lungs until a gunshot pierced the air. Bang!

One of the masked men yelled, Stop, or I'll shoot.

But Saliha didn't stop. She sped up instead.

The two thugs that darted behind her accelerated until they caught up to her wobbly legs and managed to knock her down. They returned to the metal house with the barbed-wire fence, holding her by the ankles and dragging her body across the scorching desert ground, yet right before the armed men heaved Saliha inside the house, she caught a glimpse of the third masked man passing Jerjes a stack of American dollars.

It was the price of the woman he'd just upsold.

CHAPTER SEVEN

NA'EER

any loud noise or clamour; organised yelling, for example: against a
sports team; mooing or lowing (the deep, low guttural sound of cattle)

Rijal Almaa Village. Kharar Bridge

9 Dhu Al-Hijja, 1431

5:10 p.m.

Mazen parked the black Tahoe under the bridge. After killing the engine, he glanced at his phone to examine the different coloured routes on his Google Maps, then lifted his head to confirm, That's the bridge, guys. We're here.

Faisal, who took in the gramineous surroundings sloping all around them, turned to his brother and asked, Now what?

Now, we wait for her to call us.

Instead of the optimism that had washed over Faisal upon leaving Mecca—of which nothing was left—there was now a constant quiver in his fingertips. He unlocked the door and got out of the car, his legs stiff, his feet numb. A painful sensation, which had sprouted in his neck, now shot down to the bottom of his back. He'd been sitting rigidly throughout the seven-hour drive, contemplating their rescue attempt's potential outcomes. But he was here now, where the kidnapper had specified, the whole ransom withdrawn in cash. All he needed to do from this point onward was to wait until she called his cell phone again. But could he really handle five more hours of waiting?

Where to, Bu Mishari?

Stretching my legs.

He walked around, surveying the foothills, the sandy ground, the cypress bushes, and the basil seedlings growing among the rocks. Looking up at the sky, he realised the sun was about to set, then he spotted a black bird in the air flapping its wings and thought, *Not a crow. Is it a bat?* His heart prickled, so he turned to peek at his brother from the corner of his eye.

Saud had already perched on a rocky stump and was just starting to light a cigarette.

Meanwhile, Mazen had unclasped the lid of the maamoul pastry box and was offering some to Saud.

Although Faisal wasn't hungry, when Mazen turned toward him, he accepted one of the butter cookies and immediately broke it into pieces. Faisal watched as the crumbs fell in a powdered sprinkle on the grass. Within minutes, ants began to swarm the sugared fragments, and Faisal stood there, contemplating the scene between his feet. After a while, he sensed his brother's gaze boring into him, so he asked, What?

When will you call Sumaya?

Later, Faisal said, averting his eyes.

His younger brother crushed his cigarette on a nearby rock, then pulled another and flipped it around his fingers as he peered into the distance.

Something's bothering him. Faisal wondered if he should ask, for as desperate as he was to find out—he also didn't want to know. After all, he understood that Saud was only trying to protect him. *But from what? The truth? What has the kidnapper told Saud that he hasn't shared already?*

Faisal sat beside Saud. He placed his palm on his younger brother's knee, looked him deeply in the eyes, and finally asked, What are you thinking?

Nothing, Saud said, looking away.

Don't lie.

I didn't.

You think I'm stupid?

Of course not!

Then out with it.

Out with what? I don't even get it myself.

Then tell me what you don't get.

Saud let out a deep breath and hesitated before he said, She was whispering when we talked.

Faisal raised his eyebrows. Why would she whisper?

Saud swallowed. I heard a man's voice before she got off the phone. And banging on a door.

For a moment, the three fell silent before Saud carried on in a hoarse voice, It was like she was hiding. Maybe she betrayed her partners?

Mazen added, Maybe she doesn't want to share the ransom?

Maybe, maybe, Faisal said irritably, his chest constricting in pain.

Does this mean we're now dealing with an individual instead of a group?

Saud nodded. A defector. Someone who's afraid.

Faisal looked down at his hands and his trembling fingers. I'm worried.

Mazen asked if Saud had heard her natural voice.

I did, he replied with a nod. She used her regular voice when she answered the man who was pounding on the door. I remember it very well.

As the call to Maghrib prayer jangled out of Mazen's phone, Mazen promptly got up to perform his ablutions from a bottle of water. He used his phone to determine the qibla's direction, turned his face toward Mecca, then looked back at the two brothers and said, Come on guys, time to pray.

Saud, who bounded toward Mazen, received another bottle of water to wash his hands, arms, face, and feet in the order of the cleansing ritual.

Faisal sat there, stunned. He couldn't believe he was watching his brother leap at the opportunity to pray, his brother who had never prayed a day in his life—Saud: the reckless, the entitled youth, the connoisseur of wine and women. Faisal was even more dumbfounded when he heard Saud employ the technical term for the prayer conditions during travel: jam' taqdim—shortening two prayers and combining them into a single observance performed earlier than the official timings.

Yep, Mazen concurred before he raised his hands to begin the takbir.

Saud followed suit.

Faisal's grief, which was pulling him down, made him feel as heavy as the rock on which he sat, so he remained in place, squeezing his stomach.

Mazen asked him one more time, Will you be joining us?

His brother answered on his behalf, Just let him be.

Rijal Almaa Village. Kharar Bridge

9 Dhu Al-Hijja, 1431

10:10 P.M.

It was now past ten p.m.

Why hadn't she called? Faisal trembled. His face was rapidly losing colour. Where is she?

Saud said calmly, Take it easy, brother. She'll call.

Faisal tried to calm down, but his heart was beating erratically. He even thought it might leap out of his chest. His voice sounded strangled when he said, I don't get it. Why don't we call her to tell her that we're here?

Saud said, She makes the rules.

I know. But... Why...?

Maybe this delay is a power move to show us she's in control.

Maybe, maybe, maybe! Faisal erupted. Wherever we turn, we spit this word! You know what, I hope she's dead. I hope she's rotting in hell.

Saud reached out for his brother's arm. Calm down, Faisal, please!

Don't touch me! Flailing his arms, Faisal pushed his brother away, then swerved around like a bird in a cage, fearing an ambush. Faisal glared at the mountains before bellowing, Are they watching us right now? Then he cupped his hands around his mouth, and a mad howl burst, Heyyy! He yelled a few more times before crying, Bitch! Don't you want your money? Then screaming, Mishari! Mishari!

Saud whispered, Faisal please lower your voice! You're going to get us killed!

Turning to his brother, his red eyes drenched in tears, Faisal asked, But... where is she? Why hasn't she called?

Be patient, please. She...

Faisal tried to steady his nerves, but his thoughts continued to dwell on a hurricane of possibilities, each more gruesome than the last. His arms fell loosely to his sides, and he felt his gut communicating something to him. Gazing at Mazen's face, he stammered, They found out about her.

We don't need to rush to conclusions.

But if they find out about her, we'll never see the boy again! Faisal paced in a circle, screaming at his phone, Call! Call me now, you bitch!

Saud got up, pulled the cigarette from his mouth, and gave it to his older brother. Can you please calm down?

Faisal's eyes bulged and he fixed his brother with a quizzical look. He couldn't believe what Saud was suggesting.

I know you haven't smoked in years, Saud said, as though reading his older brother's thoughts.

Tears welled up in Faisal's eyes. The day he stopped smoking and all its vibrant details flooded his memory. It had been the day Mishari was born, and Faisal and Sumaya were finally blessed with their firstborn son after a series of painful miscarriages.

On that day, it felt as if Faisal had walked on coal for miles until he reached the finish line—until he finally stood behind the glass panel to look at the nursling swaddled in a baby-blue blanket, wearing a white cotton hat, resting in a bassinet among a dozen newborns. Faisal remained rooted in the narrow hallway on the other side of the panel for hours, promising to become the best father he could be. He wanted to earn his fatherhood, which he received after years of trying and failing to sire a child. Faisal had promised to perform all his obligatory prayers at a mosque. He would do it each day without missing even one. For his son, he had also vowed to quit smoking, yet his brother was now suggesting that he take a drag for Mishari's sake.

Saud whispered, You've got to relax.

Faisal hesitated before his quivering fingers accepted the cigarette. He placed the butt between his teeth, took a deep breath, exhaled, then turned to his brother and asked, Now what?

Let me handle it.

Saud asked Mazen for the phone, but Mazen was hesitant. Thus, Saud suggested they contact the kidnapper from their Saudi line.

Mazen raised an eyebrow and said, Calling from a different number will breach our agreement.

She breached it already by not delivering the rest of her instructions on time.

Mazen handed his phone to Saud, who dialled the number immediately.

He heard it ring several times before it cut off. Then he tried again and again.

Saud and Mazen's uneasiness mounted with each failed attempt.

Should we call the police? Saud asked.

Mazen, who agreed, urged Saud to hurry.

Meanwhile, Faisal dashed to the black Tahoe, climbed into the front seat, slammed the door shut, squeezed his head in his palms, and sobbed.

Rijal Almaa Province. Haswah Police Station

10 Dhu Al-Hijja, 1431

12:05 AM

An officer cried, Come on, guys, hurry, if you want to sleep for two hours before Eid prayers!

Faisal was standing in the hallway outside the detective's office next to his younger brother. He glanced at his watch and found that it was five minutes past midnight, and he couldn't believe that it was Eid already. It was also a new day, the fourth since Mishari's disappearance. Time was intentionally antagonising him as if it were his enemy. Wondering what might've happened to his kid during the past four days, he turned to his brother and whispered, Sometimes I wish he were dead.

Saud, who couldn't believe that he heard his brother utter these words, merely gaped in silence.

Faisal wiped his eyes with his fingertips and added, Death is far more bearable than the unknown.

Saud shook his head defiantly. Never. I would never accept Mishari's death. I'll find him.

Saud's face seemed as if it had aged a decade in the past hour. His wide and aimless eyes were staring at the wall, and his weak voice felt frayed from all the shouting he did in the mountains.

When will you call Sumaya?

Later.

She doesn't know what happened.

She doesn't need to.

Did she call you?

No.

Strange.

We're just busy.

Did something happen between you two?

Faisal levelled his tired eyes at his brother. Everything happened between us! We lost Mishari.

After pursing his lips, Saud whispered, You don't blame her for it, do you?

I don't... I don't know.

Saud patted his older brother's shoulder. Don't worry. Everything will go back to the way it was when Mishari returns.

With a blank expression, Faisal asked for a cigarette. He couldn't delve into his feelings, so he stepped back, allowing his younger brother and his brother's friend to take charge. The officer occasionally directed questions to him, but Faisal spent the rest of the time tearful and dumbfounded—drowning in silence.

It was Saud who kept answering, We know that he's nearby. He has to be.

The officer responded curtly, At least now we know that we must stop searching for him in Mecca, but you should've reached out to us from the outset.

We did our best based on the knowledge we had at the time. She did threaten us, after all.

Mazen interjected, The blame game won't help anyone right now. We are closer to Mishari, and we know where to search.

The picture of Muhammad Akbar banging his head against the floor, his tears splattering against his round-rimmed glasses, flashed into Faisal's mind, so when he spoke next, his voice rattled in his throat and came out weakly, They have other kids. They might be here, too.

The officer said with a nod, We'll conduct a more comprehensive search, but now listen to me, Bu Mishari. As we do what we can, you should prepare yourself for what we're facing. He drank the rest of his teacup, then clarified, We've been suffering from a deluge of African intruders here in Saudi Arabia. Thousands are hiding in caves, dikes, sewage systems, levees, and farms, to name a few locations. What I am trying to say is that their numbers are frightening. We know of at least ten thousand.

Mazen raised his eyebrows. Just ten?

Ten thousand undocumented people in a country is a massive number! But what's even more frightening is that our land is on their side. Only a few days ago, the border patrol in Wadi Al-Juniya discovered that 450 African trespassers had been living in the valley for the past five months. This tells us we get about a hundred new intruders on a monthly basis. Of course, we quickly extradite the ones we capture. But new people keep replacing them, so it's a continual process. I guess what I'm trying to say is that we aren't up against a random mob but rather a system that is both intricate and effective.

Mazen asked, How did infiltration become this simple? Where's security? Where's Border Patrol?

As he clasped his hands together, the officer replied, It's not that simple, actually. They know where to find all the gaps in the border between us and Yemen, and new vulnerabilities keep popping up no matter how vigilant we are or how dedicated we are in patrolling and standing guard. Yemeni smugglers and Saudi brokers also help one another. They even assist those they smuggle into the country by finding them work opportunities in herding or farming. In fact, Saudi merchants prefer to employ undocumented Africans because they're hard workers and cheaper than documented labourers. Some even accept any price. And then there are those who get into banditry, theft, and the manufacture of alcohol, of course. They, too, have their cunning ways to ensure their survival. We arrest large numbers daily. Jazan's prisons already include thousands of undocumented Africans. I guess what I am trying to say is that the enemy we are facing is...

Saud, who was hanging on the officer's every word, concluded the sentence, Large.

The officer coughed, then said, Large? Yes, I suppose. The woman who contacted you probably has numerous spies looking out for her, and she probably belongs to countless branches of their criminal organisation, so if you think she betrayed her group, she must've joined another. To be honest, I've responded to reports of banditry, theft, and drug dealing in the past, but this is the first kidnapping case I've accepted. After all, it took place in Mecca, which makes it unusual. We don't get reports of this kind of activity around here.

So, now what? Faisal spoke up at last.

Now, you rent a place in 'Asir. Only God knows how long it'll take you to find your son.

Rijal Almaa Province. Haswa Police Station

10 Dhu Al-Hijja, 1431

2:32 A.M.

He counted three beeps before he heard his wife's voice. Sumaya? Faisal, who was standing at the end of the hallway, had given his back to his companions to get some privacy for the call. Hello?

Faisal?

It felt as if years had passed since their last correspondence, and though his wife's voice maintained its youthfulness on the phone, Faisal still imagined that Sumaya had aged like him. They were quiet for a whole minute. Yet, Sumaya's end was clamorous—cars honking in the distance, men calling out to one another, and infants keenly weeping.

Where are you? Faisal asked, visualising his wife's voice as a vibration in the void—but it was just the roaring of the wind colliding with the speakers, clapping against his ear, mingling with the sound of the crying infants and the murmuring brook of the worshipful crowds still praising: Labbaik, labbaik. Sumaya, where are you? he asked again. Her reticence now mimicked the gulf that had stretched between them. When did his wife become so far away, like this? Like he could see her nails clawing at the wall of silence separating them, as though she were waiting for one word—one that could transform everything from their current predicament to their relationship. But only their lack of communication remained articulate, conveying their loss, their stress, and their distance.

Hello?

I can hear you, Faisal.

Where are you?

Muzdalifa.

His eyes widened. *Muzdalifa? Was she still performing her rituals?* He couldn't believe it. *How could she lose her son, then continue with the sacred rites as though nothing had happened?* What are you doing there?

Searching.

Who said he's in Muzdalifa?

Sumaya exhaled slowly, as though avoiding the question.

What's your proof, Sumaya?

I don't have proof, Faisal. I have a feeling.

A feeling? Baffled, he shook his head. *Just a feeling?* Sumaya always did follow her intuition, which prompted her to search in The Sacred Mosque, whereas he chose to remain at the hospital. That same gut instinct had led her to Muzdalifa, even though her son was in the south: in 'Asir, or Jazan, or... Who knows, maybe the boy had reached Yemen already. How could Faisal bring himself to ridicule her maternal instinct? How could he rob her of the one thing she had not lost faith in? Faisal let out a deep breath and said, Alright. Keep doing what you're doing.

He realised when he said these words that they were heavy and wounding. *What are you doing, Faisal? What are you trying to accomplish here? Do you want your wife to lose her mind from all that aimless effort? Or do you want to demolish her only compass, however useless, however farcical? Why would you want to do either?*

Listen—

No, you're right. I don't have the slightest clue what needs to be done.

Listen to me—

No. You listen to me. I don't want to hear your voice unless you have news about my son.

Calm down, Sumaya. I'm trying to tell you something. Hello? Sumaya!

Sumaya, who didn't answer Faisal, started talking to someone else. Don't cry, baby. Just wait a little more.

Sumaya? Can you hear me?

Faisal? Why are you still on the line?

Who are you talking to?

Kali.

Who?

Exhausted from his questions and feeling the power drain out of her, Sumaya let out a deep breath, then said, This conversation is pointless and it's wasting my time.

Who's Kali, Sumaya?

You just won't leave me alone, won't you?

Who is Kali?

He's just a kid! A kid who's lost! I'm helping him search for his mom!

Faisal laughed, astonishment flashing on his face. This was his wife, alright: a woman he loathed more than he loved. And even though her behaviour was entirely nonsensical, Faisal nevertheless understood her well. Sumaya—

I'm hanging up, Faisal.

Take Kali to The Centre for Lost Children. They'll take care of him there.

Where is it?

There's one in Mina, one in Arafa, and one at The Sacred Mosque. There are a few.

Fine. I'll do that. Thank you.

Don't hang up yet.

What do you want, Faisal?

He swallowed with difficulty. There have been some developments... He could almost sense her heart sinking in fear.

Sumaya repeated after him. Some developments...? Faisal, where are you?

    'Asir.

    South?

    Yes.

    What are you doing there?

    The kidnapper called...

The Sacred Mosque's Courtyard. Centre for Lost Children

10 Dhu Al-Hijja, 1431

6:02 A.M.

Sumaya, who held the little one's hand, began penetrating the crowd of women in black abayas. Only the colourful outfits of children racing across the square occasionally punctured this tenebrous mass. The mosque's minarets were now resounding with the invocations for the Eid prayer: Allahu akbar, Allahu akbar.

Sumaya felt her blood rumble in her veins when she heard the phrase, There is no God but Allah, and her lips then began to mumble of their own accord.

Because the little one's hand almost slipped out of hers, she intertwined her fingers with Kali's and marched among the joyful slew of believers excited about Eid's sacred arrival. Allahu akbar, Allahu akbar.

While people are celebrating, my son and I...

Her eyes welled with tears.

A young girl, hopping on the marble floor, started to chant:

> Tell me why, tell me why
>
> You are sitting nearby
>
> Some have completed their rituals already

Yet, you haven't even tried.

One of the women scolded the child for singing the song.

Sumaya's eyes, by now, were drenched in tears.

The little girl, jumping even higher, continued to stubbornly chant:

> Come on by, come on by
>
> Stay here until the night
>
> Drink from our fancy cups
>
> Before you say goodbye.

The same woman now grumbled to others about the naughty girl still warbling during the holy invocations.

The call to prayer itself seemed to rumble even louder in Sumaya's body. She felt it pass through her porous physical membrane as though it wanted to touch the sky. Sumaya kept walking until she reached The Centre for Lost Children, where she was greeted by a young woman in an olive-green scout uniform. I found a missing child. He's called Kali, and he's Indonesian, from Jakarta. He can speak neither Arabic nor English well. I found him at Mount Arafa.

The young woman leaned in, but Kali flinched.

He stepped closer to Sumaya and held on to her abaya before kicking and screaming, effectively warding off anyone other than Sumaya from coming near him.

Kali! Relax, baby! Your mother will come to get you soon.

But he latched onto Sumaya's black cloak, weeping and speaking in a language she didn't understand.

I don't get it, Kali, please relax. Sumaya pressed her gentle palms on his round cheeks and spoke softly, knowing full well that he wouldn't grasp a single word she'd said. Don't worry, Mama will be here shortly, but I have to leave this place to search for my son.

Kali had a quizzical expression on his face when he peered into her eyes.

Allahu akbar, Allahu akbar!

The volume of the invocations increased all around them. Sumaya squeezed Kali's shoulders and said, Your mother is coming soon. Then, noticing his eyes searching her face, she asked him, Kali, do you understand what I'm saying?

He said something incomprehensible again.

After she let out a deep breath, Sumaya said, I have to go.

The young woman who worked at The Centre came closer. Can you please wait a little longer until Nadia arrives? She'll be here in an hour.

Who's Nadia? Sumaya turned to the young woman.

She's an Indonesian volunteer at The Centre who's on her way from Mina. She'll be able to understand him.

Sumaya shook her head. Nadia will be late because of the crowd, and I must go.

The young woman pleaded, Don't leave him now, please. He's attached to you.

The minarets kept echoing: Allahu akbar, Allahu akbar.

Sumaya looked into Kali's eyes, then asked, her voice cracking, What about my son?

One hour, please.

Sumaya, who beheld the boy's narrow Asian eyes, compared them to Mishari's wide and sleepy eyelids with their thick lashes, and wondered why she continued to see Mishari in Kali. Why did she still see a resemblance despite their different outward appearances?

Kali looked at her as though she was the only person left on earth.

The minarets still echoed the call to prayer—Glory to Allah in the morning and the evening. Sumaya finally gave Kali her hand. He curled his fingers around hers and, together, they walked across the hallway to the lobby, where children waited for their parents.

Sumaya counted twenty-one, all of whom had been separated from their families and were currently lost. Feeling a lump in her throat, she whimpered as she dropped to her knees: I am grateful to God!

Kali was still peering at her with his puzzled expression.

Sumaya steadied her nerves, grabbed his hand, then took him inside the bright and colourful foyer full of dolls and figurines. Some children were watching a cartoon, and others were engrossed in the crayons or toys spread across the floor: a variety of dolls, plastic vegetables, and tiny, metal cars. Sumaya bent down to rummage among the handful of superhero figures also on the ground. She held Superman with one hand, then dropped him to pick up Spider-Man, and she began to cry when her fingers wrapped around Batman.

Kali, on the other hand, was taken by his surroundings. Curiosity was shining in his eyes when he slowly uncoiled his fingers from Sumaya's hand.

She nudged him forward. Go on.

He took the Batman figurine from her hand and began to play with it. Within moments, it seemed that he had forgotten about Sumaya, who sat on a small blue chair, her lips reciting the Eid invocations along with the minarets outside The Centre, her eyes gradually taking in more details as she ruminated on all the missing kids engrossed in their loss, some of whom were even playing games or laughing in front of a wide screen. *Is this what we look like? Are we merely people who have forgotten that we are lost?* Sumaya then turned to the young woman and asked, How will you find his mom and dad?

When Nadia gets here, she'll ask for his name and his parents' names. After that, we'll call Indonesian Hajj caravans and ask about his parents. It won't be difficult.

Sumaya nodded.

The young woman said, You must be tired. Would you like something to drink?

Sumaya remembered that she hadn't eaten anything since the night before. However, glancing at the hem of her dusty abaya, she noticed that its luxurious black had faded, so she told the young woman, I want to pray, but I want to perform ablution first.

How about some tea?

I'm OK, thanks.

The young woman led Sumaya to the washroom, where Sumaya scrubbed her face, removed all her clothes, and lathered her body with a bar of soap. Because her abaya smelled like sand and dried sweat, she rubbed the bar on the cloak's armpits, rinsed the soap with water, and waved her cloak in the air a few times to dry the wet stains. Shortly after, Sumaya put on her abaya once more and went looking for a prayer room to perform the obligatory and optional rites. Upon completing the ritual, she found that Nadia had arrived and had already begun conversing with Kali.

Sumaya watched them both communicate behind a glass wall, Kali opening his mouth and speaking and the woman nodding encouragingly. For the first time, Sumaya thought the boy's language did not feel like gibberish.

You can leave now if you want, the young woman said.

Sumaya nodded, for she could see that Kali looked safe and comfortable with Nadia.

The young woman then added, Allah sent you to protect him.

That's right. Allah sent me.

CHAPTER EIGHT

SAREER

bed; mattress; throne

Jazan. The Farm of Sheikh Ibrahim Hijab

11 Dhu Al-Hijja, 1431

5:00 A.M.

He opened his eyes at five o'clock each morning.

In fact, his body woke him up a few minutes before the alarm even rang. The first time it happened was eight months ago, when his body became familiar with the rhythm of the land.

Nitham kicked the covers and got out of bed. He wrapped a lungi around his waist, dropped a raggedy tank over his head, then scratched his naked shoulders on his way to the sink, where he splashed cold water on his face then watched, as he brushed his teeth, the young boy's reflection in the mirror, curled like an earthworm in his bed.

Nitham hawked water and toothpaste gunk into the sink. While drying his mouth with the hem of his tank, the alarm went off, so he strolled to the corner of the room to silence the beeping clock. He then turned to the AC unit blasting warm air and made a mental note to replace the water in the storage tank. After powering it off, he went to the metal door, which made a creaking noise upon opening. Nitham left the room and locked the door behind him, placing the key in one of the cactus pots he'd recently planted. He stood up in front of the sprawling mountains, examining the vacant fields on his farm, breathing in the earthy fragrance of the ground and the saltiness in the air. He picked up his wooden stick and got to work, stabbing the ground with the sharp tip to carve straight lines across the field. Nitham went back and forth, relying on three handspans to separate the indentations. When he was done, he swept the field with his eyes to make sure that the distance between every row and the depth of each depression were generally uniform.

The soil was fertile, and the land was ready to be ploughed. He took another panoramic view of the field filled with parallel lines. Now that he was positive there was no room for another indentation, he tenderly rubbed the soil with his fingers, scooped a batch in his palm, inhaled its scent, and thought, *She's ready!*

After throwing away the stick he'd been holding in his other hand, he went to the pantry, where he used his bare brown arm to wipe the sweat off his forehead. He opened one of the millet sacks to dip his fist into the pile of seeds and cupped a handful before returning to his farm. There, he dropped to his knees slowly and pressed his cheek against the delicate loam, and in that position, he began to relax his fingers, allowing the millet seeds to trickle out of his palm into a hole. When he was done, he moved on to the next incision, and after filling them all, he returned to the first one and proceeded to cultivate it with soil, using his brown arm and its protruding veins to pat the surface of the earth.

An hour later, the sun shone brightly, and the air grew warm. Sweat was by now seeping out of Nitham's body, and because his tongue felt dry and heavy, he aimed the water hose into his open mouth to satiate his thirst, then pointed the tube at his face to wash his head and shoulders. Feeling refreshed, Nitham continued to work for two more hours. It was then that he heard successive knocks on the iron door.

The rapping sound meant that the boy had woken up. *Must've been the heat.* But the banging on the metal door abruptly stopped, and soon enough, two small arms started waving between the bars of the room's only window.

Nitham! Nitham! the little one called out.

There was no need to ask the boy to quiet down, since he couldn't understand Nitham's language anyway, but there would be ample time for him to learn Urdu in the future.

Nitham! Nitham Shuja a-Din!

Cute. Nitham smiled fondly. He was impressed by the boy's ability to remember his full name even though he'd been drowning in hallucinations throughout their first meeting. Smart kid, he muttered to himself as he returned the bag of millet seeds to the pantry. He still had a lot of work to do before returning to his room. For instance, he'd need to sprinkle water on the bulbous parts of the field for the seeds slumbering underneath to germinate over time, and he'd need to water his two mango trees and his several guava trees, in addition to the cucumber plants, tomato vines, and head lettuce. He'd also need to milk the goats, replenish their fodder, clean their barn, and clear out their faeces. *Who knows, maybe the hens have laid new eggs today.* Nitham had many tasks to accomplish, so the boy would have to wait.

He might even ache from thirst.

Jazan. The Farm of Sheikh Ibrahim Hijab

11 Dhu Al-Hijja, 1431

8:07 A.M.

He is searching for a cave, the one that the woman who kidnapped him had said she'd hide him in. She was the one who took him. And she was the one who'd return him to his parents. But even though he crosses marshes, crawls over rocks, and stumbles into cacti fields, he still cannot find it.

Mishari woke up—in a stuffy room. His head began to ache when he lifted it off the pillow. Sunrays were cascading through the bars from the open window. As soon as he got out of bed, however, he swayed, so he reached out to steady himself against the concrete wall. Once the dizziness subsided, Mishari flicked on the light switch beside the metal door. Blue neon light flashed in the cylindrical bulb.

There was a dingy look about the walls. A panel of the Kaaba handcrafted from beads and sequins hung on one of them, and a collage of naked women was duct taped to the opposite surface. Mishari approached that wall hesitantly, then stood agape before the smooth female body parts that had been cut up from various magazines and compiled into women. He passed his terrified eyes over an armpit, a breast, and two hips, but when he went lower, he panicked, and an image flashed in his mind, that of ruptured flesh between lean thighs and a young Indian girl moaning: Paani! Paani!

Mishari turned away quickly, his breathing heavy, his heart palpitating. He clapped his hands over his eyes, and when he took two steps away from the collages, he tripped over the sponge mattress, so he opened his eyes again, then wandered about, inspecting the place, while making sure that he avoided the frightening wall.

Beside a small fridge, copper bowls were piled on the floor, and a static fan drooped from the ceiling. Mishari's eyes wandered to the portable cooler, which wasn't working. He tried to pry open the metal door and leave the room, but it was locked, so he rapped his knuckles on the clanking surface and called out the name of the man who saved his life. Mishari wanted to tell him that he had woken up, and because he could recite his father's number from memory, he wanted to call his dad and tell him to come to this place and pick him up.

The stuffiness in the room had become unbearable, so Mishari returned to the AC unit and turned it on. When it blasted hot air, he powered it off again. His eyes then darted to the open window, which was higher than his reach. After stacking cushions on top of each other, Mishari climbed to the top, stretched his arms between the metal bars, and called out the foreigner's name as he waved them in the open air: Nitham! Nitham!

The foreign man didn't answer.

Nitham Shuja a-Din!

He still didn't answer.

Mishari went back down, grabbed another cushion, and added it to the pile. Standing on tiptoe, he peeked outside the window and noticed the sprawling mountains followed by a tilled field and a man spraying trees with his hose. It was the same man who rescued him.

He's busy, Mishari thought. He'd return soon, and when he did,

Mishari would tell the foreign man all the horrible things he'd endured. For example, Mishari would tell him about the foreign woman who kidnapped him, how she put him in the trunk of a car, and how she drove him to a house full of black children whose faces were wet with tears and snot, children who wanted cookies but who got pelted with sticks instead, children missing limbs. Scenes from three days of hell flooded Mishari's head. He didn't want to be lost anymore. All he wanted to do was call his father.

As he clung to the metal bars of the open window, Mishari surveyed the faraway mountains and goats roaming the field. He inhaled the warm, salty air creeping from the outside until the dizziness returned, and he almost fell, so he climbed down the cushions slowly and went to the AC unit. Last spring, his father pitched a tent in the desert which included a water tank that looked just like it. Because Mishari remembered everything his uncle and father did that day, like lighting coals and chasing the jerboas away. He also remembered pouring water into the tank, so he removed the AC unit's tank and filled it with water from the sink. Within minutes, cool air began to wash into the room, and it became easier for him to breathe. He opened the fridge, looking for something to eat, and found cucumbers, head lettuce, radishes, and cherry tomatoes. Although he used to remove the tomato slices from the burgers his mother made, this time, he ate every last one. He also devoured the cucumbers, and although neither had satiated his hunger, Mishari was nevertheless confident that the generous man who saved him would also feed him as soon as he returned from the farm.

Therefore, Mishari waited, his back to the wall of the naked women that elicited a memory of a moaning girl. Gazing at the Kaaba made of sequins, he remembered his mother the moment she let go of his hand and started to scream, Mishari! Move! Move! Move!

That's what he did, so when exactly did it all go wrong?

Jazan. The Farm of Sheikh Ibrahim Hijab

11 Dhu Al-Hijja, 1431

10:12 A.M.

He was relieved when the little arms stopped swinging between the bars. *The kid has finally learned that he must quiet down and wait.* Nitham could now continue ploughing his field and deal with the little one at the end of the day. *So what if the brat keeps banging on the door? Nobody will hear him.*

Nobody will ever know. In fact, that was the first thought that crossed his mind when he found the boy unconscious in front of a dilapidated wall a few miles away from his field. Nitham had been out to buy sorghum seeds from a nearby farm, but stumbling on the boy changed everything. The feverishly shivering child was small, scrawny—and beautiful. Nitham looked around him until he was satisfied that they were alone. *He must be lost. Nobody knows where he is.* Nitham swept the kid in his arms and went back to his room. Breathless with excitement, he closed the door behind him, for he now had a boy all to himself.

Once Nitham laid the kid on the sponge mattress, the boy's body coiled like boiled shrimp. He had soft fingers, black hair, long eyelashes, and a trembling mouth that seemed to be on the verge of crying. His dusty face smelled like salt, and his clothes, caked in mud, were torn at the edges. Because the boy had been delirious, Nitham kept shaking the little one's shoulders, but the kid was already lost in the tunnels of a distant dream. So, when Nitham lowered the latch to lock his room from the inside, he thought he could buy the sorghum seeds later. What he needed to do now was to take care of the boy he found catatonic in the wilderness, desperately wanting to be carried home.

Nitham cradled the boy in his arms, gave him some water, and communicated in his mother tongue, because he knew no other language. And as he wiped a towel over the boy's dirty face, Nitham examined the kid's features, which did not resemble those of Jazan's inhabitants. They were prettier, plusher, and paler. When Nitham traced his thumb over the delicate lip of the sleeping child, a strange thunderbolt shot through his body. He was confident that the boy was not from this area. Nobody comes to this farm anymore, not since the landlord died, not even the Africans who used to work here but who realised after the old man's passing that nobody was going to pay them.

Nitham was living in a forgotten part of the world. Yesterday, while everybody was celebrating Eid Al-Adha, Nitham did not receive a single slice of meat, because nobody asked about him anymore. The last time anyone visited the farm was seven months ago, when two men knocked on the door and spoke in Arabic. They left, because Nitham didn't understand a word, and returned with a Pashtun to interpret their Arabic. He explained that the men wanted to know whether Nitham was interested in participating in the annual mango festival, but Nitham shook his head, since he only had two trees.

This was the last time anyone had knocked on his door. The conversation itself did not last longer than ten minutes. Even then, nobody had entered his room, where pictures of naked female bodies were taped to his wall, pictures that included cutouts of Kareena Kapoor's, Zarina Khan's, and Priyanka Chopra's faces. Nobody had ever laid their eyes on his nude collage. What happened in his room stayed in his room forever.

Nitham had removed the boy's clothes to wipe the gaunt body with a wet towel. He had brushed the protruding bones, and when he had gently run his fingers over the small shoulders and armpits, the young one had giggled.

What are you laughing at, larka?

The little one had opened his eyes and said in a frail voice, pointing to his chest, Mishari.

In the beginning, Nitham didn't understand.

But the boy's voice became clearer after he'd coughed, and he said in English, My name is Mishari Faisal.

Nitham had repeated the boy's name: the only Arabic words he'd uttered in the last two years.

The little boy had asked Nitham for his name.

And, pressing his palm to his chest, as the kid had done earlier, Nitham had shared his first name before uttering it in full: Nitham Shuja a-Din.

Nitham Shuja a-Din, the boy had echoed.

Nitham now thought with a chuckle, *There will be many more words to share in the future.*

Finally, the silence was broken.

Jazan. The Farm of Sheikh Ibrahim Hijab

11 Dhu Al-Hijja, 1431

10:30 A.M.

His stomach rumbled again.

This time, Mishari devoured the lettuce and radishes. His mother would not have believed her eyes, even if she'd seen him consume the remaining vegetables in the fridge. As Mishari nibbled on a white radish, he began to think of her and what she might do upon his return, which he was sure would happen soon. She'd be twice thrilled! Because first, he'd be back and, second, he'd be eating vegetables.

Salivating, Mishari wondered whether the foreign man would prepare the food he liked: chicken nuggets and French fries with ketchup, a burger, or a pepperoni pizza. The truth is, Mishari was hungry enough to eat anything, including the chicken machboos his grandmother made, which she stuffed with raisins, cashews, cloves, cardamom, and fried onions. And he would eat all the foods that used to drive him crazy when he found them on his plate. Once he returned, he would eat them without complaining—because he was an adult now who ate grown-up meals.

Getting lost forced him to grow up.

Mishari chewed on the remaining radish and tried to recall the last time he'd felt sated. It might have been upon landing in Mecca when he'd wanted a meal from Kentucky Fried Chicken, which came with a colouring book and some crayons. However, his mother had insisted that they all eat fresh poultry from Al-Tazaj.

Mishari now regretted traveling. Had he stayed in Kuwait with Uncle Saud, he'd be satisfying his current cravings, since his uncle would buy him a meal and a drink from Shake Shack without hesitation. He'd only ask Mishari to keep it a secret from his mother, which Mishari always did. He had kept all their secrets. The ones that involved burgers and the ones that involved girls.

The day his family landed in Mecca, Mishari protested his mother's decision to eat healthy by throwing a tantrum when his father queued up behind the other customers. But, after a single bite, Mishari revelled in the taste and texture of Al-Tazaj's fresh chicken. His mouth now drooled as he recalled the taste of that chicken, dipped in tahini and lemon, and the Pepsi his mother had permitted, which had run smoothly down his throat. *She's not as strict as she sometimes sounds!* It's true that she usually grumbled about his food preferences, but she eventually conceded and made whatever he wanted in the end.

After losing her for days, Mishari wondered what his mother would do once they reunited. No doubt she'd hug him tightly, and he'd get to smell on her neck the oud oil fragrance she frequently wore—a smell he used to hate, since its pungency hurt his nostrils. He could never understand why his mother kept wearing it instead of spraying perfume from the bottles that smelled like fruits and flowers. But she had assured him he would understand her taste when he matured.

Well, now he was older, eating radishes and tomatoes, and maybe his nose was also ready to appreciate the smell of oud. Their reunion would be long, Mishari thought absentmindedly, his eyes welling with tears. Whenever his mother took her time with their embrace, he used to tell her, That's enough, Mama! This time, he wouldn't tell her that—but, suddenly, Mishari worried if his mother would punish him. *What will she do after the long hug?*

The last time he had wandered out of her sight, she'd forbidden him from playing with his iPad for a whole day. They were going to the bird market with his uncle and father. His mother had held his hand until it became clammy and slipped out of her grip. Mishari, who had tried to look for her, got distracted by a large Amazon parrot, with its vivid green and yellow feathers. He had darted into the store, first, to gaze at the colourful bird, then at the rest of the confined animals, including the carp, canaries, and the Persian cats. Mishari had also stumbled upon a monkey in a massive cage peeling an orange before tossing the peels on the ground. Mishari didn't feel the passage of time. When he was found at last, his mother's face had turned red, and his uncle's had gone yellow. Meanwhile, his absolutely fuming father had stretched an arm to slap Mishari in public.

Something similar could happen this time, since parents perform incomprehensible deeds in the name of love. His mom, for example, would hug him and then penalise him; his dad, in contrast, would slap him and then reward him. After all, his father had bought him a spectacular remote-control car that day, after slapping him in public: the original Batmobile—black all over, with fins on the side, sprinklers and a pointed nose in the front, and a latch on the back to prevent the car from slipping down the road. The toy his father bought was meant to be a gift for his good grades. Because Mishari was only allowed to visit Fantasy World three times a year—on Eid Al-Fitr, Eid Al-Adha, and his birthday—he thought, *Maybe this time my father will buy me a present, too?*

The day Mishari had gotten lost at the bird market, his family had left without buying the pair of aquatic turtles they'd promised to get him. They didn't even allow Mishari to hold a single dyed chick from the boxes outside the fence, which always filled his nostrils with the scent of guano and feathers wafting from the rooster and bulbul cages. His parents didn't even let him look at the puppies. And when Mishari pleaded for at least a box of Pop Pop Snapper Fireworks, his father had complained, while starting the engine, that Mishari had ruined his mother's mood. Still, despite their anger and disappointment, his parents had ended up parking in front of a pomegranate stall to buy two bags of the deseeded fruit.

How much have I ruined my mother's mood this time?

Will my father forgive me?

A tear slid down Mishari's cheek when he recalled a sombre tune his uncle often sang—a tune he didn't like because it pulled on his heartstrings.

His uncle, who replayed the song time and time again, kept teasing Mishari throughout the ride, You know what? You don't deserve to hear Adani songs! This, right here, is talent! What do tidbits even know about art?

The song had bothered Mishari, because he didn't want to listen to scary lyrics or to melodies that twisted his heart up in knots.

Feeling a lump in his throat, he thought, *If my mother shows up now, I'll tell her I miss her so much it hurts.* He didn't want to wait any longer. Because he wanted to call his father this instant, Mishari climbed back up the cushions he had previously stacked on top of each other, reached his arms between the iron bars of the open window, and hollered, Nitham! Nitham!

Jazan. The Farm of Sheikh Ibrahim Hijab

11 Dhu Al-Hijja, 1431

11:15 A.M.

Nitham smiled when he heard the little one's cries carrying faintly across the field. *What a wonderful thing it is to listen to the voice of another human being after all that silence.* Just one more hour and Nitham would finish ploughing the field. In a week, he'd plant corn.

He raised his head to get a better look at the arms swinging through the bars and thought, *How did that demon reach that window? He must have used all the furniture in the room.* Nitham decided to tidy the boy's mess, but only after completing his work, for he needed to focus on the farm right now and go through his daily tasks the way he had been doing for the past two years.

He had not spoken to anyone in a while—even before the old man's death. And apart from Abida Parveen's Sufi songs, which he listened to in the car on his way to the market to buy new seeds or tools for his farm, he had barely heard anybody else talk. His master, after all, had been a lonely man, deaf and mute, fond only of the earth and the trees. The old man had taught Nitham everything about managing the field without uttering a word, and he had treated him well, so well in fact that Nitham sometimes forgot that he was only a hired labourer.

The old man would sometimes enter Nitham's room to share a cup of tea with mint, and he would indicate that he'd be teaching Nitham how to grow melons in the morning. Nitham didn't understand the gesture at the time, but when he saw the melon seeds resting on his master's palm the next morning, he put two and two together. When the old man's fingers were curved as if they were holding a giant egg, Nitham figured the old man was referring to cantaloupes. When the old man spread his fingers wider, Nitham gathered it meant watermelons. And there were other signs for other vegetables that Nitham picked up over time, such as guava, lettuce, and cucumbers. The old man had devised his own signals for each vegetable, instead of relying on Arabic sign language. He merely matched the shape of his fingers to disparate vegetables. His hand communicated with Nitham as articulately as his mouth would have, allowing Nitham to acquire, in two years, his entire gestural lexicon.

Indeed, the old man had taught Nitham everything he needed to know to function in Jazan: how to cultivate grain and fodder, how to plant fruits and vegetables, how to care for livestock, and even ways to cook them. Patiently and repeatedly, the old man had shown Nitham how to make a loaf of bread the way he liked by adding milk. He had also taught Nitham how to prepare dessert by mixing bananas, ghee, and honey. And he had shown Nitham how to make a meal that became Nitham's favourite.

You ferment and knead the millet, drape the meat into the dish, pour the broth into the pot, and mix it all together.

Although eight months had passed since the old man departed, Nitham still felt pain from the loss, because it happened before his eyes. After hiring eight African men and paying them by the hour to help on the farm, for example, to mow the crops and wait for the millet stalks to dry in the sun, everyone got busy fertilising different parts of the field, and it was during this period, while each was engrossed in their individual task, that the old man indicated to Nitham that he needed to rest because he was tired. Nitham nodded, then carried on with his work, moving the box of urea fertiliser to his part of the field. The old master lied down under the guava trees, closed his eyes, and never opened them again.

As Nitham recalled the old man's features, he remembered the olive skin, delicate nose with its wide nostrils, white goatee, and white eyebrows. When he died under the shade of his trees, the old man was probably in his mid-seventies.

His children, who had occasionally visited him, tended to leave the old man either frustrated or flat-out displeased. A heated quarrel had even erupted on their final visit. Because Nitham had seen every hand swinging rapidly in the air, it seemed to him that they were all conveying their agitation. He thus surmised that they had asked their father to return to Riyadh, but their father argued that he wouldn't be able to plant corn in the city or gaze up at the mountains each morning.

So what? They had responded. Corn could be purchased from any store.

But that reply had only aggravated the old man further. He trembled and signed how shameful it was for his own children to neglect the sky, the trees, and the earth. He would never follow suit, for he could never abandon the south! He had lived his whole life on this field and he intended to die there. When I'm gone, he had signed, you can sell my land and take all my money. But know this! You bastards would have sold your mother! He had shoved them out of his way to return to the house, where he stayed, refusing to come out until they went back to Riyadh.

From then on, the old man began to view Nitham as his only confidant: the only person who, like him, was eager to touch the earth, dwell on its highlands, and breathe in the salinity of its ocean air. Nitham—the man who came from Karachi's slums—became just like the son the old man never had.

Jazan. The Farm of Sheikh Ibrahim Hijab

11 Dhu Al-Hijja, 1431

12:00 P.M.

He was sitting in the corner of the room when he heard the key turn and the hinges moan. Once the door opened, Mishari saw a dazzling light punctured by a dark silhouette. The silhouette had arms and legs, and it was stepping into the room. Mishari began to bounce and cry cheerfully, Nitham! Nitham! Running toward the foreign man, joy animating his face, he asked, Where have you been? I've been waiting for so long!

The foreigner, who didn't understand a single word, was surprised to notice the cooler working, so he opened the tank and chuckled when he found it full of water. He said a few words in a language Mishari didn't recognise before heading to the bathroom, where he washed his face, then performed the cleansing ritual for prayer.

After he left the bathroom, Nitham spread his prayer mat toward the panel of the Kaaba, hanging on the wall. He turned his back on the collage of naked women, raised both hands behind his ears, and said, Allahu akbar.

Mishari had often prayed with his dad at home, and he always attended Friday prayers with his father, who took him to the mosque to pray with other men. Mishari thought he needed to do the same with Nitham, so he hopped into the bathroom, briskly performed ablution, then hurried back to stand straight beside the foreigner, who was still reciting the takbir. Mishari thought, *When the man completes his prayer, he'll call my dad.* Thus, Mishari stood there patiently waiting until the man finished his mandatory and voluntary prayers.

Nitham then said something Mishari didn't understand. The foreigner pressed his fingers together and brought them close to his lips.

Mishari realised that the man was asking if he was hungry, but he'd already eaten the vegetables in the fridge, and what he really wanted—more than anything else—was to tell his father to come and get him, so Mishari shook his head, placed a palm on his ear, and asked, Telephone?

The foreigner looked away.

Mishari wondered if Nitham had intentionally ignored him or if he hadn't understood the signal.

The foreigner was now pushing three copper pots toward him that were stacked on top of one another. After opening the lid of the first, Nitham dipped his fingers into the container.

Mishari craned his neck to see what Nitham was eating. Because it looked like the harees his grandmother made during Ramadan, he leaned in closer to inhale the scent of the food wafting from the bowl. However, the dish smelled like flour dough and bananas.

The man scooped a mushy heap with his fingers and tried to feed it to Mishari, while saying, Kahao.

That's how Mishari learned that kahao meant to eat. Although he was at first put off by the unfamiliar texture and smell of the dish, he nevertheless considered Nitham's offer by reasoning that he did like bananas. Plus, the aroma of the pudding-like dish had by now suffused the entire room, and it was enticing enough to make Mishari's stomach rumble with hunger, so he cupped a morsel in his hand, and as soon as he dumped the morsel in his mouth, his eyes popped open. Relishing the taste, Mishari plunged his fist into the copper pot and pulled out dollop after dollop until the container was nearly empty.

At first, the foreign man chuckled, but as soon as the metallic surface began to show, he pulled Mishari's hand out of the copper pot, clasped the lid shut, and said, Bss. He then got up to wash his hands.

Mishari followed to do the same, but he panicked when Nitham peeled off the pair of pants he'd been working in, exposing his naked body. Mishari quickly closed his eyes and turned to face the bathroom wall.

The foreigner chuckled as he wrapped a lungi around his waist. He said something before leaving the bathroom in a language Mishari didn't understand, then he stretched his body out on the sponge mattress, where he patted a vacant spot to his right, and told Mishari, Aao.

But Mishari didn't want to sleep. He wanted to call his father. So, he shook his head, clapped his hand over his ear a second time, and said, Telephone?

Ignoring Mishari, the man slid off the mattress and crawled to an old television set with a logo that read: National. Nitham's TV did not resemble the flat screens in Mishari's house. This one had a protruding belly, while the rest of the receiver was encased in flat wooden planks. When Nitham powered it on by turning a round button that jutted from its side, a dance sequence from an Indian movie flashed on the convex screen. The actress in the scene, dancing amid vast green fields in a yellow sari, was one of the women hanging on Nitham's scary wall. Her smile made Mishari groan, sending shivers down his spine, even though the actress on the monitor looked different from the one on the wall, because the one on the screen was wearing a yellow sari that showed off her midriff and was swinging a very long braid.

Nitham returned to his spot on his frayed mattress, clasped his hands under his head, sunk between the cushions, and watched the dance sequence with a smile of contentment—like a king luxuriating in the kingdom of pleasure.

What is he doing? When is he going to call my father? Mishari couldn't wait for the movie to end. *Indian movies are so long!* He wanted the foreign man to call his dad immediately because he wanted to return to Kuwait: *Now! Now! Now!* Mishari demanded the foreigner's attention by pulling on the hem of his waistcloth. Then, once more, Mishari pressed palm to ear and said, Nitham! Telephone!

But the man continued to ignore him and gaze with absentminded delight at the naked belly button swaying on the bulky TV.

Jazan. The Farm of Sheikh Ibrahim Hijab

11 Dhu Al-Hijja, 1431

1:00 P.M.

He was exhausted from all that ploughing and desperately needed to nap before he went out to buy more seeds, but the boy kept nagging, tugging on his waistcloth, yanking on the cushion Nitham was leaning on, and repeating, Telephone! Although it was a beautiful feeling to hear someone else's voice in this room, the boy's unrelenting whining became annoying after a while, and Nitham had to berate him—twice—before he learned his lesson and stopped screaming.

Mishari marched to the corner where he squatted and glared through teary eyes.

Twice, the boy had refused the offer to sleep beside him. And since Nitham's intention wasn't to frighten the kid, he thought it would be better to pace himself. Besides, Nitham was exhausted from all the hours he'd already spent cultivating his field. It didn't matter that the boy was currently out of reach. Nitham would focus on Kareena Kapoor's dance now since he could always devour her in his dreams. His eyelids kept getting heavier until he finally slept to the Indian score and the little one's silence—but Nitham's eyes bulged open when he heard the door creak. He turned around.

The boy was missing.

But the metal door was locked, and the key was in his pocket! *Where's the kid?* Nitham got up to search, following the sound of running water. He opened the bathroom door and found the boy facing the toilet stall.

Mishari told him to get out.

But Nitham's lower lip trembled, and his eyes focused on the lower part of the boy's body. He stood in place, watching the little one pee.

Mishari rushed to the door screaming—urine drops splashing on the floor and splattering on his long ribbed tank. He snapped the door shut, and when he came out moments later, he sat crossed-legged in the corner, draping the tank over his knees and ankles, his small, angry eyes staring at Nitham. It was the first time he'd behaved as though the older man could be dangerous.

Nitham, who still had more time to sleep, returned to his sponge mattress. He spread his body among the cushions, then laid an arm over his forehead to cover his eyes, trying to recapture Kareena Kapoor in his imagination, and though he conjured her breasts, his thoughts immediately wandered to the scene he had just witnessed.

Telephone.

There he goes again with his nagging. Seems like he won't drop it. Maybe he'll whine forever.

Telephone, telephone, telephone!

Nitham moved his arm away from his eyes to peer at the boy who was now fixing him with a scornful look.

Mishari was still sitting on the floor, hugging his legs, his knees hiding his mouth and nose. Only his eyes, forehead, and thick hair were visible.

Wow, he really didn't like that I saw him pee.

Wonder where he came from and how he got here?

Mishari stood up and moved around as though searching for something. When he found a stack of blank letter sheets and a pencil on top of the small fridge, he wrote down a number, then gave the page to Nitham. The number started with +965.

Guess that means he's not from the north, south, east, or west of Saudi Arabia. He must be from an entirely different place.

Baba! Mishari said, pointing at the number on the sheet. Telephone, Nitham! Telephone!

Nitham beamed when an idea to forever quell the boy's irksome persistence crossed his mind. He got up to open the cupboard, withdrew his duffel bag, and extracted a 6275 Nokia from one of its pockets.

The boy, who held the cell in his hand, saw that it was a black rectangular model, which didn't look like modern phones, but seemed to work, so he went ahead and called his dad. However, the line cut off before it even connected with his father's phone, so he tried again and again, but it went dead each time. Perplexed by this turn of events, Mishari wondered if he had messed up his father's number or if his father had stopped using his line. No matter how many times Mishari dialled his dad's digits, the line disconnected. In the corner of the room, his eyes welling with tears, Mishari tried all the other numbers he had memorised, yet none worked. After an hour of failed attempts, Mishari belted an anguished scream and collapsed into a weeping fit.

Nitham ignored him. After all, he needed to buy more seeds. He thus untied his waistcloth and slipped into his outdoor pants. Nitham picked up the phone the boy had cast aside in his frustration, stuffed the phone in his pocket, then went outside, and turned to lock the metal door, twice.

Mishari did not attempt to catch up with him. By the time Nitham left, the screaming kid had already buried his head among the cushions.

He'll calm down soon enough, even if it takes a day or two. We have all the time in the world. Nitham continued strolling along the farms nearby, thinking about his field. *Getting watermelon and cantaloupe seeds might not be such a bad idea. Although summer is in three months, it might be better to get them now than to get them later, when they're more expensive.* Nitham wanted to nurture his farm. As he recalled the mango hanging from a branch of one of his trees, he thought, *Ripe and ready for picking.* Soon, he'd bite into it. Nitham salivated. When he thought of the boy locked in his room and the fruit dangling from his tree, a dopamine rush flooded his body. It was picking season, after all.

Nitham recalled those lengthy hours he'd spent aching from loneliness and became emotional, until his smile returned and he thought, *Glad I didn't subscribe to an international calling service.*

Jazan. The Farm of Sheikh Ibrahim Hijab

11 Dhu Al-Hijja, 1431

7:06 P.M.

Then he fell asleep.

After having spent hours weeping, kicking, and screaming, and after having whimpered until the pain in his chest dissipated, Mishari's body finally began to droop until he plunged into a deep slumber.

Strangers are lowering two black girls who are crying into the trunk of a car. Two massive arms then reach toward Mishari. He bites into the flesh of one, and bolts out of the vehicle, screaming.

When Mishari woke up, he saw his legs moving on the sponge mattress, while the chequered quilt was crumpled between his knees. The sound of the water flowing in the bathroom alerted him to the foreign man's arrival. His heart pounded, and he closed his eyes, thinking that if he pretended to sleep, the man might leave him alone. It then dawned on Mishari that Nitham must've carried him from the corner where he had fallen asleep behind a pillow fort and laid him on the man's frayed mattress. Since noon, the man had been telling Mishari to sleep beside him, constantly uttering: Aao. Aao. Mishari thought perhaps it meant sleep or come here.

Opening half an eyelid, Mishari observed the foreign man as he left the bathroom half-naked, his blue-striped lungi wrapped around his waist.

Nitham sat in front of the equally blue gas stove, where he opened the lid of two copper pots. He ladled out some rice from one and heavy broth from the other. The scent of spices quickly permeated the room. The foreign man then placed his frying pan on the stove to heat the food, which he later ate alone.

Mishari remembered that the last thing he had eaten was the banana purée, but he didn't have an appetite because he was afraid of something he couldn't quite articulate.

The man crawled to the TV, and the same actress appeared when he turned it on again. She had light brown skin, green eyes, and fine black hair. *He must love her,* Mishari thought. He noticed that the foreign man was stealing glances at him, so he shut his eyes, but he sensed the man scooching nearer and nearer until he lay beside him. Mishari, thus, turned around to give Nitham his back. His heart was pounding frenetically when he coiled the chequered blanket tightly around his body. He remembered sleeping in his uncle's bed and between his parents, but this man...

Nitham continued to watch the movie a while longer, his lazy fingers fiddling with Mishari's hair, scratching his shoulders, and brushing the back of his neck.

Mishari wondered whether the man enjoyed touching him. His uncle, after all, used to hug him, and he frequently asked Mishari to crack his fingers and walk on his back. Sometimes, his uncle would even peel off Mishari's shirt and bite into his naked shoulder. Mishari laughed whenever his uncle did those things, but this man...

That's when Mishari felt warm breath on the back of his ears and neck. The man, who was no longer watching the movie, was now lying on his side, peering at Mishari, who began to tremble, his eyes opening wider in fright the more he felt the man inching closer and closer.

When the man's body finally touched Mishari's, something solid pressed into his back, and two big hands crept up Mishari's thighs. Suddenly, Mishari found himself lying on his stomach and the man on top of him. Struggling under the weight of the foreigner, Mishari tried his best to slip away, and though he screamed at the top of his lungs, his face was buried in a pillow—and nobody heard him.

Day 6

He opened his eyes before the alarm went off. It was a new day.

Nitham gazed at the boy crouched in the corner behind a wall of cushions, assuming they'd protect him, but those cushions would crumble with a single huff. The boy had fallen asleep, exhausted from all his sobbing.

Nitham didn't understand why Mishari was bothered to this extent. He'd been gentle, and he had even taken into consideration that this was Mishari's first experience. Nitham had therefore eased into it. He didn't even remove his waistcloth. But when he was done, the wet spot still staining his lungi, the little one jumped up and beelined to the corner, where he started shouting in his ridiculous gibberish. He might've been hurling all the curses he'd learned throughout his pitiful life. He screamed until he ran out of tears, then fell asleep from fatigue.

Nitham left the little one alone to take a rejuvenating shower, which left him feeling energetic and light. *If he prefers to sleep on the hard floor, so be it. But if he wants to sleep on something soft and comfortable, he now knows what to do*. Nitham performed the sacred washing rites followed by the dawn prayer, while the little one snored faintly behind the cushions. It was a lovely sound, a sound that allowed

Nitham to feel for the first time that this lonely room had come to life. He contemplated the boy's features, where yesterday's tears had smudged the swollen face. Mishari's lips and cheeks were still flushed, which made Nitham rejoice over the pet fate had delivered. *I'll tame him well.* Nitham decided to feed the little boy the way he nurtured his goats and chicken. That's when he remembered that the kid had not eaten anything since noon the previous day. It upset him that he'd forgotten something this important, so he left the little one the copper pots containing rice and vegetable masala. *If he could turn on the cooler, then he's a smart kid. He'll also be able to serve himself and eat.* From this point onward, Nitham realised that he needed to cook for two, and to keep the little one healthy, he must fill the small body with lean meat.

After tending to his farm, Nitham would return to the house of his dead master the way he had always done, sweep the dust, vacuum the floor, and clean the windows. Nitham would then go into the kitchen to prepare an appetising lunch for himself and the kid. *This time, it won't be masala.* Nitham would cook a meal his master used to relish, then add a tablet of Brewer's Yeast to the pot. He'd pour some broth and whisk it until it became soft before dropping in slices of chicken or lamb. However, since he had neither in the kitchen, he'd have to make do with potatoes and pumpkins. *Either way, it will still be delicious.* He would also make more of the banana purée the kid seemed to enjoy, and this time he'd add extra ghee and honey, and he'd top it off with a sprinkle of cinnamon. His master had not originally prepared the dish with cinnamon, yet Nitham began including the spice to his recipes after trying it once and relishing its taste.

He now sat there ruminating over all the southern recipes he'd make. It was a shame that he didn't know their Arabic names, but he could always invent Urdu versions for them. Happy and cool sensations began to wash over his heart, and he thought, *It's only a matter of time. A farmer needs to be patient, or else he'd pick a sour mango.* And Nitham preferred to bite into a sweet and juicy drupe instead, so he was willing to wait his entire life if it meant picking a ripe fruit without a fuss.

It was only a matter of time until the little one realised that Nitham Shuja a-Din, the farmer hailing from Karachi, was now the only person in the whole world left to care for him.

CHAPTER NINE

HADEER

growling; rolling; rumbling

Like: water boiling or rushing down a towering cliff; the sound a camel makes in its windpipe; the cooing of pigeons; a lion's roar; or a thunder strike

Abha. Al-Raha Apartments

17 Dhu Al-Hijja, 1431

5:45 A.M.

Do you know that moment when a father tells his son, Everything's going to be alright?

Faisal crushed his cigarette on the railing to his side. He was sitting next to his brother on the empty steps leading up to the back garden of their hotel. Lifting his head, Faisal skimmed the grassy area before him. His eyes wandered over the circular basin in the middle of the garden brimming with cacti. The sun was about to rise, and a misty veil had started to spread. Dozens of cigarette butts were scattered on the steps around the two brothers.

Seven strenuous days had passed since their arrival in 'Asir. Seven terrible days lacking leads, interspersed with regular visits to security operation rooms. Seven days of waiting and more waiting. It felt as if he were dangling from a rope wrapped around his neck while still alive—kicking into the void, fighting for survival.

What if he's already dead?

Do you know that moment? he asked his younger brother.

Saud merely nodded.

Faisal exhaled smoke and continued, When a criminal is killed or captured in the movies, the Good Cop who rescues the victim tends to spread his arms and say: Everything's going to be alright. After a moment of silence, Faisal said in a quavering voice, Saud, why do adults lie?

Faisal had spent the last ten days speechless, as though his words had dried up and Time itself had stood still. Yet, sitting on the steps beside his younger brother, Faisal was unusually communicative, for he believed that the past ten days had taught them plenty, and now he found himself explaining, That moment will never come, when everything can be fine again. Just picture a policeman telling the child he had just rescued, Everything's going to be alright. Now imagine the child rushes into the officer's arms, and at that very moment, a reckless driver crashes into both of them. Faisal chuckled, then went on, Real life is truly this absurd, and the moment you believe you've survived is the moment you'll perish. He pointed the fingers holding his cigarette at his younger brother and added, You can't rely on a stable future. You can't.

Saud patted Faisal's back. Today, it seemed that the younger brother was the one who had nothing to say, for Saud could no longer assume the role of the Good Cop, the superhero, the dark knight, or Batman himself. He could no longer utter the phrase, Everything's going to be alright. How could he, after what they've been through? So, instead, he merely mumbled: Allah is gracious.

Faisal carried on. You've got no right to give your child false hope. But do you know where the actual problem lies? The problem lies in hope itself, for it's inherently false. Even if you were to hide your child in a room that you secured with a million locks so that no one could sneak in to harm him, the smallest and most despicable virus could still take your son's life. Have you ever wondered what it means to be a parent, Saud? He exhaled. We should not have brought him with us to Mecca.

Saud sighed, raising his eyes to the sky, where the first shafts of light were now shooting across the horizon.

Fatigue visible on his face, Faisal muttered, For the first time in my life, I envy you because you're single and childless.

Saud hesitated before asking, How's Sumaya?

Faisal pursed his lips. Better than me. Apparently, God is helping her. After a brief pause, Faisal added, Last night, her sister called and offered to come to Saudi Arabia to provide emotional support, but Sumaya turned her down. She said she didn't want to see anyone before she found Mishari. She hasn't left her prayer mat. Can you believe that?

Saud stammered an admonishment. Your quarrel... Everybody in the hotel heard you two screaming yesterday.

I can't help it, Faisal said lowering his head.

You two have been fighting nonstop since we came here to 'Asir. It might be better if you didn't blame each other.

The older brother shook his head.

Do you really blame her?

Faisal didn't answer.

Only crickets chirping in the grass pierced the silence between them.

Faisal gazed absentmindedly at the cigarette butts strewn haphazardly to his side. He had been smoking like a madman, hoping to burst into flames. Lifting his cigarette in front of his brother's face, he said, It was a genius idea.

What was?

Offering me a cigarette under the bridge. It was a pretty smart thing to do.

Saud, who didn't like the compliment, said, Please stop smoking once we return to Kuwait.

Faisal replied with a shake of his head, God helps only some of us. As for the rest... We need to take care of ourselves.

Are you so helpless that smoking is your only answer?

Of course! Helplessness is logical.

Saud furrowed his brow. Why are you so angry at God? If memory serves me correctly, you were on your way to performing the Hajj ritual, weren't you?

I was, Faisal said, averting his eyes.

What changed?

I don't know.

I'm only tolerating your heresies out of pity.

Grimacing, Faisal asked, Saud, do you remember the day Father died?

I do. I can't forget it.

Me neither. But I won't forget that day for another reason.

What do you mean?

Faisal said, exhaling smoke from his nostrils, Do you remember how they wrapped Father's head in a piece of cloth once they had prepared him for burial? Because they didn't want his mouth to drop open, they stabilised his jaw. But when they did that, the lower lip slipped under the upper one.

I don't remember that, Saud said.

He looked just like this, Faisal said, imitating his father's face. Do you remember now?

What are you trying to say, Faisal?

The dead look like they're smiling, but they're not. The strange thing is that all those who entered the room to say goodbye to him that day came out smiling as well, wiping away tears of affection and crying: Bless him, he's smiling! Faisal snickered as tears welled up in his eyes. Dad wasn't smiling, Saud! He was simply dead!

His younger brother flashed him a pitying look. What's going on, Faisal? What are you trying to say?

It was then that I realised that people see what they want to see, Faisal answered. And yet, I couldn't do it, no matter how much I wanted to see it, too. He wiped his eyes with his forearm and continued with a snuffle, Is this faith, Saud? Because I can't see what Sumaya sees, even though I've thought of myself as a believer my whole life. But now...

Saud, patting his older brother on the shoulder, finally managed to claim, Everything will return to normal when he returns.

Faisal smiled. What about you?

What about me?

I noticed you've been praying.

It calms me.

Prayer?

Yes.

Congratulations.

You'll stop smoking if Mishari returns, Saud said, who put out his last cigarette before he'd finished it. You must be a role model for him. There's already a bad apple in this family.

Faisal whispered, Mishari, then repeated the name over and over again. Although their lives had revolved around his son for the past few days, Faisal didn't think they used his name enough, and instead referred to the kid as though he were already dead and gone. Faisal mumbled, A week has passed.

Seven days in 'Asir and three days in Mecca, Saud murmured.

Ten altogether, thought Faisal, who counted the days. I keep wondering what he has seen in the past ten days. Then...

Then what?

I hope I get news of his death.

Saud's fingers twitched. He said with a shake of his head, No. He'll return, and everything will be alright again. You'll see.

Faisal exclaimed with a smile, The Good Cop's deception! What a wonderful lie.

Abha. Al-Raha Apartments

17 Dhu Al-Hijja, 1431

8:34 A.M.

He returned to the room and found Sumaya draped in her black abaya standing on the prayer mat. When she knelt, Faisal realised just how emaciated her body had become. Her thighs and arms had shrunk, and the fleshy chunks in her back had disappeared. She seemed like a foreign woman to him, a forbidden woman, and he felt awkward.

Faisal unbuttoned his shirt. Then he opened the cupboard to withdraw a new dishdasha for yet another day spent with Saud and Mazen, another day revolving around the same activities, the same centres, and the same operation rooms.

Faisal tried to remember what Sumaya had looked like before Mishari's disappearance. She had been chubby and tender with soft, plump arms, round cheeks, and two spectacular dimples. But he was now peering at a slender woman who pressed her forehead to an inlaid image of the Kaaba on her green prayer mat. Lately, Sumaya had been lingering during her sujood, prostrating longer than usual. Faisal also realised that she had been covering her hair everywhere she went, even in front of Saud—and it struck him that she must have decided to wear the veil.

Upon completing her prayer, Faisal heard Sumaya utter the name of God, then she asked him for forgiveness and recited other supplications: You alone are peace! Peace itself flows through you. Those steely, invisible hands seized Faisal's throat again as he watched her askance.

Sumaya flaunted an unfamiliar serenity as she sat there on her mat in deep meditative silence, whispering softly, sibilance slithering between her teeth. She no longer parted from her mat and either read the Quran or stayed up all night to pray. Her sky wasn't as quiet as Faisal's sky, as though Allah was always with her.

When she had landed in 'Asir a week ago, Faisal picked her up, his face cold, his body tense. They didn't even look at each other.

Sumaya was staring at her shoes when she asked him, What's the room number?

He carried her luggage, showed her to their suite, then to her bedroom.

Sumaya didn't comment when she realised Faisal had ordered a room with separate beds. In fact, she'd been hoping he would. It was the first time they'd sleep in different beds. In the past, whenever they quarrelled in the morning, they always returned to the warmth of their bed at night, as if they were declaring a truce. At first, they would sleep apart, giving each other their backs, but when they woke up the following day, her head would always be on his chest, his hand on her forehead. Neither would be able to recall how they had ended up in each other's arms, but their disagreement would no longer matter.

Fragrant Sumaya, whose neck smelled of oud, whose hair smelled of saffron, whose palms smelled of Bride's oil and musk; tender Sumaya, his wife, the mother of his child, the one whose desires he had vowed to satisfy—how did she become so distant?

Faisal closed the cupboard. As he was heading out, he heard her ask:

Where are you going? Then, to soften the edges of her question, she added, You didn't come home last night.

I was in the garden with Saud.

All night?

Faisal nodded.

Sumaya arched her right eyebrow.

Faisal thought she must be calculating how many hours he'd slept. Were it not for his recurrent fainting spells, that number would be nearly zero.

You must sleep a bit.

Faisal shook his head. He'd never sleep. He had made that decision a few days earlier, because he wasn't ready to enter into that dark cognitive space where reality sparkled in comparison.

After folding her prayer rug with two weak hands, Sumaya got up, left the mat on the table, sat on the edge of the bed, and hesitated before she asked him, Did you perform the Fajr prayer?

Faisal smirked. Sumaya was no longer asking whether he performed his optional prayers. She was now asking only about the obligatory ones. No doubt she questioned whether he was still abiding by the basic religious dictates or if he'd completely deviated from the path.

As he grabbed the doorknob, Sumaya said, Faisal.

Yeah?

If you don't look for him, you won't find him. She then turned to the open window to peer at the sky.

Faisal felt hot blood flowing up to his temples, flooding his limbs. Trembling, he tightly clenched his fist and tried not to punch the door in front of him. Faisal was so angry that, if he had punched the door, he'd have broken it. *How dare she plant such an insidious accusation in that statement?* Wasn't Faisal on his way to resume his search before she called him away from the door? And wasn't she the one who never parted from her prayer mat? *She thinks that if she prostrates long enough, someone will knock on her door to return her son to her. And Mishari will have been magically safe and sound the whole time. Meanwhile I... I... I'm the one who is navigating hell. I'm the one who is not sitting around waiting for divine intervention. I'm the one doing things myself. I'm the son of a bitch who...*

Sumaya... He struggled to articulate his thoughts as calmly as possible. I'm always searching for him.

As she smiled, Sumaya said, I didn't mean our son.

Abha. Al-Raha Apartments

17 Dhu Al-Hijja, 1431

8:56 A.M.

Saud was waiting in the living room when he heard the screaming.

Once the door to the master bedroom opened, Faisal rushed out.

Sumaya followed, waving her index finger at him. How can Allah answer your prayer when you don't even pray? Tell me! Faisal opened the apartment door, but Sumaya pulled him backward, yanking on his dishdasha, her eyes exuding fear. Faisal! she screamed. Are you still a believer?

Shoving her off him, Faisal yelled, Get away from me, Sumaya! But she was still clinging to him, so he grabbed her hand and pushed her away.

Although her back slammed against the wall, she rushed toward him to shake his shoulders again. How can God respond to your pleas when you don't pra—

Faisal yelled, I never even asked him for help!

Sumaya's fearful eyes bulged. Because she couldn't believe her husband's words, when she screamed next, her voice came out hoarse, Mishari won't come back if you don't pray!

Saud tried to separate the spouses. Please, enough, Sumaya, he told the wife. Just go to your bedroom. Leave him alone.

But as she admonishingly waved her finger at her husband, she reiterated, Mishari won't come back if you don't pray!

I've prayed my whole life, Sumaya! Faisal blurted out angrily. So, how come I lost my child?

She took a step backward, and as she anxiously pondered his words, Sumaya gazed at Faisal's swollen cheeks and the protruding veins on his forehead, then took a step closer to her husband and whispered, He disappeared because of our sins.

Faisal kicked the back of the sofa, punched the wall, and caterwauled, Because of our sins?!

Sumaya tried to explain gently, God is testing you.

But her husband threw pillows before he knocked over the dining table. Testing me by allowing my child to be kidnapped? And why is he testing me anyway? Why is he testing me, Sumaya?

As he wrapped his arms around his brother, Saud said, Calm down, Bu Mishari! Relax, please. And you, Sumaya, go to the bedroom. Now. Go.

Instead, Sumaya took a few hesitant steps toward her husband, her eyes still surveying his puffy, tearful eyes and dry lips.

But it was Faisal who spoke while panting, as if he found it hard to catch his breath. Listen to me, Sumaya. Faisal gazed into his wife's deep, black eyes—those eyes that were confronting him with all her fear and desperation. How could he put it as nicely as possible?

I'm listening.

His voice came out flat, almost lifeless, Nobody passes this test.

Saud loosened his grip on his older brother.

Sumaya, who began to sob, grasped Faisal's dishdasha. Her chin was trembling, and her eyelashes were wetly gummed together when she tried to touch Faisal's face, but he turned away. So she said in a whisper, Faisal. Have you become an atheist?

Faisal's cheek twitched, then he said with a grunt, Atheists possess a level of certainty I currently lack. He found himself suddenly chuckling.

With a look of confusion on her face, Sumaya peered at her husband. Faisal, do you believe in Allah?

It was a labyrinthian question Faisal couldn't personally solve.

She looked up at him imploringly, hoping he'd find his way through the maze of doubt back to the map of certainty.

And though Faisal began to search inside him for a reassuring answer, or at least a word that might dispel the fear from Sumaya's eyes, what he found instead was the same well of loneliness into which he'd already tumbled.

It is heartbreaking to lose your son, Sumaya whispered. But to lose God, too?

Faisal pursed his lips and averted his eyes. How could he explain to his wife that he was abandoned at the same time she began to see him everywhere, to talk with absolute conviction as though he were listening to every word, and to latch onto her prayer mat as though she'd found in that green rectangular rug all the bliss in the world?

How could Faisal articulate his loss?

Despite taking a step back, Sumaya reached up again, and this time, she managed to cup Faisal's face in her palms.

Faisal would have pushed her away, had it not been for the way she levelled her welcoming gaze at him: those big, open eyes capable of accepting both fear and love. Faisal...

He felt her warm breath on his face before she swallowed.

Are you aware that your disbelief has repercussions?

Yes.

Do you know what they are?

He nodded.

As a tear dribbled down her cheek, she asked, And is this what you want, Faisal? You want us to break up? After all these years? After our child?

It was his turn to envelop her face in his palms, but when he sensed her shaking her head, Faisal held her cheeks in place, and when her eyes darted to the side, he demanded, Look me in the eye, Sumaya. Then, Faisal gripped his wife's chin and lifted her face so she could be at eye level with him. He could see her fear glistening in her veiny eyes.

What child, Sumaya?

Our son!

Our son is gone.

My son is not dead! she cried, tears twisting her face.

I wish he were dead!

He'll come back.

No, he won't.

You've got to trust in God.

God?

Yes!

Faisal glared at his wife, whose mouth was open in shock. Where is he now? he asked.

Kidnapped by criminals! But we'll find him. He'll return to us.

Faisal smiled. I didn't mean our son.

Abha. Al-Raha Apartments

17 Dhu Al-Hijja, 1431

9:33 A.M.

Faisal rushed down the stairs.

Faisal! Sumaya cried as she ran after him, so he stopped. Wait! she said, sounding apologetic.

He lifted his head and saw her leaning on the railing, her puffy face looking down at him, her tears still pouring.

Will everything go back to the way it was?

He pursed his lips.

If Mishari comes back to us, will you return as well? She swallowed and added, Will we get back together?

I don't know, Sumaya, he said, shrugging before trotting down the stairs to avoid another question.

Mazen and Saud were waiting for him in the car when he left the hotel.

Saud was sitting in the backseat, his eyes red, his nose runny. He hadn't been able to stay another moment in the apartment after he'd heard Faisal and Sumaya discuss divorce. He had opened the door immediately and sprinted out. Now he sat in the backseat, wiping his nose with a napkin that he put away when his brother appeared.

Faisal forced himself to smile at his younger brother, for he understood the burden he was facing. Saud: the peaceful one, the Good Cop, the Dark Knight... Yet everything was slipping out of his helpless hands.

Where have you been? Mazen asked.

Faisal replied with another question, Any updates?

Get in. I'll explain on the way.

Faisal slid into the passenger seat.

As the car left the hotel parking lot, Mazen began to share the latest developments.

Last night, he said, the local police destroyed one of the shantytowns on a hillock that was housing dozens of African men and women from various criminal organizations. The shantytown comprised a series of adjoining rooms constructed out of tree bark, stones, and leafy branches. If one entered a room, one could exit from another into the valley about ten miles away. But as I said, the police surrounded the perimeter and asked everyone to turn themselves in. When no one came out, the police demolished the whole infrastructure with bulldozers. Many criminals escaped, and those who couldn't get out in time died in the rubble. The police extricated fifteen corpses, then captured the remaining men and women who had managed to escape.

When Mazen paused to catch his breath, the two brothers yelled, Then what happened?

Nodding his chin toward the police station, he said, The detective wants to see you.

Rijal Almaa Province. Haswa Police Station

17 Dhu Al-Hijja, 1431

10:11 A.M.

The detective, who was waiting for them, said Come in, Bu Mishari. He waved at the two chairs in front of him, then asked his aide to bring some water for his guests.

The two brothers each occupied a chair, while Mazen stood near the doorway.

Faisal believed this was the moment he'd hear confirmation of his son's death, for why else would the officer request some water? *They probably found his remains in the rubble.* Did you locate the body? he asked. Faisal was prepared to hear the worst and was ready to accept that his son had been injured or was lying somewhere unconscious in an intensive care unit. Anyway, if the detective told him that Mishari was dead, it wouldn't hurt as much as the hell he was currently experiencing. Faisal realised that Saud was staring at him in disbelief, unable to fathom how casually Faisal spoke about his son's potential death. Please don't sugarcoat anything. I know he's dead, Faisal said, turning to the detective.

Remember God, my good man, the detective said with a shake of his head.

Remember God? When did Faisal forget him?

Sir, do you have any news about the kid? Saud interjected.

This time, the officer nodded. Our detectives just interrogated the criminals they had arrested yesterday. Those who snitched kept referring to two women around whom odd tales seemed to circulate. We were told that these two women were new to the shantytown, but even though they didn't work in the fields like the others, or deal in opioids, they had wads of riyals on them when they were captured. We used your flier in our investigation, and it motivated a number of the arrestees to disclose the name of an associate of the two women, the leader of a child-trafficking ring called Jerjes.

Faisal held his breath.

Saud patted him gently on the arm to alleviate his fear.

The detective went on, Our men have just concluded their interrogation of the two women, who were told that due to the sheer number of witness testimonies we've compiled, they'd certainly hang for their crimes, but a confession might mitigate their punishment, so they cooperated.

Faisal, who winced, felt a chill shoot up his spine. His heartbeats quickened, and though he wanted to ask a question, his lips wouldn't move.

It was Saud who eventually asked, Did you find Mishari?

When the officer shook his head, Faisal felt his body deflate.

His younger brother squeezed his arm.

And the officer said, First, we isolated the two women, then we showed each of them Mishari's photograph. Although they did confess to abducting Black children, they denied kidnapping your son.

Faisal stood, then leaned against the desk to look directly into the officer's eyes, before saying, Where's the kid?

The officer replied with a shrug, They said they didn't know. They could be lying, of course. We'll know more soon enough, when we restart the investigation. I just wanted to keep you abreast of our findings thus far. We're not exactly closer to discovering the child's location—

Where are they? Faisal interrupted.

But you wouldn't recognise either of them, even if you saw them in person.

I would! Saud said. The criminal called me. I'd recognise her voice.

Where are they? Faisal asked once more.

Rijal Almaa Province. Haswa Police Station

17 Dhu Al-Hijja, 1431

10:40 AM

Here's the door opening.

An officer is now shouting at the two women, ordering them to enter. Your heart is pounding so loud you fear it might leap out of your chest. You turn to take a closer look at the two skinny, haggard women covered in bruises, whom police officers have been kicking and punching all night.

An incomprehensible rush of ecstasy floods your body, and you lunge toward the criminals, but your brother reaches them before you do. And when you stop, you watch them fearfully retreating until their backs are plastered against the wall.

Your face contorts in disdain and the blood boiling in your veins reflects your repugnance. You want them to know they disgust you. Then, a sudden, mysterious force thrusts you forward. You don't realise you've moved until a hand jerks you back. It's Mazen's hand. How come you didn't feel your body charge?

Mazen's voice, recalling you to your senses, whispers in your ear: Let your brother handle the criminals.

He recognises the shining glint in your eyes, the shortness of your breath, and your boiling blood forcing your limbs to tremble with rage. Your skin feels hot. Your nerves are twitching.

But your brother is now moving closer to the women. His hand

*becomes a fist as he approaches the one on the left. What's your name?
he asks.*

Bahati, she answers, lowering her head.

*You survey her bulging eyes, her hollow face, the thin lips that are
both chapped from all the screaming, and the fresh bruise in the corner
of her mouth. When she speaks, you notice her missing teeth.*

*Saud looks at you, shaking his head. Not her voice. Turning to the
other one, he asks, And you?*

Averting her eyes, she answers, Adania.

*You note her green-tinged teeth and the wrinkles stretching around
her mouth. Her face, resembling hunger itself, is skeletal.*

Saud, facing you, now concludes, Not this one, either.

*You don't know how your body shot like an arrow at the two criminals.
As you scream, you pound them with your balled fists, Do you know who
I am?*

Mazen and the two officers leap at you to restrain your visible anger.

Calm down, Faisal! Mazen cries.

*But not knowing the answer to your question is killing you. Do you
know who I am, bitch?*

*Your brother, who has also lost his temper, knees one of them in the
stomach.*

She leans forward and hugs her body.

Although a policeman hurries to prevent Saud from attacking the criminals, the detective belts an order, Leave them alone!

The officers' hands, which were holding you back, finally release you, so you kick the other one's thigh, and she collapses on the ground at your feet, wrapping her arms around her body and screaming in pain.

The detective rises, pulls out his billy, and says, This is the father of the boy you've kidnapped.

Snarling again, you yell, I'm his dad!

The officer continues, I promise I won't stop him if he decides to kill you.

You notice panic blooming on the faces of the two females and bellow, Which one of you did it? Which one of you kidnapped my child?

They both wail at your feet. Not me! Not me! It was Ruwaina who—

Where is she? Saud interjects.

We don't know!

He starts slapping their faces.

The detective hands Faisal the billy club, but Faisal lets it drop. He wants to batter these women with his knuckles. His fists were craving vengeance. Where's the boy?!

Writhing in pain and wailing, the two women raise their handcuffed wrists to their faces to ward off the blows. I don't know!

You start strangling one of them, then slam her head against the wall.

Where's the boy?

Mazen shouts, You're going to kill her, Faisal!

But Saud retorts, Then may she rot in hell!

So you keep asking, Where's the boy?

The officer and Mazen join in.

You bang her head against the wall again, and this time she becomes dizzy. When you spit in her face, you watch as your white foamy saliva shoots out of your mouth before landing on her eyelids, above her glazed eyes.

Her body sags, but you pull her up by the shoulders and hold her against the wall.

They went far away, her voice comes out strained.

You squeeze her neck until her face turns blue. She coughs and coughs, but you ignore her and roar, Where did they go? When you notice her opening her mouth, you loosen your grip.

They crossed the ocean, her words emerge in a breathless murmur.

Did she say ocean? You ask your brother.

Ocean? Saud screams at the criminals.

Yes, they answer in unison, both nodding.

When? you ask.

A week ago.

One of them starts to cry and mumble in her language.

The detective orders the officers to separate the criminals, then drag one of them outside the interrogation room.

You and your brother are now cornering the one they left behind.

Speak! Saud slaps her.

You slap her, too.

Now both of you are concentrating your anger on the same kidnapper. Spill! You both order. Which ocean?

The female criminal, who didn't understand the question, keeps repeating, Ocean! Ocean!

From the corner of the room, Mazen asks, Where did they go?

They went to Sinai, she says as blood dribbles down the corner of her mouth in a thin stream.

You and your brother stop moving. Your fists hang in the air, then fall of their own accord. Your legs shake as though you've lost a lot of muscle in one blow. You feel yourself dropping down a deep hole. Sinai? Your son is in Sinai while you are here?

Saud howls like an animal as he bangs one of the women's heads against the wall, refusing to believe her.

Don't kill her now! you tell him, placing an arm between them.

What will you do to the kids in Sinai? Saud demands an answer.

I don't know!

He picks up the billy club lying on the ground and strikes her twice in the belly, hollering, What will you do to those kids in Sinai?

Sobbing, she curls into a ball.

Talk! the officer commands. What will you do to them in Sinai?

Her voice cracks when she finally answers, We'll sell their organs.

Abha Private Hospital

17 Dhu Al-Hijja, 1431

2:05 P.M.

He couldn't remember much.

What Faisal did recall was a bright flash followed by a succession of images, all bursting from the same damned nightmare.

A yellowed corpse with black eyelids, a white ihram, the Kaaba's holy black stone, an amputated arm, a white shroud, green fabric, and millions of pilgrims in The Sacred Mosque chanting: Pray for the dead, may God have mercy on your souls. Faisal tries to reach the corpse—to hug it, then unshroud it—but the green fabric spreads until it covers everything in sight, and the multitudes, treading on the floor, rumbling like a flood, begin to plead in unison: Allahumma do not deprive us of his reward or distract us after his death.

The same nightmare woke Faisal up with a start.

Mazen, who sat beside him, regarded Faisal with tired, worried eyes.

Faisal looked around, searching for Saud.

But Mazen asked, How are you feeling?

He had no words to answer this question. When Faisal turned his head away from Mazen, he saw the end of a white hospital bed, a metal rod on which an IV drip was hanging, and a black screen monitoring his heartbeats and calculating the amount of oxygen in his blood.

Am I in the hospital?

Yes. You fainted.

How long has it been?

Almost two hours.

Where's Saud?

He went back to the police station.

What about Sumaya? Does she know?

Not yet.

A tear sprang from the corner of his eye. Faisal stared at the ceiling, unable to help but think his son had died. All this time, he believed the news was going to comfort him. But to be chopped up into pieces? He sobbed as he banged on his chest with his fist. Faisal, who wanted to tear himself apart from the pain, began to wail, Mishari's gone!

Mazen squeezed his arm and reasoned, It's too early to say these things.

It's been a week.

He could still be alive.

Sure. He's either already dead or about to be soon. Those monsters will slice the boy into pieces, sell his slabs like Eid meat, then cast his remains for wild dogs to devour. Mishari's organs will be given to other children. Although his body will spread throughout the world, Faisal will never again be able to see him, touch him, smell him, or embrace him whole.

At that moment, Faisal gaped at the ceiling, and his body began to shake.

Mazen held him down and screamed, Doctor! Doctor!

Three nurses rushed into the room before they strapped Faisal's body to the bed to inject his forearm with a tranquiliser.

Faisal lost consciousness.

He's floating on a red ocean filled with amputated arms and legs. He notices the organs: eyeballs, livers, and hearts. They all seem to be hovering on what looks like blood. He tries to search among those disembodied organs for the parts that belong to his son, as though Mishari would return whole once he finds them all. The rumbling waves are now carrying a decapitated head that resembles Mishari's. Spurring himself forward, Faisal reaches the head, grabs the hair, and pulls it up to look at the face, but it's dark-skinned, with thin lips and two golden hoops dangling from each dainty ear.

When the face opens its eyes, Faisal screams, drops it back into the ocean, then swims away.

Faisal woke up panting, his legs thrashing in bed.

Abha Private Hospital

17 Dhu Al-Hijja, 1431

3:14 P.M.

Faisal's bare legs appeared as he kicked away the covers, which then laid crumpled on the edge of the mattress.

Faisal! Faisal!

He opened his eyes.

Saud was gently patting his cheeks.

Faisal, who was breathing heavily, wrapped his arms around his brother once he saw him and sobbed.

Saud whispered in his ear, Hang in there, brother! I want you to be steadfast now. I need you to be resilient.

Mishari's gone!

No, he's not, God willing.

Faisal could only peer incredulously into his brother's face, for he couldn't understand how Saud could continue to hold on to that absurd, pathetic, and obstinate thing called hope. Saud would never accept Mishari's death until he saw the corpse with his own eyes. Whereas Faisal could no longer accept the illusion called hope. *It's been a week since the criminals had crossed the ocean. What's the likelihood of them not having already killed the boy, chopped him into pieces, and sold them bit by bit?*

Did I kill her? he asked his brother. Did I kill her before I fainted? Did I? Faisal wished with all his heart that he'd ended her life.

Handing his older brother a plastic cup, Saud said, Faisal, drink this. Then he poured some water on his palm and wiped Faisal's face. Remember God, brother. Recite his name.

Faisal wondered as he gawked, *While we were searching for him here, he'd already left Saudi Arabia and gone to Sinai. Who could've mapped out this labyrinth of loss? And what does arriving at the right place at the wrong time mean?* Lifting his head off the pillow, Faisal asked, She said organ trafficking, right? Did you hear her say it, too?

Saud nodded. He also couldn't believe what he'd heard, but then he added, I should've known.

Mazen asked, What do you mean?

The one I'd spoken to had said something strange, after all. She said if the police get involved, I'll chop the boy up and sell him piece by piece. I couldn't imagine for a moment that she'd meant it literally.

But we didn't contact the police! Mazen protested.

That's right, Saud said. It would appear that a quarrel had broken out among the group members. The detective called me an hour ago to let me in on one of their hypotheses. He said that the Coast Guard had found the body of an African man floating in the ocean with a bullet in the head about six days ago. When the Coast Guard searched the area further, they came upon a heavyset African woman whose body had washed up on the shore. She was wounded and had lost a lot of blood from a stab wound near her stomach. The Coast Guard neither found the gun that killed the man nor the blade that punctured the woman's belly, and local authorities found no records of the two individuals. The African man was thus briskly buried, and the African woman was rushed to the hospital. Her limbs and abdomen were bloated, and her body was covered in bruises, some days old, potentially the aftermath of somebody kicking and punching her. Some of her other injuries were caused by the haemorrhaging, both from her mouth and from the gash in her guts. She has been in a coma for the past six days. Doctors believe that she may not make it.

Is she the one who kidnapped Mishari? Faisal asked.

Saud nodded and continued, The officers drove the two female criminals they'd already apprehended to the hospital. They identified the unconscious African woman as Ruwaina, the one who had kidnapped the white child. Neither woman was aware of the call Ruwaina had made to us. And they didn't know about the dispute that had raged in the ocean between their other group members because they had already fulfilled their roles and had parted from the group.

When Faisal closed his eyes, Mariam's image painfully flashed in his head, and he felt his heart constrict.

What can we do now? Mazen asked.

The Kuwaiti embassy in Cairo has already updated the Egyptian government, while the Saudi detectives in 'Asir have communicated with Egypt's secret service about transferring our file to Al-'Arish. This way, Egyptian detectives can carry on Mishari's investigation.

When he heard the name, Faisal's eyes drenched with tears.

Saud said, as he kneaded his brother's shoulders, I want you to get up now, so we can return to the hotel. We'll pack a small bag and fly as soon as we can.

Abha. Al-Raha Apartments Hotel

17 Dhu Al-Hijja, 1431

8:15 P.M.

Saud opened the apartment door before he and Faisal stepped in.

Sumaya was in her bedroom, on her green prayer mat, the holy Quran between her palms.

When Faisal heard her warm voice reading surat Al-Rahman, his eyes welled with tears. *Should I tell her?*

He couldn't. How could he tell her that criminals had dragged her son to Sinai to kill him and sell his organs to medical colleges and hospitals? He felt dizzy.

Saud held him steady. Relax, Faisal. Then he added, You don't need to do anything now. I'll take care of things from here. His younger brother walked up to Sumaya's bedroom, knocked on the partly open door, and called, Um Mishari!

Minutes later, Sumaya came out of her bedroom, her hair covered in a veil, the Quran still between her palms. She asked in a panicked tone, Any updates?

Please join us in the parlour.

Fear glazed her face when she asked, Khair?

Have a seat first.

Taking hesitant steps into the living room, Sumaya sat on the sofa facing her husband, her eyes darting between the two men. Did you find him?

Faisal's eyes widened. *Wow! What intuition!* When he heard that there were updates about his son, his first instinct was to assume that the child had died. In contrast, his wife's first instinct was to ask if they'd found him alive. Even more baffling was her tone of certainty. *From where is she getting all this confidence?*

There have been some other developments, Saud said, shaking his head. We know now that the criminals have crossed the Red Sea and have gone to Sinai.

Her eyes bulged. Sinai? Why there?

We don't know, Saud replied with a shrug.

Sumaya pursed her lips and looked askance at Faisal. What are you hiding from me?

Nothing, Saud answered.

I'm his mother. It's my right to know.

I'm aware that you're his mother. It's why we're here sharing our discoveries.

Then why are you scratching your forehead?

Damn it, Sumaya! Are you a detective at a police station?

You're chewing your lips.

I'm thirsty.

You're not hiding anything from me?

No. Saud coughed. Nothing.

She turned to Faisal and regarded him with disbelief, because he hadn't said a word since he'd returned. What's wrong? Then she looked at Saud and added, What's wrong with him?

Nothing, Saud said, forcing a smile. He's just tired. We had a gruelling time at the station.

Her eyes studied Saud's body language as she asked, What did you find out? Tell me.

Faisal wanted to say something, but Saud jumped in.

Listen to me, Sumaya. Faisal and I will need to travel to Sinai. Could you quickly prepare his luggage? Mazen is waiting for us downstairs.

Sumaya nodded before adding, I'm coming too.

No, Sumaya. We need you to stay here.

She raised her eyebrows. Why should I stay here if my son is in Sinai?

Faisal opened his mouth and finally said, Go back to Kuwait, Sumaya.

I'll go back to Kuwait when my son returns to me.

No, Faisal, Saud interjected. She can't leave yet. Sumaya has to stay in 'Asir.

Faisal peered at Saud from the corner of his eye.

She should stay here in case Ruwaina wakes up, Saud explained.

Who's Ruwaina?

Mazen can handle Ruwaina. Sumaya should go back home. There's no reason for her to stay here alone.

Who's Ruwaina? Sumaya asked again.

The kidnapper, Saud answered. She's lying unconscious at the hospital as we speak. When she wakes up, we can learn more about what happened to Mishari.

Faisal repeated his point, Mazen can handle it. Sumaya should go back home.

Honestly, Saud muttered, I feel too ashamed to ask Mazen something like this when he hadn't even seen his family in ten days. He's already been too generous with his time. Now, we must continue our search without him.

She should at least tell her family to stay with her.

Sumaya shook her head and told Faisal, No. I don't want to see anyone.

But how can you manage without a man?

She mumbled before getting up, Allah doesn't forsake his obedient servants. I will only return to Kuwait with my child. Then, she disappeared into her bedroom.

Where are you going? Saud asked from the parlour.

To prepare Faisal's luggage.

CHAPTER TEN

JAZEER

a small, insular land; to kill or butcher (a person or an animal); the
tide returning to sea, i.e., ebbing

Day 11

Although the alarm rang for a long time, he didn't hear it.

When Nitham opened his eyes, sun rays were sliding through the window. How has he slept like this? He slammed his hand on the alarm clock to turn it off. He felt a strange headache pounding in his forehead and pain in his lower back, while the light penetrating the darkness in the room angered him. *Is it really a new day?* It was the day to plant his corn. Actually, he was supposed to have done it yesterday. *What happened to me?* The sun was already beaming, yet he hadn't performed the Fajr prayer. His body no longer woke him, as if he'd lost harmony with the earth.

After taking a deep breath, he sat upright and looked at the little boy, whose hands and feet were bound, sleeping to his right. Mishari had spent the night screaming until Nitham stuffed a sponge in his mouth. Strange red freckles had appeared all over the little one's face. Nitham's eyes now skimmed the blue bruises punctuating the young one's arms and legs. He was utterly naked, curled like a sticky snail, the bones on his arched spine protruding.

Nitham hadn't thought it would be this difficult, but the little one had spent an arduous night running and jumping around. He spat, and screamed, and threw whatever he could pick up, creating such a mess that Nitham had to restrain his limbs and gag his mouth. Only then was he able to tidy up the room. Nitham never wanted to hurt the kid. But Mishari left him no choice.

When Nitham went to the bathroom, he turned on the shower and cold water sprinkled out, so he raised his head for water to splatter against his forehead and shoulders. The night before, he had tried to bathe the little one, who hadn't showered since Nitham brought him to his farm. *The filthy boy!* But Mishari kept running around and sobbing. After catching the child, Nitham laid Mishari on the ground to peel off the dirty garment he'd been wearing the previous week, but the little fool latched onto the raggedy shirt until it ripped.

Nitham had dragged the little one with difficulty to the bathroom, yelling, You stink! You need a shower!

Yet, the little one had ignored him, even though Nitham was certain that the kid had learned a few words in Urdu and understood what Nitham meant perfectly, but he was a stubborn child who didn't know what was good for him.

Nitham wanted to rub him well, bathe his tiny body with Lux floral soap, wash his hair with shampoo twice, and massage his arms and legs with Nivea cream. Nitham also wanted to put some scented talcum powder on the little one's tummy, backside, and armpits. He wanted to dote on Mishari, to enjoy their time under the water, each washing the other, but the little fool turned everything into a vicious fight, thereby forcing Nitham to hold the sprinkler from a distance and violently hose the little one down with cold water. As soon as Nitham was done washing the boy, the little one curled up in the corner of the bathroom, still wet, gasping from the cold. Nitham couldn't shampoo Mishari's hair or scrub his body. He couldn't even touch him, since the kid slipped out of the bathroom and started to yell once more as he threw spoons, pots, and pillows. Mishari then grabbed the copper pot and knocked out the rice and masala on the ground, which stained his recently washed shins, feet, and fingers. Nitham had no choice but to punish him: to show the little one that what he did was unacceptable—that he couldn't act like a monkey or an ape.

Look what you've done! Who's going to clean up now?

Nitham unclasped his leather belt, then whipped the boy until blue ribbons appeared on his body.

The kid curled into a ball, covering his head with his hands.

Bad boy! Nitham shouted. Seeing the belt slapping the kid's tender flesh made Nitham's blood flow rapidly in his veins. A sudden electric charge shot through his body. He cast the belt aside, hurried to the bathroom, and locked the door, leaving Mishari naked in the room. Since, he'd already torn his garment, Nitham didn't think there was any point in washing it now.

Mishari wrapped the chequered quilt around him and tucked himself between the pillows.

Nitham thought it might be better to leave him in the room, inside his pillow fort, instead of hopping here and there like a plucked canary. Nitham could buy him new clothes, since he didn't want the boy to get sick, but for now, there wasn't anything wrong with leaving him naked.

Approaching the child became more difficult each day. It had been easy at first, when the kid didn't know what was happening, but now he hurried to the corner and stayed there for a while, then ran around roaring, forcing Nitham to tie him up, bury his head in a pillow, and gag his mouth. Nitham didn't want to be cruel. It wasn't exactly what he'd pictured—and yet he kept feeling that strange electricity whenever he used violence gratifying and terrifying him at once.

Nitham came out of the bathroom with the towel wrapped around his waist, quickly slipped on his trousers, faced the wall with the Kaaba panel, and skipped the optional Dhuha prayer to perform only the obligatory one.

After completing his prayer, Nitham turned to the naked child, sleeping with his arms and legs bound on Nitham's bed, teeth chattering and chin trembling.

Mishari blurted out an Arabic word Nitham couldn't understand.

Nitham untied the blue nylon rope, then covered the child with his blanket. He would leave him alone now and return in six or seven hours. Even then, Nitham would have to ruminate on his next steps, so he unlocked the metal door, got out, slammed it shut, and locked it. Then, he tucked the key into a nearby cactus pot before heading to his pantry.

Jazan. The Farm of Sheikh Ibrahim Hijab

18 Dhu Al-Hijja, 1431

9:40 A.M.

His full bladder woke him up. When he sensed silence, he opened his eyes, then relaxed. *Good. The foreigner has left.* Mishari struggled to sit up, and then examined the bruises covering his naked body. The blue injuries hurt, and so did his heart.

Noticing that the man had untied him, Mishari got up, moaning from his internal wound, and realised, as he stood before the toilet stall to pee, that the blue and red spots had spread around his member, while blood was oozing out of his asshole and dripping down the backs of his thighs. It stung to pee, and he dreaded the need to defecate.

Two days ago, the foreigner had wetted a small cotton pad in a blue bottle before chasing Mishari around the room. After catching Mishari, Nitham bound the tiny arms and feet, laid the kid on his stomach, and began to dab the cotton ball on the wound as Mishari screamed from the pain.

Mishari now walked toward the cupboard with his legs apart in search for something to wear. Although everything was too big, he picked out a singlet that reached the middle of his shins.

Famished, Mishari unclasped the lid of the copper bowl and took two bites of banana purée. His stomach rumbled and tears welled in his eyes. *The strange man will take many hours to return.* And once he returned, the pain would follow, so Mishari picked up one cushion after the other and built his pillar. Climbing to the top and clinging to the windowsill, he peeked outside, and saw Nitham hosing down the trees. Mishari's eyes wandered all over the field. There were numerous rooms beside each other. *Does anybody else live here?* Mishari started calling out, Hey!

The foreigner turned to him and shouted, Shut up!

Mishari understood this word. He got down quickly. The pain in his backside burning, Mishari moaned as he rearranged the cushions and built a wall to hide behind. It was the same fort he built every day, but the man, like the wolf in the fairy tale, kept breaking down the wall with a single touch. He'd then drag Mishari to the sponge mattress to hurt him. Mishari thus needed a knife to protect himself, but four days ago the man removed all the sharp objects from the room when Mishari waved a butter knife at him. Using the wooden shaft of his broomstick, Nitham knocked the knife from Mishari's hand. Later, a black bruise appeared in the same spot.

Mishari, after building the wall, now laid on his stomach. It was the only way for him to sleep since even sitting caused pain. Burying his head in the crook of his arm, Mishari thought of distant memories: the day he stayed up with his uncle to watch the second movie in the Batman trilogy. The Joker used to terrify him. Mishari remembered Christian Bale, Batman's excellent car, the popcorn, and his comfortable navy-blue duvet. Mishari couldn't recall the features of his uncle's face, and the faces of his loved ones had become more distant, blurry and hazy, enveloped in white mist. He remembered his father's chest hair and the oud fragrance his mother wore. But the faces...

Where did their faces go? Why do faces disappear like dreams?

Jazan. The Farm of Sheikh Ibrahim Hijab

18 Dhu Al-Hijja, 1431

2:50 P.M.

He could no longer feel the soil between his fingers.

What happened to me? Nitham grabbed a fistful and rubbed it with both hands, smelled it, then tossed it in front of him. *Yesterday, it wasn't just dirt. What happened to my hands?* He had finished sowing half the field with sorghum but hardly recalled anything he had done in the past few hours. He had been working as though hypnotised, his fingers utilising their muscle memory, his mind wandering far away. Nitham tried to recall the feel of the seeds, the water's coolness, and the earth's smell—nothing. *What happened?* he wondered as he raised his eyes to the pale blue sky. He sighed. *That devil had cursed me.* Feeling his chest constrict, Nitham sat at the edge of the field, dripping with sweat, contemplating nature.

He tried to regain his connection to the farm, the mountains, and the salty smell of the air, but it was as if his senses had been extinguished. The earth no longer spoke to him. He had lost all his pleasure in farming, and the only thing that responded to his five senses was... *Where did I go wrong?* Nitham rose and walked toward the mango tree, where a ripe piece hung from a damp bough. Cupping it in his palm, then smelling it, he thought, *It finally matured,* and realised he was smiling.

He picked the mango and sniffed its fragrance as he wiped the fruit on his face. *The long-awaited fruit. It was finally ready!* The idea that each fruit would eventually ripen reassured him. *A good farmer must always be patient.* He glanced at the window of his room. Because no one was watching him anymore, he wanted to bite into the fruit, but stopped at the last moment. He would eat the mango of course, but he wouldn't do it here. He would eat it inside, before the little one, to make the kid drool. Nitham's smile widened. *Why didn't I think of it earlier?* He figured out where he went wrong. He had spoiled the little one by doting on him, trying to feed him, clean him, and care for him, and he had even tried to treat his wound. It's true that he was harsh at times, but he was more frequently caring. *Those damn children! They confuse kindness for weakness.* Nitham found himself giggling, then shook his head in disbelief. How could he have missed it? *The little devil thinks I'm weak. I may be soft-hearted, but my tenderness can wait. This damned child will learn who's the master and who's the servant.* Nitham's body was awash with a strange sensation. *He must fear me. Even more than he does now. He must be so afraid he'd obey all my orders. Think of all the harmless pleasures the little one could provide! If only he was more malleable. If only he stopped kicking and screaming.*

The fantasies rumbled inside Nitham's head. Although he felt an overwhelming urge to return to the room immediately, he joyfully wandered, whistling an upbeat melody, tossing the mango in the air, then catching it. He figured out what to do. He would deprive the little one of food. *Sustenance for affection! Either the damned kid succumbed, stopped kicking and spitting at my face, or he'd go hungry.*

Hell, he might even starve.

Jazan. The Farm of Sheikh Ibrahim Hijab

18 Dhu Al-Hijja, 1431

3:50 P.M.

The little one was hiding behind the wall of cushions when Nitham returned, chuckling as soon as he saw the little bastard in his white ribbed tank, which looked like a cotton dress on him, revealing his pathetic chicken legs. And like every day, the pillow barricade collapsed on the little one's head as soon as Nitham touched it. The terrified look in Mishari's face as he backed up against the wall made Nitham dizzy, but the game had to wait for now.

Mishari began to scream the one word he knew so well, Chub!

Shut up... When will you learn another word? Nitham said, Idher aao—a command he always used when he patted the pillow beside him. Come here. Come to bed, boy.

The urine that streamed down Mishari's leg formed a blood-tinged pool of piss between his feet. Mishari involuntarily soiled himself whenever Nitham uttered that cursed phrase: Idher aao.

Filthy child! Nitham left him and sat down, leaning back against the wall. Peering at Mishari from the corner of his eye, he took out the ripe mango from his pocket. Raising his arm, Nitham said, It's very delicious. Do you want it? He added as he wiggled his eyebrows, Aao.

Mishari, sitting on the floor, his knees in front of his face, furrowed his eyebrows and gave Nitham a scornful look, then wrapped his arms around his legs. He swayed in place a few times before lying on his stomach.

Nitham smiled. Are you in pain? It won't hurt as much if you stop acting like an ape. By the way, I have the medicine, but I won't run after you. Come here if you want it. Nitham nodded at the cupboard with the antiseptic solution on its shelf, then raised one eyebrow. Not coming? He plunged his teeth into the mango, plucked its skin, then spat it on the floor. As he slowly peeled the skin, the fleshy yellow interior emerged. This isn't yours, he told Mishari. It's mine. Once Nitham sunk his teeth into the fruit, its juices mingled with his saliva. His eyes opened wide. It's sour! he cried, unable to believe he'd make a mistake like this. He had smelled its fragrance, touched its skin, inspected the colour, and waited long enough! He was confident the fruit had ripened! Nitham knit his brows, cast the fruit aside, and spat out the morsel. *How shameful for a farmer to eat an unripe fruit! How shameful to make this error!* Nitham stared at his fingers in astonishment. *What happened to me?* Then he glared at the boy. This is your fault! You little devil! You ruined everything! Everything!

The boy didn't seem to understand, yet he still engaged in angry retorts. Chub! Chub!

Nitham yelled back, You shut up, you damn ape! He quickly got up and left, slamming the door violently behind him, the metallic boom echoing in the empty field. Nitham was horrified. He stood panting in front of his farm. If he could not distinguish a ripe fruit from an unripe one, how would he harvest the millet, pick the ears of wheat, pack the reeds, dry the pines, or filter the seeds? How would he do anything, having lost his one strength: his sensitivity?

Nitham looked at the ground. The millet stems had begun to puncture the soil's surface and shoot upward. How could he take care of his land? The little devil had cursed and tarnished him.

Nitham buried his face in his palms, which were sticky from the sour mango. When the memory of his late master flashed in his mind, it filled him with shame.

As soon as the foreigner left, the boy rushed to the mango fruit that had been tossed into the corner of the room, bit into it, then returned to his spot to rebuild his fort, wondering what could've riled the man. Although the fruit was sour, Mishari devoured it, the pain of his hunger rumbling in his stomach. Nitham didn't bring any lunch today, even though Mishari had licked the leftover chunks that were gathered at the bottom of the copper pots. He'd also licked the last grain of rice and the last remains of the porridge. Darkness had descended outside, and still, Mishari hadn't eaten lunch, so he relished the mango, sucking on its juices until all that remained was a bony seed. Mishari cast it far away from him before opening the fridge, but it was empty. He'd eaten all the radishes, the cucumbers, and the tomatoes. The man hadn't refilled it with vegetables. He hadn't brought any eggs. And he hadn't offered Mishari any meals. *Why didn't he eat?*

Mishari tried to forget his pain. Laying on his stomach, he closed his eyes and tried hard to remember the faces that began to disappear, but his nose suddenly recognised the enticing scent of oil and onions. *So, he's cooking. He'll probably return with a hot meal soon.* Mishari stacked the cushions on top of one another, moaning in pain as he climbed, blood dripping down his thighs. He then clung to the edge of the window and, when he peered out, saw that the light bulbs were on in one of the rooms overlooking the farm. He also noticed Nitham's shadow moving back and forth. *He's cooking lunch at night.* Mishari drooled. Despite the pain wracking his body, he held on to the metal bars and stood on tiptoe, watching the silhouette's movements with two wide eyes relaying hunger.

Nitham opened the door, left the kitchen area, and sat on a bench, a pot filled with food on his lap between his hands. Mishari wondered what he was eating and if there was any meat in the container. From a distance, the dish looked like bread dipped in a stew. Mishari salivated some more when Nitham began chewing. He even saw the man's tongue roll in his mouth and his eyes bulge wide. Nitham sucked on a chicken thigh and, a few minutes later, cats showed up. Some roamed around him. Others meowed in place. When he finished sucking on the bone, he threw it among them.

I wonder why he hasn't come inside to eat.

At that moment, Nitham realised that Mishari was watching him through the bars. He looked up and asked, Bahoka?

Mishari wanted to jump down and hide, but his hunger paralyzed him, so he screamed, I'm hungry!

Nitham mimicked the little one with a snicker: I'm hungry! I'm hungry!

Mishari tried to remember what Nitham would say whenever he brought food. He tried, Kahao! Then he screamed it loudly over and over again.

Nitham chuckled and joyfully slapped his knee.

The cats had by now surrounded the bone, their meows echoing across the field. Two of them then lunged at one another, while a third slipped in between the two and escaped with the bone. The others swiftly followed.

Meanwhile, Mishari was still screaming. Kahao!

Raising his eyebrows, Nitham uttered a few words Mishari couldn't understand, yet he immediately nodded. Seeming satisfied, Nitham returned to the kitchen smiling.

Mishari yelled, Nitham! I'm hungry! Kahao! He pulled on the bars, crying, trying to break them.

Nitham returned after a minute. He had another pot with him, loaded with bread, stew, and chunks of chicken. Nitham opened the lid and spoke in his gibberish.

Mishari wanted to eat, so he kept nodding, kept saying, Yes, yes, yes.

The smile that stretched across the strange man's face made Mishari's heart drop.

Jazan. The Farm of Sheikh Ibrahim Hijab

18 Dhu Al-Hijja, 1431

9:42 P.M.

The little one was waiting for him, standing behind his pillow fort, stretching his arm through a makeshift opening because he wanted to receive the pot and eat it inside his barricade.

Nitham laughed. *Is that really what he thought would happen?* He sat on the ground, leaning against the wall, and placed the pot in front of him. When he pulled off the lid, steam drifted out, and the smell of the stew permeated the room.

The little one said behind his fort, Kahao!

Nitham shook his head. Aao.

Mishari now knew exactly what that word meant.

Nitham kept patting the place next to him. Idhar aao.

Mishari looked away.

Just like a confused monkey who only wants to grab the food and return to his pathetic cage. Nitham closed the lid, then got up slowly.

Mishari screamed, Kahao! Kahao! He sounded anxious.

Nitham pointed his index finger where he wanted Mishari to sit. Aao.

Mishari hesitated before leaving his fortress. He walked, legs trembling and spread apart, then moaned when he sat in the spot Nitham had chosen for him and saw the trail of blood drops he'd left behind.

Smart boy. Look at you, you're so well behaved.

Mishari looked up, his face covered in sores, his voice coming out as a plea, Kahao, Nitham.

Alright, Nitham said, nodding. Food will be your reward for your behaviour.

It didn't seem as though Mishari understood Nitham's words. However, he fixed his eyes on the pot. The fragrance of the food was making him dizzy.

Nitham moved to sit in front of the kid, placing the pot between them. When he opened the lid again, warm steam rose.

The boy attacked the food with his fingers.

Nitham struck him on the back of his hands to teach him proper etiquette.

Mishari pulled his hand back fearfully, then slowly stretched it toward the pot, his eyes focusing on Nitham.

In the name of God, Nitham said, reminding the boy to evoke Allah's name before devouring the meal.

Bism'Allah, the child said.

Nitham gave Mishari a thumbs up.

Mishari ate one bite before Nitham closed the pot again.

That's enough! Nitham said with finality.

Mishari grabbed the pot, hands already smudged by the stew, yelling, No! No! Kahao, Nitham! Kahao!

Nitham's right eyebrow rose. He asked Mishari, More?

Mishari nodded.

It appeared to Nitham that Mishari at least understood that word. As he got up, he picked up the pot.

Mishari tugged on his pants.

Nitham pushed him away, turned on his TV, and Kareena Kapoor appeared, dancing in her green skirt with its golden designs, moving like a snake.

The boy's features changed, as he understood what it meant for Kareena Kapoor to be present among them.

Nitham nodded. That's right, he said. You do get it. He returned to his sponge mattress carrying the container of food, then lay back, spread his legs, placed the food between his thighs, and said as he patted the bowl, Kahao.

Two reddish streams of urine slithered down Mishari's legs. Trembling, the little one hurried to his pillow fort, then ducked behind.

This time, Nitham wouldn't run after him, wouldn't hit him, wouldn't even tie him up. He'd open the lid, and the smell of the stew would do the work. If Mishari wanted to eat, and he'd have to eat at some point, he must come willingly and obey Nitham's every order. So, he ignored Mishari, and kept dipping his fingers in the pot, licking them, and watching Kareena Kapoor carry on dancing on screen.

Nitham believed he was a better partner than Salman Khan. He thought the actor's red shirt was ridiculous. In the second part of the dance sequence, the actress wore a white see-through nightgown and brushed her hand up and down her hips, her thighs, and her waist.

Nitham's body hardened. Thinking that Mishari had been punished longer than necessary, he turned to the boy.

The little one was glaring at him, pain coating his face.

Nitham removed a chicken leg from the pot and ate it.

The boy looked away. He wasn't yet ready to pay the price for the meal.

Fine. Nitham would wait. Kareena Kapoor was now flicking her hair, wearing her green skirt with a golden design and a glossy purple shirt covering her breasts and part of her beautiful shoulders, waving her small hands with bright red nail polish in the air, the same red that streamed down the boy's legs—the red he liked.

Day 13

The boy did not eat anything for three days. He became even thinner as he withered. His ribs and spinal bones jutted out and the dark area around his sockets made his eye pop. Mishari became feverish twice, and it looked to Nitham as though the child had no desire to heal.

Mishari's state worried Nitham, who examined him every night, wondering, *Will he die?* Nitham had never wanted to kill the child. He only wanted to tame him. He knew he couldn't have him forever, but he wasn't ready to give up on the kid.

When Nitham returned from the farm carrying a pot filled with warm banana dough, the little one was still asleep, and white mucus had gathered around his mouth. Nitham shook Mishari's shoulders. Wake up, kid! Don't you want some food?

Nitham wanted him to eat even if he didn't pay the price. Get up! Kahao! I made you banana purée. He opened the lid and moved the pot close to the little one's nose. Look! Wake up now and eat something. Or do you want to die?

No sooner did the boy attempt to open his eyes than his eyelids drooped, and he lost consciousness again.

Nitham felt panic crawling up his skin. *He will die!* Placing his palm on the little one's forehead, he felt it burning up. Sores had spread around his mouth while bruises covered the little arms and legs. Nitham peeled off the cotton tank Mishari was wearing. The skin below the abdomen was inflamed, and there was a trail of scars between his thighs. Nitham mumbled, He will die. Mishari hadn't eaten in three days. After rushing to the cupboard, Nitham took out a bottle of alcohol, dipped some on a cotton ball, then wiped it on the boy's skin.

Mishari felt the sting of the cold liquid and moaned in pain.

Nitham got up again to bring the boy a glass of water. He put the glass close to the boy's lips. Paani, larka.

Mishari didn't want to drink.

What's he going to do now? It had never occurred to him that Mishari's health would deteriorate this quickly, since they'd already spent ten days together that could've killed the boy—but didn't.

Larka, get up now. Nitham patted Mishari's cheeks. Larka. Larka. Nitham wracked his brain, trying to remember the boy's name, which he'd only mentioned on the day they'd first met. Mishari!

The boy briefly opened his eyes before closing them.

Nitham felt upset. The little one would die, and Nitham would have to bury him quietly in a forgettable area on his farm. Wiping the boy's nose with the edge of his lungi, Nitham said, Don't die now, then carried the child in his arms toward the bathroom, and laid him on the ground to pour cold water on the boy's face and body.

Mishari, moaning and trembling, his lips curving into a frown, began calling: Mama.

Nitham was happy to see the kid wake up and cry. After wrapping him in a towel, he lifted the child and went back to his bedroom, where he laid the kid on the sponge mattress.

Mishari screamed and waved his weak arms. No! No...

Nitham held his hands. Hush, larka.

He cupped some banana purée and, after dipping the morsel in Mishari's mouth, Nitham heard the boy's tongue roll.

When the little one swallowed, Nitham's face brightened. Kahao, larka. Kahao. He fed Mishari another mouthful.

It seemed to Nitham that the little one's unconscious body had begun to shake off the layers of death it had collected, regain some of his vitality, and wake up.

You must eat. You're very thin.

A rosy flush returned to Mishari's cheeks. He ate half of the purée, then went back to sleep, breathing softly.

What a stubborn child. Nitham was applying a wet towel to the kid's forehead. *As stubborn as an ass.* He combed the little one's bangs with his fingers.

When he felt something touch his body, Mishari woke up kicking and screaming, the cover crumpled into a heap at the edge of the mattress. Mishari tried to run to his pillow fort, but Nitham embraced him and muttered in his ear, Hush, larka. Hush.

The boy didn't.

CHAPTER ELEVEN

NASHEER

to spread or to expand; to broadcast; fabric tied around the waist

Sharm El Sheikh International Airport

18 Dhu Al-Hijja, 1431

6:15 A.M.

The plane arrived at Sharm El Sheikh International Airport.

As passengers stood up, some began retrieving their leather bags and laptops from the overhead bins while others picked up nylon bags or backpacks before waiting in the aisle for the airplane door to open.

Faisal, whose body felt like a log on his seat, was staring at the screen on the chair in front of him. Its glazed surface reflected the terror in his eyes and the wrinkles around his mouth, perfectly capturing the nausea visible on his face, for he was battling a sinking sense of dread, feeling simultaneously as though he were still suspended in the air and as if a powerful force were pulling his bowels into his aching heart.

Another uncharted territory awaited him.

A map of the area appeared on the screen. Faisal moved his finger to trace the cities and countries he had crossed in the past few days: Kuwait, Mecca, 'Asir, Sharm El Sheikh, and soon enough, North Sinai. *Could Mishari have travelled all that distance as well?*

A young cabin crew member approached Faisal and whispered, Detectives from the Egyptian Criminal Investigation Unit are waiting for you.

Faisal's heartbeat quickened. He didn't want to know what this place had in store for him.

Would you like to leave the airplane before the other passengers?

Faisal shook his head.

Saud asked, Does your stomach still hurt?

Faisal settled for another shake of his head.

You've been afraid of flying your whole life, Saud said.

True. I also hate the smell of airplanes.

Beating around the bush was their new way of conversing about the missing boy.

Saud, who received a phone call from the Kuwaiti embassy in Cairo, informed the representative of their arrival. The detectives are waiting for us, he told his brother when he got off the phone. How are you feeling now? Better?

Faisal's heart had been pounding in his ears for the past six hours, ever since they'd set foot in Abha's International Airport, all through their flight over King Abdulaziz Airport in Jeddah, up until they reached Sharm El Sheikh. *Three cities in six hours. How many hours did the kidnappers take to cross the sea?* Faisal moved his finger from Jazan to the Suez Canal, then across the Red Sea. *How many hours?*

Faisal felt his brother's palm rest on his shoulder and his brother's eyes analyse his face.

It was clear to Faisal that Saud wanted to get off the plane and reach the desert immediately to excavate the organs of the boy who...

Ready? Saud asked.

No.

Then get ready.

Saud's tone changed after the plane landed. This time, when he
ordered his brother to calm down, it sounded more like a command
than a plea. Saud was also more proactive on this trip. He opened
the paper bag for Faisal when his older brother started to puke.
Saud brushed Faisal's back with his other hand and reassured him
that they were very close and that the end of this chapter was near.
He described their arrival in Egypt as: Development. Because it was
difficult for them to talk about the child directly and to keep their
language and tone neutral, they began referring to what happened to
Mishari as: The matter.

The matter began when...

The matter will conclude when...

There have been some developments in the matter.

Faisal thought of all the words he could use to express the matter
more accurately: calamity, nightmare, bereavement.

But he needed a neutral language, something dull to filter his pain.
It was a laughable attempt to control his sorrow.

You must be ready.

Faisal nodded. *The matter isn't up to you anymore. Your level of
preparedness has no impact on the matter. The world will trample you
and even crush you under its hooves, regardless of whether or not you're*

ready to face what lies ahead.

The question remains: How do you prepare for the possibility of finding your son dead or on the verge of dying?

Saud got up and looked at Faisal, who was still plastered to his seat, even though the other passengers had already vacated the aircraft.

Saud reached down to unbuckle Faisal's belt. Come on. Get up.

Faisal stood up heavily, as though pulling his body out of a swamp. He laid his hand on his brother's shoulder, before allowing Saud to usher him out of the plane.

On the Way to Al-'Arish

18 Dhu Al-Hijja, 1431

6:30 A.M.

A slender, brown-skinned young man in his twenties rushed toward them as soon as they descended the airplane steps. Wearing a white shirt and grey pants, a folded coat dangling from his arm, he stretched his free arm to shake both Faisal and Saud's hands and said, My name is Mustafa Wajdi. I'm the detective who's heading your case in the North Sinai division.

Saud greeted him, then said, I'm the kid's uncle. He's the father.

Nice to meet you.

Faisal nodded quietly, because speech had dried up in his mouth and his lips wouldn't part.

This way, the young detective said, preceding the two brothers to his car.

Faisal sensed his fatigue returning, so he leaned against a wall beside a red cylindrical trash can. Blonde women passed in front of him and his brother. The morning breeze was cool and the sky a bright blue.

Saud whispered in Faisal's ear, How old do you think he is?

Don't know.

Saud, who seemed annoyed, told Faisal, He looks young... A

mere fledgling. What does this youth who has just hatched from his university egg know about organ-trafficking gangs?

Faisal examined the young investigator's hurried walk, stern expression, and knitted brows. Then, feeling increasingly lightheaded, he mumbled faintly, I don't know.

Hang in there, Faisal. Are you dizzy?

The young detective opened the door of his white Toyota. When the two brothers came over, he politely asked them to go in.

Once the car began to zoom between the sprawling grasslands, the investigator informed them that it would take them about six to seven hours to drive from Sharm El Sheikh airport to Al-'Arish. He added, Sometimes, it takes longer because of the police and army roadblocks, but as long as you're with a criminal investigator...

It was a meaningless remark.

He went on to explain that he had received their case only two hours ago because the person who was initially in charge had an emergency. He didn't say what kind.

Frustration became visible on Saud's face. So you don't know anything about the case?

Shaking his head, the detective said, I read the file, but it really doesn't say anything. How about you bring me up to speed during our drive?

Saud clicked his tongue and said, No.

The detective gave him a puzzled expression. No?

Saud looked the detective in the eyes and said defiantly, We'll talk about the case at the police station.

They drove silently for an hour, the car coasting along Sharm El Sheikh Dahab Road. Trees swayed on either side of the paved street before they moved past a chain of hotels on their right, while the blue sea was to their left. Faisal breathed a sigh of relief. *The ocean!* He muttered, I haven't seen it in a while. It was a fleeting remark outside the context of their calamity.

This is Naama Bay, Mustafa explained.

The area was teeming with tourists in swimsuits surfing the waves. Others lay on golden sand. And some were even hanging from parachutes. After a while, the sea disappeared, and mountains sprang up to their right, followed by the desert, where Faisal spotted a boy with thick bangs wearing a shabby jalabiya tending a caravan of camels. The boy's hair reminded Faisal of...

Tents had been erected near the main street behind bamboo bushes that had grown on the slopes of the mountains, and colourful attire hung on clotheslines connecting the tents to one another.

Faisal leaned his head back. There was a question that kept reverberating in his chest since yesterday: *Why Sinai?* The location brought up several things: a demilitarised zone, Camp David, and a power vacuum—words one tends to read on newsreels. Apart from the sports section and updates on Kuwait's National Assembly, Faisal didn't read much else.

The fine golden sand stretching between boulders reminded Faisal of the dunes he'd taken Mishari to last spring near Subbiyah. His son had climbed up the sand hill before sliding down, giggling. Faisal recalled other details from that trip. Mishari would sit cross-legged next to his mother on the sadu rugs in front of their portable fire pit, burning chestnuts and warming their teapot. This was followed by another memory. Faisal was standing two steps away from Sumaya, who had a cashmere shawl draped around her shoulders. Her long black hair was curled and clipped at the back of her head. She was chasing Mishari with worried eyes, cooing, Slowly, slowly, honey. Be careful, darling. Faisal recalled another scene: Saud whispering in the little one's ear while standing on the top of a dune. Faisal didn't need much to decipher the content. Your mom is a scaredy cat! Ignore her. Saud embraced the child and they rolled down the sandy incline together.

It was a year with heavy rain that filled the land with a local yellow crowfoot called Nuer. The memory trampled Faisal's heart. It was a simple life. Just like any other life. *How come it now feels like a fairy tale?*

The radiant turquoise sea appeared on their right for a second time before they reached the city of Nuweiba. The investigator explained that the Nuweiba seaport was connected to the Jordanian port of Aqaba and appeared on the opposite bank, adding that pilgrims passed through it during the Hajj season.

Even in Sinai? Faisal felt persecuted by the Hajj, as though no matter where his body went, he remained in Mecca, circumambulating the Kaaba he couldn't see. He looked down at his trembling hands and could hardly believe that he'd embarked on his Hajj journey eleven days ago. It felt like a whole year had passed since the last time he'd found himself believing in something. He looked up confrontationally at the sky and its unbearable silence.

As the car passed by several resorts, it cut through the city of

Taba. The sea disappeared and the land appeared: a vast desert with uplands on its periphery.

Mustafa, the detective, pointed in the direction of the mountain. This is Jabal Al-Halal.

The two brothers looked out of the window.

Halal means goatherd for the Bedouins.

Saud cried: Naama Bay, Nuweiba Port, Jabal Al-Halal... Do we look like tourists?

A mysterious smile crept over the young detective's face. Calm down, bashmohandes. I didn't mean to offend you. He swallowed before continuing, I was going to explain that numerous armed conflicts are waged here.

Saud cried again, Armed conflicts?

The detective nodded. Between local authorities and armed militias. This happened several years ago after the Taba and Sharm El Sheikh bombings. Jabal Al-Halal is one of the most dangerous zones because jihadists, escaped convicts, human traffickers, weapons smugglers, and drug dealers use it as their hideout.

What about local authorities?

The ghost of a smile loomed on the detective's lips. What authorities? The Egyptian army is prohibited from entering these areas. Not even a single tank can get in.

How come?

The detective's smile widened. What do you know about Camp David, bashmohandes?

Saud shrugged. He didn't know anything.

Faisal asked, What if my son is trapped on that mountain?

The detective pursed his lips. Let's hope he isn't.

Faisal felt his heart fall. How would he find Mishari in Sinai?

The detective uttered words the brothers couldn't digest: Area C, Hilton Bombings, tourist kidnappings, opium plantations. He mentioned terrifying details that seemed entirely out of place compared to the luxury hotels and hip surfers populating the scene, as though the words belonged to another world entirely.

After about an hour, Mustafa pointed right and said, That's Israel.

Faisal felt his heart beating hard. It was the first time he'd heard Israel mentioned outside the context of a news bulletin, and it became tangible for him.

All he wanted was to perform the Hajj ritual.

How did he end up here?

Al-'Arish's Security Directorate (First Division)

18 Dhu Al-Hijja, 1431

12:32 P.M.

They entered Al-'Arish through an empty desert road, where olive trees lined the bank and a few small houses occasionally popped into view.

The detective drove the rest of the way in silence.

When they passed Al-'Arish's International Airport, Saud cried, Hang on! Why didn't we fly here directly if there's an airport?

Mustafa explained that there were no flights between Al-'Arish and Sharm El Sheikh. There were weekly flights to Cairo and an international trip to Saudi Arabia that transported Al-'Arishi pilgrims and Palestinians. The detective glanced in the rear-view mirror and saw the boy's father cringing. Whereas the boy's uncle was staring at him with eyes full of suspicion. Mustafa thought there was nothing he could do or say to make Saud trust him.

As the car penetrated the city's heart, it passed tall palm, olive, and acacia trees.

The two brothers gazed absentmindedly at the concrete buildings and the expansive balconies, skimming varicoloured clothing hanging from ropes and chords.

How long until we get to the police station? Faisal asked the detective.

Ten more minutes.

Shortly afterward, the car parked in front of a beige building with a sign that read: Al-'Arish's Security Directorate (First Division).

The yard was bustling, as usual, with dozens of vehicles.

Saud asked, What are all these cars?

These vehicles have been confiscated for their lack of license plates. The detective opened the car door and got out. Follow me.

The two brothers stood in the yard, scanning their surroundings and nearby buildings. There was a university campus, which included student housing and apartments with plants and clotheslines on the balconies.

Exhaustion was visible on both their faces as they followed the young detective through the entrance. They greeted the policeman guarding the gate, as he was searching one of the applicants.

The detective walked two steps ahead of Faisal and Saud until he reached his office at the end of the hallway. The main foyer was teeming with people. Mustafa turned the key and opened the door, calling one of his aids. He sat down, then invited his guests to join him. Please, have a seat.

Faisal collapsed on a nearby leather sofa.

Saud remained standing.

Bashmohandes, please sit.

Saud refused and said, We need to discuss something first.

What would you like to discuss?

Saud unloaded what was piling on his chest, Mister Mustafa, I don't want you investigating my missing child. After referring to Mishari as his own son and briefly pausing, Saud added, With all due respect, you're still a child yourself, and I won't risk my son's safety with an inexperienced detective who thinks this case is his opportunity to earn professional glory. Saud's voice became louder. The embassy informed us that it had assigned a team of experts to investigate the matter. To be honest with you, you don't seem qualified. Not even remotely.

The detective tried to assure him that he would do everything possible to solve the case. When Mustafa asked for enough time to at least start the investigation, Saud began to scream.

Despite asking to speak to the manager of the police station, he meant the chief of police. Where is your manager? he kept shouting. Where is he? Saud had also started to speak in an Egyptian accent, reproducing the dialect of Cairenes even though Mustafa came from Sinai and he—a son of the Sahara—did not find the Khaleeji accent difficult to understand.

Saud threatened to contact the detective's superior, even though the North Sinai Security Director was the one who had entrusted Mustafa with investigating the matter in the first place.

Mustafa glanced at Faisal, who was covering his face with trembling hands. Even his head was quivering. He then fixed his gaze on the younger brother shaking with anger, pain, and fatigue. Spit was splattering out of Saud's mouth and veins had protruded on his forehead. *The guy is calling for a team of organ trafficking experts. Maybe he's expecting something similar to American movies.* How could Mustafa tell Saud that he was lucky the director even assigned anyone to the case in the first place? What would you like to happen now?

Saud, the Kuwaiti engineer, calmed down momentarily and said, I want a team of experts on organ trafficking.

The detective gave Saud a sympathetic nod. I'll pass your request on to my superior. He pressed a chat button and asked his secretary to write an official letter to the North Sinai Security Director expressing Saud's request.

The office aide arrived holding a tray with glass tea mugs and water bottles.

No, thank you. Faisal and Saud declined despite the excessive dehydration that chapped their lips.

Okay, Mustafa said, as he began to survey from the corner of his eye the boy's father, sitting on the sofa, unaware of anything transpiring around him, seeming small. Mustafa then turned to the uncle and said, We have two options, bashmohandes. Either we sit and wait for a new team to be assigned by the criminal investigation department, which could take hours, perhaps days, or we could go to the morgue and continue working on our case until the new team arrives.

The brothers seemed confused.

Faisal's eyes bulged in fright. Morgue?

Al-'Arish Hospital, to be exact. Most dead bodies in the desert are transported to the mortuary department.

Dead bodies? Saud asked.

Yes.

Dead bodies in the desert?

Yes. Mustafa struggled to maintain his neutral expression and tone.

Saud swallowed with difficulty, then said, Oh God. OK. Let's go.

As soon as Mustafa picked up his car key, Faisal began convulsing. His body shook all over before falling flat on his face.

Saud rushed to embrace him, yelling, Faisal! Faisal!

His older brother's face was hollow, as though a force was yanking out his soul with pliers.

Al-'Arish. Swiss Inn Resort

18 Dhu Al-Hijja, 1431

1:46 P.M.

I'm sorry, Faisal. I'm sorry.

Saud kept apologising as he tucked his older brother beneath the hotel bed's white duvet. Don't worry about a single thing, he said after kissing Faisal's forehead. I'll take it from here. And though Saud had promised that he wouldn't cry anymore, tears now soaked his eyes. His lips were dry, and his tongue was heavy. Saud felt responsible for what had happened, as though he had personally pushed his older brother toward the unbearable.

Mustafa ran out to bring a bottle of water. When he returned and brought the bottle nearer to Faisal's lips, he told Saud, We need to take him to the hospital.

Faisal shook his head. No. There's no time. He looked at his brother. Saud, he said.

I'm here, Faisal.

Go ahead. Take care of things. Faisal closed his eyes. He wanted to go toward the end of this damn tunnel, to delve into the bottom of his wound and investigate. Faisal muttered faintly, Please find out if my son is dead or alive.

Saud wanted to reassure Faisal by saying, Your kid is alive. Visiting the hospital mortuary department is just a precautionary measure. Don't lose hope. Trust in Allah. But he realised that these words no longer...

Faisal, on the other hand, wanted neither hope nor despair. He only wanted the truth. And Saud, the Good Cop, felt unable to give his older brother false hope by telling him that things would be alright. All he could do was go out to uncover what had happened, then return to tell Faisal how awful the matter truly was.

How can I leave you alone? Saud said. You're tired.

I'm fine.

Saud carefully examined Faisal, who looked painfully pallid. Wrinkles had formed around his mouth, and white streaks had appeared on his sideburns.

Saud wondered, *Will I lose him too? I might be able to handle losing one of them but not both.*

Mustafa placed his palm on Saud's shoulder. Don't worry. Some of my colleagues can stay with him.

Saud, who was breathing heavily and wiping his nose on his sleeve, resolved not to cry.

Faisal ordered his younger brother again, Do what you must.

I will.

Saud kissed Faisal on the shoulder, then left.

Al-'Arish General Hospital

18 Dhu Al-Hijja, 1431

2:05 P.M.

Saud and Mustafa were waiting for their ride at the hotel gate when Saud turned to the detective and asked, Is the hospital far from here? The idea of walking away from his brother frightened him.

The detective shook his head. Just ten minutes.

Saud glanced at the tall palm trees along the shore. Watching the ocean gave him incomprehensible solace. His chest filled with a warm salty breeze, which he hadn't tasted since he'd left Kuwait.

Bashmohandes?

Saud realised that the detective standing beside the car was calling him. He fixed him with a look that urged him to hurry, and said, Won't you get in?

Saud didn't realised that their ride had arrived. He pulled the door handle and got in.

The car drove through a walled gate and entered a yard full of cars and ambulances. The detective parked in front of a vast concrete building bearing slender windows with reflective glass between balconies with handrails. In one of them, a nurse wearing a white dress, a white veil, and a white niqab stood watching the crowd of people below.

Several women and children were sitting on the grass under the aluminium awning. People crowded the entrance to the hospital while a child, playing with a water hose, giggled as his younger brother ran into the splashing water.

Saud looked away. There was a stretcher to the right of the stairs. Its green paint had peeled off and now showed a rusty, brown interior.

When Saud walked in front of the detective, Mustafa stopped him and pointed at a small building to their side. The morgue is this way.

After following Mustafa inside the building, Saud watched him speak with one of the employees. A doctor in a blue surgeon's uniform then accompanied them to the morgue, and once Saud descended the four-step ladder, the odour overwhelmed him, so he covered his nose with his arm as though the smell had smacked his face.

The doctor gave him a mask.

But he cried, What's this smell? The stink was gnawing at his head. Saud glanced at the detective and saw that Mustafa was covering his nose with his sleeve. Saud's stomach convulsed from the heavy rancid smell filling the air.

The doctor explained with an apologetic shrug, Most of the corpses we receive are already decomposed. These bodies are either torn apart by wild animals or riddled with bullet holes.

Saud's pupils widened. The smell stung his eyes. Although he understood what the doctor had said, he couldn't digest its meaning.

The doctor took a step toward the freezer with three metal drawers. He opened the lower drawer and found two bodies joined together. The doctor said apologetically, The authorities found seven bodies yesterday at the border. We don't have enough refrigerators. Sometimes, we must squeeze two or three bodies in one drawer.

Saud still struggled to comprehend the meaning behind the doctor's words. What exactly happens here? Was there a massacre?

The doctor removed the cloth to reveal one of the bodies. It was an African male with chiselled cheeks, hollow eyes, and an open mouth. He had been burned to death with a flame thrower. We found his body at the border a few days after the time of death, the doctor said.

What border? To Saud, everything felt booby-trapped with loss. He looked at the exposed corpse, its black skull almost decomposed, still hungry. Who is this man? He doesn't look Egyptian.

The doctor and the Egyptian exchanged glances.

Even though masks covered half of their faces, Saud nevertheless saw traces of incomprehensible smiles.

The doctor said, You don't know anything about what goes on around here? He pulled out the rest of the drawers. Each of them included two or three bodies. Then he walked around, removing masks and revealing the dark faces underneath, all of which looked hungry, from the first dead body to the last.

Stop! cried Saud. Enough!

The detective chimed in, We're looking for a Kuwaiti child.

But we rarely receive white bodies, the doctor said.

The boy was smuggled about a week ago.

I'd remember a white boy if we got one.

Saud and Mustafa looked at each other while the doctor hurriedly covered the faces of the dead and returned the drawers to the belly of the freezer.

Saud climbed the four steps leading out of the morgue's exit. He leaned his back against a wall in the hallway, gasping, unable to believe what he'd just seen: an Egyptian hospital full of African corpses, some shot with weapons, some torn apart by wild predators. *What did I witness in a forgotten place only four steps below ground level? All those people... What were they doing here? And why were dead bodies showing up one after the other?*

A few minutes later, Mustafa followed. Peeling the mask off his face, he peered into Saud's eyes and asked, Are you OK?

I am.

He was lying.

Al-'Arish. Swiss Inn Resort

19 Dhu Al-Hijja, 1431

7:00 A.M.

I'd feel better if you stayed at the hotel today as well, Saud told Faisal while buttoning his older brother's shirt. You're not ready, Faisal. You should rest. I can't focus on the investigation if you're with me.

The trembling hadn't left Faisal's fingers since yesterday's seizure. When he couldn't button his shirt, he asked his younger brother for help. Faisal had recently been unable to perform the simplest tasks, yet his eyebrows still rose. Mishari is my son, though.

Saud looked deeply into his brother's eyes. Your son is my son.

Faisal interrupted him, But it's my responsibility as his dad—

It's not about responsibilities, dumbass.

Faisal pushed Saud's hand away and reached out for his final button. He turned around and went to the mirror. The button was shaking between his fingers.

The last time Saud insulted him, Faisal was ten years old. He taught Saud a lesson by knocking one of his teeth out of his younger brother's mouth.

This time around, it wasn't the insult that bothered him. In fact, Faisal would have laughed had it not been for his current state. He muttered to himself, I'm OK—even though the button kept slipping from his fingers.

Come here.

Saud was now ordering Faisal around, which was strange. *He's acting like he's the older brother.*

Sit here.

Faisal sat on the edge of the bed.

Saud opened the drawer, took out a sock, then mumbled, Sumaya only packed three pairs!

A half-smile appeared on Faisal's face. We only packed three pairs for the whole trip. One cannot search in the desert for a missing son while sporting Najdi sandals. Come to think of it, when our grandparents were herding in the wilderness, what were they wearing? Adidas?

Saud says, I'm surprised you're joking.

What about you?

What about me?

You came to Mecca in your engineering uniform.

Mazen bought me the rest.

How is he?

He called yesterday and wanted to know where we've been. He sounded worried.

Faisal shook his head. He's a decent man.

Kneeling at his brother's feet, Saud put on Faisal's socks before getting up to close the last button. You're ready, he said, placing his hands on his older brother's shoulders, and, as he stared into Faisal's eyes, Saud added, Listen to me now.

Faisal felt the faint smile stretching across his face. But it was a peculiar smile: out of context and barely perceptible.

Saud raised his eyebrows. You've had more than one seizure and haven't yet gotten a diagnosis.

Faisal looked away. Does the matter require a medical label?

I said listen to me. We don't know if what's happening with you is temporary or chronic. I can't risk your health. If you come with me, you'll witness things I can't protect you from.

OK, Dark Knight, you can chill. Faisal gently pushed his brother away.

I'm not joking, Saud raised his voice.

Neither am I.

Saud sat on his knees. He put his palms on his brother's hands to steady their involuntary tremors. Stay here, Faisal, for Mishari's sake and mine. You can stay here. I'll be your eyes and ears. I can handle everything. I promise to go out into this damned desert and bring your boy back. Just let me make sure you're safe.

Distress wriggled into Faisal's chest. Saud, he said.

Yes?

What happened yesterday?

Saud swallowed.

You didn't update me.

I told you what you needed to know.

You're making me angry.

Please don't. Saud grabbed Faisal's hand.

What did you see in the morgue yesterday?

Nothing that concerns you.

I can call the detective and find out everything from him.

But you won't.

Why not?

Because I forbid it.

Since when did you start acting like my older brother?

Since you started acting like a child.

You're crossing a line.

Faisal, please. I'll do anything if you just stay.

You're an ass, Saud.

Fine.

Do you seriously think I'll wait in the hotel while you look for my kid alone?

Your son is my son, dumbass.

You're the dumbass.

Faisal. Please.

Tell me what you saw at the morgue yesterday. What are you afraid of?

I'm worried about you. Your fingers are quivering. Why?

What? It's probably the fatigue.

What if it's something else? Parkinson's? M.S.? Or some other damned thing?

Faisal raised his trembling hands and said, You a doctor now?

No, but you're an ass who's refusing medical attention.

You're the ass.

What if you get your boy back but can't hug him? Did you even consider that? Did you think about it?

Struck by a glimmer of hope, Faisal said, I'm willing to pay the price.

And who said your health is the cost of Mishari's return?

Faisal shrugged. Who knows?

You've become as delusional as your wife.

Faisal smiled. Can we go back to normal where I'm the older brother and you're the one who does my bidding?

Saud got up, and mumbled as he opened the door, We can go back to normal when I find Mishari.

Al-'Arish's Security Directorate (First Division)

19 Dhu Al-Hijja, 1431

8:05 A.M.

They're here, Detective.

The head of one of the officers was peeking through the half-open door.

The whispered statement distracted the detective from the papers and pictures scattered before him. He began picking up the documents on the desk and, after stuffing them in a drawer, stood up, stretched, then turned to the clock that was fixed to the wall on his left. It had just passed eight o'clock. Mustafa had spent the past ten hours among empty glass tea mugs and cigarette butts, reading like a madman. His neck and shoulders were stiff, and he was as lost as he had been when he'd started this long night of reading. *How does a child disappear in Mecca? And how have they ended up searching for him in Sinai?* He spent the entire night reading about cases of organ trafficking. Mustafa had heard about such issues in the news like anybody else in Sinai. The more stories he'd heard, the less he believed, but now he was starting to feel there was more to it than the images and cases he had filed through all night. He thought about that desert far from the sea, outside 'Arish. *What secret are you hiding?*

Skimming the map of the Sinai Peninsula hanging on the wall in front of him, he thought, *All those corpses no one had noticed...* Bountiful deaths. Free of charge. Mere miles away from where he stood. Lives ending in absolute silence and buried quietly—the sand that swallowed the dead is hiding their bodies in its depths, where no one could hear anyone else's screaming.

Mustafa remembered yesterday, when he was assigned the case. He had accepted the mission because he was grateful for the rare opportunity. His eyes had gleamed with excitement as he pondered the world's interests in the subject, the political sensitivity of Sinai, the Egyptian government's reputation in international arenas, and the mobilization of Khaleeji populations. It was his opportunity to make a name for himself. But now, after ten hours of staring at pictures of corpses with sutured bellies, he couldn't avoid the same question the Kuwaiti engineer had asked him the day before: *Why did my superior choose me?*

The Kuwaiti brothers entered his office.

Good morning, Saud said, shaking Mustafa's hand. He didn't seem as angry as he was the day before. Saud placed a copy of *Al-Ahram* newspaper on the detective's desk. A statement by Egypt's Minister of Interior said on the front page, Egypt Recruits a Team of Experts to Investigate the Disappearance of a Kuwaiti Child.

Mustafa tried to hide his smile. *A team of experts!* His secretary, his aide, and himself.

Saud asked, Has the team arrived?

Not yet. Mustafa had decided to keep the Kuwaiti brothers in the dark—to keep them waiting for the team of experts that would never come.

When will they get here? Saud asked.

Mustafa knew that he had to look the man in the eye. Not to cough or rub his nose or forehead, but to answer in a confident tone instead.

May it be a blessing, Saud mumbled.

The Kuwaiti engineer didn't seem as bothered as he was yesterday about Mustafa remaining in charge.

You look tired, he told the detective. Did you leave the office?

Mustafa smiled. I was reading. He peered at the father, who was both smiling faintly and on the verge of tears, then asked, How's your health?

Better.

Mustafa gestured to the two chairs next to his desk. There's a man I want to introduce you to. Please have a seat.

Saud and Faisal sat down.

Saud asked, Who do you want to introduce us to?

Clasping his palms and intertwining his fingers on his desk, Mustafa answered, A Bedouin called Huwaishel. A former smuggler.

The father echoed, A smuggler?

Former smuggler. He has since repented, as they say.

Faisal glanced at his brother, who seemed nervous.

The detective rested his elbows on his desk, his fingers covering his mouth.

Faisal asked, Weed smuggler? Gun smuggler?

Saud answered, Human.

Where does he smuggle people into?

He smuggles them into Israel.

Israel? Faisal frowned, naive astonishment coating his face.

Whenever that look of shock appeared on either brother, it filled the detective with distress. It was like they were separated from the real world. Or was the real world separated from them?

Why was he destined, purely by virtue of being born and raised in Sinai, to live a brutal life worthy of crazy headlines: gas pipe explosions, jihadists hiding in caves, bombs, tourist kidnappings, destruction of opium plantations, corpses at the border...

Faisal turned to him. Do you think my son was smuggled into Israel?

The detective shook his head. It's too early to say that. We first need to determine how the boy was transferred and to gather information about it from desert tribes.

The two brothers nodded in agreement. Saud seemed impressed by the speed of the detective's response and the logic of his plan.

Satisfaction gleamed in Mustafa's eyes when he pressed the button on his desk to tell his secretary: Call Huwaishel.

Al-'Arish's Security Directorate (First Division)

19 Dhu Al-Hijja, 1431

8:33 A.M.

Khair, I hope, detective.

The Bedouin who had just walked into the office asked before sitting on the sofa. His head sunk between his shoulders as he apprehensively examined the faces of the detective's guests.

The Kuwaiti brothers sized him up.

Huwaishel, a man in his forties, had a hooked nose and terrifying eyes and he was wearing a white jalabiya with red chequered headgear.

The Bedouin clasped his palms between his thighs, looking at the investigator, waiting for his questions.

Well, Huwaishel... The detective paused for a moment, put out his cigarette, then said to the man. Huwaishel, you've been involved in smuggling—

But I've repented! he interjected seriously. Raising three fingers to his face, he added, Three years ago!

We're glad that you've repented, Huwaishel. Now, let's get straight to the point.

Go ahead. Tell me.

Mustafa gestured toward Faisal. This man's son has been

kidnapped.

Huwaishel pointed at Faisal. This man?

Yes, the detective said.

No way, the Bedouin said, shaking his head.

What do you mean by that?

He's not African.

We know he's not African, Mustafa remarked.

Sighing and leering at Faisal, the Bedouin asked again, How?

But what he was really asking Faisal was: Why are you here? The unspoken question pierced Faisal's chest. *What made you come down here? This isn't your hell.* Faisal did not know before this moment that discrimination existed even in hell, which segregated its inhabitants based on their skin colour. An area for Whites. An area for Blacks. And one for those who are crushed daily under the wheels of the modern world: those who cross the geography of thirst and the labyrinth of loss, to find a livelihood and not...

But since Mishari did not belong to that infernal roster, Faisal didn't know if he should rejoice or drown in shame.

Mustafa said, We need you to help us find the boy.

At your service, Huwaishel said, regarding Faisal with a steady gaze.

The detective added, We need to learn how you've smuggled

people.

That depends, Huwaishel said. Where was the boy kidnapped?

In Mecca.

In Mecca?

Our reports indicate that he must've reached Sinai by now.

That means they crossed the ocean!

Huwaishel seemed less nervous as he sat upright. Clasping his hands over his knees, he said, Look, Sir, there are only three smuggling routes in Sinai. You won't find a fourth. He got up and walked to the map hanging on the wall. With his long, skinny finger, he pointed at the Suez Bridge. You either cross via the Suez, then take a four-wheeler to the border area of Al-'Ajra south of Rafa', passing the coastal road... Are you following, Sir? Huwaishel moved his finger across the route he just mentioned and added, Then Balootha, Rummana, Bir Al-'Abd, Al-'Arish, and Sheikh Zuwayed. In other words, away from the main roads. Sir, every smuggler is an expert in these routes, since there aren't any security checkpoints. Huwaishel moved his finger on the map.

Or you take the second way via Al-Salam Bridge or Qantara ferry. Here.

Huwaishel moved his finger south of the Suez, mumbling, The third way is this, and it's the one you want. Criminals would take small boats to the eastern shore from the south of the Suez. From there, they'd sail to the middle of Sinai. Nikhel Centre, specifically, then through the valleys and from there to the border fence.

Border fence? Saud asked.

It's between Sinai and Israel.

Mustafa nodded, then asked, Where do you go afterward?

The Bedouin, who scanned the faces in the room, hesitated before answering, To Ghost Houses.

Faisal felt panic creep under his skin. His voice, coming out hoarse, disappeared at the end of the phrase, Ghost Houses?

Huwaishel nodded. It's what the Africans call them.

My son isn't African, Faisal said, his blood boiling, his head pounding.

The Bedouin murmured, I know, as though he couldn't believe the kidnapping story.

Saud asked, What do they do in the Ghost Houses?

Huwaishel pursed his lips before answering, They hold them hostage. Some sell their prisoners to one another. Because each tribe controls an area, when an African hostage is sold to another tribe, that hostage's price increases with each new deal.

I don't get it, Faisal murmured. His head filled with pictures of his son being bought and sold and passed on from one kidnapper to another. From south to north Sinai, from the Red Sea to the Mediterranean, and from Mecca to Israel.

Was this even possible?

Sinai. Al-'Arish

19 Dhu Al-Hijja, 1431

11:24 A.M.

Smuggling was my only choice, Huwaishel said. People who perform these dangerous operations are usually unemployable. He was gazing at the sea through the window to his right as the white Toyota, navigating Al-'Arish, cut across roads flanked by palm and olive trees. I wasn't a trafficker. As a smuggler, I was doing the Africans a service, since I knew this land like the back of my hand. I was their best bet to cross the border safely. And I certainly have nothing to do with those Ghost Houses.

Mustafa interjected, But that's where you delivered them. Isn't that right?

I had no idea what went on inside.

Mustafa cast a penetrating gaze through the rearview mirror, a gaze full of suspicion. Perhaps you didn't want to know.

Huwaishel waved his arms in protest. Pardon me, Sir. Do you think Africans begin their journeys in Sinai? Haven't you ever wondered where that journey begins?

What do you mean?

Africans leave Eritrea, Sudan, Nigeria, and Ethiopia behind for a better life. Russians, Chinese, and Georgians made the same trek before them, crossing every border by land, by sea, and by sky. Our authorities have never truly deterred immigrants or smugglers. Have you ever wondered why we don't take severe measures to protect our borders?

It's because the criminals are armed, Mustafa said. And they know all our geographical vulnerabilities, so they know where to hide.

Huwaishel let out a derisive snort. That's not the main reason.

What do you mean?

There are things one cannot say in this country, especially to authorities, Sir. After a minute of silence, Huwaishel calmed down, then added, When have you ever interfered on behalf of the victims? These cases happen daily. When have you offered to help? Look, there are twenty different paths to cross the border between Ismailia and Sinai alone. Have you ever asked yourself why the local authorities do not patch up these vulnerabilities?

Mustafa said irritably, There's corruption everywhere, so that's no excuse for your smuggling.

That's right! Huwaishel cried. But when you find yourself having to choose between smuggling to live or starving to death, and when you actually choose hunger, you can come back here and judge me!

Mustafa lowered his gaze.

More silence transpired between the two men until Huwaishel muttered, I'm an educated man. Did you know that? Although I only graduated from middle school, I speak my mother tongue, Hebrew, and English, all fluently. But I have six children. I had to feed them. I worked on a farm until the government raised the price of pesticides. What would you have done if you were in my shoes?

Saud asked, Was smuggling a lucrative business?

Huwaishel's head bobbed. Of course. I lived like a king, sometimes making ten thousand dollars a day!

Mustafa whistled. Ten thousand, you son of a—

Huwaishel added, An African immigrant would pay between one to twenty-five thousand dollars just to cross the border with some aid.

But if these immigrants had all that money on them to begin with, why would they choose the illegal route? Saud asked.

It's not their money, you see, Huwaishel clarified. They'd borrow it in six or seven-thousand-dollar instalments, hoping to pay it back upon finding a job in Israel.

I don't understand, Saud said.

What don't you understand, bashmohandes? Huwaishel thought momentarily, then added, Imagine you're planning on sneaking into Israel, yet your mere presence on Egyptian soil is a crime. Your entry into Israel is likewise illegal.

Mustafa nodded.

Huwaishel continued, There are no official documents that show who you are, where you come from, and where you're heading. In legal terms, you're no one.

Saud swallowed.

The smuggler you asked for help, Huwaishel continued, doesn't need to fulfil their end of the bargain. He could just sell you to a human trafficker, who'd sell you to a criminal, and so on. Your price will increase with each transaction, but you won't be considered an unauthorised immigrant any longer. From then on, you'd be a slave. And to repurchase your freedom, you'd have to repay your owner.

But how could they repurchase their liberty if they're broke? Saud asked.

The kidnappers would call the parents so they could hear their children being tortured. Then, the parents would reach out to their community for help in raising thousands of dollars to cover the ransom, which usually amounts to twenty-five thousand dollars.

Only twenty-five? Saud cried.

Astonishment flashed on Huwaishel's face. Is that a small number to you?

Saud shook his head, still unable to fathom the amount. We offered a million dollars for Mishari's return.

Huwaishel's eyebrows arched. A million dollars? And they didn't call to make the exchange?

Nodding, Saud explained, The kidnapper did call. But she was found stabbed and unconscious a few days later. We gathered that the boat she was on was leaving Jazan and heading to Sinai.

Huwaishel's eyes narrowed. So they're supposed to have arrived in Sinai a week ago? Why would they call you now? If I were in their place... I mean, pardon me, bashmohandes, but do you think it likely that the kidnappers would simply ignore a child for whom the parents are willing to pay a million dollars?

Al-'Arish. The New Generation Foundation for Human Rights

19 Dhu Al-Hijja, 1431

2:14 P.M.

Mustafa parked in front of a middle school building.

The Kuwaiti brothers got out of the white Toyota to look around. They skimmed the concrete structures followed by students waiting at the gates and cars haphazardly idling across the sandy expanse.

The detective pointed at a small, shabby building with a sign on the top that read, The New Generation Foundation for Human Rights.

Mustafa explained, There's someone in there with whom we need to speak. His name is Hamdi Al-Azzazi. He's an expert in the war on organ trading.

Saud was comforted by these words and believed that the investigation was finally heading in the right direction. He even gazed upon Mustafa with admiration before surreptitiously peeking at his older brother. The tremor in Faisal's fingers was getting worse. Stress aggravated it even more.

Huwaishel apologised and said he wouldn't be able to join them.

Mustafa winked. An old acquaintance?

The Bedouin smiled without commenting.

Hamdi Al-Azzazi's office was in an apartment on the ground floor. It was average in size, neither cramped nor spacious. There was a desk around which a group of young men and women had gathered. Images of a chunky white-haired man with a grey moustache surrounded by young Black kids smiling to the camera hung from a corkboard on one of the walls.

Mustafa whispered to Saud, This place offers workshops and lectures on human rights.

Where's the expert? Saud asked.

But Mustafa continued, When it first started, this place was merely an online project where forum members published under pseudonyms. Look at them now!

Wow, Mustafa, that's amazing. Now, once you've curbed your enthusiasm, maybe you can tell us where we can find our guy.

The detective pointed his chin at a man behind the desk. That's him.

Saud scrutinised the man's face. He was a plump man in his forties, like any man one would encounter on the street, and reminded Saud of Egyptian teachers who taught in schools in Kuwait. Al-Azzazi was a man who did not resemble any superhero.

Suddenly turning to the newcomers with a perplexed expression, he asked, Can I help you?

Mustafa apologised for the interruption. I'm so sorry, Mr. Hamdi Al-Azzazi. My name is Mustafa Wajdi. I'm the detective who called this morning.

The Human Rights expert got up to shake Mustafa's hand. Welcome. Gesturing to his group of students, he told them, We'll resume our lesson later. Then he peered into the faces of the Kuwaiti brothers and asked, Which one of you is the father?

Faisal raised his hand.

Mustafa cut in. Mr. Al-Azzazi, with regards to the case of the boy who went missing in Mecca, which I mentioned earlier, our evidence now suggests that he has been transferred to Sinai. The Criminal Investigation team in Saudi Arabia has surmised that we are dealing with organ traders.

Faisal's face paled. Hamdi Al-Azzazi offered him a bottle of water, but Faisal declined with a shake of his head. He didn't want water. He wanted answers. His eyes fell upon the documents cluttered over the expert's desk, which included photographs of black corpses whose bellies were sewn and whose sockets were stuffed with fluffy white cotton balls. What the hell is this? Faisal cried anxiously.

Excuse me, Al-Azzazi said, quickly flipping over the photos on his desk.

Faisal began to hyperventilate.

Al-'Arish. The New Generation Foundation for Human Rights

19 Dhu Al-Hijja, 1431

2:32 P.M.

Hamdi Al-Azzazi explained that he could predict the next steps in most smuggling cases because he was well-versed in them. However, he didn't possess the same level of expertise in organ trading. For example, he told Mustafa and the Kuwaiti brothers, We know that there are forty-four detainees in a village in Mahdia, in Rafah. Someone called Musa is ready to let them go. Al-Azzazi shook his head. These are forty-four lucky Eritreans whose parents have raised the money for their ransom. Al-Azzazi reached for a bottle of water and chugged it all before continuing. We lack that intel when it comes to organ trading. We cannot predict the criminals' next moves, so we keep stumbling on decomposing corpses several days after their death, and by then some would have already been torn apart by wild dogs. Most bodies that we have delivered to Al-'Arish's Hospital are of this ilk.

Faisal turned to his brother.

But Saud looked away.

The human rights activist continued, You must understand that black market organ trading is highly profitable, with little to no overhead. Do you know what traders make in this business? Teeth rake in fifteen thousand dollars, a single kidney is worth thirty thousand, eyes go for twenty grand each, one lung is about forty, so is a uterus or a testicle, and hearts go for a hundred thousand. The spare parts, ready for harvest, are worth more than the living human being. And if we're talking about children, we're dealing with even more significant transactions because there's a shortage of children's bodies in the black market, so their organs go for triple the price of their adult counterpa—

But we offered a million-dollar ransom! Saud interjected. A million dollars, Mr. Al-Azzazi! If smugglers demand ten thousand dollars from Eritreans to buy back their freedoms, Mishari's ransom is therefore worth a hundred Eritreans! Saud fell quiet momentarily, then pointed his index finger at the detective's face. And if we calculate the cost of Mishari's organs... Rummaging in his pocket for his iPhone, he pulled up the calculator, and began tapping—three thousand for a kidney. Hang on, was that for just one of them? So, let's say sixty thousand for two, a hundred thousand for the heart, and—

What do you think you're doing? Faisal asked, looking squarely into his younger brother's face.

Forty thousand for his testicles, Saud rattled on.

You son of a bitch! Are you pricing my son's organs in dollars and calculating their worth?

Forty thousand for both lungs, twenty for each?

Shut up!

Twenty for his eyes, ten for each?

Stop it, you ass!

Fifteen for his teeth...

Saud finally faced his brother who screamed, Are you insane? You think you're selling slabs of meat?

Faisal, Saud said, the total is two hundred and seventy-five thousand dollars. It's way less than a million! Saud turned to the others open-mouthed, the expression on his face showing how he was struggling to make sense of the numbers. Why didn't they call? He deleted the number on the calculator screen to redo the calculations. Then he repeated the process a third and a fourth time.

Faisal, who lost it, started screaming, Will you now believe me when I tell you my son's already dead?

No! I won't believe it unless I see it with my own eyes!

Because you're an ass! Faisal lunged at his brother.

Grabbing Saud's shirt, Faisal smacked his younger brother against the wall.

Saud, trying to resist, shoved his older brother off him.

Faisal tripped backward and fell to the ground, but he was ready for more, so he sprang up immediately.

The two brothers waved their balled fists and slammed them against one another's faces while hurling insults and profanities. When one of them stepped in closer, they both reached out to strangle one another. It was hard to tell who was succeeding when Hamdi Al-Azzazi and Mustafa Wajdi stepped in. The detective untangled Faisal from his brother, while the activist pulled Saud away.

Don't you dare say that again! Saud roared. Mishari's not dead! You hear me? He's not!

Faisal, who wriggled out of Mustafa's grip, ran to his younger sibling, and caught him by the collar before he slammed Saud against the wall again, shouting, You ass! You absolute ass! When are you going to understand? When? We've offered them a million dollars! And we can raise even more than that! We can pay in Kuwaiti dinars! Do you know how much that's worth? That's three million American dollars! We're talking about the ransom of three hundred enslaved Eritreans! You ass! But that's not all! We could raise even more than a million if they'd asked! And they know that! So why didn't they call? Do you not get it? Are you that stupid? Saud! Mishari is dead! He's dead! Dead! Dead! Dead!

Saud stood petrified, eyes closed, trying to fight back the tears, while his brother kept slapping him and saying: Dead.

Al-'Arish. Swiss Inn Resort

21 Dhu Al-Hijja 1431

7:15 A.M.

Saud came out of the bathroom, his waist wrapped in a white towel.

His older brother was still lying on his bed, his eyes staring at the ceiling.

Saud felt the weight of silence pressing heavily on his chest. It was their fourth day in Al-'Arish. He shouldn't have counted the price of Mishari's organs. What made him do such a thing? He couldn't stop thinking of their fight the day before yesterday, how they'd insulted one another, and all the times his older brother had slapped him.

Faisal collapsed on his bed as soon as they returned to their hotel.

Though his eyes were open the whole time, it was clear to Saud that Faisal wasn't present, so he turned off the lights, leaned over his older brother, and kissed his head. I'm sorry, he whispered to him before running outside to spend the night on the shore with his tears, alcohol, and cigarettes.

Then, yesterday, Saud went to the Security Directorate to spend the whole day with Mustafa and Huwaishel. They accompanied him to the hospital morgue a second time and even visited the border, walking along the fence, searching for new corpses.

They went to Bedouin resting areas when they couldn't find anything resembling Mishari's body. In these oases, Saud and his companions tried to assess the level of the nomad's involvement in the organ trafficking case, but nobody knew anything about Mishari or the other missing kids.

Saud returned to the hotel to find his brother precisely as he'd left him, still lying on his back, gazing at the ceiling. They barely exchanged greetings. Saud summarised their day's activities, then left the room again, escaping to the sea. Saud stayed on the shore until he heard the call to Fajr prayer. Back in the hotel room, Faisal was still awake. Once more, they exchanged superficial pleasantries. Then Saud asked, How long have you been awake?

How long have you been drunk?

Ignoring his older brother, Saud dropped into bed and slept for two hours.

Faisal, on the other hand, remained awake.

And though another day had arrived, Faisal remained bedridden, which simultaneously comforted Saud and broke his heart, for Saud believed he'd search more effectively without Faisal's pessimism.

Saud went to the tea kettle, pushed the button, ripped into the sugar packet with his teeth, then poured the fine powder into a mug. I'm going to see Al-Azzazi again, he said without turning.

Faisal said nothing.

Saud quickly peeked at his older brother's trembling fingers, then poured the boiling water on the tea bag. Sitting on the edge of the bed, he stirred, then handed the mug to his older brother and said gently, Drink some tea, Bu Mishari.

Faisal sat up.

He received the mug from his brother and quietly sipped until Saud said, It's Day Four. But nothing's changed. The experts are still as baffled as they were at the start.

Looking into the cup in his hands, Faisal muttered, People die. They don't need a breaking newsreel to announce their passing.

Faisal has avoided mentioning his son to Saud since their quarrel at Hamdi's office. Faisal needed the time to grieve his son's passing, but Saud's denial held him back. Even though Saud was still confident that Mishari would survive his ordeal and return, there was nothing he could do other than head out into the desert daily, armoured with his certainty, searching despite all the evidence they'd accumulated thus far.

Is this how the labyrinthian map of loss is drawn? One person descends into despair? The other haemorrhages from hope?

Peeking at his brother, Faisal noticed Saud's severe weight loss, the deep ridges rippling around his mouth, and the piercing sadness in his eyes. Did Faisal have a right to ask Saud to relinquish his delusion? Faisal should give up trying to make Saud accept that destiny was dark and arbitrary. Melancholy is thus mercy for people like Faisal, who were ready to accept that life was always unknowable. Saud, on the other hand, thrived on the idea that he might be Mishari's only saviour and had thus decided to shoulder the entire burden himself.

Saud got up to make himself a cup of tea. By the way, he told Faisal. Mazen says hi.

That's kind of him.

And Sumaya called last night.

Faisal didn't respond.

Don't you want to hear her updates?

Did she return to Kuwait?

No.

Has anyone from her family come to stay with her?

She doesn't want anyone.

Did she need anything? Money?

No.

Faisal went quiet, as though he didn't want to hear anything else about his wife.

She goes to the hospital every day, Saud said.

Did she come down with something?

No.

Then what's wrong with her?

Saud swallowed, then forced a smile. Sumaya takes a Quran with her, sits by Ruwaina's head, and reads holy verses. She's waiting for the kidnapper to come out of her coma.

Sumaya is reading Quran beside Ruwaina? Faisal's eyes bulged for a split second before he chuckled cheerfully. His demeanour changed, and he beamed, but his laughter quickly mingled with a coughing fit. Tears began to stream abundantly out of his swollen sockets down his now flushed cheeks.

Faisal turned to his brother as if drowning in the deluge, pleading for help.

CHAPTER TWELVE

JAREER

a leash; someone or something pulled against their will; guilt of a
crime (for which one has to be punished)

Day 19

It was evening and Nitham was sitting under the guava trees, sweat drenching his face and armpits. Wiping his forehead and cheeks with the hem of his waistcloth, he leaned back against the slender tree trunk. Despite the refreshing weather and the fragrant, earthy smell he loved, his mood was sour.

Tossing an absentminded glance at the newly sprouted millet stalks, he thought that the date of their first harvest was on the horizon, and if he experienced last year's fortune, he'd be able to cut and bale at least three batches of this year's crop, which reminded him that he needed to buy more urea, but no sooner had his mind wandered to the fertiliser than it flitted away toward the window at the far end of the field.

Nitham tried to make sense of yesterday's events. He had cared for the boy, fed him, given him plenty of fluids, bandaged his wounds, and even provided him with necessary medication. Yet the boy regained his stubbornness as soon as he recovered, roaring like an animal whenever Nitham tried to touch him. The only difference this time around was that Nitham now delighted in the hunt: from running, to squirming, to kicking and screaming, all the way to the bloodstains! The chase made Nitham dizzy with desire. It made his own blood rumble in his veins.

Nitham couldn't understand why he relished the resistance. When the boy kicked him away, like a buckling, or when he bit into his arm, or when Nitham fell upon the kid, snapping a palm over Mishari's mouth, pressing the tiny shoulder against the sponge mattress with his other hand, Nitham felt the ache of raw hunger. His craving was bloody and dark, like discovering a different self inside of him tucked away deeply—a whole new continent of darkness.

Last night, Nitham had dreamed of his mute employer. The Southern man was standing under the guava tree. Nitham couldn't believe it when his old master spoke, though the sound differed from the grunts and hums he'd heard in the past.

But the old man suddenly shouted, Jili jao! For some reason, the Saudi employer screamed it in Urdu, ordering Nitham to go away, to leave the farm, to get lost.

Nitham looked at the goats he had just released from the barn. After head-butting the doe, the buck pressed the female goat against the wall, but she replied in kind, forcefully resisting his advances.

Nitham's thoughts reverted to the little one. Each morning, when Nitham examined the young body, he discovered new blood and bruises on top of the old sores and whipping-related injuries. Because the sight always distressed him, Nitham would promise every day to be gentler with the kid, but the dark spirit within him would take over, and the only thing he could focus on in that demonic state was instant gratification. Just the mere memory of that locked room and the boy inside it would send a shiver down his spine.

That kid would never obey him. Nitham understood this, and while it used to bother him, he now looked forward to watching the nude boy flee into the cage he had built for himself. Nitham wanted

Mishari to scream like a monkey, to kick and wave his hand until Nitham used the boy's body to relieve himself. And he liked to see blood stains on the boy's soft skin.

Exhaling and seeking refuge from the devil, he whispered protective invocations. *How come the pleasure I experience in my body is simple and clear, but the thoughts that follow are riddled with confusion?* He couldn't quite pinpoint what exactly was bothering him. Nitham lowered his head and saw, between his bare feet, an army of ants swarming another, tearing one of them into pieces.

He had witnessed a similar scene many times before. After losing a mandible, an ant would be unable to defend itself. Other ants would rush to chop up the remaining legs. Some might even devour the corpse. This had nothing to do with hunger or sustenance because these ants would be retaliating against weakness. Animals understood this principle very well.

Nitham peered back at the billy goat. The female's attempt to escape the buck's advances was infuriating the male, who bleated angrily before ramming his horns into her stomach, then mounting her. The doe stopped resisting after this happened. This was a daily occurrence. At first, the doe would ignore the buck, but then she would realise that, if she tried to escape, she'd have to pay the price of her fragility.

It's a natural law: The frail must pay the price of their weakness. Our world doesn't forgive vulnerability. It doesn't even tolerate it. And since God is the one who created nature, and since this is a natural law, who am I to break it?

Day 21

28 Dhu Al-Hijja, 1431

7:20 A.M.

He woke up late, then looked at the child, who had new bruises on his body, swelling in his eyelids, congealed blood in the corner of his mouth and blisters all the way down to his stomach. These details no longer bothered him.

Nitham went to the bathroom and thought that he was almost getting used to starting work later than usual. *What would happen if I didn't wake up at five? The farm will remain as it is, and so will the seeds, water, manure, sun, and moon.* Nitham's consistency had been a remnant of his old master's habits. But the old man was forever gone. And though Nitham still had local employers, who regularly wired his salary from Riyadh, he had now become his own master. This meant he needn't be hard on himself because of two hours of added sleep, especially since he had stayed up the past two weeks.

Recalling last night's events sent an exhilarating rush through his body, like a blue electrical charge coursing along his intestines, making every cell dance with pleasure as though Kareena Kapoor existed in every one of his atoms, twirling in a red sari. His lust had become so intense that Nitham had begun associating it with a sheer bright flash followed by a black sky and glittering stars. Last night was the best yet, and he refused to feel guilty for a brief interlude of pleasure in an otherwise dreary life of loneliness and silence.

Nitham completed the cleansing ritual, performed the obligatory Fajr prayer, then entered his farm with a swagger. He felt a freshness and smelled a saltiness in the air that pleased him. The southern sun was casting its warmth upon the distant mountains. It had been two whole weeks since he first planted the millet seeds. Today was their second fertilization day. Nitham carried the urea bag out of the pantry. He dipped his hand, cupped the white grains, then scattered them on the soil, but that's when he noticed fluffy white spots on the surface of the leaves. Nitham caressed the millet. *Impossible!* He thought in disbelief. *Rotten?*

He kneeled between the stalks to take a closer look. His eyes flashed open in fright. Nitham pushed himself off the ground before galloping all over his field, examining the rest of his millet, moving on to the corn, the vegetable beds in the corner: the onions, cucumbers, lettuce, potatoes—everything was sick, withering under the effect of white mould.

His farm has become useless.

This had never happened to him before, since he'd never had to contend with worms or insect eggs in his flowerbeds, he'd never had to deal with beetles, moths, locusts, mice, birds, or weevils, and he'd never had to struggle against excessive dryness or humidity, either. Nitham was familiar with his foes: the farm's enemies.

So how...? These spots...? How did they manage to infiltrate his farm? Where had he been? And how come he hadn't noticed their encroachment before it was too late?

Nitham felt the weight of two massive hands clamping on his chest. The pain reminded him of his dream when his mute old master opened his mouth and shouted, Jilli jao!

Nitham ran around his farm like a madman, inspecting his plants repeatedly, smacking his head and screaming, Damn it!

He dropped to the ground. Although it felt like he was sinking into the abyss, he nonetheless lifted his head and raised his arms to the sky, wondering, *What am I to do now?*

It was a catastrophe, for Nitham understood the impact of this agricultural disease. The only solution was to uproot and burn all the infected plants. And since the mould was ferocious, he could no longer plant new seeds in the same infected soil, as the mould had contaminated the entire farm! Nitham dropped to his knees clutching his head. Then, he began to pound the soil with his bare hands, as though he were performing chest compressions on someone experiencing cardiac arrest.

The farm had spoken—and it wanted him out. But who could he be outside the farm? And what would he be if not a farmer? How could he lose his focus? His touch? He got up again, snarling, and, as he pulled the rotten plants, he cursed and screamed at the sky.

Then he heard laughter, so he turned to the gate. Four young African men were standing outside his field, trying to muffle their amusement.

Panic set in his heart. *Why are they here? What do they want?* He ran at them, shouting, No! No! Who are you? What do you want? Why are you here?

Unable to understand his language, they signed as though they were carrying shovels with which to plough the earth.

They're looking for a job. Jilli jao! Jilli jao! Nitham shook his head and shoved them backward through the bars of his gate. Jilli jao!

Some of them left pouting. Others mumbled and laughed.

You better not return! Nitham cried before swivelling around to gaze at the locked room at the edge of his field. Fortunately, the little one had not stuck his arms between the window bars and screamed. Nitham felt his heart drop to his stomach, and it dawned on him that keeping the boy around was becoming increasingly dangerous.

He had to get rid of him.

Quickly.

Jazan. The Farm of Sheikh Ibrahim Hijab

28 Dhu Al-Hijja, 1431

11:20 P.M.

He stood before the metal door for several minutes, calculating his next steps. Only the pale light of the crescent moon above challenged the totality of darkness that had enveloped him. Despite his red eyes and erratic breathing, he knew what he had to do—for there was no other option.

What did you expect? he asked himself. *The kid was never meant to survive. You knew it was only a matter of time. Just look at that skinny body full of sores! You knew that, if you carried on, you'd wake up one morning to find him lying dead beside you, a cold expression on his cadaveric face, his jaw loose, apprehension blaring from his wide-open eyes. You'll place your hand on the little chest to feel his pulse. His body will be cold and stiff. You'll wrap him in a towel, then bury him under the guava tree, and his decomposing body will fertilise your grove. And just as well, the field will prevail in the end, taking in the flesh, blood, skull, and bones after you took your fill of your transient delight. The little one's miserable existence will come to a discreet end and remain hidden forever.*

Why is your hand shaking? You know that you could instantly crush the kid's frail and frivolous life with your bare fists. And you also know that the weak have to pay the price of their weakness to those who are more powerful. This is a natural law. A self-evident truth. And you were always going to present him as an offering to your one true love—the land that is pregnant with your millet and corn. Eventually, we all return to it. Some of us rejoin her sooner than others. That's all this is:

a loving reunion.

So why is your hand shaking? You are facing an inevitable moment, and you know it. Did you really think you could keep him forever?

How did you feel when the African labourers showed up unannounced with their rags and mocking laughs? Squeamish? Terrified? What brought people back to your quiet place after all these lonely months? Your quivering fingers caress your neck.

Damn it. You just never imagined it would end this soon. You had such a wonderful time together. What a shame to give it all away. But you've got to come out of your drunken stupor now. The sooner you get it over with, the better.

Unclenching your fist, you take in the discolorations on the back of your hand and fingers. You had spent the day cursing and screaming at the sky, plodding across the length and breadth of your field, denuding your crops, and burning them in a massive fire. Your farm has become your ruin. You've got nothing left to harvest. What will the heirs of the deceased master do when they find out?

White mould destroys the earth. It destroys everything.

Like the white boy.

Would the old master's heirs give you another chance to revive their land? Or will they sell the farm when they hear of the mould? Can you risk them finding out? What if potential buyers flock here and discover the kid in the locked room? You were almost exposed today when those young men came asking for work. You'll wind up dangling from a rope, a noose around your neck.

You shake your head. You must get it over with quickly. Your trembling fingers remove the key from the pot beside the door—so why are you still hesitating?

You mull over everything that had changed upon the boy's arrival. He had lit the flame of a never-ending hunger. Kareena Kapoor no longer suffices. Everything pales in comparison to the touch of the little one's skin and the sound of his screaming, everything pales including the texture of the soil, the fragrance of the air, and the freshness of the water.

After inserting the key into the lock and twisting, you hear a clack followed by the creak of the door as it opens. You step into the room filled with blue light, suffused with the smell of curry and rice wafting from empty copper bowls.

Your ears pick up a soft whimper. Your eyes lock on the little one huddled in the corner, dipping a cotton ball into your antiseptic solution—which he must've stolen from your cupboard—and wiping the wet cotton ball over the trail of sores between his thighs.

He jumps like a monkey when he senses your presence, balling his fists and waving them at you, ready to punch.

Your heartbeats accelerate. Could you be weaker than you think? And would you pay the price of your fragility? You turn to the boy with the black bruises.

Although every part of his body is smarting from the pain, he seems prepared for yet another battle...

Day 22

Jazan. The Farm of Sheikh Ibrahim Hijab

29 Dhu Al-Hijja, 1431

12:03 A.M.

The foreigner had never looked at him this way.

He often gazed at his eyelashes, nails, arms, legs, and between his thighs. But this time, Nitham's red and veiny eyes were looking Mishari squarely in his. Mishari waved his arms and shouted, hoping to strike fear in the man's heart and force him to walk away.

The man muttered calmly, Aao, larka. He didn't pat the sponge mattress this time, and Kareena Kapoor wasn't dancing on the screen. The man took two steps closer to Mishari, grabbed his arm, then dragged him out. It was the first time Mishari had left the small room since his arrival. He breathed the outdoorsy air, which was warm and humid, and though darkness had encompassed the entire farm, stars glittered in the sky.

Eyes still gaping in admiration at the sparks of light above, Mishari allowed himself to be led by the foreigner clutching his arm. They crossed the now-empty field, where remnants of the massive fire, which Nitham had built earlier in the day, caught Mishari's attention. Whereas the sores between his legs stung, and though he was walking awkwardly, legs somewhat far apart, Mishari was nevertheless captivated by the sky and the way his heart started beating manically once the night air touched his skin.

The man headed toward three trees adjacent to his farm's brick wall, dragging Mishari by the arm. He then shoved the kid against the middle bark.

Mishari stood in place, goggling at the foreigner, unable to discern his intention.

Nitham rattled on in the language Mishari didn't understand, then bent down to pick up something from the ground. The man's eyes widened as he inspected the metal glistening in his grip.

Mishari gasped when he realised it was a cleaver. Warm liquid trickled down his legs, irritating his injuries. A filmy glaze coated his eyes when he spotted the foreigner's lips and moustache reflected in the blade. Mishari willed his legs to move, to run away, but his knees buckled. He fell curled into the foetal position, tucked his head under his arms, and screamed.

Nitham leaned over Mishari. With his left hand, he grabbed the little one by the hair and yanked the head upward, exposing Mishari's frail neck, readying him for the slaughter.

Mishari, who closed his eyes, bitterly sobbed and babbled in Arabic.

The foreign man, who didn't understand Mishari's language, was likewise babbling in his mother tongue. Nitham nodded, and began to threaten Mishari, If you do not—

But Mishari offered absolute obedience. I'll do anything you want! Even the things you love! I'll be your servant! Just let me go! He repeated his vows until he opened his eyes and the two looked at each other.

For a moment, it seemed that they both understood.

Mishari scanned the man holding the cleaver. With a slight tremor in his hand and tears stinging his eyes, Mishari said breathlessly, Nitham Shuja a-Din... When he noticed a little twitch in the man's mouth, Mishari thought if he kept calling Nitham's name, it might stop him from...

So, he whispered again, Nitham Shuja a-Din! Tears now streamed in a heavy flow down his cheeks. Nitham Shuja a-Din!

Please, don't kill me.

Jazan. The Farm of Sheikh Ibrahim Hijab

29 Dhu Al-Hijja, 1431

12:21 A.M.

At that moment, Nitham's fingers loosened and the cleaver fell. He stared at his hands in disbelief. Could it be possible that he wasn't capable of killing the kid? What had become of him? What made him soft? He couldn't forgive himself. *The only thing worse than murdering someone is the realization that you can't go through with it.*

Vulnerability pulsated in his chest and his heart felt an unusual heaviness, so he leaned back against the tree trunk beside the boy who was curled on the floor, protecting his head with his arms. Nitham looked up, gazing wondrously at the stars glittering above. He raised his open palms and said, God, help me. But when he regained his composure, he realised that Mishari had darted away, so he bolted after him.

It didn't take long for Nitham to catch up with the kid, grab a fistful of Mishari's hair with one hand and his thumb with the other. Nitham made his way back toward his room, kneeing Mishari in the back whenever he wanted the boy to keep moving.

But Mishari went wild when he recognised their route. Because he felt like he was being dragged back to hell, he flailed his arms, sobbed, and screamed.

Nitham let go of Mishari's wrist and clasped his hand on the little mouth. He tossed the kid into a corner as soon as they entered the room.

Mishari leaped up at once and began to pace frantically, banging his fists on the walls, thunderously roaring.

What could Nitham do now? Mishari had tasted freedom, had inhaled the fresh air, had gaped at the star-spangled sky, and had even overcome death. Mishari felt that he had gone up to the edge of a cliff, then turned back—so he screamed like a feral animal. Sounds of pure anguish, empty of human language, came out of his mouth. What could Nitham do now? He couldn't keep the kid. He would have killed him instantly had Mishari not opened his big eyes that reflected the darkness of the night and the kid's unbounded fear. Why did Mishari's terror frighten him?

He had to do something quickly, for the boy had lost his mind.

Mishari was throwing anything he could find: pots, pans, spoons, tissue boxes, the medicine bottle, and the videotape of Kareena Kapoor's movie. Then, dashing to the wall where the collage of naked women hung, Mishari ripped them off, and openly declared his defiance, even though his small, bloody body looked like a festering pimple, by tearing them into shreds, one by one, right in front of Nitham.

After opening one of the cupboards, Nitham pulled out the blue nylon rope he had been using to bind Mishari at night. Although the kid put up a fight, Nitham still managed to secure the tiny wrists and ankles, but he made the knot so tight that blood congested under the skin. Then, he removed a pillowcase, scrunched it into a ball, stuffed it into Mishari's mouth, and taped his lips. Returning to his cupboard, Nitham pulled out a white cotton tank, grabbed the hem, and bit into it to cleave the undershirt into a strip with which he blindfolded Mishari, who was curled like a foetus, the way he'd been when Nitham first laid his eyes on him.

Once more, Nitham carried the boy out of the room, but he laid him in the back seat before climbing behind the wheel. Jabbering and cursing, Nitham felt adrenaline stirring in his fingertips when he turned the key in the ignition. The roar of the engine rose to a crescendo. When Abida Parveen's voice streamed out, Nitham quickly turned off the in-dash stereo. Needing profound silence to think, he slowly navigated a familiar road until he reached a sandy path that branched to the right. Nitham then drove across long stretches, passing by various fields, some cactus mobs, and prickly pears.

His car rattled along the bumpy, dusty road, through layers of darkness. Searching for a remote and uninhabited location in Jazan was simple. What Nitham needed, however, was to find somewhere far from home. *God forbid—if the child survives this ordeal, he must not be able to figure out how to return to the field. But he should not survive.* Nature was fully capable of accomplishing what Nitham had failed to complete. The wolves were probably going to stumble on the little one first.

Nitham considered all the areas he'd seen since arriving at Jazan three years earlier. *What's my best choice? The cave!* He remembered a cavernous hole two hours' drive from his field. It was located in a mountain he used to frequent during the rainy season when he went out to gather cade. Nitham smiled contentedly. *Why didn't I think of it before?* That cave was hollow, dark, and quiet, only inhabited by bats—a perfect place for a boy to die alone.

Jazan. The Cave

29 Dhu Al-Hijja, 1431

2:15 A.M.

Nitham was carrying the boy on his shoulder when he reached the cave.

Because Mishari's blindfold had loosened, he was able to see what was happening.

As soon as Nitham stepped into the cave, a cold, moist breeze slapped his face. His nostrils picked up a sour stench, and he heard the sound of flapping wings, which he knew came from above, where bats were roosting, hanging upside down, their talons clenching the rocky ridges like black hooks. Nitham's arms, thighs, and the back of his neck suddenly felt itchy, so he began to scratch, thinking that he better leave this place as quickly as possible. Pressing a palm to a wall to steady himself, Nitham lowered the boy against it, then shined a light from his mobile phone.

Mishari was staring at him, teary-eyed, horror-stricken, whimpering despite the cloth stuffed in his mouth, muffling his pleas.

Nitham wouldn't have understood Mishari's Arabic gibberish even if he had removed the tape. Nevertheless, he told the kid, These are bats that eat fruit and honey. Your blood will not appeal to them. But there are wolves in the area. I've been hearing them howl in the distance for years.

Mishari was nodding as if he understood.

Nitham exhaled and said, It's over, larka.

Mishari shook his head as if he both comprehended and disagreed with Nitham's statement.

Nitham aimed his phone's flashlight at the boy for the last time. I'm going to leave you now, he said, combing his fingers in Mishari's muddy and matted bangs. Nitham peeled off the sticky tape, then extracted the pillowcase he'd previously jammed in there.

At once, the kid began to repeat his name, Nitham! Nitham Shuja a-Din! Nitham!

A sad smile crept over his face when he said, Mishari. It was only the third time he'd ever used the boy's name out loud throughout the eighteen days they'd known each other.

The bats above began to flap their smooth, leathery wings.

And fearfully, with his still-bound wrists, Mishari dug his nails into Nitham's arms.

Goodbye, larka. Khoda hafez. Nitham retreated, crawling on all fours to avoid the bats until he'd left the cave.

Mishari looked up and a ghastly scream escaped his mouth.

Nitham, who exited in a hurry, was followed by a cloud of bats as he jogged down the slope toward his car, then hit the ground running as he pictured the bats trailing above his head. He stopped only when he'd passed the juniper bushes and tried to catch his breath. Nitham believed that he'd left ample distance between himself and the cave, for he could now barely hear the little one's screaming.

Nitham! Nitham!

Gritting his teeth, Nitham thought. *Fool! He's calling the wolves right to him!* Hobbling down another slope, he meandered through trees, using his phone as a flashlight. Although the boy's cries grew fainter, Nitham thought he could still hear Mishari, who was no longer repeating Nitham's name. *I wonder what he's saying.* With some effort, he recognised Mishari's plea: Aao!

For the past two weeks, Mishari had understood this word to mean: the shabby mattress, navy and green chequered blanket, Kareena Kapoor's bare midriff, and Nitham's hand stroking Mishari's skin before clutching, kneading, and pounding resistance out of him. Mishari was now offering himself, showing utmost submission, begging to return to the locked room, because anything was better than the dark cave packed with black roosting bats. Nitham's legs felt heavy, so for a moment he stopped moving. He couldn't believe that the little one had finally submitted to him. *After I'd decided to get rid of you? Too late!* He remembered his ravaged field and his grass speckled with white mould, and he realised that he was giggling in disbelief. He had finally tamed the feral boy. He had finally won— but after losing everything.

The whole land is ruined, his Saudi employers would fly over as soon as they found out, and other African labourers might show up unannounced at his doorstep, and him... Himself... Would he ever be able to love someone else without craving to hurt them?

Aao! Mishari was still pleading. Come. Drag me back to hell. I'm yours.

Nitham shook his head apologetically. *What a shame, larka.* He plodded down the slope like someone was chasing him. Only when he hopped in the car and started the engine did he realise that he hadn't been running away from the bats but from Mishari's voice. That aao resounded in his chest, rattling against his rib cage, breaking his heart. Nitham swerved and sped away from the mountain, heading back to the road from whence he came. This time, he repeatedly glanced at the empty backseat through his rearview mirror. Mishari's voice still reverberated, so Nitham turned on the in-dash stereo. Abida Parveen's voice—the most captivating in Pakistan—spilled out, but her soothing voice was interspersed with the anguished pleas that echoed from afar: Aao! Nitham! Aao!

When Nitham returned to his farm, he found Mishari's face, printed on a leaflet, taped to his gate.

The boy on the flier was standing behind a metal fence enveloped in vines, smiling with a missing tooth, wearing a red T-shirt.

Nitham's heart pulsated faster and sweat poured down his forehead. He felt fortunate to have gotten rid of Mishari. As he studied the image of the missing boy, who looked nothing like Nitham's emaciated kid covered in bruises, the prize money caught his attention, so he tore the sheet and thought, *It would be insane to risk bringing him back only for the reward.*

Nitham unlocked the door to his room and went in, but he found it emptier and wider than he'd imagined. Though the chaos the little one had left behind remained, Nitham was too tired to tidy up the mess from the past few days. Would he ever forget what happened here? Nitham could pretend that he had never stumbled upon a famished and feverish kid, that he had never carried him to his sponge mattress, that he had never done what he did to him. But the silence was deafening, and it was interrupted by the cries of the little one bursting out of Nitham's own chest.

He turned on the faucet just to hear something else, performed ablution, prayed the optional rites after Isha, then tried to sleep, but the little one's voice kept echoing in Nitham's head and heart. He even felt the shrieks rattling in his eyes and mouth. Nitham felt it everywhere. In the Lux soap and the water trickling out of the faucet. He felt it when he thought of the row of bats in the cave, in the voice of Abida Parveen, Kareena Kapoor's midriff, in the mountains, and the silence. The screeching was bursting out of his body like blood gushing out of a wound. Nitham found himself muffling his ears with his palms. He opened his mouth to scream louder than the sound that was exploding out of him, but he felt as though his throat was becoming rough and his veins were drying up. The boy's face appeared everywhere he turned, haunting him like a jinx.

Because of his fatigue, Nitham fell asleep for a few minutes before frantically waking. In the brief dream, he saw his old master standing under the guava trees, replanting the boy's agonised pleas inside Nitham's chest.

Aao! Aao! Aao!

When he woke up, Nitham jumped out of his chequered quilt, grabbed his car key, locked the door, and drove back to the cave like a madman. He arrived in two hours and stood doubtfully at the entrance of the cave. *Why am I here again? Damn it!* Larka! Nitham turned on his phone's flashlight, got on his knees, and crawled inside. *Why am I doing all this for you, boy? Why? Where are you? Damn it!* Nitham's hands navigated the dark terrain. Turning to the wall on his right, he shuffled forward a few more steps before stumbling on the little one, coiled like an earthworm, his bound wrists shielding his head, his knees bent against his stomach.

Nitham touched Mishari on the shoulder. Because he found it

cold, he brought the light of his mobile phone close to the little one's face, who was shuddering like a hatchling, his eyes gaping and his mouth clenched. Nitham whispered, Larka?

Mishari didn't look up.

Larka, I'm back. Aren't you thrilled? Nitham wondered if Mishari lost his hearing, so he said a little louder, What's wrong with you? Can't you see I've come back for you? It's me! Nitham.

Nitham shook Mishari's shoulders, but the kid was unconscious even though his horror-stricken eyes were wide open. Nitham had completely lost the boy now, who must've experienced something terrifying in the past two hours to shatter his nerves in this manner. *It's like he's lost it and gone mad. Is he now deaf? And has he really lost his ability to speak?* What happened to you, little one, that would make you forget me so quickly?

Mishari's eyes were fixed on the ceiling, his pupils trembling.

No, larka. No… I didn't return to find you like this. What am I to do now?

The boy didn't move.

Nitham exhaled. Why did he return? He no longer wanted to keep the boy. The daunting task of revitalising his farm weighed heavily on him. Nitham had more important matters to worry about than this kid. He couldn't understand why he returned when he'd been willing to murder the boy a few hours earlier.

Nitham wanted to sleep at seven, wake up at five, plant his millet and corn, and never miss the Fajr prayer. He could not fathom what had happened to him in the past few hours.

Larka? He caressed the boy's head, hoping to extricate Mishari's awareness from its cage. Larka, I'm back. We'll leave this place now. Do you hear me? Mishari? Nitham whispered a hairbreadth from the boy's ear, but the kid didn't respond.

The face, petrified by terror, remained as is, until, after a few moments, Mishari's eyelids loosened. When Mishari closed his eyes, he lost the last shred of awareness and passed out.

Don't worry! I'm here now. Nitham carried the boy in his arms and rushed out of the cave, following the same track from earlier, then descending the valley toward his car, where he stretched Mishari in the backseat, and hopped in the front. As Nitham started the motor, he raised his eyes, saw a cloud of bats bursting back into the cave, and murmured:

It looks like a hundred bats must've smacked you in the face, larka.

CHAPTER THIRTEEN

MAS-EER

Guts or intestines; fate; the final destination—i.e. heaven or hell

Al-'Arish. Swiss Inn Resort

26 Dhu Al-Hijja,1431

6:36 A.M.

You open the door slowly, taking care not to disturb the darkness within, hoping your brother is sleeping, but you find him lying on his back, wide awake, staring at the ceiling. You approach him gradually, kiss him on the forehead, and say, Good morning Bu Mishari.

Faisal doesn't respond. He has been stumbling through a maze over the past three days, never parting from his silence.

Although this is your eighth day in Al-'Arish, your brother remains shrouded in eloquent speechlessness, the kind that conveys adequate information about the dangers of false hope, the inevitability of pain, and everything in between.

Your voice doesn't reach him anymore, and neither does your love. He is completely gone. Only you remain. All the desert now belongs to you. It's there waiting for your endless wandering. And it's never going to release you.

You've only now understood the magnitude of your endeavour. Nobody can rescue anybody else. Not even you. Even though you're the only one left to help Mishari, you can't even help yourself. Since you arrived at Sinai, you've been spending every night awake at Al-Nakheel Beach, leaning against a tree stump, accompanied by your cigarette pack, your whiskey bottle, and your tears, surrounded by hundreds of seashells, the waves serenading your ears, the night weighing heavily on your chest.

Scenes of Al-'Arish are a painful reminder of Kuwait: a city that is part desert, part seaport. It seems that you can't escape your hometown. The Bedouin features on people's faces, their red chequered headgear, their white dishdashas—everything keeps reminding you of a time when life was possible.

You stare absentmindedly at the Mediterranean Sea, calmly rumbling before you. Some still call it the White Sea, and it makes you realise just how far you are from the blue Arabian Gulf. You chug the rest of your whiskey, a teardrop dribbling down your cheek.

Mazen calls like he does every night. You stay on the phone for hours, discussing what you've seen and heard during the day, then hang up before you break down and cry.

The power struggle you've witnessed daily in Sinai seems bigger than you. Even Mazen couldn't believe what you were telling him.

Imagine, you had said, we comb the border every day. We pretend to be looking for Mishari, but we're really searching for his corpse.

Your friend exhales. What makes you so sure he's dead?

I don't want to lie to myself anymore.

But there's no evidence—

Try to understand what I'm saying.

I'm listening.

I called the head of Egypt's Forensic Medicine Authority, yesterday. He explained that one could not carry out an organ transplant in Sinai.

Then why would the kidnappers go there?

The process requires advanced equipment that isn't available in Sinai. Yet, we've been finding scores of bodies missing organs. I've seen some myself, their bellies stitched, their eyes gouged out, their sockets stuffed with cotton.

If that's the case, then why would you still believe organ transplants are carried out elsewhere?

Saud exhaled. Surgeries are performed in the cities.

No way! cried Mazen.

In Cairo, you say before swallowing. Or Tel Aviv.

Your friend's silence is telling.

One of the tribal elders who used to work as a smuggler told Huwaishel that disposing of the dead bodies they receive from Israel is a lucrative business. In other words, crimes aren't being committed at Sinai's border. That place is just a cemetery, a human dumpster for crime networks. Sinai's border is perfect for criminals because none of the countries on either side wants to tackle criminals head-on. Do you understand?

Hang on. Are you saying the children you're looking for might've already been smuggled into Israel?

Exactly. We're just waiting for their corpses to show up in Sinai.

Does Faisal know all this?

No, but I don't know why I'm hiding it from him. He accepted the possibility of Mishari's death days ago.

What about the human rights expert? Does he know?

Of course.

What did he say?

He said, What did you think was going on? Hamdi Al-Azzazi believes that the criminal organization's leaders include a cabal of global elites comprising ministers and generals from different countries and a rabbi. He says similar crimes have been occurring since 1992, when Palestinians first noticed their martyrs' bodies disappear then reappear with missing organs. He says their organization has documents that prove Israeli soldiers have been stealing organs from dead Palestinians, but it seems that it wasn't enough. They needed more bodies. The kind that wouldn't make a fuss.

You stop talking momentarily, then take a deep drag on your cigarette. Hamdi has said that his organization counted tens of thousands of unauthorised immigrants. But the number officially recognised by Israel is much lower. So, where did the rest of the immigrants go?

Saud, I don't understand.

Let me break it down for you. Say an Israeli broker accepts unauthorised immigrants from a Bedouin smuggler, the Israeli would then assure the immigrant that they're just going to the hospital for a regular checkup, that there's nothing to worry about, that they've reached their final destination, and that this procedure is only for their wellbeing. When African immigrants close their eyes, thinking that they have at last left their status of illegality behind, true crime takes place. They are anesthetised so that their healthy organs can be snatched from their bodies. Afterward, their corpses are cast in the desert to gradually decompose. Huwaishel says that the Israeli broker pays the smuggler large sums of money to get rid of the body emptied of organs, and the latter would throw these cadavers in the desert to act as their place of death, like thousands before them.

You hear your friend gasp. Afterward, he begins to ask a question he interrupts with a stream of insults ending with a curse.

As for you, none of these invectives impact you anymore. Only silence satisfies you now.

Mazen finally asks, What's your next step?

Hamdi Al-Azzazi is calling different human rights organizations in Tel Aviv to inquire about the missing kids. Whereas I...

Tears overpower you. You go quiet because you feel suffocated.

Hello? Saud? You ok?

You catch your breath. You don't want to go back to the hotel to see Faisal, but you go back anyway.

Your older brother resembles a statue more each day. Apart from his quivering fingers, he lies in place.

You shower quickly, open the closet, and pick out this morning's attire.

It's a new day where anything can happen to anyone.

Yesterday, you and a group of volunteers received a message from Hamdi Al-Azzazi, who wanted you all to come to Sadaqah Cemetery to rebury exhumed corpses that wild dogs had mangled.

*You exhale. Sadaqah Cemetery, Rummana Prison, Rafah Crossing…
You learn of another violent episode in this dark hell daily. Sadaqah
Cemetery is where the unknown are buried and where anonymous
individuals pray for those they've lost. It lies on the other side of the
official cemetery's fence, where those who can be identified congregate
in death. You consider this separation an expression of ignorance, but
you've been swimming in that lately.*

*Yet maybe there's a glimmer of hope at the end. At Sadaqa Cemetery
two days ago, you dug your shovel into the earth and asked yourself,
as sweat oozed down your skin, Am I still doing this for the kid? Or
has this journey become about me and my desire to make an impact,
however small? You're frustrated because you keep losing every thread
and stumbling upon a perennial end.*

*You sit on the edge of the bed, bend to put on your socks, then straighten
up and look at him. It's hard for you to speak to Faisal.*

*I know you don't want to talk. Your throat hurts, but you continue, I
mean, I know you cannot communicate, Faisal. I get it. I won't judge you
for it. But I also know you can hear and register everything I tell you.
And I have updates that matter.*

*Your eyes are fixed on the door in front of you. Like every morning,
you share your experiences, narrating what you've seen and heard. You
start with news from Kuwait, and tell Faisal about your mother who…*

*Then you share news from the local papers, Twitter, and Facebook,
and you update him on Sumaya, Mazen, and Ruwaina—who's hanging
between life and death. Then you divulge the latest information from
your activities in Sinai.*

I didn't tell you what happened yesterday, Faisal. I met with Hamdi

Al-Azzazi at the human rights foundation. He was on his way to Rummana prison, so I tagged along.

Closing your eyes, you swallow, and your mind fills with images of black, angular faces, red eyes, and missing teeth. You blink, but there's no trace of Mishari's features in your imagination. It frightens you that you've lost him in your memory.

Yet, you go on, Hamdi Al-Azzazi asked prisoners to draw what they'd seen or experienced in the Ghost Houses. I've seen those pictures, Faisal. They're heartbreaking. You pause momentarily and peek at your brother, who looks like he hasn't heard a word. What can you say to get him out of his deadly silence?

You stubbornly continue, We've got news of a young Sudanese man who managed to escape from one of those Ghost Houses and hide in a mosque in Rajah. His name is Mohamed Ramadan. He was kidnapped in Aswan and locked in a small house outside Al-'Arish. His jailers were asking for a thirty-thousand-dollar ransom. They threatened to extract his kidney if nobody paid his fee. He says he's witnessed four murders. When you hear about these deaths, don't you wonder who these four victims were? Have we already buried their bodies? Or are they still out there, decomposing on the ground?

You exhale. The details you've been collecting in your memory are like jagged shards: all those names, colours, and faces—overwhelmingly black.

The investigation of the children who disappeared eighteen days ago has stalled. Because you feel helplessly impotent, you've been volunteering to wash and shroud lacerated or decaying corpses that emit an unbearable odour.

In the beginning, their stench used to keep you away from the washing area. You'd stand there, covering your nose with your sleeve, before apologising to the human rights activist—I'll help bury them! He'd nod and smile understandingly, but you'd feel the sting of shame anyway before running out. A few days later, you turned around, came back, grabbed the hose, and watched water flow over the lifeless bodies as a cold feeling crept into your chest. There's a strange beauty in washing the corpse of someone whom no one knows has died. You scrub bullet-ridden torsos and chests with metal rods sticking out, then pour water mixed with sidr leaves. The smell of camphor fills the washing area and wafts into your nostrils.

Starting with the head, then the right side of the body, then the left, and keeping the white cloth on the body's privates, you aim the cold water on the stomach before washing the legs.

One of the bodies bearing traces of bite marks from wild animals lost an arm during the cleansing ritual. The activist tucked the arm inside the shroud anyway. One should be buried whole not missing parts, Hamdi Al-Azzazi said.

These washed and shrouded corpses are then carried to Sadaqah Cemetery, where Al-Azzazi prepares to pray. After standing to his right, you follow his lead, feeling as though you could follow him to the end of the desert, and when you're done with the prayer, you pick up a shovel and a bucketful of sand and begin to bury the dead, marking the top of each grave with a nondescript brick.

Allahumma do not deprive us of his reward or distract us after his death.

You now explain to your older brother as your eyes well with tears, Bodies must be buried, Faisal. I believe in honouring the dead! When

I perform that sacred ritual on an anonymous corpse, I feel it's the only thing holding me together after what we've experienced.

A lump in your throat makes you stop talking for a moment. Then you utter with resolve, *If I find Mishari dead, Faisal, I promise you I'll be happy.* As you wipe your tears away, you add, *I swear I won't cry.*

Faisal's face twitches.

Because you notice a glint in his eyes, you wipe your tears with the tip of your shirt, and think, *I mustn't be weak*—but you say, *Faisal, I'm really worried.*

Then you get up, fill your empty kettle with fresh water, and press the button before continuing: *Hamdi Al-Azzazi is also worried. Imagine, Faisal, the bodies that arrive at the morgue are already missing organs. And the permits that are later issued describe the cause of death as: Ongoing Investigation, yet bodies are buried without examination. And nobody ever mentions the missing organs. Neither the public prosecutors nor the medical examiners. How can they say they're busily investigating when they bury the bodies themselves before compiling any report? And what's the rush?* You rip into a coffee sachet, empty it in a mug, then pour boiling water. *Huwaishel is also worried. Actually, he is panicking the most. When I asked him yesterday about the proliferation of weapons among Bedouin tribes, he exploded in my face, Because authorities are incompetent! I'm talking about all of them! The army, police, and border patrol!*

You stir the coffee in the cup. *Did you know that Camp David encompasses this area? If the smuggling routes are known to all the national authorities who are impacted by the illegal activities that take place here, why is no one putting an end to this genocide? And who does it benefit? Damn it!*

You sit on the edge of the bed. The steam wafting from the mug touches your face before moving it closer to your brother.

Would you like some coffee, Faisal?

His eyelids drop. The silence remains.

You let out a deep breath. Listen to me carefully, Faisal. I may never repeat these words, so I hope you appreciate what I'm about to tell you. You're right. Maybe there's no hope. Maybe all our efforts to rescue Mishari end here. Maybe it's the end of your fatherhood, marriage, and even faith. But just because these things are ending, it doesn't have to mean the end of everything. That's certainly not the case for me.

You put the cup on the table close to your brother's head, hoping the steam will persuade him to drink a little later, then say, I'm going out now. You get up and walk toward the door, where you turn around one last time, hand on the doorknob, and add, Faisal? If you started thinking of another missing child, a child who wasn't yours, someone like Mariam Akbar, perhaps it would be easier for you to get up and make a difference.

Al-'Arish Security Directorate (First Division)

26 Dhu Al-Hijja, 1431

8:47 A.M.

Saud was in a cab, heading toward the cemetery, when Mustafa called and asked him to come to the station as soon as possible.

Khair? Saud asked, his heart palpitating. Something in his colleague's voice alarmed him. He had a feeling Mustafa had essential updates to share.

There have been some developments.

Saud answered immediately. On my way! He arrived at the police station in half an hour. Mustafa and Huwaishel were waiting for him. Saud's heart dropped when he didn't see a comforting expression on their faces. Did you find his body?

Have a seat, Mustafa said, gesturing toward the couch.

Saud hobbled over to the edge of the sofa and peered into his colleague's face, urging him to speak.

We've got some updates.

About what?

Mustafa and Huwaishel looked at each other.

Say something, Mustafa! Saud's heart was pounding.

Bashmohandes, Huwaishel said, let me tell you what happened.

After our last meeting, I contacted several smugglers and asked them about the kids who crossed the Red Sea. Then I told them one of these children was Khaleeji, and his parents would pay a hefty sum to anyone who'd provide them with information on his whereabouts. I kept hitting dead ends until last night, when I got a call from someone who introduced himself as The Sultan. He's a powerful criminal with money and weapons who usually hides Africans in a cave about forty kilometres from Nikhel City, in a remote, uninhabitable area about 93 miles from Al-'Arish, which includes an abandoned house frequented by white vans that resemble delivery trucks or ambulances—

Mustafa, who interrupted Huwaishel, elaborated, We already checked The Sultan's records. He's a fugitive dodging a life sentence. The people from his village have shunned him because they suspect his involvement in a mafia specialising in organ trafficking, but no one knows where he is.

We know about the cave's location, though, right? Saud asked, feeling two heavy hands clamping on his chest.

Won't you tell him? Huwaishel asked Mustafa, who shook his head and said, No. There's no need. He straightened up and told Saud, We've got to head out now.

Saud wanted to reach the end of their damn tunnel—to dig up the desert's own torso and extract from its belly the rest of the small bodies, so he could wash them, shroud them, bury them, and perform the prayer over the deceased. He understood the point of this meeting. It was too late. The kidnappers wouldn't have postponed the murder of those lost kids. No. They'd have dissected their bodies over the past eighteen days and already removed their organs. Their tiny eyes, livers, lungs, and hearts were probably on their way to America by now in plastic refrigerators filled with crushed ice.

Sinai. The Cave

26 Dhu Al-Hijja, 1431

12:04 P.M.

They reached a simple one-story edifice built of bricks and cement, a metal roof, and windows covered in bark. Like a solitary plant, the house stood in a quiet, empty desert amid roof tiles and wooden poles, a short distance from a mountain range.

As police patrols surrounded the building, officers prepared to storm in. One team swarmed the house, and when Mustafa kicked down the door, the second team burst through.

Without waiting for an official command, Saud stepped in as well. Canned beans and peas, onion peels, juice cartons, dried garlic cloves, and empty plastic plates were strewn across the floor. Saud followed Mustafa into another room, where he saw a desk and an office chair, and when he peered into the open drawers, he found receipts of orders from Tel Aviv. Turning to Mustafa, Saud said, It's probably where he kept the kids before smuggling them across the sea.

The detective nodded.

Didn't Huwaishel mention white vans?

Yeah, he did. Vans with fake business logos.

Saud studied the documents he found in the drawers. That's a lot of money. Way more than they'd get from only smuggling.

He must've sold them alive, then recovered their dead bodies to dispose of in the desert.

Saud's pupil dilated. But where are they?

Hurrying outside, images cascaded in Saud's head with each step, as if he could watch the whole scene unfold before him: *A well-lit and sterile operation room. Hospital beds with belts. Airtight plastic containers full of crushed ice, ready to store warm human organs straight from their living ovens. Scissors, scalpels, and surgical staples—science in the service of crime.*

Closing his eyes again, Saud saw the following scene: *Men drugging children, fastening their little wrists and ankles to the bed, and sending them to sleep. A door opens. A surgeon wearing green scrubs enters, stretching out a gloved hand. The nurse passes him a scalpel, which he uses to puncture the tiny abdomen, and while slicing into flesh he informs his nurse which organs he plans on salvaging and which he plans on discarding. In this particular scene, the doctor chooses to extract the heart, the lungs, the livers, and the kidneys. The nurse holds the scalpel as the doctor moves to the head of the boy, who'd been dead for the past few minutes, and opens the eyelids with his fingers. Once the doctor asks for the scalpel again, he plucks out the eyes, wraps them in white cloth, and shifts to another bed.*

The doctor will be done soon, and in two hours or less, he will have made a fortune, with ample time to return to his home, enjoy a delicious, early meal with his wife and children, and even plan a trip with the money he's made from this side-hustle.

Saud wasn't angry. He could feel all those serene thoughts running through his head, broadcasting from the heart of the action. He didn't miss a single detail, not the smell of the blood, the clattering of the scalpels, or the crushed ice sprinkling over two brown eyes. Saud stood still, lost in thought, traveling through time and space, then heard Mustafa asking:

Where are you going?

Although Saud didn't answer, his legs moved on their own accord, kicked down a door, and left.

Mustafa and Huwaishel followed.

Saud who became an undertaker marched like someone was calling him. He couldn't help but keep searching for the gravesite—a single hole for all the kids—until someone unearthed this mass grave and reburied each child in their little hole. Saud imagined Mishari's face. *He'll have his own pitiful grave as well.* Wiping his tears with the back of his hand, he ran toward a steep rock face about half a mile from the house. *What have you got for me, dear mountain?* Saud pictured the mountain opening its mouth and revealing a cave. Then he saw, down below, a hollowed-out section at the edge of the cliff.

Saud, Mustafa, and Huwaishel reached the cave by traversing a narrow trail. They entered the cold, dark mouth, cautiously following an unmistakable scent. Cans of beans and peas, sacks of onions, and juice boxes were scattered beside skeletons and corpses decomposing on the ground. The three men covered their noses with their sleeves. Wading deeper into the cave, they came upon earthy protrusions that barely covered the bodies underneath.

Saud dropped down on his knees, brushing the sand away with his palms until a small, black, amputated arm appeared, so he dug in, throwing heaps of sand left and right, burrowing into the belly of the cave, screaming, Mishari! I'm here! I'm here!

Al-'Arish. Swiss Inn Resort

26 Dhu Al-Hijja, 1431

7:04 P.M.

Faisal was still lying on his back when his younger brother returned to the resort.

Saud stepped into the room, his eyes wet, his nose red. After turning on the lights with a sigh, he sat on the edge of the bed and called his brother, Bu Mishari.

Because Faisal sensed, under all those layers of silence weighing on his chest, that his brother was getting ready to share important details, he paid attention to Saud's every word: on the abandoned house, the wire transfers, the cave in the rocky ridge, and the mass grave within. His younger brother explained that the team uncovered twenty-seven bodies. Some of them were adults. Others were children. The forensics team estimated the time of death of five young, semi-decomposed bodies as having been four days ago. Some of the bodies were missing arms.

Saud's voice trembled. These were, most likely, the kids we've been searching for.

Faisal felt his numbness and his silence subside, but his ability to experience pain returned when he bent his arms and tried to push himself up. Because his body was weak, he said as he extended his hand to his brother, Saud, help me sit up.

Slipping his arm around his older brother's back, Saud propped Faisal up against the headboard.

I'd like some water, Faisal muttered.

Saud rushed to get a bottle of water and gave it to his brother, who chugged it in two gulps, streams trickling down his chin. Faisal's lips then arched into a frown, and he started to cry like a boy who had just realised that he was lost.

They both felt they had reached the end of the tunnel he had previously thought was endless.

The investigative unit discovered the crime scene and the victims' remains. After the forensics team members identify the dead, they can deliver Mishari's body to his parents. Then we can all return to Kuwait for the funeral.

So, that's it, then? Faisal asked.

Not yet. There's just a little more work to be done.

Faisal stretched his arm to Saud, and the two embraced, crying over the child's tragic end—dead at age seven before he'd even had a chance to live. The tears they'd been resisting for days, nineteen to be exact, and those tears that overcame them during vulnerable moments of invocations and circumambulation, now flowed in a singular rush, a Biblical flood, an all-encompassing sadness.

Faisal banged on his chest before letting out an exasperated cry: It's so unfair! He imagined the kinds of torture his son would've had to endure only to die in the end. If he had only perished! Faisal cried, Perished without suffering!

Saud, who was sniffling, got up to bring a box of tissues that he placed between his older brother and himself, then said, I don't want to visualise how Mishari could've been tortured. Wiping his eyes with a tissue, he carried on, I want to remember him before his kidnapping when he begged me to take him to the bird market; hopping over waves on the beach; skating on dunes in Al-Subbiya; or running through the sprinklers in the yard. And... I want to remember the look in his eyes when he saw Batman overcome his fears and emerge from the cave with his supportive cloud of bats.

Saud and Faisal cried for hours, their tears flowing in waves, their contemplative silences followed by uncontrollable weeping. They had been building dams along their journey to prevent themselves from falling apart, now they began to rupture these dams, one by one—to finally welcome their physical expression of unbearable grief.

They stopped only after thoroughly exhausting themselves. Faisal lay on his back again, whereas Saud got up to make hot tea for his brother.

Did you tell Sumaya? Faisal asked.

Saud said with a shake of his head, I'll tell her tomorrow when they identify the bodies.

Al-'Arish. General Hospital

27 Dhu Al-Hijja, 1431

7:06 A.M.

The next day, Mustafa was in the hotel lobby to take Saud and Faisal to the hospital morgue to examine the dead bodies they had discovered. When Saud and Faisal came down at last, their eyes were red, and their sockets were swollen. Saud took shorter, faster steps while Faisal lingered, taking care not to trip and fall. Mustafa remembered how he'd met them the first time at Sharm El Sheikh's Airport.

Why have you taken so long?

Why? Saud asked. What's going on?

Follow me. I'll tell you in the car.

When they all got in, Mustafa explained that the hospital had issued burial permits for the human remains they had uncovered the previous day.

Eyebrows knitted, Saud asked, This quickly? Did they at least record the cause of death?

Mustafa shrugged. They wrote: Ongoing Investigation.

Saud cried, his eyes bulging, What the hell is going on, Mustafa? Why are they rushing this?

You know exactly why. Mustafa sighed, then added, We're talking about twenty-seven corpses, some of them had been rotting for months. There aren't enough spaces in the morgue. In fact, some of our refrigerators have recently broken down. And the smell—

Saud interjected, But how will we discover the identity of the victims? How will you guys conduct your DNA analyses? How will you figure out the details of the crimes?

What are you asking, Saud?

What do you mean what am I asking? Saud felt betrayed. Did you tell Hamdi?

Mustafa nodded. He lost his temper as well.

When's the burial?

They confiscated the adult bodies last night, but we managed to keep them from burying the kids to give you a chance to identify...

He didn't go on. The brothers went quiet as well.

Ten minutes later, they arrived at the morgue, where the stench of the dead was overwhelming. The children had been taken out of the refrigerator drawers, and the corridor was filled with forensic investigators and detectives. Both Saud and Faisal looked at each other in astonishment. The small bellies were covered in stitches and their eyes were stuffed with cotton—but they were all black.

Where's my son? Faisal yelled, staring at the corpses in disbelief. This time, too, there was no sign of Mishari. *Could he still be alive? Or did the police dig up the wrong grave?* Faisal felt painfully unsteady, unable to discern whether he was happy or sad. Feeling lost, Faisal absentmindedly gazed at the tiny bodies as his brother shared his testimony with the forensic investigator. They had that distant look of the dead, unfathomable, beyond reach. Five children have been kidnapped and murdered, their bodies violated, and their organs stolen, then dumped into a mass grave without anyone noticing. Faisal found himself wondering out loud, Where's Mariam?

The others turned around, but said nothing.

Faisal didn't know why she crossed his mind. Yet, none of the bodies on the drawers resembled her photograph: Mariam Muhammad Akbar, an Indian girl from Delhi... *Where was she?*

Saud and Faisal followed Mustafa out of the morgue. While the brothers sat on guest chairs, Mustafa remained standing, his right shoulder leaning against a wall, staring at the ceiling.

Faisal asked, Are these the kids we were looking for?

I'm not so sure anymore. Mustafa added, I'm so sorry. I really thought we found them.

Saud's voice cracked when he said, They only died four days ago.

Mustafa lowered his head. Bashmohandes, do you understand what this means? Four full days stood between us: between saving their lives or failing them.

But where's my kid? Faisal whispered as if he hadn't heard the detective.

Saud's face was flushed and the veins on his forehead and the back of his hands were bulging. He got up, then kicked at the wall. Mishari could be anywhere! And this damn nightmare will never end!

We need to start considering other possibilities, Mustafa said. Maybe non-Black bodies are treated differently? Maybe there's a different market for white slaves? Maybe we're looking at child prostitution? Or... Maybe they just died on the way? Mustafa's voice was dripping with shame.

The brothers peered at each other.

Alright, so what does this mean for us? Faisal asked. Are we going to search for another mass grave? He conjured up the hellish tunnel they'd been traversing, the one he recently believed had reached its end, but there was no end to their pain for the road to eternal damnation was paved with suffering.

Unlike yesterday's uncontrollable deluge, Faisal's throat clamped up and his eyes became unbearably dry. Burying his face in his palms and feeling an affinity with the others' silence, he sat quietly until his phone buzzed in his pocket. He pulled it out and stared at the screen. It was Sumaya. His eyes bulged when he asked, Why is she calling? Faisal hadn't heard her voice since he'd departed from 'Asir. He swallowed and pressed the phone to his ear. Hello, Sumaya?

Ruwaina has woken up from her coma, she said breathlessly. The police are interrogating her now, and she just confessed that Mishari escaped before the boat even sailed. Faisal!

Her perplexed husband asked, What are you saying?

Sumaya raised her voice, I'm saying Mishari didn't leave the province! He's here! Right here in Saudi Arabia! So, why are you wasting time in Sinai?

CHAPTER FOURTEEN

NAMEER

clear; wholesome; panther

Jazan. The Farm of Sheikh Issa Muftah

29 Dhu Al-Hijja, 1431

11:43 A.M.

Ruwaina's interrogation revealed the site of the boat and the shore through which Mishari had fled. That land, shortly afterward, began to swarm with people. The expedition that commenced on the beach yesterday evening consisted of men and boys brandishing phones, a few dressed in their respective law enforcement uniforms, and the rest sporting varicoloured, civilian outfits. Everyone was ready to inform police officers of Mishari's whereabouts. The volunteers advanced steadily, combing every inch of the area until they reached the millet farms.

Faisal, Saud, and Sumaya were among them. So was Mazen, who had flown in from Jeddah and who arrived with relatives and friends. They ended up forming smaller volunteer groups to aid in the search party's efforts. Many came from Kuwait to lend a hand, including Faisal's and Sumaya's cousins, neighbours, and friends.

While the search party moved uniformly, its smaller groups veered off to investigate the shoreline, foothills, caves, dams, deserts, and fields. Knocking on doors and farm gates, they shared the flier that showed Mishari, smiling in his red Ferrari T-shirt, outside the yard with the green gate and the crimson bougainvillea vines.

But no one said that they'd seen him around.

Faisal's health was deteriorating. Though his fingertips continued to quiver, he sensed numbness crawling up his arms. Twice, the numbness reached his head, and he collapsed on his knees when he lost his bearings. Faisal relied on his younger brother's assistance for the remainder of the expedition.

Marching beside Faisal, an arm wrapped around his older brother's shoulder, Saud led Faisal forward as though his older brother were blind.

Sumaya trailed behind them, reciting the holy verse to aid in recovering whatever was lost.

Twenty-two days after Mishari's disappearance, and after two days of searching—while the search party had gone back to comb the shore a second time—an officer approached Faisal and whispered, Bu Mishari, we've got news.

Faisal felt his heart drop and the earth spin.

Saud whispered, Hang in there!

Head buzzing and pounding in pain, Faisal peered searchingly into the officer's face and asked the one question gnawing at him from the inside:

Dead or alive?

Watching the officer's lips move, Faisal's vision clouded, and he couldn't hear a single word. But Saud, still holding his older brother upright, carefully led Faisal to the nearest police car to tuck him into the back seat. Sumaya had sprinted behind them, and was now sliding in beside her husband, as Saud hopped in through the passenger door. When the police vehicle took off, Mazen followed in his car.

The officer explained on the way that the Saudi authorities had received a phone call from a small farmer, who said that he'd found a boy on his doorstep upon his return from the mosque, where he'd been performing the Fajr prayer. The kid, about five or six years old, was naked, his wrists and ankles bound, and his body covered in a chequered quilt.

Mishari! Sumaya gasped. Her hand clamped on Faisal's. Their fingers intertwined. She swerved toward him, buried her head in his chest, and sobbed. Thank God! Thank God!

Faisal remained wide-eyed and stiff. He refused to believe the implications of this latest development until he saw his son with his own eyes. The past few days had taught him nothing if not to distrust those ruthless glimmers of hope that fed off bleeding, broken hearts.

Saud asked the officer, Didn't the boy tell you his name?

No. The officer hesitated before adding something in a dialect the others couldn't understand. He cleared his throat when he realised this and said in the dominant dialect, Since the kid hasn't uttered a word, the old farmer assumed he was deaf.

Deaf?

They drove silently, each in their stupor, their heads bent low, their chests heavy with doubt: *Could it be someone else?*

Forty minutes later, the police car parked in front of a brick wall with a green metal gate beside a small cornfield. The old man was waiting for them at the gate. He was a stooped, frail brown man with slicked-back hair and a white goatee. Hello! he said when they came over. My name is Issa Muftah. I'm the one who called the police.

Saud immediately asked, Where's the child?

Over here, he said, before leading them inside the house. He's asleep now. My wife fed him some sweetened crumbs and a glass of milk earlier. But he hasn't said a word since he appeared on our doorstep. I asked him his name. How he got here? Who tied him up? Who hurt him? But it doesn't seem like he understood anything.

Are you saying he looked injured? Saud asked, choking up.

The old man, furrowing his thick, white eyebrows, said, There are scars on his body, sores between his thighs, and blisters around his mou—

Faisal interjected, Where's the boy?

Issa Muftah opened a bedroom door.

Sumaya burst right in.

In the corner of the room, an old, niqab-wearing woman sat on a bed, her back to the wall, cradling a boy in her lap, reciting Ayat Al-Kursi, her fingers playing with his hair.

Faisal, Sumaya, Mazen, and Saud took slow steps toward the bed, their lips trembling and their eyes darting to Mishari.

Saud then dropped to his knees, clasping both hands to his mouth and struggling to muffle his weeping.

Mazen bent down to embrace his friend.

Sumaya, who kneeled over the bed, gently cupped Mishari's face in her palms, before pressing kisses all over his cheeks, forehead, nose, mouth, and chin.

Mishari's eyelids opened slowly and blinked twice before wandering around the room to scan the faces of the people present.

He seemed lost.

Faisal went to the other side of the bed, hugged the little one's legs, and buried his face in the tiny feet. He felt grateful that he hadn't lost his sense of touch, although his fingers still trembled. Mishari, baby, I'm here.

I'm here.

EPILOGUE

LETTERS

21 Dhu Al-Hijja, 1432

17 November, 2011

Dear Saud Al-Saffar,

Al-Salam alaikum, my honourable friend. May all your family and loved ones be in good health. I'm writing this email a year after we first met in November. Bashmohandes, can you believe that a whole year has passed?

Two days after you left Al-'Arish, our local newspapers ran a story on the missing Kuwaiti child who was found on a farm in southern Saudi Arabia. Needless to say, this announcement thrilled our authorities for reasons that are unrelated to your nephew. Almost instantly, our establishment media began denying the existence of an international network of organ traffickers operating in Sinai. They used Mishari's case to obfuscate the evidence of the human trafficking crimes we'd uncovered. Huwaishel, the ex-smuggler, Prof. Hamdi Al-Azzazi, and I were equally frustrated.

Additionally, an order from the higher ups forcibly closed our case, despite there still being other children whom we hadn't yet been able to locate or learn more about. A year later, America's FBI published a report on the involvement of the former interior minister of Egypt in an organ trafficking network run by an Israeli rabbi residing in Brooklyn named Levi Yitzhak Rosenbaum. The FBI's report, which *Al-Wafd* and *Rose El Youssef* quoted, explained that the rabbi had been arrested three years earlier, in 2009, on charges of organ trafficking. However, the FBI had struck a deal with the rabbi, which entailed a reduction of his sentence to only five years in prison in return for providing information on the details of the organ trading process and the members involved. I need not remind you that the member list included the interior minister of Egypt.

At least four thousand human organs have been sold through this specific network. These include African and Egyptian organs, especially after the January 25th Revolution and the fall of Hosni Mubarak's regime in February 2011.

The Sultan was murdered in the desert by the al-Tiyaha tribe, who decided to take revenge on him for smuggling human organs to America, probably because he lost the protection the minister had afforded him.

I've been reading about these developments and pondering the question you first asked me. Why did my superiors assign an inexperienced detective, someone who, in your words, was merely a fledgling, the task of investigating such a daunting case? My theory is that they didn't want us to succeed. It's really unfortunate, bashmohandes, that we, in fact, did not.

I guess I must also admit that I never sent the official request for a team of organ trading experts. Maybe you already knew that. And perhaps you already knew why I didn't file the request.

Looking forward to your updates.

Faithfully,

Mustafa Wajdi

22 Dhu A-Hijjah, 1432

18 November, 2011

My dear friend Mustafa,

I was happy to see your email in my inbox. And Faisal says Hi!

Like most people in Kuwait, we've been following the latest developments in Cairo, The Protected City. We rejoiced in your victory on January 25 and hope this will rejuvenate Egypt. Imagine the impact it'll have on a global scale if Um al-Dunya is reborn. Our hearts go out to you all. Mine, in particular, goes out to Al-'Arish. Not a single day goes by without me pondering what I'd witnessed there.

Four days after the investigation, I began doubting whether you filed the report requesting specialised assistance. But rather than feeling disappointed, I felt reassured, because I had started to fear what someone occupying a higher position would do to the case. They could've been clandestine members of the same criminal network we were trying to investigate, which turned out to be bigger than we had imagined.

Two weeks ago, Mazen, my Saudi friend from Jeddah, informed me that the female criminals they caught would be executed. Shortly after his message, Ruwaina, Adania, and Bahati were hanged from a crane in Jazan's Al-Qasas square. I asked him if the police had captured Jerjes. He said they'd lost every trace of the man like he had never existed.

After we found Mishari on the farm of the old Southerner in Jazan, we admitted him to the hospital. The medical examination revealed that he'd been repeatedly raped and that his body had suffered bruises and belt marks. The kid was pale and skinny, and his bones stuck out. At first, he didn't recognise any of us. It took him eight months to say his first word. He's still afraid of the dark and refuses to sleep alone. I'm the one who spends the most time with him. Mishari kicks in his sleep and screams words that don't sound Arabic. Of course, I rush to comfort him—hold him and tell him it'll be alright—but I'm not so sure I believe these words myself.

He still hasn't told us what happened, though we've ascertained some things from his reactions. For instance, a few days ago, our neighbours decided to renovate their house. When Mishari saw an Afghani mason laying bricks, he stopped still, then wet himself.

I tried to remind him of his favourite activities, so I bought some popcorn, and we got ready to watch the Batman movie, but he hid his head under a pillow and started screaming when the bats flew above Christian Bale.

Despite these post-traumatic stressors, Mishari will resume his schooling next year. I often take him out with me to the ocean, because I think the long hours of silence aid in his recovery.

He is gradually getting back to normal, but it's not an easy feat, especially in light of his parents' divorce and his father's disease. Faisal has been diagnosed with Parkinson's.

Our emotional scars are too deep, my friend. I fear we may never return to the way things were.

In response to your letter, I'm excited to share that I registered my name at Kuwait's Transplant Society as an organ donor. Not a day goes by without me thinking about all the bodies I washed, shrouded, and buried, and over which I prayed. Their poor Black faces have not left me.

Sometimes, I wonder if there was a deeper meaning behind our ordeal. When we were in Sinai, for example, Mishari was in Jazan. When we returned to Mecca, Mishari was already in 'Asir. It all seems meaningless on the surface, but when I think this, a daunting thought flashes, and I wonder perhaps we're the ones who assign meaning to events.

This ordeal has changed us all, for we are carrying scars larger than our hearts.

Sumaya, for example, has become a full-on dervish. She sees Allah everywhere, speaks in his name, communicates with him, and never stops talking about him. She is thoroughly convinced that Mishari's disappearance was all a big message from God.

On the other hand, Faisal now occupies a lonely world empty of divinity. His sky is always silent, where nothing ever makes sense.

As for me, my friend, I am still lost. But if you give the matter more thought, you might realise that all of us must be trying to find our way out of the same labyrinth.

With love,

Saud

The End

Translator's Note

To discuss some of the translation choices I have applied in this book, it might help to begin with the title of the original— خرائط التيه —a phrase consisting of two words. The first, *khara'et*, is easy to translate into English because it articulates the plural version of the noun: map—hence: Maps. The second word poses the kind of difficulties I have faced throughout the novel. For example, *al-taih* means both wandering or getting lost, as well as a particular space in which people find themselves astray, i.e. a labyrinth or a maze. A literal rendition of the title's lexical and syntactic components thus produces, on the one hand: *Maps of the Wandering* or *Maps of the Getting Lost*; and, on the other: *Maps of the Labyrinth* or *Maps of the Maze*. Translating *al-taih* as a gerund (*Maps of the Wandering* or *Maps of the Getting Lost*) foreignises the target language. However, beyond conveying one single meaning, it is unclear what this defamiliarization aims to communicate, whereas translating *al-taih* as a noun (*Maps of the Labyrinth* or *Maps of the Maze*) ascribes to the book a title that echoes stories from young adult fantasy novels. In other words, neither formation encapsulates the deeper meaning of the original, nor do they evoke the plot's mood and tone, reflect the author's voice, or situate this novel in its literary landscape.

I settled on *Lost in Mecca* because I felt that, linguistically and emotionally, it captured the impact of the original. "Lost," after all, retains the linguistic and emotional significance of the Arabic's *al-taih*, while "Mecca" specifies the location, which was implied but not explicitly communicated in either word of the original title:

map or maze. Mecca offers, in addition, other layers of significance: narratively, it is where the story and the traumatic confrontation with privilege begins. Physically, it is where Muslims flock to perform their pilgrimages and where they turn their faces to during prayer; figuratively, it acts as Muslims' moral compass; historically, it points to the place Islam emerged; and, lastly, it links this historical past to a contemporary city in a nation-state that has contributed to the economic network the book alludes to in its critique of neoliberal inequality, systemic racism, and various forms of violence.

It became vital for me to decide from the outset which categories of meaning I wanted to represent faithfully in the English manuscript. Put differently, I asked myself whether I was singularly translating the way lexical and syntactic items appear on the page (i.e. the shell of the book) or if I was entrusted with conveying their deeper functions and their overall impact (i.e. the flesh, the bones, the liver, the kidneys, the eyes, and the heart)? Text-related pun aside, because readers of the Arabic version often praise how it makes them feel, I decided to prioritise the author's voice, the tone of the book, cultural and psychological significance, and the overall hypnotic cadence and rhythm of the source material. I rendered the lexical and syntactic elements as literally as possible whenever a denotative representation reflected these values. However, I deviated from the surface when a denotative representation damaged the original's voice, tone, context, or rhythm.

My translation approach involved familiarising myself with the source material's logical goal: its content and its underlying ideas. What is the story about? And what might its scenes signify or thematically communicate to a reader? Here is my summary:

When a seven-year-old Kuwaiti boy is lost in Mecca during the

Hajj pilgrimage, his loss spurs his parents' confrontation with their own privilege, which they discover is built on racist foundations that link their local past to a contemporary global financial network. The book's thematic concerns (its variety of violence upon women, children, undocumented immigrants, and people with darker complexions) are staged through scenes of battery, abuse, murder, and international criminal activities, especially organ trafficking.

Yet people do not only engage with this book's content and ideas. Rather, readers of the Arabic version also engage with the book's affective goal, and it is this category of meaning (the emotional impact of the book) that I decided to underscore in my translation. Thus, I investigated the way various readers of the original felt upon completing this book. Based on the logical aims of the plot and its thematic concerns, one might assume anger, repulsion, disgust, or even guilt—if they recognised themselves in that privilege. Yet, the many reviews of the book and the interviews I conducted showed that readers of the Arabic version expressed those sentiments in addition to an equally powerful sensation of marvel and splendour. In a similarly paradoxical vein, readers of the Arabic have frequently mentioned how the original made them feel as though they were rushing toward an impending doom, on the one hand, and, on the other, toward claustrophobia, as though the story was never going to end. To recreate this book in a different language, I decided to convey the novel's logical aim (what happens first, what follows, and why) and the story's contradictory, emotional aims (awe and anger, stress and delight, etc.).

After familiarising myself with the book's logical aims as an intimate reader, I unpacked the novel's storytelling mechanism as a prose writer and poet. I discovered that the original employs a series of stylistic choices to achieve its affective aims. First, it relies on suspenseful elements to generate urgency: countdown effect, escalation of stakes and action, division of long chapters into short sections that end with cliffhangers, and oscillating POVs that complicate the thriller's more stable roles of victims and villains. But if these were all stylistic choices to speed up the action and generate stress (the sense of impending doom), the original novel employs several other formal strategies to slow down its page-turning action. These include: (1) Not enclosing direct speech in quotation marks; (2) not typographically distinguishing direct thought from indirect thought or even from speech; (3) allowing multiple characters to converse in a single paragraph; (4) not always identifying these characters by name, which makes it unclear when gendered pronouns appear in these multivocal paragraphs; (5) occasionally italicising or using boldface but not doing so consistently or systematically; (6) altering tenses arbitrarily, sometimes in the middle of a paragraph or a section; and finally, (7) jumping from third person narration to second person narration mid-paragraph or mid-section without a particular plan. Put differently, the stuffy and unpredictable manner in which the fast-paced narrative is told creates that incongruous feeling readers experience in the original, where the story seems to be both rushing and circling the same spot. This very idea, in fact, is referenced in the first chapter of the novel when it is said that Faisal, who was running in the courtyard of the Sacred Mosque in search of his son, was "sprinting as fast as one could in a dense crowd."

When I reproduced the Arabic paragraphs verbatim, however, I lost the book's logical aims because very little made sense in English with its stricter grammatical rules. I also lost the book's emotive goals, and instead of generating a paradox of wonder and disgust only a tremendous sense of uncomplimentary confusion remained, which beta readers struggled to power through. At that point in my process, my challenge then became to figure out ways to honour the various building blocks that exist in the source material while also systematically deviating from the way in which they were originally applied. Therefore, in my version, (1) like the original, I did not enclose direct speech in quotation marks; however, (2) unlike the original, I italicised direct thought, dreams, and narration told from the minds of characters perceiving the action; (3) I broke paragraphs apart when multiple characters spoke to one another; (4) whenever I felt that it could aid in comprehension, I added or removed characters' names; and (5) I decided against using boldface because, for a book criticising the way blackness is exploited in the Middle East, I thought that using boldface strategically might make it seem as though the author had intended to claim things that do not, in fact, exist in the original. The last two points (regarding grammatical tenses and pronouns) deserve their own list, hence:

I set the time before the trauma (i.e., "Before that moment") in the third person; past perfect

The time of the plot: in the third person; simple past

Memories: in the third person; past perfect

Dreams: in italics; third person; present

Direct thoughts and minds of characters perceiving the action: in italics; first or second person depending on the context; present

And documentation (such as surveillance screen footage or phone recordings): in the third person; present

By systematising some of the stylistic choices originating in the source material, I aimed to facilitate readability and comprehension (to allow the story to flow based on its page-turning elements) as well as to generate a feeling of claustrophobia (to reproduce stuffiness and overwhelm via shifting tenses, pronouns, and typography).

But what of the sense of wonder and disgust that the book achieves through its reliance on rhythm and visual representations, such as metaphors or cinematic descriptions? Put succinctly: the way sentences show vividly distressing scenes in a melodious language? My earlier section underscores the importance of form in meaning-making. I now want to focus on syntax, moving from how paragraphs fashion affect to how this emotional impact is generated at the sentence level.

Sometimes, finding a word-for-word equivalence felt like a glorious undertaking. Consider the following:

لم يكد يعرفها.

بدت مثل شبحٍ شاحبٍ، هزيل وأصفر.

A literal translation produces:

He hardly knew her.

She looked like a pale ghost, gaunt and yellow.

A lexical equivalence instantly loses the author's employment of the half-rhyme (شبحٍ شاحبٍ / shabahin shaahebin), which, as I mentioned earlier, is not a merely decorative device, for it is at the sonic level that the original produces the reader's sense of wonder. Thus, the usual Arabic-to-English concerns may not be relevant here. I am referring, for example, to the consideration of "pale" and "ghost" as redundant synonyms and, due to this consideration, feeling the need to excise one for the other; or, eschewing the option

"She looked like a ghost" because it smacks of cliché; or thinking that "She looked pale, gaunt, and yellow," might be considered bad writing because it strings three adjectives together; or leaning toward a more literary-sounding solution, such as "She looked translucent" instead. Rather, in my translation, I have endeavoured to find sonic solutions for sonic problems to retain a paradoxical affect of wonder (conveyed through rhetorical and figurative devices) and disgust (conveyed through the plot's content, where I reframed, when necessary, passive sentences into active ones, and where I utilised more specific nouns and verbs). I ended up translating "شـبح شـاحبٍ" as "almost ghostly," thereby retaining the Arabic rhyme sh-b-h (as most/ghost) as well as the phonic variation provided by its *alif mamdooda* and its *tanween* (as al/ly). Moreover, the sonic solution, which nudged the meaning of the original, did not veer far off or betray the initial message the text was communicating (pale ghost/almost ghostly).

Altogether, my translation became:

He barely recognised her.

Sumaya appeared almost ghostly: thin and frail—

In addition to the sonic solution, in other words, I also paid attention to verbs and the way they added to the overall visual and sonic landscapes of the manuscript. In the example above, for instance, I replaced "knew her" with "recognised her" and "looked like" with "appeared."

That said, I also frequently stumbled on phonic areas in the original where a word-for-word translation proved impossible. Consider the following:

كانـت التفاصيـل فـي رأسـه تتدافـع، تتواثـب، تتهافـت، تتكالـب، تحتشـد فـي قيامـةٍ كبرى.

It is a sentence with five synonyms of which four are half-rhymes. Stringing together as many similar-sounding synonyms in English falls short of awe and wonder. Take the following example:

The details in his head were jostling, jumping, collapsing, colliding, gathering in a great resurrection.

Hence, when I found that a literal rendition might damage the authorial voice, narrative tone, cultural or psychological contexts, or the sonic landscape of the original, I frequently stepped away from the surface. My solution to this particular four-rhyme conundrum became the following:

...the vibrant minutiae of his memories, flashing in succession and lashing at his heartstring, kept crashing into one another—like the fated clash at the end of days.

In other words, I introduced three full rhymes and one half-rhyme: flashing, lashing, crashing, and clash. More importantly, I spaced them out rhythmically and wove them into a fabric of consonantal echoes: sh, k, l, and n. What I am trying to communicate here is that I viewed the sonic landscape of the source material as a fundamental part of meaning. In my view, the mechanics of rhyme, phonic echoes, and beats or stress employed in the original do not act as a frivolous cover to an otherwise self-evident tale but are rather the very building blocks through which the story itself is told. And, just as with formal choices, the overall impact of these phonic decisions matters.

After all, what is خرائط التيـه if not a beautifully written book that problematises the limits of storytelling? It bears emphasising, however, that although this book challenges artistic limits, it is not simultaneously purporting its limits as its own moral, social, or political standpoints. Bothayna Al-Essa has spent her whole creative life, on the one hand, pushing margins on the page to allow for more artistic freedom in a conservative society and, on the other, challenging the political fabric of that society to be more inclusive. For example, Al-Essa mobilised local creatives and civil society members in an effort to dismantle the censorship branch of Kuwait's Ministry of Culture. Her efforts yielded success in 2020 when the government abrogated the entire department. Al-Essa also established a bookstore and cultural platform that provides opportunities for artists and intellectuals whose voices and experiences were not welcomed in other literary venues in Kuwait. In addition, Al-Essa has engaged in cultural exchange by personally translating books into Arabic and supporting other translators' efforts through her publishing house, inviting international writers to share their stories and their views on storytelling, and traveling elsewhere to speak with various communities. Moreover, she has taught a generation of Arab writers elements of the craft through her numerous workshops. Finally, she continues to invest financially in diverse programs that help foster a love of reading, creativity, and critical thinking in Kuwait.

That said, I fell in love with this book during a translation workshop at Columbia University and would not have been able to produce this work or even think in the terms I have laid out above without the tremendous love and support I have received from Katrina Dodson and Katrine Jensen, my classmates in both workshops; Kareem James Abu-Zeid who was my thesis supervisor; Susan Bernofsky who encouraged me to try a translation class when all I wanted to do was bathe myself in poetry; both Hannah Kauders and Shyanne Figueroa Bennett, who read recent versions of the book and who have had a profound impact on the way I worked through the novel's knottier issues; and my peers who agreed to work with me when I was too afraid to confront my traumas that were reflected in specific portions of the story: Shelby, AJ, Afrah, Razi, Moos, Haidar, Athbi, Hawraa,

Ruqia, Sarah, Amal, Johanna, Showg, Dima, Alice, Mehsen, and Mark. A warm note of gratitude goes to Sefi, whose words of wisdom helped me reach the finish line.

Finally, I am especially grateful for Nasser Al-Badri's patience and compassion throughout this project and for Dar Arab UK's commendable work both in translating and publishing new Arab voices; Marcia Lynx Qualey for her insightful edits and all the work she continues to do to elevate Arab Literature herself; Hassân Al Mohtasib for accepting the author's and my ideas for the cover of this manuscript; and to my dear author, Bothayna Al-Essa, who entrusted me with her vision and voice.

Author's Bio

Bothayna Al-Essa is a novelist from Kuwait. Born in 1982, she holds a Master's in business administration from Kuwait University. She is the co-founder of Takween (a cultural platform, bookstore, and publishing house) and the author of ten novels, the most notable of which include: *Lost in Mecca* and *All That I Want to Forget*, which have been translated into English; *Under the Feet of Mothers*, which has been translated into Persian (as بهشت مامان غیضه); and *Guardian of Superficialities*, which will be published in English in 2024. Furthermore, Al-Essa has written books on writing and has offered writing workshops throughout the Arab region. She has been writing full-time since 2013 and won Kuwait's National Encouragement Award twice for her fiction: in 2003 and 2012.

Translator's Bio

Nada Faris is a writer and creative writing teacher from Kuwait. In 2018, she received an Arab Woman Award from *Harper's Bazaar Arabia* for her impact on Kuwait's creative landscape. She is an Honorary Fellow in Writing at Iowa University's International Writing Program (IWP) Fall 2013; and an alumna of the International Visitor Leadership Program (IVLP) April 2018: *Empowering Youth Through the Performing Arts*. Faris holds an MFA in Creative Writing (Poetry & Literary Translation) from Columbia University. She is the author of multiple books in different genres, and her shorter works have appeared in: *The Norton Anthology for Hint Fiction, Gulf Coast Journal, Indianapolis Review, Nimrod, Tribes, One Jacar, The American Journal of Poetry,* and more. *Lost in Mecca* is her first literary translation.

HEDDA

BY PETER HADEN

The Angry Island
The Silent War

The Jan Trilogy:
Book One: Jan
Book Two: Hedda

HEDDA

Peter Haden

The Book Guild Ltd

First published in Great Britain in 2023 by
The Book Guild Ltd
Unit E2 Airfield Business Park,
Harrison Road, Market Harborough,
Leicestershire. LE16 7UL
Tel: 0116 2792299
www.bookguild.co.uk
Email: info@bookguild.co.uk
Twitter: @bookguild

Typeset in 11pt Minion Pro

Printed and bound in the UK by TJ Books LTD, Padstow, Cornwall

ISBN 978 1915603 517

British Library Cataloguing in Publication Data.
A catalogue record for this book is available from the British Library.

To my daughters
Vanessa Haden and Belinda Haden

PROLOGUE

England, March 1940

After escaping from wartime Europe they went their separate ways[1]: Jan redeployed, Hedda would stay in London for a while and Tadzio volunteered for the Army. He suspected that Hedda's value to the war effort, with her fluency in German and Polish, would be far greater than his own.

Tadzio's first posting was an intense language course at a military school in Buckinghamshire. Because he spoke virtually no English he was escorted to the station, where his guide exchanged a railway warrant, handed him a ticket, found the right platform, and eventually showed him to a seat. He knew the name of his destination, and that he would be met. The carriage soon filled up, but when a fellow passenger attempted to engage him in conversation, he used some of the few words his escort had taught him, just in case.

'I am Polish. No English.' After which his fellow passengers ignored him. That is, until a ticket inspector appeared.

'Fellow says he's a Pole,' said another passenger, his thumb indicating Tadzio. 'Perhaps the police should check.'

Tadzio had not understood, but the gist was obvious. Slowly he produced a temporary identity document from his inside pocket and handed it to the inspector, together with his ticket.

---

1   See '*Jan*' by Peter Haden.

'Gentleman is a volunteer, sponsored by the War Office,' he told the passenger, 'but thank you for your concern.' He smiled politely with a friendly nod as he handed the ticket and document back to Tadzio.

'Sorry old chap,' said his fellow passenger, 'but you can't be too careful these days.' Sensing that he might not have been understood, he also tapped his chest by way of apology.

Tadzio smiled. Fortunately, he had a window seat. He looked away over the countryside.

CHAPTER 1

London, March 1940

Hedda's billet was a handsome terraced house in Pimlico. 'My name is Mrs Ecclesworth,' her elderly hostess began, as Hedda's driver set down her suitcase on a small square of black and white tiles. 'Come in, my dear.' She beckoned, stepping back from the doorway. 'Put your case here in the hall for now, and we'll have a cup of tea. Or would you prefer coffee?'

Hedda followed her into a beautifully furnished lounge where two sofas sat either side of a long coffee table. 'May I call you Hedda?' she asked. 'And you must call me Clarissa!' she exclaimed, without waiting for an answer. She rang a small hand bell. 'Doreen Jackman from the War Office arranged for you to stay here,' she went on, 'and as you know I am to work on your English. I'm aware of your background,' she added, 'but don't worry, Doreen and I are old friends – in fact, she used to work for me and was promoted when I retired.'

A few minutes later, a maid appeared carrying a tray. There were tea and coffee pots, together with a plate of biscuits. 'Thank you, May,' she said, then, turning to Hedda, 'What will you have, and shall I pour?'

As she and her fiancé Tadzio had suspected, Hedda learned that her potential value to the war effort was indeed rather greater than his. So as a precaution and to preserve the secrecy of her identity, she was being schooled privately on a one-to-one basis by someone the department knew to be utterly reliable.

There was but one rule: only English would be spoken, although it seemed that French was also a common language. However, in response to her hostess' query, Hedda confessed that her French was, at the moment, rather the better of the two. 'It was the first foreign language we learned at school in Germany,' she explained, 'and my father, who spoke it almost fluently, also taught me a lot so that I could be top of the class. But I had five years of English lessons before…'

She stopped, reluctant to explain why her parents had committed suicide. But Clarissa had already been briefed. So she smiled sympathetically and paused, drinking tea to give her new guest time to set aside painful memories and collect her thoughts.

Hedda stayed at the Pimlico house for almost two months. She had a lovely single room on the first floor and sole use of a bathroom. A younger maid, Florence, assisted May with household duties such as the fireplaces and laundry. There was also a housekeeper and a cook, although Mrs Kent and Mrs Lewis did not live in.

Meals were strange, but Clarissa made a point of explaining their preparation. Hedda could not believe her good fortune: she was living a life of luxury, more so, even, than when she had been a young girl and her parents were alive. Her eyes grew visibly moist when she mentioned this to Clarissa.

'Enjoy it whilst you can,' she replied gently. 'Doreen told me what you have been through, and I think she wanted you to have a reward for what you did in Poland. She knows I am well able to afford a guest, but even so, don't feel guilty about it – her department insisted that I would be very well remunerated for looking after you.'

They passed a couple of hours each morning in conversation, and Hedda spent a lot of time reading, often aloud, so that Clarissa could correct her pronunciation – almost every word at first, but Hedda had an ear for languages and improved rapidly. They sometimes visited a park or exhibition in the afternoons, but the trips were taken for educational purposes. Occasionally they went shopping, and Clarissa added some items to Hedda's meagre wardrobe, insisting that her former department would pick up the bill – although Hedda had a strong suspicion that this was not the case, but rather her hostess was both kind and extremely generous.

In the evenings, they listened to the wireless, and soon Hedda was asking less and less frequently about the meaning of a word or phrase. Hedda's parents had been academics, and Clarissa soon realised that her guest was extremely intelligent. Best of all, Hedda automatically absorbed the social customs and manners of upper-class English society – she was no longer bewildered by the array of silver cutlery and crystal glasses that adorned a dinner table. It was a million miles away from her former existence as a partisan.

Towards the end of April, after almost two months, Clarissa reluctantly concluded that her job was almost done. 'It's been lovely having you here, my dear,' she told Hedda that evening as they enjoyed a glass of sherry, 'but as soon as this weekend is over, I am going to have to phone Doreen.'

Keen though she was to move on to the next stage of her life, Hedda had known this point could not be far away. 'I shall be sad to leave you,' she replied with a small sigh. 'I confess I was worried about how things would work out in England, but you have been so kind. I have lost my family, and I know we are not related, but I think of you almost as if we were… I hope I may look upon you as a very dear friend.'

Clarissa leant over to pat Hedda's knee. 'And I, you,' she responded, clearly a little emotional at the thought of their parting. 'But I insist that you come and see me from time to time. And if ever you need help, you must know that I shall always be here. I fear that we may be in for a long war… I do not subscribe to the view that everything will soon be over. I know that you faced great danger in Poland, and I pray that you will be safe in times to come.'

'We are going to treat ourselves,' she announced a few days later. 'Let's have a drink. Then there's a special dinner for your last evening here. Usually, I make do with ration coupons, but I asked our family estate manager to put a hamper on the train for tonight. It was delivered this afternoon. First, there's some smoked salmon, and Cook has rolled it into those cones that you stuff with trout and horseradish. After that, it's roast beef and an apple tart with cream – your favourite English dishes.'

A large black Humber saloon arrived at ten in the morning. Whilst the driver took her suitcases – she now needed two – they hugged tearfully on the doorstep. Clarissa waited until Hedda had waved and the War Office Humber had drawn away before using her handkerchief to dab at her eyes. Then, softly, she closed the door.

*

'So, how did you find the Honourable Clarissa?' asked Doreen Jackman as Hedda settled into one of two chairs in front of a desk. She took the other so that the heavy piece of furniture would not come between them. Two cups of coffee sat on a small side table.

'The Honourable…?' returned Hedda, puzzled.

'Yes, her father held a minor title, so she's an "Honourable". But she married a commoner and stopped using it. Then she had to divorce Ecclesworth. We go back a long way,' she offered without further explanation. 'Now, tell me all about your stay. I want to know every detail.'

Hedda could not help but smile. 'She's absolutely delightful. And so kind and generous. But I rather think you already know about my stay,' she replied. 'Clarissa must have told you, so I think you just want to put me to the test – to hear my English for yourself?'

'Sharp as ever,' admitted Doreen with a wry smile. 'But it seems Clarissa was right – you are almost fluent, hardly any trace of an accent. In fact, if you didn't know, you might not even realise… she's done a great job, you could fit in anywhere.'

'So what happens now?' asked Hedda. 'When we first arrived from Poland, you said that I might be employed within one of your intelligence services after my language training.'

'That is what we have in mind,' Doreen replied. 'We have set up a new listening organisation at a place called Bletchley Park. It's north-west of London, not far away. We need top-class translators. You were largely brought up in Germany, so your absolute fluency will be a godsend. There might be some Polish-English translation, too, although I'm not sure about that. Either way, they know you are coming, and I suspect they'll welcome you with open arms. Your cases are still in the car, so if it's all right with you, I'd like you to travel on this morning. Have you heard from Tadzio, by the way?'

'Yes, someone kindly brought round a couple of letters. He did a short language course, just the basics, then he was posted to something called the Armoured Fighting Vehicles School – apparently, they have a Driving and Maintenance Wing at Bovington – Clarissa said it's near the south coast, west of here in the county of Dorset. He's hoping to take some leave as soon as he can.'

'Where you are going is a top-secret establishment, so he probably won't be able to visit you there. But don't worry,' Doreen hastened to add, seeing the look of concern on Hedda's face, 'they will brief you in more detail when you arrive, but if necessary, get in touch with me, and we'll sort something out. That's why you will both have to continue writing via this department – everything is so secret, you can't even tell him where you are.

'We'll stay in touch,' she added, 'and you will always be able to phone me here or send a message. Now, if you are quite content, I'll walk with you down to your car and see you off.'

It was early afternoon when the Humber pulled up at an imposing set of gates. Two soldiers checked her identity documents, and the driver was instructed to take out her suitcases and return to base. 'It's a bit of a three-day camel ride up to the house, Miss,' one of them said cheerfully, 'so we'll keep these here till you know where you're going to be billeted. Most of the young ladies live in the village.'

After being collected by a messenger, she was shown to a small office occupied by someone who stood as she entered and introduced himself as Lieutenant Commander Hawkins. He was tall and slim with pleasant features. Somewhat awkwardly, he offered to shake her hand. He did not seem at ease meeting young women, or perhaps, she thought, it was because she was half Polish and half German.

'Good afternoon,' he greeted her, indicating the only chair in front of a desk. 'Won't you please be seated.' Then, opening a file, he glanced through it as if to remind himself who she was. 'Miss Sommerfeld, I know our security services have cleared you,' he began, 'but there's hardly any information in here. I gather that German is your mother tongue?'

'I have two,' she replied confidently, silently blessing the intense tuition given to her by Clarissa. 'German from my father and my mother was Polish. When I was in Germany, I was Hedda Sommerfeld, and when I was in Poland, I took my mother's maiden name – Hedda Agnieska Szymborska. So I use both surnames, and I am fluent in both languages.'

'Where did you learn to speak such good English?' he asked curiously.

'First of all, at school in Germany. I got to quite a reasonable level before my mother and I had to return to Poland.'

'And your father?' he queried.

'He was a lecturer in classics at the university in Berlin. Because he was Jewish and my mother Polish, the Nazis took away their citizenship, our house and land, and finally, his employment. We were destitute.' Hedda looked down at her hands. She usually managed to block out her past but had to blink away her sadness at this sudden recollection. She continued, hesitant but resolute, 'My father hanged himself, and my mother took me back to Poland. She is also no longer alive,' she added quickly to forestall any further query.

His face reddened – the reality of her suffering in Hitler's Germany had both shocked and embarrassed him.

'However, your English is much better than school English, if one may call it that?' Clearly, she thought, he was anxious to move away from her past life. But Hedda saw no reason to hide her background. 'When the Germans invaded, I joined the partisans. Our group lived in the forest. Conditions were terrible, but then I moved onto a small farm – the owner was one of many who supported our group. We killed Germans,' she said flatly, 'but eventually, we had to escape to England through no fault of our own. I was told that you need translators fluent in German – maybe Polish, too – but first your security service decided to improve my English. Well, you have been kind enough to offer a compliment about that, so here I am.'

For the first time in his career, John Hawkins felt very humbled. No longer fit for service at sea because of injury, he had been grateful to accept a posting to this administrative position. But the young woman before him had seen more active service than any English person of his generation that he could recall.

Hedda learned that she was to be assigned to a translation section in Hut 3 and billeted near Bletchley village. It turned out to be a comfortable house with several bedrooms. The owner, Mrs Willis, was a widow and only too happy to receive the extra income for her keep. Hedda was currently the only boarder, although her hostess thought more young ladies would arrive soon. For now, she had a large room with two single beds, a wardrobe, a writing table and a couple of chairs. The windows, at the rear of the house, overlooked farmland.

As a translator, she was to be paid two hundred pounds per annum. The salary meant little to Hedda, who had virtually no

7

time to spend it anyway because the hours proved to be punishing. She worked a six-day week, with shifts of four o'clock to midnight, midnight to eight in the morning and then eight till four. At the end of the third week, there was an additional four till midnight shift which meant a sixteen-hour day. The other girls in the team were friendly enough – mostly upper-class academics who had studied German at university – but Hedda was eternally grateful for Clarissa's brilliant instruction, without which she might not have been accepted so readily into their group. However, they lacked her natural fluency in German and sometimes consulted with her to confirm an exact word or idiom. But despite the hours, they sometimes managed an evening out in London.

Every weekend she wrote to Tadzio with the letter addressed to 'Room 47, Foreign Office', although Tadzio was a less regular correspondent. But their plans for a summer reunion and a serious discussion about their future were shattered when he wrote that he was being sent to France.

One May afternoon, she returned from her shift to find a young woman unpacking a large suitcase lying open on the spare bed.

'Hello,' she offered, extending her hand, 'Charlotte Fitzgibbon's my name. But everyone calls me Charlie. It seems we're to be roommates.'

'Hedda,' she replied, then remembered her manners, 'Hedda Sommerfeld.' Charlie Fitzgibbon was about her own age and height, slightly above average, with blonde wavy hair cut to curl on her shoulders and, like Hedda, piercing blue eyes. She was, thought Hedda, very good-looking, although perhaps handsome rather than pretty. The suitcase and the clothes in it, plus what she was wearing, looked to be extremely expensive. Not for the first time, Hedda was grateful for Clarissa's taste and generosity, even though she felt a little awed and perhaps plain compared with Charlie's rather aristocratic air.

'There's only one wardrobe,' said Charlie, 'so I hope you don't mind if I put a few things next to yours.' She looked down at a second, equally large case standing unopened by the bed. 'I'll just hang my everyday items – the rest will have to stay where it is.' Charlie's voice sounded much more refined than her own, although she had a warm smile as if she hoped that they would be friends. But it was as though she was welcoming Hedda to the room rather than the other way round.

'I'm sure we'll be fine,' Hedda said quickly, wanting to make up for a relatively subdued beginning. 'I didn't have much to fold away. Two of the three drawers in the bottom are empty, so you should have plenty of room. Do you need a hand with anything?'

To Charlie's surprise, Hedda admired the clothes as she passed them up from the case. 'Beautiful,' she said rather wistfully. 'We had fashions like these in Germany when I was younger. The designs from Paris and Rome are so much better...'

With everything stowed away, as Charlie put it, she announced that she was hungry. 'There's a common room with a small canteen at the Hall,' Hedda told her. 'You could get something there – I'll show you the way if you like. But I won't stay – I had something there after my shift.'

'Do come,' Charlie replied. 'And please stay – you might be able to introduce me to a few people, and I can drive us both back afterwards.'

'Drive us...?' queried Hedda, surprised. 'I saw a car outside – surely it's not yours?'

'No, it belongs to Madeleine,' came a cheerful reply without further explanation. 'But Daddy set this job up for me, and apparently, the people he spoke to said that although petrol's been rationed since last September, we can get extra coupons if I use it to drive people to and from the Hall and for any other duty runs. Between you and me, I suspect he's hoping that there will be a few left over – coupons, I mean – that he can use for his Bentley, but we'll have to wait and see.'

Hedda knew what a Bentley was – Clarissa had told her about the life of the English upper class – but the only car journey she had taken previously was in the back seat of a War Office Humber. Charlie's Austin Sherborne was smaller, but the seats were leather. She took in the three windows down each side as her roommate slid back the sunshine roof. Clearly, Charlie came from a wealthy family.

Hedda had no idea who had arranged it, but she and Charlie, plus two other slightly older men who had occupied the remaining two single bedrooms, were all on the same shift. The following morning, they assembled alongside the Austin.

'Would you like me to drive?' asked a quietly spoken academic called Maurice.

Charlie ignored him, opened the driver's door and settled behind the wheel. He walked round the bonnet and opened the passenger door. Then, his hand still on the handle, he began to pull open the front of the door so that he could settle in. 'No,' said Charlie firmly, her arm fully extended across the car, her hand raised to stop him. 'This is Hedda's and my transport. If you two gentlemen would care for a lift in our ladies' carriage, you are very welcome, but please take the rear seats.' Maurice blushed, visibly taken aback, but he held the door open for Hedda.

'I thought they would refuse,' said Hedda after the men had entered the main hall.

Charlie was still grinning. 'I don't accept the old-fashioned idea that it's a man's world,' she replied firmly. 'And anyway, what a cheek to think he could drive my car.'

'They might have argued,' Hedda persisted. 'What then?'

'What then, as you put it, is that they would have walked a mile or so in the rain,' she said with a laugh.

Hedda realised that she had met a kindred spirit.

10

CHAPTER 2

They were strictly forbidden to discuss their duties, but Hedda knew that Charlie worked in one of the cryptoanalysis huts, and Hedda saw no reason not to mention that she was part of a translation section in Hut 3.

'Does that account for your surname – it's not English, is it?' Charlie had asked one evening. By now, they were firm friends – co-conspirators when they wanted to break some minor rule and escape for a few hours. Hedda explained her dual nationality but spared Charlie her life history, just mentioning that she was fluent in German and Polish, which was why she was now a translator.

'Your English is superb,' said Charlie in genuine admiration. 'At first, I didn't realise it wasn't your mother tongue.' Hedda did not tell her about her time in London; it might have raised too many questions.

It was not quite high summer when they finished a Saturday shift at four in the afternoon. Mrs Willis made them beans on toast for tea, after which Charlie suggested that they treat themselves to a drink in the local public house.

Hedda picked up her handbag. Unusually, it had an extra strap, two short ones and a much longer one that Charlie noticed she liked to put over her head and on to the other shoulder, although the leather of this strap was a slightly different shade to the others. Clearly, it had been added as an afterthought. Perhaps it was a Polish custom…

'Let's walk,' she suggested. 'I'm a bit low on petrol, and anyway, I feel like a few decent drinks, so it might be better if I didn't have to drive back. The exercise will do us good,' she added, 'and we can take the path through the fields.'

The lounge bar was full of men stationed at Bletchley Park. 'Please, let's not join them,' Charlie suggested. 'We see them every day, and they'll only try to flirt with us. And in any case, I suspect most of them are already married.' Hedda was only too happy to agree, so they turned right into the snug. 'The drinks will be cheaper in here,' Charlie told her, suspecting that Hedda would not be well versed in the traditions of an English public house.

It was still early. Thinking about that night in London, when she had first tasted English beer with Jan and Tadzio, Hedda had drunk a pint of bitter. She asked for the same again. To the surprise of the landlord, a middle-aged dark-haired, well-built man, Charlie went for a large gin and tonic. They sat at a bench seat curving round a table in one corner. The landlord was busy helping a barmaid in the saloon but came back from time to time to make sure that the girls were all right. Charlie stood up to buy another round, but she had already paid for the first, so Hedda intercepted her. 'Let me,' she offered.

Charlie placed a hand on her arm. 'Look,' she began, 'please don't be offended, but I can't let you pay for gin and tonics when you have barely started on a pint of beer. The landlord will probably top you up for free – I don't suppose he sells all that many spirits in his snug.'

Charlie was standing at the bar, leaning over it in the hope of catching the landlord's eye as he served along the corridor in the saloon when three young men walked in. From their appearance, they were farm workers or labourers. When the landlord returned to serve the new arrivals, he turned first to Charlie. 'Yes, Miss?' he asked politely.

'Same again for me, please,' she answered, 'and can you just top up this one for my friend? She's not quite used to English beer!' Even as she said it, clearly in the hearing of the new arrivals, Charlie wondered if she had just been horribly indiscreet. Hopefully not, but it was too late now. She carried the drinks back to their table. The three other drinkers could have sat anywhere, but after a nudging of elbows and a few glances between them, they chose an adjacent table, one nearer to the centre of the room.

The three strangers were on their second pint, whispering and laughing amongst themselves. The girls looked at each other. They were beginning to feel uncomfortable. Charlie was about to suggest that they drink up and move to the saloon bar after all when one of the men, who seemed to be a year or two older than his companions, stood up then sat down again alongside Charlie, setting his drink on their table.

'Thought you'd fancy a bit of friendly chat, 'lung a we, like,' he began, nodding towards his companions, 'seein' as you two young girls be on your own.' They both winced at his voice. Charlie caught a whiff of body odour, and she was acutely aware that his thigh was deliberately pressing against her own. She shuffled towards Hedda, but there wasn't much room to move.

'Don't be like that,' he said as if she had been guilty of some misdemeanour. His right hand settled on her arm.

'Thank you, but we did not invite you to join us,' Charlie replied, trying to sound more relaxed than she was feeling.

'Oity-toity then, is it?' he replied. 'Come on, give us a cuddle,' he went on, lifting his right arm to put it over her shoulders.

Hedda stood to let Charlie move away. The other two men watched intently, grinning and making encouraging remarks to each other. Hedda moved round the table to stand in front of their interloper. 'Leave her alone, and go back to your table,' she said quietly. 'You are not invited to sit with us.' But under the stress of the moment, she lost her hard-won English accent and pronounced the 'w' as a 'v' sound.

The man grinned back at his companions. 'Posh one an' a furriner bitch,' he told them. His free hand patted Hedda's thigh. 'Nice bit o' meat, though…' There was no one behind the snug bar, and quite a lot of noise and the sound of someone playing the piano coming through from the saloon.

He pulled back his arm and cupped his right hand over Charlie's mouth. Hedda thought she might have to face the other two first. This did not worry her unduly, but there might not be time to shout for help, and much as she didn't doubt Charlie's spirit, she didn't think she could count on her for much…

His hand still gripping Charlie's face, suddenly he was halfway to his feet but leaning over the table, off-balance. The other two had not moved. Hedda seized her chance and put both hands behind his head, which she smashed down on the table with all her strength. His glass fell to the floor and shattered. She moved to stand back as he tried to sit up, his hand no longer on Charlie. He was dazed, with blood running freely from his nose. Hedda thought he might try to strike her, but before he could come to his senses, hearing the smashed glass, the landlord had hurried through to the snug, snatched up the counter flap and rushed into the room. He looked fit and strong – as if moving a full barrel of beer would not present a problem. He grabbed their assailant's collar, pulled him to his feet and swung him round so that he was facing all three young men.

'You lads be off home,' he shouted angrily at them, 'and as for you, Jimmy Jenks, any more trouble and you be banned from this pub. And I'll tell all the other landlords round here. See you dry till bloody Christmas.'

Still visibly annoyed, he shoved all three of them towards the door. A young woman came through the counter carrying a dust tray and broom. The landlord turned back towards them. 'I'm really sorry about that, ladies,' he apologised, still breathing deeply but calmer now, 'and pardon my French. They were in here at lunchtime, so they weren't that sober when they arrived. I wanted to pop back more often, but we were getting right busy next door. I'm only sorry I served them now. Are you both all right?'

Charlie was still a bit shocked, but Hedda was perfectly calm. 'Thank you for what you did,' she answered quietly. 'It saved us from any further problems.'

'Won't you go through to the other room?' he asked them. 'Before she sweeps up, I'll get Betty here to clear a table for you, they won't mind, and I'll make sure nobody bothers you.' Betty walked quickly towards the saloon. 'Have something to settle you down,' the landlord offered, 'and it will be on the house.' He stood to one side. 'Please come through, behind the bar.'

They were soon seated in much more comfortable surroundings. Betty must have said something because although the saloon bar was quite full, there was an empty table near the fireplace and nobody disturbed or even spoke to them.

'Tell you what, Betty,' the landlord said to his barmaid a few minutes later, 'I don't know who she is, but I never thought I'd see a slip of a girl give that Jenks lad a bloody nose.'

'He's always been a bad 'un,' she replied, 'but I'll tell all my friends in the village. He'll never live it down.'

They decided not to stay till closing time. Leaving their table, they gave Betty a small wave as they headed for the door. It was a warm night and still not quite dark. Following a path alongside the field in companionable silence, they were about halfway along when two men emerged from the hedge about twenty metres to their front. Hedda looked back quickly. A third man had appeared a slightly shorter distance behind them. 'Quick, with me,' she hissed to Charlie, and walked away from the hedge and onto the stubble. All three men turned to follow them. Whatever their intention, they were in no hurry. But Hedda doubted that there was any chance they could outrun them in their low heels.

15

To Charlie's surprise, Hedda stopped, turned to face them and reached into her bag. She was even more surprised when Hedda dropped the bag and adopted a steady, two-handed grip on some sort of automatic pistol aimed firmly at the nearest man, whom she could see clearly now was the one called Jenks, the troublemaker from the public house.

'Stop, and leave us alone,' she commanded, her voice loud and clear in the still air.

'You dursn't dare use it, even if you knows how,' he sneered. He had not stopped walking. 'Probably not even loaded…' By now, he was only about three metres away. She lowered her aim slightly, which he took as a sign of surrender and kept coming. His grin widened.

The sound of the shot deafened both of them, but it was much more of a shock to Charlie. Jenks was on the ground, both hands clutching his left thigh. A red stain began to thread through his fingers. The other two had stopped. Then, to Charlie's surprise, Hedda left her and walked almost up to Jenks.

'Turn on your side, away from me, and let me see the back of that leg,' she ordered briskly, 'before I put a bullet in your other one.'

Jenks, clearly in a state of fear and shocked disbelief, did as he was told.

She leaned forward slightly then straightened up. There was a hole in the back of Jenks' trousers.

'Not a bad shot,' she told him, her voice still perfectly calm. 'You have an exit wound, and it's bleeding but not spurting, so nothing vital.' She backed off to stand next to Charlie. 'Take this piece of manure away,' she told the other two. 'Get him cleaned up with disinfectant and then bandaged.' Together they hauled Jenks, still clutching his leg, to his feet. Hedda picked up her bag but kept the automatic in her hand. 'Let's go,' she said to Charlie, and led her well clear, back to the path. Hedda checked only once – the three men were heading clumsily back to the village. She locked the slide and returned the weapon to her bag. They did not see or meet anyone else on the rest of the way back. And even if it had been heard, which was unlikely, there were always poachers in a rural area. The occasional single shot would not be unusual.

Back in their room, Hedda removed the magazine and the round still in the chamber, then deftly stripped off the barrel assembly. Next, she fished in her bag for a small tin containing a pull-through, some more cloth and a bottle that looked as though it might once have held perfume but now contained oil. Charlie watched, fascinated, as Hedda set to work. They had been quiet the rest of the way home, but now she was bursting with questions.

'Where did you learn all that?' she asked.

'All what?' said Hedda, not wanting to give too much away if at all possible.

'Back in the pub – you weren't frightened like I was. You took that Jenks thug out, and if the landlord hadn't rescued us, you looked as though you were quite happy to take on the other two as well. Then the weapon,' she went on in a hurry. 'Where on earth did it come from? That shot was no fluke. You obviously know exactly how to use it. And look at you now – the way you are taking it to pieces. You've been through military training, haven't you?'

Hedda put down the weapon. 'All right, I probably owe you an explanation,' she replied, 'but it stays strictly between us, fair enough?'

Charlie just nodded her agreement.

'You might as well know,' she said, 'I'm half Jewish on my father's side. We were persecuted by the Nazis. Papa committed suicide, and eventually, so did my mother, after taking me back to her family in Poland. When the Germans invaded, I joined the partisans. We had many ex-soldiers with us, and those of us who volunteered to fight were well trained – unarmed and knife combat, as well as with weapons. I took this pistol off a dead German officer we killed in an ambush.'

She paused, thinking of the overturned armoured car and the column of enemy lorries. 'When I and two others escaped,' she went on, 'through Poland and Germany and finally on an American ship from Sweden to England, I kept it hidden. Before we left Germany, I would have shot myself rather than been taken alive, but it never came to that.' She watched Charlie's eyebrows lifting as she spoke. 'And because we were refugee partisans,' Hedda went on, 'and had someone with us working for the British government, it never occurred to anyone to search us. Apart from the first few days at work, I have always kept the weapon in my bag in case anyone breaks into or searches my room. So now you know,' she finished quietly.

Charlie was silent for a moment. 'That's quite a story,' she said eventually, 'and you have probably told me only the half of it. What about that Jenks fellow?' she went on. 'Won't he be reported to the police for having a gunshot wound?'

'He might,' Hedda shrugged carelessly, 'but he should be all right if he treats it properly. I imagine his class is pretty used to looking after themselves if they can. Otherwise, he'll just have to make up a story. I suspect they had it in mind to rape us – I can't see them admitting to that.' Both women shivered at the thought. 'But I doubt we'll hear any more about it,' Hedda continued, 'and even if we do, all I'm guilty of is having a weapon and firing in self-defence. I doubt the authorities would even take formal action, especially after what the landlord would tell them. And there's a war on – I bet the senior officers at the Park would stick up for us.'

'Just one small detail,' Charlie said with a smile. 'Your English is great, but can I offer you a tiny correction?'

Hedda just looked at her. 'It's when you told them to remove that piece of manure,' Charlie went on. 'Whoever taught you that word was far too refined. You should have told them to take away that lump of shit.'

Hedda thought for a moment, then realised that it was the English word for the German *Scheiße*, with which she was only too familiar. After the stress of the evening, both girls collapsed into giggles.

Nothing was said when they reported for duty on Sunday morning. The only unusual activity came when Hedda's supervisor, a rather prim but kindly lady in her thirties called Miss Morris, asked whether she would like to think about taking a short break. 'You haven't been here all that long,' she told her, 'so you are not due for annual leave just yet. But you worked over Whitsun, so we wouldn't mind if you wanted to take a couple of days off – besides, we find that it's quite a good idea after the first few weeks of settling in. Many of our girls' – she pronounced it *gels* – 'have husbands or boyfriends away in the forces, so we are not short of staff. You can stay here if you like, perhaps just relax, or if you want to get away for a couple of days, it won't be a problem.'

Hedda was reluctant to tell her that she had no relatives in the country. But perhaps she might be allowed to stay with Clarissa. 'I need to write to someone,' she replied. 'Would it be all right if I gave you an answer in a few days?' Apparently, this was not a problem, and Miss Morris moved to another group of translators.

'I need to write a letter,' she said to Charlie that evening as she settled at the table.

'That boyfriend of yours?' she asked with a smile.

'No, my supervisor wants to know if I would like to take a few days off. I have a friend in London I could probably stay with. She's retired now, but she was my English tutor before I was posted here – that's where the manure came from,' she finished with a grin.

'Tell you what,' said Charlie, 'let's ask if we can take a break together. I'm sure your friend in London is jolly nice and all that, but an elderly tutor doesn't sound like much fun. If I can get time off too, come home with me. My people would love it, and the two of us will have a great time.'

Charlie obviously had some influence because the following day, Miss Morris announced that her supervisor had spoken with the Lieutenant Commander, and the two girls were to be given leave at the same time – a precious two days, either side of a weekend. And on Friday morning at the end of that week, their cases on the rear seat, they set off in high spirits.

Her people had to be well off, but even so, Hedda was taken aback when Charlie steered the Austin through imposing double gates set on tall stone pillars. 'Nice of someone to leave them open,' she remarked. However, Hedda was not really listening – a gravel drive bordered by mature trees led through what seemed like parkland until they rounded a bend and drew up outside a huge country house. A man in a tailcoat descended a flight of steps and hurried to open the driver's door. 'Welcome home, Miss Charlotte,' he greeted her politely but with an obviously genuine smile of pleasure and just the hint of a bow.

'It's good to see you too again, Brook,' she returned his greeting, also with a smile. Hedda let herself out of the car and stood rather nervously by the bonnet.

He turned towards her. 'And welcome to Stonebrook Hall, Miss Sommerfeld.' Also just the hint of a bow. He turned back to Charlie. 'I will have Jacob attend to your cases, Miss Charlotte.'

She took Hedda's hand. 'Come on, you must meet the family,' she told her, pulling her gently towards the steps.

They walked through a hall with a broad, curving staircase. Charlie led the way into a drawing room.

Her father was a tall, distinguished-looking man probably in his forties, his dark hair beginning to turn grey at the sides. To Hedda's surprise, his wife, who introduced herself as Madeleine, seemed much younger – too young, in fact, to have been Charlie's mother, and they hugged and kissed as close friends. Then, a boy ran into the room – he must have been about ten, not quite adolescent. Whereas his mother had the classic good looks of a fair-haired beauty, the boy was handsome – he would turn ladies' heads in years to come. 'Hedda, this is Peregrine, my stepbrother,' she told her. 'Perry, this is Miss Sommerfeld.' So Madeleine had to be Charlie's stepmother, Hedda realised.

'How do you do, Miss Sommerfeld,' he said formally.

She smiled and offered her hand. 'How do you do,' she answered equally formally, once more blessing Clarissa's lessons in etiquette.

'Everyone calls me Perry,' he offered with a smile.

'If you will excuse us,' Charlie addressed her father and stepmother, 'I'll show Hedda to her room.'

There must have been at least eight rooms on the first floor. Charlie opened a door. 'I'm dead opposite,' she told her, 'so my guests are always in here.' Two sets of windows looked out over farmland to the side of the house, but Hedda was amazed to find a young girl in a black dress with a white apron and cap in the process of unpacking her suitcase. She bobbed a curtsey, and with an 'I'll come back later, Miss', quietly closed the door behind her.

They did not dress for an early dinner. Charlie had asked for this concession because, as she had told Madeleine, Hedda did not possess a formal wardrobe. There were no other guests for the same reason, and as a special treat, Perry was allowed to join them. Father, it came out in conversation, spent most of his time 'at the ministry', although he did not say which one.

'You're a German,' Perry blurted out when they were enjoying a fish course of sea bass with a creamy prawn sauce.

'Enough,' said his father sternly. 'You may not be discourteous to our guest.'

'It's all right,' Hedda said gently, anxious to defuse the situation. Then, turning to Perry, she went on, 'I'm actually half Polish *and* half German,' she explained. 'My Polish name is Szymborska, and we Poles are on the same side as the English people.'

Charlie was embarrassed. It was her fault. She had told her parents about Hedda, and either they had told Perry or he had been eavesdropping.

'You'd be surprised,' she turned to her half-brother. 'Hedda is very accomplished, and she knows about lots of exciting things that you can't do.'

He was curious now. 'Like what…?' he asked.

'Well, for a start, Hedda speaks four languages,' Charlie began, but Perry's face suggested that he was not overly impressed.

'I'm doing Latin and Greek,' he responded, if a little defensively, 'and we start French next term.'

'She's also an expert shot with a pistol,' Charlie added. 'And she can take one to pieces and put it back together again faster than you can say *abracadabra*.'

This did seem to impress Perry, who returned to his fish course.

'This is quite delicious,' Hedda said to Madeleine, a little concerned that Charlie had let out a secret and anxious to change the subject. The polite manners of upper-class dinner party convention automatically accepted the diversion. But the exchange was not lost on Sir Manners Fitzgibbon.

CHAPTER 3

Two Years Previous – August 1938

'She should be thinking about coming out next year,' Sir Manners said rather firmly. 'After all, she's of an age to marry. Charlotte can be presented in March, as was her mother, and hopefully, she will meet someone suitable during the season.'

Madeleine chose her words carefully. 'Manny, you know I love you dearly. But in terms of years, I am a few nearer to Charlie than you are. So sometimes our conversation is more one of sisters – there isn't much of a generation gap at all.'

He twirled his wine glass by the stem. They were lunching privately, Brook having been asked to leave them. He thought of Hermione, his first wife, who had died in childbirth. Then of the day when Madeleine had been hired as governess and tutor soon after Charlotte's fifth birthday. One of the few young ladies who had been allowed to attend university, she had a good degree from Oxford. But business and the civil service were almost a closed world to young women in the 1930s. So her progressive but middle-class parents were relieved when Brook, at a Labour Party meeting, had mentioned that Sir Manners had sought his advice on the best way to recruit a suitable person. It was a better position than that of a junior teacher, and not just financially.

Manners had to be in London during the week but found increasingly that he looked forward to weekends, finding more and more excuses to be with Charlotte in the presence of her governess. Hermione had been a society beauty. Madeleine was no less alluring – her pretty, comely face was framed by chestnut hair styled almost to meet under her chin – and he could not help but notice that her conservative dress did not conceal an hourglass figure. But Madeleine was a different young lady from his late wife. She was, he realised immediately, intelligent to the point of being gifted. Yes, Madeleine had classical, academic learning. However, she was also highly interested in politics and world affairs. They often disagreed, but despite their employer-employee relationship (she did not consider herself to be in service), and although she was always careful to remain courteous, she was more than able to hold her own. As his grief disappeared over time, Manners came to realise that she was not just an indispensable asset for Charlotte. He was falling in love with her.

She did not accept his proposal immediately. Madeleine discussed her concerns with brutal honesty. There was an age difference, although ten years was not that unusual. He countered that they shared a love for Charlotte, who needed a mother. She told him that much as she cared for Charlie, she wanted a lover and the companionship of a kindred spirit, not money and a title, which his circle would assume to be her reason for their marriage. And she was not sure that she had the background to assume the wifely duties that society would expect. 'I'm honoured that you ask this of me,' she had responded, 'but equally, I would be grateful if you allow me a short time to consider.' His reply, as always, was unfailingly courteous.

Rescue from her concerns came in the unlikely form of Brook. She had her own rooms that were not on the servants' top floor, and she did not often venture into the kitchen – the preserve of cook and the junior staff – but they occasionally enjoyed conversation over a nightcap in Brook's small study. He noticed that she was becoming increasingly withdrawn and ill at ease, and not for the first time he asked if she was all right. 'Sir Manners has asked me to be his wife,' she told him late one evening. 'I know it's an honour to be asked, but…'

'You have a different station in life,' said Brook, not unkindly. 'And you're worried whether or not you would fit in. Assuming, perhaps, that you are mindful of accepting in the first place.'

'He's always been very kind to me,' she replied, 'and we both love little Charlotte. I couldn't bear to lose her.'

'You probably think of him as just a senior civil servant, perhaps?' he queried. 'A few years older than you, and rather conventional, perhaps even a bit set in his ways?'

'Well, he's always very correct – even formal, which makes him seem somehow rather distant. But I do like him, really I do. Of late, I have been increasingly drawn to him – I love the time the three of us spend together as a small family.'

'I'm going to let you into a few secrets,' Brook told her. 'We go back quite a way, me and the master.'

He put down his glass and settled to his story. 'We met in 1917, not long before the end of the Great War. I was a platoon sergeant at the time. He was a newly commissioned second lieutenant, straight out of officer training: a bit older than some, he volunteered at university, but still hardly more than a schoolboy, really. And in those days, a young officer's life was measured in a few short weeks, sometimes even in days.

'I had served under several officers,' he went on. 'The worst thought they had some hereditary right to command. They made stupid mistakes, and as a result, men died. On his first night with the platoon, Mr Fitzgibbon, as he was then, called me into his dugout. I can see it now as if it was yesterday – the smoke from a single candle, the stench of rats in the trenches and just a blanket to hide the light and keep out the cold.

'I want you to know,' he said to me, 'that I need your help. I shall have to rely heavily on your experience – because that's all we have between us. When I seem uncertain, please do not hesitate to tell me what I should do or say. And I don't care if some of the men do hear you. When I give an order, if you think it's hopeless, or even just not quite right, the same applies. In fact, the first order I am going to give you, right now, is that you are always to do precisely that – no ifs or buts.

'I found out later,' Brook went on, 'that his elder brother had given him that advice in no uncertain terms. He had learned it himself, the hard way. And he wanted to give his younger brother at least a chance of survival.' He paused. 'Unfortunately, though, it was Major Fitzgibbon who did not survive the war. It was just bad luck, an artillery shell…'

He paused, then, 'That night, before I was dismissed, I was ordered to form up the men in sections after stand-to at first light. It would have been difficult to assemble as a platoon in the trench system. He spoke to all the junior non-commissioned officers, and by the end of the week, he knew every single man's name. But he never asked any of us to do anything that he wasn't prepared to do himself.' He hesitated. His mind, thought Madeleine, was back in the trenches.

Suddenly, as if on cue, it returned to the study. 'The next time we were ordered to send out a fighting patrol at night to take a prisoner, he led the raiding party himself. I told him we needed a platoon commander and asked if he would send one of the other non-commissioned officers or me. I'll never forget what he said. He nodded towards the men along the trench and said, "How will sending you or one of the junior NCOs help me to earn their respect?"'

Brook took another sip of brandy. 'When we went over the top, I managed to persuade him to carry a rifle and leave his pistol in its holster. That way, he wasn't the immediate target for their machine-gunners. But he never let the platoon run into a hail of fire. He took my advice. We fought in sections, one trying to keep the Huns' heads down whilst the others advanced, one shell hole to another, till we could use our grenades and storm their trenches.

Yes, we lost good men, but the casualty rate in our platoon was the lowest in the battalion.'

He gave a sad smile. 'We all got parcels from home, but the officers fared better than we did. Most of them just enjoyed what they had, but I remember when someone sent Mr Fitzgibbon a bottle of brandy. There wasn't enough for everyone, but he worked out that there were at least ten good tots, so he organised a raffle. The winners shared the bottle poured into their mess tin. Afterwards, I went through all the pieces of paper that he had put into my tin hat. His name wasn't even in it. And I know now, although I didn't back then, that it was one expensive bottle of brandy.'

They sat in silence for a few seconds. 'Whatever you decide,' Brook went on quietly, 'don't worry about your situation. You have always been very considerate and polite to the staff – not like some governesses who try to lord it as if they were the equal of the aristocracy. You are both liked and respected. If you were to become mistress here,' he emphasised the 'were', 'I would do all I could to help you, and I know the staff would feel the same way.

'I know you will respect my confidence,' he said finally, 'but I just wanted you to know what sort of a man he is.'

Madeleine set down her glass. 'Thank you so much,' she replied, rising to leave and, in a gesture of thanks, touching his shoulder as she passed. If she were strictly honest, she thought to herself, perhaps she was more than a little in love with Sir Manners anyway, and Brook's kindness had certainly eased her concerns.

The Times in June 1927 reported that in a quiet ceremony at Chelsea Registry Office, Miss Madeleine Amelia Wood, daughter of Doctor and Mrs Samuel Wood of Framlingham, Suffolk, married Sir Manners Hubert Oswald Fitzgibbon of Stonebrook Hall, Leicestershire.

'It's 1938, Manners,' she insisted. 'Yes, girls still come out. Of course, most of them look for no more than a suitable marriage, but times are changing. And anyway, our Charlie isn't like that.' Manners smiled – he always called his daughter Charlotte, but her step-daughter was now always Charlie to Madeleine. And he loved the fact that since their marriage, she often referred to her as 'our Charlie'.

'You know as well as I do, we have talked about it often enough,' she persisted. 'Charlie has absolutely no ambition to wear a dress with silly puffy sleeves, as she calls them, then to lock one knee behind the other and just hope she doesn't catch a heel in her underskirt and fall on her bottom when it's her turn to makes a curtsey to the King and then the Queen. To her way of thinking, it's too trivial. She would rather go to university, and she wants a career, not a husband and a brood of children before she's twenty-one.' But, out of kindness to Manners, she did not tell him how Charlie had confided that 'doing the season' sounded like something more appropriate for a bitch on heat – which socially was precisely what it was.

They compromised. Charlotte – or Charlie – would not formally come out. Instead, she would spend some time at finishing school in Switzerland to improve – among other things – her languages; then they would consider the possibility of university.

*

The Berg Institute, set in a large country house in the hills above Geneva, provided a half-year course for the education of young ladies. Many – although not all – of its students were English. Without exception, however, they came from wealthy, upper-class families. The young ladies assembled in September and dispersed the following Easter. They would not have been presented at court but would attend most of the season after having spent two terms learning French and German plus the etiquette of society in three countries: England, France and Germany. Madeleine escorted Charlie to the Institute, stayed overnight in the best hotel in Geneva, then returned to England via Zürich airport the following day.

A maid showed Charlie to her room. From the Berg Institute's literature, she knew that it would be a spacious room with its own bathroom, still a novelty in England. However, she would share with one other student who would, whenever possible, be of a different nationality – the more to encourage language skills.

Her trunks were already on the floor. A young woman of similar age, who had been seated in an easy chair, put down her book and rose to greet her. 'I'm Anneliese Hoffmann,' she introduced herself. 'How do you do?'

'Charlie Fitzgibbon,' she replied automatically, taking Anneliese's hand. 'How do you do? And I say, you speak English.'

'Some,' said Anneliese with a smile. 'I come from Germany to learn French and English.'

Charlie was acutely aware of her inadequacy with languages. 'I have some French,' she replied, 'but only a little German – *nur ein wenig Deutsch.*'

'Then we will learn together – my English is not so perfect,' she replied. Charlie suspected that Anneliese's English far exceeded her knowledge of either French or German. 'Would you like a hand with your things?' she was asked, as Anneliese indicated the two trunks on the floor.

Although strangers, they formed an instant friendship. Anneliese was as tall as Charlie and had the fair hair and blue eyes typical of so many of her race. But it was not set in the plaits so favoured in Germany at that time – it settled luxuriously on her shoulders. She had a slightly sharp nose which gave her an aristocratic but intelligent appearance, but this was softened by a wide, sensuous mouth with full lips. She also had an excellent figure.

They settled into the routine of the Institute. Tuition was either in small groups or one-on-one tutorials. Anneliese suggested that they spoke English and German on alternate days, and they agreed to be unfailingly strict with corrections. Charlie compensated for her lack of fluency in German by helping her roommate with French, a language with which she had far less

29

experience. By December, Charlie's language skills had improved dramatically.

Anneliese, Charlie learned, came from a prosperous business family. 'My surname was originally associated with being members of minor landed gentry,' she told Charlie, 'but *Vati* is a manufacturer – we make electrical and military equipment, mostly radios and small weapons, in our factories in Germany. My uncle Berndt manages production, and Father handles the export agency, which is more easily run from Switzerland rather than back home.'

One morning Anneliese asked Charlie what she had planned for the Christmas break when they would have two weeks' holiday. She had, she told Charlie, already spoken with her mother. The family planned to leave their apartment near Zürich and drive over the border to the family home near Munich. Charlie was most welcome to join them if she did not wish to travel to England and back.

She wrote to her stepmother that same afternoon, pointing out that not only would it be much simpler administratively, but also that she would really like to go, and being immersed in a foreign language could only improve further her spoken German.

Madeleine replied that Perry would be disappointed. In fact, they all would, but her father also felt that they should not deny her such an exciting opportunity that would greatly broaden her horizons.

On the morning of Saturday 18th December, precisely one week before Christmas Day, Herr Hoffmann's Mercedes-Benz saloon drove through the arch and into the courtyard of the Berg Institute, her father at the wheel. Both parents alighted to greet and hug Anneliese. Charlie, who had been politely standing back, had always been teased at home because of her love of cars and all things mechanical. She took a moment to study the Mercedes. It was a four-door saloon, long and low, with a burgundy body and black wings and running boards. The solid wheels were also burgundy, inset with black hub caps centred with a silver

Mercedes star. A spare wheel was strapped into the clamshell passenger front wing, and at the front of a long bonnet sat a silver radiator also adorned with the Mercedes star and with two huge, silver headlamps sweeping back from either side. It was the most beautiful motor car she had ever seen.

Charlie was shaken from her reverie when Anneliese disengaged herself to make an introduction. Frau Helga Hoffmann was a tall, elegant woman – very much an older version of her daughter. She wore sensible flat shoes for travelling and a tweed suit with a mid-length skirt. Her long jacket suggested a hacking or hunting style. A small, trilby-like hat sported a coloured feather. Anneliese's father, Herr Dieter Hoffmann, must have been six foot tall and slim, with handsome features and light brown hair. He was clean-shaven and wore a well-tailored suit. He gave her a broad smile. Then, taking her hand, he gave her a slight bow and told her how much they were looking forward to her visit. Settled into the car, they all agreed that they would continue to speak only German for the duration.

The drive, Herr Hoffmann told Charlie over his shoulder, was about three hundred kilometres, and they would make a stop for lunch so that it would take the best part of the day. Charlie loved the new-car smell of leather and knew that if Herr Hoffmann were anything like her father, it would be his pride and joy. 'I do like your car,' she replied.

'It's a 230 saloon,' he told her. 'Six cylinders, if you are interested. This model was new last year.' Charlie couldn't help thinking that the Germans were probably more than their equal in automotive engineering.

A few kilometres before Munich, they turned off onto a road signed for 'Starnberg'. They passed through a good-sized village before eventually turning off again into a drive that led to a large country house built in a copy of the gothic style, with a red roof and white, timbered and stone walls. It was smaller than Stonebrook Hall, Charlie's home, but it was still a substantial dwelling. As they approached, Charlie caught a glimpse of a lake within the grounds to the rear of the house.

The Hoffmanns employed a housekeeper rather than a butler, and like Stonebrook, some footmen had been replaced by maids. The days passed quickly. They enjoyed walking – there was a hotel in the village, the Hotel Adler. It boasted a coffee room that served delicious cream tarts. Both young ladies were competent horsewomen, and in the evenings, they played cards or listened to the wireless. Presents were exchanged on Christmas Eve – Charlie's mother had sent a hamper from Fortnum's full of English delicacies for Herr and Frau Hoffmann, and Charlie had sent it on in her trunk that the Institute had despatched to await her arrival. That afternoon, she had placed it under the huge tree in the hall. The Hoffmanns were thrilled – the hamper turned out to be a great success.

They were joined for luncheon by Herr Hoffmann's elder brother and his wife on Christmas Day. Unlike Herr Hoffmann, Berndt was dark-haired, and although with similar looks to his brother, he was running to fat. His rather round-faced wife also had what might kindly be described as 'a generous figure'. By now, Charlie could follow the conversation almost perfectly. And unlike at home, there seemed to be no convention that business would not form part of the discussion.

'The Nazis are good for the economy,' Berndt confirmed, in response to a query from Anneliese's mother, 'but more and more of our production is being demanded by the Party, and we are in no position to refuse.'

'Surely we can decide what we do with our own production?' she argued. 'The export side is important: we have diversified away from a purely domestic market, and not least, we earn Swiss francs. Let us not forget what happened to our currency after the Great War.'

'I'm not sure how much you have been able to follow events here, living in Switzerland,' Berndt replied. 'Financially, our company has contributed generously to the Nazi Party, but although it has been encouraged, I am not of a mind to become a member.'

The Hoffmanns, Anneliese included, all nodded or murmured their agreement. But Charlie sensed underlying reasons that she should try to understand.

'I would never wish to be impolite or too inquisitive, Herr Hoffmann,' she addressed Berndt, 'but as a guest in your country, I do not understand?' The lift in her voice at the end of the sentence clearly indicated that this was a tentative enquiry.

'Do you mind...?' he asked his sister-in-law, presumably, Charlie thought, because politics was perhaps not normally a subject for conversation over Christmas lunch.

Helga shook her head. 'Clearly, it would be good for Charlie to understand what is happening to Germany,' she replied.

'Hitler and his Nazi Party have always been very anti-Jewish,' Berndt began. 'They blamed them for the loss of the Great War, even though they comprised less than one per cent of the entire population. Now, they are no longer allowed to be citizens – just 'subjects'. They are not allowed to marry non-Jews, and since 1936 they have been banned from the professions. They are also banned from working in any government or political roles. In November,' he went on, 'after the son of a deported Polish Jew shot the third secretary to the embassy in Paris, *Kristallnacht* saw the smashing of Jewish shop windows and widespread looting across the country. Hundreds of homes and synagogues were burned down. Some ninety Jews were murdered, and in the days that followed, thirty thousand more were arrested and transported to Nazi camps. Finally, earlier this month, a law was passed forcing them to sell their businesses – always for ridiculously low prices – to Aryan Germans.'

He set down his knife and fork and steepled his fingers. 'Some of our best engineers and designers are Jewish,' he told her. 'So far, my financial support to the Party has meant that we have been able to retain them. But for how long, I don't know...' His voice trailed off despondently.

'We don't think the rest of the world has much idea, if any,' Anneliese's father took up the narrative, 'about the persecution, or the camps.' He looked very directly at Charlie.

'We know who your father is,' he went on, speaking slowly and very deliberately, 'and our enquiries in Switzerland have given us an idea of where he works and the nature of his duties. When you have an opportunity, and it can only be very privately and verbally, never in writing, you would be doing a great service if you could make him aware of the situation here. Not just of what is happening to the Jews and others such as intellectuals seen as a threat to the Nazi Reich, but also of the fact that we are convinced Herr Hitler intends to take Germany to war.'

Charlie was stunned. It occurred to her that these people, whoever the 'we' were, knew more about her father than she did.

'Thank you for the explanation,' she said quietly. 'Please be assured that I shall do as you ask.'

Anneliese, her mother and her aunt also seemed shocked by the turn of the conversation, which clearly they had not been expecting.

'Enough,' said Helga Hoffmann firmly. 'Dieter, this is supposed to be a Christmas celebration. Let us finish lunch. Afterwards, I know you have decanted a fine bottle of port from that lovely hamper. We will all take a glass. I shall play the pianoforte, and we will sing carols. Perhaps we should start with "*Stille Nacht, heilige Nacht*" – Charlie is our guest, so just this once, as an exception, we will sing "Silent Night" in English.'

And they did. To Charlie's surprise, they all knew the words by heart.

CHAPTER 4

France, Late May 1940

'Stop,' ordered Tadzio. Their tank rocked briefly, fore and aft, on its axis. They were somewhere west of Arras. German ground forces had attacked through the Ardennes, threatening to cut off the British Expeditionary Force from the French Army. Their assault on Arras had been defeated, and they were retreating in some disarray. The Mk I Matilda was well armoured and could often survive a hit from a German tank, but not from 88mm anti-tank artillery, which had finally broken the attack.

He knew only too well that British doctrine had failed to keep up with the German development of blitzkrieg. Between the wars, tanks were still seen as an adjunct to trench warfare, so their 'Mattie', despite having the heaviest armour on the battlefield, was equipped only with a Vickers .303 heavy machine gun. Its four thousand rounds were ideal in an infantry support role, leading troops across trenches or defending strong points. But it was absolutely useless against enemy armour. The new Matilda Mk IIs had a two-pounder anti-tank gun as the main armament, but rumour had it there were only just over twenty of them available. And with the Matilda Mk I, as an infantry support weapon, the designers had not anticipated a need for speed. On the road, it was flat out at eight miles per hour. Cross-country, it could just about manage five and a half.

Tadzio had been deployed as part of a reconnaissance screen, reporting on the German advance as they pushed the British Force back towards the coast. The General Staff intention was to hold the enemy by day, then fall back to a new pre-prepared position overnight. But, in practice, there was a substantial degree of chaos. Worse still, Tadzio had only a vague idea of where they were, and the radio had given up the ghost twenty-four hours ago. Not that it had ever been much use in the first place.

Still, 'orders is orders', as he had voiced to Ted Hughes, his driver. They would stay where they were until they had something worth reporting, then fall back and either try again to radio a report or wait till they found some of their own units who could pass on a message. The trouble was that the German Panzer Mk IVs *did* have an anti-tank round for their 7.5cm main armament, not to mention two auxiliary 7.92mm machine guns. And it was hard for the Mattie to run away from a tank that could touch twenty-five miles per hour on a good surface, and pretty much ten even off road.

Well camouflaged up on a track and facing into the wood, the branches overhead gave excellent cover. Behind their tank, they overlooked a shallow valley of undulating farmland. Then, about half a mile away, the other crest came to life. First, a line of Panzers halted hull down on the horizon, showing only their turrets, then supporting infantry formed up alongside them.

'We're in the shit,' said Ted Hughes, his cockney accent still strange to Tadzio's ear. 'Must be at least a battalion plus coming at us, armour and infantry.' The enemy began their descent into the valley. 'We'll mount up,' Tadzio decided quickly. 'As soon as we're through the wood, we can find cover again before they see us. After that, we head west and look for our own line.' They cleared the wood and soon entered a small village. On the other side, they would still be screened from the advance. Some villagers stood at the roadside, sullenly watching the retreating British tank. Now they were out of the village and into farmland. Tadzio decided to sacrifice speed for cover and made good use of the thick hedgerows and occasional patches of scrub and woodland.

*

Oberleutnant Conrad Fuchs was badly shaken, as was his gunner, Helmut, in the rear seat. The sortie had started so well. Their Junkers Ju87 Stuka dive bomber had unloaded its main 250-kilogram bomb onto an enemy heavy artillery emplacement, taking out at least one eight-inch howitzer and killing its crew instantly. But no sooner had they recovered from a near-vertical dive angle than an RAF Hurricane bounced their flight. It scattered, and to Fuchs' dismay, the Hurricane closed in for a kill. They were vulnerable. He threw his aircraft all over the sky, but it was probably just a matter of time… until a shout of triumph over his headphones told him that against the odds, his gunner had found his target. Trailing white smoke, the Hurricane peeled off and headed for home. They had been incredibly fortunate. Resuming their original course, they were alone in the sky when, from four thousand feet, he saw the lone tank that looked to have avoided the leading elements of a distant advancing force.

It was a perfect target, and he still had four fifty-kilo bombs under the wing mounts. He would attack from a rear quarter, and if he did not use the siren, the tank's commander might not hear him above the noise of the engine and tracks, at least not until the last minute. This time he favoured a shallower approach – not entirely trusting the automatic pull-out mechanism, designed to take over if the pilot blacked out under the six times gravitational force recovery from a near-vertical attack. He turned into a gentle dive, aiming for the turret. But if he only managed to damage the unprotected caterpillar track and wheels, at least he could cripple the tank.

Tadzio heard the Stuka, but by the time he had screamed a warning to Ted, the pilot had already released. He ducked into the turret as the aircraft screamed overhead, pulling up from its dive. There seemed to be a double crump of explosions before a massive detonation from the tank's front, forward of his driver. Tadzio's head was thrown against the hatch as they lifted and slewed violently sideways. He blacked out.

He came to minutes later, heavily bruised and with a splitting headache. Miraculously the tank was not on fire, but the engine had stopped. Only half-conscious, he climbed out through the turret hatch and, supporting himself as best he could, stumbled alongside the tank to check on Ted, who had been driving with head and shoulders exposed, the rectangular hatch open behind him. His driver's head lolled to one side. Tadzio climbed onto the glacis plate. There was what looked to be a serious head wound from a shard of metal. He checked Ted's bloody neck for a pulse, then closed his friend's sightless eyes. Tadzio jumped down and crossed the front of the tank to see the mangled wheels and track. Mattie was going nowhere.

Tadzio knew that his priority was to put distance between himself and the tank. Entering Mattie for the last time, he retrieved his small pack and stuffed it with their remaining rations, some clean underwear, a small medical pack, his washing and shaving gear, and, finally, a map and compass. He fumbled in the bin for the belt and holster containing his Webley & Scott Mk IV .38 revolver, together with four boxes each containing twelve cartridges. Finally, he opened the fifth box and pushed six of its contents into the chambers. He reckoned that with a total of fifty-four rounds, he would either survive any encounter or be dead.

He knew the enemy axis of advance and thought that they had probably watched it from somewhere near the Germans' left flank. The fastest way to avoid meeting them would be to head east, but that would take him away from the British lines and the coast. That said, if he went west, he would almost certainly not clear the enemy formation. He might be able to hide whilst it passed by, but that was by no means certain. Tadzio decided to head inland.

38

After a while, he felt confident that he had avoided the German advance. Staying close to hedges as much as he could, he watched the first main road he came to for some time. A Mercedes open staff car drove by, left to right, with two officers in the rear seat and a small swastika fluttering from a front wing. It confirmed what he already suspected: the Germans had passed through at this point unopposed. He was behind enemy lines.

By dusk, Tadzio thought he had put probably ten miles between himself and the remains of his tank. He had no fear of pursuit – there was no way the enemy would detach from a major assault to search for a solitary survivor, who might not have lived for long anyway. His immediate aim was to avoid being taken as a prisoner of war. After that, he would try either to make his way to the coast, which he realised would be almost impossible because of the defensive battle still being fought by the British Expeditionary Force, or perhaps he could find another route, either south through Spain or east into Switzerland. He settled for the night in the barn of a deserted farm. The small cottage was tempting, and although the larder had been looted, it was otherwise undamaged and deserted. But he knew that if German troops turned up, the barn would offer the best chance of either concealment or escape. He opened a tin of bully beef for supper, then settled into a pile of straw and fell fast asleep.

It was still dark when he woke. But the pre-dawn could not be far off. It was the habit in the British Army. When they were in the field, it was always 'stand-to' at first and last light. Statistically, these were the most likely times for an enemy assault. Then he remembered. Something had caused him to wake up. Had it been the end of a dream, or the unmistakable sound of a door shutting, perhaps accidentally, with a slight slam?

Tadzio was thankful now that he had been so tired he had not even taken off his boots. The belt, holster and weapon had been by his side throughout the night. He raised the flap, withdrew the revolver and cocked it. The barn door he had left slightly open, the better to hear if anyone approached. There was a flickering light from a candle in the kitchen overlooking the farmyard; a shadow passing over the window told him that someone was moving inside. Tadzio knew the cottage had been empty the night before, so quite possibly one or more of the German invaders, wanting a comfortable billet, was still inside, although there was no sign of any vehicle. Still, not all of their infantry had transport...

He watched for several minutes, but there were no other lights in the building. Tadzio moved to stand outside the door. It had not been locked previously, so it was probably still unlocked now. He could hear noises that suggested someone might be opening and closing cupboard doors, but no conversation. He would have the advantage of being in shadow, and whoever was there would have lost their night vision. Very gently, he unlatched the door and pushed it open, at the same time lifting his revolver as his eyes swept the room.

A young woman turned with a sharp intake of breath, one hand raised to her mouth. Tadzio lowered his weapon, then winked at her and raised a forefinger to his lips in the international gesture for silence. He waved his hand to indicate the rest of the cottage. The trouble was, he hardly knew a word of French. 'Germans?' he asked softly, raising the inflection to make the word a question.

'*Je suis seule,*' she whispered. Then, more confidently, in heavily accented English, 'I am alone.'

'You speak English?' he asked, relieved at his good fortune.

'A little,' she replied haltingly, 'I learn at school.'

He took a moment to look at the young woman. She was bedraggled, and her coat was filthy with mud, as were her shoes, which were really small boots. Her hands and face were heavily grimed with dirt. Twists of dark, chestnut hair fell to her shoulders in rats' tails. Beneath her striking green eyes were streaks clearly made by tears. She was slim and quite tall. Underneath that coat, he suspected that she had a good figure. And undoubtedly, despite all the tear marks and grime, she was pretty.

40

'Tommy,' she said, looking at his uniform. If she wanted to call him that, thought Tadzio, it would do for now.

'You?' he asked, pointing a finger.

'I am called Liliane,' she replied. Her voice did not rise or fall. He sensed that there was absolutely no feeling in the reply. In response to his next question, Liliane explained in broken English and with some hand signing that she and her parents had left their farm, fleeing from the advancing Germans. They had taken their small car, heading for Paris, where they had relatives. But two German aeroplanes had fired on the refugee column. Afterwards, someone said they were Messerschmitts. She had dived to the roadside, but her parents had not been quick enough. She stifled a sob.

'Papa try to help *Maman*. He shot in head. She die, two, three minutes, in my arms.' Liliane wiped her eyes and nose on her sleeve. 'The car... finished.' She told him that she could have gone on, but it was a long way and dangerous for a young woman alone. Already some of the men were not behaving well... She trailed off.

'I leave column,' she went on, seeming to pull herself together, 'go home. Have friends, neighbours, some still there. I have house to live,' she said with some resignation, 'so take chance with Germans.'

'Where's home?' he asked.

'Five, six kilometres.' Her index finger pointed in an easterly direction. 'Small farm, like this. I look for food – not eat today.'

Together they finished searching the kitchen. Although the larder was empty, a more thorough search than Tadzio's the previous evening uncovered some bottled fruit stowed away at the back of a shelf under a long, wooden preparation board. She unscrewed the metal ring and lifted the glass top off a jar of plums. 'You want eat?' she asked nervously.

'Wait a minute,' he said quietly, 'I have some meat.' The sky was brightening, and in the yard, it was much lighter now. Returning to the barn, he looked out over the countryside, but no Germans were in sight. From his small pack, he extracted the last tin of bully beef. But at least they would have a good breakfast. By the time he returned to the kitchen, Liliane had found two small plates and some cutlery. They ate quickly, in case they had to leave in a hurry. But they were not disturbed.

Afterwards, Tadzio pushed his chair back and lit a cigarette. 'What are you going to do now?' he asked her.

She shrugged. 'Go home, stay there,' she said matter-of-factly, 'if Germans not find me and house good.'

'I'm going that way – we could go together,' he offered. 'But I have to find some clothes and get rid of this uniform. We could look upstairs – there might be something useful for you, as well.'

The main bedroom yielded a wardrobe, half of which contained a couple of cheap dresses and one good, warm jacket that Liliane thought would be better than her filthy overcoat. A man's working clothes hung in the other half – patched and worn but clean. The refugees had obviously taken their best things with them. Not that it mattered – even if he could have fitted into them, the trousers would have ended a good two inches above his ankles. He went into the second bedroom. From the model aeroplane hung on a wall and the football on the floor in one corner, it had clearly been a boy's room.

On a dressing table stood a photograph of a well-built young soldier in uniform. In a drawer, he found a French identity card. The picture on the left-hand page was of the same person, a young man of about Tadzio's age. On the right-hand page was a fingerprint. It had been issued by the local *Préfecture*. Presumably, it was left behind because its owner would have been given military identification. The photograph looked nothing remotely like Tadzio, but he put it in his pocket anyway.

This time the wardrobe contained a good selection of civilian clothing, and it was more or less the correct size. Tadzio avoided what must have been the young man's Sunday best, settling for a pair of heavy working trousers, a good shirt, a sleeveless pullover and a well-worn jacket. Best of all, he found a pair of boots that were almost the right size. His Army ones would have been a dead giveaway.

Tadzio kept his ID discs – they would identify him as a soldier and might just save him from being shot as a spy. He discarded everything else, including the Webley, and threw the lot, the bundle weighted with a couple of heavy stones, into a rainwater barrel in the yard. Liliane seemed to have accepted his suggestion that they travel together – presumably, if she had even considered it, thinking that the safety of having a male companion outweighed the risk of being with an Englishman.

They set off, following narrow country lanes, often scrambling through hedges to take to the fields. But they were not troubled by passing traffic. It was as if, after the intensity of yesterday, the enemy had passed on and peace had returned to the land. The only activity was in the air, but the planes were much higher today, on their way to and from supporting the now distant advance.

They had left at ten. Tadzio checked the time. They had been walking for almost two hours. To his horror, he realised that he was still wearing his British Army issue watch. He began to undo the strap.

'Do you have the time?' he asked Liliane.

Without thinking, she pushed back the sleeve of her jacket to show him her wristwatch. Thankfully, he threw his own into the long grass.

'There,' she told him, pointing to a bend and making a curving motion with her right hand. They rounded it and turned onto a wide track of dry, packed mud. In places, potholes washed out by the rain had been filled with stone chippings. It was a long drive, bordered by the occasional tree and a sparse hedge. As a precaution, they crossed through it and approached slowly, going back onto the drive only when they were almost at the front of the house. It was a solid, brick-built two-storey farmhouse with a slate roof. It looked rather more prosperous than the cottage they had left earlier. Tadzio could see a large barn behind and to one side of the house. The farmyard and outbuildings were to the rear of the property.

They crossed an open area of cobbles about ten metres deep. 'The front door is still closed,' Liliane whispered, although there was no one within earshot. She produced a large key from her pocket. 'I take from Papa…'

A few steps behind, he waited as she moved forward to unlock the door. It was opened, suddenly, from the inside. Liliane gasped and stepped back. An officer in the field grey uniform of the German Army stood facing them, a pistol in his right hand held waist high and aimed towards them. Two more Germans appeared, one at each corner of the house, holding at the waist what looked to Tadzio to be one of the new MP40 Schmeisser sub-machine guns. There could be no escape.

CHAPTER 5

The officer turned his back on them, walked along a short hall, then turned right. The two soldiers closed up behind them, using their barrels to nudge Liliane and Tadzio to follow. They entered a good-sized dining room. The soldiers took station just inside the door. A long table – it looked to be mahogany – was covered with maps and a manpack radio, its aerial almost touching the ceiling, had been placed on the floor beside it. Tadzio was thinking furiously. Unless he took the initiative, they were finished.

'*Gott sei Dank sind Sie angekommen*,' he said. 'Thank God you have arrived.' The officer was surprised to hear what seemed to be an excellent command of German.

'Who are you,' he asked in the same language, 'and who is the woman?' He looked at her clothing. 'Is she French?'

'My name is Gerhard Huber,' he replied, using the first name that came into his head – a German friend from his schooldays. 'I'm also German, brought up in Bromberg, which used to be part of Prussia until the Allies gave it to the Poles after the Great War...' his shoulders lifted, as if in disbelief, 'even though about eighty per cent of the inhabitants were German. After that, it was called Bydgoszcz.'

45

'So what are you doing here,' asked the officer, 'and I ask you again, who's the woman?'

Tadzio recognised the rank epaulette of an *Oberleutnant*, but flattery never did any harm. On the contrary, he promoted him to captain. And besides, a civilian would not be familiar with *Wehrmacht* military ranks.

'*Herr Hauptmann*,' he went on, 'I am an engineer. A few years ago, when it was not easy to find work in Germany because of the recession, I took a job at the Citroën factory near Paris. When war was declared, the police confiscated my *Ausweiss*. I think they were going to intern me, but when I heard of the invasion by our forces, I decided to return to my homeland and offer my services to the Reich. Yesterday I met this French woman – her parents were killed in a refugee column heading south, and she was trying to return home. Today we travelled together, and now we have arrived. This is – or was – their farm. My intention is to stay and rest for a day or two, then continue my journey.'

A private soldier knocked and entered, wiping oily hands on a piece of cloth, but stopped between the two guards. 'Excuse me, *Herr Oberleutnant*,' he apologised, 'but you said to let you know as soon as possible.'

'Well?' replied the officer calmly, obviously not annoyed at the interruption.

'I'm not really a mechanic, sir, like I said. I tried my best, but it's no go. I just can't get the damn thing started.'

The officer turned back to Tadzio. 'You said you are an engineer. What sort?' The question was asked abruptly, but even so, the *Oberleutnant* did not seem at all threatening, perhaps just impatient.

'Automobiles, sir,' he replied politely. 'At the car factory,' he added for good measure. 'I don't know what it is that won't start, but maybe I can help?'

'*Ja bitte*,' said the officer, 'yes please.' He looked at the soldier who had been trying to wipe the oil from his hands. 'Go with him,' he ordered, 'and tell him what you have already done. You too,' he added, nodding at one of the two guards. Obviously, thought Tadzio, he was trusted, but not completely.

There were two *Kübelwagen* in the farmyard behind the house. One had the cover over its rear engine hinged up. 'Bastard thing fired at first,' said the soldier who had been working on it, 'but wouldn't keep running. Now, it won't even do that.'

The only two things Tadzio knew about the *Kübelwagen* was that Ferdinand Porsche had designed it, and it was based on a Volkswagen. He knew absolutely nothing about the detailed innards of this particular vehicle's mechanics, but his training at Bovington's Driving and Maintenance Wing had been thorough. It kicked in now.

'I'm going to make sure there's a spark,' he told the soldier, who said his name was Willi. It took only seconds to remove a spark plug, reconnect the lead and hold the base of the plug against the engine block. 'Just give it a quick turnover, Willi,' he instructed. A big fat spark jumped the gap. The problem probably wasn't electrical. Tadzio disconnected the fuel line from the carburettor. 'Same again,' he called out to Willi. The fuel should have spurted out. It barely dribbled.

It didn't take long to trace the trouble to the strainer underneath the fuel tank. Willi came round to the front to watch. It was full of bits of muck. Thanks to the use of Willi's finger, they lost some fuel, but not much. Tadzio cleaned the strainer, replaced part of the fuel line and, as a precaution, blew back till he heard the sound of bubbles in the tank.

With everything reconnected, he borrowed Willi's rag and wiped his own now-filthy hands. 'Give it another try,' he suggested. 'You might need the choke.'

After a couple of turns, they were rewarded with the breathy sound of an air-cooled engine as it spluttered to life then settled to a steady tick-over. Tadzio gave the connections one last check and closed the hatch. Willi returned to stand beside him. It had been straightforward, but the young lad was clearly impressed. 'It should be all right,' Tadzio told him, 'but when you have a chance, clean out the tank. And you saw what I did, so if it happens again, you know what to do.'

Tadzio returned to the house, followed by his guard, who had not said a word. But by now, the weapon was on his shoulder. 'Dirty fuel blocked a filter, sir,' he informed the *Oberleutnant*, 'but it's running now. And I've shown your young soldier how to fix it if it happens again. He seems a bright lad,' he added, hoping to put Willi back in the officer's good books.

'Thank you, Herr Huber,' the officer said courteously. 'We are reconnaissance troops, so we must catch up with the advance. I have released the young woman – I think she is in the kitchen. But, unfortunately, I do not speak French, and she has no German, so please tell her that I hope there is no damage to her home, other than a broken lock when we forced the kitchen door. And I wish you a safe journey back to the Fatherland.'

Tadzio was relieved. His one worry, all along, was that he might be ordered to translate from German to French, which would have blown his cover. But it had not happened.

The *Oberleutnant* collected his cap from the table and shouted for his men to follow. Seconds later the two vehicles disappeared down the drive. Liliane appeared at the door. 'They take some food,' she said haltingly, 'but they not take all. And is much mud in bedrooms. I think because from upstairs is view.'

He followed her into a good-sized kitchen. Liliane opened a tin of meat and prepared a few vegetables left in the larder. She also fetched a bottle of wine from a cellar that the Germans had seemingly not had time to explore. After a modest supper, towards last light, she beckoned that he should follow her upstairs.

'This one for you,' she indicated. It was a single guest room that overlooked the farmyard and the fields beyond. The bed was already made up. 'I sleeped next door,' she explained, 'but now I take the room of my parents. It gives view on the front.'

For now, the only sensible option was a good night's sleep. They were safe, thought Tadzio, but for how long, and where on earth would he go from here?

*

Almost a year after the outbreak of war, Captain (Acting Major) Charles Kaye-Stevens, the Royal Worcestershire Regiment, applied to return to regimental duty. As he told his superior officer, the defence attaché to the embassy at Bern, he was not comfortable holding down a desk job whilst his regiment was on active service, albeit that it was now reforming in England after the Dunkirk disaster.

Brigadier James Summerton invited him to sit down. 'I applaud your sentiment, my dear chap,' he began, 'but your request has come at what I can only describe as an awkward moment.'

'Sir?' he queried.

'You were selected for this appointment because you studied languages at Oxford – French and German, as it happens, two of the three widely used here.'

'Yes, sir,' he argued, 'but my duties are largely pushing paperwork and social. There must be plenty of civilians with my language skills, and if I may say so, they would probably enjoy the social side much more than I do. First and foremost, I'm a soldier. Wouldn't I be more use in the field, perhaps commanding a company?'

'Don't do yourself down,' said the brigadier kindly. 'You have developed a lot of useful contacts since you've been here. But something new has come up. We want you to move to Zürich.'

'May I ask why, sir?' he queried.

The brigadier pushed a photograph across his desk. 'Take a look at that,' he ordered.

'A very pretty young lady,' observed Charles, 'but I have no idea who she is.'

'Her name's Anneliese Hoffmann. She's a German national. Her father's an industrialist living in Zürich. The family comes from somewhere near Munich, where they manufacture military weapons and electronics. Her father, Herr Hoffmann, handles the export side of the business. According to London, they are probably loyal Germans, but we know that they are definitely anti the Hitler regime.'

'But where do I come in, sir?' asked Charles.

'Some eighteen months ago,' came the reply, 'the family opened a channel of communication with us. At the time, its purpose was to let us know what Hitler was doing to the Jews and to warn that the damn house-painter was almost certainly planning on another war in Europe – there was quite a lot of useful detail.

'Anneliese was at finishing school here in Switzerland with the daughter of one of our people in London,' he went on. 'It seems she intends to apply for a job with the German administration in Paris. I don't want to stray too much into the background, but if she does, we need to know as much as possible – what she will be doing, who she will be working for and, most important of all, when she will take up her appointment.'

'It sounds like you want me to be a spy,' said Charles somewhat uncertainly. Like many of his class, he looked upon this sort of activity as unbecoming for a gentleman.

'Not really,' came the reply. 'Yes, we want you to befriend the family, particularly Anneliese, and yes, we need the information, but there's nothing sordid about it. Just try to establish a close, ongoing friendship. We're not asking you to tup the damn woman; we just want to know what's happening.'

Charles winced at the rather coarse farming analogy, but otherwise, he recognised that the request was not unreasonable as part of his duties.

'What do I tell her?' he asked. 'Presumably I'm not going to introduce myself as a member of the embassy?'

'That's exactly what we want you to do,' said the brigadier. 'Anneliese Hoffmann shared a room at the Berg Institute, a finishing school here in Switzerland, with a young British woman called Charlie Fitzgibbon. They got on well. So well, in fact, that Miss Fitzgibbon spent Christmas with the family at their home near Munich. Over the holiday, Charlie Fitzgibbon was asked to pass on the information about Hitler's regime. That was how the Hoffmann family opened their channel of communication.

'We think,' the brigadier continued, 'that were you to introduce yourself to Miss Hoffmann, the approach would not be entirely unwelcome.'

Which was why, the following Tuesday morning, Charles found himself standing on a Zürich street corner outside an office block, looking at a selection of small brass plates mounted on the brickwork alongside a glass door. One, on the second floor, simply stated the name: Hoffmann. From his briefing notes, he knew that Anneliese was working for her father. Unfortunately, there was no nearby coffee house within sight of the building. He spent an uncomfortable hour standing on the same side of the street so that he could not be seen from a window above.

He was rewarded just after twelve when Anneliese Hoffmann left the building and walked away from him. She wore a light grey close-fitting pencil skirt and a slightly flared, tight-waisted short jacket that made no secret of a very trim figure. He followed her for perhaps five minutes till Anneliese entered a fairly small but rather smart restaurant, clearly not one intended for junior office workers. She took a table for four by the window and ordered from a waiter.

He entered and approached, standing back just a little to not seem intimidating. '*Bitte darf ich hier sitzen?*' he asked politely, with a slight smile, indicating one of the chairs opposite. Her jacket was now on the back of the chair beside her, next to the window. The two top buttons of a rather formal white blouse were undone, showing just a slight swell of her breasts.

Surprised, she looked up to see an impeccably dressed, dark-haired young man, perhaps a little older but not much. He wore a beautifully tailored charcoal-grey suit with a crisp white shirt, the

51

cuffs fastened with plain gold links. His silk tie was pale blue, and a white handkerchief showed from his breast pocket. An aquiline nose above slightly full lips and a well-defined chin added to his good looks.

'There are plenty of other tables,' she replied, without dismissing him completely.

'This one is the most attractive,' he answered in English. She could not help a slight intake of breath. She knew intuitively that this was no accidental meeting. The waiter returned with a tray bearing a glass of white wine that he set before her. Charles's head inclined towards her glass. 'May I join you?' he asked, still in the same language.

She was intrigued, wondering where this was all leading. And unless she agreed to his request, she was not going to find out. Seeing another customer, her waiter had returned. '*Noch ein Glas Wein bitte*,' she ordered, indicating with her hand that the stranger should take a seat opposite. Anneliese said nothing till the waiter reappeared and set down a second glass. Her new companion was also content to wait.

She took a sip then looked at him directly over the rim. He was struck by the intense blue of her eyes. 'All right,' she said, 'so who are you, and what do you want?' Her English was educated and accomplished.

He said, 'My name is Charles Kaye-Stevens, and I am attached to our embassy in Bern. As for now,' he continued, 'I wish only to make your acquaintance.'

'I'm not sure that I believe you, Mr Kaye-Stevens,' she said directly.

It was essential to earn her trust, something he felt that only a degree of honesty would achieve. 'It's Major Kaye-Stevens,' he offered. 'And I am talking to you because over a year ago, your family sent us a message through Miss Fitzgibbon.' He paused, but there was no reaction. 'Of course,' he pressed on, 'we were grateful to receive it. But now, airmail from Switzerland to England is suspended, and although sea mail is possible via Madrid or Lisbon, as you know, it is a long, tortuous process. Plus, of course, it may be subject to interception or censorship. So I am asked only to say that should you – or your family – wish to contact Miss Fitzgibbon or her family again, the facilities of our embassy would be at your disposal.'

Their waiter returned, clearly assuming that they would wish to order lunch. Anneliese ordered *Schnipo* and a side salad. Seeing that he did not understand, she explained, 'It's a childhood favourite, a Swiss contraction of the words *schnitzel* and *pommes frites*. The better ones are made with veal, as they do here, rather than pork. Why don't you try it?'

The ice had been broken. Two intelligent young people enjoyed an excellent lunch. Again, being perfectly honest, he told her that he had been ordered to Zürich to meet her, and he was living in a serviced apartment owned by the embassy. But he knew absolutely no one in the city. The conversation was easy but general until they discovered a mutual love of music. 'There is a concert on Saturday,' she told him. '*Vati* has a permanent balcony box, so we will be going. The main item is the Brahms second piano concerto. If an *Engländer* doesn't mind listening to German music, would you care to join us?'

As soon as she had spoken, Anneliese wondered whether the invitation had been too obvious. And it had been what the English would call 'fast', to say the least. But she knew her father would wish to meet Charles Kaye-Stevens. No… he had made the first move. She could have rejected him, but every instinct told her – at this stage – to reciprocate.

The concert, she informed him, would be at the *Tonhalle Zürich*, a hall with perhaps the finest acoustics in Europe. The orchestra would be the Berlin Philharmonic, under the famous conductor Wilhelm Furtwängler. What's more, the pianist would be Edwin Fischer, famous for his interpretation of Brahms. 'Furtwängler is known to be Hitler's favourite conductor of Wagner,' she added, 'and Fischer usually likes to conduct unconventionally from the piano, so I suspect this concert has been put together as a spectacular propaganda coup. Still, it should be quite something, so I would not want to miss it. And it's what you English call white tie,' she concluded.

'That is an extremely kind invitation,' he said without hesitation, 'and I would very much like to accept. But perhaps it would be more correct, if not to say courteous, if I were first to introduce myself to your parents – or at least to your father?'

She was only too aware that he was absolutely right. 'I hope you will not think me too forward,' she asked, 'if I suggest that we have a light supper together this evening? You could call for me at the apartment. My parents will be at home... perhaps at seven?' They exchanged addresses and telephone numbers. Anneliese did not try to analyse the reason for her suggestion. Perhaps it was to pursue the connection with England. But she also rather liked the young British officer.

Afterwards, for his part, Charles could not help wondering how much events had been driven by circumstances or to what extent it had been more of a thoroughly enjoyable lunch with a charming young woman. So it was still with mixed emotions that he paid off a taxi in an upmarket residential district and was admitted by a uniformed concierge to a low-rise block of apartments. He was expected, and invited to take a lift to the penthouse. Another elevator, he noticed, served the floors beneath. He emerged into a spacious hall to find Anneliese waiting for him.

'Come and meet Mother and Father,' she greeted him with a smile and led the way from the white marble-tiled hall into a large lounge with a breathtaking view over Lake Zürich. It was expensively furnished. A large, oriental carpet almost covered a parquet floor. Herr Hoffmann rose to shake his hand. 'Anneliese has told us about you,' he said in German by way of introduction, 'and this is my wife, Helga.' Charles turned slightly to face an elegant blonde woman – unmistakably an older version of Anneliese.

Helga Hoffmann smiled and remained seated on a chaise longue. He closed his heels in the German fashion and made a slight bow. 'How do you do,' he said politely in the same language.

If Herr Hoffmann felt in any way embarrassed by the presence of a man with whose country his own was at war, he was too civilised to show it. They made polite conversation for a few minutes, after which Herr Hoffmann remarked that he was pleased Charles would be able to join them on Saturday. Anneliese thanked her father – clearly, there had been much discussion beforehand – and excused them both so that they could depart for their evening. The introduction and their brief meeting, Charles thought, seemed to have gone well. But he was acutely aware that it had been important more for what had not been said. He had been accepted as a friend of the family, which indicated that Herr Hoffmann was, at the very least, content to retain his channel of communication.

CHAPTER 6

Tadzio was woken by a cockerel crowing. He didn't know what time it was, having had to throw away his British Army watch, but it was not fully light, so he guessed somewhere around five in the morning. Looking over the fields, then to the horizon and up at the sky, it promised to be a fine day. The countryside seemed deceptively peaceful, but England and France were at war.

He pulled on the shirt he had discarded last night. It did not smell too fresh on its third day now, but there was no alternative; it was the only one he had – just one of the many problems to be faced that day.

The kitchen was empty, but the door to the farmyard was open. They had closed it last night, so Liliane had to be somewhere outside. He found her in a henhouse, searching in the straw for eggs. A few birds scratched at the dirt floor.

'Father turned them loose before we left,' she explained, 'but some of them have come back because they're hungry. There's more feed in the barn. I'll fetch some now and leave the door open. Perhaps we shall be lucky and rescue a few more.' She had spoken in French, then realised from his expression that he had barely understood a word. So she explained again, in broken English.

56

They toured the outbuildings and saw that several cows had found their way into the dairy and were waiting in stalls, ready to be milked. Tadzio found a clean bucket and churn, rolled up his sleeves, and settled onto a stool. Liliane was surprised and delighted to discover Tadzio knew what he was doing. He told her, wistfully, about his farm in Poland. Only then did she learn his nationality and real name.

They soon had a full churn. Liliane explained, not without difficulty that she would make butter, but for now, they had fried eggs and potatoes. After breakfast, she took him to what had been her parents' room. 'He take some, but not all,' she said, showing him the clothes left in her father's wardrobe and chest of drawers. The underwear and shirts were, to his relief, more or less the correct size.

Over the next few days, they worked hard to bring a semblance of order back to the farm. Tadzio reckoned that he was reasonably safe for the moment, but they agreed that if any Germans arrived, he would hide in the copse behind the barn. It could be reached unobserved by anyone approaching from the drive and cobbled area to the front of the house. He also resolved to learn as much French as he could and as quickly as possible. Liliane proved an adept teacher, and after a few days, they could make themselves understood in a mixture of French and English. Then she resolved to use only French, after which his progress improved rapidly.

They listened to the BBC's Empire Service on the wireless in the evenings, and Tadzio keenly followed the Dunkirk evacuation and subsequent events in England. But for now, in an occupied country, without papers and still able to speak only the most basic French, he was, he realised, pretty much stuck on the farm.

They settled into a routine. The Germans announced that they would take about eighty per cent of all food production and from farmers half of their livestock and twenty per cent of all other produce. But as Liliane observed, that was only a half or a fifth of what they could identify. And they were in a fairly remote area. So far, they had not been approached by the invaders, although they expected to see either a German or a collaborator at any time. In the end, it turned out to be the village police sergeant, who handed out a leaflet instructing all food producers on how to declare and make available their produce. 'I am not collaborating,' he told Liliane over a glass of wine in the kitchen, 'but if I don't do this, they will replace me with someone who will be far less sympathetic. For now, this is the best way I can try to protect people I have known all my life.'

For Liliane, it was a difficult decision of what to do next. She was torn between the need to obtain papers for Tadzio – if he were caught on the farm without them, she faced severe reprisal – but on the other hand, if he had documents, he might attempt to return to England. And she wanted him to stay on the farm, because she could not survive independently; she needed him. And without him, the Germans would not let a prosperous small-to medium-sized farm go to waste: they would impose some other solution.

In the end, she decided, it would have to be papers. A good friend from her school days worked in *La Mairie*, the local town hall. So as July morphed into August, she arranged for Tadzio to visit a trusted photographer. A week later, he had documents identifying him as Louis Chevrolet. To Liliane's undisguised amusement, historically, his surname was that of a goat farmer. But papers solved only half of her problem.

It wasn't only Tadzio's help on the farm that Liliane liked. He was good-looking, above average in height and well muscled from heavy work on the farm, not to mention his time in the British Army. His light brown hair was growing longer than its previous regulation length – the fairly tight waves suggested that he might lose most of it in his middle years, but for now, it fell forward onto his face and curled attractively just over the top of his ears and collar. When he smiled, which was often, his big brown eyes twinkled, and tiny pleasure creases broke from each corner.

However, she knew very little about him. Only that his family had farmed in Poland, his father and sister were dead, and he had lost contact with his mother. Oh, and there was a brother somewhere who had also escaped to England, but Tadzio had not given his name.

She asked him outright, one evening after they had enjoyed a supper of casseroled rabbit – trapped on the farm – and a bottle of wine, whether he was married or there was anyone else in his life. After all, she pointed out, he did not wear a ring.

'There was someone,' he replied, looking into his glass. 'We fought in Poland and escaped to England together. But we have not seen each other since, which was several months ago. And now there is no way of making contact.'

She turned over this information in her mind. He had not been specific about the relationship, if indeed that was what it had been. But a few months, to a healthy young man, was quite a long time. They had been together for some weeks now, and she knew her feelings had deepened. Liliane's parents had been strict, and she was still a virgin: as much through lack of the right person and an opportunity as for any other reason. But if she wanted to keep him on the farm, as she was beginning to realise, all else aside, this was a sacrifice that she would have to make. She sipped her wine and smiled very gently. Though perhaps it would not really be a sacrifice at all.

*

In Zürich, Charles was thoroughly enjoying the concert. The Brahms, particularly, was superb. The first movement had long been a favourite, not least with the languorous opening of the French horns leading to the thrilling, rhythmic statement by the piano early in the same movement. Since the overture, he had been acutely aware of Anneliese's presence, as their two chairs were set closely side by side behind those of her parents. Now, in an involuntary reaction to the crashing piano chords, his hand settled on her forearm. He was about to remove it, but she placed her free hand over his and held it there for a moment. She did not turn her head away from the orchestra, but it was a subtle touch of encouragement. Gently he withdrew his arm in case one of her parents should choose that moment to glance around. He knew that whilst being welcomed as a messenger was one thing, a closer association between their daughter and an English officer might be viewed entirely differently.

After the concert her parents announced that they would walk home, taking a drink at what they called 'the hotel' on the way. Charles and Anneliese were invited to join them, but she politely declined, saying that she would prefer a drink at the Katzen Club, where they could listen to jazz played by a band of black, American musicians. 'Brahms to jazz,' said her father with a sad smile, 'is like taking a mouthful of vinegar after a glass of fine wine.' Charles thanked Herr Hoffmann for the invitation to the concert, which he had thoroughly enjoyed. In fact, he told him, it had been absolutely outstanding, something to remember for a lifetime. *Which in my case, with a war on*, he thought to himself as they left the concert hall, *might not be all that long.*

It was difficult to talk above the sound of an excellent band, but they enjoyed the music and a bottle of wine, and then another. They were not entirely sober when she suggested that they might walk home, and it took him a while to realise that they were not going in the direction of her parents' apartment.

'I have my own,' she told him in response to his query. 'I made it a condition of staying in Zürich and working for my father. Otherwise, I would have applied for a position back home in Germany, probably Munich or Berlin. With so many men joining our armed forces, at last, there will be career opportunities for us women. I can type, you know I speak excellent English and I have good French. Financially I don't have to work, but I want to, and I know I could find something more exciting than doing office work for my father. So at the moment, I'm making enquiries.'

It was a short walk, and they were still in the older part of the city, where there were plenty of clubs, cafés and restaurants. Even though it was quite late, many mostly young people were still walking the streets or sitting at outside tables enjoying a drink on a warm summer's evening.

In what had once been a grand, older residence now converted to flats, her first-floor apartment was spacious and well furnished. 'But apart from the kitchen and the bathroom,' she explained once they were inside, 'I have only two rooms.'

Whilst he looked down at the street from a full-length window, she returned from the kitchen with a bottle of wine and two glasses. She poured, and they sat at opposite ends of a large chesterfield. She draped an arm over its high side. He was not sure that still more wine would be a particularly good idea, but he took a cautious sip. She noticed, took a full measure from her own glass, then moved to draw the curtains.

'If you are thinking of returning to your hotel,' she told him, 'there is a taxi rank in the next street alongside this building. But you don't have to.'

She disappeared into her bedroom, and he heard the sound of a zip, followed by a rustle of clothing. Anneliese reappeared wearing a blue silk robe which she had not troubled to fasten. It covered her nipples, but neither the inner sides of her generous breasts nor a mound of dark blonde curls below. She stood right before his knees. 'Come on, my Englishman,' she said softly, extending her hand to lead him to bed.

At his suggestion, agreed instantly by the defence attaché, Charles settled into a routine of working in Bern during the week and leaving for Zürich on Friday at midday, returning after the weekend on Monday morning.

*

Sir Manners Fitzgibbon steepled his fingers. There were just three of them round the table in London. Operation Dynamo had provided at least a modicum of comfort and a much-needed tonic to the national morale. But the losses had been horrendous – so many killed at Dunkirk, so many POWs till the end of the war, and so much vital equipment destroyed or left rotting in the countryside and on the beaches.

'Well, they entered Paris unopposed on 14th June,' he observed, 'and now Hitler has taken his sight-seeing tour. They have the occupied zone in the North of France, with Pétain's Vichy-based French government in the South. They are nominally in charge of the whole of France, but in the occupied zone, the Germans have total authority, and the French authorities and civil services have to do exactly as they are told. In sum, it's a Nazi dictatorship.'

This was nothing new, although two others at the meeting, his assistants Doreen Jackman and Bill Ives, listened attentively. They had been Tadzio's brother Jan's controllers for his mission to Poland the previous year, and had debriefed all three of them: Jan on return from his second mission only a few weeks previously, and Jan, Tadzio and Hedda when all three of them had escaped from Poland via Germany and Sweden earlier in the year. Doreen kept a watching brief on Jan and Hedda – the former on leave and Hedda at Bletchley Court. Doreen and Bill had prepared the detailed plan, a copy now on the table before each of them. They were the only three copies in existence.

'Let me sum up,' said Sir Manners. 'Dieter Hoffmann has twice written to me, but only to report on Germany's situation, particularly Hitler's intentions and the Nazi persecution of Jews. However, Anneliese corresponds with my daughter Charlie from time to time. She is anti-Nazi, as are the family, and has no intention of volunteering for the armed forces.

'That said,' he went on, 'she is a patriotic German and would like to serve her country. So she has enquired about the possibility of joining their equivalent of our Foreign Office. The

German embassy in Paris is heavily involved in establishing the administration of the occupied zone, and they are desperately short of staff. Anneliese speaks good French and excellent English, and has agreed to accept a position at the Paris embassy in any administrative capacity, not least as an interpreter. All she is waiting for, at the moment, is her security clearance.'

'And we know from our man in Bern,' put in Doreen Jackman, 'that this should not take too long. His assistant, Charles Kaye-Stevens, thinks that it will come through any day now, and she will probably be assigned to her new post at the beginning of September. Either way, he is confident that he will be able to give us a least a short period of notice.'

'I have a reservation about allowing anyone from Bletchley Park to go abroad,' said Sir Manners slowly. 'It's a policy laid down from the very outset when it was established.'

'It's a chance we can probably afford to take,' offered Bill Ives. 'First, Hedda has not been working on any highly classified stuff, just routine Army and Naval signal traffic. So even in the very worst case, she probably couldn't tell the Germans anything they don't suspect we are doing already. Second,' he ticked off on his forefinger, 'we could transfer her immediately to the Foreign Office here in London. She would only have to walk in and out of the building a couple of times. That would establish the bona fides to her back-up cover story – if it all goes wrong, at least she could claim to have been just a minor civil servant. Even if the Germans know about Bletchley, which I very much doubt, they can't get anywhere near the place – but I wouldn't mind betting that they photograph the staff entering or leaving from or to King Charles Street. And finally,' he concluded, 'she is probably our only candidate. Her German is fluent, she looks quite like Anneliese Hoffmann and she has already proved herself in the field with the partisans. There isn't time to train up another agent, even if we could find one, but Hedda already has most of the skills she is likely to need.'

'And if anything goes wrong, we will have sent her to an almost certain death,' added Sir Manners.

'She will have to be a volunteer,' put in Doreen Jackman after a few moments' silence. 'But let me talk to her. I know her background. Her German-Jewish father eventually committed suicide because of Nazi persecution. Her Polish mother took her back home, but then she, too, took her own life. Hedda has always blamed the Germans for the death of her parents because, in 1934, they gave Hitler a ninety per cent vote of approval. So she hates her fellow countrymen with a passion, and she has already killed enough of them to prove it.'

'Action immediate,' said Sir Manners, closing his folder. 'Let me know how you get on.'

*

Towards the end of her day shift, Hedda was a bit surprised to be asked to report to Lieutenant Commander Hawkins' office. It was a warm, sunny afternoon, and she enjoyed the short walk from her hut to the main building. His door, on the first floor, was open.

'Hedda,' he greeted her with a smile. 'Won't you sit down, and how are you?' He carried on speaking as she settled herself onto a not very comfortable office chair. 'It hardly seems any time at all since you arrived. But I have heard good reports of the work you have been doing for us.'

'Thank you,' she said pleasantly, recognising the English habit of polite small talk, 'but you haven't asked me here just to give me a kind word of encouragement.'

John Hawkins had not forgotten her history, and he remembered how perceptive she had been during their one previous meeting.

'You're right,' he said. 'I had a phone call from Doreen Jackman today. It seems you are to travel to London for a meeting. She has arranged it for midday tomorrow, so we'll give you a warrant, and you can catch a train in the morning. Also, you might not be coming back to us, so you should pack your things and take them with you.'

'Is that all you can tell me?' asked Hedda.

'You know as much as I do,' came the reply. 'I did not like the idea that you might not return, and I tried arguing for you to stay here, or at least for a promise that you would come back after whatever it is that they need you for. I wasn't just being polite. I meant what I said a few minutes ago about your work. But I got nowhere. It seems our Miss Jackman is a rather powerful lady,' he grinned ruefully, 'and I got my ear somewhat chewed off, as it were. So either we let you go tomorrow or I shall find myself having an interview without coffee with some admiral or other.'

Hedda had a feeling where all this might be leading. She thanked him, he wished her good luck and she returned to hand over her work in progress to her supervisor. No questions were asked, and she did not say goodbye to the other girls in her section.

But she had to tell Charlie, of course, over a few drinks in the local public house – the same one where she had faced down Jimmy Jenks. Apparently, she had acquired a considerable degree of respect – or notoriety – amongst the locals, and the fact that Jenks had been off work for some time afterwards had not gone unnoticed. At the time, there was even rumour of a gunshot wound. Either way, ever since, Jenks had been too embarrassed to show his face in the public bar and now drank elsewhere.

Charlie drove her to the station to catch an early train. They hugged and promised to keep in touch. 'Although I might not always be able to do that,' Hedda told her without further explanation.

'It's all right,' Charlie replied. 'Father says he should be able to pass on any messages.'

She reflected on Charlie's words as the train chugged slowly through the countryside. If Sir Manners could do that, he had access to Doreen Jackman. Which also meant that despite his bland assurances, he was not just some senior civil servant in the City.

*

'I'm sorry,' Doreen Jackman said to Hedda as soon as they were seated with a cup of coffee. 'There is still no news of Tadzio. But don't despair,' she went quickly, seeing the sadness in Hedda's downcast expression, 'he could well be a prisoner. In which case, he'll be transported back to Germany then allocated to one of the POW camps. It could be a few weeks yet before the Red Cross can send us all the names.'

'Thank you,' Hedda said. 'But so many men died on the beaches… I have seen some of the radio traffic. But now,' she went on, trying desperately to put a brighter note into her voice, 'you have asked me to this meeting.'

Doreen Jackman had already decided that blunt honesty was the only way. 'We want you to volunteer for a mission in France. If you succeed, you will have access to people and hence intelligence that would be priceless to our war effort. We think there is a good chance of success. But if you are discovered or betrayed, almost certainly, you will be tortured and probably shot.' She tried, but failed, to discern a reaction. 'If you would rather return to Hedley Court,' she went on, 'no one could possibly blame you, especially after all that you have been through already. Your work there might be a more passive role, which you might prefer, but it is still vitally important.'

Doreen hesitated, then said, 'I've arranged for you to stay with Clarissa tonight. I hope that's all right? Would you like to think things over and come back and tell me tomorrow morning?'

Hedda had crossed her legs. She stared at the toe of her shoe for a full minute. Wanting to give her as much time as she needed, Doreen Jackman began to read a document from her 'in' tray. She finished reading and put it down. 'Come back tomorrow,' she urged kindly. 'I'll get a car to take you to Pimlico.' She saw that when Hedda looked up, her eyes were moist.

'First my parents,' she said softly, 'and now Tadzio. Even if he's alive,' she emphasised the 'if', 'I won't see him till the war's over. And if not…' Her voice faded away. There was a moment's silence. 'I'll go to France,' she said resolutely, 'better than just sitting and hoping at Bletchley Park. I felt I was really doing something back in Poland. It was very good. I know what I'm doing now is helping the war effort. But if I can play a more active part, maybe I can feel like that again.'

'You can still change your mind,' Doreen Jackman told her. 'But have a pleasant evening. If you are still of the same decision tomorrow, we can talk about the mission. And you will need a bit more training, although not much, I suspect.'

Hedda was sent to a local Territorial Army unit for a range day with one of the department's instructors. 'All I did was introduce her to the weapons,' he reported, 'the main one being the Browning semi-automatic 9mm. If she carries anything, a Browning HP would be her best bet. She worked out how to strip and reassemble in no time at all. And does she know her way around firearms! She put five rounds into a target at twenty yards, and I could almost have covered the grouping with one hand.

'Next,' he continued, 'I went through the Thompson sub-machine gun. She was just as good with that. Although she announced that the Schmeisser was a better weapon – quicker to reload. And finally, damn me if she didn't produce a Walther P38 from her shoulder bag. I had already loaded the Browning magazine for her, but she thumbed rounds into the Walther as fast as you like. And her grouping was even tighter. After that,' he concluded, 'there was nothing more I could teach her, so we binned the rest of the session.'

'So then what did you do?' asked Doreen Jackman. 'I had that range booked for a whole day.'

'Went for a damn good pub lunch,' he said, grinning unashamedly. 'And the department's going to pick up the bill!'

It was the same with unarmed combat training. After the first hour, her instructor gave up. 'I thought we fought dirty,' he said later. 'But from the way she's been trained, those Poles are something else.'

There had been no news from Switzerland, so there was time to arrange a crash course in basic espionage techniques – surveillance and how to lose it, dead letter boxes, brush passes and so forth. Hedda was even able to spend a few days at Ringwood for parachute training. But just as she thought she was getting the hang of it, a phone call instructed that she would be driven back to London immediately.

CHAPTER 7

Charles Kaye-Stevens spent the last full weekend of August in Zürich. During the coming week, Anneliese would pack, vacate her flat, place her furniture in storage and move in with her parents. Then, on Monday 2nd September, she would take the express for Paris.

'I wish now that I had not applied,' she told him after they had made love for what they both knew might be the very last time. Apart from a meal in a local restaurant and a walk in the park, they had spent most of their time together at her apartment and much of it in bed. The previous weekend, when Anneliese had taken a shower, Charles looked through a file she'd left in the living room. The contents of one of the envelopes were of particular interest.

'An English officer and a German Fraulein, but there is no future for us,' she said sadly, turning on her side and supporting her head with one hand, her elbow on the pillow. 'Sooner or later, you will have to rejoin your regiment. I am surprised we have been lucky enough to have had these past few weeks…'

'It's been wonderful,' he spoke softly into her silence, 'and I shall never forget you. Perhaps it will be a short war. Let's just be grateful that we have known each other and wait and see what happens. Switzerland has announced that it will stay strictly neutral, so we may be able to make contact again when this ghastly war is over.'

She kissed him and rolled off the bed. He never ceased to admire her body. She slipped on a robe. Already the sky was lightening. It was Monday morning, and he had a train to catch.

*

Doreen Jackman opened the meeting with Hedda. Bill Ives was the only other person present. It took less than fifteen seconds to confirm that Hedda was firmly resolved to return to the field, whatever that might involve.

'We want to insert you into the German administration in Paris,' said Doreen bluntly. She looked for a reaction. There was none. Hedda just held eye contact and waited for more.

'There is a young German woman,' Doreen went on, 'her name is Anneliese Hoffmann. At the moment she is living in Zürich, Switzerland, as are her parents, although she has her own apartment. She has been befriended, if I may use the term loosely, by our assistant defence attaché to the embassy at Bern – Charles Kaye-Stevens, a rather dashing young major in the Worcestershire Regiment.'

'Dashing?' queried Hedda. This use of the word was not in her English vocabulary, excellent though it was. 'Do you mean he is in a hurry?'

Doreen smiled. 'In a way, he has been,' she replied. 'They have been acquainted for some time now. And I mean acquainted in the sense that they are lovers.'

'But they are in Switzerland, and you want me to go to Paris,' said Hedda impatiently.

Bill Ives held up a hand, palm towards Hedda, asking for a pause.

'Anneliese Hoffmann has applied for a position with the German equivalent of our Foreign Office,' he told her. 'They are administering the occupied area of Northern France through the

Paris embassy. It's a huge job, and they are short of staff. This particular Fraulein is about to leave Switzerland to report for duty. Our intention holds that she will not arrive: you will take her place.'

Hedda tried to let this information sink in. 'I have so many questions,' she began. 'How will the switch be achieved? Do I look like her? Languages, papers… will anyone know her in Paris?'

Doreen Jackman replied, 'This is a dangerous operation,' she began. 'We don't think she will be known to anyone in France, but to be honest, we can't be absolutely sure. We will arrange the switch. Anneliese Hoffmann will get on a train in Zürich, but you will meet with one of our people at the station in Paris. Hoffmann is a German national, but you also speak it fluently. Anneliese speaks excellent English and good French, but again, so do you. And although you studied English for a different reason, I have long had it in mind that this ability might be essential for some even more important undertaking.'

She looked at a folder and then went on, 'As for appearance, she will obviously have submitted documents with her application. Thanks to Major Kaye-Stevens, we have several passport-type negatives. These we have given to our boffins, and they have melded them with yours. You will have an *Ausweiss* and other papers that will pass any examination. The photograph will certainly resemble Anneliese, but it will also bear more than a passing likeness to you. Plus, we'll give you a set of French identity documents – they might help you escape in case of emergency.

'Needless to say,' she continued, 'if we can pull this off, and we think there is a good chance we can, the people you are likely to meet and the information to which you will have access would be absolutely priceless to our war effort.

'Just think,' she concluded, 'one of our own people at the heart of the German administration in Paris. But you must be aware that if you are betrayed or discovered, you would almost certainly not survive – although to guard against what they might do to you, we will give you a suicide pill.'

To Doreen's surprise, this did not seem to worry Hedda at all. But, she thought to herself, the young woman had carried a Walther through Germany. She would have used it to take her own life, so a suicide pill was just another means to the same end.

Hedda turned to more practical matters. 'You brought me back from Ringwood in a hurry,' she pointed out. 'So you must have some idea of timing, how I get to France and all that?'

'Today's Tuesday,' Doreen replied. 'You have to be in Paris and fully operational by close of play Monday next. So we want to send you over on Thursday, Friday or Saturday. At the moment, weather-wise, the met. is looking good for Friday night, and it's a fairly full moon, so you'll be able to see the ground.'

'It's a parachute drop, then,' Hedda confirmed.

'Shouldn't be a problem,' Bill Ives broke in. 'According to Ringwood, you seemed to enjoy jumping. And they *did* manage to fit in a practice night drop before we had to send the recall. You will be jumping from a Mk IV Armstrong Whitworth Whitley – exactly the same type of twin-engined medium bomber used in training. It will be taking part in a leaflet raid for the benefit of the local civilians but will drop you off in the countryside on the way, somewhere south-west of Paris.'

'So how do I get there – Paris, I mean?' she asked.

'The locals will mark the DZ, the dropping zone,' he told her, 'and you will be met by a French woman, codename Marie, whom we put into France before the war. You will be known to her only as "Chaffinch". She is an experienced operator, and most importantly, she is wireless trained. It's how you will send messages back to us here. In fact, it will be one of your former colleagues at Bletchley who will receive them, although she will have no idea who is providing the information because she will recognise only Marie's fist.'

You don't train to be a parachutist without learning what a DZ is, she mused wryly. *Typical of a man, to want to explain it.* 'So what happens next?' she asked bluntly.

Sensing her reaction, and she could have kicked Bill under the table, Doreen intervened. 'Marie will have everything organised. We know where and with whom you will be billeted in Paris. You and Marie will travel there together on Monday, and you report for duty the following day.' She pointed to a folder on the table. 'You have two days to master quite a hefty brief, and we also have to fit in time for you to be kitted out. There's a car waiting to take you back to Clarissa's so you can get started. And be warned, the old girl knows better than to ask, but she has spent years in this business, and she's only human. She's bound to be curious, but you say absolutely nothing. And we have installed a small secure cabinet in your bedroom. When you are not working on it, that brief stays under lock and key. We'll collect it once you have left.'

Hedda would have liked more time to study her background brief, plus all the information on Anneliese Hoffmann. Then there were the details of how and where she should report for duty in Paris, plus pages of administrative instructions. But by Thursday evening, she felt she was pretty much on top of the paperwork. Over a glass of champagne, Clarissa mentioned that the Germans had now commandeered eighty per cent of all sparkling wine production. 'There are some consolations for being an old secret squirrel, though,' she told Hedda. 'We saw this coming, and I have laid in quite a few cases.'

'Who exactly is *we*?' asked Hedda curiously.

'This intelligence business was all very ad hoc in my time,' came the reply. 'But needs must, and the war has focussed our minds. Assets were combined under Hugh Dalton, the Minister for Economic Warfare, only a month ago. You, Doreen and Bill are all part of what is now the Special Operations Executive. I don't know who the top brass are, but Doreen and Bill are pretty senior. Some of my old chums tell me they even have direct access to Winston.

'Hope I haven't been indiscreet,' she added quickly, perhaps, thought Hedda, just a little embarrassed. 'Let's eat and enjoy ourselves, my dear.' She stood, indicating that they should move to the dining room. Clarissa gave her the best farewell dinner that she could secure. The ingredients mainly were estate-produced – soup, grouse, a gooseberry tart and finally a ported Stilton. On Friday afternoon, Hedda was driven to Tangmere Cottage, opposite the airfield. It had been set up specially to dispatch and receive agents travelling to or from France. One room had been fitted out as a wardrobe facility. Hedda was asked to step into a curtained cubicle and remove and hand over every item of clothing, plus her watch and any other items of jewellery or personal possessions, including her handbag.

The curtain was partially drawn back, and she was handed a basket containing a fresh set of clothes. 'Mostly bought from German refugees,' a slim, middle-aged woman told her once she had dressed. 'Now, you will need a warm jacket.' She looked at Hedda, then took one from a rack. 'This should fit,' she told her, 'and I have been instructed to give you only chic clothes of good quality. The label is French, but I'm told that melds well with your background.' Hedda tried it on then promptly handed it back.

'It won't do,' she said firmly. 'One of the buttons does not quite match, so obviously it has been replaced. That would not matter, but the stitching is criss-crossed. On the continent, the French do it from side to side. That English version would be a dead giveaway.'

Her dresser looked at Hedda with new respect. She handed the jacket to an assistant. 'Fix it,' she instructed curtly.

*

Just under 160 kilometres south-west of Paris, Marie pedalled north-west from the beautiful medieval town of Nogent-le-Retrou, home to some seven and a half thousand souls in an otherwise under-populated and very agricultural area. It was, she thought, set in lovely countryside, astride the Huisne River. In her basket lay six freshly baked croissants in a paper bag, wrapped inside a cloth. She hoped they might still be just a little warm when she arrived back at the isolated estate a few kilometres away.

The owner, Jean Renaud, allowed her to use one of the cottages on his land. It stood perhaps half a kilometre from the main farmhouse. They had spent two days digging a shallow trench into which they had laid a cable protected by lengths of rubber hosepipe, bringing electricity to the old cottage so that she could use her radio.

Jean had dual nationality. Born in London to a French wine merchant father and an English mother, he had been sent to prep and public school in England, but the family spoke French at home. Most importantly, his birth was registered in Nogent, his address the family estate and he had genuine French papers, as did his wife. He had left school, aged eighteen, in 1916, and had volunteered for and been commissioned into the Intelligence Corps, formed only recently on 5th August 1914. He spent the last months of the Great War behind enemy lines.

In 1925, following the death of his father, Jean had appointed a manager to oversee their London operation and moved to France. Most of the land was already let to tenants, and Jean assumed the wine-purchasing responsibilities of his late father. In 1927, he met and subsequently married Monique, the daughter of another local landowner. When he judged war to be a forthcoming certainty, Jean purchased a return ticket to Paris. There, he had informed a surprised British defence attaché that he was both well trained and bilingual and would assist in any way they might wish. Jean was quite prepared to enlist again: he was extremely fit for a forty-year-old. But he suspected that his embedded position in France, plus the facilities he could make available, might be even greater use to the Allies during the conflict. The point was well taken. Marie took up residence on his estate even before the invasion of France. Her mission was to plan and eventually establish one of the earliest resistance cells of the war.

She asked Marius and Edouard to the cottage on Thursday evening. The air was thick with fumes – both men were heavy smokers. 'It came through on the BBC Empire Service last night,' she told them. 'The drop is set for Friday, onto the field we have already selected. We set out five lights to form an "X", with one light at the centre of the DZ.' Marius and Edouard were the same generation as Jean and had been recruited at his suggestion. But they were unaware that he'd passed their names to Marie, and since her arrival, he had not been involved in any of her resistance activities.

But both Jean and the two Frenchmen were excessively grateful for the Thompson sub-machine guns she had provided from the small cache she had brought with her. Marie, Marius and Edouard would set out the lights and meet the woman arriving from England.

*

Hedda settled down near the exit hole as her pilot fired up the two Rolls-Royce Merlin engines. Flight Lieutenant Johnny Barnes had introduced himself at the final briefing. 'Should be an easy run,' he told her confidently. 'Good met., an almost full moon and the DZ's a good one. Just north, the river takes a marked turn to the south. We're on dead reckoning, which can be difficult, but once we find the river we identify the bend, head south to Nogent, then turn to starboard till we see the lights in the field.'

Once again, she was feeling sick from the dreadful smell of the lacquer they used on the inside of the fuselage. Twin Rolls-Royce Merlin engines roared into life, and minutes later, they were taxiing round the field. She always felt anxious till they were safely airborne. They picked up only very light flak. Johnny had mentioned that the route was planned this way, and they were so far south from Paris that they would be very unlucky to be caught by a night fighter. Once they had sighted the river, she shuffled over to the hole cut in the aircraft's underbelly. It wasn't easy to move around, wearing her parachute and with a kit bag strapped to her thigh. The lights changed, and her dispatcher gave her a firm pat on the back. She remembered to jump well forward so that there was no chance her chute could catch on the rim of the hole and slam her face into the other side. Then she was out, stable, her kit bag lowered, and she could see the white dot in the centre of the 'X'.

As soon as Hedda had jumped, Marius and Edouard ran to extinguish the outer ground lights. Marie walked towards the centre one and waited whilst her arrival landed about twenty-five metres away and sorted herself out. These meetings were always tense moments. In order not to cause alarm, Marie was armed only with her automatic, which she had left holstered.

'*Bravo, et bienvenue en France,*' she said as she approached her new arrival. 'Leave your bag and chute,' she continued in English, 'the men will sort everything out. Please come with me. I know what it's like in those draughty bombers – what you need are a hot coffee and a large cognac.' Together, they walked to the cottage.

Once round the kitchen table, Marius handed over a small package he had brought from the drop bag. 'Just a few personal things and a change of clothing,' she explained. 'I gather I shall only be here for a day or two.'

'We take the train to Paris on Monday,' Marie confirmed.

*

Anneliese's parents took her to the *Hauptbahnhof*. The embassy in Paris had sent a second-class rail warrant, along with instructions on what to do once she arrived, but when she had bought her ticket she paid the difference so that she could travel first class. Her father placed her two cases on the luggage rack then they returned to the platform. All three embraced. Both Anneliese and her mother had tears in their eyes. But it was time to board again and take her seat. She stood at the window and waved frantically till they were out of sight, unaware of the man and woman seated in the next compartment. Then, finally, the woman said, 'See you later,' and went to join Anneliese. She knew that there would be no one else in the compartment. The British embassy had reserved all the other seats.

Anneliese's fellow passenger greeted her with a polite '*Guten Morgen*' but settled to reading a magazine. After that, they exchanged only a few words of conversation from time to time until the woman stood to look out of the window. Anneliese had a window seat, and the woman had taken an opposite corner. But now she was now standing sideways-on in front of Anneliese. 'Just look at that,' she said conversationally. Automatically, Anneliese turned her head to the right. The other woman's hand moved towards her, and she was aware of a sharp sting in her neck.

The woman looked down at her. 'Don't try to fight it,' she said encouragingly, 'I promise, you will be all right. But we need you to rest for a while.'

Anneliese tried to speak, but her vision was blurred, and she was so, so weary. She could hardly move. Then, slowly, everything went black.

The woman banged on the panelling between the two compartments. Her companion appeared at the door with a wheelchair. The train was approaching the ancient city of Basel, standing on the River Rhine near the border between France and Germany. But importantly, still just inside Switzerland. As soon as it stopped, they wheeled an unconscious Anneliese, now heavily cloaked in a blanket under which her body was strapped to the chair, to the carriage door. He stepped out first, and she was lowered gently to the platform. The woman pushed Anneliese away from the door whilst he returned for her cases. She took a white armband bearing a red cross from her pocket and placed it above her right elbow. It was amazing how authoritative such a simple device could be. At the exit, the man was careful to place himself between the ticket inspector and the wheelchair when he handed over three Zürich-to-Basel tickets. The inspector barely gave them a second glance, not wishing to appear discourteous to an invalid. The man picked up the cases again, and they continued outside to a waiting ambulance.

The woman removed her armband and stuffed it into a coat pocket. Next, she took off her dark blue overcoat and threw it into the ambulance behind the wheelchair. She was handed a smart, shorter-length beige coat and a matching cloche-style hat of the style made famous by Greta Garbo. Importantly, it followed the fashion of having a veil – worn in daytime only, of course, for at night, the veil signified a rather different class of woman. Moreover, this veil had the added virtue of being patterned in places, further obscuring her face. The ambulance drove off, and she picked up the two cases. They were heavy, but she was young and fit. Although as she returned to the entrance, a porter was quick to offer his services. 'The buffet,' she told him. She would enjoy an early luncheon before the next train for Paris arrived. The change of clothing had been a wise precaution, but it was a different inspector when she found another porter and settled into her first-class compartment.

CHAPTER 8

Not once had there been the slightest hint of intimacy between them, not even a brushing of hands, accidental or otherwise. But Liliane knew he found her attractive. Often she had caught him looking at her when he thought she would not notice – he liked to sneak a glance at her body. Now back at home, with a modest wardrobe to choose from, she took care with her appearance. It was very different from the bedraggled, grimy, tear-streaked apparition he had found when he caught her searching that farmhouse kitchen. But she sensed that he was biding his time, trying to find some way to escape back to England. His French had improved significantly over the weeks. Now, it was the only language they used. He still had a slight English rather than Polish accent, but a German with only limited French would probably not notice the difference. And now he had his Louis Chevrolet papers.

Perhaps the mill stream would be the answer. The mill itself was not on her property, but the source of its energy, crossing their farm, had always been called that. And there was the place where it passed through a copse and slowed almost to a standstill as it entered a small pool, just right for a cool dip on a hot summer's day. Although strictly forbidden by parents, she and her girlfriends had often skinny-dipped in it when they were children.

Despite the German announcement that they would have to surrender produce, the farm had not as yet been raided by the invaders. So Liliane was able to produce a delicious Sunday pot roast of chicken and vegetables. It was a scorching hot day. Tadzio had spent the morning dividing their small herd of cows and driving the animals in ones and twos to isolated fields, where he had constructed makeshift barns in the most remote and least visible parts of the farm. Now, if – or perhaps when – the Germans came, hopefully there would only be a few beasts to be seized nearer the farmhouse. But there was not much he could do about the chickens.

They had no ice, but she had chilled a bottle of white wine by wrapping it in a cloth repeatedly dipped in cold water. Liliane took only one glass, and after he had thanked her for the meal, she invited him to finish off the bottle whilst she washed up.

'It's a lovely day,' she remarked afterwards, 'let's go for a walk. I want to see where we might set another snare or two for rabbits – even the Germans can't seize those from us.' Tadzio was quite content to go with her. They had nothing planned for the rest of the day and it would be good to walk off a fine lunch. They strolled as far as the mill stream, although some way from the copse and pool. There was a hint of a narrow path on the bank, where she and her parents had often followed the watercourse, hoping to spot kingfishers and sometimes even a mallard. Liliane took the lead. She was wearing a cotton skirt and a short-sleeved blouse, and she sensed that he was watching her hips. They followed the path into the copse and she stopped by the pool.

'It's incredibly hot. Would you like to swim?' she said in an excited whisper. 'No one else comes here anymore.'

'It's a nice idea, but we don't have costumes,' he pointed out. 'And I don't know about you,' he went on, 'but I don't even own one.' Although from the way he looked at the water, she could see he was tempted.

'We can swim in our undergarments,' she offered. 'It will be quite respectable. Turn your back for a minute.' Without waiting for a reply, she began to unbutton her blouse. Next, she stepped out of her skirt, folded both garments neatly and put them on the grass. Now she was wearing what she thought of as her secret weapon. Her mother had given them to her last Christmas, with instructions that they be put away as part of her trousseau: a pair of knickers and a slip. They were satin, not silk, and only the shoulders of her slip were trimmed with the tiniest amount of lace, but they were very different from the plain cotton she wore every day. There was even a brassiere to go with them, but she had deliberately left that in the drawer.

She knew that just here, by the bank, the water would barely come up to her waist, so she took a good jump out to where it would be deeper. Standing on the bottom with her head just above the water, she looked over her shoulder. Hearing the splash, Tadzio had turned round. He undressed down to his undershorts and jumped in. He took a few breaststrokes past her to the centre of the pool, where he duck-dived to check the depth. His head surfaced and he wiped a hand over his face to clear water from his eyes.

'Must be nearly three metres,' he spluttered. She turned and made her way back to the bank. He followed, then stood up and walked. Still in the water, she turned to face him. They were less than a metre apart. The slip was clinging to her breasts, the dark shape of her nipples clearly visible underneath. He lifted one hand out of the water, then hesitated. She moved towards him, so that it was almost touching her breast, then placed her own hand over the back of his and pulled it towards her. His hand closed, and the thumb and forefinger began to rub her nipple, which was fully erect. She glanced down – as was his penis, bulging and straining against his undershorts. His other hand moved to her bottom, and he pulled her against him.

'On the grass,' she said softly, and climbed up to sit on the bank. She knelt, eased off her slip, then stood to take down and step from her knickers. He, too, had climbed the bank and pulled her towards him again. Her forearms on his chest, she eased away. Raised on a farm, Liliane was no stranger to animal reproduction, but pushing down his shorts, she looked for the first time at a man's penis, engorged and erect. Curious, she could not resist taking its shaft in her hand. He moaned, and with common consent, they sank to lie on the grass. She opened her legs and guided him towards her. Thanks to years of riding, there was barely any resistance, then he was completely inside and her legs were crossing at the ankles behind him. She felt him shudder his seed, but he kept moving strongly till her own orgasm subsided. Afterwards, as they lay there in silence, still coupled, she was sure she had achieved her aim. She could not help a gentle smile. He might have papers, but he would not, she was reasonably certain, be going anywhere any time soon.

*

'Edouard will take us to the station in Nogent,' Marie explained. 'It'll have to be a horse-and-cart job, but it's better than walking the best part of ten kilometres. We'll travel in the same carriage on the train, but to anyone else, we don't know each other. I have French papers, and you can use your Hoffmann ones. If you are asked, the fact that you are reporting for duty at the embassy should see you through. You can always tell them that you spent a few days in the country with old friends to brush up on your French. I doubt they'll ask, but you can give them Jean Renaud's address if they do. He has a cover story that you met when he supplied wine to your estate in Germany in December 1938, but quite honestly, I doubt if that will ever be necessary.'

Their tickets were inspected, but there were no identity or other checks during the journey. They arrived in Paris late in the afternoon. Marie took Hedda to the station buffet. They sat at a table nursing a soft drink and waited for the arrival of the late train from Zürich.

A well-dressed young woman seated herself next to them. 'I've checked, and it's all in there,' she said softly, indicating two suitcases half under the table. 'You can study the original reporting instructions tonight, but I have put the billeting stuff on top of the file. Now we go outside to a black Citroën. It looks like a Gestapo car, but the driver is one of ours. We don't use it much because it's hard to get petrol, but I'm told this is high priority. Read the billet paper in the car. It will drop Fraulein Hoffmann off near the address, then take Marie and me to the safe house. I shall go back to Switzerland tomorrow. Any questions?'

There were none. For the moment, if she needed to send information to England, Hedda would leave a chalk mark on a park bench to alert a messenger, then either use a dead letter drop or arrange a meeting. Her unknown courier would travel to Nogent and contact Marie. They were all well versed in the tradecraft necessary to counter surveillance, and they had a proven method of passing the information. It was the best – it was all – they could do.

*

Simone Faucher lived on the ground floor of an apartment building half an hour's walk from the German embassy. She had found work there as a cleaner, from Monday to Friday, from 6pm through to however long it took her to clean most of the offices and toilets, usually till between ten and eleven each evening. She felt doubly resentful. They had led a comfortable if plain existence till her husband Marcel died prematurely of a heart attack a few years ago. The flat they had inherited from his mother, their modest savings she was determined to keep for her old age, so it had been a case of having to find work after he passed away. They had married young, and she had never worked till then. She was unskilled but resented that she was obliged to take a job, and one that she considered very much beneath her.

Now in her thirties, she had retained her good figure, but with the war and the occupation, her chances of finding another husband were slim. She knew men looked at her, and some of the diplomatic staff would have taken her to bed, but that would have been all. Although her meagre wages put food on the table, prices had rocketed, and there were ever-increasing shortages. She could barely afford her ration of not much more than one thousand calories a day, and it was humiliating to have to hand over tickets to buy basics such as bread or cooking oil. Moreover, soap was almost impossible to come by.

The Germans she had found loud and brusque before the war. Since the occupation, they had become unbearable. And because they had known about her, that she lived alone in an apartment with two bedrooms, they told her she was to make her spare room available to a new employee at the embassy. She would not have to provide food, they said, and normally she would have been expected to support the Fatherland without remuneration. But as she worked for the embassy, they would pay a modest sum for the accommodation – which they were sure would help in these difficult times. Their condescension, their assumed right to do as they wished with her life and home, she just had to accept. She could have said no but feared for her job. So it came as no surprise when there was a knock on the door.

'Madame Faucher? My name is Anneliese Hoffmann. I believe you are expecting me,' a well-dressed young woman said in excellent French. She stood politely in the hall, waiting to be invited through the door, two suitcases on the floor beside her.

Leaving the girl in her room, Simone returned to her small kitchen. A few minutes later, there was another knock, the gentle tap of a knuckle on the open door to the kitchen. 'May I come in?' Anneliese Hoffmann asked politely. 'I shall understand if you would prefer that I had not been imposed upon you,' she said immediately, 'and frankly, I have no choice either. But I hope that we shall reach a friendly understanding. I have brought a small offering from Switzerland.'

From behind her back, she produced a good-sized packet of coffee. Simone Faucher could not help a sharp intake of breath.

Even if she had been able to afford such a large amount, it had not been in the shops for weeks. The German girl was trying very hard to be pleasant and agreeable. Much as she hated the occupation, perhaps their relationship would not be so bad after all. Her fingers touched the top of the packet. 'Thank you. I have not had the luxury of coffee for a long time,' she said quietly. 'Shall I make some for both of us?'

Her folder included a street plan showing the way from her lodgings to the embassy. As she walked, Anneliese reflected that last evening had gone as smoothly as could have been expected. If Simone was hostile, she was hiding it well.

The building was guarded by two soldiers, each with a sub-machine gun. She showed her papers and letter of appointment and was directed to the main entrance, where two more soldiers made a second examination of her documents. Finally, she reported to a glass window and was invited to take a seat in the entry hall. Shortly afterwards, a door opened, and a fashionably dressed young woman in a black pencil skirt and white blouse introduced herself as Irmgard Stein.

'I'm the personal assistant to the administrator,' she added. 'He's trying to sort out where to place all the extra people we are having to employ. He'll be very pleased to have another German national – we can use you where we need people we can trust. So follow me, and I'll take you to his office.'

Herr Schulte, the administrator, moved with a pronounced limp as he courteously moved from behind his desk to shake her hand and draw back a chair. He was a middle-aged, short, slim individual, balding with dark hair going grey at the sides. Round-rimmed glasses made him look like some sort of clerk. 'The last war,' he explained as he returned awkwardly to his own chair behind the desk. Perhaps, thought Hedda, an old soldier's psychology needed to justify why he was not taking a more active part in this one. But she felt a frisson of excitement. If she were allotted to a position *where she could be trusted*, then the information to which she would have access might be as invaluable as London had hoped.

He studied her file as if to remind himself. 'Excellent French,' he said out loud. 'Can you type?'

Hedda had no intention of finishing up in a typing pool, not if she could help it. Deliberately she adopted a slightly affronted tone. 'Of course I can type,' she replied abruptly. 'But before I applied to come here, I was running the export office of my father's business. I handled the contract side of things with a staff of twelve people. I am an experienced administrator with a good knowledge of commercial law.'

Herr Schulte looked at the file again. 'Armaments,' he said to himself.

'And electronics,' she corrected. 'Military radios and such. In addition to export, we supply the *Wehrmacht*, for which we have the appropriate security clearance.' She had no way of knowing if this was true, but she was sure that Herr Schulte didn't either.

He was silent for a good thirty seconds. Then, at last, he seemed to make up his mind. He scribbled a quick note on the document in her file.

'I was going to allocate you to a typing pool. Then when you reminded me of your experience, I thought you might make a good supervisor. But you are, I think, a very capable young woman.'

Hedda thought it best to remain silent, to see what came next.

'How would you like to work with the ambassador's personal staff?' he asked her. 'The Head of Chancery needs a deputy. He's been ringing me every day for a week. You would be the number two in a large secretariat. It's a responsible position – you would be in charge of all administrative functions, including reports that go to Berlin. You would also be expected to contribute to policy discussions and implement them as ordered. Under you, there would be a staff slightly larger than the one you managed for your father. They might not like the idea of a woman, at least not at first, but right now, I don't have another suitable candidate. It would be up to you to prove your competence and establish your authority.'

'It sounds an excellent opportunity,' she said guardedly, 'and your confidence in me is appreciated.'

'It's quite a challenge,' he said evenly. 'Do you feel up to it?' She wondered if he would have asked the same question of a man. Hedda was at pains to show no emotion, no delight. But in such a position, the intelligence, she realised, would indeed be priceless.

'Yes, Herr Schulte,' she replied formally, 'and I shall be honoured to serve the Fatherland to the best of my ability.'

*

Liliane and Tadzio had just finished supper and cleared away when they saw two men walk up the drive and across the gravel. 'It's fine,' she reassured him quickly. 'I know them both. Yves is a friend of a friend – my contact at the *Mairie* didn't say so, but I'm sure he was the one she persuaded to produce your French identity papers. Jean-Claude you met when he came here, but this time he's not in uniform.' Tadzio recognised the village policeman, whom he judged to be in his early forties. Yves was probably only in his late twenties, although he carried an air of greater authority.

Liliane invited the visitors to be seated at the kitchen table and produced two more wine glasses. They responded to her toast – 'To France'. 'We are aware,' Jean-Claude began, looking at Tadzio after they had set down their glasses, 'that you are in the British Army.' Tadzio said nothing, waiting for them to continue.

'We heard de Gaulle's speech on *Radio Londres*,' Jean-Claude continued. 'France cannot remain forever under the heel of the Germans. For the moment, England fights on alone. But what they call the Battle of Britain continues. We listen to the BBC's Empire Service, and the Luftwaffe has not defeated the Royal Air Force. Without air superiority, the Germans cannot invade. And we have to hope and pray that this is something they will never achieve.'

'So why are you here?' asked Tadzio warily. 'What's the point of your visit this evening?'

'We have to hope that at some stage the war will again be fought on mainland Europe,' came the reply, 'and we wish to disrupt the German war effort: for now, as a resistance, in any way that we can. But, eventually, come the great day when France can be liberated, we will rise, united, as a fighting force.'

Tadzio thought for a minute. 'I admire your spirit,' he said. 'There is also a resistance in my homeland.' It was their turn to be surprised. 'I am from Poland,' he told them. 'Our resistance operated from the forests and sometimes from my farm.'

'But now you are a British soldier,' came the reply. 'You have been well trained. Our problem is that we have volunteers but no weapons or equipment, save the odd shotgun or small calibre hunting rifle. We have no military experience and no leader who can train us in the use of weapons or explosives. And the other problem is that we have no way of asking for help from Britain. We have simply no way of contacting them.'

'So, what do you want from me?' Tadzio asked, although he had an idea where this conversation was leading.

'We want you to go back to England,' came the reply. 'It will be dangerous, but we can help. First, we want you to tell London about us, then to return and lead our cell. But you must bring arms and ammunition back with you – explosives, too. Then you can teach us how to use them, and we will be able to fight back against the *Boche*. The more damage we can do to them in France, the less harm they can inflict upon England. And the more we can help towards our eventual liberation.'

Liliane was not at all happy with this turn of conversation. 'I need Tadzio here,' she protested. 'I can't manage this farm on my own, and if I can't, the Germans will take it away from me.'

It was Yves' turn to speak. 'We have anticipated this small difficulty,' he replied. 'We, too, want Tadzio back here. But whilst he is away, one of our number will help you to work the land. He was brought up on a farm, although he was a younger son, so he had to make another way in the world. He is retired now but still fit and healthy. He has offered to stand in until Tadzio returns.'

Liliane was not happy but saw that she had little alternative.

Tadzio was excited at the prospect of returning to England. Although what would be decided when – or if – he got there, he had no idea. 'So how do I escape from France?' he asked.

Yves began to tell him.

CHAPTER 9

Herr Schulte took her through what looked to be a typing pool and administrative area to a good-sized outer office containing two desks, only one of which was occupied. On the other, which was bare of any paperwork, stood only a telephone and a small black intercom extension.

Herr Schulte entered and approached the diplomat's desk. Hedda waited just inside the door. Although there were chairs in front of each desk, Herr Schulte stood deferentially, Hedda's file in hand. A rather distinguished-looking man of about forty looked up from a document in which he had clearly been engrossed.

'Herr Richter, if you have a moment, may I introduce Fraulein Anneliese Hoffmann. She has volunteered to come to Paris and work for the Fatherland. I think she would make an excellent assistant. Let me tell you about her—'

'Is that her file?' he interrupted, extending an open palm to indicate that Schulte should hand it over. Hedda studied the diplomat. His features were regular rather than handsome, and his wavy black hair, swept back over his ears, was beginning to silver, adding to an air of authority. His dark suit, she noticed, was beautifully tailored – in London, at a guess – and his snow-white double cuffs showed a pair of pearl links.

'Thank you, Schulte,' he said, 'I will decide. That will be all for now.'

The administrator made a slight bow and turned to leave. Hedda had remained where she was. 'Come and sit down, Fraulein Hoffmann,' he said, indicating a chair in front of his desk, 'whilst I read through your file.'

It took him half the time it had taken the administrator. 'Where did you learn French?' he asked her in that language. He seemed to speak it quite well, but his command of the language was pedestrian compared with the mellifluous sonority she had absorbed from her late father. And his accent would have been stamped out ruthlessly by Anneliese's finishing school. She gave him the Switzerland explanation for her fluency. He seemed satisfied and reverted to German. 'Please, no false modesty,' he went on brusquely. 'Your father must have travelled a lot – you ran the business for him, in his absence?'

'I did,' she said succinctly. 'And to save you asking, I handled all of his correspondence, even when he was there.' She repeated the management experience she had given to the administrator, including a mention of armaments and electronics, plus her knowledge of commercial law.

'Being my assistant is a very senior position, especially for a woman, let alone one so young,' he said, not unkindly.

'My father is an enlightened man,' Hedda replied, sensing that she would have to overcome his conservative views. 'I am well educated and well trained,' she said in her best no-nonsense voice, '*and* I have considerable commercial experience in the real world.' However, she wondered immediately whether she had gone too far by inferring that her 'real world' was more challenging than diplomacy.

His eyebrows lifted, but he could not, she noticed, suppress a faint smile. 'I wanted a professional, up-and-coming young diplomat,' he told her. 'But we are at war, so the Fatherland has other needs of such men. So...' He paused as if making up his mind. Hedda waited anxiously. 'I have a feeling,' he said at last, 'that we will work well together.'

She had made it. He had decided to accept her. But again, she was careful to hide her exhilaration. 'What would be my duties, sir?' she asked politely.

'We call the ambassador "Your Excellency",' he informed her, 'but I am addressed as Herr Richter, and you are Fraulein Hoffmann.

'The worst thing,' he went on, 'is that even though we are fighting a war, Berlin is insatiable for information. The ambassador has to sign off a detailed report each week. It covers just about everything, from commerce through to agriculture, details of the occupation, security – I could go on. But you take my point. Of course, the military put in their own reports, but the Führer insists on a civilian view to add balance. Your job is to read all the material that comes in, liaise with other agencies, including the military and the intelligence services, and then write the report. It has to be ready for my approval by Thursday evening. I will look at it first thing next morning, and the ambassador will sign it off that same day so that it can go by courier each Friday. I will write the report for this week, but you will be very much alongside me. Next week, it would help very much if you were to take over.

'I'll give you a couple of old reports to study, and my secretary, who works out there,' his thumb indicated the outer office, 'can make a list of all the people you need to see each week. She will also do a preliminary weed of the incoming paperwork so that you don't have to read too much routine correspondence. I'll call her in now and introduce her.'

He pressed a button on his black box. 'It will look better if you sit behind the desk,' he said with a smile. 'I don't usually share an office,' he added, 'but with so many additional staff, this is the most efficient solution.' The secretary, introduced as Frau Becker, also wore the uniform of dark pencil skirt and white blouse. She was a rather plain-looking mousy blonde, probably in her mid-thirties.

But if she was surprised by Hedda's lack of years, she was at pains not to show it.

With only a short break for lunch in the embassy canteen, she read throughout the day till by five in the afternoon her head was aching.

He noticed that she was increasingly rubbing her brow. He looked at a gold wristwatch. 'I have to see someone on the other side of town,' he told her. 'I have a car and driver waiting. I know where you live. Let me give you a lift home, and we can start again tomorrow.'

Hedda accepted gratefully. She wondered whether Simone Faucher would be at home or whether she would have left for her cleaning job. No matter, she had been given a key. When she let herself into the apartment, she was surprised to find Simone had company. She and a man were in the tiny kitchen. They looked startled, almost guilty, when she walked into the room.

'This is Monsieur Courbet,' said Simone quickly. 'He is a chemist,' she added gratuitously.

'Lucien Courbet,' he introduced himself, then stood as if to leave. He was tall and slim but not particularly well dressed. His jacket was stained and had seen better days.

'I'm sorry, I did not mean to interrupt,' Hedda said quickly. 'I'll be in my room so that you will have privacy.'

As she turned, Simone said, 'Thank you, but there is no need. We were about to leave anyway. It is time for me to go to work.' They walked past her to the hall, and a few moments later, Hedda heard the front door close.

Lucien Courbet was about Simone's age, she reflected, and quite handsome... if they were more than just friends, then good luck to her.

She settled down to a light supper of chicken and salad sandwiches together with a bottle of red wine, all bought at the canteen, and after some searching – they had changed the frequency yet again to try to avoid German jamming – she found *Radio Londres*.

*

A slim, middle-aged man of medium height wheeled two bicycles across the cobbles and leant them against the farmhouse wall. He introduced himself as Claude Boulier and a friend of Yves. The sun was barely up, but Tadzio had been expecting him. He had not bothered to dress beyond his underclothing – the rest of his clothes were in a small haversack on the kitchen table. Liliane had announced that she would stay in bed till he had gone. She was still sulking because of his departure. Claude handed him a pillowcase. Rolled up inside was a uniform identical to the one he was wearing. 'Today, my friend,' he said with a smile, 'you are a ticket inspector of the *Société Nationale des Chemins de fer Français*. The *SNCF* is the finest railway company in Europe,' he added proudly.

Tadzio put on the uniform and peaked cap. It was all a good fit. 'It's about eighty kilometres in a straight line to the coast,' Claude told him, 'but we will have to make one change, at Amiens, so it will be nearly twice as far. Then, from Amiens, we take the train to Boulogne. Both of the usual inspectors will enjoy a day tending their roses. There will probably be guards at the station, and as we are going to the coast, there will probably be Germans inspecting the travellers' papers, but they never bother with the railway staff. I think we are beneath their attention.'

There were soldiers at the entrance to Arras station – it was a main railway hub – but they were ignored. They boarded at the rear into the guard's van. Claude smiled conspiratorially. 'It will look odd if we just sit here,' he said. 'We'll walk to the front of the train, see who's on it, then work our way back.'

All went well during the trip to Amiens. But there were several Germans in uniform on the train to Boulogne. Although it was only lunchtime, some of the soldiers were drinking wine. From their somewhat dishevelled appearance, it looked as though they had spent the previous night enjoying rest and recuperation in the bars and brothels of Amiens. Most of the officers were in first class, but a fresh-faced young *Leutnant* appeared to have been placed in charge of this second-class carriage. Judging by the boisterous behaviour of his men, he was out of his depth.

'Same as in first,' said Claude. 'Just check the civilian passengers.' As they walked down the carriage, an old woman with a lined face and wearing a peasant headscarf rounded on Tadzio. Despite the attempted restraint of a younger woman at her side, possibly her daughter, she screeched at him. 'You check us, respectable French people,' she protested, pointing to include the French passengers around her, 'but you don't ask them for their tickets.' A wavering hand with an extended forefinger embraced a group of Germans more or less opposite. Whether one of them understood a few words of French or the woman's gestures had made clear her meaning, Tadzio was not sure.

Either way, a young private, obviously the worse for drink, unbuttoned his fly and took out his flaccid penis. 'This is my ticket, you old bag,' he shouted in German, waving it at her. He looked at Tadzio. 'You can inspect it if you want, Monsieur ticket inspector, then that young bitch next to her can suck me off. It could probably do with a clean after last night.'

His companions laughed with him. The two Frenchwomen looked away. Even if they had not understood the German, they must have had a good idea of what was said. The *Leutnant* stood but seemed uncertain what to do next. Tadzio did not want to involve him. That risked bringing them all to the attention of the authorities. But he was anxious to defuse the situation.

Humour was probably his only chance. 'If that is your ticket, Monsieur,' he said clearly in German, 'then I'm afraid it will probably not get you much beyond the next station. But I can't really tell because I don't have my magnifying glass.'

They were all surprised to be addressed with such fluency, but his companions thought it uproariously funny. They punched his arms. 'You asked for that, Hans, you stupid fart,' one of them, a little more sober than the others, told him. He, too, had half an eye on the *Leutnant* hovering nearby. 'Now put it away, and don't get us into any more trouble.'

Hans pushed his member back into his trousers and took another swig from his bottle of wine. He had not bothered to do up the buttons, but the danger had passed. 'Thank you,' said a clearly relieved young officer. 'You handled that very well. But where did you learn to speak such good German? I recognised the accent. I, too, am from East Prussia.'

Tadzio almost panicked. Had he given himself away? Frantically he cobbled together an explanation. 'F-French father, G-German mother, sir,' he stammered, hoping that his haste would be mistaken for nervousness at having to address a German officer. 'They met when he was working in Germany before returning to France after the Great War. But she came from the Free City of Danzig. We spoke German at home, hence my accent.'

The *Leutnant* considered this. '*Sehr gut*,' he responded, apparently satisfied with the explanation. He thanked Tadzio again and returned to his seat. Tadzio saw that the offending soldier had fallen asleep. He turned to the younger woman. 'Please try to restrain your companion,' he said pleasantly but loudly enough for the young officer to hear. 'We do not want any more trouble, and the *Leutnant* does have the authority to order an arrest.' The older woman made a defiant shrug with her shoulders but said nothing and turned to look out of the window. Tadzio had his back to the Germans. He winked at the younger woman, who gave him just the faintest smile. Then, he turned to face the officer, who gave him a nod of appreciation.

A relieved Claude was waiting at the rear end of the carriage. 'You had me worried back there,' he said softly, 'but well done. That was brilliant.'

He left the station at Boulogne. Claude went with him to the staff exit. As Tadzio thanked him, he looked relieved to be free of his charge. A question to a waiter outside a café gave him directions to the harbour. He did not have a map, but given sight of the sea, he knew he had to head south. Leaving the town, he found what was little more than a country lane that ran parallel with the coast. He changed into civilian clothes in a field behind a hedge and left his uniform bundled up underneath it.

His destination was Étaples, an estuary village just north of Le Touquet nestling in a nature reserve. It was where the Canche river entered *La Manche*, or the English Channel, as they called it. It was a popular holiday destination and something of a centre for enjoying either the river or the estuary in small boats. The principal harbours such as Boulogne or Calais were closely guarded, but it should not be difficult, they had assured him, to steal something in this much less supervised rural area.

He was only vaguely aware of a bicycle approaching from behind. He moved closer to the hedge. 'Good evening,' said a woman's voice loudly, in English. He had already turned automatically to look over his shoulder before he realised his mistake. 'I thought so,' said the cyclist as she braked to a halt alongside him and stepped through the frame. It was the younger woman from the train. She was quite tall and handsome rather than beautiful but still attractive to look at: she had a good figure, and trim ankles emerged below a midi-length skirt.

'Do you want to speak French or English?' she asked, still in that language. She had a slight French accent but sounded fluent.

'You startled me,' he answered, buying time by speaking in French.

'Monsieur,' she replied in the same language, 'I studied at the Sorbonne. Possibly the finest language school in France. You speak it well, but you are no Frenchman, although a German would probably not be able to tell. And I heard your German. You *do* have an eastern accent. But you did not learn French as a German,' she went on, 'your accent is much more like one of an Englishman. And if you learned French when your everyday language was English, and you are now in France, then you must be something to do with the English war effort – probably a member of their armed forces.'

Tadzio, heart racing, thought for a moment. She was obviously highly intelligent but not a threat – at least not to him. Had she wished, she could have betrayed him on the train or immediately afterwards at the station. He switched to English. 'So how did you know where to find me, just now?' he asked.

'Easy,' she replied. '*Maman* lives in Boulogne, not too far from the station. She walked home whilst I followed you. Once I had realised that you were taking the coast road south, I went back to her house, where I had left my bicycle earlier today. You were unlikely to be offered a lift – hardly anyone can get petrol these days. So either you were on foot or in a horse and cart. Sooner or later, I was sure I would catch up.'

Tadzio cursed himself for being careless – after the train journey, he had not thought to check whether he was being followed. 'All of which begs the question,' he went on, 'of why you are so interested that you take the trouble to follow me and make this approach? What do you want of me, Mademoiselle?' he asked.

'It's Madame,' she replied automatically, then added, 'although I think I am now almost certainly a widow. And let me guess, then I'll answer your question. You are going to the area of Étaples, are you not?'

'And if I am?' he queried. 'After all, that is where this road leads, does it not?'

'You are trying to get back to England,' she stated bluntly, as a matter of fact. 'The major ports like Boulogne or Calais are closely patrolled and guarded. But Étaples is quite remote. There are no Germans stationed there – the nearest are in Le Touquet, further south. So,' her shoulders lifted, 'either you are trying to find a fisherman who will take you across the channel, or perhaps you hope to steal a boat. But someone has given you good advice on this part of the coast and where you might have the best chance of success.'

Tadzio was surprised by the accuracy of her deduction, but he was not quite ready, just yet, to confess the truth of his intentions. 'Why should I trust you?' he asked bluntly.

'You don't have to,' she replied. 'You can walk on, and I shall ride away and forget even that we have spoken. But I live in that area. Like many French people, I have good reason to hate the Germans, perhaps more than most. You would not be the first English person we have tried to help. So, it's your choice. Do I ride on?' she concluded.

They walked for a few paces, then he stopped and turned to face her. 'My name is Tadzio,' he began. 'I am from Poland, but now I am fighting with the British Army. And yes, I am trying to get back to England.'

'Nicole Chevalier,' she said, extending her hand. 'I can offer you somewhere to stay, and we will work out how best we can help *you*.'

They turned off onto an even narrower lane. There was a healthy hint of ozone, so they could not be far from the sea. After about half a kilometre, they came to a two-storey house, set well back on what appeared to be a smallholding. Nicole led the way around the house and left her bicycle leaning against a windowsill. Taking an old-fashioned-looking key from her skirt pocket, she unlocked what turned out to be the kitchen door. Tadzio was invited to be seated at a large wooden table. Nicole disappeared into what appeared to be a larder and came back with a bottle of wine. She opened it and took two glasses from a cupboard. After raising her own glass in salute, which Tadzio reciprocated, she took a generous gulp. 'I needed that,' she said, then after a moment's pause, 'so, you had better start by telling me what you want to do.'

'Quite simply,' he replied, 'I want to get back to England. I was told that in this area I might be able find a fisherman who would take me.'

'Won't work,' she said bluntly. 'First, the fishing fleets are monitored by a patrol vessel when they are out. And second, the fishermen have all been told that if any of them are caught trying to escape, they will be shot, and even if they succeed, their family will still be sent to a concentration camp in Germany.'

'So I have to steal something,' he said, thinking out loud.

'Anything with a motor and capable of crossing the channel has either been requisitioned or is guarded,' she told him. 'But we have helped one of your countrymen before. He set sail in a small dinghy. I don't know if he ever arrived, but he knew how to sail – it was his hobby, apparently, before the war.'

'I can steer a boat,' said Tadzio, 'but I know nothing about sailing. I have never even set foot in a sailing boat.'

'Then that's going to be your next challenge,' she said enigmatically. 'But for now, we have to think about supper. I prepared a chicken casserole to heat up, which I was going to have with some cabbage. But if I add some potatoes, it will stretch for two. Would that be all right?'

Tadzio affirmed that it would. 'But why are you helping me?' he asked. 'You know you are taking a huge risk.'

'My husband is a pilot,' she explained. 'Or perhaps I should say "was". He flew a Morane-Saulnier, but he told me it was underpowered and under-armed, so no match for the Messerschmitt 109. His squadron fought the Germans as they invaded, but one of his colleagues wrote to say he was shot down. His aircraft was on fire. They did not actually see him crash, they were in action at the time, but no one can recall seeing a parachute.' Nicole shrugged her shoulders in a sad expression of acceptance. 'So, almost certainly, I am a widow.'

'How will you live?' asked Tadzio. 'I mean, how will you manage?'

Again, a Gallic shrug. 'We – or I – own this house,' she explained, 'and in the countryside, we are a lot better off for food than the unfortunate city-dwellers. Also, I work. Before the war, I was a teacher. Now, the Germans in Le Touquet have told me I must work for them as a translator. Also, I am required to give French lessons to some of their officers. I hate them, but I have to live, and I am well paid. I have a lot of information – I would be happy for you to mention that if you manage to reach England.

If anyone wants to contact me, just have them say your Christian name, then I shall know that they are genuine. I sent the same message with the person I shall call your predecessor, but there has been no reaction so far.'

'Maybe he didn't make it,' Tadzio suggested. There was no reaction from Nicole. 'And he was a sailor. So what chance do I have?' he wondered out loud.

'Before the war, Maurice and I were members of a local sailing club,' she answered. 'From the back of this house, there is a path to the estuary. If we turn inland, about a kilometre upriver, there is a barn set well back from the bank. When war broke out, we moved the boats from the hard standing by the clubhouse further along the river and put them inside it. So far, the Germans do not know they are there. Tomorrow, I will show you. Also, I will tell you how to sail. After that, if you are prepared to take the risk, and the weather is right, a night sail should get you inside English coastal waters.'

CHAPTER 10

At first, it was the light, so bright – even with her eyes closed. Then, as consciousness returned, Anneliese was aware of being in a bed. There was a hospital smell of antiseptic. Slowly she opened her eyes to an aura of whiteness, from the colour of the walls and ceiling to the sheets and pillows. The overhead light was switched on, although sunlight streamed through a window. Anneliese lay still for a few moments, trying to gather her thoughts. The last thing she remembered was being on a train, and then with something of a panic, she recalled that a woman had stabbed a needle into her neck. She lifted her arms first, then moved her legs. She was in bed but not restrained.

Exhausted, she lay still. There was a rustle of clothing. A nurse in a white uniform walked forward into her field of vision. 'Welcome back, Fraulein Hoffmann,' she said kindly. 'How do you feel? You will be thirsty. Can I help you to some water?'

Without waiting for an answer, the nurse poured from a small glass decanter on a bedside cupboard and, her arm round Anneliese's shoulders, raised her gently and held the glass to her lips. She sipped gratefully.

The nurse let her lie back. 'Where am I?' Anneliese asked anxiously. 'What happened?'

'You are in a private nursing home in Switzerland,' the nurse told her. Her voice was soft and reassuring. 'We are taking very good care of you, and someone will be along tomorrow to explain everything. But for now, it would be best if you could try to take another rest.' Anneliese still felt overwhelmingly tired. She closed her eyes.

The next time she stirred, the curtains were drawn, and the light above her head seemed less bright and focussed away from her pillow, illuminating the room. 'You will be hungry.' Again, it was the same nurse's voice. 'Would you like supper? Perhaps scrambled egg or a salad? If there is anything else you would prefer, please tell me, and we will do our best.'

She felt much stronger now. Anneliese raised herself onto her elbows. She was beginning to feel on more equal terms with the nurse standing before her. And she was also beginning to feel angry.

'Why am I here?' she demanded. 'What time is it? And where are my clothes? I should be in Paris, not Switzerland. I wish to leave immediately and contact my parents.'

She pulled back the one sheet covering her and swung her legs over the side of the bed. She was wearing a white nightdress that was not her own. The nurse made no attempt to stop her. She stood, carefully, not steady on her feet, and held on for a few seconds to the metal frame of an over-bed table. Her balance returned, and she took the few steps to the door. It was locked.

She turned to look at the nurse, who had returned to her seat. 'Please calm yourself, Fraulein Hoffmann,' she said quietly. 'To answer your question, it is Tuesday evening. You have been unconscious since we brought you back from Basel late yesterday in a Swiss ambulance. We are not treating you as a prisoner, but for your own safety, you must stay here overnight.

'Now,' said the nurse, 'please go back to bed and allow me to order you some supper. I promise all will be explained to you in the morning. And there is a wireless on one of the side cupboards, should you wish to listen.'

The nurse picked up a telephone. Shortly afterwards, there was a knock on the door, which was unlocked from the outside, and an orderly wearing a white jacket entered with a tray which he set down on her bed table. He lifted a domed cover to reveal an omelette, separate mushrooms, buttered asparagus and a few *pommes frittes*. Bowing slightly, he knocked on the door, which was opened for him, and left the room. The door was re-locked from the other side. Anneliese realised that she was indeed hungry. This was a meal intended for a patient who might still have a delicate stomach, but it was not ordinary hospital food. On the contrary, it had been prepared by a competent chef. There was even a half bottle, already opened, of a good Rhine wine.

The nurse picked up a book. After the meal, Anneliese found a Swiss radio station playing classical music – the slow movement of a Beethoven piano sonata. She did not object when the nurse switched on a small table lamp and turned off the overhead light. Soon, after the meal and the wine, she drifted off into a comfortable sleep. Her last thought was to wonder whether they – whoever *they* were – had put anything into the wine.

There was a knock on the door. 'You have a visitor,' the nurse announced after breakfast the following day. Until then, she had ignored all Anneliese's demands that she explain what was happening.

'Hello, Anneliese darling,' said a very familiar voice.

'Charlie Fitzgibbon!' she exclaimed, amazed, as her visitor deposited a massive bouquet on the table, now at the foot of her bed. Charlie rushed to embrace her old friend, and they hugged for a full half minute. Then, finally, she stepped back.

'It's lovely to see you,' said Anneliese, 'but what on earth are you doing here? Are you going to tell me, at last, what *im Himmel* is going on?'

'Yes, that's why I have been sent here,' came the reply. 'To tell you what in heaven, as you put it, is going on. You might be cross – in fact, I think you have every right to be. But we have been friends for a long time. So please try to stay calm, and remember that I am only the messenger.'

Anneliese realised she had no choice. She sat up, turned, bunched her pillows, then folded her hands on her lap, waiting for her friend to speak.

But first, Charlie turned to the nurse. 'Thank you,' she said politely, 'but I would be grateful if you would now leave us.'

To Anneliese's surprise, the nurse rose from her seat and knocked for the door to be unlocked. Then, removing it from the outside, she handed the key to Charlie and left without another word.

'Right,' said Charlie, tossing the key onto the bed table next to her flowers. To Anneliese, this seemed a small change in status – perhaps, with the arrival of her friend, she was no longer completely alone nor quite such a prisoner.

'First off,' she began, 'I have a message from Charles – as in Kaye-Stevens, in case you had forgotten.' She smiled almost conspiratorially as she mentioned his name. 'He realises that you will probably be both hurt and angry, but he wants me to tell you that he loves you. What started out as an official assignment changed completely, but by then he was trapped, despite his feelings for you. It might help you to know that yesterday, when you left for Paris, he put in a formal application to leave Switzerland immediately and be posted to active service with his regiment.'

'Where is he now?' asked Anneliese.

'Still in Switzerland,' came the reply. 'The application won't be forwarded just yet, if at all. But we can talk about Charles later. What you need to know is that another person, another Anneliese Hoffmann, is now working in Paris in your place. Which is why you were sidelined, as it were, and then returned to Switzerland in an ambulance.' She hesitated, then, 'You will realise that for us, the United Kingdom, this is a massive intelligence coup against Hitler's Nazi regime.'

Anneliese was quiet for a moment, finding it hard to come to terms with such a blunt revelation. 'And where does that leave me?' she asked eventually.

'With conflicting loyalties, I suspect,' said Charlie honestly. 'You volunteered to go to Paris and help the war effort, but were you helping your country or Hitler's Third Reich? We know your family is not sympathetic to the Nazi Party; otherwise, they would not have sent us a warning message when you and I spent Christmas together in '38. So I think you have to choose.

'And there is another thing,' she went on, 'I happen to know the woman who, with incredible courage, has taken your place. In fact, she is a close friend. If you betray her, she will be tortured and shot. I, for one, would be heartbroken.

'And finally,' she concluded, 'perhaps you could give some thought to yourself and Charles. He told me that you both despaired of a life together, but he loves you, and he is sure you feel the same way about him. Nothing is impossible – although you and Charles would need to talk. But should you wish, we have the means and authority to establish a life for you both. So, will you talk to him?'

'When?' asked Anneliese.

'Now, if you wish. The last time I saw him, he was along the corridor, pacing up and down like an expectant father outside a maternity ward.'

*

'I gather it all worked out well in the end,' said Sir Manners Fitzgibbon to his wife as he drew the curtains against the English rain rattling in the dusk against the windows. 'Although when he first walked in, apparently she told him that she needed the radio; otherwise, she would have thrown it at him.

'But they had a very honest discussion,' he went on. 'Anneliese wanted to know what would happen if she did not cooperate, and he told her as gently as he could that for security reasons, she would have to be interned in England. Kaye-Stevens explained that it wouldn't be a concentration camp like they have in Germany, but nevertheless, although she would be well treated, she would lose her freedom. I don't know what was said after that,' he said apologetically, 'only that they talked for the best part of an hour before he went down on one knee, and she accepted.'

'I think that's lovely, but what will happen now?' asked Madeleine. 'Do you really believe that she's genuine and can be trusted, or just avoiding the alternative only to betray us the first chance she gets?'

'Charles had a long discussion with James Summerton,' he replied. 'It got him into a certain amount of hot water as he hadn't previously revealed the full depth of the relationship. It seems that but for the war, they would have been thinking about marriage anyway, even though with a German wife, Kaye-Stevens would have had to resign his commission. But with the war, they had to conclude that a life together was out of the question.

'Then the brigadier spoke to both of them,' he went on. 'This Paris job was more of a career-come-adventure thing – she had volunteered before Kaye-Stevens came along. Anneliese wrote to Charlie and she passed the news on to me. She didn't want to work for the military because of her intense dislike of the Nazi Party. Sommerton's judgement is that she truly does love Kaye-Stevens. So as for whether Anneliese can be trusted, his feeling is that her views on the Nazis plus her genuine love for Kaye-Stevens means that she can. She won't betray Charlie Fitzgibbon's close friend – apparently, she told him that this would be almost as bad as betraying Kaye-Stevens himself, and although she is a German national, this she would never do.'

'So where are they now?' asked Madeleine.

'Spending the night at the embassy,' said Manners. 'The ambassador's wife insisted that they have separate bedrooms,' he added with a grin, 'but the brigadier happens to know that there is a connecting door between them! As for bringing them home, our American cousins have access to a DC3, and they'll fly the pair of them to Gibraltar for us, no questions asked. From there, we'll use an RAF Catalina on its way back from the Malta run for the last leg. Just extra insurance – Anneliese will not have contact with any non-military personnel.'

'Then what?' she asked.

'Then they get married,' he told her. 'And I have a gut feeling that at least one, if not both of them, could make a very useful contribution within my organisation.'

*

The next morning was cold and blustery with low clouds threatening showers, if not driving rain. There were whitecaps on the waves in the estuary. 'Got to be a good force four north-westerly,' said Nicole, 'so you won't be going anywhere tonight. We have to have a wind somewhere between south-east and south-west. But we'll check over the boat, and I can explain how everything works.'

They walked upriver for about twenty minutes till she turned left and followed a well-defined path along the edge of two fields to a good-sized barn. She unlocked a heavy padlock, and Tadzio helped open one of two heavy wooden double doors. There were about ten dinghies inside, all set out on the floor. Some had their rigging and sails inside them. There was a gap in the front row. 'That's where mine used to be,' she told him. 'I gave it to the last person we helped, your predecessor.' She touched one next to the space. 'This one belongs – or belonged – to Maurice. I don't mind giving it to you...' She hesitated. 'He would have approved.

'The design dates back to the early twenties,' she told him, pulling off a canvas cover, 'and it was used when France hosted the 1924 Olympics. It's not a bad choice for a channel crossing – as you can see, the foredeck is covered, which will help keep you dry. It's quite a heavy boat, and although I wouldn't normally cross the channel in a dinghy, five metres is a good length – she'll give you more than a fighting chance. And I'll rummage around in the other boats for a bucket.' She smiled at him. 'It's a standing joke that nothing bails faster than a frightened sailor.' Faced with the seeming complexity of the dinghy, with all its ropes and sails, Tadzio did not return her smile.

'It's what we call a *houari*,' she went on. 'I remember the last Englishman told me you call it a Gunter rig. Anyway, it has a foresail, then a large four-cornered sail behind the mast. The mainsail fastens to a boom at the bottom and a gaff spar at the top.'

'Are you sure I will be able to manage this?' asked Tadzio nervously. 'It looks complicated.'

'It is, a bit,' she conceded. 'I've been giving it a lot of thought. It's about sixty kilometres to the English coast or thirty-seven and a half of your English land miles. I suggest you do away with the mainsail and just run under a jib. That way, you'll only have one line to contend with in the cockpit, plus, of course, you will be steering with a tiller.' She ran a finger along the varnished woodwork. 'Without the mainsail, you won't be able to point up towards the wind, but if we wait until it's more or less behind you, then given a good breeze, you should make about three knots, maybe four. Which means that if you leave at last light, you should be off the English coast by dawn.'

Nicole spent some time searching the other dinghies in the barn. She did indeed find a bailing bucket with a long lanyard attached, which she tied off inside the cockpit – also, a large yellow oilskin cape. 'When we sailed downriver from the clubhouse,' she explained, 'a few people took everything home that they could, but most of us were in a hurry, so we didn't. Pity about the bright colour, though,' she told him, 'but you won't need to wear it unless it's raining, and in poor visibility, it probably won't matter.' She taught him how to raise and lower the mast and centreboard, and she demonstrated how he would need to move the sail from one side of the dinghy to the other – a gybe, she called it – if the wind changed direction. They could not finally rig for the journey until they were outside the barn. 'But don't worry, I'll be with you on the night to make sure that everything is all right before you set off,' she told him.

'My main worry is navigation,' she told him that evening over a glass of wine. 'Your predecessor had a torch and a compass. I can give you another hand torch, but I don't have a second compass. So we'll have to have a night with the right wind and not too much cloud. You need to head pretty much north-west. At first, you'll have sight of land, but after that, it will be a case of keeping the wind in the right place and hopefully with a star to follow.'

'I can find the pole star,' he told her. 'I was taught how to do this crossing from Germany to Sweden. And if I have to navigate only on wind direction, come sunrise, I shall have confirmation of where east is, so if the wind has shifted, I can make a correction.'

Nicole took this in. Perhaps he could make the passage...

'But don't let yourself get set too far to the east,' she cautioned, 'otherwise you'll leave Dover to port and find yourself sailing up *La Manche*.' She smiled. 'That's what you presume to call the English Channel, even though half of it is ours.'

It was two days before Nicole judged conditions to be right. Tadzio paid for his keep by doing a lot of heavy digging on the smallholding. But that evening, they walked to the barn. Nicole had given him a warm, heavy jumper that had belonged to her husband. It was not a bad fit. It took two of them to lift the dinghy onto a launching trolley, which they dragged over the fields to the estuary shore, by which time they were both sweating.

In the fading light, Nicole rigged the mast and bent on the one sail. Leaving it on the deck, she led the sheets back to the cockpit. When they were ready, she took off her plimsolls and pushed the dinghy into the water. She turned it round and stood knee-deep at the stern, holding it steady. 'Take off your boots and everything below the waist, then wade out and climb aboard,' she told him. 'At least that way, you can start off with dry clothes.' She politely looked away from the estuary.

When he was in and dressed again, she launched herself into the cockpit. Nicole sorted out the centreboard and tiller, raised the jib with the halliard and made it fast on the mast. She showed him how to pull on the sheet till the sail's leading edge stopped shaking. 'Then you can usually edge it out a bit,' she explained, 'but don't let it shiver at the luff – that's the front bit.' The sail set, she turned a couple of figure of eights round a cleat and sat back.

'Take the tiller,' she instructed as the wind took them along the estuary. He found the steering incredibly sensitive, compared to his only other experience, a fishing boat in the Baltic. But he soon had the hang of it.

'It's a good steady southerly,' she raised her voice above the wind, 'so keep it on the port quarter – the left-hand side of the stern of the dinghy – and you should be all right. You happy now?'

'As happy as I'll ever be,' he told her, 'but how do I set you ashore?'

'You don't have to,' she said. 'When we leave the estuary, and you settle onto your course, it will only be a short swim to the beach.' She took off her dress to reveal a swimming costume.

Nicole rolled the dress tightly round her plimsolls and stuffed it down the back of her costume. She moved to sit next to him, gave him a firm kiss on the lips, then stood and jumped over the centre of the transom to surface behind him. She waved once before setting out with a steady breaststroke for the shore. She was soon out of sight.

Tadzio made sure the wind was coming from the right direction, then re-set the jib. The dinghy was moving along quite nicely, not too much splash from the waves and just heeling steadily. For a while, he could see the coast of France, but then that, too, disappeared. There seemed to be a lot of cloud cover, but he was not too worried. Perhaps it was a confidence born of ignorance, but keeping the wind on his stern quarter, he settled to his task of sailing for England.

He didn't have a watch, but Tadzio reckoned that it was past midnight when he first heard the rumble of an engine or engines. Then he saw it – a fast patrol boat not showing any lights. But, unfortunately, it was coming from the direction of France. He had heard of the German E Boats. At first, he thought it would pass well clear, but to his dismay, the engine note dropped, and it turned in a wide circle to stop in front of him, about fifty yards away, across his course. After all this, he thought sadly, he was about to become a prisoner of war.

CHAPTER 11

Hedda studied the list of contacts given to her by Frau Becker. The Gestapo input came from one *SS-Sturmbannführer* Werner Scholz – who had the fanciful rank of Assault Unit Leader, which they claimed to be equivalent to that of major in the army.

Frau Becker offered to telephone 84 Avenue Foche to set up an appointment. It was, she added, the headquarters of the *Sicherheitsdienst*, the counterintelligence branch of the *Schutzstaffel*, or Protection Squadron, Hitler and the Nazi Party's major paramilitary organisation. She returned a few minutes later to report that the *Sturmbannführer* had suggested a meeting at his headquarters. 'It's just childish power-play,' she added. 'When Head of Chancery was writing the report, he was so senior to Scholz that the *Sturmbannführer* stiffed his arm out over here, in this office. But he undoubtedly knows who you are,' she went on, 'and that you are more or less equal in rank, although if anything, the fact that you are embassy means you have the edge. Shall I tell him not to play games and get his Nazi backside over here?'

Hedda thought for a moment. She liked Frau Becker's attitude. And not least the opinion the secretary had inadvertently revealed of the Nazi Party. 'No,' she said thoughtfully. 'I appreciate your support. But I would quite like to see the Avenue Foche, and it would be good to meet him on his own ground – please just ask for an appointment.'

'He said he'll send a car for you,' said Frau Becker a few minutes later, standing in the doorway. 'Ten o'clock tomorrow morning.' She smiled. 'I think the offer of a car was by way of an olive branch.'

At one minute to ten, the reception desk phoned to say that her transport was waiting. Hedda had taken some care with her choice of outfit. Herr Richter had already complimented her on her appearance and smiled approvingly when she told him why she had dressed for where she was going: a Chanel suit, sheer blouse, heels, plus a little additional make-up – not what Werner Scholz would be expecting from an embassy civil servant.

A tall, good-looking man in a well-tailored suit was waiting for her at the reception desk. 'Werner Scholz,' he introduced himself. No Hitler salute, she observed, just the more traditional click of the heels and slight bow. 'I hope this is in order,' he said politely. 'It seemed discourteous to ask you to travel with just my driver and an escort. Shall we…?' He indicated towards the door he opened for her.

The driver and escort, seated in front, were also in plain clothes. As she settled into the Citroën's rear seat, she noticed that the front seat passenger held a sub-machine gun below the level of his side window. Scholz closed her door and walked quickly round the rear of the car to sit beside her. Each turned to look at the other. He was, she thought, quite unlike the image she had of the Gestapo. Most upper-class Germans regarded them as little more than thugs, men recruited from the lower classes after the Great War, many of them unemployed former soldiers who now enjoyed positions of power that would have been unthinkable a few years ago.

But Werner Scholz was different. For a start, he could afford a decent tailor. He dressed and behaved like a gentleman. And he was blessed with aristocratic good looks: unusually tightly curled blond hair, blue eyes, high cheekbones and a firm, slightly cleft chin. His lips were, if anything, a little thin, but he had an engaging smile. Altogether, she thought, he was an attractive man. Hedda was quite tall at just under 173 centimetres, what the British called five foot eight, but even with her heels, he was still a little taller.

At the entrance to a large house in the Avenue Foche, the front seat escort hurried to open the door for her. Werner Scholz took her elbow and guided her gently through double doors, returning the salute of two armed, uniformed guards at the entrance with a finger casually touching the brim of his hat. Another uniformed guard at a reception desk stood quickly to attention and greeted him with, '*Guten Morgen, Herr Sturmbannführer.*'

'Fraulein Hoffmann, from our embassy. She is with me,' he said briskly.

'*Jahwohl, Herr Sturmbannführer,*' came the automatic response.

She walked with him along a corridor to a large office at the rear of the building. It held a partner-sized desk near the window behind two upright chairs, but slightly to one side of the room, on an expensive-looking carpet, were four comfortable armchairs around a highly polished low table.

'Would you like coffee?' he asked. 'Or something stronger, perhaps a glass to welcome you to our headquarters?'

'Just coffee would be fine, thank you,' she replied, thinking of all the work that awaited her back at the embassy.

He pressed a button on a box on his desk and ordered, not waiting for a reply.

'Let me tell you about this building,' he offered. Raised eyebrows indicated her interest.

'The routine administration takes place on this floor,' he began. 'For your information, there are five. Above us is the wireless unit, known as Section IV. Their job is to search for enemy radio operators. Then we use captured sets to transmit false messages.

'Above them are the *Standartenführer's* people. They identify people we wish to send back to Germany. The Reich needs labour, although not all of them are suitable.' He did not, she noticed, mention what happened to those who were not acceptable.

'On the fourth floor are the offices and private quarters of the commander of this building. And finally, on the top floor, we have facilities for holding suspects brought to the building for interrogation.'

She managed not to show the slightest sense of disapproval. 'By the way, Fraulein Hoffmann,' he added casually, 'I have read your file. I think my people know of your family, although I don't think we have ever met.'

She thought 'my people' might refer to his own relatives, but there was just a hint of uncertainty. Did he, perhaps, mean the Gestapo? She decided to take his remark at face value and said nothing.

There was a knock on the door, and a waitress entered with a tray of coffee. Werner Scholz poured from a cafetière and handed her a china cup and saucer. She declined cream and sugar. It was excellent coffee – but then, the Nazi Party would have access to all that Paris had to offer.

'How are you enjoying the city?' he asked her.

'I have not had time to see much of anything,' Hedda replied. After that, she decided to stick purely to business. 'I have to produce my first report by the end of this week, so I hope you have some input for me?'

He walked behind his desk and took a large envelope from a top drawer. 'You should find this helpful,' he told her, setting it on the table in front of her. 'It is very much the usual contribution we have provided for your Head of Chancery.'

'Thank you,' said Hedda. 'It has been good to meet you, and thank you for telling me about your organisation here. Presumably, from now on, you will send the weekly reports over as usual?' She finished her coffee.

'Indeed,' he confirmed. 'But you said you have not had an opportunity to enjoy Paris. I was going to suggest dinner this evening, but clearly, you have much to do before the end of the week. Would you perhaps consider dining with me on Saturday? I would very much look forward to introducing you to Paris and also to the pleasure of your company.'

She thought quickly. He was *SS*, but a different class of Gestapo… perhaps a useful contact. And it was a very gracious invitation. 'Thank you,' she replied, after only the briefest hesitation. 'How very kind – something to look forward to after a week's hard work.'

'I will pick you up at eight, if I may,' he said. 'I hope you will enjoy the Ritz.'

He was telling her in the most subtle way that they would be dining formally. She would dress to the occasion. Hedda picked up the envelope. 'Till Saturday,' she said with a smile.

'The streets are not entirely safe,' he told her after she thanked him for the coffee and stood to leave. 'I have my car available. Please allow me to escort you back to the embassy.'

He was far too well mannered to make it obvious, but, Hedda thought to herself, he was definitely interested.

The next problem was that when Herr Richter had produced the report, he had written it in longhand and handed it to Frau Becker to be typed. But for what she had in mind, Hedda had to type the report herself.

'Herr Richter,' she began, 'you may recall that during my interview, I mentioned that I handled all my father's correspondence, even when he was there.' She had his attention now, although he made no comment. 'Well,' she went on, 'we did not have the luxury of a typing pool. I took a course – it was much more cost-effective. I am a competent touch typist. If it is all right with you, I would like to type the report myself, first as a draft that I can proofread and then its final version. There are two advantages. First, I can work twice as fast – I don't have to hang around whilst somebody else transcribes my handwriting. And second, there is less chance that I will overlook any silly typing mistakes. I automatically check my own work as I go along.' She paused for a minute to let this sink in. 'The only problem,' she concluded, 'is how would you feel about a typewriter being used in our shared office? Surely that would be a nuisance?'

She did not get quite the answer she was looking for. At best, she was hoping for the use of a separate room. If not, that Frau Becker would at least find her a space in the outer office where she could work on the report.

'This is a large enough office,' he replied after thinking for a moment. 'I don't see that it will be a problem. If it is, we'll think again. But for now, just ask Frau Becker to find you a really top-quality machine' – he smiled at her – 'perhaps the quieter, the better.'

Her second concern was more easily solved, and here Hedda had one item of good fortune. The stationery supplies for the embassy had been procured locally before the war, and no one had seen any reason to change this arrangement. There were only two copies of the weekly report: one went through Herr Richter to the ambassador, and the other was retained on file. She was required to number the copies and enter their details and final destination into the classified register. A clerk checked the carbon papers into a bag of classified waste for disposal. During a lunch-hour break, it had not been difficult to find a shop and purchase a pack of the same carbon paper used by the embassy.

Hedda deliberately worked late, alone in the office on Thursday evening, to meet her deadline. She inserted a double layer of carbon paper. When she had finished, one set went into the waste bag, as usual. The extra carbon paper she folded tightly into a small square, and it left the embassy under the circular puff in her powder compact.

Herr Richter had complimented her on the report, as had, half an hour or so later, His Excellency. Hedda announced that if it was all right, as it was a nice day she would treat herself to a glass of wine and lunch. 'I know you worked until very late last evening,' Herr Richter told her. 'When I came in this morning, I saw that it was almost midnight before you signed out. So there's really no need to come back this afternoon.'

Hedda thanked him, and he wished her a pleasant weekend. But it was time to put her recent instruction into practice. As Marie had briefed her, she walked to a nearby park. There, she sat at a particular bench, and when there was no one else in sight, she placed three chalk marks on the edge of the top, slatted back rest.

She sat there for some time, seemingly enjoying the sunshine, before rising to her feet and walking to a nearby café with tables on the pavement. She ordered a simple salad and a glass of red wine. But, remembering her tuition, she did not set down her knife and fork neatly side by side, as would have been polite in England. Instead, she left them carelessly apart on the plate and mopped up the last of the dressing with some bread.

Simone was still at home when Hedda returned mid-afternoon. She took a parcel wrapped in brown paper from her bag, and set the parcel and two bottles of red wine on the kitchen table. 'I told the head chef in the canteen that I wanted to cook for myself this evening.' She smiled. 'I think he rather fancies me. I asked him to be generous. There's almost half a kilo of steak, *surlonge*, some mushrooms, and a few tomatoes and potatoes. I had lunch not long ago, but take all that you need. I'll cook for myself a bit later, if you don't mind, after you have gone to work.'

'Thank you so much,' said Simone, genuinely appreciative. These were rations that she could neither afford nor obtain for herself. Hedda noticed later that Simone had taken just one glass of wine and somewhat less than half of the rations. She made her own meal, washed up, then settled to another glass of wine, a Beethoven concert on the wireless. It was strange, she mused whilst enjoying her final glass, that the Germans could be so brutal yet so gifted musically. Tomorrow, if all went well, she would hand over the carbon paper concealed in her powder compact.

Simone had not appeared the next morning when Hedda let herself out of the apartment. She had been vaguely aware of a door opening and closing some time after midnight. Perhaps Simone had been for a drink with her chemist friend after work.

She looked up and down the street and began the routine designed to ensure she was not being followed. Several times she paused to look in a shop window, she took a coffee in a building that allowed her to leave by a different exit, and finally, she sat in a park and read a newspaper for at least twenty minutes. Then, satisfied that she was not being observed, she headed for the restaurant specified by Marie. It was mid-morning. The only other person who entered was an elderly woman. She ordered coffee and cake. Precisely fifteen minutes later, she settled her bill and made for the exit. A stranger with a yellow bow tie entered as she was leaving. As they passed, Hedda's hand, close by her side, held out a small envelope containing the carbon papers. It disappeared between his fingers and immediately into his coat pocket. The stranger settled on a stool, leaned his elbows on the zinc, and called for a coffee and cognac. Hedda walked into the street. In the unlikely event that he would be asked, the proprietor could report only that she had been entirely alone and had neither spoken nor made contact with anyone. It had been a perfect brush-pass.

Back at the safe house, the bow-tied man inspected the contents of the envelope. One chalk mark signified a routine message that could probably be transmitted by radio. Two would have indicated one too long for the radio, but not that urgent. Three meant lengthy but also highly sensitive and – or – urgent. Holding the first page up to the light, he began to realise the significance of the sheets of carbon paper. He re-folded them, returned them to the envelope and slipped the envelope into the inside pocket of his overcoat. That way, if necessary, he had at least a chance of getting rid of evidence that could see him tortured and shot. He took a lunchtime express to Switzerland. A King's Messenger took an American DC2 flight to Dublin, from where the precious envelope was flown overnight by a small private aeroplane to Croydon, although the pilot was a serving officer in the Royal Air Force.

'This is absolute gold dust,' said Sir Manners Fitzgibbon to Doreen Jackman and Bill Ives, waving a typed transcript. 'The latest and accurate figures of German aircraft losses and, I might say, the first absolute confirmation we have had that Hitler postponed his *Unternehmen Seelöwe* on Tuesday last – Operation Sea Lion will not now take place, so we now know for definite that the United Kingdom will not be invaded. Moreover, this will allow us to redeploy scarce resources desperately needed elsewhere. And there's a hell of a lot else besides: living conditions in France, their perceived threat from the resistance and how they are trying to counter it, the extent to which all this is tying down their troops and resources… brilliant!' he exclaimed, setting down the document with a flourish.

'I agree,' said Doreen Jackman with enthusiasm. 'Chaffinch has exceeded all expectations. And our responsibility, now, is to put this information to the best possible use. I only wish we had more resources on the ground.'

*

'*Où allez-vous*, Froggie?' called a voice from above. A seaman in a white polo-necked pullover leant over the side of the patrol boat. But the Germans would not have called him 'Froggie', and the accent was definitely English. Tadzio was overwhelmed with relief.

A second white pullover appeared alongside the first. 'Don't you Froggie me,' shouted Tadzio, as he turned the dinghy to drift alongside the other craft. 'I'm Sergeant Janicki to you, and I'm trying to get back to England.'

'In that case, old chap, try not to scratch the bally paintwork,' said an officer-like voice. The first sailor threw down a scrambling net, and seconds later, Tadzio had climbed aboard. The dinghy painter, which was long enough to reach the gunwale, was still in his hand. The first sailor took it from him and walked aft to tie it off somewhere astern.

The officer held a revolver that was pointing at the deck. But he was a couple of yards from Tadzio and could have brought it instantly into the aim. 'You don't sound English,' he said suspiciously. 'Any identification?'

Tadzio quoted his Army number, rank and name. 'Polish,' he added, as he took his identity disks from round his neck and tossed them gently to the officer, followed by a brief one-minute outline of his time in France.

'Have to hand you over to the authorities, old boy, but we can give you a lift home,' came the reply. 'Pity to waste a good dinghy – we'll tow her gently, but if we meet any opposition, we'll have to cut her away so we can either fight or run.'

The first sailor had returned. 'Do you mind if we search you?' asked the officer politely. 'Just a precaution, you understand, seeing as you don't sound very British.'

Tadzio thought back to the incident in the railway carriage all those months ago. It seemed like a lifetime. 'Don't mind at all,' he said, 'but I am unarmed. I don't even carry a knife.'

The sailor patted him down efficiently enough, not forgetting his ankles and the small of his back. Then, satisfied, he stepped back and nodded to his officer.

'I'm Lieutenant Waldron, the number one, Sergeant Janicki,' he said. 'We'll take you below and give you a hot drink – I expect you could do with one. All being well, we'll be in Pompey within the hour.

'We'll look after the dinghy for you,' Lieutenant Waldron told him as they shook hands before Tadzio was handed over to two uniformed members of the Military Police. 'We're based in Plymouth – the headquarters will be able to tell you where to find me.' Tadzio had no idea where Pompey was. Only when he was ashore did he learn that he was in Portsmouth.

His escort was not officious, but neither were they friendly – which considering all that he had been through to return to England was, thought Tadzio, disappointing. He told his story to an unsmiling captain, his escort standing behind his chair, without mentioning any names or precise locations. 'So I need to reach certain contacts in London,' he told him, 'to pass on all the detailed information I have learned about the beginnings of a resistance movement. It will be invaluable to people that I know.'

'We have to check out your identity,' said the stony-faced captain. 'Meanwhile, I'm afraid you will have to be detained in custody overnight. We'll probably return you to your unit under escort tomorrow or the day after.'

Tadzio was frustrated, but there was no point in losing his temper.

'Captain,' he began, his voice firm but very level and unemotional, 'not long ago, I was fighting with partisans in Poland. I escaped with other people via Sweden. We were sponsored by a department in London that controls events so far above your security clearance level that you probably don't even know of their existence. I don't doubt you can do as you say and send me back to my unit. I shall then make an immediate phone call.' The captain was clearly taken aback by Tadzio's tone and information. 'But I urge you not to delay my information,' he pressed on rather more gently. 'I am going to give you a London number. Please ring, and tell them that you have Jan's brother, Tadzio, here. They will tell you what to do via your own chain of command. And whilst you are doing that, I really would appreciate something to eat and drink.'

The captain, a Scotland Yard officer but also a reservist called up for the duration, had known the fringes of the sort of organisation that the young sergeant was urging him to contact. 'Very well,' he agreed amiably enough. 'I'll make the phone call. But, in the meantime, please wait here with your escort. I'll see if we can rustle up something for you, probably be only tea and sandwiches at this time of night – fair enough?'

'Thank you,' said Tadzio simply.

Attitudes seemed to be changing. One of the escorts disappeared, the other offered him a cigarette. Tadzio was not really a smoker, but after the events of the last few days, the nicotine was a welcome distraction. The second escort reappeared, bearing a plate of cheese wads – buns and margarine with a thick slice of cheddar inside – and three tin mugs of tea. He also set down a jar of pickled onions and a fork. 'Nicked these from the kitchen,' he said, grinning at Tadzio. 'Help yourself.'

Tadzio had not long finished the first food he had eaten since a late lunch the previous day when the captain returned. 'Sergeant Janicki,' he said rather formally, extending his hand, 'I'm Captain Townsend. The number you gave me rang back. I have spoken to a lady called Miss Jackman, whom I believe you know well. After that, I had another phone call from my brigadier.' Townsend put his other hand over his and Tadzio's as they shook. 'I don't know much,' he said, 'but from what I have heard, honoured to meet you.

'I'm to put you on a train to London first thing in the morning,' he went on. 'Sergeant Jolliffe,' he addressed one of the escorts, 'do you have access to the sergeants' mess at this late hour? I think we should all take Sergeant Janicki for a drink – and if you could square it away, they will all be on me.'

'Duty Sergeant has the keys, sir,' he replied. 'Give me five, if you will, then the lights will be on, the shutters will be up, and I shall be delighted to invite you and Sergeant Janicki to join me as guests in our mess.'

They gave him a good breakfast, and a car took him to the station, for both of which he was grateful. Tadzio Janicki and his hangover boarded the train for Waterloo.

CHAPTER 12

Hedda looked out of the apartment window and watched the black Citroën draw to a halt. Rather than involve Simone, she left the building before Werner Scholz could ring the doorbell. She smiled appreciatively – he had chosen black tie rather than a uniform. He looked resplendent, from a beautifully tailored dinner jacket with expensive rippled silk lapels to a matching cummerbund and patent leather shoes.

He, too, smiled as he held open the rear door. Hedda had felt guilty, shopping in Paris for a mink stole. The Franc was now a subsidiary currency of the Reichsmark, with the exchange rate set ludicrously at twenty to one. Quite simply, this allowed the Germans to plunder occupied France. But Anneliese Hoffmann was wealthy in her own right and would have afforded the clothes Hedda was wearing. The black Elsa Schiaparelli cocktail dress, obviously bought just before the war and unearthed from Anneliese's suitcases, showed Hedda's figure to perfection.

Following the head waiter, Werner took her directly to their table. On the way, he nodded to several acquaintances. Most of the men were in uniform, quite a few of which showed the insignia of the SS. Their partners, she observed, were all younger and pretty, but their clothes did not quite match the hotel or the occasion.

They were Frenchwomen prepared to accept the attentions of German officers offering a meal in exchange for their company – and whatever else besides.

Even so, it was a glittering scene of white linen, silver cutlery, crystal glasses and table flowers. A small orchestra played – she recognised Offenbach, a French composer but German-born. Werner drew back her chair and she settled at the table. She rather liked that he had done this personally, politely indicating aside an attendant waiter. He ordered champagne, not generically but by name and vintage. The sommelier clearly approved. Perhaps, she mused, they were pleased to welcome guests who would have been at home here before the war rather than a more boorish element of falsely affluent occupying military.

'May I order for you?' he asked.

Yet again, Hedda mentally thanked Clarissa Ecclesworth for her tuition in London. But Anneliese would be a strong, confident woman. Hedda gave a slight shake of her head.

'I would like some oysters, please,' she replied. 'Nine, if I may. I always find six too few and a dozen too many! No fish course – but I like my filet de bœuf à point. Dauphinoise would be perfect. But please choose a green vegetable.'

Werner had the good grace to smile ruefully at the way he had been so neatly side-stepped, allowed to choose only one small element of her meal. He dutifully ordered the same for himself plus a selection of 'anything green'. The waiter tried hard to conceal his amusement. Werner did not bother to consult the wine list – the sommelier, attentively to hand, was invited to choose a fine claret.

'You are a lady who knows her mind, Fraulein Hoffmann,' he said admiringly. 'But now that you have so beautifully put me in my place, may I call you Anneliese?'

'Yes,' she replied, 'indeed you may, and I shall call you Werner. And by the way,' she added, 'I'm pleased that you are not in uniform but also curious to know why?'

'I knew I would have the pleasure of a beautiful German lady's company. And please allow me to say that you look absolutely exquisite. I wished to set us apart.' He indicated the rest of the room. 'I doubt if some of my fellow officers even own a dinner jacket, and none of their ladies have your class.' Then he added with a grin, 'If they even qualify for that title in the first place, which somehow I rather doubt.'

She smiled gracefully at both his compliment and the irony. 'So, Werner Scholz,' she replied, 'other than you have been described to me by the ladies of the embassy as both dashing and a heartbreaker, I know nothing about you.'

'Is that what you see?' he replied evenly.

She was somewhat taken aback by his question. 'I'm going to choose my words carefully,' she said. 'I have not made the acquaintance of others within your organisation, but you must know that it has a certain reputation. Although politically, you hold a tremendous amount of power and influence.' Hedda decided that this was as far as she could reasonably probe, so she let her observation hang in the air.

'I know how the traditional German officer class regards us,' he replied. 'I, too, am of that class.' He smiled at her as if to lighten the conversation. 'The only reason I don't have a duelling scar is that I am very good at it. But perhaps,' he went on more seriously, 'instead of my class sticking together and despising my organisation from the outside, it might make sense for at least some of us to share that power. Perhaps, even to offer a balance from within.'

Almost as soon as he had said it, he wondered whether he had been indiscreet. But no, he rationalised, he knew Anneliese Hoffmann's family background: wealthy and very much part of the establishment. 'I understand,' she said quietly. 'And thank you for sharing a confidence. Although I think I had pretty much worked that out for myself.'

They were interrupted by the arrival of their oysters. After that, the conversation turned to more congenial matters: families, what they had been doing before the war and leisure interests. They discovered a shared love of classical music, not least opera. After the beef, strawberry parfait gave way to coffee and, for Werner, a brandy. Hedda wanted to keep a clear head. She had to keep reminding herself that this was rather more than a dinner date.

Werner had mentioned that he lived in a requisitioned apartment, but he made no more mention of it when they left the hotel. His driver was instructed to take them to Madame Simone's address. On the pavement, Hedda thanked him for a lovely evening, which she had genuinely enjoyed. He kissed her hand. 'May I ring you during the week?' he asked, still holding her hand for longer than was decorously necessary. 'I would very much like to see you again.' The inflection in his voice clearly made it a question.

'I would like that too,' she found herself saying without thinking. 'Please do – telephone me, I mean.'

He released her hand, and she extracted a key from her evening bag. He waited by the car whilst she opened the door. Only when she was safely inside did she hear the sound of the engine as the Citroën accelerated away.

Simone was in the small lounge enjoying a cup of coffee from the beans 'Anneliese' had brought from Switzerland. 'I hope you don't mind,' she said, indicating the cup, 'but you did give them to me.'

'Not in the least,' said Hedda. 'They're yours. But tell you what, I have a bottle of brandy in my room. So if you wouldn't mind making me a cup, I'll change into something more comfortable and bring it back with me.'

'You look like a million dollars,' said Simone wistfully. 'But I would love a brandy.' She stood and walked towards the kitchen.

Later, alone in her room, Hedda tried to analyse her thoughts. A year ago, she had been a partisan fighting in Poland, intent on killing every German in her sights. Because of anti-Jewish legislation, her German father, a highly respected university academic, had been reduced to poverty. She recalled with a shudder that he had soiled himself whilst slowly choking to death hanging from a doorway in their Berlin apartment. With no choice but to return to her family in her native Poland, eventually, her mother had also taken her own life. At Bletchley Park she had not heard from Tadzio for some time before her deployment to France. They had been lovers, but now she was unsure what she felt.

And she had just enjoyed an evening with a charming SS officer. To be fair, he had shared something of his political views but not his ideology. Nevertheless, she found it hard to believe that Werner Scholz was a genuine Nazi. Hedda found *Radio Londres* on the wireless and poured another glass of brandy. She reminded herself sternly that she was here as part of the British war effort, not to enjoy dinners at the Ritz. She would develop her relationship with *Sturmbannführer* Stolz for professional reasons. But Hedda ignored the small voice in the deepest recess of her mind that suggested this might not be entirely the truth.

*

Tadzio knew his hangover would soon fade with the resilience of youth. His spirits were also buoyed when he discovered that someone, probably Doreen Jackman, had sported the funds for a first-class ticket. At Waterloo, a man held a sign in front of this chest that said 'TJ'.

'Are you looking for me?' he asked him.

'You the Polish gent, sir?' the man replied. Tadzio confirmed that he was and followed the man to a car parked outside. Twenty minutes later, he was seated in a comfortable chair, a cup of good coffee alongside, whilst he told Miss Jackman all that had happened since a German aircraft had destroyed their tank and killed his driver.

'We had a standing instruction,' she told him, 'that because of our involvement with your brother and Hedda, if your return was reported by any of our authorities, we wanted you to be directed here rather than to your unit, which would have normally been the case. For some reason it obviously didn't reach the Military Police, so I'm relieved that you insisted on making contact.'

'Where are Jan and Hedda?' he asked. 'And how are they?'

'Both well,' came the reply, 'and both deployed. However, you will understand that I can't tell you where or pass on messages, for security reasons. But if there is any change to that news, I give you my word you will be the first to know. But back to you,' she pressed on. 'Tell me all about your time in France; I need to know every detail.' With questions, the debrief lasted for a good half-hour. 'So,' Doreen Jackman concluded, 'you have been on the loose, surviving in France for the entire summer. You now have good French, as well as German, you have established a cover identity with this woman Liliane, and her friends want you to train and lead a resistance group. And you have genuine French documents – we would like to borrow those, if we may, just to make sure that any we forge for someone else are up to date. Then there is Nicole, who gave you the dinghy and helped you escape. You say she openly hinted that she would be happy to pass on information gained through her enforced position with the Germans. It seems to me that you have set up at least one if not two embryo resistance cells.'

She paused, then, 'This department is now called the Special Operations Executive,' she informed him. 'We're quite a new organisation – we were formed officially on 22nd July this year under the Minister of Economic warfare, one Hugh Dalton. Our brief is to conduct espionage, sabotage and reconnaissance in occupied Europe. I think you are wasted as a tank commander,' she told him bluntly. 'You are now a much more accomplished asset than the man who landed with Jan and Hedda earlier this year. We take only volunteers. Would you be prepared to join us?' Tadzio told her that his mind was made up. He wanted to return to France. If SOE had deployed Hedda, he could do no less.

'Think it over carefully,' she advised quickly. 'Spend the night at a safe house, go out and have a few beers, then come and see me in the morning. But I'm going to be brutally honest. We will train you. But unless they are outstanding, or perhaps extremely lucky, I fear that not many of our operatives are likely to see the end of this conflict.'

The next morning she told him, 'I have already spoken to your Commanding Officer. 'Colonel Wylde sends his best wishes and congratulations. He was delighted that you survived and made it back. Although he was less than pleased when I said we were going to poach you, as it were. Seems you are well thought of – they were going to put you up for a commission.'

Tadzio thought for a moment. 'So what happens now?' he asked.

'We don't want to waste time hanging around whilst you go through officer training,' Doreen replied. 'So we'll have you honourably discharged from the Army, and you will join us as a civilian volunteer. Look on the bright side. Instead of being an officer cadet, you will have officer status and pay. The staff at your old mess have already packed your things, not knowing whether you were just missing or something worse, so they will send them on.

'But you will need training for your new role,' she explained. 'We now tailor courses for individuals. It's a new concept, sort of modular. Although we'll give you a one-day refresher, you won't need weapons training, but you will require explosives and demolition instruction. Then we'll give you the basics as a radio operator, including Morse. Next, you will have to learn tradecraft. And to return to Europe, I'm afraid there's also a parachute element. You will have to earn your wings.'

'His brother thoroughly enjoyed the training,' Sergeant Hathaway confided to Doreen Jackman afterwards, 'but Tadzio absolutely hated it. I've been doing this training for a long time. Know what to look for. However, there was never the slightest hesitation. You tell him to jump, and he's out. That takes a different sort of courage. Not my place to say so, ma'am, but he'll be all right. He's a good man.'

132

Some of his instructors had also helped train Jan, Marie and Hedda, but Tadzio was entirely unaware of this. They all knew better than to risk the lives of those training to be SOE operatives. There was no careless talk to cost lives. As the Army put it, 'no names, no pack drill'.

One month later, Tadzio made a night exit towards a remote field in occupied France. As his parachute opened and he lowered the attached drop bag, he heard the pilot pull on the power and turn for home. He did not know that it was the same reception party that had welcomed Hedda only a few weeks previously.

Safe in Marie's kitchen with his drop bag – Marius and Edouard had already buried his parachute – Tadzio enjoyed a hot coffee and a cognac. 'How will you travel to your base on the farm?' she asked. She knew it was somewhere on the other side of Paris, but for safety, that was all she wished to know.

'Train to Paris,' he told her, 'then another one further north. It'll be a long day, but I should make the farm somewhere around nightfall.'

'I know you have genuine French papers,' she said, 'and your clothes and things are authentic. But even so, it's dangerous,' she reminded him. 'You are carrying a radio. If you are asked to open your luggage, it will be a firing squad.'

'I'll have two items,' he told her, 'the radio in its suitcase, and a holdall with my clothes and a few other things – including a Browning HP. The radio I'll place away from me, the holdall immediately to hand. Then, if necessary, I can open it whilst they try to determine who owns the suitcase. But I have to have the radio at the farm, so there's no other way. I will just have to take a chance. Worst case, I might have to shoot it out.'

The radio was heavy, some thirty pounds in a two-foot-long suitcase. Doreen Jackman had mentioned that female operators had to practise carrying it so that they did not attract suspicion by obviously hefting its weight. Still, for Tadzio, this was not a problem. The next morning he checked and reloaded the Browning, which he stuffed into the left-hand side of his trouser belt. His heavy jacket would conceal it. Marie took him in the pony and trap to the station at Nogent. 'Your French is excellent,' she told him, 'but you do have a slight accent.' So to avoid anyone remembering a possible foreigner and using a few of the not inconsiderable funds he had brought with him, she purchased his ticket. Finally, she kissed him on the cheeks and wished him luck.

He had, however, left her with a problem. Having briefed London on his contact with Nicole at Étaples, London were keen for Marie to develop her as an informant, with a view to building up a cell in that area. But Tadzio had travelled to the coast in the uniform of a French railway conductor. That was hardly an option for Marie. Moreover, rumours were rife that the coastal areas were being developed into a forbidden access zone. She would talk this over with Jean Renaud, but for the moment, she had no idea how to reach Nicole.

Midweek in early October, the train was not crowded. Tadzio was asked for his ticket, but there were no other checks. In Paris, he changed for Arras. Again he was lucky, only a French inspector, and he arrived there late afternoon. But he still had to walk the last few kilometres to the farm. There was always the possibility of running into a German patrol. Just to be sure, he walked through the town, but once into the countryside, he settled behind a farmer's hedge and rested until dusk.

It was late evening when he reached the farm. He set down the suitcase and his holdall and withdrew the Browning. A light was on in the kitchen and the curtains had not been drawn. He approached from a side angle, to avoid its loom, till he could take a cautious glance through the window. Music was playing on the wireless. Liliane was seated at the kitchen table, a glass of wine to hand. Tadzio moved to stand in front of the window and tapped it with a forefinger. She looked up, startled, then rushed to open the door. Hastily he pushed the Browning back into his belt and turned to greet her. They did not embrace – she grabbed his upper arm and pulled him into the kitchen before kissing him briefly on the lips and stepping back. 'What the…?' she began, but he held his finger against his lips in the universal gesture for silence.

'Are you alone in the house?' he asked. She nodded. 'Then I have to bring in my luggage,' he told her. 'First thing in the morning, we have to find somewhere to hide this one,' he added, setting both pieces on the floor. 'It's a radio.'

'So you came back,' she said in a quiet voice. 'Jean-Claude was convinced you would. I wasn't so sure. Even after I tried my hardest to keep you here, I thought that if you made it back to your own kind, you would want to rejoin the war and fight for England again.' They both smiled at the memory.

'Pour me a glass of wine,' he asked her, 'and I'll tell you as much as I can about what's happened.' She also refreshed her own. 'A toast,' he said, raising his glass. 'To France, and to the Resistance.'

CHAPTER 13

'I, Anneliese Brunhilde, take thee, Charles Edward…' Even as she read the order of service for the first time, by way of preparation for her marriage, Anneliese could scarcely believe what would soon happen. The wedding would take place, by special licence, in the small, private chapel on the Fitzgibbon estate, one almost fallen into disuse but, they had been assured by the local priest of the parish, still in a good state of repair and – more importantly – a consecrated building.

From Switzerland to Southampton, her journey, at first in an American DC3 and then a Royal Air Force Catalina, had been an interesting if slightly unnerving experience. However, it was made bearable with Charles at her side and also the company of Charlie Fitzgibbon. In Gibraltar, they had been accommodated overnight by the RAF Station Commander before take-off for England early next morning. Charlie had arranged for her father's driver to meet them with the Bentley, and they had arrived at the family estate with time only for brief introductions and a nightcap before taking to their rooms. Anneliese had been grateful for Madeleine's welcome. 'Let me show you the way,' she said, giving her guest a hug with an arm round her shoulder. 'My son is home for half term – you'll meet Perry in the morning. I have put you and

Charles into two singles.' She gave her another squeeze as if she were a fellow conspirator. 'But don't worry, he's only next door.' Anneliese was both pleased and relieved that her hostess was not that far divorced from her own age.

She unpacked her meagre belongings. Most of her things, she now knew, were in Paris. As suggested, she left her new Swiss passport on a dressing table. 'It's genuine,' Charles had said, handing it to her on the plane. It was a couple of years old and had stamps indicating travel to France and Italy, but not Germany. 'The staff are only human,' he said, 'so they're bound to look at it.' Her English was excellent, but she had a slight but well-defined German accent. 'They won't like it if they know you are German,' he told her, 'and they will probably gossip, which is the last thing we want. But if they see for themselves proof that you are a neutral Swiss national, you will be accepted, so that won't be a problem.'

Next morning Anneliese experienced the breakfast ritual of an English country house. All manner of ingredients were set out in chafing dishes on a sideboard. The household did not take this meal together. Instead, they wandered in and out at a time of their own choosing. Anneliese found herself seated with Charles and Sir Manners, who suggested that they meet at ten for a conference in the library. Remembering the good times at her finishing school and being introduced to the English breakfast, she helped herself liberally to bacon, eggs, mushrooms, a sausage and – her absolute favourite – devilled kidneys.

Brook set down a tray in the library. There was a fresh pot of tea for Sir Manners and Charles and a pot of coffee. 'May I pour for you, Miss Hoffmann?' he asked with a warm smile.

'Just black, please,' she accepted gratefully. Either Sir Manners had said something, or the chambermaid had looked at her passport – perhaps both. Hence the coffee. But although in a strange country and household, she felt both welcomed and at ease.

'The problem now,' Sir Manners began, 'is what we are going to do with you. I am a member of a security committee,' he went on, 'and we have talked long and hard about your future.' He did not explain that it was a 'committee' of three, Doreen Jackman and Bill Ives with himself in the chair. Better that she believed he was acting under orders rather than being the arbiter of her future.

'Because of the all-consuming importance of our operation in Paris,' he confided, 'the committee is obsessed with security. I hope you will understand their concern,' he added, looking at Anneliese, who inclined her head in acknowledgement. 'More particularly,' he continued, 'I am to tell you that they do not for one moment doubt your sincerity, but nevertheless, I am instructed to ask if you will remain as our guest in this household, at least for the time being. I need hardly add,' he continued after a moment's pause, 'that you would be most welcome. Madeleine has tasked me particularly to tell you how much she would enjoy your company. Perry will return to school after his exeat, and with me away in London all week, she finds herself somewhat alone. She would love to have you stay here as a companion.'

It could not have been put more courteously, thought Anneliese. But the British intended to make sure that she could not betray their agent in the German Embassy. Charles had explained the alternative: an internment camp, possibly on the Isle of Man. Humane, certainly, compared with a concentration camp in her own country, but a form of imprisonment nevertheless. However, in return for her cooperation, she was being offered a very comfortable lifestyle and the freedom to marry the man of her choice. Anneliese would have preferred to have been trusted unconditionally, but she understood their reservations. She would accept, not least for the sake of their forthcoming marriage.

Later that morning, she and Charles went for a walk in the grounds. 'I've had another chat with Sir Manners,' he began. 'One thing concerns me. I have met your parents, and although the war separates us, I think they would accept and even approve of our union. But I am an only child, and I think my parents would be devastated if we suddenly turned up and I announced that we were man and wife. So how would you feel if I suggested that you meet them? Sir Manners said that he would have absolutely no objection if we stayed with them for a weekend.'

They had been walking a little apart, but she moved closer and hooked her arm underneath his. 'I would like that very much,' she said simply. 'I am sad for my parents, but it is only right that you should introduce me to your own, and I think they have to be there when we are married. I only hope that they will approve. But what will you tell them – that I am German?' she asked.

'I'll have a word with Pater,' he told her. 'He's a wise old bird. I can tell him that you have dual nationality. Although you were born in Germany you are undertaking important work for our government and also have a Swiss passport. He'll know not to press for too much detail. I'll give them a ring and tell them we will arrive on Friday evening and come back here on Sunday.'

Anneliese was disappointed when Charlie announced that she would drop Perry off at Uppingham then return to what she called her rather hush-hush administrative duties. But, unfortunately, her leave of absence was at an end. 'I'm sure they'll give me time off for the wedding,' she said, 'but we probably won't meet again for a while after that.' She did not mention that her father had already arranged this with her superiors. As he had said to her privately, it was important to support Anneliese as much as possible during what had to be difficult and strange times for the young German woman.

'The trains are awful,' said Sir Manners when Charles mentioned that they would like to spend the weekend visiting his parents. 'Tell you what, take the Bentley.'

'Sir, that's extremely generous,' responded Charles, 'but what about petrol coupons? I left my MG at home when I left for Switzerland, but I'm not sure if I will have been given enough to pay you back.'

'Don't want to sound pompous,' replied Sir Manners, 'but I helped set up this Paris thing. We must look after Anneliese,' he smiled kindly towards her, 'and I don't think a crowded stop-start train to London, a traipse across the capital to change stations, then another kangaroo session up to Worcestershire quite meets that remit. I do have a little authority, and I can put these coupons down to a very worthwhile duty.'

Sir Manners' Bentley was a 1938 Park Ward, four and a quarter litre, two-door pillar-less sports saloon. Resplendent in deep red, with its long clamshell front wings and separate silver headlights, it was the most beautiful car Charles had ever seen. 'It's the uprated model,' Sir Manners told him, handing Charles the keys. 'Four forward gears and an overdrive. Have a good weekend and my compliments to your parents.'

They arrived at a small country house between Bromsgrove and Redditch in time for tea. Anneliese felt nervous. Charles's parents came out to greet them as they drew up alongside a plain single front door. His mother rushed to embrace her son whilst Charles's father shook his hand. But his eyes were glued to the Bentley. Anneliese found herself alone for a moment, but she need not have worried. 'I'm Muriel,' Mrs Kaye-Stevens introduced herself, stepping back from her son and taking one of Anneliese's hands in both of her own. It was not a handshake, more a gentle hug of welcome.

Charles's father, a tall, rather distinguished-looking man still with a good head of hair, although it was more silver than black, ushered them into the house. Mrs Kaye-Stevens was a little shorter than Anneliese, and it was clear that Charles had inherited his father's good looks, but she was still an attractive woman with a slim figure. 'I've put you in your old room,' she told Charles. 'Why don't you bring your things whilst I show Anneliese the way?' The guest room was at the rear of the house, overlooking the countryside. A small fire burned in the grate. It was both warm and cosy.

'We're simple country people,' Muriel explained, 'and from what Charles has said over the phone and in his letters, I rather suspect that your background is, may I say, rather more elegant.

But you are very welcome here, and I hope you will enjoy your stay.'

Anneliese had already deduced that Charles came from a good family, one that Clarissa would have described as upper-middle class, and she was touched by the warmth and kindness of his mother. As if on cue, he appeared in the doorway with her suitcase.

'Put it on the bed, Charles,' his mother instructed, 'then Anneliese can come and join us when she is ready.' There was no maid to unpack this time, but she did not care. She reminded herself that it was not all that long ago that she was living in a small one-bedroomed flat. Charles's father, James, offered sherry and proposed a toast 'to the new member of our family'. Muriel excused herself and disappeared into the kitchen. Later they moved to the dining room for what Charles explained was a traditional Friday supper of fish, parsley sauce and vegetables. 'My own produce,' said James. 'Being a country lawyer is not a physically demanding occupation, so the exercise in the garden does me good.' He moved to the sideboard for a bottle of white wine.

Conversation also flowed. They were interested in Anneliese's family and background but too polite to ask too many questions. She explained that she had a Swiss passport and had lived there, as had her parents. She would not lie to such decent people. 'And I gather you now work for our government,' James observed, without questioning further.

'I am to be a translator,' she told him. 'In Switzerland, we speak German, French and Italian, but German is my mother tongue.' James deliberately turned the conversation to Charles's MG and asked what he intended to do with it.

'What's an MG?' asked Anneliese, turning to Charles.

'It's an MG TA – a small sports car,' he explained. 'I left it in the garage before leaving for Switzerland.'

'Do you have petrol?' she asked quickly, an idea forming in her mind. Charles confirmed that he did.

'The tank's full,' he told her, 'and I haven't used any of my coupons. I'll introduce you to her after breakfast.'

He spent the first hour of Saturday morning thoroughly checking over what he referred to as his mistress. Anneliese busied herself with a large yellow duster borrowed from Muriel and removed all the dust from the – now – shining green paintwork. It was a lovely October day. They drove the few miles to Redditch with the roof down, and he showed her the county high school where he had been educated. Standing with their back to the imposing front entrance topped by its stumpy dome, they looked over playing fields to the farmland beyond, and to the gentle crest of the skyline far in the distance.

'This was – is – a state school, what you would call a *gymnasium*,' he told her. 'I was happy here. But before the war, most Army officers were from public schools, which in England means that they are private and fee-paying. Then I went to Oxford. That and the fact that I studied modern languages were probably the only reasons I was accepted for a commission. When I joined, I was one of the few officers in the regiment without a private income. The MG was the result of a fortunate inheritance from a bachelor uncle,' he explained with a rueful smile.

She was quiet for a moment. 'One day, I would like to show you my school,' she said wistfully. 'Like yours, it is set in beautiful countryside and not too far from *München*.' She hesitated, then said softly, 'I wonder where we will educate our child?'

It took a second or two for Charles to realise the enormity of those few words. He moved to stand in front of her, hands on her shoulders. 'You mean...?' he began.

'Yes,' she broke in gently, 'I am going to have a baby.' Tears formed in her eyes. 'Now seems as good a time as any to tell you. I'm sorry, I know I told you that I was being careful, but things didn't quite work out as I thought they would.'

'*Liebling*,' he said quickly, deliberately using the German endearment. 'That's wonderful news.' He pulled her gently into an embrace.

'I didn't know what you would say,' she told him nervously, managing to extract an arm and dab at her eyes with a handkerchief.

'How long have you known?' he asked her.

'Not long,' she replied. 'But I have always been very regular. And now I'm not. But I don't think attitudes will have changed in Germany,' she added. 'I know my parents would stand by me, but they would be mortified. And from what I have seen of your lovely parents, I think you would also be in for a talking-to,' she finished with a faint smile.

'Can't we wait?' he queried. 'I mean, not say anything just yet. Perhaps a honeymoon baby, just a little early? I confess I don't know about these things.'

'That will be fine,' she reassured him. 'It will be our secret.'

They walked, hand in hand, back to the MG.

'I love your car,' she said as they settled into the seats. 'Why don't we take it back to Stonebrook Hall with us? Then you would have your own transport. Even if we could just go out for a drink from time to time, that would be lovely.'

'But I have to take the Bentley back,' he argued.

'I could drive the Bentley,' she said mischievously. 'After all, I have driven Father's Mercedes often enough. But I would hate to have to tell Sir Manners if I scratched it. So why don't we take both cars, and I'll drive the MG?'

'You never told me you could drive,' he responded, surprised. 'Young ladies don't, as a general rule.'

'Well, I'm not a "general rule", as you put it,' she told him bluntly. 'Father never wanted a chauffeur; he always enjoyed driving himself. And he was quite happy when I begged him to teach me. Tell you what,' she added, 'let's swap. Then you can find out whether you're content to let me drive your precious mistress.' She resisted the temptation to enjoy herself too much with the MG, which was, he warned – rather unnecessarily, she thought – capable of eighty miles an hour. Still, she pushed along briskly, and, he had to admit, she handled it perfectly. 'There you are,' she said as she parked in his parents' drive, 'you can be a gentleman and put it in the garage.'

On Sunday, they went to morning service at St Bartholomew's in Tardebigge, with its impressive spire. After a lunch of roast pork – Charles's father mentioned that a farmer friend had given him a whole leg – they set off for what she now thought of as her second home. Anneliese was mindful that although she was trusted, there was still a concern for the total security of the Paris operation, so she drove carefully and at a pace that tested neither the MG nor the following Bentley. They arrived in time for the habitual cold collation of Sunday supper.

'Technically, Charles, you are still the assistant defence attaché to Berne,' Sir Manners pointed out as the two of them took tea in his study after an early breakfast on Monday morning. 'But how do you see the future panning out?'

'Brigadier Summerton has kindly authorised a few days' leave effective after the wedding on Saturday, but as things stand, I will be due to return to Switzerland at the end of next week,' he replied.

'I'll give your brigadier a ring as soon as I'm back in the office,' said Sir Manners, 'but I can't see the Army supporting the luxury of an experienced officer staying with the diplomatic service, what with the war and everything.'

'In which case, I'll be posted back to regimental duty,' Charles observed. 'Probably to command a company of one of the Territorial Battalions after the losses at Dunkirk. I know it'll be a worry for Anneliese, but I have already told Brigadier James that I would like a transfer to more active service.'

'Does you credit,' said Sir Manners, 'but doesn't a first in modern languages suggest that you could make a more important contribution?'

'You might think so,' responded Charles, 'and if they insisted on a transfer to something like Signals or Intelligence, I wouldn't say no. But I'm an infantryman, first and foremost. It's what I always wanted to do, and I enjoy it. Or at least I did until Hitler started this damn war, and I can hardly back out now. Like everyone else, I have to do my bit.'

'Would you consider working with me?' asked Sir Manners, rather quietly.

'What, working inside some sort of ministry?' responded Charles, clearly taken aback by the invitation. 'I'm a soldier, sir, at the very least for the duration.'

'And so you would remain,' came the immediate response. 'And I am not part of "some sort of ministry", as you put it, despite the impression I may have given. My role is to build up and supervise a particular adjunct to the war effort. Our brief comprises espionage, irregular warfare – mostly sabotage in enemy territory – and special reconnaissance. We are recruiting both military and civilian personnel. So you can see why someone with your language skills would be of interest to us. You would be making a far greater contribution than ever you could with your regiment. But before I say more, what's your reaction?'

Charles paused for thought, taking his time. He was about to be married and to become a father. If he agreed, was he being selfish? Or would it be wrong not to make the best use of his talents? Sir Manners did not press him, but after a while, he added quietly, 'By the way, the training is arduous, and any mission will be dangerous.'

But, thought Charles, he was just as likely to get his head blown off fighting as infantry. And he and Anneliese would be separated anyway. What's more, the affair in Switzerland had whetted his appetite. He looked up from the carpet.

'I would like to volunteer,' he said quietly.

'Very well,' came the reply. 'Follow me up to town tomorrow. There's a spare room in my apartment. I'll arrange for you to see some people on Wednesday. Also, as soon as I'm in the office, I'll have someone phone your brigadier.'

*

Madeleine and Anneliese were taking coffee in the morning room when a Humber staff car appeared in the drive and Sir Manners joined them. 'Darling,' she began, 'what a pleasant surprise. It's only Thursday. We weren't expecting you till...' She broke off, seeing the look of anguish on her husband's face. He walked over to Anneliese, who put down her cup and saucer.

'My dear,' he said gently, one hand on her shoulder. 'I'm so very, very sorry... it was the blitz. The flat took a direct hit. Charles died instantly.'

Anneliese sat, silent, for several seconds. 'Thank you for telling me,' she said in a small voice. There were huge tears in her eyes, but she stood, holding her composure. 'Please excuse me,' she whispered, then, with a knuckle pressed to her lips, she rushed from the room.

'I'll give her a little time,' Madeleine said, 'then go to her. Forgive me for saying so, but thank God at least you are alive.'

'I was working late,' he replied. 'When I got back, they were beginning to pull people out of the rubble. Eventually, I was able to identify the body.' He exhaled audibly in sorrow. Then added, 'I've arranged for an officer and a padre to inform the poor lad's parents.'

CHAPTER 14

Liliane, Tadzio, the policeman Jean-Claude and Yves sat round the kitchen table. 'It seems a long time ago,' said Yves, 'since we were here together and I was telling you how to try to escape from France to England. Truly, we did not think we would see you again.'

'You were a great help,' said Tadzio, 'but the idea of a fishing boat turned out to be a non-starter. I was extremely fortunate to meet someone who helped me sail back in a dinghy. Best I leave it at that.

'*Eh bien,*' he went on. 'Let me bring you up to date. First off, I have a radio. Using it is not without risk, but I can send messages to London. They have agreed to a small arms drop.'

Yves and Jean-Claude looked at each other. 'Why only small arms?' asked Jean-Claude.

'At this stage, it's all we need,' Tadzio replied. 'Let me explain. Back home, by which I mean the UK, there is very little knowledge of what is now going on in occupied France. They get the odd snippet from soldiers like me who escaped after Dunkirk, or from downed airmen who also make it back, often via Spain, but it's very little. So I have been given a list of tasks in order of priority.

'London is only too aware that we are a long way from when major action from the resistance will be required,' he went on. 'So for now, heavy weapons – mortars, anti-tank rifles – are not as important as small arms and explosives, which will be sent in our first drop. After that, our number-one priority will be any task set by London, which might be a specific target or just reconnaissance.'

'Any other priorities?' queried Yves.

'Any form of sabotage that will hinder and tie down German troops,' Tadzio replied. 'Also, assassinations, particularly of key personnel, whenever possible. And, of course, the weapons are available if you decide to liberate supplies for your own use. These latter activities are left pretty much to our discretion.

'And one last point,' he added, 'the free French in London are developing a similar resistance over here. But unfortunately, there is pretty much zero cooperation between them and us. So if you learn of any activity in this area, it would be enormously helpful if you could let me know. Apart from avoiding any conflict of interest, we would surely be far more effective if we could work together.'

Yves and Jean-Claude nodded their assent accompanied by a murmured '*Oui*'.

'So what will you do now?' asked Yves.

'Contact London,' he replied. 'Use my sked tomorrow.'

'Use your what?' queried Liliane.

'My radio schedule,' he explained. 'All operators create one so that they never transmit at the same time of day or on the same day of the week. So the Germans can't track a pattern.'

'But isn't that dangerous?' she asked. 'They say the Germans can trace a radio signal to the place where it is being transmitted.'

'That's true,' he told her. 'But with only one detector, all they can establish is a position line. The sender could be anywhere along it but over quite a distance. To pinpoint a position, they need two detectors. Then, where the lines cross, they have the sender. But in a city, it takes about twenty minutes to do this. In the countryside, to have even one detector van in the right place at the right time is not that likely. To have two is much more difficult. If I'm quick, we should be safe enough, although to be honest, there's always a risk because even just a position line would pass through or be very near to the farm. If at all possible, I would rather not transmit from here.'

'I think I can help,' offered Jean-Claude. 'A lot of families fled south when the *Boche* came. There are several empty and boarded-up properties in the village, but most still have electricity. So you wouldn't even need to use the same one each time.'

'That would be ideal,' said Tadzio, relieved.

'But what about the drop?' Yves asked. 'Where will we do it?'

'Not on the farm,' he reassured them. 'We'll choose an isolated field not too far away but on someone else's property. Of course, if you know or suspect anyone who might be a collaborator, that would be even better – throw suspicion on them. But I can tell you from my experience in Poland, it's absolutely vital to collect the drop and clear the area quickly. Back then, we used pack horses.'

'Not a problem, this is a country area, plenty of horses,' broke in Yves. 'I can arrange it.'

'In which case,' Tadzio replied, 'I'll ask for four containers tied in canvas kit bags as two loads of two. That should be plenty for some small arms and explosives. We'll just sling them over a couple of horses, and we can be clear of the drop zone in no time.'

Tadzio carried the radio into the village the following morning. Liliane rode ahead on her bicycle. If she needed to tell him there might be a problem, she would stop and remove her beret. But Jean-Claude had chosen well. The three-storey house was detached, and Tadzio would be able to hang some eighty feet of aerial out of a rear attic window that faced out over the countryside. For now, they left the radio concealed in the house. Even if a tramp or some refugee used the building for shelter, it would be safe. And Jean-Claude would replace the window boarding.

Tadzio and Liliane left to return to the farm before dark. There was no formal nine-till-five curfew in the countryside, as was the case in Paris. Still, the Germans sometimes had patrols or roadblocks near villages, and being stopped after dark would always invite attention and unwanted questions.

'Mother will send two. Mother will send two.' The repeated BBC message confirmed that Tadzio would receive his drop to the designated field at the appointed time two days from now. It was a cold, clear night. They met at the farm, Yves leading two horses as promised. Keeping to the fields, they were well onto an adjacent property by midnight. Tadzio was concerned that, armed with only his pistol and a shotgun with each of the other two men, they were hardly well placed to defend themselves from any German intervention. But an 'X' of battery-powered lights was switched on when they heard the sound of aero engines, white parachutes billowed from less than a thousand feet, and seconds later, the field was once more in darkness.

Tadzio had prepared a hide under a pigpen on the edge of the farm. He turned out a disgruntled boar. They lifted a wooden flap, covered in turf and straw, to reveal a cavity lined with tarpaulin into which the canvas containers, each with individual items wrapped in oiled cloth, plus the parachutes, were concealed. With the boar herded back into the pen, they left the horses in the field and returned to the farmhouse for the night. Liliane had prepared a cassoulet. Tadzio opened two bottles of wine, and Jean-Claude produced a bottle of brandy. They toasted their operation, the resistance and France, in that order. Liliane chose not to mention the uses to which she would put the highly valued parachute silk.

The following day was fine and dry. Tadzio set to the task of unwrapping and examining the contents of the canvas kit bags. The first was one-third filled with plastic explosives, detonators, fuze cord and wired detonator boxes with the traditional T-shaped plunger. Tadzio had been taught how to use Composition C, which was mostly RDX mixed with a small amount of plasticiser so it could be moulded to any shape. More importantly, it would cut through metal such as railway lines. Underneath the explosives kit, he found a box of hand grenades plus ammunition for Thompson machine guns and six of the weapons. The other container yielded the same weaponry, more ammunition, half a dozen standard Enfield No. 2 Mk 1 .38 calibre revolvers and a couple of Very pistols. And he was relieved to find a couple of boxes of ammunition for his own Browning HP. It took the rest of the morning to re-pack the containers and return everything to the hide.

A couple of days later, Yves turned up. 'I think we should divide the weapons cache,' he offered after Liliane had produced a pot of coffee from her now almost finished stock of beans. 'Also, someone has hinted that he would like to join any organisation that's prepared to take on the Germans. He suspects that I'm involved, but he doesn't know for sure. His name is Serge Moreau, and he runs a small garage and blacksmith business in the next village. He repairs anything from motorcycles to farm machinery. Before the war, his father also had an agency to sell new motorcycles, but obviously, that's gone now. Serge and I go back a long way – were at school together,' he finished.

'Can you prepare a good hide on your property?' asked Tadzio. Yves confirmed that he could. 'We grow apples and make cider,' he replied. 'One barrel for half of the cache in a cider cellar should be safe enough.'

'Let's go and see your old school friend,' Tadzio suggested. 'And I agree, we don't want all our assets on one farm. So we'll make a plan – perhaps eventually a three-way split.'

Yves had deliberately not said much about his friend, he wanted Tadzio, as their unofficial but de facto leader, to form his own opinion. The property was isolated but just half a kilometre from the edge of the village. It stood in about a hectare of land. They found Serge in a large barn behind his cottage and adjoining forge. He was swarthy and quite short, heavily muscled and with black hair. A slightly hooked nose also hinted at North African Arab ancestry. He did not seem at all surprised when Yves turned up with a stranger.

There was no introduction. 'Yves tells me you want to oppose the Germans,' Tadzio said bluntly.

'Who are you?' came the reply, equally abrupt.

'I wouldn't be here if I didn't have Yves' trust,' Tadzio told him, 'so for now, who I am doesn't matter. You can tell me about yourself, or not, as you prefer, in which case I simply walk away.'

'He's all right,' broke in Yves. 'It's safe to talk.'

Some empty metal oil drums were lying on their side. Serge sat on one and waved his hand, indicating that they should do likewise.

'Very well,' he began. 'A few years ago, this place belonged to my parents, and it was my father's business. I was living in Paris at the time. Not to put too fine a point on it, but we were a small syndicate of criminals. A larger group tried to take over.' He shrugged. 'We survived. Most of them didn't. But I was known to one of our attackers who reported me, out of revenge. I was on a police wanted list, on the run, and it was a matter of time, so I volunteered for our Foreign Legion.'

'But you're a Frenchman,' said Tadzio.

'Didn't matter,' Serge replied. 'They were always relaxed about this. Invent a name, tell them you're from a French-speaking country. I said Belgium, and it was a case of no questions asked. I signed up for five years.'

'So then what happened?' Tadzio asked.

'The *Boche* invaded. That's what happened,' came the reply. 'I was about to be discharged: a new name with French citizenship, a clean start… instead, I was dug in with the 11th Foreign Infantry Regiment near Verdun. We held for a while, and then we were forced into a fighting retreat. But in one week, we lost three-quarters of our strength. Eventually, we were at Toul, on the banks of the Moselle. After the armistice was signed, we were disarmed, but some of us slipped away. I was lucky to make my way back home, only to find that my parents had fled south. So I am slowly picking up the remains of my father's old business.' He grimaced.

'The only good thing that has come out of all this is that the case against me in Paris is forgotten – it's history.'

Tadzio was quiet, thinking, for several seconds. 'Obviously, you are more than competent with weapons,' he said. It was more a statement than a question.

'Pretty much all small arms,' came the reply. 'Plus, I was trained to handle explosives. And my father had already taught me all he knew about engines and vehicles. That enough for you?'

Tadzio was not sure whether he was being deliberately confrontational as a challenge or that it was the traditional legionary contempt for authority. Nevertheless, it was an issue to be settled immediately.

'Your skills would be invaluable,' he said quietly. 'And yes, I am building up a resistance force. But my country is supplying all our equipment, and for the moment, it is up to London to decide how best to confront the *Boche*. If and when your Colonel de Gaulle can return to France, he will obviously assume command of all French forces. But for now, I must have your assurance that you will obey my orders. I'll make it even clearer. We will arm you, but you do nothing without my approval. Is that understood?'

The Frenchman looked at him for several seconds through narrowed, hooded eyes. Suddenly he broke into a grin and extended his hand. '*Absolument, mon ami,*' he replied. Tadzio's grip was equally firm. He just hoped that Serge would be as good as his word.

*

They had enough from the drop to divide the cache three ways. As good as his word, Yves produced his hide in a barrel – in fact, two barrels. After some experiment, he even weighted them with stones and lined them with cloth packing so that, given a casual push or a tap, they did not appear too different from the others. Serge had the benefit of a fair amount of woodland on his land. He lined a shallow pit with a wooden box, well inside one of several copse areas, and covered it with a superficial layer of earth and leaves.

Their target was the marshalling yard at the regional railway hub of Amiens. Claude Boulier, Yves explained, was reluctant to join the resistance. He was middle-aged, married, and had a wife and five children to support. Too young for the Great War and now in an occupation vital for the German war effort, he had no military experience. And as he said, he had never even held – let alone fired – a gun. But his station at Amiens had access to the routing and timetable of the *Société Nationale des Chemins de fer Français* – the French railway system. On the other hand, and as he had proved already, he was more than happy to help the cause of occupied France.

A consignment of aviation fuel intended for Juvincourt airfield, north and slightly west of Reims, would arrive overnight in three days' time. Captured during the invasion, it had been an unmanned peacetime practice landing field for the French air force, but it was now being enlarged rapidly by German engineers, to become a significant base in north-west France for the Luftwaffe. The loss of a complete consignment of aviation spirit would certainly reduce the effect of Hitler's recent decision to switch to the bombing of London. Rather than risk strafing – albeit not that frequent – by the Royal Air Force, the consignment would remain in the heavily defended yard complex by day and reach its final destination the following night. With a major airbase nearby and a heavy concentration of Flak 18s that could throw up fifteen to twenty high-explosive rounds per minute, the Germans were obviously hoping that the Royal Air Force would not mount a suicidal daytime attack.

The two of them were in Serge's barn, discussing the raid. 'We really need to mount a nighttime operation, but the depot will be heavily guarded. We don't have the manpower for that,' pointed out Tadzio.

'Agreed,' came the response. 'Perhaps we should blow the track as soon as it reaches open countryside after it leaves Amiens, derail the train and fire the contents. That would only need two people – perhaps you and me. We are the only ones who can handle the explosives, and two of us gives a better chance of success in case one person doesn't get through.'

'But that means we have to get to the other side of Amiens,' said Tadzio. 'It must be more than twenty kilometres.'

'Been thinking about how we are going to get around, ever since we first met,' Serge replied. 'Come and see.'

He led the way to the back of the barn and, with something of a flourish, removed a large sheet of canvas to reveal two motorcycles. 'Gnome et Rhone three-fifties, both 1937,' he said proudly. 'One belonged to my father. The other was probably brought in for repair just before the invasion because it wouldn't start. I fixed it the other day. There used to be another motorcycle with a sidecar, but I suspect my parents used it to go south. I found these two under some bales of straw – obviously, my father hid them before he left.'

'What about fuel?' queried Tadzio.

Serge nodded. 'There's plenty for this trip. There's a small tank behind the barn – the Germans missed it. Sooner or later, we'll have to steal some more, but that's tomorrow's problem,' he said with a grin. 'Now, take a look at the fuel tanks,' he invited.

Tadzio looked closely. 'I don't know anything about motorbikes,' he admitted, 'but this one looks normal enough to me.'

Serge unscrewed the filler cap. It seemed to take longer than usual. Then he lifted the top third of the tank clear of the filler pipe. It was hinged at the front and had been cut laterally to where the last of the tail section disappeared under the saddle. Only a thin rubber seal marked the division, which did not look at all out of place from the outside. Underneath, a new top below the empty compartment sloped from front to rear. 'Cuts down the range,' he said proudly, 'but still leaves plenty of room for our needs. I've done both tanks. We can hide the explosives and detonator wire, plus a Webley and a few spare rounds. Also, the firing handles from the detonator box. The rest of its innards I've disassembled and left inside it, now painted up and marked "spares". We can tie that to the luggage pannier. Even if they look, the Germans are not going to recognise the bits. We can tell them they're for the bike's electrics. I've thrown in a couple of bulbs just to make it look authentic.'

Tadzio was impressed by the ingenuity and workmanship and complimented Serge profusely. He just shrugged. 'I reckon we take the back roads but drive by daylight, starting early in the morning. We'll travel well apart. If one of us is stopped, the story is that we can't get any more petrol, so we are going to offer the bikes to the *Wehrmacht*, hopefully in exchange for some food and a few cigarettes. Depending on the reaction, the one behind can either follow on or turn round and make a run for it. But with any luck, at least one of us should get through.'

'Just the two of us, then,' Tadzio offered. It was more of a statement than a question. 'Your French is perfect; mine isn't. Perhaps you should ride in front.'

'We could just as easily be stopped by a German roadblock as the French police,' Serge pointed out. 'I picked up a few words in the Legion, but I'm not as fluent as you.'

Liliane was put out when Tadzio would not say why, telling her only that he would be spending two nights away and would not be back until the following morning. 'You're doing something with the resistance,' she said suspiciously. 'Surely I have a right to know? And why are you wearing all those clothes on a sunny afternoon?'

'Better you don't know, for your own sake,' he said gently. Then, his hands on her shoulders, he went to kiss her on the cheek. To his surprise, she took his head in her hands and pressed her lips to his. 'Just be sure to come back,' she said, quite harshly, Tadzio thought.

Obviously, there was still some feeling there, he mused, walking across fields to come out behind Serge's property. He would spend the night there, and they would set off in the morning.

CHAPTER 15

With Operation Sea Lion cancelled, France was a relatively inactive theatre – an absolute treat for those fortunate enough to be stationed there. And Berlin produced a constant stream of senior officers able to invent a plausible excuse – however thin – to visit, enjoy themselves and shop for their wives in the French capital.

Sometimes Hedda walked through the park on the way to the embassy; other days, she took a stroll during her lunch break. It was over a week since she had sent a copy of her first report. She would not send another until she had further information of significant interest to London. Her position was too valuable to risk for anything less.

So it came as a surprise when a chalk mark indicated a meeting. The arrangement was simple. That evening she would call at a small café on her way back to Simone's apartment. It was early in the week, so routinely, she would leave work at about half-past five. She smudged out the mark with her fingers.

She recognised him from their sole brush-pass. He was seated outside, well wrapped up against the slight chill of an otherwise pleasant autumn evening. She chose a table next to his and took a chair. They were not quite back to back. Only one other outside table was occupied, an elderly couple chatting quietly. They were well beyond earshot. She ordered a pastis, and he waited until the waiter had set down her glass and a small jug of cool water. She paid immediately, declining a few small coins of change.

'You have a commercial section at the embassy,' he said quietly.

Hedda did not respond immediately, making a show of diluting her aperitif. 'We do,' she said eventually, the glass at her lips to conceal any movement.

'London urgently needs information on French factories making vital items for the German war machine. Vehicle production, weaponry – complete or just components, whatever you think might be important. If you can identify them, we have bombing targets.' Out of the corner of her eye, she could see that he had unfolded a newspaper. She took her time finishing her drink then walked away.

It made sense. Without air superiority the Germans could not invade, and the British Army had lost most of its equipment at Dunkirk. So, for now, it was up to bomber command to take the fight to Europe. And the embassy *did* have a commercial sector. From their contribution to her first report, she knew that they had been commenting on French production facilities. Herr Richter's secretary, Frau Becker, had passed on their information, although it had all been rather broad brush, not in any detail. Merely that some factories had already been taken over, and their output switched to supporting the Reich's war effort.

As head of the outer administrative office and typing pool, Martha Becker had her own cubicle. 'Who and what do we have in the commercial section?' asked Hedda, closing the door behind her.

'It's the largest section in the embassy,' she replied. 'The older men are still there, although two younger ones have been called up. And all the girls have stayed on, some German, a few locally employed. The head is Herr Weigelin. He's a pompous old fart – too important to bring me their input himself, although I know he edits it. The draft is produced by his secretary, Irmgard Neumann.

She's the same age as me, and we're friends. It's Irmgard who delivers the final version.'

'Do you think you could ask her to come and see me this afternoon?' asked Hedda, trying to sound as casual as possible, as if the question were not that important. She knew that Herr Richter would be out of office. He always declared a 'sports afternoon' on Wednesdays, although she suspected that this comprised a good lunch with his cronies rather than anything more energetic.

She had not long returned from her walk in the park when Frau Becker tapped on the open door. 'This is Frau Neumann,' she announced.

'Come in, both of you, and sit down,' invited Hedda.

'I hope our report is satisfactory,' said Irmgard Neumann nervously.

'It's fine, and I'm grateful for it,' Hedda replied to put her at ease. 'It's just the detail that we need to discuss. But so that I have my facts straight, do you mind running through how the local procurement system works when we take over French industries for our own use?'

Frau Neumann took a moment to gather her thoughts. 'There are really two systems,' she began. 'Take Gnome et Rhone for an example. Before the war, they made motorcycles and aero engines. BMW has decided that they will make their 801 aero engine under licence. With a major project like this, they will put in their own engineers to supervise the tooling up. They report back to their own people in Munich, but we also report progress and production figures to Berlin.

'The other system,' she went on, 'is when, say, the *Wehrmacht* needs spare parts that can be produced locally. We find a French factory. They are ordered to switch their production to what we want. Our military engineers monitor quantity and quality, and the items are sent directly to our depots here in France.'

'And do you monitor and report on this?' asked Hedda.

'Not in any detail,' came the reply. 'Only to make mention of the extent to which we can help the *Wehrmacht*, as you will have seen.'

Hedda steepled her fingers and paused for a moment. 'Industrial production is vital to the success of our war effort,' she went on, 'and as you have reported, we are rapidly bringing French production on line to support the Fatherland. But, as you say, at the moment, the *Wehrmacht* here in France tells us what they need, then leaves us to find a factory that can produce it. But it would be helpful to our planners in Berlin if we could offer them this information. And more importantly, what they also need to know is what the factories here are *capable* of making, should the need arise.

'It's like this,' Hedda went on. 'The RAF has switched to bombing our cities whilst we are blitzing theirs to rubble. But if we know exactly what can be produced in France and where, Berlin can make a decision. If it's an essential item – take ball bearings, for example – they can make sure there are additional production points here in France. More dispersion, if you like, whilst any bomb-damaged facilities in Germany are restored. That way, we make the very best use of all our captured facilities. Perhaps you could continue with your reports on the major projects but then add a list of what else is already being produced and where, and finally flesh this out with details of potential production. That would be ideal, and we will pass it on. Do you think Herr Weigelin will agree?'

'I'm sure he will,' came the reply. 'But he's very set in his ways. If it's all right with you, I won't mention our conversation. Then he'll pretend that it was all his idea so that he can take the credit.'

Hedda felt that the meeting had gone well. The following week Frau Becker was in the room when Herr Richter complimented Hedda on the report's additional information. 'We called a meeting,' replied Hedda deliberately vaguely, a hand and arm gesture including his secretary in the praise for the initiative. 'We both think this might be useful.'

Outside the occupied zone in South West France, a little over two hundred kilometres east of where the U-boat facilities at La Rochelle were under construction, the Gnome et Rhone aero-engine factory was already supporting the Luftwaffe. Allied intelligence had been well aware of La Rochelle, but Hedda suspected they had not known about the Limoges facility. *Not until now*, she mused as she walked home that evening. Her illicit copy of the report would already be in London. An annex to the report gave a full list of all military production facilities in France – what they were already making and what plans were in train for other well-known firms such as Renault, Citroën and Hotchkiss. The RAF wouldn't be capable of neutralising all of them immediately, but Hedda was equally sure that plans would be made eventually for all of them to be razed to the ground. In the meantime, the resistance would be tasked to deal with the more modest targets.

Werner had not produced the Gestapo input for her following report. His duties had taken him out of town. She did not know who had created the draft, but it was competently done if rather short. A despatch rider had delivered it, and she had included it verbatim. She came back from a meeting with the assistant defence attaché to be met by Martha Becker. 'You must have made quite an impression,' she said with a conspiratorial grin. Despite the difference in status, a bond of friendship was forming rapidly between the two women. 'Your arm-stiffing friend,' reported Frau Becker, still smiling broadly, 'is back from wherever he went to terrorise the locals, and he's been on the phone twice this morning already.'

*

Eventually, they decided that Serge would ride a hundred metres or so in front of Tadzio. All went well till they approached the village of Houdain, where there was a crossing of four quiet country roads. It was an ideal spot to set up a checkpoint. Serge disappeared round a bend. Tadzio followed, then braked sharply to a halt. Ahead, a *Kübelwagen* had been parked to block half of the narrow road. Tadzio rapidly took stock of the situation. One German soldier stood in the other half of the road alongside the vehicle. Two others were deployed on either side, and all three were armed with Schmeissers. Serge had coasted to a stop and was being ordered to dismount. He pushed down the stand and lifted the machine but left the engine running. The soldier in the roadway gave him a sharp poke in the stomach to push Serge aside.

Tadzio thought fast. He had a choice. They had spotted him, but he had every chance to turn and run. On the other hand, Serge did not speak German. So he would not be able to explain what they were doing with the motorcycles. If he made a run for it, they might go over Serge's machine with a fine-tooth comb. Alternatively, he might just be arrested so that he could be interrogated later. His decision made, Tadzio put his machine into gear and approached slowly. His left hand unscrewed the filler cap on his fuel tank. He lifted the top a fraction with his finger to ensure that it was free before letting it fall back. Replacing the cap, he gave it just a quarter turn, then cruised to a halt a couple of metres behind Serge's motorcycle.

'*Guten Morgen*,' he called out cheerfully. '*Wie geht's?*' The soldier was obviously surprised to be wished good morning and to be asked how he was in his own language. He took a couple of steps towards Tadzio. 'Are you German?' he asked.

'French father, German mother,' Tadzio responded, choosing at this stage not to go into the story he had used on the train to the coast. Instead, he pointed out that Serge spoke only French before explaining what they were doing.

'Please also dismount,' came the order. 'We will look at your papers.'

From the corporal's tone, Tadzio sensed that he had been only half-believed. But once away from his motorcycle, he would have no means of resistance. He shrugged his acceptance, dismounted and put the bike on its stand. But before he could be prodded away, he flicked off the cap, lifted the top of the tank, grabbed the Browning and put a round into the German's chest.

The soldiers on either side of the road had relaxed, their weapons pointing down at forty-five degrees. His machine offered some cover from the one to his right. The soldier on his left was also lifting into the aim. Tadzio dropped flat to the ground but simultaneously loosed off two rounds. His target spun away, obviously hit in the shoulder. As he turned to check on the remaining German, he heard the bark of a .45 Enfield. The German to their right had been concentrating on Tadzio. Serge had seized his opportunity. 'They took their eyes off me when you were riding up,' he said quietly. 'I half turned towards my machine as if I were watching you. They couldn't see my hand as I unscrewed the tank.' He walked over to the German who had been Tadzio's second target. He wasn't moving, but as a precaution, Serge put a round into his head.

'What do we do now?' he asked, looking around. 'We have three dead Germans – the uniforms might come in handy. Plus their Schmeissers, a good amount of ammunition and one *Kübelwagen*. Sooner or later, they will realise their patrol hasn't returned, and they will start looking.'

'Too good a bonus to leave behind,' Tadzio replied. 'There's a decent-sized wood about two kilometres back the way we came. Let's hide the lot there. The patrol won't be missed until this evening, by which time we'll be on the other side of Amiens, so I doubt our mission will be compromised. And if the Germans do eventually turn up here, they'll have no idea what has happened. Like as not, they'll just go away.'

They hefted the bodies into the back of the *Kübelwagen* and lifted Tadzio's motorbike on top. It looked dangerously obvious, ridiculous even, but they had only a short distance to go. Tadzio drove, a sub-machine gun next to him on the front seat, and Serge followed, now also armed with a Schmeisser. They reached the wood without incident. Tadzio forced the vehicle between trees and through undergrowth till it was completely hidden from the road. Next, they stripped two of the bodies – one uniform was too soaked in arterial blood to be worth taking – and pulled all three of them into a shallow dip well clear of the vehicle. The Schmeissers and uniforms they left on the rear seat. Finally, they covered both bodies and the vehicle with enough branches and greenery to ensure nothing would be seen from the air.

'We have lost a good hour,' Tadzio observed as they wheeled both motorcycles back to the road. They set off again, using the quieter roads north of Amiens to move round the city until they identified the main line running south-east to Reims. After that, it was simply a matter of following it on roads running more or less parallel till they were a kilometre or so into the countryside. After several dismounts and reconnaissance on foot, they found a suitable site. The line entered a shallow cutting. It was only two fields from the nearest lane, and the area was lightly wooded. They left the motorcycles just off the lane and walked to the lip of the bank. 'Ideal,' said Tadzio. 'We'll get some protection from the blast, and by the time anyone recovers, we will be well away.'

Tadzio invited Serge to set the explosives. He proved as competent as his word. They would blow the line in front of the locomotive. Serge agreed. They had no wish to kill a French engine driver and his fireman. But, hopefully, they would survive a derailment, which was necessary because it would then take days to restore the line. Plus, the fuel had to be destroyed.

The afternoon light was beginning to fade when they heard the approaching locomotive. Looking along the track with a slight height advantage, Serge could see into the open freight cars. 'There's an anti-aircraft flak gun on a platform immediately behind the engine,' he said quickly, 'then a long line of wagons. Looks like they are all stacked with two hundred-litre fuel drums.'

When the locomotive was almost up to the explosive charges,

Serge pressed the plunger. They detonated a split second later. A significant length of track was suddenly no longer there. The engine driver had no chance. Wheels crushed into the hardcore. The engine and tender swayed both ways then, almost in slow motion, leaned away from them, coming to rest with an almighty crash, side-on against the opposite bank.

The flak car buckled against the derailed tender and slewed sideways across the track. Its crew leaped for the far bank as the wagon behind slammed into it, throwing several fuel drums onto the track immediately below Tadzio and Serge. Those behind simply bunched, partially damaged as couplings compressed under the shock of collision. They watched the driver and fireman jump from the engine and run forwards to escape the carnage. 'The attack's a failure,' said Serge bitterly. 'The fuel hasn't ignited.'

'Cover me,' shouted Tadzio. He ran down the bank and, from a range of less than twenty metres, fired six rounds from his Browning HP into the two nearest drums. In the fading light, he was sure he could see arcing streams of fuel. Ridiculously, it reminded him of a boys' pissing contest up a toilet wall. Then he could smell vapour.

He ran back up the incline and flung himself down alongside Serge, who said, 'You throw a match on that and you'll be blown to kingdom come.'

Tadzio grinned at him and extracted a Very pistol tucked into his waistband underneath his heavy jacket. 'Very thoughtful of London to drop this.' He grinned at Serge. It was pre-loaded with a cartridge. He fired the red flare at the leaking fuel. At first, there was just a soft 'whoosh', but then the heat exploded the first drum. They watched the beginning of a chain reaction as the explosions and fire began to spread back down the train. But in the light from the blazing fuel, the crew of the flak wagon emerged from around the front of the locomotive. Sub-machine gun fire was hitting the bank all around them. Serge and Tadzio returned a few rounds, although it was extreme range for a handgun. But it would discourage any immediate charge up an exposed slope.

'OK to run?' Tadzio shouted, patting Serge on the shoulder. The two of them turned and sprinted for the motorcycles. It was almost dark now. If – or when – the Germans followed, they would have no idea of direction. Tadzio, younger and faster than the stockier Frenchman, reached the machines first. To their relief, both started first kick. Riding without lights, with Tadzio in the lead, they roared safely away.

He came to the wood where they had hidden the *Kübelwagen*. Waving his intention to Serge, Tadzio pulled off and stopped by the camouflaged vehicle. In the distance, they could see a rising orange glow. 'These Scheisssers and uniforms are too good to leave,' he suggested to Serge.

The Frenchman agreed. 'We could risk taking them on the bikes,' he suggested, 'but if we are stopped we are in the shit. We might as well take the *Wagen*. The *Boche* will be busy back there,' he thumbed over his shoulder at the blaze behind him, 'and anyway, they don't like doing roadblocks in the dark. I reckon we leave the bodies, take everything else and put one bike in the back. You drive, I'll follow on my machine, and we'll both have a Schmeisser and plenty of ammunition. Plus, you'll be driving a German vehicle. I reckon that if we hit trouble, there is every chance that we can shoot our way out in the confusion.'

'Let's do it,' Tadzio agreed. Minutes later, they were back on the road.

They approached the village from the far side, so there could be no chance of two men in civilian clothes, one driving a *Kübelwagen* with a motorcycle sticking up from the back seat, another riding a second machine, being seen and reported. Tadzio parked inside the barn so that the vehicle could not be seen from the road. Back in the kitchen, relief and adrenalin combined. They were laughing like schoolboys. Serge produced a bottle of calvados, and both took a deep draught.

'What we haven't worked out,' said Tadzio eventually, 'is how we will hide that *Kübelwagen*. Let alone what we are going to do with it.'

'First thing in the morning,' came the reply, 'I'll take it to pieces. Most of the bits are Volkswagen. I'll put them in the store with the rest of our spares. Anything incriminating, I'll hide. At some stage in the future, a German vehicle might come in very handy. For now, we have some valuable weaponry and uniforms.' He raised his glass again. '*Mon ami*, let's drink to a bloody good start to our resistance!'

An RAF Spitfire reconnaissance flight recorded the carnage on the Reims line just outside Amiens. They were grateful for almost a week of much-reduced air opposition from Juvincourt field. It was reported to SOE. 'Looks like that drop to Tadzio's lot has paid off,' observed Sir Manners Fitzgibbon to Doreen Jackman and Bill Ives. He produced a bottle of single malt from his desk drawer and three glasses.

CHAPTER 16

Anneliese twirled the stem of her wine glass. It was only a few days after Charles's death, and they had just finished Sunday lunch. 'It's a strange thing, losing someone you love,' she said rather abstractly. 'I have come to terms with the fact that Charles is gone – that I shall never see him again. I also know my family has never been supporters of the Nazi Party,' she went on. 'But for me, it's more personal now. Hitler decided to bomb your cities – innocent civilians, women and children. To my way of thinking, he is as guilty of killing Charles as if he had held a pistol to his head and pulled the trigger.'

Madeleine reached out and touched the back of Anneliese's hand with her fingers. Anneliese withdrew her hand, then placed it over Madeleine's and squeezed, almost too firmly. 'I want to strike back,' she said vehemently, drawing herself upright in her chair.

'Perhaps that's something we can discuss,' said Sir Manners, after a moment's silence. 'But for now, you must continue to think of this as your home.' He waved a hand intended to encompass not just the dining room but the entire building. 'We love having you here, and for my part, you're doing me a favour, keeping my wife company whilst I'm away all week. And when you feel the time is right, we can look at what else you might be able to do. I could certainly make use of your language skills, and it may even be possible for you to take a more active role.'

'I would like that,' she replied. 'But there's something I need to tell you. Please don't think ill of me...' she hesitated, 'but I'm pregnant. I am expecting Charles's child.'

'Oh my dear,' said Madeleine softly. She left her chair to stand alongside Anneliese, leaning to give her shoulders a gentle embrace. 'Did he know?' she asked quietly.

Anneliese nodded. 'I told him the weekend before he died.'

Madeleine thought for a moment. 'Do his parents know?' she asked eventually.

Anneliese shook her head. Madeleine, still embracing Anneliese, raised herself to look very directly at Manners. 'We would never feel anything but affection for you,' she said softly to Anneliese. 'As for what I think, it's that something good – something wonderful – can emerge from this tragedy.' She paused whilst Anneliese dabbed her eyes with a handkerchief.

Madeleine returned to her chair. 'You'll stay here, of course, and when you are ready, I'll take you to see my man for a check-up. He was marvellous when I had Perry, wasn't he, Manners?'

'Er... yes,' he replied automatically, only too aware from how his wife had looked at him that she expected his immediate and absolute agreement. But in truth, he had every sympathy for the German girl, away from her parents in a strange country, and now left on her own and with child. He, too, had become rather fond of Anneliese. He smiled at her and raised his glass. 'Here's to *good* news, for a change!'

'Thank you,' Anneliese said quietly, 'thank you both so much.'

'But I think you should tell his parents,' Madeleine said, now that Anneliese looked more composed. 'They will have a grandchild. It will be a huge comfort to them.'

She wrote and asked if she might visit the following weekend just for one night. Sir Manners had filled the MG's tank – Anneliese was only vaguely aware of the rationing system, so it did not occur to her to be curious about how he had managed to obtain the coupons. She arrived late morning on Saturday. James and Muriel came out to greet her. She was made no less welcome than before, but the sadness in the household was painfully clear.

'It was good of you to come and see us, my dear,' said Muriel, as they sat with a glass of sherry before lunch.

'Gift from a grateful client, just before the war,' stated James. 'Probably regrets it now – doubt there will be any more after this.'

Anneliese set down her glass. She had thought long and hard about how and when to do this. 'I have something to say,' she began. She looked at his parents. 'We all loved Charles very much,' she went on. 'And our grief is still raw. You have lost your son, your only child,' she added, turning to Muriel. 'I…' She hesitated, unable to continue just for a moment. She gathered her courage. 'I have to tell you that before he died, Charles knew that I am going to have his baby. I am carrying your grandchild.' She could not hold back her tears. Neither could his mother, who turned and buried her head in her husband's shoulder. It took several minutes and much use of handkerchiefs before they all recovered. James distracted himself with half a glass of sherry at one gulp.

'Oh my dear,' said Muriel eventually. 'How can we ever thank you for coming to tell us?'

'If all goes well, it will be a late spring baby,' said Anneliese.

'What will you do till then?' asked James. 'I mean, where will you stay, and will you be all right, financially? If there is any way we can help…' He turned to his wife, who, still too tearful and emotional to speak, vigorously nodded her approval.

Anneliese explained that she would be staying at Stonebrook Hall. 'Sir Manners has an official position,' she said, deliberately vaguely. 'He will arrange for me to use my language skills to help the war effort. So yes, I am provided for financially. Obviously, there will be a period when I cannot work, but otherwise, I shall carry on as planned.' Lost in their own thoughts, they accepted her explanation at face value. 'But I want you to know,' she went on, 'that I will write and tell you the news. The future is horribly uncertain for all of us, but after your grandchild is born, if it is humanly possible, I want you to know and love Charles's baby as much as you can. Half German, half English,' she said reflectively, 'but he – or she,' Anneliese added with a faint smile, 'will be raised by a loving family. And exactly as Charles would have wished.'

'My dear,' said Muriel, sitting on the arm of Anneliese's chair and putting a hand round her shoulders, 'we were in the depths of despair. Nothing can bring our beloved Charles back. We had no hope for the future. But now, thanks to you, we have so much to look forward to.'

'She'll be knitting from now till Easter,' said James, unashamedly wiping a tear from his eye. He finished his sherry in one more swallow.

Anneliese offered to return Charles's MG, but James would not hear of it. 'You'll need a car,' he argued, 'and anyway, if it were here in the garage, it would knock me back every time I opened the door. So you take it, my dear, I know it's what Charles would have wanted.'

It was a crisp sunny morning when, with the hood down, she waved goodbye. It was too soon to be happy, she thought, pottering gently along the lanes, but perhaps now that she had told everyone, particularly after Charles's parents' reaction, she was not quite so sad.

*

Jean Renaud was surprised to be summoned to the garrison commander's office in Nogent-le-Retrou. Thus far, he had stayed well clear of Germans. Tall, dark-haired and swarthy, at forty-one years of age, he was extremely fit from a combination of riding and working the land. His classic Roman nose made him look fierce and impressive rather than handsome.

Much of Renaud's family estate was let to tenants, but they had retained their vineyards. Although the war had halted their wholesaling business as exporting wine merchants, they were still busy selling to their domestic clients, including the German military and restaurateurs throughout central and northern France.

There were extensive cellars beneath the estate. After the Great War, Jean's grandfather had partitioned them, building a dividing wall from the same stone used for the original construction. These walls separated off roughly one-third of the original floor area. The larger parts were still served by the same entrances, but separate, concealed doors were constructed for what Claude, the head cellar man, always referred to as 'them new bits'. By the 1940s, the additional internal walls were indistinguishable from those of the original cellars.

In his father's time, Claude had been the only other employee on the estate who knew of these cellars and their entrances. Jean had followed this tradition. Sometimes they worked late into the evening when all other estate workers had gone home; the best wines remained hidden in these 'bits'. Although, to be fair, the Germans in Nogent-le-Retrou had not looted; they had paid for the ordinary wine collected by the garrison quartermaster – albeit that the imposed exchange rate was little more than state-sponsored theft.

'I don't like it,' said Monique, as she gave his jacket a quick brush with her fingers. Because of his upbringing in England, he thought of height in terms of feet and inches. At five foot six, she was considerably shorter than his six foot, but a more determined woman he had yet to meet. They had played together as children during his holiday visits to France. When he returned permanently to France, he found a beautiful young woman living on a neighbouring estate. He courted her, and they were married within six months. Sadly, there were no children.

'Even so,' he replied, 'I'm quite keen to introduce myself to this German. From what I have heard, he has the reputation of being a reasonable man. He probably wants a meeting because this is the largest estate for miles around, but let's see. I've put a case in the trap. Not our best stuff, so he won't be suspicious, but a cut above what they have been buying off us till now. No way will I ever be a *collaborateur*, but it might be useful if he looks on me as someone who might be prepared to cooperate with our German masters. You never know what we might learn.'

Monique knew that her husband had been a British intelligence officer behind German lines in the Great War, although he had never – out of modesty, she suspected – offered any further detail. '*Sois prudent, mon cher*,' she urged, pulling his lapels to bring him to her lips.

A non-commissioned officer showed him into what had once been the hotel manager's room before the Germans had requisitioned the building as their garrison headquarters. A uniformed captain rose courteously from behind a desk as he entered.

'Monsieur Renaud,' he greeted him in French, 'thank you for coming to see me.'

'Friends have spoken of you, *Herr Hauptmann*,' he replied, 'and I am pleased to make your acquaintance.'

'You may know that my name is *Hauptmann* Horst Brandt,' he responded. 'Would you like coffee? And…' His hand indicated that Renaud should take a seat on one of four armchairs set round a low table before pressing a button on his intercom. As Brandt seated himself, the door opened and a waiter in a white jacket set down a cafetière. 'Please,' said Brandt, 'help yourself. There is cream and sugar.' It was good Colombian, thought Renaud, as Brandt also helped himself. No shortages in the Garrison headquarters, then.

'You must be wondering why I have asked you to come and see me,' Brandt began.

'Indeed,' Renaud replied. 'But before we go any further, you might like to ask someone to take a box from my trap outside – I took the liberty of hitching my horse to your hotel railing. There's a case of wine – of rather a better quality than your quartermaster purchases. I hope you will enjoy it – call it an appreciation of the fact that you do actually pay for your wine. I am aware that German forces have been, shall we say, more inclined just to liberate whatever they require in other parts of France.'

'You put it very courteously,' Brandt replied, 'but I have given orders that there is to be no looting or theft in this district. Our high command sees France as a long-term ally. Under German control, perhaps, but with only a light hand. France will be a valued trading partner and an important southern extension to the Third Reich. I am sure that after the war, many of our citizens will wish to visit your delightful country.'

Not if we can throw you lot out first, thought Renaud, but he kept his counsel.

'And I thank you for the wine,' added Brandt. 'It brings me to the purpose of your visit.'

You mean why I have been summoned, thought Renaud, but again he contented himself by complimenting the officer on his ability to speak such good French.

'I am not a professional officer,' Brandt replied evenly. 'I was a teacher, before the war – languages, although I was also a reservist and ran the local cadet cadre. That is probably why they have given me command of a peaceful garrison well away from the coast, somewhere I can't do too much harm. I don't envisage that Nogent-le-Retrou will be a target for the British Commandos.'

Renaud was aware that there had been raids along the coast further north, although, from all accounts, they had achieved very little.

'Now, to my purpose,' he went on. 'You are by far the most prominent landowner in this region. Also, I have no doubt, a man of influence. And, of course, you have extensive vineyards. But it is your previous, pre-war activity that interests me.'

Renaud was instantly concerned that somehow the Germans had learned of his Intelligence Corps past, but his face showed not a flicker of response. 'You were a wine merchant,' the German went on, to his relief. 'But of course, part of your business has ended with the war.'

'You are correct,' he conceded. 'We exported to many countries, England and Germany amongst them.'

'The Reich requires as much French wine as we can obtain,' Brandt continued. '*Vin Ordinaire*, for our soldiers, but also those of better quality for our officers and leaders. I am told that Herr Hitler, even though he does not drink alcohol, has the finest French wine in his cellar. The trouble is, quality wines are proving difficult to procure. We know that your countrymen are withholding their best vintages.'

'And you think I may be of assistance?' queried Renaud.

'I do,' came the reply. 'To improve procurement, in each region of France, we are appointing a *Weinführer*. He will have the authority to source and purchase wine, but where there is refusal and concealment, he also has the power to search and seize without payment. And those responsible are being disciplined.'

'But I have always supplied what your quartermaster has requested,' pointed out Renaud.

'Accepted,' came the immediate response. 'However, I have now been appointed the *Weinführer* for this region. I suppose they think my military duties are so unimportant that I have time to undertake this additional responsibility.'

'But first,' he said with a rueful smile, 'let me explain. Schoolmasters are not well paid at home. My wife and I do not often afford a bottle of wine. And so I know next to nothing about it. Second, I have to consider the reaction of your fellow growers when I try to insist on their better vintages. It is a recipe for confrontation.'

Now he understood the purpose of their meeting. 'You want me to act as an agent for you,' he observed.

'They would listen to you and cooperate. If it were me, there would be only mistrust and hostility. But I propose that, through you, I will ask only for that which is reasonable and which the vineyards are prepared to provide. I hope this will sustain an element of peaceful co-existence between us that would avoid both violence and confrontation, to our mutual benefit. There need be no searches, no seizures and no arrests. The growers would retain at least some of their better wines, and I shall satisfy the demands of my masters.'

Brandt stood to extract from a desk drawer a bottle of cognac and two glasses. He poured. 'I would welcome your views,' he said, lifting his glass.

Renaud thought on the proposal for several seconds. 'I would be happy to help,' he said eventually, and lifted his glass to signal a silent toast. 'But I can see one or two problems.

'First,' he went on, ticking off one thumb with the other, 'if I procure wine, then unless you wish to set up your own warehouse and distribution facility, you will need my company to undertake this. We have the ability to do it, but not the fuel for our vehicles.

'Second,' he continued, his thumb moving the forefinger, 'there is a financial aspect. At the moment, because of the exchange rate, we are struggling to survive. I have no wish to take advantage, but we will need additional funds to underwrite the costs of this exercise. For a start, I shall have to employ at least one or two additional personnel.

'And finally,' he added, thinking with an inner smile of a previous conversation with Marie, 'some of my suppliers and many of the destinations to which you will want the wine to be delivered are in our coastal areas, to which we are denied access. Without some sort of access permit for me and Marie, my assistant buyer, much as I like the idea of cooperation, I could offer only minimal assistance. In which case your plan, civilised and admirable though it is, just would not work.'

Jean Renaud took a second sip of cognac. He could imagine the German's train of thought: that of a reasonable and seemingly honourable man thrown into an administrative situation, with heavy military and political overtones, that was completely beyond his experience and abilities. Jean was offering him a lifeline.

'Very well,' he said at last. 'Fuel in this region is under my direct control. The permissions you seek, and I can understand why you need them, are not. I will need to speak with my contemporaries in other regions. But when I explain the situation, I think they will be only too happy to facilitate.' He smiled. 'After all, you will be making a most important contribution to their quality of life and those under their command. Let me see what I can do, then we must speak again.'

Having finished the coffee and cognac, they parted on what, at least from the German's perspective, were promisingly good terms.

'He'll contact me again,' he told Monique and Marie, 'once he's consulted with his fellow commanders in our adjacent districts. I'm fairly sure those in the coastal areas will be only too willing to cooperate.'

'When he does,' Monique offered tentatively, 'he'll almost certainly ask you to return to Nogent. But I have an idea. Why not invite him to come to the estate instead? Show him round, tell him about the wine industry. It's a perfect pretext. And Marie could join us, perhaps for lunch?'

She looked anxiously at Monique. 'But then I would become known to the Germans,' she protested. 'As it is, living alone in my cottage, they are not even aware of my existence.'

'You wish to travel,' Monique replied, 'to places where your presence, your reason for being there, will inevitably be questioned. If Jean's reading of Brandt is correct, and I am sure that it is, you will have the right papers. But if you are known personally to Hauptmann Brandt, you will be able to invite anyone who is suspicious to telephone him. Think about it, as a back-up, you could not have a better reference. It's a classic example of hiding in plain sight!'

When he rang and asked for Monsieur Renaud, Monique replied that her husband was tending the vines. She asked if she could take a message. Brandt told her that he had obtained the documents her husband would require, and they were ready for collection.

With her husband seated beside her, his ear also close to the telephone, Monique began a carefully scripted invitation. Perhaps the *Herr Hauptmann* might like instead to be their guest for luncheon? They would be only too delighted to show him round the estate. Moreover, it would be helpful if he were to see firsthand what they would be undertaking on his behalf. He would also meet Marie, who often travelled with her husband and sometimes acted as his deputy.

A small-town schoolteacher would never have been invited to be received by the social equivalent of the Renauds in Germany and even less to be invited to luncheon. That there might be a hidden agenda did not even form part of his thinking. He accepted immediately.

After an impressive tour of the vineyards and the estate facilities, which included tasting some of the better wines of the type that Renaud intended to procure, they assembled in the drawing room. Jean introduced *Hauptmann* Brandt to his wife and Marie. The German could not help comparing this fine country house, the elegance of the ladies, with the apartment back in German that he shared with his wife – a once-pretty young woman now, with a ring on her finger, letting herself lapse into a rather dumpy *Hausfrau*. He was utterly taken with Marie, who told him that she was originally from Nantes but that her parents were dead, and she had no brothers or sisters. From how he looked at her with spaniels' eyes, she doubted that he would even remember what she had said. But if he checked, it was all true. Except that the real Marie had died in England before the war, her death unrecorded in France.

Lunch was delicious, but as Monique had insisted, deliberately modest. She served a fish course and then venison, shot on the estate and therefore not something that contravened any of the new agricultural regulations. However, Jean did offer two fine wines. For the German, it was both a social elevation and a most enjoyable interlude from his military duties. Before thanking his hostess profusely, he produced an envelope for Jean Renaud. 'These documents will allow you both to travel,' he stated, placing the envelope on the table, 'along the coast south from Boulogne and throughout the Cherbourg peninsular. Should there be any queries, the person concerned is invited to contact me immediately.'

They waved from the steps as Brandt departed in his *Kübelwagen*, a second one behind acting as an armed escort. Monique had arranged for its occupants to be given a good lunch in the servants' kitchen.

'I think,' she said to Marie as they watched the departing vehicles, 'you have our garrison commander eating out of your hand. I would not be surprised if you hear from him again.'

'Perhaps,' she replied evenly. 'But as soon as possible, I intend to go to Étaples.'

CHAPTER 17

'Anneliese Hoffmann, from the embassy,' she replied to the switchboard operator's query when she asked to be put through to *Sturmbannführer* Scholz.

'Anneliese, thank you for returning my call.'

'I'm sorry I missed both of them,' she said. 'I had a meeting. As soon as I got back, Frau Becker told me you had been ringing.'

He hesitated. 'I wanted to tell you how much I enjoyed our evening together. Now that I am back in Paris, I am hoping we might meet again.'

She could not help smiling. 'Yes,' she replied. Hedda remembered that Anneliese had a rather forthright way of speaking – she did not beat about the bush. 'I shall be working on the report this week, but I am free on Saturday.'

'I shall be out of the office from Thursday,' he told her, 'back some time Saturday morning. Could I pick you up, say, six o'clock? But much as I enjoyed the Ritz, would you allow me to make supper? Perhaps not up to their standard, but I promise not to poison you.'

She laughed, recognising that it was a subtle way of asking if they might be alone together.

'Six o'clock on Saturday, then. I will look forward to it.' She was still smiling when she replaced the receiver. She had enjoyed his company at the Ritz. And after all, she had invited him to ring her again.

'You look happy,' Frau Becker remarked as she placed a folder of documents in Hedda's in-tray. Her hand was still on the telephone, now back in its cradle.

'That was my arm-stiffing friend, as you call him,' she told her. 'We had dinner at the Ritz not long ago. I'm seeing him again on Saturday.'

The older woman raised her eyebrows and gave Hedda a knowing look but left the office without comment.

With the report safely away on Fridays, Herr Richter habitually encouraged her to take the afternoon off. She had lunch in the canteen and, as she did most days, then asked the head chef if he would kindly let her have something to cook for herself that evening. After lunch, she purchased a couple of bottles of wine from the small kiosk set up in the embassy and enjoyed a walk home through the park. To her relief, there were no chalk marks on the bench. As Simone Faucher was leaving for work, Hedda told her that she was welcome to help herself to anything left over in the larder – as always, the chef had given her far more than she would need. And by the way, she said, she would not be in for supper the following evening – a certain *Sturmbannführer* had offered to cook for her at his apartment. He would be collecting her. 'I'll try not to wake you when I come in,' she added.

She chose a plum-coloured flared skirt and the type of white blouse worn under a traditional Bavarian dirndl dress – it had puffed sleeves that fell to just above the elbow and a rather deep neckline. Since they would be indoors, she opted for comfortable dressy pumps that matched her skirt. As before, she let herself out of the building when his car drew up outside. In the front seats were the same driver and bodyguard that had taken them to dinner at the Ritz.

His modern apartment building was in a fashionable neighbourhood not far from the Avenue Foche. 'We took over the entire building,' he explained as they passed two armed guards at the entrance. 'A section of men are billeted in what was the caretaker's lodging on the ground floor, and there are always two sentries on duty. Most of the eight apartments are occupied by senior military personnel. He opened the door to his own on the first floor and stood aside so that she could enter a small hall. She suppressed a smile as she removed her fur jacket, which had been buttoned almost to the neck. He reddened slightly as she caught him looking at her blouse. 'I'm sorry,' he said quickly, 'I hadn't meant to stare.'

'That's quite all right. I imagine that's the reason these blouses were designed like this in the first place,' Hedda added mischievously.

The apartment looked out onto a courtyard at the rear of the building. It was comfortably if anonymously furnished. 'I'm afraid I'm not senior enough to rate a view of the avenue,' he explained, 'and my boss lives in the penthouse. But it's much better than being in some third-rate French hotel, and at least I have my independence. The kitchen's small, but the lounge and bedroom are quite generous. Now, what can I offer you to drink?'

She accepted a glass of wine, and he put a record on, the music at a low volume. To her surprise, it was American jazz. 'I thought the Gestapo disapproved of this music,' she observed.

'The Führer does; he says it's degenerate,' he replied, 'so that's the party line. But I like it, even though it's probably safer not to play it too loudly.' Again, she noticed, an indication that his underlying beliefs were not those traditionally held by the Gestapo.

A table had been set for their meal. Werner excused himself and disappeared into the kitchen. A heavenly aroma of something roasting drifted into the lounge through the open door. He returned, carrying two plates.

'I hope this is all right,' he said almost apologetically. 'I have made a Bavarian *Wurstsalat* – I believe it should be thin slices of soft sausage with slivers of onion and sliced tomato. I'm not sure how you like it, so I'm serving the paprika and vinaigrette separately. But I did make the dressing myself.'

'It's delicious,' she told him. 'You weren't to know, but it's a family favourite. You are making me feel quite homesick.' As she said it, Hedda was sorry to have to lie – despite her personal history, she knew she was developing affectionate feelings for this German. But, she admonished herself, it was vital to maintain and build her cover.

'I'm flying under false colours,' he admitted as he served the next course. 'I'm not really a chef, but I have had to learn to cook for myself.' He set down two bowls. 'Roast duck with potato dumplings served in a gravy reduction,' he announced proudly. It was absolutely marvellous, and she said so.

He opened a bottle of dessert wine before disappearing into the kitchen to return with a glass jug of cream. Finally, he set down two more plates with something of a flourish. 'Your Bavarian *Zwetschgenkuchen*,' he said proudly. Hedda hoped he had not noticed her relief when he mentioned its name. Otherwise, it might have been a problem because she had absolutely no idea what a *Zwetschgenkuchen* was. It turned out to be a plum tart with a sugary crumble on top – not a dish native to northern Germany or Poland.

'Don't tell you made this?' she asked, after a first exquisite mouthful.

'Would you believe me if I told you I did?' he countered with a grin. 'But I didn't,' he went on quickly. 'Part of my department's job is to identify German nationals in Paris – they almost always have local information that is useful to us. Believe it or not, I found one who runs an upmarket *patisserie*. I traded butter and flour, and in return, he suggested this. I hope you like it!'

She thanked him profusely for such a lovely and thoughtful dinner and offered to help with the dishes, but he would not hear of it. He cleared the table then put on another record – Franz

Schubert's song cycle of *Dichterliebe*, words loved by a poet and set to music. They settled side by side on the sofa, glasses in hand. She wondered whether he would make a pass at her. More to the point, she wondered what she would do if he did. Tadzio had been missing for three months before she volunteered to go to France. He might be dead. At best, he was interned until the end of the war, and then what? She wondered, now, whether they had ever been in love, or whether their affair had been born of desperate circumstances in Poland and fuelled by her determination not to die without ever having sex.

He did not even put his arm round her, just rested his hand gently on her wrist. 'I hope we will have many such happy times together,' he said gently. 'But perhaps tonight, you might prefer that I take you home?'

Again, she was touched. It was a very oblique way of saying that he wanted to sleep with her, but he was not putting her under pressure.

At this point, her desires, inclinations and mission seemed to meld. She stood. 'I think that would be best, Werner. After all, this has been only the second of two lovely evenings together.' She hesitated for a moment, then added, in all sincerity, 'But please don't stop asking.'

They were in his Citroën and not far from Simone's apartment when the first shot was fired. From somewhere in front, a round shattered the windscreen and hit their driver in the face. Blood, bone and grey matter spattered into the back of the car. A second shot took their bodyguard in the chest. Werner rose and tried in vain to take the wheel over the driver's shoulder. They veered to the right, mounted the pavement and the nearside front wing crumpled with some force into a building. Werner and Hedda were thrown forward by the impact of the collision. A shot from behind shattered the rear window. Werner was hit. As he fell back, he tried to pull Hedda down to safety. But she had caught the muzzle flashes of their first assassin. They were from an open ground-floor window across the road and about thirty metres further on. The ambush site was well chosen. It was a fairly narrow street, with only locked apartment blocks on both sides. There were no shop doorways or alleyways into which they could dive for protection.

Slumped forward, Werner was not moving. Another round – it sounded as though it had also come from across the street – crashed into the back of the car, somewhere at the top of the boot. It did not penetrate the interior. She knelt in the footwell, managing to manoeuvre Werner onto his back, lying on the seat with his knees raised. They were safe for the moment, but it was a matter of time before their opponents closed for the kill. Hedda opened her door, crawled onto the pavement and scrambled forward. The angle at which the Citroën had come to rest after hitting the building gave cover from both snipers. Reaching up, she half-opened the bodyguard's door. He was slumped against the fascia. Pushing him back and ignoring the blood soaked into his jacket and trousers, she managed to tug the Schmeisser from his lap. It had been her weapon of choice in Poland, taken from the bloodstained corpse of an ambushed motorcycle courier.

A quick feel told her that the weapon was cocked, but the bolt handle had been lifted into the safety notch. She flicked it down. All she had to do now was pull the trigger. No further rounds had been fired from the front, but she fired over the bonnet as a precaution, putting a short burst of three rounds into the sniper's window.

For a full minute, there were no more shots from either direction. She waited, continuously checking both ways. Eventually, a tentative shot from the rear hit the wall above her head. But now she knew exactly where the round had come from. Hedda stood and, in a brief few seconds, returned a short burst. It was a stalemate. Neither of the snipers could approach without facing her machine-gun fire. But she could not attack either of them without the risk of being shot by the other. She called out to Werner, but there was no reply.

She leant inside, still looking to both front and rear. Flicking up the bolt handle to safety, she rested the Schmeisser in the footwell. With some difficulty Hedda managed to lift and pull Werner's jacket from his left arm and shoulder. The exit wound to the front was leaking badly, but not from arterial damage. It had to be the same underneath, but he would still bleed to death at this rate.

She took off her own jacket, all the time risking another glance around. Next, she took off her white blouse, then wriggled out of her stockings. She wrapped the blouse over his shirt around the front and back entry and exit wounds and used both stockings to bind the dressing as tightly as possible. Finally, she covered him with her fur jacket. She was wondering what to do next when, to her relief, she heard the rumble of a heavy truck engine. Headlights illuminated the scene as a section of German soldiers jumped down from the rear. They had obviously heard the sound of gunfire. A young officer approached the car, pistol in hand.

'We're German,' she shouted frantically. 'We were ambushed. The *Sturmbannführer* has been hit. There were snipers behind and in front. I fired at both. You can see the open windows. I doubt they are still there, now that you have arrived. Your men can check. Except detail off two as an escort, and use that lorry to rush this officer to the hospital before he bleeds to death.'

He looked at her, not knowing who she was, but she had given clear military orders that made absolute sense.

'Get on with it,' she shouted angrily. 'Quick, now! If he loses his life, I will ensure that the Gestapo holds you personally responsible.'

The young officer had frozen from inexperience, but her words galvanised him into action. Werner was lifted gently onto the back of the truck and covered with a couple of greatcoats. At that point, Hedda realised that she was almost naked from the waist up, wearing only her brassiere. She grabbed her jacket from the back of the Citroën and ran back to climb up beside Werner and the two soldiers. Within minutes they were at a small hospital staffed exclusively by German medical personnel.

Two hours later, a surgeon entered the waiting room. 'He will live,' he said quickly before she could speak. 'There's quite a lot of damage, but I have stitched him up as well as I could. Fortunately, the bullet just missed his lung. He's lost a lot of blood, but your emergency dressing saved his life.'

Hedda slumped onto her chair. 'Thank you,' she said after gathering herself for a moment. While waiting, she had realised that it would not be safe for her to return to Simone's apartment that night, indeed, if ever. 'Have you emptied his pockets?' she asked. 'And did you find a set of keys?'

The surgeon confirmed that they had. 'Can I see him?' she asked.

'Tomorrow,' he said kindly. 'Right now, he's still unconscious from the anaesthetic.'

'Perhaps you could telephone the Avenue Foche for me?' she said. 'They will have a night-duty officer. I need to tell them what has happened and ask them to provide a car to take me back to the *Sturmbannführer's* apartment.'

An *SS-Untersturmführer* and an armed guard and driver in the front of another Citroën drove her back to Werner's apartment block. But this time, there was a *Kübelwagen* with three more armed SS men as an escort. The *Untersturmführer* briefed the building guards then escorted her to the door. He stepped back and gave the Nazi salute when she thanked him. Hedda leant back against the front door and exhaled, then searched the apartment where, only a few short hours ago, she and Werner had spent such an enjoyable evening. She found a bottle of schnapps and poured a good three fingers into a tumbler. It would be light in three or four hours. She was too tired to change the sheets. Instead, she turned over the pillow, pulled back the eiderdown and fell into bed.

Hedda was vaguely aware of someone knocking on the door. Pulling a hand through her hair, she looked at an alarm clock on the bedside cabinet. It was almost ten o'clock.

'Who's there?' She called through the door.

'*Untersturmführer* Krüger, Fraulein Hoffmann,' came the response. 'I escorted you here earlier this morning. I am ordered to take you to the hospital.'

She opened the door and, taking his arm, pulled him into the entranceway. 'How is he?' she asked anxiously.

'I am told he is conscious and recovering well, Fraulein,' he replied courteously. 'There is nothing to worry about. But our commander thought that you would wish to see him.'

'I fell asleep,' she explained, her hand gesturing over her rumpled clothing. 'Can you wait whilst I bathe and change? I'll be as quick as I can. Please, would you take a seat in the lounge?'

She started running a bath then dashed back to the bedroom. She had no change of clothing. Knickers she could do without. She borrowed one of Werner's shirts and a pair of socks to replace her stockings. Fortunately, they did not look too bad with her pumps, even if her skirt was a bit creased. She used his toothbrush and powder, but twenty minutes later, she was ready and looking reasonably refreshed and composed, even if she did not feel it after the stress of last night's combat.

Werner was sitting up in bed when she entered. An elderly officer stood to greet her. 'My name is *Brigadeführer* von Scheuen,' he introduced himself. He smiled. 'I am Werner's commander. Sadly, we lost two good men last evening, but I believe I have you to thank for saving this officer's life. I shall leave you to talk privately,' he added, 'but I hope, Fraulein Hoffmann, that we shall meet again.' With that, he gave a courteous, old-fashioned bow, picked up his uniform hat and left the room.

Werner gestured to indicate that she should take the chair vacated by his commander, but she stood next to the bed and took his hand. 'Thank heavens you are all right,' she said, 'but how are you feeling?'

'Bit weak,' he replied, 'but they tell me that's only to be expected. Also, I'm on some strong painkillers, so I hope I'm not drooling or sounding like a drunk.'

She took the chair, still holding his hand. 'You were the only one still conscious,' he went on, 'after the initial attack. Young Krüger has already briefed the *Brigadeführer*, but it would appear that by the time he got there, you had taken Schmidt's Schmeisser, wounded one of the attackers through a window and the other fled. After that, Krüger said that you took charge like a professional, threw out orders, got me sent here fast enough to save my life and all he had to do was mop up afterwards. Anneliese, I have to ask you, where in hell did you learn to do all that?'

She almost panicked, then her mind flashed back to her detailed and thorough brief on Anneliese Hoffmann. Forcing herself to appear outwardly calm, she smiled. 'I'm a country girl,' she replied, 'and a bossy one at that. Father loved to shoot, and since he did not have a son, he decided to teach me. I had a lightweight sixteen-gauge shotgun when I was in my teens, as well as a .22 rifle for rabbits.'

'That still doesn't explain what you were able to do last night,' he replied gently.

She could read the doubt in his eyes. 'Don't forget,' she invented hastily, 'our factories make light weapons, side-arms and radios. When we were in Germany, I loved going with Father to see Uncle Berndt at work.' She hesitated deliberately, as if thinking of home…

'The factory has its own firing range,' she pressed on. 'Whilst they were talking business, I was allowed to go with one of the senior armourer technicians and try out all sorts of weapons, but the Schmeisser MP36 and then the MP38 were always the ones I liked best. When I grabbed poor Herr Schmidt's weapon, everything flooded back. And I'm so sorry you lost your two men,' she added gently.

She managed to conceal her relief when he nodded, appearing to accept her explanation completely. 'I understand you are babysitting my apartment,' he said, changing the subject. 'Obviously, it's too dangerous to return to your old place. My

Brigadeführer said he has spoken with your Head of Chancery to sort something out. Your original lodgings were meant for someone much more junior. But when you were appointed to be Herr Richter's most senior assistant, effectively his deputy, your security arrangements should have been automatically reviewed. Unfortunately, they were not, and this serious error has cost two good men their lives.'

'So what happens now?' she asked.

'I gather your boss is somewhat mortified,' he told her, 'and whoever is head of security at the embassy will endure what we military call a rather one-sided conversation. In fact, he will be lucky to keep his job. *Brigadeführer* Von Scheuen has suggested that you be moved into an apartment in our Gestapo block, and you will be provided with transport and an armed escort to and from work, at least for a while. I hope that will set your mind at ease?'

'I'll have to collect my things,' she said without thinking. 'I had to borrow one of your shirts this morning, and since you are in no position to take advantage, I don't mind telling you that I didn't have any clean knickers, so I'm not wearing any!'

He laughed, but clearly, it caused him pain. He drew breath. 'I suggest you ask young Krüger to take you there this morning with an escort. I shall be here for a day or two, by which time I understand that another apartment will have been made available. Until then, you are more than welcome to make use of mine. And I haven't told you,' he added, 'I almost forgot: Madame Fauchet won't be there. The first sniper, the one who put those rounds through the windscreen, did a runner. But the second shooter, the one behind, took a hit from your Schmeisser. We picked her up not far from the back of the building. It was your own landlady who put a bullet into my back.'

Hedda gasped. A hand flew automatically to cover her mouth.

'I don't think you were the target,' he went on. 'They obviously knew who I am, and a *Sturmbannführer* would have been quite a coup for the resistance, not to mention a bonus of two of my men. But if you had been killed or, perhaps even worse, taken alive, God knows what they might have done to you – under torture, everyone breaks sooner or later, and they would have assumed what you have in your head to be priceless. It doesn't bear thinking about.'

He relaxed back onto his pillows, tired from talking. Hedda rose and kissed him on the cheek. 'I'll settle myself into your flat,' she said, 'and you must rest. But I'll come and see you again tomorrow.'

CHAPTER 18

The journey to Paris was uneventful. But when Marie asked for a ticket to Le Touquet, there came an immediate, '*Un moment s'il vous plaît, Madame.*' Seconds later, there was a French policeman at her elbow.

'Le Touquet lies within a controlled zone,' he told her, not unkindly. 'Your papers, please, and why are you going there?'

Marie allowed herself to appear a little flustered, as might any country girl questioned by a Paris policeman. She explained her role as a wine merchant's assistant and produced the papers signed by *Hauptmann* Brandt, *Weinführer* for his district of Nogent-le Retrou. To her relief, they were accepted without question. 'It is good that our wine commerce continues,' he said blandly. She smiled at him but inwardly felt nothing but contempt for an obvious collaborator.

It was early evening when she arrived in Le Touquet. Marie took a room for one night in a modest *pension* well back from the seafront – she would resume her journey in the morning. Tadzio had given her a good description of Nicole and where she lived. She would be looking for a tall, slim, dark-blonde with strong, striking rather than good-looking features. Also, he had mentioned that she taught French to German officers stationed at the headquarters in Le Touquet. But, he confessed, she had never mentioned her surname.

It would be too dangerous to loiter outside a hotel taken over by Germans. So Marie found a bicycle repair shop in a run-down area of the town. With his income almost decimated by the imposition of the security zone, the ageing Frenchman was only too happy to let her rent a bicycle for a few days at what she knew was a well-inflated price. He also demanded a ridiculously high deposit. But, he explained, bikes had become a valuable commodity now that there was virtually no other means of transport. Her small overnight bag fitted clumsily into the wicker basket.

She had to cross the estuary. It was several kilometres upstream before she came to the first bridge. By the time she had cycled back towards the coast and found Nicole's smallholding, she was tired, sweating and thirsty. She pushed her bike round to the back of the building, sat on a rusting garden chair and waited.

Despite her best intentions, Marie had almost dozed off in the late autumn sunshine when a woman answering Nicole's description stood in front of her. 'Who are you,' she asked bluntly, 'and what are you doing in my garden?'

'Tadzio told me to mention his name,' she replied, squinting up at Nicole. 'You will be pleased to know that he got home safely thanks to you. He wanted me to tell you that the Royal Navy is looking after your dinghy. It will be returned to you, with grateful thanks, after the war.'

Nicole reached into her coat pocket for a key. 'You had better come inside,' she replied.

'I'm so glad he made it,' she told her. 'I had often wondered. He was the second one we helped. I never knew what happened to the first.'

'Who is "we"?' asked Marie?

'A small number of acquaintances from the sailing club,' came the reply. 'When the Germans invaded, we hid our dinghies in a barn belonging to one of our members, a farmer. Not long afterwards, he found an English pilot who had bailed out from his Hurricane hiding in one of his outbuildings.' She hesitated, before reminding herself that the young woman had just quoted Tadzio's name. 'The farmer speaks only French,' she continued, 'but knew that I am a linguist. He also knew that my husband – my late husband – was a pilot, shot down and killed in the first few days of the invasion. So he felt fairly safe coming to me. Together we organised an escape by dinghy.

'I met Tadzio purely by chance,' she went on. 'He very cleverly defused an ugly situation on a train. His German is fluent, but not his French – which he spoke with a rather strange accent – that of someone who had spoken only English more recently. Perhaps because I am a linguist and am aware of nuances in speech, it was obvious that he, too, was trying to escape, so I offered to help.'

'And you gave him a message,' said Marie. 'Provided someone mentioned his name, you have – or had – information that might be useful to us.'

'This time, it's my turn to ask,' said Nicole. 'So who is "us"?'

'I'm as French as you are,' stated Marie. 'You must be able to tell. But I was trained in England, and I work for London. That's all you need to know.'

'Did Tadzio tell you that I was a teacher before the war, but now the Germans force me to work as a translator and teach French to their officers?' she asked.

Marie nodded to confirm that she knew.

'When I am not working in the hotel in Le Touquet,' Nicole continued, 'I am allowed to use the officers' recreational facilities – the bar and dining room. They have become accustomed to my company. Most of them are lonely and like nothing more than to spend time with a young Frenchwoman.' She glanced at her finger, from which, to avoid obvious questions, she had removed her wedding ring.

'I have been there so long,' she went on, 'that they have become careless and often speak of matters that have security implications. Did you know, for example, that the Luftwaffe is using the former civilian airfield at Le Touquet? I think it's just an emergency landing ground, not one of their main bases. Probably a bit vulnerable, being so near to the south coast of England.'

'Yes, we are aware of this,' said Marie. However, she was beginning to suspect that the promised 'information' might be so low-level as to be of little interest.

'And the radar and radio station in the woods nearby, but still within the perimeter, where they also undertake coding and decryption?' came the response.

Marie exhaled slowly with a soft, sibilant whistle and raised her eyebrows. 'Now that really *is* of interest,' she voiced quietly.

'I think there are three types of German officer at the hotel,' Nicole went on. 'First, some ordinary administrative types who liaise with the locals and generally tell them what to do. Then there are a couple of Gestapo officers. And finally, there are four captains and majors who I think are from some sort of wireless or signals organisation. Their badge is a zig-zag lightning bolt, like an arrow pointing downwards.'

'Definitely signals,' said Marie.

'All the officers command soldiers billeted in the town,' Nicole added. 'They have a small motor pool kept in the hotel courtyard to the rear. The bottom two floors comprise the mess facilities and the administrative offices, and the accommodation is on the three floors above. Needless to say,' she added, 'the whole building is well guarded.'

'I can see three possible opportunities here,' replied Marie. 'First, there is the airfield. Perhaps London already knows all about it, but maybe not exactly how or to what extent it is being used. Second, there is the hotel building itself – to destroy it together with most of its occupants would be a significant setback to the Germans in this area. And finally, there is this signals facility. I think London would give their eye teeth to lift it, lock, stock and barrel – perhaps together with at least some of its personnel – back to the UK.

'I think this is the sort of target I need to discuss with London,' Marie said after a moment's pause. 'Also, I need to see as much of the ground as I can. I have no wish to impose,' she added, 'but would it be possible for me to stay here for the night so that I can make a reconnaissance in the morning?'

'No problem at all,' came the reply. 'I would be glad of the company. The bed in our spare room is already made up. I'll light the fire and pull back the covers to air it.'

'And are you all right for food?' asked Marie. 'I'm well provided with funds. I can leave you with more than enough so that you won't be out of pocket.'

'Not a problem,' said Nicole. 'This is a smallholding. If necessary, I could be self-sufficient. But what with my wages from the Germans, plus the rations they often give me, I live well enough – far better than they do in our towns and cities, from what I hear. I think at least half of the hotel inhabitants,' she added with a mischievous grin, 'including their head cook, have a secret ambition to see what's under my skirt. A mild flirt is a small price to pay for a bottle of wine or a mound of butter. But that's all they get,' she added firmly.

Changing the subject, Marie asked about the people known to Nicole who might form the nucleus of a resistance group.

'Well, there's the farmer,' she began. 'And all the men and women in the sailing club who helped to hide our dinghies in his barn. I haven't approached any of them, but I know several who would almost certainly volunteer if asked. Of course, we have a wide range of skills: a doctor, a chemist, an electrical engineer, to name but a few. But we are all civilians. I know the farmer has a shotgun, but as for the others, I doubt they have a single weapon between them.'

'Let me think about it, but at the end of the day, it might be just a few volunteers that we need,' Marie reflected. 'Weapons, and the people who know how to use them, we can provide.'

After a fine supper of casseroled sausages and vegetables, Nicole opened a second bottle of wine. With the table cleared, she produced a map and opened it out. 'The airfield's here,' she said, pointing to a densely wooded area about three kilometres to the south and east of Le Touquet. 'You will have to cycle across the nearest bridge over the estuary, the one you used today, but then it's more or less on your way back to the town. I have to report for translation duties in the morning, so we can leave together.'

Once across the bridge they went their separate ways, Marie having told Nicole that she would return if London authorised any form of action against the Germans in Le Touquet. She found the airfield easily enough, set not too far back from the main road, with gently undulating woodland away to the rear. The entrance to the deserted airfield appeared to be unguarded, but even so, she pedalled past it, cycling on round a gentle bend till she was out of sight and past the end of a tall perimeter fence, topped with barbed wire, that looked to be reasonably new. When it turned away from the road, she stopped a couple of fields further on, lifted her bicycle and then her overnight bag over a chained gate, and hid both behind the thick hedge so common in that part of France. Fortunately, she had a stout pair of shoes.

Staying two fields away, she walked parallel with the perimeter. At first, she could see onto the empty airfield, with its two hangars and a small control tower. A tattered windsock fluttered in the light breeze. Next to the control tower stood what looked to be a rather large and sophisticated radar antenna for a small airfield. It was, she thought, very cleverly hidden in plain sight. When the fence disappeared into woodland she was able to close up and walk alongside it. Clearly, this section of the fence had been added only recently. She suspected that originally it had stopped at the edge of the grass strip but had then been extended to include the wooded area. Finally, after perhaps another hundred metres into the trees, she heard a faint hum that grew louder as she walked. Then the sound began to fade. Somewhere, on the other side of that fence, was an engine. Almost certainly, she reasoned, it was powering a generator.

She walked back to the point where the sound was loudest then studied the fence. There were plenty of trees on both sides standing next to it, with overhanging branches. At first, she thought this was a security oversight, but she then realised that the Germans had been forced to compromise. Had they cleared away the adjacent forestry, the fencing would have been evident from the air, clearly inviting closer inspection.

Marie made sure she had a good escape route, then climbed a broad-leafed tree, moved hand over hand along a branch and dropped to the ground. She double-checked that another tree provided an easy climb to re-cross the fence then moved slowly and carefully towards the sound of the generator. There were several clearings in the forest, which she avoided, but eventually, through the trees and undergrowth, she could see an unusually large one. It contained a line of six half-buried, long bunkers, each with a domed roof above ground, all covered with fallen leaves, grass and low bushes. They would be absolutely invisible from the air. The forest came almost up to the bunkers, but edging forward on her stomach, through the undergrowth she could see a track leading away towards the airfield. There were two vehicles on the track, a lorry and a *Kübelwagen*, well under the trees – obviously transport for the shift on duty. Two uniformed guards with automatic weapons patrolled the area. There were probably more inside one of the bunkers. The nearest trees had been used to support an impressive array of aerials, some of which were interconnected with additional wires to serve long-range frequencies. This was clearly a significant facility and superbly camouflaged. She had seen enough. Marie edged back on her knees and elbows till she was out of sight. Minutes later, she was back over the fence.

She was a bit dishevelled, but having returned her bicycle she retreated to the ladies' rest room at the station and removed most of the evidence, not least the mud stains on her shoes. After an uneventful return journey she had to walk from Nogent, but by late evening Marie was back in her cottage on the estate. Gratefully she threw her bag onto the table. Then she removed her shoes from blistered and bleeding feet, placed a bowl of warm, salted water beside her favourite kitchen chair, poured several fingers of calvados, settled her feet in the bowl and quietly collected her thoughts.

*

Brigadeführer von Scheuen was as good as his word. Werner was released from hospital forty-eight hours later, by which time Hedda had been allocated a small, one-bedroomed apartment on the same floor, although she had yet to move in. She settled Werner into his armchair, poured him a glass of *pils* and herself wine. He sipped the lager appreciatively. 'Been looking forward to this,' he said, smiling, 'they refused point-blank to give me any alcohol at the hospital!'

'Herr Richter has been very good about time off,' she told him. 'I don't know what the *Brigadeführer* said to him, but he seems to think I have been much more affected by the ambush than I really am. He and Frau Becker are doing the report between them this week, and I don't have to go back to work till next Monday.' She sipped her wine. 'So it gives me a few days and another weekend to look after you,' she added. 'I have made my bed up in the other apartment, and we can share a casserole here this evening. I'll finish moving out tomorrow morning.'

'Which reminds me,' Werner replied, 'the *Brigadeführer* has asked if you would be so kind as to report to his office in the Avenue Foche tomorrow morning. He'll send a car for you at ten. I gather he wants your help with that French woman we picked up – your former landlady.'

'We had to wait a couple of days before she was conscious enough to face interrogation,' the *Brigadeführer* told her next morning after being served coffee in his office. 'Thus far, she has been questioned quite strongly, but there is a risk that she might

200

not survive what I'm afraid I must refer to as our somewhat harsher means of extracting information.'

You mean torture, thought Hedda, but she was at pains to appear expressionless. Clearly, Simone had to be a member of the resistance. And under severe distress, she would almost certainly betray other cell members, which might include persons providing her courier and message service, leading back to Hedda herself. But, as yet, she was still undecided about what she might do. Nevertheless, she had slipped her cyanide capsule into an inner jacket pocket as a precaution.

'However,' the *Brigadeführer* continued, 'although you may find her appearance distressing, we have to weigh our methods against the actions of the resistance. Two of my men were murdered. There are two widows back in Germany, both with children, who must now survive as best they can. She will not give us information willingly, but on the other hand, she might not survive further interrogation, which would not suit our purpose. But you have been on excellent terms with her for quite some time. It is just possible you can persuade Madame Faucher that her only hope of survival is to cooperate with us. Hence my request for your visit here this morning.' He went on to describe how the interrogation must otherwise proceed.

Hedda was shocked. Not so much by the *Brigadeführer's* words – she had been briefed in London on what to expect if she were taken alive – but by Simone's appearance when she was admitted to the interrogation room. A bloody bandage covered one shoulder, where one of Hedda's rounds had struck home. Otherwise, Simone was naked to the waist. She seemed barely conscious. Had not both her body and legs been tied to the chair, she would have fallen to the floor. There was one other chair set facing her. Simone slowly raised her head as the door was closed, leaving Hedda alone with her in the otherwise bare room. Dark stains surrounded a drain set in the concrete. There was a shower rose overhead. Carefully she looked at all the walls and the ceiling.

There was no sign of a camera, although she was sure their conversation was being monitored. She would have to follow the *Brigadeführer's* instructions. But if Simone talked, it could mean the end of her own mission. And potentially her own life. She would have to make a run for it.

'You,' said Simone softly. 'Have you come to make me confess?'

'I want to help you,' she replied quietly. 'We have been friends. I can't bear to see you like this.' She paused. 'Look,' she went on, 'I know I have never discussed my job at the embassy, but I am in a senior position, one of influence. I have direct access to the ambassador, and he has at least some influence over the head of the Gestapo. The *Brigadeführer* has agreed that if you cooperate, you will receive medical treatment. If not, to put it bluntly, you will be tortured. I doubt if you will survive. For a start, they will pull out your finger and toenails. Sometimes they cut off a woman's ears or her nipples. If they do not die, everyone talks sooner or later. Personally, I do not approve of this interrogation. But more than that, I fear you could never survive such treatment. Please... I can protect you. Tell them what they want to know.'

'We have never been friends,' Simone said bitterly. 'If you thought that a bag of coffee or some extra rations could buy your way into my feelings, you were very much mistaken. I had no choice; you had to be tolerated. But I knew you were dating that Nazi. We have people everywhere. Your night at the Ritz was reported to me. It was obvious you were going out with him again on Saturday. It was only your second date, so we suspected that you would return home that night. You were both a target, and the men who died were a bonus.' With that, she raised her head and spat a bloody gob of spittle onto Hedda's face.

Hedda faced the most difficult decision of her life. She could spare Simone the agony that would surely follow and at the same time protect the remainder of her cell. And one way or another, after what she had just said, Simone would die anyway. She had the pill in her pocket. If Simone did not bite down on the capsule until the torture began, a heart attack would be the obvious conclusion. She extracted the pill and held it in front of Simone, then drew a finger across her own throat to make it clear what would happen. 'You are a brave and foolish woman,' she said slowly. 'There is nothing more I can do for you.' But she shook her head from side to side, indicating that this was not true.

Gently she pushed the pill into Simone's mouth and was relieved when a slight bulge in one cheek indicated that she had pushed it to one side with her tongue. Hedda barred her teeth and made an exaggerated biting gesture. Then she pointed to her own cheek before brushing a finger down her throat to tell Simone that she should try to swallow the capsule after she had bitten it. There was a mixture of surprise, understanding and relief on the Frenchwoman's face. Her tears began to flow.

'*Au revoir, ma chère. Vive la France!*' she whispered very softly into Simone's ear. Then she placed a finger under Simone's chin, lifted it slightly and kissed her briefly on the lips. Without another word, she walked away and banged on the door. She, too, was in tears as she left the room.

Werner was well enough to call in at the Avenue Foche by the end of the week, although he would not return to full duties for several more days. That evening they were together in Hedda's apartment. Although living separately, they were spending most of their off-duty time together.

'I can update you on your former landlady,' he told her over a glass of wine. 'I hope this won't upset you too much, but she is no longer alive.'

'How did it happen?' asked Hedda anxiously.

'Well, the *Brigadeführer* was extremely grateful for what you tried to do,' he replied. 'He told me so himself. But after you left, there was still a lot of concern that she might not survive further interrogation, given her condition. And we did need to know who her accomplice was, not to mention details of her cell contacts. So it was decided to send her to the prison at Fresnes, on the outskirts of the city. It has a small medical wing. The idea was that after a couple of days' rest, she *would* be strong enough to undergo further interrogation. But unfortunately, after admission, she died sometime during the night. Her death was only discovered the next morning.'

Hedda looked down at her hands, desperately trying to hide her feelings. She had been briefed that there would be a smell of almonds on the lips or mouth for a couple of hours after taking a cyanide capsule. There was a chance it might be noticed, but a heart attack under torture would have looked so obvious; it was a chance Hedda had been prepared to take. But if brave Simone, knowing what lay ahead, had simply crushed and swallowed it overnight, there would be no evidence by morning. Neither would it show up in the unlikely event of an autopsy: there was absolutely nothing to incriminate Hedda.

Mistaking her silence for grief, Werner placed his arm round her shoulders. 'I'm sorry, *mein Schatz*,' he said gently. 'You knew her well and liked her, I think. But try not to be upset. I have some other news,' he said brightly.

'Because of your courage last Saturday and the help you have tried to give the Gestapo, you are greatly admired – by your colleagues in the embassy and throughout the Avenue Foche. The *Brigadeführer* was keen to show our appreciation. We have organised a week's Christmas leave at home for certain deserving people. A Junkers Ju 52 will fly to *München* and then on to Berlin. I have been added to the list for the flight to Munich, to complete my recovery. To show our appreciation for what you have done, so have you. Is that not good news, Anneliese? You will be home for Christmas!'

CHAPTER 19

'Sir, how do we stand with the letters?' asked Doreen Jackman.

'Anneliese wrote home as soon as Hedda was in place,' Sir Manners replied. 'The letter was posted from Paris. We asked her to say that her new role was a senior position, and the workload was very heavy. She did not say so, but by implication, there would not be frequent correspondence. Her mother replied, just family news, and Hedda passed the reply to her courier. He, in turn, asked the cousins to pass it on to us. I must say the Americans have been extremely helpful. Anneliese will reply soon, but that's where we stand now. She has also passed on the news about being sent home on leave for Christmas.

'But that can wait,' he went on. 'In the meantime, what do we do about Marie's latest report?'

'I have been talking to some of our boffins,' offered Bill Ives. 'They would give their eye teeth to have that equipment.'

'So far, raids on the French coast have not been a success. They were ineffectual – not even a boost to morale,' Sir Manners observed. 'But if we could pull this off, it really would be one in the eye for the Germans. The question is, how?' he added. 'Any suggestions?'

'I called a fairly low-level planning meeting the other day,' put in Bill Ives. 'Didn't give anything away, just posed a hypothetical scenario: unused airfield next to a radio and radar site, an estuary available nearby, that sort of thing, with the stated aim of lifting the equipment.'

'And…?' queried Sir Manners.

'Quite useful, really,' replied Bill Ives, looking rather pleased with himself. 'The Navy is prepared to try putting something into the estuary, but that still leaves the problem of getting to and from the airfield and loading and offloading the equipment. The RAF had the best answer. First, secure the field, then drop in a transport with enough men to do what's necessary. They can put everything on the aircraft, and provided nothing goes wrong, they would be airborne again as soon as possible. That way, we won't need much of a local presence on the ground.'

'We need to talk with Marie,' said Sir Manners. 'We can't plan a complex operation like this at arm's length. Either we send someone to France, or we recall Marie then drop her back in to organise the locals. I favour the latter.' He closed a file and looked at Doreen and Bill. 'I leave it in your capable hands. In the meantime, I will give some thought to Christmas.'

*

Sir Manners delegated the Christmas problem to Brigadier James Summerton. After all, he reasoned, Hedda would be less than convincing if she tried to avoid going home for the holiday. And her family had already proved themselves to be anti-Hitler, willing to offer information to Britain. Therefore it was logical to assume that they would help with this new dilemma. The downside was that they would have to be briefed on the operation in Paris, a risk that would preferably have been avoided. However, their loyalty could surely be secured with the offer of up-to-date information on their daughter's situation and wellbeing.

Summerton was an old hand. And he spoke excellent German. He was hugely saddened by the news of his former assistant attaché's death, and with a war on, there had been no question of a replacement for Charles Kaye-Stevens. He ordered surveillance on the Hoffmann office, and it was a bleak, late autumn morning when he took the train from Bern to Zürich. Not wanting to risk a telephone call, he simply followed someone into the building, took the lift to the first floor and asked a receptionist in the outer office if he might have a few words with Herr Hoffmann.

As was the way with so many personal assistants, she tended to assume an authority that went not with her position but that of her superior. In a rather frosty tone, a sharp-featured middle-aged woman asked for his name and that he state his business. A door behind and slightly to one side of her desk was just slightly ajar. He ignored her, walked round the desk and gently pushed the door open.

She rushed from her seat to stand beside him. 'I'm sorry, sir,' she said quickly. 'He just barged past me…'

The brigadier smiled at her, then turned to the man behind a large partner's desk. 'It's about Anneliese,' he said in German.

'Thank you, Liesel,' Herr Hoffmann said quietly after a moment. 'It's really quite all right.'

As she returned to her desk, the brigadier made a point of closing the door behind her. Then, sensing that Hoffmann was about to ask a question, he held up his hand, palm forward. 'Rest assured, she is safe and well,' he told him. 'But I would like to speak where there is absolutely no chance of being overheard. Shall we take a walk, or would you care to recommend somewhere suitable for lunch?'

In the event, it was the latter, a private and rather exclusive club where the tables were well spaced – not that the adjacent ones were occupied at this slightly early hour *zum Mittagessen*. Herr Hoffmann ordered a bottle of wine but declined the menu for the moment. He had already calculated that his visitor was a person of some importance. 'So,' he said as soon as the waiter had poured and departed, 'who are you, and why have you named my daughter?'

The brigadier had planned this conversation carefully. 'First of all, Herr Hoffmann,' he began, 'I hope this will not come as too much of a shock, but your daughter is alive and well and in England.'

'But we had a letter from Paris—' exclaimed the German.

'Anneliese wrote it, at our request,' he broke in. 'But she is being very well looked after on one of our country estates in England. The very courageous woman posing as Anneliese in Paris is one of our agents. The information she is providing to us regarding Hitler's war effort is priceless.' The reference to Hitler had been deliberate.

Herr Hoffmann was clearly taken aback. He was silent for several seconds, then, 'How did all this happen?' he asked quietly.

'You knew my former assistant attaché, of course,' he replied. 'And I am sure you are aware that he and Anneliese had formed a relationship.'

'*Ja, Ja*, she confided in her mother much more than she told me,' he replied. 'But yes, I gather they had developed strong feelings for each other. According to my wife, with hindsight, had she known this would happen, Anneliese would not have applied to go to Paris. As it was, she almost didn't go. I think in the end, she was persuaded only by a sense of duty.'

'Anneliese left the train at Basel, and Charles persuaded her to accompany him to England,' the brigadier continued, avoiding the detail of how she had been drugged and removed in a wheelchair. 'My masters had decided that Charles's language skills made him too valuable to be allowed to return to his regiment, although that was his wish. He was working in London,' he said, being deliberately vague, 'and he and Anneliese were planning to marry.'

'*Were* planning,' said Herr Hoffmann. 'I fear you are not the bearer of good news…'

'Charles was killed in an air raid,' the brigadier said quietly. 'Anneliese was in the country. They had just spent the weekend with his parents – he came from a good family,' he added reassuringly, 'his father is a lawyer.'

Taken aback by the news, he studied the table for several seconds, then looked up. 'So what will happen now to my daughter?' he asked.

'For the moment, I fear she has little choice but to stay in England,' the brigadier replied gently. 'Anneliese has agreed to do this. She blames Hitler's indiscriminate bombing for Charles's death and is willing to help us protect our Paris operation.' He hesitated, but it was only right that Herr Hoffmann should know. 'And second, on a more personal note,' he continued, 'I hope this also doesn't come as too much of a shock, but she is expecting Charles's child. Their baby will be born in the spring. You would wish to know that this has proved a huge comfort to Charles's parents. He was an only child.'

Herr Hoffmann's hand covered his eyes. '*Mein Gott*,' he said very quietly, 'but what is this war doing to us?'

'Please rest assured,' the brigadier added quickly, 'your daughter will receive the finest care and attention that can be provided. The lady of the house where she is staying is not much older than Anneliese, and they have become firm friends and companions. Anneliese wants you to know that under the circumstances, she is healthy and content.'

'And now, I have something to ask of you…' said the brigadier.

*

Marie was quite enjoying herself, although she wished that *Hauptmann* Horst Brandt would not keep pressing another beer into her hand, albeit that she had insisted on a smaller, more ladylike glass. There was no way, she told him, that she would emulate his officers and drink from a huge *Stein*.

As garrison commander, he had decided to hold an *Oktoberfest* party. The Renauds had been invited, and he had been most insistent that Marie accompany them. 'Please,' he had argued, 'there will be so few ladies. It will be a pleasure for my officers to have the company of yourself and Madame Renaud, plus that of another charming young lady.' Under the circumstances, Jean Renaud thought it politic to accept. Several long tables had been placed in the hotel ballroom, as they would be set out in Munich. But there was still room to dance to a small 'oompah' band that had somehow been recruited. However, it was obvious that *Hauptmann* Brandt had little intention of sharing Marie's company with his officers despite his former comments. Already, some of them appeared to be the worse for drink, so she was not sorry when Jean thanked their host, saying that now might be a good time to allow the officers to enjoy their celebrations. *Hauptmann* Brandt had clicked his heels rather formally, taken Marie's hand and expressed the sincere hope that they would meet again soon.

'Told you so,' said Monique with a grin once they were safely in the car. Fortunately, her husband's wine duties brought with them a reasonable allowance of petrol. Marie did not reply. But she had been worried all evening about returning to the cottage in time for her late-night 'sked'.

'I'm going to be away for a while,' she told Jean the following day. 'If anyone asks, I'm on a long wine-tasting trip all over Bordeaux vineyards. So you don't know where I'm staying. And for real, I can't tell you when – or even if – I'll be back.

'The pick-up's set for the day after tomorrow,' she added. 'It'll be a Lysander – from the usual DZ. It's not long enough for anything else.'

'Don't worry about the radio,' he told her. 'Anything compromising, I'll put in one of the hidden cellars. It'll never be found.

'Do you need any help with the field?' he asked.

She shook her head. 'Marius and Edouard will be fine,' she replied. 'But best if you are somewhere else with witnesses that evening, although the DZ is isolated enough. I doubt the aircraft will even be reported.'

*

He called her 'Lizzie', as in 'Lizzie the Lysander'. Johnny Metherwell loved the aircraft, a high-winged monoplane with an incredible short-field take-off and landing ability, thanks to its extremely low stall speed of fifty-six and a half knots, or sixty-five miles per hour to the non-aviator. He had volunteered for dangerous and challenging night flights for the embryo resistance, always on or near a full moon, with only a map, a compass and his mark one eyeballs to enable him to reach a field anywhere in occupied France. His black painted aircraft could bring out a downed airman, saving the weeks and months otherwise necessary for a dangerous and sometimes unsuccessful journey through France, into Spain and finally Gibraltar. Of course, the aircraft was vulnerable to an enemy fighter, but at night, Johnny was content to accept the risk.

He refuelled at Tangmere. The met. was good, and he wasn't too concerned about navigation: a sharp river bend should point the way to Nogent-le-Retrou, and after that, it was simply a starboard turn to pick up the lights. He was humming to himself, Vera Lynn's 1940 recording of 'A Nightingale Sang in Berkeley Square', a favourite on the mess gramophone.

When, by dead reckoning, he was very near to the field, he gave Lizzie a touch of rudder and stick to put her into a gentle turn. Less than half a mile to the north, the lights came on. He started a gentle approach. There was quite a high hedge – small trees, probably – on the glide path, so he used opposite stick and rudder to flutter down in a steep, side-slipping approach. Kicking it off at the last minute, he flicked on the nacelle lights above his wheels and flared out for a perfect short-field landing. He gave a burst of engine to turn Lizzie round and return to the edge of the field, which would give him the maximum length for take-off, conscious of the old maxim that anything behind you was wasted runway.

A figure ran to the plane. Metherwell opened the canopy as she climbed the ladder on his starboard side and dropped into the rear seat. With the canopy closed again, he did not wait for his passenger to strap in. Throttle wide open, and Lizzie bounced across the field. She was airborne and climbing well in not much more than three hundred and fifty yards.

Marie wriggled into her straps and put on the headset dangling in front of her. Johnny's voice sounded in her ears. 'Welcome aboard your private flight to England,' he began, imitating a commercial airline captain. 'We have a headwind, so your flight time will be about one hour. We are ascending to four thousand feet. Unfortunately, refreshments will not be served, but your pilot will be more than happy to offer you a drink upon our arrival.'

'Thank you kindly, sir,' she replied. 'It was bloody cold in that French field. I have a hip flask. You fly, and I'll drink for both of us.'

They crossed the French coast. Visibility was good on a bright, clear, moonlight night. They were about halfway over the channel when Johnny picked up the outline of an enemy bomber, a Heinkel He 111. It was just under their height and flying on only one engine. He couldn't be sure, but it looked as if it was slowly losing altitude, although it had every chance of making it to an emergency field in France.

'Going to take a look,' he said grimly. The Heinkel was well armed, with both cannon and machine guns, much more heavily so than his Lizzie, but the only gunner capable of firing upwards and to the rear was housed in a cupola on the upper fuselage. So far, he had not fired.

He pushed on the power and curved to take station well above and behind. Still no reaction, and as he closed, he could make out the line of the protruding barrel, its muzzle resting down onto the aircraft. Almost certainly, the gunner had been killed in the same exchange that had taken out the port engine. Johnny executed an 'S' turn to search the sky behind. It was empty. He closed to less than one hundred yards. Marie thought they would ram the German aircraft. Johnny poured a burst from the two .303 Browning machine guns in Lizzie's wheel fairings into the Heinkel's starboard wing and was rewarded by a flash of flame. He just had time to switch to the cockpit before pulling a tight climbing turn away from the Heinkel. Looking over his port wing, he saw that the German's second engine was well ablaze. Slowly it turned onto a wingtip and dived vertically into the sea.

'That was for Flossie and little Jimmy James,' she heard him whisper. He did not speak to her again until they landed.

Mechanics attended to the aircraft. A jeep was crossing the field towards the hangar. 'Do me a favour,' he said as they stood beside the Lysander. 'Please don't mention the Heinkel.'

'But you did wonderfully well,' she exclaimed. 'Don't you want to add to your score?'

'My orders were to bring you back to Tangmere,' he replied. 'I should have stayed well clear of that German. But with their gunner out of action, you weren't in any danger. I would have broken off otherwise.'

'Who are Flossie and Jimmy James?' she asked intuitively.

'Who *were*,' he said quietly. 'My sister and her son, my nephew. They live – they lived,' he corrected, 'in London. They were bombed and killed two weeks ago. I'm sorry if I alarmed you, but no way was that bomber going to make it back only to fly again.'

The jeep was parking in front of them. 'I'm so sorry,' she said. Marie stood in front of him and pulled down his head, kissing him on the cheek. 'Thank you for the ride,' she said softly. 'And don't worry, I have no idea what happened,' she replied. 'I must have had my eyes shut.'

'You're very pretty, and I know I'm not supposed to ask your name,' he said with a smile. 'But mine's Johnny Metherwell. I'm stationed at Stradishall in Suffolk – it's near Bury St Edmunds. If you can, drop me a line at the officers' mess. I really would like to buy you that drink.'

*

Some livestock had been commandeered, plus chickens and almost their entire stock of eggs. But Tadzio's makeshift lean-to buildings in the outer fields had escaped detection, not that their village policeman had taken the trouble to look over the farm. The accompanying German civilian had asked for his papers, but they were accepted and handed back without comment. Tadzio had explained that as he was half German, there was no way he would fight against the Fatherland. But neither would he fight for the French or the British. He was simply a farmhand in an essential agricultural industry producing food for the occupying forces.

He and Liliane lived together amicably but still with separate bedrooms. There had been no repeat of the intimacy she had initiated to try to keep him on the farm. Occasionally, however, he absented himself without telling Liliane where he was going. She was sure it had something to do with the resistance, but only after one of her fairly infrequent shopping trips to the village did she broach the subject. 'We're hearing about an attack not too long ago on the other side of Amiens,' she began. 'A trainload of fuel destined for Juvincourt airfield near Reims was attacked. Apparently, the engine was derailed, all the fuel was set alight, and the two attackers escaped. That was when,' she said pointedly, 'you were away from this farm for two nights and refused to tell me where you had been. I'm not stupid, Tadzio. Some time ago, you returned to England, and now you're back in France. Then there's a major attack on the Germans. You live here, so my life is on the line, too. I think you owe me an explanation.'

He was quiet for a moment. 'You're right,' he agreed eventually. 'I had thought perhaps that the less you knew, the safer it might be if anything went wrong.' He shrugged. 'What you don't know they can't make you tell. But as you have pointed out...

'Yes, I am setting up a resistance cell,' he admitted. 'That was our first operation. Just two of us, and it might be better if you don't know who the other person was. That way, no matter what happens, you can't give them his name.'

'I don't want to dent your male ego,' she told him. 'But I am quite capable of working out that there is only one villager who could have helped you pull it off. You would have needed another trained soldier. And everyone knows that Serge Moreau has only just returned from active service with the Legion. Am I right?' she asked defiantly, arms akimbo, fists on her hips.

'Serge is a good man,' he conceded. 'And yes, it was our operation. So now you know. Where do you want to take it from here? Do you want me to move away from the farm?'

'You know I can't manage without you,' she said. 'And I can't afford to employ a replacement.' He was still seated at the kitchen table. Liliane opened a bottle of red wine and produced two glasses. She stood alongside him, one hand on his shoulder, and poured before walking round the table to sit opposite. She raised her glass. '*Santé.*'

She went on, 'I think there's one thing you have forgotten. The Germans machine-gunned my parents. Innocent civilians. All they were doing was fleeing from the front. I know you were only trying to protect me, and I'm grateful for that. But I want to be involved. If I can help the resistance to kill Germans, then I will.'

'I understand,' he said eventually. 'And you will be. We can talk again tomorrow, but for now, let's finish our wine.'

She smiled at him. 'Can I ask you a question?' she replied. 'Were you offended when I seduced you by the mill stream pool? You obviously know why I did it. Is that the reason you haven't been near me since you returned? But I want you to know it wasn't entirely without feeling – at least not on my part, and I think not on yours either. So, when we have finished our wine, will you come to bed?'

'I… er… have a concern about making you pregnant,' he said. 'I have to tell you, I do not have anything…'

'That's something you don't have to worry about,' she responded evenly. 'Because I already *am* pregnant.' She tapped the table with her palm for emphasis. 'God knows what the future and this horrible war will bring, so we might as well make the most of the present.'

CHAPTER 20

Sir Manners, Doreen Jackman and Bill Ives sat round a table with Marie, who had arrived from her safe house.

'Good trip back?' asked Doreen, since she was the one who arranged the flights.

'Exciting,' said Marie. 'My pilot was someone called Johnny Metherwell. I'm not good on Air Force ranks, but I think he's a flight lieutenant. We met a Heinkel on the way back. He managed to get behind it and shoot it down.'

'One more to his score!' exclaimed Bill Ives.

'He's not claiming it,' said Marie. 'Apparently, he should have left it alone because his priority was to get me back to England. But his sister and her son were killed in a recent air raid, and there was no way he was going to let a damaged bomber return to base, only to fly again. He asked me not to tell the RAF, so this has to remain just between us,' she added firmly.

'Agreed,' said Sir Manners. 'But a good show, all the same. Now,' he went on, 'the purpose of this meeting is to begin working up an outline plan for a raid on that airfield near Le Touquet. We really do want that radar and decoding equipment. Bill,' he turned to one side, 'you have done the preliminary work, so perhaps you will share your initial thoughts with Marie.'

'May I say something,' Marie put in, 'before we even start pulling things together?' She took a moment's silence for assent. 'This operation has to look like a raid organised by British forces.' She placed a strong emphasis on the 'has'. 'Otherwise, the reprisals against my countrymen will be terrible. That's all,' she said, turning her hands over to indicate that she had made her point.

'I don't see that as a problem,' replied Bill Ives. 'So this, in broad outline, is what I have in mind…'

The discussion continued for another hour, after which Doreen Jackman took Marie back to her office. 'How are you coping?' she asked once they were seated. 'I'm only too aware of the constant stress and strain our agents are under, living in France.'

'It's not so bad for me,' Marie told her. 'I was born and brought up there. Plus, I get to travel – the local German commander has given me passes that allow me to visit the coastal regions. Apparently, *Hauptmann* Horst Brandt has been appointed *Weinführer* for the local area, and the travel permits are all to do with Jean Renaud's role helping him out. Jean's wife Monique is convinced that he's sweet on me, so there might be some possibilities there.'

'So you are happy to go back?' asked Doreen gently.

'Yes, but I wouldn't mind a few days off in London if that's all right?' she replied. 'Nothing immediate will happen over there, and it would be absolute bliss to take a little time to unwind.'

'If you hadn't asked, I would have insisted on it,' Doreen replied with a sympathetic smile. 'Let's have an agreement. You have the use of the safe house, and don't use your own funds whilst you are in England. His Majesty can pay for your break – you have more than earned it! Here…' She took an envelope from a drawer and pushed it across her desk. 'If there's nothing pressing, please come back to me when you want to return to France. Or if anything urgent crops up, I know how to contact you. But otherwise, I want you to have a couple of weeks of rest and relaxation. I know you don't have family in this country, but how does that sound to you?'

Marie told her that it sounded absolutely fine. The first thing she did back at the safe house was to pen a note to Johnny Metherwell at 'The Officers' Mess, RAF Stradishall'. If he was still prepared to honour his offer to buy her a drink, she could take the train directly to Bury St Edmunds from London. She signed it: 'Your recent passenger'.

Other than a change of underwear, she had only the clothes she was wearing when she had climbed into the rear seat of Johnny Metherwell's Lysander. Marie spent a day shopping in London using the funds Doreen had given her. However, she bought only the absolute minimum of clothes for her short period of leave. Unfortunately, she would not be able to take any of them back to France.

The next morning but one brought a reply. Johnny was due a few days off, so if she could ring the mess and leave a message, he would pick her up at the station on Friday morning. Also, he would book her accommodation.

Johnny pushed forward as she stepped from the train, kissed her chastely on the cheek and took her small case. 'You know who I am,' he said, 'and I am so glad that you could come. But daft as it seems, I don't even know your name.'

'It's Yvette,' she told him. 'It's not the name I use in France, but it's better that you don't know that one. Yvette's my real name.'

Parked right in front of the station – 'Nobody's going to object,' he told her – was an Austin Ten RAF staff car with its dun grey paintwork and RAF number plates. 'The CO's a really good egg,' he told her as they settled into the front seats. 'Petrol's tight, but he lets us use his staff car so that the few coupons we have for our own can be saved for leave or whatever. I can drop you at your hotel,' he said, 'then take this bus back to the mess. I have plenty of petrol for the weekend, so I suggest that you check in whilst I'm doing that, then we can have dinner this evening and perhaps spend a day out tomorrow. Oh, and by the way, there's a bash on at the mess tomorrow night. I'm not flying, so you have to come,' he said with almost boyish enthusiasm. 'The other chaps will be so jealous. Sorry...' he added quickly, 'didn't mean to be quite so forward...'

'You English,' she said with a smile. 'So very correct, but I thought it was charming.'

They had dinner in a local restaurant. She recognised that there was a mutual attraction, but best of all, it was so easy to share her thoughts. They talked for a long time after their meal. She learned that Johnny had been at Cambridge on a scholarship studying modern languages, but desperate to learn to fly, he had joined the university Air Squadron. 'No way I could have afforded it, otherwise,' he told her. 'My people aren't well off.'

With the outbreak of hostilities, rather than complete his degree, he had volunteered for the Royal Air Force and was eventually selected to fly the Lysander. 'It's more of a meritocracy than the other two services,' he told her. 'I was a grammar school boy, but all that matters now is whether I can fly an aeroplane.'

A waiter coughed alongside their table, where the bill had lain unattended for at least half an hour. They moved to a nearby public house for the rest of the evening. Being a Friday, it was noisy and full. She told him that she had an English father and a French mother and had been brought up in France. 'But I have to go back,' she told him, 'so it is safer for me if I don't say too much. You'll just have to take me on trust,' she finished with a conspiratorial grin.

He walked her back to her hotel. 'I'll not come in,' he told her, 'but can I pick you up around ten-ish tomorrow?'

'Thank you for a lovely evening,' she said simply. He moved to kiss her on the cheek, but her hand guided his face, and their lips brushed. '*Jusqu'à demain*,' she said softly.

'Until tomorrow,' he repeated.

The bar was still open when he entered the mess. Johnny decided that a nightcap would be in order. 'How was your evening,' asked his squadron leader, 'with your new popsie?'

'Er… my new what?' he replied.

'Well, you didn't have a girlfriend before, so either you have one now or you have joined the WAAFs and taken to wearing lipstick!'

Johnny wiped his lips with the back of his hand, and sure enough, it came away bearing traces of deep pink. He finished his quick half to the general laughter of those standing around. But he didn't mind. He was, he knew, very taken – perhaps smitten might be the right word, if he were honest – with a young French woman called Yvette.

He had booked her into a fairly upmarket country hotel a mile or so from the edge of town. There was enough in his bank account to cover the bill, but not much more. The following morning he picked her up in his own car, a modest Morris Eight two-door saloon. They spent a couple of hours admiring the ruins of Bury St Edmunds Abbey and its gardens. A local hostelry served them a cheese and pickle lunch, and he was about to pay when she placed a hand over his.

'The people I work for have given me quite a generous allowance to cover the time I am in England,' she explained. 'I know that an English gentleman always thinks he should pay the bill, but it would not be fair. *Alors*,' she said, handing a one-pound note to a slightly surprised barman. 'And I shall also pick up my hotel bill,' she added whilst waiting for change.

They walked round the town centre for a couple of hours in the afternoon, by which time they had just about exhausted Bury St Edmunds. 'Come and have tea at the hotel,' she invited. 'There's no point in driving back to the mess and then coming all the way back here to pick me up. I'll change, then we can have a drink and go to the party.

'Will you wait for me down here?' she asked, setting down her cup. Marie collected her key from the lady receptionist, who watched with an indulgent smile as the pretty young foreign lady headed for the stairs while the rather handsome pilot in his uniform watched her before heading for the bar.

There were a lot of cars parked all over the place in front of the mess. 'You're my guest, so I have to introduce you to the president of the mess committee,' he explained as they walked to the entrance. 'Apparently, that's the form. He's a squadron leader, but not mine.' She noticed that there were other ladies there, wives or girlfriends, but they were far outnumbered by the officers.

He took her hand and walked towards a group of officers. She noticed that one of them, a rather portly individual, had more rings on his arm than the others. However, he was not wearing either a pilot's wings or the single one of a navigator on his chest. Johnny suddenly realised that he did not know Yvette's surname. 'Yvette,' he said lamely, 'this is Squadron Leader Hoskins. Sir, my guest Yvette.'

His face was florid, she thought. He wasn't drunk, but neither was he completely sober. Her black cocktail number showed just a little décolletage, and he was looking at it. 'Er... welcome,' he managed. The officers around him were trying hard to smother a grin. '*Merci*,' she responded, with a half-smile that Johnny knew was not genuine. 'My English, eet is not good,' she said with a heavy accent that he knew she had put on deliberately. 'But sank you.' She switched to French. '*Johnny, veux-tu m'emmener rencontrer tes amis?*'

'Yvette has asked to meet my own squadron friends, sir,' Johnny said evenly. 'So please excuse us.' Without waiting for a reply, he took her elbow, and they moved away.

Ralph, David and Hugh were steadily downing pints at the end of the bar. Johnny accepted a half and Yvette a glass of wine. She thought the three of them looked barely older than schoolboys. 'So you have met Hoskins the Horror,' said Ralph with a grin.

'Look, chaps,' said Johnny, 'we have been out all day, and I need to freshen up. Would you look after Yvette for me? I shouldn't be more than twenty minutes.' He turned to her. 'And whatever you do, don't let them sneak off with you whilst I'm away.'

'As if...' exclaimed Ralph innocently, 'but then again, we might try, so you had better hurry up.'

Johnny had not returned when it was announced that a finger buffet was served in the dining room. The trio was about to escort Marie when the squadron leader joined them. 'I see you have been deserted by your host, Miss Yvette, so may I take you in to the buffet? But forgive my familiarity; I'm afraid Flight Lieutenant Metherwell did not offer your surname.'

'Thank you,' she replied. 'You are very kind. But we will, I think, wait for Johnny. He will be back in a minute, and in the meantime, these gentlemen are very kindly looking after me. As for my surname, I'm afraid it is known only to London.'

He gave no sign of noticing the difference between her previous use of English and this sudden fluency. 'If you are sure,' he said, somewhat red-faced, leaving the rest unfinished. 'He couldn't take offense,' said Ralph with a grin, 'but that was quite subtle, a beautiful put-down!'

'And now for another one,' she said mischievously. 'Johnny will join us. But let's wait for just a minute, then perhaps you young gentlemen would be kind enough to escort me towards something to eat?' When he joined them in the dining room, glass of wine in hand, the glance that came their way told Johnny they were extremely fortunate that none of them served under the squadron leader's command.

After supper, there was drinking and dancing to a gramophone. She noticed that Johnny drank sparingly, just a couple of halves. They danced, not closely. 'Please don't mind,' she said to him, 'but your three friends do not have a partner. I shall dance with each of them in turn.' And he was not at all jealous. On the contrary, he admired her thoughtful and endearing nature.

Later in the evening, couples began to drift off, and the unaccompanied officers settled to the bar for the duration. 'It's been a lovely evening,' she told him, 'and I have really enjoyed seeing something of your life and meeting your friends. But would you mind taking me back to my hotel, please, *mon cher*?'

He parked outside and was about to open his door when she

placed a hand on his arm. 'I have to go back to London tomorrow,' she said quietly, 'but I would like it if we could meet after breakfast, and perhaps you would take me to the station?'

'Of course,' he said quickly. 'But when will I see you again?' he added quickly. 'We will see each other again, won't we?'

'Trust me, I'll write. And next time you have a night off, please come to London.' With that, she pulled him towards her, and Johnny Metherwell received the first truly passionate kiss of his entire life.

*

A follow-up meeting was planned for Monday, but only Marie, Doreen Jackman and Bill Ives were present.

'First, timing,' he began. 'We want to take aerial photographs of the target. Then we can build a display model. Also, we have to pick and brief the people we need to use for the raid. Marie, you will need to set up your group on the ground. They have to secure the area so that we can land an aircraft safely. The RAF Special Operations Squadron is keen to help, but we seem to be at the height of the Blitz, so they are asking for a breathing space. They have only recently been bombed out of North Weald, and they are barely operational at Stradishall in Suffolk.' Marie chose not to mention that she had just spent the weekend there.

'We're well into November now,' he went on. 'So we think the raid could take place sometime in January. It'll be called "Operation Quick Spark".'

He saw the look on their faces. 'Don't blame me,' he said apologetically, 'I don't choose the bloody names!'

'Really, Bill,' admonished Doreen. 'Come along, Marie,' she rose to leave, 'we have things to discuss. Let's leave this rather vulgar gentleman to his own devices.'

'Did you have a pleasant weekend?' she asked, once they were back in her office and she had poured coffee. 'Obviously, we need to get you back so that you can organise things at your end. But how do you feel about that?' she asked solicitously.

'I didn't want to say anything in front of Mr Ives,' she replied, 'but I had a lovely weekend at RAF Stradishall. Flight Lieutenant Metherwell took me to a party in the mess on Saturday evening. If I could stay in London for just a few days, I would like us to have another weekend together, assuming that he is not flying, that is. Otherwise, I'm happy to go back whenever you wish. But I was going to ask you if it would be all right to ask him to stay at the safe house?'

Although single, Doreen Jackman's past life had certainly included its fair share of moments, and she could read between the lines. 'I think, my dear, you will find that as one of our few Royal Air Force officers with special operations experience, Flight Lieutenant Metherwell will be requested to attend a planning meeting on Friday, with a warning to his squadron leader that it could well extend into the weekend.' She smiled broadly, warming to her conspiracy. 'Almost certainly till Sunday,' she added. 'So just tell him that your superiors have rented the house for you.' Doreen reached over and patted Marie's hand. 'We girls have to stick together. After that, if it is all right with you, we will send you back to France some time towards the end of next week.'

Marie met the first train from Bury on Friday morning. It turned out that having parents of modest means, he had hardly ventured at all beyond East Anglia, where he had attended school and then Cambridge. They dropped off his case at the safe house then did a typical tour by bus and Tube: Big Ben, Buckingham Palace, the Oxford Street shops and Green Park. They had an early tea in Lyons Corner House in the Strand and wandered back to the safe house before dark. Marie carefully drew the blackout curtains.

'What would you like to do this evening?' he asked.

'I was tempted to use some of the funds I have been given,' she replied. 'Perhaps the Savoy or the Café Royale. But maybe tomorrow. Tonight I am going to be selfish. I want you to myself, so we will have an evening at home, if you don't mind. The lady I work for has been wonderful. She arranged for everything I needed to be delivered, even though I do not have a ration book.

'We French take our food seriously,' she said emphatically. 'So I can offer some oysters, *un boeuf en croute avec pommes de terre fondantes et une réduction du vin rouge*, and a simple *tarte tatin* for what I believe you English call pudding. *C'est un désert*,' she added firmly. 'To me, pudding – *ce n'est pas un mot gentil*.'

Whilst she was cooking, they enjoyed a glass of *fino* in the kitchen. Unusually for London at the time, there was a refrigerator. It was American, so she assumed the safe house was also used by their ally. It had chilled the Montrachet to perfection, so it was superb with the oysters. Doreen's hamper from Messrs Fortnum had also included a good claret and a bottle of Armagnac. It was the finest meal he had eaten in his life.

'You must let me help with the washing-up,' he said, utterly replete.

'No,' she replied. 'You have to return to your squadron on Sunday. I can do it in the morning. Then we shall have another whole day together. But, for now, put your case in my room and get into bed. I shall go to the bathroom and then join you.'

She had made her decision after the weekend at Stradishall. Living as Marie, she had been lucky so far. She was falling in love with Johnny Metherwell. But there was no guarantee that either of them would survive the war. She urgently needed a memory to take back to France. Johnny was just looking at her. It was impossible to read his thoughts. Perhaps they were both nervous.

Yvette hesitated before continuing. 'I hope you don't mind, but I can't afford to fall pregnant. There is a packet of American condoms in the drawer of the bedside table.' She did not tell him that Doreen had asked if she should provide them. 'It will be my first time,' she added quietly.

'Mine too,' he said softly.

CHAPTER 21

Hedda and Werner spent most evenings together and always weekends, either in one apartment or the other. They often dined out in some of the better, smaller restaurants, usually with a good band and a small dance floor – venues favoured by the military and made safe with armed guards. The cosy nights in developed into a competition of cooking skills, usually declared a draw, whilst they listened to the wireless. As a Gestapo officer, it was perfectly in order for Werner to listen to *Radio Londres* or the BBC. The latter, Hedda particularly enjoyed. By mid-November, Werner's shoulder was healing well, and he was back to light duties.

She knew that one of his chief responsibilities was the identification of French nationals, particularly of the Jewish faith, for deportation by rail to work within German factories supporting the Fatherland's war machine. He had not said as much, but she sensed that he found the work distasteful. It was as if his sense of honour and devotion to duty were in conflict.

Hedda also thought a lot about Tadzio. She had no idea whether he was still alive. There had been no news for months. Surely London would have sent word if they had heard anything…? Much as she had loved him at the time, she had begun to think of him more and more like someone from her past life. At the beginning of December, after a night out of intimate dining and dancing, then a glass of cognac in her apartment, she took Werner to her bed. He was an accomplished lover – but so he should have been, she reflected happily afterwards, if there had been only an element of truth in his reputation amongst the ladies at the embassy.

Her greatest fear was the flight home to Munich for Christmas. She had no idea whether she would be met at the airfield or by whom. Werner would leave the aircraft with her and had offered to arrange transport to her home if necessary. Then the seventeen-seater tri-motor Junkers Ju 52 would fly on to Berlin.

With her heart beating heavily and from her briefing photographs back in London, Hedda recognised Herr Hoffmann standing with a small group of people in front of the terminal. She had resolved to rush up to him and, with a quick embrace, whisper into his ear that she was Anneliese, adding, 'For God's sake, pretend that I'm your daughter.'

She need not have worried. As they walked across the grass, the roar of the tri-motor's engines as it taxied to take off again drowned out any chance of a conversation being overheard. Herr Hoffmann ran towards her, both arms extended for an embrace. Instead, he spoke frantically into her ear.

Werner waited for a moment, then as the aircraft took off, he introduced himself with a correct bow, his heels clicking together, even though he was in uniform and by rights should have offered a salute. He turned to Hedda. 'I'll let you settle in with your family, then perhaps I may telephone you after a few days. It would give me great pleasure for you to visit my home and family.' So saying he took his leave to join a uniformed chauffeur. A baggage handler stood patiently to one side with Hedda's suitcase.

'*Komm, Anneliese*,' he said not too quietly for the benefit of those within earshot, his arm still around her shoulders as he led her towards his Mercedes. He took the suitcase from the handler and placed it on the rear seat, then held the front door open for her.

He walked quickly round the long bonnet and almost collapsed into the driver's seat, exhaling a loud exclamation of breath. 'Well, Anneliese,' he said with relief, 'I know about your situation in Paris. And I think that went as well as we could possibly have expected.' He told her about his visit from Brigadier Summerton.

'The staff have been told that Anneliese is in Paris but cannot be spared from her duties to come home for Christmas,' he explained as they drove from the airfield. 'You are simply a distant relative from northern Germany with the same Christian name. They have not been given any details because that's all they need to know.'

She asked whether he and his wife would go back to Switzerland after the holiday.

'Things have changed a bit since the start of the war,' he told her. 'Now, nearly all of our production is dedicated to orders from the government. With only a few exceptions, we are not allowed to export. We now make some military radio equipment, but mostly we turn out rifles. I still travel to Switzerland, and we have kept our apartment and business premises there. But really, that side of the business is much reduced. I find myself spending more and more time back here in Germany, helping my brother Berndt with production. He and his wife will join us for lunch tomorrow.'

'But they will know I am not Anneliese,' she replied, clearly alarmed.

'They do already,' he replied flatly. 'I had to tell them. But don't worry, as a family, we are opposed heart and soul to Hitler. That is why we contacted your people, through Miss Fitzgibbon, in the first place.' He turned to face her and smiled. 'But let us leave that subject for the moment. Helga and I wish to welcome you to our home. Despite this terrible war, I hope we will have a good Bavarian Christmas and a thoroughly enjoyable evening tonight.'

Hedda was intrigued by the substantial manor house with a lake in its own grounds. Her father had been an academic, but this was wealth and substance far beyond her own family background. Dinner that evening was a relaxed affair, just the three of them present, but they were served by uniformed staff directed by Helga, as Hedda had been asked to address her hostess. Afterwards, they retired to a drawing room for coffee and a liqueur, something which, back in London what seemed a lifetime ago, had not been included in Clarissa's otherwise extensive instruction. She had served wine to ladies at dinner, and then they had withdrawn for coffee, nothing stronger. Not knowing what to choose, Hedda asked for *wodka* – fortunately, it was the same word in German.

'Certainly,' Herr Hoffmann replied smoothly. 'I know we have some somewhere. But that's an interesting choice. Forgive me for mentioning it, and your command of our language is perfect, but it's not something for which any young German woman would ask.'

She saw no point in being other than honest. They were already fellow conspirators, so Hedda reasoned that she had nothing to fear.

'My father was German,' she said quietly. 'He was a professor in Berlin. Under the Nazis. They took our small farm. Then he lost his job. Finally, he committed suicide. My mother was Polish – a student of chemistry at the university when they met. She took me back to Poland, but everything became too much for her. Working as a chemist, she had access to all sorts of medicines. She, too, took her own life.'

She paused for a moment, hands before her resting on the table. Helga very kindly placed her own above Hedda's. 'I fought with our partisans against Hitler's army,' the younger woman continued after a moment to pull herself together. 'At first hiding in a forest, then from a farm. Eventually, we escaped to England. But now you know – I am half German, half Polish and fluent in both languages. I also speak good French. Hence being chosen for this assignment.'

Helga was silent for a moment. 'You have had a hell of a life,' she said eventually. Then, she turned to her husband. 'Dieter, go check that all the staff have gone home or to their rooms.' He returned a few minutes later to confirm that they had. 'Right,' she went on, 'go find that *wodka*,' she copied Hedda's pronunciation. 'Berndt and his wife will be here tomorrow, and we have much to discuss. But tonight, we will drink a toast to your bravery.'

Her husband served two measures from a silver tray, then, placing it aside, took his own. '*Prost*,' he said firmly. And then, 'To freedom.' They took a sip. Hedda drained her glass then set it down. They laughed and followed her example.

The staff were all off duty on Sunday afternoons. Once lunch had been served and cleared, Helga checked that they were all off the premises or two floors upstairs in their accommodation. She served coffee in the drawing room. Dieter and Berndt had said little during the meal because, Hedda reasoned, they were waiting till they were all together but free of servants before beginning their discussion. His wife, Krista, had said hardly a word. Blonde, probably in her thirties, although she looked older. She was the dumpy epitome of a German *Hausfrau*, interested only in *Kinder, Kirche und Küche*, children, church and kitchen. Hedda was not to know that she had been a junior secretary in one of Berndt's father's factories, common but blousy and sexy enough to tempt advances from an inexperienced young man learning his way in the industry. She got herself pregnant and insisted on marriage. To his parents' fury, Berndt had little choice – the family could not afford such a scandal in their small, tight-knit rural community. Three children later, they led comfortable, almost separate lives, and Berndt took his pleasures elsewhere.

'Berndt,' opened Dieter Hoffmann, once they were settled, 'do you want to begin?'

'Anneliese,' he said, 'I do not even know your name.' He paused for a moment, hoping that she would respond, but Hedda remained silent. 'All *I* know,' he continued, accepting that his brother might have more information, 'is that you have somehow replaced our Anneliese to become deputy to the Head of Chancery in Paris, but you are a British agent. Of course, it goes without saying that you can pass information to London.'

Dieter took up the conversation. 'We still have our property in Zürich,' he said, 'but the government here now has total control over all production in Germany, and we are told what we must produce. In my case, our factory here produces radios and similar electronics for the *Wehrmacht*. In our other one, Berndt supervises the production of rifles, thousands of them.'

His brother nodded in confirmation. 'So, as I also mentioned in the car,' Dieter continued, 'our export function in Switzerland is much reduced, although there is still some activity there that needs my attention from time to time. But I no longer have a valid reason to live there permanently. It has recently been suggested that my patriotic duty is to remain in Germany and, as a qualified engineer and industrialist, assist with production for the war effort.

'But I want to return to my conversation with Brigadier Summerton,' he went on. 'You now know that he called at my office when I was last in Switzerland. But your visit was not the only subject we discussed. I took the opportunity to update him on the situation here, including information on Dachau and the use of forced labour.' Berndt moved his head slowly from side to side, indicating his support for his brother's disapproval.

'Afterwards,' Dieter resumed, 'he returned to his office in Bern. But he was back in my office forty-eight hours later, asking for my help on the subject of Lend-Lease. As he explained, it has to succeed. And we can provide evidence that will go a long way towards helping Roosevelt persuade isolationist Americans in Congress that they must support Britain in her fight against the Nazis.'

'Let's start with Lend-Lease,' said Berndt. 'Have you heard of it?'

Hedda admitted that she hadn't. 'Don't forget,' she added, 'I've been holed up in Paris for the past few months.'

'At the moment, under their 1939 Neutrality Act,' he told her, 'the sale of American war materiel to Britain has to be on a cash and carry basis, and all purchases have to be transported to the United

Kingdom by their merchant navy. The brigadier told my brother that earlier this month, or possibly even in November, Churchill warned Roosevelt that with dwindling gold and currency reserves, this arrangement was no longer affordable. Fortunately, Roosevelt is only too aware that a Nazi victory will, in time, pose a direct threat to the United States.

'Churchill, therefore, appealed personally to Roosevelt,' he went on, 'and in exchange for a ninety-nine-year lease on British bases in the Caribbean and Newfoundland – they would become US air and naval bases – the Royal Navy would receive more than fifty obsolescent but desperately needed destroyers.'

'So,' Dieter took up the narrative, 'President Roosevelt is about to embark upon a campaign to persuade Congress that the United States should lend, rather than sell, military supplies to the United Kingdom. Payment will be deferred indefinitely and will be in any form that the United States government deems acceptable. This initiative has to succeed,' he stated, his hand striking the table for emphasis. 'If it fails, the United Kingdom will probably lose the war. At the very least, Great Britain could be forced to sue for peace on Hitler's terms,' he stated dramatically. 'And as for France, Poland and the rest of Europe…' He tailed off, the final outcome too dreadful even to contemplate.

'That is what Lend-Lease is all about,' he continued eventually. 'But persuading Congress is not a foregone conclusion, and the debate will go on for at least a couple of months. If we supply evidence that Roosevelt can use to support his argument, it could mean the difference between success and failure. It could determine the war's outcome: it is that important,' he finished, his final words spaced, staccato and heavy with emphasis.

He nodded to his brother as if exhausted by the explanation. Berndt took up the conversation.

'We consider ourselves good Germans,' he stated firmly. 'In Switzerland, my brother agreed to help the British by accepting your Christmas visit here as much for his daughter's sake as for our opposition to Hitler and the Nazis. I can tell you that we have talked long into the night about the British Lend-Lease request. We would already be considered traitors for what we are doing now,' he went on. 'But for the sake of Germany, Hitler and the Nazis cannot be allowed to win the war. So we have decided to help the British.

'Does the word *Dachau* mean anything to you?' he asked.

Hedda thought for a moment. 'Just before he died, when we lived in a rented flat in Berlin, my mother and father often had heated discussions. They were usually after I had gone to bed, and they thought that I was not listening, although I could hear everything through the thin walls. I was little more than a child, but I think it was something to do with a punishment that the Nazi Party inflicted on those they did not like. Whatever it was, I sensed that it really frightened my parents.'

'*Es ist ein Konzentrationslager*, a concentration camp,' he added in English, in case her German vocabulary was not up to date. 'Dachau was originally a disused munitions factory, but the site was converted in the early 1930s to house people considered by the Nazis to be politically undesirable. More to the point, it is not far from here – the camp is about sixteen kilometres north-west of Munich. You know that we manufacture weapons and electronic equipment. Both of our factories are near Dachau.

'Originally, most prisoners were German nationals,' he went on, 'but now the camp houses people from all countries overrun by Germany, most of them Jews.'

'I understand,' said Hedda, 'but I'm not sure how this is relevant to me.'

'We need labour for our factories,' Dieter answered her. 'Most of our former employees have been conscripted. In addition to Dachau, the Nazis have begun to construct adjacent sub-camps, *Arbeitskommandos*, they call them. They have just completed the first one for women. But the point is, not only are we forced to employ what is effectively slave labour, but conditions, we've been told, in all of the camps are brutal and appalling.'

'For a start,' Berndt broke in, 'their rations are hopelessly inadequate. As a result, they quickly become severely malnourished. I have tried repeatedly to explain that once we have trained someone as a machinist or an assembly worker, it makes no sense to let them die from starvation or some associated disease. The Nazi attitude is that it is cheaper to let them die and just provide replacements, many of them Jews from Poland.

'I remember telling someone who was a guest here for Christmas two years ago – an English lady, a Miss Fitzgibbon, I recall…' He looked at Hedda, who did not react. 'Anyway,' he said, 'I mentioned that we had several Jewish employees. Now only a few senior ones are considered indispensable. The rest have all been taken to the camp. They still work for us, but they are no longer free.

'They tell us what is going on in the camps,' he told her. 'Sometimes, they are forced to stand for extremely long periods. Beatings are common. A favourite punishment for infringements, which are often imagined, is being hung by the arms when they are tied behind a man's back. It is excruciating, usually resulting in dislocation and permanent damage. It often amuses the guards to jiggle the rope. The victim screams until he passes out.

'And it is no better for the women,' he went on. 'The guards are both male and female. I am reluctant to go into detail, but you can imagine the suffering that the women must endure to receive their rations.'

There was a lull in the conversation as Hedda took in what Berndt had said.

'We have been asked to provide evidence,' he told her eventually. 'Full details of what is happening in Dachau and the *Arbeitskommandos*, and most importantly, there will also be photographs – absolute proof of our allegations. It will be up to Herr Roosevelt how he uses them.

'Those of our senior Jewish people who have not been interned,' he added, 'our most specialist engineers and top scientists, have close contact with their fellow workers from the camp. In practical terms, the company provides additional food for the Dachau people when they are at work. The camp guards are bribed substantially to overlook this. And we have photographic evidence of money being handed over to ensure their silence.

'We have two volunteer internees who have agreed to carry cameras,' he went on, 'the smallest we could buy. Their mission will be to photograph as much of life in the camps as they can, particularly any brutality they can witness. The date set for returning these cameras is the day after Christmas. The internees are being given one day off: not for any religious reason but to boost the morale of the guards by allowing them to celebrate. Sadly we fear this will include an orgy of drink and abuse, but it will aid our cause. Then we will produce a report. We want you to take it, together with the original negatives, back to Paris. And then to ensure that it all reaches London.'

'This is a high-risk operation,' said Dieter. 'We are using only two cameras, one for a male volunteer and another for a woman. One of our members, a chemist, has manufactured two cyanide capsules. He says they are crude but effective, causing death within seconds. Otherwise, if caught, the volunteers would be tortured. Few can resist for long, and that would risk the Gestapo tracing the cameras to us, and if we were arrested, that could lead to a further betrayal of our movement.'

'And if they do not take the pill?' asked Hedda, knowing that she had agonised over whether she would have had the courage to take this step. It had been almost a relief to donate hers to the unfortunate Simone Faucher.

'They have sworn that they will,' Dieter replied grimly. 'Both of them have said that it might even be better than the life they are living at the moment. Nevertheless, in the unlikely event that something goes wrong, we have a back-up plan to run for Switzerland, but that need not concern you.'

'And if we are successful, and the report and negatives reach London, what do you imagine will happen?' she asked.

'We are confident that Sir Manners Fitzgibbon will know how to make best use of it all. Imagine, for example, that an influential congressman favours isolationism and is opposed to Lend-Lease. I believe even some of the Jewish members take this view. A leader can be taken aside by Roosevelt or one of his aides. Then, under the Official Secrets Act, they can be shown irrefutable evidence of Nazi atrocities. It is hard to believe that they would not then change sides and use all their influence to support the President's bill.'

Their after-lunch discussion was interrupted by a telephone call. As the staff were off duty, Dieter moved quickly into the entrance hall to answer it, leaving the door open.

'*Moment, bitte*,' they heard him say. 'It's for you, Anneliese,' he said from the doorway. '*SS-Sturmbannführer* Werner Scholz,' he added, closing the door behind her. 'He travelled with Anneliese from Paris,' he explained for the benefit of the others, 'and introduced himself at the airport.'

'Is he a threat?' asked Berndt.

'No reason to think so,' Dieter replied, 'but let's wait until Anneliese comes back.'

As she resumed her seat, he remarked, 'That was a short conversation.'

She took his remark for the question it really was. 'I have been invited to spend a couple of days in Munich,' she told them. 'A night at his apartment so that we can have an evening out in the city, then another with his parents in the country. He has suggested that he drives me back to Starnberg on Monday afternoon so that I shall be here for Christmas.'

'I do not wish to pry or be invasive,' Dieter replied, 'but there had to be a reason why this Gestapo officer introduced himself at the airport. Given what we have just told you, I think we need to know what your relationship is with this Nazi.'

Hedda thought for a moment. 'He provides the Gestapo input for the monthly reports I prepare for Berlin,' she said eventually, 'and we live in the same block of apartments.' She did not go into detail of how this came about. 'Please do not think too badly of me,' she went on, 'but I seduced him, in part for the sake of my mission. We do not live together, but we are lovers.'

'On the contrary,' said Helga, 'I admire what you have done. It does not sound as if he is a threat to us, but I would be interested to know what you make of him. Is he as stupid or fanatic as some of his kind that we have met?'

'Thank you for what you have just said – I am grateful,' she told Helga. 'But to answer your question, he just does not seem like a normal Nazi. There appears to be a conflict between his duties in the Gestapo and his conscience. It's something I am hoping to explore, but as you will appreciate, it's a delicate issue that we have not talked about so far.'

'What did you say to him, just now?' asked Dieter.

'I said that I would very much like to accept his invitation, but obviously, I had to make sure that it would be all right with my family. So I hope you don't mind, but I promised to ring him back in the morning.'

Dieter and Berndt looked at each other. Berndt gave a slow but firm nod of agreement.

'If it is your wish, we both think you should accept,' said Dieter. 'It can't do any harm, and perhaps the more we can learn of their local organisation, the better.'

Dieter drove to the factory every day except on Sunday. It was, he explained, no great distance to drop her off on Saturday in an expensive and fashionable suburb of Munich. Hedda gave her name and a uniformed concierge admitted them. 'You are expected, Fraulein Hoffmann,' he replied formally, and showed them to a lift. But, again, it went only to a penthouse. There was a separate lift for the other apartments.

'I'll leave you here,' said Dieter, as its door opened. He set down her case, raised his hat, nodded politely to the concierge on the way out and returned to his Mercedes.

Werner greeted her in the hallway, relaxed in civilian clothes. She almost dropped her case as they kissed and embraced. His hand was inside her coat, and her tongue slipped between his lips. They urgently wanted more.

CHAPTER 22

Getzel Bergman had once lived in an artisan's house near Dachau with his young wife. The son of a schoolmaster, he was a rather scholarly-looking young man, slim, swarthy and with a round face and equally round glasses. He was nevertheless determined to succeed in life. Unfortunately, after school, there was not enough family money to send him to university. Still, he benefitted from considerable training at the Hoffmann electronics factory, rising quickly to a well-paid position as a foreman. This was despite his lack of years, although he was not as senior as a fully qualified electrical engineer. He married Eva at the beginning of 1938. Getzel had never understood why such a lovely, chestnut-haired, green-eyed young woman agreed to be his childhood sweetheart and then his bride. She could have taken her pick from all the young men of the village. So he thanked the Lord every day for his good fortune. They were looking forward to starting a family.

But after *Kristallnacht* in November of that year, he and Eva had been just two of the thirty thousand Jews rounded up and sent to concentration camps, many to Dachau. It had been a terrifying experience. They had been separated. Along with other men, he had been forced to hand over all personal possessions – wallet, money, watch, clothes – till he stood naked with fellow Jews, all strangers. They were issued with vertically striped prison uniforms. What had happened to his wife, he had no idea.

Even so, amongst his fellow inmates, he considered himself fortunate. Because of his employment, he was one of a separate detachment who stood together at roll call. They were one of the first groups to be checked because they had to be marched to work. Usually, they avoided having to watch the beatings that followed the most minor transgressions, whether real or imagined. And they were not required to stand for prolonged periods inadequately dressed in their flimsy prison uniforms hopelessly unfit for the freezing weather. Not, that is, except for Sundays, when the factory was shut for maintenance. Sundays were reserved for witnessing the most severe punishments meted out to those guilty of more serious crimes, including any attempt to escape.

Another small blessing was the extra rations given to the factory inmates by Herr Hoffmann whilst they were at work. The diet at the camp was hopelessly inadequate. Slop, mostly, with bits of gristle and vegetable and lord knows what else with one slice of poor-quality bread per man per day. Typhoid came and went, and many succumbed to minor ailments simply because of malnutrition or for want of the most basic medical attention. Even so, it was hard to endure a day that began before daylight, followed by a two-kilometre walk to the factory, then a ten-hour shift, only to face an even more exhausting walk back to the camp. One thought kept him alive: Getzel was determined to survive and find his beloved Eva. Once, he would have been considered a healthy young man. Now, he had lost at least two kilos in weight. His regular features were tight against his head, and his skin had developed eczema. His once-lustrous black hair was dull and lank. And he had lice.

But he was an experienced foreman in the electronics family. And his seniors often consulted him on how best to manufacture and assemble components. So it was not unusual for the guards to see him deep in conversation, a blueprint held jointly, or perhaps weighted down on a machine bench. They took no notice when Dieter Hoffmann stood next to him, then beckoned to Getzel Bergman to follow him into his office. Bergman's senior engineer accompanied them. It was an ordinary, everyday factory occurrence.

Getzel Bergman was fiercely loyal to the Hoffmanns. The previous year he had mentioned his concern for his wife to his supervising engineer, who had spoken to Dieter Hoffmann. A few days later, he was told that his wife was alive and as well as could be expected; that is, for someone assigned to one of the many sub-camps or *Arbeitskommandos* located throughout southern Germany. She had been traced to the one allocated to women forced to labour in the weapons factory managed by Dieter's brother Berndt. The female workers were housed in the factory and controlled by a handful of guards. At least, thought Getzel, his wife was spared the daily forced march. Each took comfort from the knowledge that the other was still alive. Very occasionally, the kindly Hoffmanns passed on messages or snippets of information.

Dieter Hoffmann took the chair behind his desk and invited the other two to be seated. He took a small camera from his desk drawer and placed it in front of him. 'It's a *Voigtländer* Bessa 66,' he announced quietly, 'otherwise known as a Baby Bessa.' He returned the camera to his drawer, reached out to a bookcase behind him, extracted a folded technical drawing of a radio and placed it in front of the two engineers. 'In case anyone walks in unannounced,' he said quietly.

'As you know,' he went on, still speaking softly, 'we need pictures of what life is like inside the Dachau camp. The more embarrassing to the Nazis, the better. You take my meaning?'

Getzel nodded to indicate that he understood. 'The most unpleasant,' he stated flatly.

'The camera has an f3.5 lens, so you should get something even if the light is not too good,' Dieter informed him, 'and the 120 film roll should give you at least twelve shots, maybe a few more.'

'*Ja,*' said Getzel. '*Ich verstehe.*'

'No, you don't understand,' Dieter continued. 'First, if we can pull this off, these pictures might help defeat the fascists and determine the outcome of the war. Second, if you are discovered, you will be tortured and executed. We are also giving you a suicide pill, but you must have the courage to use it. Otherwise, the pain will be unbearable, and eventually you will be forced to betray us all.' He did not elaborate on who, precisely, was 'us all'.

'There's more,' said Dieter. 'We know there are atrocities committed in the women's camps. We need photos from there, too. Your wife has agreed to try to provide them. She also has a camera, although its lens and film have been modified to give at least acceptable results in low light. Her message to you is that she is determined to make the attempt. If she has to take her cyanide pill, she wants you to know that she died with her love for you in her heart. I am also to say to you, her message is that, if it is necessary, please do the same. And that she sends you all her love.'

He was silent for several seconds, till a tear rolled slowly down each cheek. Roughly he brushed them away. 'How do I get the camera into the camp?' he asked.

'Your friend Dov has a tattered old jacket he wears over his uniform. He will lend it to you for the march back to the camp. The camera will be in one of the pockets – it would be too conspicuous in that thin uniform. The guards are used to seeing the jacket – they won't worry about who's wearing it. But take these,' he pushed a few small bars of chocolate across the desk, 'and share them out on the way. Tomorrow, when you have your midday break, I have arranged for you all to receive hot soup and a slice of bread covered with honey. The guards won't like it, but I can promise you they will look the other way.'

'May the Lord bless you,' said Getzel, rising to leave.

*

Although Eva Bergman had a camera, she had concealed much of her situation from her husband. The women were guarded at their *Arbeitskommando* by a section of older SS, men no longer suitable for more active service. The guards had their own barrack room in the disused factory and a similar facility set aside for them at Berndt's works. All the women, particularly the younger ones, dreaded the hours when they were off duty. The guards would select a few of them every night to be taken to their quarters. First, the men would consume beer or wine – sometimes spirits, if they had just been paid. Then the women would be ordered to undress. If they were lucky, it was just sex. But when the guards were really drunk, the perversions were nothing short of bestial. Most of the women had been brutally and painfully penetrated at every orifice. And not always by human flesh.

She had, of course, not passed any of this information to Getzel. At the very least, it would have enraged him sufficiently to endanger his own life. It might well have driven him to suicide. It came to something when she counted it a blessing that she was too malnourished to menstruate. So at least she had not become pregnant. When Berndt asked her to try to obtain photographic evidence, she had not hesitated. She would do anything to help defeat the Nazis, who were worse than animals. And if she had to take the capsule, it would be a relief to escape from hell on earth, which is why she had encouraged Getzel to follow her example. Perhaps they could help the war effort against Hitler. If not, she hoped that Adonai would be kind enough to let them be reunited in a very different and much kinder place.

Friday nights were the worst. It was not unusual for Eva to be chosen. She had probably lost a couple of kilos, but she had always had good breasts, and with a much smaller waist, she now had an hourglass figure. She was also tall for a woman, which they seemed to like. That night, seven of them were ordered to follow a guard, one for each of them not on duty and one more who might not be forced to have sex. Sometimes this would be the luck of the draw, but there was always the chance that if they were drunk enough, three of them would want a fresh body and all use her simultaneously.

As the sergeant in charge, the *Unterschafführer* would have first pick. Eva simply undressed for him. She was not carrying the camera because she was always the first to be chosen, and she knew they would all be looking at her. She dropped her clothing. They all knew from experience that any resistance would only invite a beating, and the outcome would be the same anyway. The other men would not watch for long – aroused by the sight of her naked body, the *Rottenführer* ordered another girl to undress in front of his chair. Once their corporal had made his choice, the privates were not far behind. But undressing together in a huddle, one of the girls was able to set down the precious camera under a pile of clothes.

Tonight the sergeant kicked off his uniform trousers and pants, then stood to lift Eva against the wall. She wrapped her legs around him and felt herself penetrated, fortunately without too much pain. She made a pretence – gasping sounds of satisfaction – and his orgasm came quickly. Then, without bothering to dress again, he took his seat at the table and poured another glass of wine.

Seemingly, for the moment, he had lost all interest in her. Eva began to pull on her clothes. To her relief, he did not object. Shira, the girl who had not been chosen, was still dressed. She gave Eva the briefest nod. Some pictures had been taken. To distract the sergeant, Eva asked him for a drink. Keeping hold of his glass, he pushed the bottle towards her. She drank deeply, keeping herself between the sergeant and Shira, giving the girl a chance to hide the camera behind a cardigan, just lifting it quickly to take more photos of the orgy in front of her. The sergeant was too drunk to hear the faint clicking of the shutter, but the sound terrified Eva. The other men in the room were far too preoccupied to notice.

Sometime later, with all of the guards dressed and some still drinking, although two of them were slumped on the table, the girls knew they had served their purpose and could leave the room. Tonight, Shira would not be abused, although she had already passed on the camera as a precaution. Occasionally, the guards would toss something as a reward, perhaps chocolate. Tonight it was a bag of apples. The other girls would know what the seven had been through. But fruit was not included in their rations. 'Come on, girls,' said Eva when they were safely back in the dormitory. 'At least my hands are still clean. Someone find me a knife. I think we can all get a share.'

*

Werner and Hedda walked around Munich's city centre on Saturday afternoon. It seemed totally unaffected by the war, except that many men were in uniform. But the shops and their merchandise did not quite match up to Paris. They settled for a coffee in one of the smarter '*Kaffee und Kuchen*' establishments, although Hedda declined a slice of tart piled high with cream. But all around, heavy, fashionably dressed ladies wielded a fork with gusto. Once safely married and producing children, thought Hedda, *Mutti* was not overly concerned for her figure. That night they dined in the *Ratskeller*, the municipal restaurant situated underneath the city council's administrative building and a source of immense pride to every German town and city. Hedda chose a steak with a piquant sauce defined as *Zigeuner Art*. Illogical, she thought, since the Hoffmanns had told her the Nazis were sending gypsies and Romas to the concentration camps these days.

They were back at Werner's apartment by half-past nine. He made coffee, and they enjoyed a nightcap of cognac brought from France.

In the morning Werner left Hedda at the apartment to fetch his car, currently housed at a local rented garage. Back at the apartment, he took their cases whilst the concierge rushed to open the building's front door. At the kerb stood a most extravagantly beautiful silver sports car. 'It's a 1936 Mercedes-Benz 500K Special Roadster,' he said matter-of-factly, 'with the optional five-speed gearbox.' She walked to the front and almost gasped at the massive silver radiator, the Mercedes star centre top and an array of lights in front, not to mention two enormous chromium trumpet horns.

'Werner, it must be worth a fortune,' she exclaimed.

'Probably is,' he replied evenly. 'But production of civilian vehicles has stopped for the duration, so it'll have to see me through the war.' He opened the passenger door, and she stepped inside, managing not to stand on the running board, despite its protective black strip, for fear of leaving a mark. To her front, the bonnet seemed to stretch away forever. A group of young boys had assembled on the pavement to point excitedly at the cabriolet.

Once out of the city, the sun came out. They were well wrapped up, so despite the cold, he stopped briefly and dropped the hood. Hedda's thoughts were a riot of conflicting emotions. Here she was, a Polish/German girl, working for British intelligence in Germany's Paris embassy as a spy, and living a life of absolute luxury with a Nazi officer whose wealth and background were totally atypical of his military background. It was, she knew, quite illogical. Every instinct told her that it was not right: it did not make sense.

From the sun in their eyes, she knew that they were heading in a more or less easterly direction, the other side of Munich from Starnberg. Eventually, after driving for about an hour, they were in open countryside when he turned right through tall, pillared gates. Hedda was not too surprised when a long drive led eventually to a large roundabout, surrounded by a wide circle of cobblestones, and Werner parked in front of a huge old house. It was built in the same style and almost a carbon copy of the Hoffmann residence but decidedly more imposing. It looked like two wings had been added, each styled as a perfect copy of the main building. Vast expanses of black timber and white stonework looked to be in pristine order. A middle-aged lady in a black uniform and white apron and cap rushed down the steps and waited for Werner to open his door. Hands together in front of her, she bobbed a small curtsey.

'Welcome home, Herr Werner,' she said, but her eyes swept to Hedda, who was opening her own door. 'Thank you, Anna,' he replied, but as Hedda walked round the bonnet, he seized Anna by both shoulders and planted a kiss on her cheek. 'Anna is our housekeeper now,' he explained as Hedda approached, 'but she used to look after me when I was a *Junge*. Any news of your husband?' he asked more seriously.

'His ship sailed four weeks ago,' she replied, 'I haven't heard.' The concern in her voice was unmistakable.

'Ludwig was our head gardener,' he explained to Hedda, 'but he was in the Navy as a young man. Now, he's been called back to the *Kriegsmarine*. Anna,' he turned to indicate Hedda, 'this is my dear friend Fraulein Hoffmann.'

Anna bobbed another small curtsey. 'Shall I bring your cases, sir?' she asked.

'Thank you for greeting us,' Werner replied. 'But no, please go back inside, and I will introduce Fraulein Hoffmann to my parents. I'll bring the cases in when I park the car.'

He took her elbow as they mounted the steps. 'Would have been a different reception eighteen months ago,' he said absent-mindedly, 'before we were taken into this disastrous war.' It was a strange remark, she thought, for an *SS* officer.

His parents crossed the room to greet them. Werner made the formal introduction. So his father was the '*Herr General*', she learned. 'Fraulein Hoffmann,' said an older version of Werner, 'welcome to Buchbach Manor. I hope you will enjoy your stay with us.' Hedda noticed that he was leaning on a cane. He caught her glance. 'Last war,' he said rather loudly, tapping his leg with it. She guessed he might be a little deaf. 'Keeps me out of this one.'

Frau Johanna Scholtz was nearly as tall as her husband, but she seemed much younger. Slim, with fair hair and blue eyes, she was still an attractive and rather aristocratic-looking woman. She took Hedda by the elbow and smiled. 'Come and sit on the sofa and tell me about yourself whilst Werner puts that dreadful car of his away – we don't have footmen in the house these days, they are all at the front, and he won't trust any of the girls to do it, even though some of them have learned to drive because we still have to run the estate.'

The General and Werner excused themselves. 'Please be so kind as to ring on your way out, Gustav,' she asked. 'I'm going to offer Anneliese a drink before luncheon, and I'll have my usual. But first,' she turned to Hedda, 'would you care to freshen up? I'll have Anna show you to your room.'

It was a huge guest room in one of the wings, with views over the drive and the countryside beyond. There was a fire burning in the grate, and on top of a marble-topped washstand stood a ewer of water alongside a matching, flower-patterned bowl. Werner arrived with her case and thanked Anna, who bobbed another curtsey and left. 'Separate rooms, I'm afraid,' he said ruefully. 'But at least we are in the same wing, and my parents sleep in the main house.' A kiss made his intentions perfectly clear.

'Anna has arranged for one of the maids to look after you,' he told her. 'But Father is old-fashioned. He doesn't hold with modernising, so if you would like to take a bath, just ask, and one will be brought in and filled for you. At least there's a toilet along the corridor. Mother put her foot down and refused to have chamber pots in the bedrooms.'

There was a knock on the door. Werner opened it to a uniformed housemaid. 'I'm Gertrud, Miss,' she said with a smile. 'Come to unpack for you.'

'Come down when you're ready,' Werner told Hedda. 'Same drawing room, then we'll go in for lunch.'

Two uniformed maids served a hearty beef soup, Hedda's Gertrud being one of them. After the first course had been cleared, Johanna indicated a sideboard. 'I thought we would have a cold collation,' she offered. 'We can serve ourselves, so Gertrud and

Herta can take the afternoon off, and we will be able to enjoy a private conversation. Come, my dear,' she invited Hedda. 'And Gustav, please pour wine.'

Eventually, they were all seated again. Johanna Scholtz lifted her glass. 'To you, Anneliese,' she said. 'I hope I'm not betraying a confidence, but you are the first young lady whom Werner has invited to meet us.'

General Gustav muttered a 'hear hear', and Werner looked embarrassed as he and his parents sipped a toast.

'We didn't have much chance to chat before luncheon,' said Frau Scholtz. 'And my son has told us almost nothing about you.'

'Never says much about anything,' the general interrupted.

'Now then, Gustav dear,' Johanna responded. It was softly spoken but clearly an admonishment. For all his 'Herr General', thought Hedda, Frau Scholtz was clearly mistress within her own household.

She turned to her. 'Anneliese, I gather your people come from Starnberg and that you work at the embassy in Paris.'

'Bit more than that, Mama,' said Werner, rather proudly, thought Hedda. 'Anneliese is the number-two to the Head of Chancery. It's a senior position, and she writes the weekly reports to Berlin. I am one of her contributors, so she could probably claim that I am her subordinate.'

His mother was clearly impressed. 'At such a young age—' she began.

'What do your people do in Starnberg?' her husband broke in.

'We are manufacturers,' she replied, wondering whether the general had the old-fashioned attitude of looking down on 'trade'. 'There are two factories, and we make weapons and electronic equipment,' she explained. 'Before the war, we exported through our office in Switzerland, but now, almost everything we produce has to go to the *Wehrmacht*. So it's just as well I volunteered to go to France,' she added. 'Otherwise, I might have been out of a job.'

'So, are you a party member?' asked the general.

'Gustav, that is not courteous,' said Johanna firmly.

'It's all right,' Hedda responded quickly, 'I don't mind, Frau Scholtz. No, I'm not.' She turned back to the general. 'And neither are my people. If you don't mind me saying so,' she added to lighten the mood, 'I don't think my political views are Werner's principal concern. But I hope you will not disapprove too much because I haven't joined the Party.'

'Let us put politics aside,' said Werner, clearly and deliberately changing the subject. 'Anneliese, what would you like to do this afternoon? I would love to show you the estate. I never thought to ask in Paris, but you do ride?'

Hedda was not about to tell him that she had learned on her father's smallholding and improved her skills on a Polish farm horse travelling to meet partisans in the woods.

'I'm not a keen equestrian,' she replied. 'I haven't ridden for years – I was too busy running my father's business in Zürich. If it's a gentle mount, I won't fall off, but I haven't any clothes...' she pointed out.

'We always have things for guests,' put in Frau Scholtz. 'We'll sort you out after lunch. Gustav, ask one of the girls to saddle up Werner's horse and my mare. Beatrix is a very gentle ride,' she added to Hedda.

Two horses were led into the courtyard. 'This is Garin,' said Werner proudly, 'he's a great hunter.' The nut-brown stallion was massive, at least 173 centimetres at the withers, if not more. Beatrix stood quietly, almost dwarfed by her stablemate. 'Don't worry,' said Werner cheerfully, 'she's not big, and we won't be jumping, but she's very nimble and goes like the wind.'

They enjoyed a fine ride through fields and then a forest track, eventually cresting a rise that looked out over the countryside. 'Most of what you can see is part of the estate,' he told her, 'although it's a struggle to keep it up financially now that we are at war. But at least we have food,' he said reflectively.

'Which brings me to tomorrow,' he went on. 'My folks are

throwing a bit of a lunch party in your honour. I meant to tell you, the Lindermanns are coming, amongst others, and so is Sarah. It's a kind gesture. Mama thought you would enjoy seeing her again, as I gather you were at school together…'

CHAPTER 23

Tadzio had not been expecting a message. It was a long one, but he didn't mind. He was in no danger with his radio set to receive. He would decode it back at the farm where Liliane had promised a cassoulet for their evening meal. They lived well, but he was only too aware that those in the towns and cities were not so fortunate.

Back at the farm, and replete with slow-cooked chicken, pork, cannellini beans and a glass of red wine, he settled at the table whilst she washed the dishes.

'So what's it all about?' she asked, putting away the last utensils and drying her hands as he set down his pencil.

'Something's up,' he replied, looking curiously at the message. 'I'm to try to recruit and train a force of preferably about ten men for an operation not in this area. Unfortunately, they don't say what, where or when,' he added with some exasperation. 'But I have a feeling this might be rather important, so I'll go and see Serge tomorrow.'

'He lives on his own, and I bet he drinks more than he cooks,' she responded. 'Ask him over for supper tomorrow, and we'll talk here.'

It was, he realised, a subtle hint that she was not prepared to be excluded from his resistance activities, but it was also a kind thought, and he knew Serge would be only too keen to accept.

He turned up with a bottle of calvados. 'It's from Yves' place,' he announced, 'and it's good stuff.' Liliane had made enough cassoulet for three more generous helpings, and the leftovers had spent twenty-four hours on a marble slab in her meat safe. It was as good, if not even better, the second time around.

Liliane cleared away, but instead of attacking the dishes, she joined them at the kitchen table. 'London wants to know if we can have a section – about ten men, he interpreted for them – for a specific operation. All I know is that they need to be small arms-trained, and I shall be in command. There's you, me and maybe Yves and Jean-Claude,' he said to Serge, 'although the other two will need training. But where we find six more, I just don't know.'

'Pour another glass of that calvados,' said Serge. 'I think I might be able to solve your problem.'

He explained that former legionnaires tended to stay in touch, often belonging to an informal veterans' organisation because so many fell on hard times. They tried to help each other as best they could, and when they occasionally met, it was usually quite local, at a particular bar or café run by one of their number. There was one in Amiens, another in Reims and he knew there were several in Paris, although they were not known to him personally. 'What's more,' he added, 'many are my age. We might not be as young or as fit as we were, but when it comes to fighting and weapon-handling, we can more than match those bastard Kraut conscripts. If I know my former Legion comrades, most of them will jump at the chance of a mission. I'll start making a few contacts tomorrow.'

'I suggest a cell system,' said Tadzio. 'You contact one legionnaire, he contacts another and so on. We need to set up a communication system, but until we all come together, each will know only of two others – the one who contacted him and the next one he recruited.'

'An old mate of mine, Hector, runs a bar in Reims. I'll go and see him tomorrow,' Serge offered. He went by train.

Hector's bar was a twenty-minute walk from the station in a run-down, working-class area. He was astonished and delighted when Serge walked in. 'So you made it back home after we escaped from Toul,' he exclaimed, rushing from behind the bar to embrace his old friend. 'It does my heart good to see you again.'

'And you're as ugly as ever,' answered Serge with an equally broad grin. 'Brought you a small present from the countryside,' he said, handing over a canvas bag. Hector set it on the zinc bar and looked inside. 'A rabbit, a chicken and a few eggs, courtesy of some friends,' Serge added.

'*Mon Dieu*, but that's welcome,' said Hector. He indicated a relatively private corner table. 'Eloise,' he called to someone out of sight, 'come in here and take over.'

Serge took a moment to study his friend. Hector was short but built like a barrel, with huge hands and arms, an unkempt black beard with hair to match, and a nose broken at least twice to Serge's knowledge. He exuded his usual odour of cigarettes and – if you were anywhere near close enough – more than a hint of onion and garlic. To Serge's eye, Hector had put on a bit of weight, but he had been a first-class non-commissioned officer and, like Serge, an absolute expert with weapons and explosives.

A rather plump woman in her thirties with a round face, a mess of blonde curls, a stomach almost a match for Hector's and an equally ample bosom emerged to stand behind the bar. 'Bring us two coffees,' Hector told her, grabbing a bottle of brandy and two glasses that he set on the table. They raised a glass in mutual salute as Eloise came over with the small, demitasse cups of robust, Turkish-style coffee they preferred in the Legion.

Serge explained his mission. He didn't even bother to ask whether his friend wanted to volunteer. Hector would have been insulted. So, instead, he just passed on the instructions given to him by Tadzio, together with the recommendation that as they were a few years older than the enemy, a little work on personal fitness, and perhaps not too many cigarettes, could soon pay dividends and might well save lives. Two weeks later, Serge reported that eight men had been recruited, all experienced former legionnaires. Once the order was given, they could assemble within forty-eight hours.

Tadzio's next sked was well received in London.

*

As before, Marie was inspected thoroughly at the Tangmere airfield cottage, but she was experienced enough not to risk her life by wearing or carrying anything that might suggest she was anything other than a native of France. She was surprised, however, when her pilot breezed into the room. It was Johnny Mertherwell. To the astonishment of her female dispatcher, she rushed to give him a hug and a kiss.

'My squadron leader never knows who my passenger is,' he replied in answer to her question. 'But whilst I was enjoying a weekend in London, Ralph, David and Hugh had to take up the slack. So when we were tasked to Nogent-le-Retrou, it was my turn to fly, and I knew it could only be you.'

The dispatcher looked at her watch. 'You have half an hour to take-off, so I'm away to make a cup of tea,' she said kindly. They held hands and talked earnestly till she returned.

They flew in silence across the channel, low under German radar. Night flying over water at this height demanded concentration. So it was a relief when Johnny confirmed their position crossing the coast of France, and he was able to climb to just under cloud base, the umbrella of which would give them instant cover. But it was not an enemy aircraft that was their undoing. Suddenly they were surrounded by black explosions. The pencil beam of a searchlight wildly combed the sky, intent on illuminating them.

'Shit,' she heard him exclaim over her headphones. 'That lot wasn't there a couple of weeks ago. We should be OK now,' he said with relief as cloud enveloped them, and he was flying on instruments. But no sooner had he spoken than the Lysander was rocked violently by a near-miss. Marie screamed, she couldn't help it, but Johnny had Lizzie back under control in seconds.

'Think that's it,' he said to reassure her. 'Behind us now, but I'll have to report that flak battery when I get back.' They flew on for several minutes. 'The tank's been holed,' he said calmly. 'We're losing fuel quite fast. Don't want to risk a dead stick landing at night. There's just enough ambient light, so I'll have to use what we have left to try to put us down safely in a field.'

He throttled back, and the nose dipped as they began their descent. At least, with every second, they were nearer their destination.

'We must be flying on fumes,' she heard him mutter as they circled what looked to be an expanse of grass. Marie kept quiet, only too aware that he needed every last ounce of concentration. Johnny had a good idea of wind direction, and he was making a wide circle at about seven hundred feet when the engine coughed, picked up once, then began to splutter intermittently. He was not quite perfectly positioned, but after a frantic side-slip under opposite stick and rudder, he slammed Lizzie onto the ground, a bit too near the far hedge than he would have wished. They hit it with a bump, the tail lifted, then slammed back down, but they were on the ground.

'You all right?' he asked urgently.

'I'm fine,' she said quickly, although the harness had bruised her shoulders.

The prop, or what was left of it, had buried itself in the hedge. The engine had stalled, but he switched off anyway. 'No fire risk,' he told her, 'the fuel's nearly all gone. So take your time, make sure you have everything you need, then climb down the ladder. I'll follow you.' He tucked his service revolver into a flying boot before checking the box containing the rest of his ammunition was in one jacket pocket, stowing his map in the other.

On the ground, he put one round from a Very pistol into a small puddle of fuel underneath the aircraft and another into the cockpit. Once the aircraft was well ablaze, he threw the Very pistol and his last flares underneath it, then turned to Marie. 'I have a good idea where we are,' he said quickly. 'But we have to get away from here. There will be a search, and they might have dogs.'

He looked up at the night sky. 'Nogent's roughly that way,' he told her. 'Fortunately, we seem to be in the middle of nowhere, so that should buy us some time. I think we should split up. I'm in uniform, and they won't know I had a passenger, so at worst, I will be captured as a prisoner of war. But if they catch you with me…' He trailed off, not wanting to put the probable outcome into words.

'No way,' she said quickly. 'You will be interrogated. I know these people. In the end, you will have to tell them who I am and where you were headed. Our best chance is to find you some civilian clothes. Come on, let's get clear of the area. If we can do that, we have a good chance of reaching our destination.' They set off across fields. After quite some time, they came to a stream. Marie had sensible walking shoes. Johnny was more fortunate still, with flying boots. But she insisted that despite the discomfort, they pushed through the shallows for a good kilometre before pulling themselves hand over hand onto a low bridge not far from a small village. 'I don't think a dog will be able to track us along the stream and now over these cobbles,' she affirmed. 'But, as I said before, we need to get you out of that uniform.'

Johnny glanced at the notes he had made and then at the map salvaged from the aeroplane. 'I'm sure it's Langny-au-Perche,' he told her. 'We were almost there – another dozen or so miles, and we would have made it.'

'Look on the bright side,' she replied. 'At least the burnt-out wreck will be far enough from Nogent. The Germans won't be looking in our area if we can make it.' He had to concede that she had a point.

It was barely a village, more of a hamlet. They waited in a field, out of sight from the lane, till it was almost light, then she walked on alone. The first cottage she came to was considerably larger than its neighbour. An oil lamp somewhere within, probably placed in the hall, was spreading its loom into the other rooms. Marie made sure her Browning was safely tucked into her skirt under her jacket and went round the back to a kitchen door. She was relieved that there was no dog to challenge her presence.

'*C'est qui?*' called out a woman's voice in answer to her gentle knock.

'*J'ai besoin de l'aide,*' she called out softly. So someone was in trouble. The woman knew that the Germans would have kicked the door open and walked right in, so there was no threat. Even so, the door was opened but just a little. Marie realised that she had no choice. 'Can you help a French woman and a British airman?' she asked. 'If not, please say, and you will never see me again.'

A tall, slim, late-middle-aged woman with grey hair set in a traditional country plait slowly opened the door. 'Come in and sit down,' she said calmly, indicating a chair by the kitchen table.

'The less you know, the better,' said Marie. 'But I am with a British pilot. The problem is, he is in uniform. For your safety, we can be gone within minutes, but I need some French clothes.'

'Where is he?' she asked evenly.

'Not far,' said Marie guardedly.

'My name is Elise. I am going upstairs,' she told her. 'I can provide a coat and a pair of trousers for your pilot. They were my husband's. But it would be better if I took them, and he walked back here with me, rather than a stranger. I doubt anyone will see us at this hour, but it would be safer even so.'

Marie had little option. She had to trust this woman, and what Elise had said made sense. She nodded her assent. Minutes later, Elise was back with a bundle under her arm. Marie told her exactly where to find Johnny. 'But he's armed, and he's on edge,' she cautioned, 'so call out his Christian name before you get too near.'

Ten minutes later, all three sat at the kitchen table.

'I am certain we were not seen,' said Elise to Marie. 'We stayed in the field and pushed through the hedge to the back door. But my Etienne was a tall man. The coat is not too bad, but those trousers look ridiculous.'

'I can put some string round them, under the coat,' Johnny offered. 'Because we need to be on our way. You are in danger whilst we are here, although I have to tell you that we could not be more grateful for your assistance.'

'My husband fought in the Great War,' Elise replied. 'He was gassed by the *Boche*. Afterwards, I watched him die in this house, slowly, as he coughed up his lungs. So I am grateful that you have given me a chance to do something back, something for Etienne. How far away is the wreckage of your aircraft?' she asked.

'Probably about ten kilometres,' Marie replied. We crossed a lot of fields, then paddled and waded in a stream for a long time before coming to the road and hauling ourselves onto a bridge. Even if they have dogs, they won't be able to track us.'

'You have done well to be clear of the crash site,' said Elise. 'And you could have gone in any direction, which means they will have to cover a huge area. But they will know that you can't be too far away so the roads will be patrolled. Public transport will be checked. And especially people on foot. But they won't keep this up for long. A few days and they will be back in barracks. That is when it will be safe for you to leave, to continue your journey.

'Besides,' she went on, looking first at Johnny, 'you are risking your life as a pilot.' She turned to Marie. 'And you are a French woman. At best, if they catch you, it will be a German concentration camp. More likely, you will be tortured and shot. So compared with the risks you are taking, hiding you here for a day or two till the Germans have given up and gone away is nothing. I would despise myself if I did not do it.'

'Madame,' said Marie politely, 'thank you so much.' She looked at Johnny, who nodded his agreement.

'And in the meantime,' said Elise with a smile, 'I shall fetch out my sewing basket. At least when you leave, Monsieur Johnny, you will not look like a circus clown, with your trousers bagging round your ankles.'

They spent their days sitting in a spare bedroom in case, as Elise explained, one of her neighbours popped round. Each evening she drew the kitchen curtains, locked the doors and they gathered round the table. Marie offered money to Elise, who took some of it so that she could replace her rations on the black market. 'But not until long after you have departed,' she added wisely. And in the meantime, as this was the countryside, they ate simple but adequate fare and listened to *Radio Londres* each evening.

They saw German vehicles driving through the village, but only for a couple of days. There were no house-to-house searches. The area was too big, and the enemy simply did not have the manpower. Finally, on the evening of the third day, Marie announced that they would be leaving in the morning.

It was about ten kilometres to Nogent, which they could by-pass, and just a few more to the Renaud estate. All country lanes, but they would be vulnerable to a chance German patrol or roadblock. The search might have been called off, but the enemy would be only too aware that an English pilot was almost certainly still somewhere in the general area.

Again, it was Elise who came to the rescue. The local doctor – he too had fought in the Great War so had no love for the Germans – had been a close friend of her late husband. More importantly, he was able to get around. Although a limited supply of gasoline was available to physicians, it was never enough, so he drove a Citroën Berline Gazogene, converted to run on coal. After two containers attached to the bodywork had been alight for about half an hour, there would be enough methane gas to feed an adapted carburettor. The car's range was only sixty kilometres at best. Then it was a case of adding more fuel and being patient for a while. It had only about two-thirds of the original gasoline version's speed, but it enabled the good doctor, who did not offer his name, to visit his patients.

Elise pointed out that they would be looking for a pilot, therefore a young man. They rubbed white ash into the dark brown curls above his ears, and Elise found an old cap to cover the rest. The doctor provided three medical masks, and a red rash was dotted and smeared on Johnny's forehead. Naturally, he would not bear close inspection. But from a short distance away, slumped against cushions on the rear seat, his old clothes half covered by a blanket, at a glance, he would pass for sick, older man.

It was a good roadblock, barely two kilometres from the village. The *Kübelwagen* closed off half of the lane just around a blind bend. One soldier had taken cover behind it, and another stood alongside, his arm raised to halt the Citroën. There was no alternative. The doctor braked to a halt and wound down the window. Glancing in the mirror, he saw two more Germans, also armed with Schmeissers, had emerged to take station behind them.

But the doctor was known to some of the local Germans. Unlike many of his medical compatriots, he had not refused to offer attention when the occupying forces requested it. Even so, they were suspicious. He wound down his window.

They were in luck. 'Herr Doctor,' the young soldier greeted him, 'where are you going, and who are these people?'

'My patients,' he said evenly. 'This man,' he thumbed over his shoulder, 'farms on the other side of the village. He seems to have caught some form of disease, perhaps a case of smallpox, or it might be something he's caught from his cows. But I can't identify it, and it could well be contagious. His daughter brought him to me, barely able to stand. I have to run some tests, and the nearest clinic is in Nogent.' The soldier took a pace back from the open window. 'But don't worry,' he added, 'I am aware of the regulations. If it is contagious,' he emphasised the 'is', 'and I have to isolate him, I will be sure to inform the authorities.'

Marie made a point of opening her handbag and taking out her papers, but the doctor's explanation was accepted – perhaps not least because the young conscript had no wish to be exposed to any form of some nasty French infection.

'Thank you, Herr Doctor,' he responded. Marie was not asked to show her papers. But her hands were trembling until a cursory wave indicated that they could drive on.

'You did the right thing there, lad,' said his non-commissioned officer, putting his Schmeisser on the bonnet of the *Kübelwagen* and lighting a cigarette. 'Didn't like the look of that one in the back seat, not one little bit.'

'Please drop us off just before the town,' Marie said eventually. 'We still have a few kilometres to go, but it is better for us all that you do not know our final destination. We can walk from there, staying off the roads.'

'I am happy to be of assistance,' he replied courteously, 'but you may need medical skills in the future, even though supplies are very difficult to obtain. I want you to know that you can always reach me through Elise.'

'Let's not have any pretence,' replied Marie. 'Tell me now what you need. Then, if possible, I will have it included in a supply drop. Perhaps we can help each other.'

Top of the list was any form of anaesthetic, followed by morphine, disinfectant, needles, sutures and bandages. 'And one more thing,' he added. 'I have read that there is a new medicine, an antibiotic that fights infection. It is made by a British firm, May and Baker, and it is registered as MB693. It would be wonderful to be able to treat wounds and conditions that might otherwise prove fatal.'

During their conversation, Johnny removed all signs of his supposed contagion. They shook hands with the doctor and headed off to the north-west. Once out of town, they took to the fields. By lunchtime, they were back at her cottage on the Renaud estate.

That afternoon she informed Jean and Monique that she had an unexpected guest. They agreed that the cottage was sufficiently isolated – there was no reason for it to be of interest to the Germans. In the meantime, Jean would give some thought to obtaining French papers for Johnny, and Marie would ask London if he could be picked up, or at least be fed into the pipeline sending downed Royal Air Force personnel back to England via Spain.

With Jean having departed to retrieve her radio, Marie confided to Monique that there was an attachment between herself and her guest. Ever practical, Monique took her into the kitchen and filled a large wicker basket with fresh provisions before adding several bottles of wine.

'Take it,' she said with a smile, pushing the basket along the table, 'because you should never make love on an empty stomach.'

CHAPTER 24

Marie made her transmission regarding Johnny in very few words, offering no chance of an intercept. 'Flak, crashed, both OK, made it home. Advise pick-up M or instruct for Spain.' The reply was 'M to follow'. She was then tasked to contact N at E. Clearly, this was Nicole in Étaples.

Jean and Monique Renaud were happy enough for Marie to shelter Johnny Metherwell in her cottage because it was about as remote as it was possible to be in a well-wooded estate. But he was cooped up by day because other workers were present around the main house, the winery and farm buildings. And much as Marie enjoyed their time together, she knew he was anxious to return to his squadron. There had been no further news from London. Presumably, one airman was not that significant in the greater scheme of things.

'But you will take care, won't you, darling?' she urged him at the table after supper that evening. 'I have to leave tomorrow, and it's best you don't know where I am going, but it should only be for a day or two.' She reached out to place her hand over his. 'At least, just this once, I have something to look forward to when I return.'

'I would like to think,' he replied with a mischievous smile as he placed his other hand over hers, 'that I am about to have something extremely precious to remember you by until you do.'

There was the same access issue when she changed at Paris and asked for a ticket to Le Touquet, but her papers and explanation were again accepted without question. The owner of the bicycle shop recognised her but did not comment. Finally, late in the day, she found Nicole at home.

'You said that they are entirely used to your presence and often speak freely over a drink or a meal,' Marie reminded her over a simple supper of sausages, potatoes and cabbage, together with a bottle of wine gifted from the officers' mess. 'London has asked for as much information as possible about the airfield set-up,' explained Marie. 'How often it's used, size of the guard force, arms carried, changeover times, routes from Le Touquet, et cetera, anything you can think of.'

'I don't want to pry,' Nicole replied, 'but that information begs an obvious question.'

'The short answer is that I honestly don't know what or when,' Marie told her. 'All I can tell you is that it can't be that urgent because I'll be told to contact you again sometime after Christmas.'

They finished the wine, then a second bottle, and Marie enjoyed an uneventful return to Nogent the following day.

*

Nicole spent some time thinking about how best to meet Marie's request. The small hotel occupied by the officers provided a comfortable home from home, staffed by locals who were only too pleased to have kept their jobs during the occupation. The soldiers were billeted separately, as were the non-commissioned officers. The hotel's civilian staff tolerated her, knowing that she was French, but illogically there was also thinly veiled hostility because she was seen as *une collaboratrice*. No, she mused, it would be unwise to confide in the staff, which left the officers.

The officer commanding the guard force, who reported directly to the detachment commandant, was a relatively junior infantry

Oberleutnant of approximately her own age. He was not usually at the hotel by day, unless attending one of her language classes, but he was always there in the evenings and at weekends – at least he was on Saturday mornings, when she usually gave conversation tutorials, although he did not attend them himself. Moreover, *Oberleutnant* Klaus Huber had always been friendly. This was in contrast to some of the other officers who'd made unsubtle advances she tried to deflect whilst causing as little offence as possible. Huber was slim and wiry, and not much taller than her. His features were unremarkable rather than handsome, but he had a pleasant smile. There was little to dislike about him, although his tight blond curls and piercing blue eyes were just a little too much in the Aryan mould for her taste. Klaus Huber was certainly intelligent – he already had a good if basic grasp of French from just attending classes.

'*Herr Oberleutnant*,' she addressed him one evening, having stayed for a drink to await his return. He had been only too pleased to find her reading a newspaper in their lounge bar and had asked courteously if he might join her. They made polite conversation for a while, but now she turned to her purpose. 'You are doing well in class, somewhat above average,' she said with a smile to accompany her mild flattery, 'but I would be failing in my duty if I did not tell you that your French would be very much better if you were to attend tutorials – either conversation classes in small groups or one-on-one instruction. In either case, we would speak only French.'

He thought for a moment, clearly a little taken aback. Huber had always rather liked the young French woman and had not approved of the way some of his fellow officers had tried to come on to her. It was not his style. '*Das wäre sehr gut...*' he mused out loud, inwardly very tempted by the possibility, and at the same time wondering whether this rather attractive young woman might just possibly be interested in him. '*Ja, ja,*' he added, 'that I would like to do. But when?'

266

'My Saturday-morning schedule is already full,' she replied. 'But if you would like individual tuition, which I recommend, I would not mind extending it into the beginning of the afternoon – say for the first hour after lunch?'

'I shall look forward to it,' he responded with evident enthusiasm. 'May we start this Saturday?'

'*Bis Samstag,*' she replied, 'until Saturday.' She often spoke German to make the officers feel that she could be accepted and, more importantly, trusted.

On Saturday, she took lunch in the dining room with a few of the officers, some of whom had attended tutorials that morning. Wine was served, and there was a general air of jollity. Nicole declined a second glass, commenting that she had to be able to concentrate during her final tutorial first thing in the afternoon. *Oberleutnant* Huber, she observed, also placed his hand over his glass.

They settled into the comfortable chairs she had installed in one of the hotel's single rooms, now converted to be her office. Nicole had given a lot of thought to her information-gathering process. Had she just asked questions outright in a purely social setting, they would have invited suspicion immediately. So she would ask only one or two questions per session, and each would be wrapped in a cloak of covering a particular topic in the French language.

Also, she used a technique she had learned at the Sorbonne. By way of example to her student, she pointed at herself she said, '*Je m'appelle Nicole.*' Then, pointing at him, she followed with: '*Et toi?*' Her rising inflection clearly indicated a question.

He managed a very respectable '*Je m'appelle Klaus*'. This had already been taught in class, but he now understood how the tutorial would be conducted. This one, she had told him, would cover the French way of expressing times and dates. So it was perfectly logical when she asked him what time he went to work in the morning and at what time he returned to the hotel. She was confident that by Christmas, and entirely without arousing suspicion, she would have all the details of the airfield, the guard force and its routine.

It had been fine, setting out from Étaples on her bicycle. But all morning the barometer had been dropping, with low pressure bringing clouds and rain off the Atlantic and into the Channel. When they finished the tutorial, it was lashing down.

'What will you do now?' he asked in German, conscious that she did not live in the hotel.

'Have a cup of coffee,' she replied in the same language, because Huber's French was still limited, 'and hope that this lot blows over. Otherwise, it will be a wet ride home. But don't worry, I have a cape that will keep off the worst of the weather. I have to cycle every day, so I'm quite used to it.'

'If you would permit,' he said with just the hint of a bow, 'I would be happy to drive you to your home. I have the use of a car, and I can change out of uniform, so you would not be compromised in any way.'

She walked to the window and looked at the sky. It was as black as ever, with no sign of improvement. And it had to be blowing a near gale. 'That's so tempting,' she replied, 'but would it be safe for you?' She knew that Germans rarely drove anywhere except armed and in convoy.

'*Ja*,' he told her. 'Because it is not a military vehicle. It belongs to the owner of this hotel. When we entered Le Touquet, I was tasked with finding a headquarters. I chose this man's hotel. He has a car, but now he can't get petrol for it. I can. We have come to an arrangement. I have the use of it, and I leave him enough fuel for an occasional personal journey. Right now, it's garaged in the hotel courtyard.'

'But how would I get back to work on Monday?' she asked.

'It's a Peugeot 402 Légère,' he explained. 'Quite a large four-door family saloon. I'm sure we could put your bicycle behind our seats, even if it means taking the front wheel off.'

'Would that be safe?' she asked, knowing that her compatriots were not above staging the occasional ambush with the hope of killing Germans.

'I think so,' he said thoughtfully. 'I could order up a *Kübelwagen* with an armed escort, but a French car, a driver in civilian clothes and a Frenchwoman beside me to speak for us… I don't think there would be any danger.'

'Then I accept gratefully,' she replied. And an opportunity presented itself immediately. 'In return,' she went on, 'if you would like a break and a change from your officers' mess, perhaps I could offer you the hospitality of a simple French supper before you have to make the return journey?'

'Give me ten minutes,' came the response. Huber returned with a large baker's basket covered with a cloth. He had changed into a Loden coat and civilian slacks that shouted 'German' as much as if he had stayed in uniform. But it would pass muster in the driving rain unless they were stopped, and that was a situation she believed she could handle. Her bicycle they managed to disassemble and squeeze into the car. It was late afternoon when he parked on her property after an uneventful journey.

They entered through the back door and into the kitchen, with his coat and her cape bundled over heads and shoulders. It was cold. Her first priority was to put a match to the range, which she had laid that morning. He set the basket on the table. 'Thank you so much,' she told him. 'Otherwise, I would have arrived like a drowned rat. Please sit down whilst I change. But first, would you prefer coffee – I still have a little left – or a glass of wine?'

He took the cloth off the basket. There were two bottles of white and two of red, plus a bottle of cognac. There were also several wrapped packages. 'I did not wish to consume your rations,' he told her, 'particularly as I know food is difficult for the civilian population. Our cook has given me a chicken and some lamb. Please take it all – there is no need for me to return anything to the hotel. And if you please, I would enjoy a glass of white wine.'

She settled two glasses, a corkscrew and a bottle of wine on the table. 'I'll only be a few minutes, please help yourself,' she told him, 'and if you don't mind, please build up the fire with some more wood and then coal. There should be plenty in the scuttle. In her room, she changed into a pair of slacks and a white blouse. Neither made any secret of her figure. When she returned, he had poured for both of them. 'May I?' she asked, beginning to unpack the basket. There was also butter, cheese, a packet of coffee and a mix of vegetables, all rare luxuries to the civilian population in wartime France. If it was a bribe with a hidden agenda in mind, she thought, it was impressive.

'Klaus, this is very generous,' she said, looking at him directly. He had the good grace to redden slightly. But he recovered quickly. 'Please,' he said simply, waving his hand over what was on the tale.

'This is a lamb shoulder,' she said, unwrapping the joint. 'If you don't mind waiting, I could make you a very traditional French supper. In the old days, before we had home ovens, housewives would put meat and vegetables into a pot. Because the baker made only one batch of loaves on a Sunday, he would take the pot and for a few coins put it in his still-hot oven. It has become known as lamb *boulangère*. Originally they would have used a leg, but we will have your shoulder. I think it is better because the fat cooks out into a delicious thin sauce and the meat is more tender. I hope you don't mind lots of garlic?' she added with a smile.

She assembled the dish in a large, round, black cast-iron pot – thickly sliced potatoes in the bottom, well seasoned and just covered with stock – a little precious jelly from her dripping pot and some liquid. 'This is made by boiling vegetable peelings,' she explained casually, 'we can't afford to waste anything these days. I need some parsley,' she added, 'but I know where it is, just outside the kitchen door, so I'll grab a pair of scissors.' It was still raining heavily, and she was very quick, but by the time she returned, her wet blouse was clinging transparently to her brassier, as she had known that it would, although, in the heat of the kitchen, it soon dried off. But not before she noticed that much as he tried to hide it, Klaus could hardly stop looking.

She chopped a complete bulb of peeled garlic and then the parsley. Most of it she spread over the potatoes before setting the lamb on top. The remainder she sprinkled over the joint before replacing the lid. Hanging it by the thin, curved metal handle from a large hook, she swivelled it over the open fire. A glass of wine later, she wrapped the handle with a thick cloth, lifted the pot and pushed it into the range oven. 'Now you have to be patient,' she told him with a smile. He poured two more glasses of wine.

Conversation came easily as the kitchen slowly filled with a delicious aroma. She was careful to drink slowly, refilling both glasses when hers was still more than half full. By the time she had lightly boiled some greens from her vegetable garden, the second bottle of white was half empty. She asked him to open a red. The meal was superb, and he complimented her generously. Afterwards, he suggested a cognac.

'I would love one,' she told him, 'but would it be wise if you are going to drive home?'

'You are correct,' he said, with a hint of slurring. He stood carefully, obviously doing his best to compensate for the alcohol.

'Sit down, Klaus,' she told him firmly. 'I don't think it's safe for you to drive. But I have a spare room. I don't know what time you have to be back on duty, but it's Sunday. You could always make an early start in the morning. Besides,' she finished lightly, 'it would be a shame to spoil a pleasant evening.' To her surprise, she had enjoyed his company.

'Thank you,' he said, and sat down again. Then, after a large glass of cognac, which she accepted because she no longer had to think about the meal, she said, 'Let me show you to your room.'

She always kept the bed made up. It was not particularly well aired, but he would not be in any condition to notice. She turned him gently by the shoulders to face into the room. As he walked towards the bed, she closed the door. Closing her own, as she always did these days, she turned the key in the lock. For good measure, she thumbed a couple of cartridges into her late husband's twelve bore and set in on the floor beside her bed.

She was vaguely aware of an engine starting but turned over and went back to sleep. When she eventually put on a thick, warm robe and went downstairs, the car was no longer there. The front had passed and the rain with it. Her bicycle was leaning against the back wall. He had replaced the front wheel.

She took the tin bath off its hook in the wall and carried it indoors to light the range. At least she had running cold water from a tap above the sink. The first kettle she would use for washing up. Whilst it was heating, she thought about the previous evening. It had made a pleasant change from being on her own. But she had not told him about her husband, only that she was widowed, implying that he had died before the war. Klaus mentioned that he had lost his only brother when his medium bomber had failed to return from a raid over London. Had it not been for the war, she mused, they might have been good friends. Now, she would let their friendship develop, despite her feelings for the Germans, but it would be for one purpose and one purpose only. In all other respects, he would be kept strictly at arm's length.

*

Hedda lay in bed, wide awake. Throughout the afternoon and dinner, she had been thinking frantically. Werner's announcement that this Sarah Lindermann and her parents would come to lunch was a bombshell. It would wreck everything. The bottom line was that she could not possibly stay and have her cover blown, which meant that somehow she had to escape before they arrived. She reasoned that the only explanation likely to be accepted would be if her 'father' telephoned with an excuse to collect her the following morning. Perhaps an emergency at home... her mother suddenly taken ill? There was a telephone in the hall. Of course, Dieter

Hohfmann would have to be given instructions, but they were all together for dinner and afterwards all evening in the drawing room.

She excused herself, pleading tiredness after an unaccustomed ride in the fresh air, but she knew Werner would come to her bed within the next hour once the family had retired for the night. Fortunately, she could hear his footsteps as he passed her door and closed his own, along and on the other side of the corridor. There was not much time. Pulling on a robe, she left her door slightly ajar and sprinted barefoot to the bathroom, where she reached in and turned on the light before shutting the door. If he came to her before she returned, he would see the light and just wait for her on the bed in her room.

The operator did not seem surprised when she asked to be put through to the Hoffmann's number. Her prayers were answered when Anneliese's father came on the line. Thank heavens they had still been up. Hastily, using heavily veiled speech, she half-whispered her problem, disguising it as best she could in case the operator was listening. But he got the message. With equally obscure speech, he tried to sound reassuring. First thing in the morning, he would telephone the Scholtz residence and report a riding accident. Her mother was unconscious. The prognosis was very uncertain. He would apologise for any disruption to whatever they had planned for the day but would ask to collect Anneliese around mid-morning as a matter of urgency. She replaced the handset with a genuine sense of relief, entirely unaware that Werner had listened to her every word from the landing.

CHAPTER 25

He was waiting for her in her room but not on the bed. Instead, he was sitting in one of the two easy chairs by the window, a low table between them. On it, he had placed a bottle of Ansbach Uralt and two glasses. 'Brought from my room,' he said, not unpleasantly, 'because I didn't believe that tiredness routine, and you, most certainly, are going to need a nightcap.'

He poured. Hedda's heart was pounding, but outwardly, she managed to appear calm. She took a generous sip of brandy.

'That's an odd thing to say,' she responded.

'There are no Lindermanns,' he said matter-of-factly. 'I made them up. And I listened to your conversation with Herr Hoffmann from the top of the stairs.' Slowly he ran his index finger twice round the rim of his brandy glass. 'I have been wondering for some time, and now I know for certain. Whoever and whatever you are, you are most certainly not Anneliese Hoffmann.'

'How did you find out?' Hedda asked simply. She felt strangely unafraid. He was hardly likely to shoot her in his family home.

'Many things,' he replied. 'It started that night of the ambush. Afterwards, I had a lot of time to think, lying in that hospital bed. When you made an application to be employed at the embassy, my people at the Avenue Foche checked you out thoroughly. You were supposed to be from Starnberg. When you came for supper, I served a Bavarian *Wurstsalat*, and you said it was a family favourite. But when I produced a slice of *Zwetschgenkuchen*, you seemed not to know what it was – yet it's another speciality of the region. With hindsight, this did not add up.

'Then we were ambushed when I was taking you home. You were as brave as a lioness when you took that Schmeisser and fought back. You had complete confidence with the weapon. You saved my life. According to my doctor, in fact, twice, if you count your field dressing. You knew exactly what you were doing. Your firing-range story was clever, but nothing in your previous life could have given you all those skills – born, I suspect, of considerable experience.

'Finally, there was the death of Simone Faucher,' he continued. '*Brigadeführer* von Scheuen asked you to speak with her. She subsequently died in a prison hospital. But her condition, although serious, was not that life-threatening. Because of the time frame after death, we could not prove it, but I think she may have taken a cyanide pill. She did not have one when she was arrested. The Gestapo is very efficient. Believe me, her clothes were examined and every body orifice inspected. I think perhaps you gave her one because who else could have done it?'

He opened his hands, palms uppermost. 'I was so sure you were not Anneliese Hoffmann that I invented the Lindermanns. And now I have proof.'

She returned to her brandy, then, 'So what happens now?' she asked calmly.

'Phone Herr Hoffmann first thing in the morning,' he told her. 'Tell him that everything is all right. I don't want to disappoint Mama, so I'll drive you back to Starnberg after lunch. But we need a conference, you, me and the Hoffmanns. Because although we are not all on the same side, we are working to the same end.'

It was an enjoyable family lunch. General and Frau Scholtz had taken to the young woman they believed to be Anneliese

Hoffmann. Hedda liked them, too, but could not help wondering how they would have felt had they known that their son was virtually living with a mixed-race Polish-German-Jewish woman. She said as much to Werner as they were driving to Starnberg.

'I'll go into more detail when we talk to the Hoffmanns,' he replied. 'But the attitude of educated Germans is very different from that of the Nazi Party. We would judge you as you are: a lovely young lady, highly intelligent, from a professional background. It is just so sad that the war has made such a mess of your life.'

'I love you for saying that,' she said, 'but don't feel too sorry for me. After all, I volunteered for what I am doing.'

Dieter and Helga Hoffmann welcomed Werner warmly. They were taken aback when Hedda told them Werner knew she was not their daughter but relieved when she added that he had no intention of reporting their secret. Helga announced that she refused to talk business until she had served *Kaffee, Apfel-Tarte und Sahne*. Dieter did not mind. Coffee was welcome and especially apple tart and cream.

'So,' said Herr Hoffmann eventually, setting down his cup, '*Sturmbannführer* Scholtz, I think we both have some explaining to do.'

'Dieter, sir, please, and absolutely no use of my Gestapo rank. This is very delicate for all of us,' he went on. 'If you wish, I am happy to begin.'

Dieter Hoffmann nodded his approval.

'I must start by saying that I am a loyal German,' he stated firmly. 'You may be aware that my father is a retired general, and whilst I have absolutely no wish to boast, it is true to say that as a family, we are wealthy, long-established and influential landowners. Nevertheless, many like mine believe that Hitler is leading us to disaster. So some of us have formed an alliance.

'We believe that sooner or later Hitler will have to be deposed,' he went on. 'Either that or he will continue to prosecute a war that we believe Germany cannot win. The turning point was the failure of Operation Sea Lion. Göring could not defeat the Royal Air Force, so Hitler cannot cross the channel. And our Führer ignores the history of the Great War at his peril. We are now trapped in Europe, waiting to see if America will enter the war.

'Those of us – loyal Germans who oppose National Socialism, Hitler and all that the Nazis stand for – have long realised that we must know what is happening from the inside. I am rising rapidly through the Gestapo ranks,' he opened his hands, palms deprecatingly uppermost, 'and I have an important appointment in Paris that allows me access to much highly classified, Nazi-eyes-only information. I am not alone. There are more like me, in other cities, other military appointments. But what I have said should explain that although I became aware that Anneliese is not, as it were, who she claimed to be, I saw her at least as possibly a valuable channel of communication, and, at best, an ally to our cause. I should add that I am very emotionally attached to this courageous young lady – also, and I won't embarrass her with details, but we were ambushed in Paris, and I owe her my life.

'I know that she is not Anneliese Hoffmann, and you,' he inclined his head towards Dieter and Helga, 'are complicit in this deception. I hope that now we are aware of each other, we can explore our common aims. But please rest assured,' he concluded, 'neither Anneliese nor yourselves are in any danger of exposure by me. And as you now know enough to realise that my activities and intentions are not those of a Nazi officer, I trust that I, in turn, may enjoy the same confidentiality from you.'

There was silence for several seconds whilst Dieter took in what had been said. 'That goes without saying,' he began eventually. 'I, too, have a story to tell. Before the war, we were very aware of the direction in which Herr Hitler was taking this country. We saw the unjust anti-Semitic laws, *Kristallnacht* and so forth. We had a guest for Christmas in 1938, you do not need to know her name, but we knew she was connected to an important and influential family within British government circles. So we asked her to pass on all the information we had about the true situation within Nazi Germany, together, of course, with a warning to the British that we believed Hitler intended to take our nation to war.

'This is not easy for me,' he said, turning to his wife. 'Helga, perhaps we could have some more coffee?' He went to a cupboard and returned with a bottle of very fine Armagnac and four glasses, pouring for each of them. 'Help yourselves,' he invited. 'If you don't want any, Dieter and I will finish it. I suspect we are going to need it.' The ladies did not take a glass. However, Dieter and Werner did not hesitate.

'We lived in Switzerland before the war,' he told Werner. 'Once it had started, Anneliese applied for a post with the diplomatic service. She speaks excellent French, so specifically to the embassy in Paris. She wrote to tell her former roommate at finishing school, the same young lady who had spent Christmas here as our guest. She told her parents. Then the British were incredibly clever. My daughter was abducted and is now in England. She was replaced by the young lady you originally thought to be our daughter and who is seated beside you. Even now, I, and I assume you, have no idea who she really is.' He chose not to mention the British Dachau request.

'Like you,' he concluded, looking at Werner, 'I am a loyal German. But I was visited not too long ago and asked to assist with this British deception because apparently "our daughter" had to return home for Christmas. I went along with it for three reasons. First, I value the communication with London that people of our political persuasion have established. Second, it may give those who share our beliefs an opportunity to challenge Hitler and his Nazis in the future. And third, I am not ashamed to tell you that although there has never been the slightest hint of any threat, I would never do anything to jeopardise the wellbeing of our only daughter who is now in England, widowed and – God willing – will presently give birth to our first grandchild.'

They were all looking at Hedda, indicating that they clearly thought it was her turn to say something. 'I hope you will not mind if I don't give you my real name,' she began. 'At least that way, there is no chance of Werner using it at the wrong time and in front of the wrong people. You all know that I am half German and half Polish. My father was a university lecturer in Berlin, and I was raised in Germany.'

'Was?' queried Werner gently.

'My parents are no longer alive,' she responded simply. 'They were persecuted by the Nazis and committed suicide. My mother and I were staying with my maternal grandparents in Poland when she died. Last night you commented on my combat skills. After the invasion, I finished up fighting with our partisans. Subsequently, I and others escaped to England, where I was recruited and trained for what I am doing now. But obviously, I was not sufficiently well prepared.

'You were very clever to notice that I did not recognise a *Zwetschgenkuchen*,' she told him. 'But what about Simone Faucher? Did not your *Brigadeführer* also have his suspicions?'

'Few of the Nazi hierarchy are well educated,' Werner replied, 'and Von Scheuen may be jumped up, but he's not overly bright either. I knew enough chemistry to work out what you did for that French woman and that after a while, there would be no residual evidence. I just kept the information to myself.'

He turned to the Hoffmanns. 'Apologies, we are talking about the past, but are we agreed that we will all guard our secrets and, for the moment, just wait and see what happens? Thanks to your cooperation, Herr and Frau Hoffmann, it looks as though Anneliese and I will be able to return safely to Paris to continue our work.'

Anneliese's parents were only too happy to agree. It was a relief when they all waved goodbye to Werner as he left to drive back to Buchbach Manor. They would meet again at the airport after the holiday.

*

Berndt arrived at Starnberg two days after Boxing Day. Seated in comfortable chairs around a low table, the three of them were closeted in Dieter's study, a heavily furnished room the size of a small library. 'Before we look at the evidence,' he began, addressing Hedda, 'I have to confirm whether, given what we now know about Werner, you still have secure communications with London?'

'Yes,' she replied, 'I can arrange for a radio message to be transmitted. And I don't know how it works, but there is also a courier system that I have used only occasionally to send a longer, hard-copy document back as well.'

He took a large envelope from his desk drawer and placed it on the table. 'It contains my photos, negatives and a short report, just explanatory notes,' he said. 'So, Berndt, what do you have?' he asked his brother.

Berndt produced a matching envelope from his briefcase. Dieter laid out the two reports, two smaller envelopes containing negatives and all their photographs on the table. 'We had our chemist make only one set of prints,' he told Hedda. 'You need to be aware of them to understand the full impact of our mission. But after that, we must burn them. Just the negatives and the notes will go to London.'

'And I must warn you, Anneliese,' said Berndt, 'that some of the images are truly shocking, to the point of being pornographic and disgusting.'

'If I must see them, so be it,' she responded calmly. 'I have seen combat, which is also obscene. But, please, if this will help the war effort, let us proceed.'

They looked first at those taken by Getzel Bergman. There was a not very clear indoors view of a hut with tiered bunk accommodation, another of the gruel they were served and one of a column of half-starved men being marched by SS guards to forced labour. The most telling image was of a gibbet, with the corpse of a prisoner in his striped uniform hanging by the neck.

'He worked in the cookhouse. It's in the notes,' said Dieter. 'His crime was to steal potatoes to feed starving fellow inmates in his hut.'

Eva's pictures were even more shocking. The first showed the back of an SS guard, his trousers and undergarment round his ankles, with a naked Eva hoisted up against the wall, her arms and legs wrapped around him. Her head, over his shoulder, seemed to be dipped as if to urge on the photographer. There were others, a girl lying on the table, another German between her legs, a third bent over it, being taken from behind. There were yet more, but Hedda had seen enough. She scooped the photographs together. 'Please throw them on the fire,' she asked Dieter. 'I will take everything else to Paris.'

Not long after her return, a full report on the Dachau operation, together with its supporting photographic evidence, was on its way to the American president.

*

Tadzio and Serge were enjoying a bottle of Yves' home-distilled calvados. It had been cooled in the pool where, last summer, Liliane had successfully seduced him in a vain attempt to keep him permanently on the farm. Tadzio had asked Serge to meet him here because after their previous conversation there was no way Liliane would have allowed them to meet alone at the farmhouse. And the less she knew about the coming operation, the safer for them all – herself included.

'Last night was the longest sked I have ever had,' he told his friend. 'Mostly, I wasn't transmitting, so no problem there, but by the time I got back to the farm and did the decoding, it was broad daylight.

'First off, we have to get the men to an address in Étaples. They can't travel as a group, and it's inside the coastal zone, for which none of them will have papers.'

Tadzio was becoming accustomed to the Gallic shrug, almost a complete language of its own. 'We are legionnaires,' Serge said, almost contemptuous of the problem. 'You just tell us to be there, where and when, and leave the rest to us. The *Boche* cannot stop a legionnaire from moving across his own country, even if we have to break the curfew and do at least some of it at night.

'Won't be safe to do it carrying weapons, though,' he added.

'Agreed,' Tadzio replied. 'London is sending someone to Étaples to organise a drop. Everything we need, including a radio for me to use, will be provided on-site. All we have to do is get there.'

'And when we do?' asked Serge. 'Then what?'

'The Germans have a radar detection site hidden inside Le Touquet airfield,' Tadzio told him. 'London would give their eye teeth to get hold of it. Apparently, if they have the equipment, our boffins can develop countermeasures. And there's bound to be other radio equipment, not to mention codebooks and such. So we take everything we can find. It's a high-value operation.

'The airfield's a few kilometres outside the town itself, where there is a small garrison,' he went on, 'which includes the technicians who operate the site and those who guard it. It seems we know all the details of numbers and shift timings for both, including how they move between Le Touquet and the airfield, although how we got hold of that information, I can't imagine. The airfield is not in regular use – it's an emergency landing strip. Obviously, I'll do a full briefing once we get there, but our job is to secure the strip and the radio site, including neutralising the guard force. After that, the Royal Air Force will fly in an aircraft and a couple of technicians. They take what they want, we load it onto the transport and quite simply it flies back to England. Afterwards, we withdraw to our mounting base and, in the same way as we arrived, we return to our normal lives.'

'Any idea of timings?' Serge asked.

'The operation is scheduled for a week today, weather permitting. If it has to be postponed, it will take place on the following night and so on. Now, I have written this down, but memorise it, and when you are absolutely sure you won't forget it, burn the note. Tell the others to do the same. They all have genuine papers, but the last thing we want is an Étaples address, and details of how to get to the house, found in someone's pocket.

'I'm going to Paris tomorrow to meet up with someone who did the original reconnaissance. She's been back since then to collect information, and now she will help organise the drop. The site has already been chosen. So by the time you and the others arrive, everything will be in place.'

'What about Liliane?' said Serge with a grin.

'I'll tell her tonight, but only that I'm going to be away for a while,' Tadzio said grimly. 'She won't take it well. And if she tries to grill you for information, don't tell her anything. Understood?'

Serge nodded his agreement.

His news had indeed not gone down well, Tadzio reflected the next morning as he walked to the village station to take the train for Paris. The journey was uneventful, and he met Marie as planned in a bar opposite the station. She handed him an envelope. 'It's a pass granted by a certain *Hauptmann* Horst Brandt. He commands the small garrison in Nogent. He gave another individual and me a document that allows us to go into the coastal zone, ostensibly selecting and procuring wine. My pass is genuine. Yours inside that envelope is a forgery, but it's a very good one. It'll serve its purpose, and it's in the name of Louis Chevrolet to match your French identity document.'

He stood beside her as she purchased their tickets. Again she showed her pass. 'My colleague Monsieur Chevrolet has the same document,' she told the counter clerk, giving him her best smile. He did not even ask to see it. It was getting dark by the time they pulled in to Le Touquet.

'There's no public transport out to Nicole's house, and it's too far to walk,' she informed him. 'There's a shop on the edge of town that sells and rents out bicycles. They're like gold dust now that we can't get fuel. But I've been there twice, and I'm sure the old man was suspicious the second time. I dare not risk him reporting me just before the operation, so we will steal two of his bicycles. He uses the upper floor as a stock room. I'm not particularly eager to hurt a fellow French national; things are hard enough for all of us as it is. So I'm going to leave him an envelope of money to cover the cost. We just have to hope that he will be able to replace them eventually.'

They walked to the shop. It was in darkness. The rear backed onto an alleyway, and there was a small courtyard enclosed by a shoulder-high wall and a locked door. Properties on either side were also in darkness. Tadzio was able to sit astride the wall without difficulty. At the rear of the shop, as well as a door leading into the courtyard, there was also a window, presumably giving access to a small back office. He leant down and opened his hand.

'Give me the cases,' he offered, 'then come up yourself. I don't think this is going to be a problem.' An elbow removed a small pane with no more than a quiet tinkle. Tadzio flipped the catch, and the sash window was up and open. They were in.

He drew the curtains, and Marie turned on the light. They were indeed in a small office, furnished with a desk and two chairs. Tadzio opened the door into the shop, with its selection of second-hand bicycles – for sale or rent – and shelves of accessories. The shutters were down, and the curtains were drawn, but he turned on only the staircase light so that they could explore the floor above. Here they found a selection of new machines.

'I think we take a couple of second-hand bikes,' he suggested. 'Less conspicuous than a brand new one. And it won't hurt the old man as much, financially.' They each made their choice.

'And now?' he asked.

'We wait,' she said bluntly. 'I don't know the local curfew times. So I suggest we try to sleep in those chairs in the back, then we leave as soon as it's light, and we see the first people walking in the street.' Which, from the upstairs window, turned out to be immediately after six in the morning. Rummaging in a desk drawer, Tadzio found the keys to the back door and the courtyard. Marie left an envelope on the desk. Tadzio locked up behind them and tossed the keys back over the wall. Then, with their small cases each in a basket, they pedalled unchallenged out of Le Touquet and towards Étaples.

CHAPTER 26

Nicole welcomed them. Thanks to her continued friendship with *Oberleutnant* Klaus Huber, she was well stocked with food and drink. That evening they chatted over a thick onion soup to which she had added pieces of chicken, root vegetables and dried pulses. Afterwards, over a second bottle of red wine, she told them how she had obtained all the information on the operation at the airfield.

'How do you stand with this *Wehrmacht* officer?' asked Marie.

'I ask him for supper about every two or three weeks,' Nicole replied. 'Usually, he stays the night.'

Marie could not help raising her eyebrows.

'In the spare room,' Nicole said quickly. 'For two reasons: first, he has the use of a civilian car, but even in civilian clothes, it's safer if he drives back to Le Touquet in daylight; and second, he likes to drink. But that works to my advantage. He often lets slip information that he wouldn't if he were stone-cold sober. I know what you must be thinking,' she added. 'He has made it clear that he would like to advance the relationship, but he also understands that only friendship and the occasional meal are on offer, nothing more.' She left it at that.

The next morning Nicole departed on her bicycle for Le Touquet, and Marie and Tadzio set off to the drop zone, which

Marie had already transmitted to London. She had selected it based on advice from Johnny Mertherwell and a careful study of the map. They walked upriver along the bank of the estuary to a stretch of land beyond the barn holding the remaining club dinghies. It was ideal, being on land owned by a friendly farmer and several fields away from the nearest country lane.

The problem was they were operating without a radio. It had been too dangerous for either of them to travel with one. They were dependent upon messages pre-arranged by Marie with *Radio Londres*. But had the DZ not been suitable, there would have been time after the recce for Marie to return to Nogent and radio an alternative. The drop was arranged for Sunday, weather permitting.

'When we set up the lights, we'll have to choose a spot well away from the river,' Marie pointed out. 'And hope that nothing lands in the water; otherwise, we'll just have to fish it out.'

'On the other hand, we can stash the stuff in the barn,' he suggested, 'because we don't have the means to move it very far.'

Fortunately, they could access the rear of Nicole's smallholding without being seen from the one adjacent property. Next, they checked the cross-country route and distance to the airfield, stopping at the point where Marie had left her bicycle in the hedge. 'Probably not quite five kilometres,' she said as they stood there. 'Say two hours from the house to here, even at night across fields.' They strolled back the same way. That night a message was broadcast by *Radio Londres*. The drop was on for the following night.

She had brought three powerful torches. If asked, she would have explained that they were helpful for looking around dark wine cellars. Two they positioned on the ground, a diffused beam pointing vertically upwards. The third Marie used to flash a recognition letter – the single dot, 'E' for Étaples, repeated every few seconds. Finally, the pilot flicked his landing lights on and off, then turned and settled for his final run.

There were three parachutes. Two came to earth quite quickly. They were heavy, obviously containing weapons and munitions. The third drifted towards the estuary but fortunately came down just short of the water. The first two they carried to the barn between them. The last one Tadzio hefted back to Nicole's house. It contained a radio, hence the over-sized parachute to ensure a soft landing, and a second box containing every possible spare that might be needed, including five glass valves, enough to replace each one in the set, all packed round copiously with straw. Marie and Tadzio finished unpacking the radio and set it up in a bedroom, the aerial trailing from the window. She turned it on and tapped out a call sign. The response was immediate. It worked.

As arranged, Serge arrived a day before the others. The rest had been told to report to Nicole's address as near as possible to a specific time the day before the operation. Tadzio explained to Nicole that they would arrive in the same order that they had been recruited. Serge would be able to vouch for his next contact, but he would not know them all. So the identity of each former legionnaire could be confirmed in sequence. And once they had sighted Nicole's house, the first on the edge of the village, their orders were to leave the road, take to the fields and enter only via the kitchen door. That way, Nicole's neighbour would not see a procession of arrivals.

It was a merry evening. Nicole declared that after a hard day teaching French to a bunch of German non-commissioned officers, she did not fancy cooking supper. So Marie and Tadzio took over. Marie roasted a large chicken in the oven alongside the open fire in the range whilst Tadzio prepared vegetables, washed up as they went along and generally did as he was told.

Serge opened two bottles of wine. He and Nicole sat heads together at the table, deep in conversation. Although he was somewhat in awe of this highly intelligent graduate of the Sorbonne, for her part, Nicole could not help being attracted to the former legionnaire. He alluded only briefly to his criminal career in Paris and his time in the Legion, but he was, she realised, equally intelligent. It was just that life had not offered him the same advantages. He talked of his plans for the garage business: 'After we have kicked these bastard *Boche* out of France.' She was a widow. It was too soon… but she knew that she could all too easily develop feelings for this stocky, swarthy, North African-looking former soldier.

Knowing what was planned for the night after next, Serge also pointed out that it would be unwise for her to remain in Étaples, regardless of how the raid panned out. Although any evidence against her would be circumstantial, *Oberleutnant* Huber was bound to have his suspicions. And he was too junior to protect Nicole from any Gestapo interrogation. He paused to let this sink in. 'Come with Tadzio and me and join our cell,' he offered. Then, seeing her hesitation, he added, 'Or I'm sure you could go with Marie.' There was a nod of confirmation to confirm that she would be welcome. The more Nicole thought about it, the more it made sense to be well away from the area.

After dinner, Serge produced a bottle of calvados. 'I carried this all the way from home,' he announced. 'Made by a friend of mine – Tadzio can vouch for him, and we can both recommend the quality of what's in the bottle.' By the time it was half empty, they were all a little the worse for wear. Serge insisted on singing a rather risqué marching song from his Legion days, after which they collapsed into giggles. Tadzio countered with 'Mademoiselle from Armentières', which he had learned in England, and they all roared out the '*inky-pinky-parlez-vous!*'. But the line about the innkeeper's daughter, 'with lily-white tits and golden hair', prompted Nicole to suggest that it was time to call it a night. Serge took the single bed in the room sometimes occupied by the *Oberleutnant*. Marie and Tadzio took the two singles in the third bedroom. But it had been, reflected Nicole as she settled into her own bed, the most enjoyable evening since she had been informed of the loss of her husband. Perhaps she might have a future after all.

They began to arrive the following morning. Some were out of sequence, others had travelled in pairs, but all eight of them were there by late afternoon. Only two had been subjected to a casual identity check as they made the initial part of the journey by train. Some might have put on a bit of weight since their time in the Legion, and Marie guessed their average age was late thirties, but there was no doubt that they were all hardened men who quickly melded into a group. And they were all extremely polite to the two ladies.

They had crowded into the kitchen, but as darkness fell, Nicole drew the curtains in the lounge, her largest room, so that Tadzio could begin his briefing.

'Gentlemen, before Tadzio begins, I have an announcement to make,' said Nicole. 'When Tadzio has finished, Marie and I will make a simple supper – just bread, soup and cheese, I'm afraid. Don't ask how, but I have access to rations so we will be all right for tonight and tomorrow.'

One of them raised a hand. 'I still have some food with me, Miss, and I expect most of the other lads will have as well.' There was a general murmur of confirmation. 'I suggest we put everything on your kitchen table. Then you will see how much more you need to put out so that we can all have supper. Save using up more of your food than you need.'

'Thank you,' she said. 'The best news is, I also have a reasonable store of wine, so we can raise a cup or two as we eat – I don't have enough glasses for all of us.'

She sat down, and Tadzio had the floor. 'If I were you,' he began, 'I think my two biggest worries would be first, what have I got myself into, and second, if he's going to lead this operation, does that young man talking to me know what he's doing?

'All of you have a lot of military experience,' he went on, 'so it's a fair question. It might help you to know that I was fighting with our partisans in my own country from the day the Germans entered Poland. After that, the British Army trained me, and I was commanding a tank until we were taken out during the retreat to Dunkirk. Afterwards, I remained undercover in France for a while and set up the beginnings of a resistance cell. I then went back to England for further training so that I could return to France as a British agent, and Serge and I have conducted one very successful raid that severely restricted Luftwaffe activity for quite some time.' He grinned at them. 'Knowing Serge, he wouldn't be here if he wasn't content to work with me again. Marie here has been back to London to plan this raid, and I have been tasked to implement it. Any questions so far?'

There were none. 'Right,' he continued, 'now for the details of the operation itself.' He concluded a lengthy and detailed briefing by telling them that Marie would guide them to where they could enter the airbase. Next, he asked for a few volunteers to collect their airdrop of weapons and ammunition and bring them to Nicole's house in the morning before first light. Finally, Tadzio asked if they had any questions or comments.

'Just one,' said Marie. 'You said that I would guide you to where you can cross the perimeter fence. But it seems to me the most dangerous moment is taking out the guards that are on duty outside their hut when you make the initial approach. Unless you can achieve a silent kill, a whole section of Germans will spill out to join the fight. I have an idea that might help here...'

Tadzio objected. Once she had shown them where to cross the fence, her part was over.

Marie was having none of it. Besides, as she pointed out, she was the only one who had actually seen their target. Serge agreed with her suggestion. So did the rest of the men. Tadzio was overruled. He had the common sense to give in gracefully.

Nicole did not have anything like enough mattresses and bedding. But they had all brought a blanket in case they had to spend a night in the open on the way to Étaples. Besides, as Serge pointed out, they were legionnaires. They might be getting on a bit, but they had not gone soft. A chair, a sofa, cushions, rugs and blankets meant they all managed to bed down somewhere warm and dry to enjoy a reasonable night's sleep.

Very early next morning, before breakfast, they retrieved the rest of the airdrop from the farmer's barn. When their small party returned, Nicole had a breakfast bar of eggs and bread up and running. 'I have to work today,' she told them, 'but I'll be back in plenty of time for tonight.' She did not see Klaus during the day.

After she had set off, they opened the canvas containers. There were only eight Thompson sub-machine guns, but there were two fifty-round drum magazines for each, together with several hundred rounds of ammunition. There were also Browning HP pistols with boxes of nine-millimetre rounds, plus grenades, smoke canisters and a Very pistol in case they had to wave off the aircraft. It would also come in handy if they needed to set fire to the establishment after the raid.

Tadzio gave them a quick lesson on the Thompson, with which they were not familiar, but they were all old soldiers and so used to small arms that they were quickly at ease with the weapon. They shared out the rest of the containers, then rested up for the afternoon. Tadzio transmitted and received confirmation that an aircraft would land at one in the morning. So they would set out at nine, leaving them two hours in hand.

Nicole returned soon after six, and she and Marie prepared another huge saucepan of hearty broth. Some men were seated at the kitchen table cleaning weapons; others were doing the same in the lounge. The distinctive smell of gun oil hung in the air.

There was a loud knock on the kitchen door, which Nicole realised to her horror that she had neglected to lock. 'C'est qui?' she called out anxiously.

'It's me, Klaus,' came the reply in German. Tadzio made a hand signal to tell her that she should open the door and bring him in. As she lifted the latch, they heard him say, 'I'm sorry to have missed you today, but…'

He broke off as Nicole stepped aside. He found himself facing a group of men, all with weapons that emitted an audible click when the working parts snapped forward as they were cocked and lifted into the aim. Tadzio extended the index and middle fingers of his left hand, then curled them together, repeating the motion several times to beckon the German into the room. It was a deliberately intimidating gesture.

'I wanted to tell you that I will not be able to come on Saturday,' he said flatly to Nicole. 'But what is this?'

'*Oberleutnant* Klaus Huber, I presume,' said Tadzio. He did not reply, but Nicole nodded her confirmation.

'Search him, then tie him to a chair,' Tadzio told the others. 'Nicole, Marie and Serge, follow me. We'll discuss this in the other room.'

Serge was all for driving the Peugeot halfway back to Le Touquet, driving it off-road, then putting a bullet in the German's head and torching the car with him inside it. Nicole protested, but in any case, Marie had other ideas. 'Gentlemen, change of plan!' she said. 'For now, all we have to do is keep him here and hide the car.' Nicole and Serge volunteered to drive it into the barn and put it inside with the dinghies.

They set off as planned, taking the *Oberleutnant*, gagged and with his hands tied behind him, in the midst of their group. Serge had told him that if he tried to escape or make a sound, he would personally cut his throat, and they would just carry on without him. Tadzio, Serge and six of the Frenchmen carried a Thompson. The rest were armed with a Browning. Everyone, Marie included, had a couple of grenades. Only Nicole had been left behind. She was not concerned that Kurt might be missed at dinner in the mess. By now, his nights away were common knowledge. But when Tadzio and Serge had again urged her to return home with them after the raid, she had agreed.

They reached the field where Marie had originally parked her bicycle with two hours to spare. She led them to the point where they could climb the tree, crawl along the branch and drop down inside the perimeter fence. It was not quite so easy in the dark, and the German's hands had to be untied, but he too dropped to the ground.

They halted twenty-five metres short of the main clearing. Two of the legionnaires, both volunteers confident of their knife skills but also armed with Brownings, worked their way round the clearing. They emerged behind and alongside the guard hut, one on either side. The door faced into the clearing. Marie edged forward, Klaus behind her, followed by Tadzio, pistol in hand. Serge and the rest of the group took up a position from where they could engage the guard hut if anything went wrong and the men inside came rushing out.

As she had seen before, there were two Germans armed with Schmeisser MP38s patrolling the clearing, which was perhaps twenty-five metres in diameter. Tadzio reminded Klaus of what he had to do. And also, that if he deviated in the slightest from their plan, the first round would enter his spine. Slowly, the three of them stood and walked to the edge of the clearing. The two German guards instantly lifted their weapon but relaxed visibly when Klaus called out, 'Good evening, men. These two good people have lost their dog on the airfield. It's a small spaniel. Have you seen anything?'

Before they could reply, the two legionnaires had moved up behind them, clamped a hand over each mouth and pushed a blade hard into the Germans' throats. Semi-beheaded, with vocal cords cut, blood spurted to their front as they were lowered to the ground.

Silently, four of them moved to the closed door of the radio room. The other legionnaires joined their two colleagues to take station in front of the guard hut. At a signal from Tadzio, Serge opened the door to the radio room and walked right in, followed by Klaus, Marie and Tadzio. He saw about seven or eight men inside, some wearing headphones, others attending to radar screens. One after the other, they turned to face the intruders. Not one of them was holding a weapon. Slowly, they raised their hands.

'You will be searched,' Tadzio told them in German, 'after which you will sit on the floor against that wall with your elbows on your knees and hands on heads.'

There was a blast of exploding grenades followed by bursts of machine-gun fire. 'That was your guard force,' he told them, 'but if you follow my instructions, you will not be harmed.' One by one, they were beckoned forward, expertly searched and directed to the wall. Klaus was the last one to be seated.

They still had an hour to wait before the arrival of the aircraft. Marie, Tadzio and Serge moved to the airfield. It was a clear night with a gibbous moon. Commissioned from the ranks, Flight Lieutenant Ian Rosewell had reached his ceiling. But he had thousands of hours on transports and light bombers and had volunteered not to take his now overdue retirement to serve on for the duration. He had flown the ageing Avro Anson transport low over the channel, then climbed to circle Le Touquet. They had not been troubled by night fighters, but although not the newest of its type in service, the Avro could give a good account of herself. Four .303 calibre Vickers-type machine guns fired forward from the fuselage, sideways from the cabin, and also from a dorsal fin. For which reason tonight, including his navigator, they were a crew of five.

He picked up the recognition signal, which confirmed that the site was secure, and there was enough moonlight to give him a glimpse of the windsock. The ground party was in the right place. He hand-cranked the undercarriage down and lined up on finals. The Anson touched down just past where Tadzio and Serge were standing. A light held by Marie blinked, showing him where to taxi. He guided the Anson to the edge of the field, next to the wood, and cut the two Armstrong Siddeley 350-horsepower Cheetah engines.

Two uniformed technicians jumped down to meet Marie, who confirmed that the site was secured. They set off into the wood, with Tadzio and Serge running to catch up. The crew stayed with the aircraft, ready to man the machine guns if necessary. It took less than an hour for the technicians to indicate to the legionnaires which equipment items they should load onto the aircraft. Meanwhile, Tadzio and Marie searched the building for documents, manuals, codebooks and anything else that might interest London. Finally, with the aircraft loaded, Flight Lieutenant Rosewell started his engines and taxied back to the edge of the strip. The Anson lifted off into the night.

Tempting though it was for the Frenchmen, Tadzio had insisted that the technicians were not foot soldiers, unlike the guard force, so they should not be executed. 'You lot set off,' Serge suggested to the others once they had destroyed the telephone switchboard. All the German radios were already aboard the Anson. 'I'll guard this lot for half an hour, just to ensure they can't raise an alarm from anywhere else on the airfield. Then, once you are all well clear, I'll follow.' It made sense to Tadzio. In the unlikely event that there was any follow-up, one man would be harder to detect than their group.

The usual covered lorry and *Kübelwagen* were parked on the track. Tadzio checked that the keys to the *'wagen* were in the ignition, then knifed the tyres on the lorry. He and Marie would drive to Le Touquet – Nicole had assured them there would not be any other traffic, military or civilian, on the road at that time of the morning.

Alone with his prisoners, it was now Serge's turn to leave. But there was a problem. Nicole had agreed to flee Étaples to avoid the inevitable investigation in which she was bound to fall under suspicion. But her association with *Oberleutnant* Klaus Huber had to be known to his fellow mess members. Her future absence might be suspicious, but it would be only circumstantial without Huber. If he lived, vengeful after being played and humiliated, the Gestapo would move heaven and earth to find her.

'I am going now,' he told them in French, reasonably sure that at least one of them would understand. He looked at Huber, shrugged his shoulders apologetically and fired a short burst into the German officer's chest. Then, whilst they were still recovering from the noise and the sight of Huber's bloody and shredded corpse, he backed out through the door and walked calmly away. War, he reflected, was more often than not a shitty business.

CHAPTER 27

The airfield was a reasonable distance from the centre of Le Touquet. No one from the hotel saw the Anson land or take off again. And if anyone heard the sound of its engines, they would have assumed it to be a German aeroplane. By the time a technician reached the hotel to raise the alarm, Marie and Tadzio, having left the *Kübelwagen* behind a factory building, were already boarding the early train to Paris.

Serge decided to hide their weaponry under the cover of one of the dinghies at the back of the barn. Whilst they all had genuine French papers, it would be foolish to chance being arrested for carrying a firearm. Finally, they returned to Nicole's smallholding. They could not risk the Germans finding and then using the radio, so Serge threw it into the estuary. At first light, the legionnaires set out in twos and threes, ten minutes apart, on the return journey. Serge and Nicole were the last to leave. Retracing their now-familiar route, the legionnaires rested up in the same barns and buildings they had used on the way south. It was not safe to board a train until they had passed through the coastal zone. The Germans mounted as intensive a search as they could in the immediate area around the airfield, but they had only limited manpower, and by this time, all involved in the raid were well clear.

It took a few days, but at dusk, footsore, weary and smelling somewhat less than savoury, Serge and Nicole finally reached the edge of his village. Serge checked the house and garage buildings thoroughly, but all the telltales he had left behind were intact. No one had been inside.

He drew the blackout curtains and switched on the lights. Nicole found herself in a comfortable family home. The furniture left behind by Serge's parents was plain but of good quality, and the kitchen was similar to her own at Étaples. The thought of what she had left brought a tear to her eye. Serge noticed but did not feel it would be quite right to put an arm around her shoulders.

'Don't be sad,' he said gently. 'It's all going to seem strange at first. I want you to feel comfortable and at home – you might like to explore, whilst I light the fire in the kitchen and warm the place up a bit.' A finger pointed above. 'There are three bedrooms, my parents' room at the front, you'll see which is my old room and then there's the guest room. The bed's made up, but I hope you won't find it too cold and damp. The fire is laid, and there are matches on the mantel shelf. We'll have a glass of wine when you come back down, then think about supper – I laid in some food and drink before I left.'

Knowing that she would not be able to return to her own home for a long time, if at all, Nicole had packed her late husband's rucksack with as many clothes as she thought she could carry. As soon as she picked it up, she knew she had over-estimated her ability, but Serge immediately off-shouldered his own, smaller pack and hefted her larger one as though it weighed next to nothing. But now, unpacking in his spare room, she was particularly grateful. The trouble was, in her present state she was reluctant to put on clean clothing. Nicole lit the fire, waited till it was well alight, put on some coals from the scuttle, turned down the bed and went back downstairs.

'Is there any chance of a bath, or just some warm water so that I can have a strip wash?' she asked him. Serge was seated at the table, glass in hand, an opened bottle of red wine and another, empty glass at his elbow.

'Sit down, have a drink,' he invited. 'I'll bring in the tin bath, boil up some water for you and wait in the front room. Do you have everything you need?'

'Thank you,' she said. 'Yes, I brought two bars of soap with me. Klaus gave me several from the hotel. I have not yet had to resort to mixing fat with caustic soda or wood ash.'

Afterwards, wrapped in a dressing gown and with a second glass of wine, she felt human again. She called to Serge that he should join her. 'I must do the same,' he told her. 'It's cold next door, though – you will need your coat.'

'Then I shall stay here,' she replied mischievously. 'When you are ready, I shall turn my chair away. You will just have to trust me not to peep.' Which she didn't, even though she was tempted. Afterwards, now also in his dressing gown, he made a simple supper of tinned meat from the stores left behind by his mother, together with a few of his own vegetables. They drank a second bottle of wine. Nicole was weary to the bone after their journey. It didn't seem to have affected the former legionnaire, but they settled for an early night.

Next morning, they walked to the farm. Tadzio and Liliane were in the kitchen. Nicole was made welcome, but Liliane glared at Serge. 'As for you,' she almost spat the words at him, 'you're as bad as he is. He won't even tell me where you've been.'

Nicole took an immediate liking to the spirited, rather pretty, obviously pregnant young woman. 'May I say something?' she asked the two men.

Without waiting for an answer, she turned to Liliane. 'When Tadzio went to England, I helped him escape in a dinghy. I live... lived,' she corrected, 'near Étaples – it's a few kilometres from Le Touquet, alongside an estuary close to the sea. London tasked Tadzio to acquire some secret German equipment near my home. His was the only resistance resource available. He was forbidden to tell anyone in advance, because it could have cost several lives, my own included.' She looked to Tadzio, who nodded his confirmation. 'We were successful,' she concluded. 'The equipment is now in England. But I was compromised. Serge rescued me; hence I am now here. I hope that puts your mind at rest and that we shall be friends.'

Somewhat mollified, if only a little, Liliane thanked her then turned again on the two men. 'If ever you disappear from me again like that,' she said firmly, 'without at least telling me when you will be back, you, Tadzio, can start looking for a new home because neither of you will be allowed back here.'

She turned aside and, in a softer tone, asked, 'Would you like coffee, Mademoiselle? I still have a little left.' But Serge and Tadzio noticed that she took four cups and saucers from the cupboard.

'It's Madame,' Nicole said quietly as at Liliane's invitation, she drew back a chair from the table. 'My husband was a pilot. But according to those who were flying with him at the time, I am now a widow. So you will understand why I wanted to help the resistance.' Liliane recounted her own story of the loss of her parents and how she had met Tadzio. The war had touched them all. They were, they agreed, four of a kind.

'Pity we had to leave the drop behind,' mused Serge the next time they were together.

'What drop?' asked Liliane sharply.

'We were a small group of ex-legionnaires,' Serge explained. 'It was too dangerous to move to Étaples carrying our weapons and equipment, so the RAF dropped what we needed before most of us arrived. Afterwards, we had to escape on foot through the controlled coastal zone before we could take a train. So we left the weapons stashed away where the Germans probably won't find them.'

'That said, I'm reluctant to just leave them there,' Tadzio admitted. 'All right, it's a controlled zone, but the Germans can't man every road and lane that leads in and out. And even if we do meet a couple of them, think about it: we have a *Kübelwagen*, two German uniforms and a couple of Schmeissers.'

'You'd be crazy to try,' said Liliane anxiously.

'I like it,' Serge agreed, slapping the table with the palm of his hand. 'You speak German. We'll either talk or fight our way through any roadblock. They're not going to be pointing weapons at what they'll assume to be two of their own in a German vehicle.'

'You have to get there first,' pointed out Nicole. 'I was brought up in that village. I know every lane and off-road track in the area. The Germans can't cover them all; they just haven't the manpower. You would stand a much better chance of not stumbling into a roadblock guarding the coastal zone if I were there to navigate.'

'But you're a woman,' Serge exclaimed.

'So you had noticed,' came the bemused reply. 'Thank you for that glimpse of the blindingly obvious. But seriously, I can make myself look like a man, especially with a uniform. And I also speak German.'

'But you have no military training,' countered Serge. Clearly, he was not warming to the idea of Nicole returning to Étaples.

'I can use a hunting rifle,' she argued. 'Have done since I was taught as a girl. And it can't be difficult to learn how to use a Schmeisser. If you men can do it, so can I.'

'I'm going to give it some more thought,' said Tadzio. 'We are quite well off after our local drop, but the resistance desperately needs more weapons, and it's a better option than having to ask the RAF to fly another sortie,' he concluded, bringing the subject to a close.

*

Before the Great War Albert Krämer's mother worked as a kitchen assistant to the Sutherland family's cook. Sir Magnus was a director of an English shipping company based in Hamburg and responsible for all European business. Only Frau Köhler, the cook, lived in.

Frau Krämer walked the five kilometres from and to her apartment in the St Pauli district alongside the harbour. They had to put up with the noise from the bars and bordellos. But it was all that she and her husband, a dock labourer, could afford.

When her firstborn came along, her employers were very understanding. They allowed her to bring the infant Albert to work. As a toddler, he played in the garden with the two Sutherland children his age, twins, a boy and a girl. Completely unaware of the difference in status, they were inseparable. Lady Sutherland, a socialist who supported the votes for women movement, eventually suggested that the five-year-old Albert might join her own children for lessons given by their newly engaged private tutor.

When other children came along, Frau Krämer could no longer remain in service. The Sutherlands gave her a generous parting gift. She used some of the money, plus what they could scrimp from her husband's wages, to pay for Albert's tram fares. The Sutherlands had kindly offered that Albert was still permitted to knock at the tradesman's entrance to continue his studies. All came to an end when the twins were packed off to boarding school in England at the age of nine. But by this time, Albert had an excellent command of the English language. After a few more years at a local German school, and by virtue of a better than average education, he was taken on as an engineering apprentice in the shipyard.

Albert Krämer survived the Great War. Because of his engineering background, he was set to work on the German fleet of tanks, armoured cars and vehicles. Benefitting from what he had learned during his military service, he found work as a mechanic in a vehicle repair shop in his native Hamburg. Ilse, his childhood sweetheart, left her small house in a middle-class suburb, where she had lived with her parents and older brother, to marry Albert and move into their tiny rented flat near the docks area. But hyperinflation in the early 1920s of the Weimar Republic made life difficult to the point of impossible. Only very occasionally, for they were trying hard to build up their savings, Albert particularly enjoyed practising his English in the bars of the docks area with sailors from England and America. He was determined that he and Ilse should have a better life.

Albert, tall and dark with a thin nose and high forehead, and Ilse, shorter, blonde, and pretty if a bit dumpy, talked long into the night. It would be better to make the move before children came along. Albert knew little about their chosen country, except for what the sailors had told him. Was it not a young country of great wealth and opportunity, the land of the automobile? Better by far, the sailors had said, than a benighted Germany broken by defeat and the reparation demands of the Treaty of Versailles. And immigrants were welcomed.

They had enough money to buy steerage-class tickets with an American line, with just a little left over to see them through no more than a few days once they had landed. But they were young and full of hope for the future. At Ellis Island and tagged with information from the ship's registry, they queued to pass medical and legal inspections and were at last released onto the streets of New York.

Albert was better prepared than many of his fellow immigrants. One of the sailors from Washington, DC, had given him advice on places to stay for the least money. And although no promises had been made, he was given the address of an uncle who ran a similar sort of business to the one in which Albert had worked back in Hamburg. The young couple would have to hitch a ride.

Paddy Reilly was a short, tubby, kindly man who wiped his oily hands on a rag as he looked the German up and down before asking a few questions. Of Irish heritage, he held no grudge after the Great War, and in any case, he had been too old to take part. But German engineers and mechanics had a good reputation. Moreover, he understood the hardships many immigrants faced, particularly those like Albert and his wife, with no relatives already in America who could support them. And besides, now he was getting on a bit. He could use an extra pair of hands.

'Can't pay you more'n sixty dollars a week,' he offered, 'but we got plenty of trade and overtime's double. Give you a week's trial,' he said, extending his hand. Albert was so grateful he clasped it with both of his own. Back in the one room that shared a bathroom and toilet facilities with the rest of the tenement, Ilse said that she, too, would look for work as soon as possible.

After a week's trial, Paddy Reilly wondered how he had managed before without the German mechanic. Albert and Ilse began to plan for the future. He was earning a good wage. They would spend only on absolute essentials. Their only entertainment was a small wireless or whatever was free in local parks and plazas. Ilse's limited education ill-equipped her for a job in their adopted country, so initially she applied herself to learning English. She also acquired a second-hand spirit stove, on which she could cook the simplest of one-pot meals that also saved them money. Their only other expense was contraception: if they were to make their way in the world, starting a family was, for now, out of the question.

Soon, her English, if basic, was good enough for her to be taken on as a waitress in a family-run restaurant. Slowly, the balance in their savings account began to mount up. Then, one morning, the blow came out of the blue when Paddy called Albert into the partitioned area he used as an office.

'I'm retiring,' he told him. 'Me and the wife haven't been blessed with children, and we want to enjoy our last few years together. I've had a very good offer for the business that I can't afford to refuse.'

'May I ask, Boss, where does that leave me?' asked Albert anxiously.

Paddy Reilly looked decidedly uncomfortable. 'My buyer is an American,' he said at length. 'He asked about you when my wife Pauline showed him the books. He was in the war – lost two brothers. I'm sorry, Albert, but he won't have a German in the business. Said there are plenty of good Americans who could use the work. A condition of sale is that I let you go before he arrives, which is a week from today. I'll pay you up to your last day and give you a week's wages on top.'

The hardest part was breaking the news to Ilse. 'My wages and tips will put food on the table,' she said, 'and you are a good man. You will find other work.'

But finding other work in 1920s America proved not so easy. Having failed to find anything similar to his previous job, Albert took to walking the suburbs looking for any opportunity. One day he saw two men offloading garden equipment from the back of a truck parked in the drive of an upmarket, single-storey home. Not expecting any joy, nevertheless he asked if they needed an extra hand, even just for a day.

'You're in luck,' said the older of the two men. 'Flanagan didn't pitch up. It'll be the drink again. I warned him last time, so he's off the payroll. I need to get this place done real quick. Got a good new contract and I need to get over there first thing this afternoon.'

The pay was only just over half of what he had been getting, but it was better than nothing. He spent the next two hours pushing a lawnmower and trimming edges. Then the three of them, Gus, their boss and Chuck, the other garden hand, squeezed into the cab and they set off for their next job out of town.

Albert continued to look for a better job, one where he would be paid for his experience, but for two weeks, nothing was forthcoming. He quite enjoyed the outdoor work, but his wages and Ilse's combined did not equate to his former earnings. Their savings no longer mounted up.

'It's some politician's place, a state senator,' Gus had told him the first time he had been there. It was the largest house on their books, one which reminded Albert of the Sutherland mansion back in his native Hamburg. The doors of a double garage were closed, and the longest automobile Albert had ever seen sat under a carport. It had four doors, but there did not appear to be any side windows. Instead, light-grey canvas covered a frame from the top of the windscreen all the way to the rear and then down to the bodywork. Fascinated, he paused from weeding a rose garden to watch as a tall, slightly portly middle-aged man, dressed in a beautifully cut suit, settled himself behind the wheel.

The starter whirred, but the engine did not even fire. After numerous attempts, Albert detected a slight slowing of the starter motor. He walked over to the vehicle, hoping that he would not offend.

'Excuse me, sir,' he said politely, removing the straw hat protecting his head, 'but the battery will soon be exhausted. Would you like me to find out why it will not start?'

'You're a gardener. How would you know anything about a Cadillac Custom Phaeton?' came the terse reply. Obviously, the man was still irritated.

'Sir, gardening is all I can find, but I was an apprentice engineer and I have worked as a motor mechanic.'

'In that case, be my guest,' said the somewhat mollified politician, climbing out and leaving the door open for Albert.

'First, sir,' said Albert, 'we look under *die Motorhaube*, what I believe you just call the hood.'

It was obvious. There was an overwhelming smell of gasoline. 'A big V8,' said Albert admiringly. 'It must be more than five litres. But on a morning like this, you did not need a rich mixture. Maybe I can clear it. Sometimes it works, sometimes it doesn't. If not, I will remove the spark plugs and dry them off.'

He identified the choke and set it to normal mixture. With his foot on the clutch to ease the friction load and with the throttle wide open, he tried a couple of short bursts. The engine roared into life at the third attempt, a huge cloud of petrol-smelling vapour making both of them cough, even in an open carport.

The politician thanked him profusely, then added, 'Let's just hope I can drive the goddam thing.'

'You do not know how?' asked Albert incredulously.

'Driver let me down. Told me last night he'd got a better job. Didn't pay him enough, I guess. Sure, I've driven her before, but only a couple of times. Kept meaning to learn properly, but always too busy.'

'Sir, if Mr Gus will allow me, I could drive for you. I have much experience.'

It was a short, one-sided discussion. Gus had no intention of jeopardising his biggest contract, and Albert immediately mastered the three-speed manual synchromesh gearbox. The Cadillac was an absolute delight to drive, far superior to anything he had driven before, and his passenger directed him to stop outside a huge building. Albert rushed round to open the passenger door.

'Tell Gus I want you back here at noon,' said the politician, who had introduced himself as Chester Freeman. 'And thanks again, Albert.'

Albert contented himself with a polite 'Sir'.

Mid-morning, a maid came out to say that the master wished to speak to Gus on the telephone. He came back out of the house but said nothing. As ordered, Albert was waiting at midday when Chester Freeman walked down an imposing set of steps. They drove to a smart restaurant. 'Be back in two hours,' came the instruction. Then, 'You got any money with you?'

Albert confessed that he hadn't. Freeman peeled off a five-dollar bill. 'Find yourself something,' he said before disappearing into the restaurant. Albert bought a sandwich and a cold drink from a street vendor. He had used hardly any of the money.

'By the way, sir, he said as he drove Chester Freeman home after what had obviously been a good lunch, 'I have your change.'

'Keep it,' came the curt reply. 'You earned it this morning.'

Again Albert opened the door. 'Park up,' he was instructed, 'then I want you to come round to the back door. Someone will show you to my study.'

Ilse was a little surprised when Albert returned bearing four bottles of beer and two steaks. 'We can't afford this,' she said anxiously as he placed them on the table.

'So I have been offered a position as chauffeur to a senator,' he concluded after recounting the day's events. 'Also, I must maintain two other vehicles as well as those on a farm in a place called Virginia. Senator Freeman asked me what I was earning. I told him that when I found another job as a mechanic, it would be about sixty a week, as I was earning before. He said he would pay the same, but best of all, there is a small cottage, one of three for the staff, at the rear of the property. It's very fine. I have seen it, and it is ours without any rent as part of my employment.'

They drank their beer, feasted on the steaks, went to bed happy and made love. Only the following day did she remember to tell him that there was a letter from her brother. 'He is coming to America,' she told him. 'He says he does not need any help or accommodation from us. I think he must have a job already, but I will write quickly and give him our new address.'

CHAPTER 28

Johnny Metherwell was still at the cottage when Marie arrived home. No one from the resistance had been in contact regarding an escape through Spain. 'Mind you, it's early days yet,' observed Marie as they enjoyed Sunday lunch at the estate's farmhouse. 'I suspect there aren't many cells up and running. The people I spent the last few days with has to be an exception, and even then, they had to enlist the help of some former French legionnaires to pull off what was really quite a small operation.'

'That's all well and good,' observed Johnny, 'but I should be flying, not taking a holiday in France. You know I have to go back, darling,' he added quickly, anxious not to hurt Marie's feelings. He placed his hand over hers and gave it an affectionate squeeze.

'You have to do your duty,' said Jean Renaud, supporting the young airman. 'But make the most of your time here. And you will be most welcome to come back, after the war. Marie will still be here.' They all knew that this was a statement bordering on the over-optimistic, but all they could do was hope for the best.

'I forgot to tell you,' said Monique to Marie, 'whilst you were away, we pretty much had to accept a dinner invitation from Horst Brandt – he's the *Hauptmann* in charge of the small garrison in Nogent,' she added for Johnny's benefit, 'and we think he's taken a fancy to Marie.'

'Not that I've ever given him any encouragement,' she put in quickly.

'True,' confirmed Monique, 'but anyway, he phoned and asked us to dinner – that very nice restaurant in Nogent where we went for my birthday. Naturally, he assumed you would be with us. When Jean explained that you were away for a couple of days, he was obviously too embarrassed to withdraw the invitation.'

'It was a good dinner, even so,' added Jean. 'But he wasn't too subtle about letting us know that he would like to see Marie again, and in the end, Monique felt it would look too suspicious if we kept him at arm's length.'

'So he's coming to dinner, the day after tomorrow. Just the four of us,' Monique announced, glancing apologetically at Johnny.

Cooking was not Metherwell's forte. But, with Marie away at the farmhouse for the evening, he made himself an omelette, adding some field mushrooms she had gathered that morning. Then he settled to a bottle of the estate's red wine and *Radio Londres*.

Horst Brandt removed his greatcoat, hat, belt and side arm before accompanying Jean into the drawing room, where he bowed to the ladies before accepting a glass of white wine. Monique soon excused herself 'to attend to some last-minute touches', as she put it. She had made an effort to entertain their German guest. They were fortunate to have their own produce, although the garrison quartermaster, who acted as its commissar, collected what he stated to be their required contribution. But she suspected that Horst Brandt had given instructions that he need not be over-zealous in his duties when dealing with the estate.

She served a chicken casserole flavoured with pigeon breasts from birds shot the previous evening by Jean, although he was now down to his last box of twelve-bore cartridges. But they gave the dish a delicious gamey taste. Potatoes they had aplenty, plus green vegetables from the garden. Afterwards there was a crème brûlée. Eggs, cream and milk for the custard had not been a problem, and she had used some of her precious sugar for the scorched and brittle topping. *Hauptmann* Brandt very much enjoyed what she explained was France's most traditional dessert.

Afterwards, he complimented his hosts generously on the food and the wine. But he was a little disappointed with the demeanour of Marie. She was perfectly polite, smiling at his lighter remarks and even initiating conversation from time to time. But he sensed that he was not making progress into her affections. Much as she had an alluring figure and had to be considered a beauty, neither had she quite dressed for the occasion as he had hoped. Moreover, the woman seemed to be at pains to offer him no encouragement, which, considering the favours that he, as the senior local representative of the occupying power, had afforded this estate, he rather resented.

The ladies withdrew for coffee, and Jean and Brandt enjoyed a glass of port before joining them. The *Hauptmann* had driven himself to the farmhouse. It was safe enough in a backwater like Nogent, where there had never been open hostility to the occupation. And although he was driving, he accepted when offered a glass of brandy with his coffee. Obviously, Jean Renaud had his sources for such luxuries whilst travelling widely through the wine districts.

When she thought she could do so politely and without arousing Brandt's suspicion, Marie thanked her hostess for a lovely meal but said she would be working tomorrow, so it was time to take her leave. Brandt immediately followed suit. Jean returned with his greatcoat and accoutrements together with Marie's fur jacket, which she slipped over her shoulders. He made a point of leaving alongside her as they descended the small flight of steps at the front of the house.

'Please, Fraulein Marie, you must allow me to drive you to your dwelling,' he suggested politely. Marie had not wanted to tell him where she lived but saw little alternative.

'Thank you, that's kind,' she replied, 'but I have a cottage on the estate. It's not far to walk, just along a path through some trees and bushes. I shall be perfectly all right. But thank you again for the offer. Goodnight, *Hauptmann* Brandt,' she said, smiling with a warmth she did not feel and extending her hand.

He did not take it. Instead, his hand closed on her upper arm. 'Then I shall escort you to your door,' he announced firmly. 'You cannot possibly walk alone through the woods at this time of night.'

She could have refused but had no wish to make a scene. Then there was Johnny. He might still be up, reading or listening to the radio in their small living room. They did not draw the curtains. What if he were discovered? In the end, it was the lesser of two evils. She offered a quiet, 'Thank you.' They set off along the path towards some trees. Hopefully, if she spoke loudly to Brandt as they approached her cottage, Johnny would realise that she was not alone. It was scarcely a five-minute stroll. 'You have left a light on,' he pointed out as they approached the front door.

'I always do if I know I shall be coming back late,' she explained. 'It can't be seen from the air, surrounded by trees and in the middle of nowhere.' Without lowering her voice, she thanked him for walking her home and wished him goodnight. To her concern, his hands went to both shoulders and he leant forwards to kiss her. She turned her head to offer him a cheek. His right hand took her jaw, turned it to face him and his lips were on hers. Then his hand released her face, pushed under her jacket and grabbed her breast, squeezing painfully.

Her training kicked in. She kneed him, hard, in the balls. As he gasped and broke away, both hands pressed over them, he automatically bent slightly forward. Using the palm of her hand, she struck upwards at the underside of his nose. The blow could have pushed the nasal bone back into his brain, but that had not been her intention. She just wanted him on the floor so that she could escape into the cottage. With her right foot she kicked into the side of his left knee, although not too hard, the joint having very little lateral strength. As the leg collapsed under him, she gave him an almighty shove that sent him to the ground.

She wrenched open the door and scrambled inside. Brandt was still down but now on one knee. She turned the key in the lock to see Johnny alongside the door, his back to the wall. She raised a vertical finger to her lips. A minute later, Brandt was pounding the door.

'You will open it, bitch,' he almost screamed. 'Now it is my turn.' The door shook on its hinges. Obviously, he had recovered sufficiently to use his shoulder or good leg, and he was a big man. Johnny's hand waved her away to the far side of the room. As she moved, another blow splintered the lock from the surrounding woodwork. Brandt stepped forward into the room. She saw blood running from his nose, and he was limping, but he was no longer in a blinding rage. He wiped the blood away from his mouth with the back of his hand and drew his Walther from its holster. It was pointing at her feet. 'Now you will remove that coat,' he said softly, 'or—'

Johnny pushed the door away from him and cocked his revolver, at the same time telling the German in his own language to drop his weapon. Brandt spun round, lifting his pistol into the aim. Johnny's first round took him centre mass, in the chest. A second kicked high and slightly right, taking him in the left eye. Marie had dived for the floor. As he fell backwards, the German tripped over her. Johnny kicked Brandt's gun from his hand, but he had died instantly. He rushed to take Marie in his arms.

He held her until she stopped shaking. There was another shout from outside. It was Jean, shotgun in hand. 'Heard gunfire,' he said as he came to the door then looked down at the prone figure on the floor. 'Now we really do have a problem,' he said quietly.

*

Albert enjoyed his new job and the time spent on the family farm in Virginia. Having brought its neglected machinery up to standard, he even enjoyed helping out on the land when not needed for driving duties. Fortunately, however, the senator and his family spent most of their time in Washington, DC, because Ilse remained there permanently.

In the restaurant one of the junior cooks had handed in her notice, leaving them short-handed in the kitchen. As an interim measure, Ilse was asked to help out. She offered to make a number of German dishes, which turned out to be extremely popular with the regulars, so she was promoted permanently, no longer a waitress but a member of the preparation and cooking team. Not only did it pay more, but her employers were also generous in allowing staff to take home unused food and ingredients that would otherwise spoil.

Alfred scarcely knew Gerd, Ilse's elder brother. They had met only once before the wedding and a couple of times afterwards at family gatherings. Apparently, he had a reasonably good job in Hamburg, some sort of junior manager in the banking or investment industry. Towards the end of February, they were invited to take lunch with him on a Sunday, Albert's day off. Inevitably, Gerd chose one of Washington's German restaurants. It was the next best thing to a *Ratskeller*, the restaurant beneath the municipal building that was the pride and joy of every German town and city. And it was not cheap.

Albert listened as Ilse's brother passed on news of her family. There was nothing from his own parents. Gerd had not bothered to contact them, even though he knew he would be seeing their son in America. In response to Albert's question, Gerd told them that he had been sent to their Washington office by the bank, specifically to study the American banking and investment scene. It was a three-month attachment. Fortunately, he had studied English at school, so his knowledge of the language was passable and improving daily.

Conversation turned to the situation at home, and to the improvements in the economy before the war under Herr Hitler. Now, vast tracts of Europe were under German rule. 'But you are also under the thumb of the Nazi Party,' observed Albert. 'The Fatherland is now a one-party state, and I know some of our people have been sent to camps. There is also forced labour.'

'Foreign propaganda,' countered Gerd.

'Not so,' replied Albert. 'Many of our politicians do not favour the President's proposal for Lend-Lease. So, apparently, he has a dossier of what life is like back home to support his argument that Hitler has to be stopped. And to do that, both Houses have to approve this new policy. Although he has not seen them, the senator I work for said there are even photographs of what it is like in the camps, including pictures of hangings, forced labour and women being used for sex. Many Lend-Lease doubters change their minds in favour when they see the evidence. The senator was telling a colleague about it in the back of the car, only the other day. I heard every word he said.'

Gerd was about to deploy his usual argument: that Germany had not been defeated in the Great War, only stabbed in the back by republicans, socialists and Jews. But he thought better of it. He would not reveal his actual status to his sister and her oily-handed husband, whom he despised. Ilse had thrown herself away on a loser. She could have made a much better marriage, even been, as was he, a senior member of the Party.

Lunch was enjoyable more for the food and the setting rather than any feeling of celebrating a family reunion. Albert and Ilse thanked her brother. But he did not, they noticed, make any arrangement that they should meet again. They were happy to return to their cottage. Gerd was also glad when their lunchtime meeting was over. It had been wise not to argue too strongly against Albert's information. Had his brother-in-law's views been different, he might have confided his position as *SS-Sturmbannführer*, but he suspected that Albert's and Ilse's sympathies no longer lay with their country of birth, unlike those of many of their fellow countrymen now in America.

Gerd had been thoroughly briefed on the situation in the United States. He knew that in the years leading up to the war, Germans living abroad were encouraged to associate within groups designed to sustain German nationalism and ideals, and to lend their support for the Nazi Party. Formed in 1936, the *Amerikadeutscher Volkbund* began operating youth training camps across the country, staffed by sympathetic German dual nationals or Americans of German descent. Just before the war, its membership numbered tens of thousands. In February 1939, some twenty thousand rallied in New York's Madison Square denouncing – amongst other things – President Roosevelt and Jewish plotting.

Whilst it was true that Gerd had been sent to study the American financial system, it was also the case that he was tasked with encouraging the activities of the Bund, to organise the recruitment of anyone from within its membership who might be useful to the regime back in Germany, and not least, to raise financial support for the Party. American dollars, banked in Switzerland, secured access to goods and services not available to the Reichsmark. The following morning he filed a report on the Roosevelt dossier with the Party's representative at the German Embassy in Washington.

*

Albert folded his *Washington Post* and placed it on their kitchen table. 'Well, he's done it,' he said to Ilse.

'Who's done what?' she asked.

'Roosevelt,' he told her. 'He's signed Lend-Lease into law. Apparently it's called "*An Act to Promote the Defense of the United States*". He signed it yesterday, March 11. We supply Britain and other allies with warships and aircraft, as well as other weaponry. The United States gets leases on army and naval bases on Allied territory in return.'

'Gerd won't like it one little bit,' was her only response.

Her brother reported through the embassy that the Dachau Report had clearly proved decisive in persuading reluctant, isolationist politicians in Washington to support Roosevelt's bill.

Whilst he had not been able to obtain a copy, Gerd had been able to describe the contents in general terms, including the fact that there were photographs of sexual abuse and brutality.

It was a bitter blow to Berlin. Not only did it give the lie to any pretence of American neutrality, it also ensured that Britain had the means to defend herself for as long as she wished to continue the war. Moreover, it cast serious doubts on whether the German U-boat offensive, much as it worried Churchill, would ever completely starve Great Britain into surrender for lack of food and military equipment.

'But that,' fumed *SS-Oberführer* Lothar Winkler, seated at his desk in Prinz-Albrecht-Straße 8, the headquarters in Berlin of the Gestapo and the SS, 'does not offer any clue as to how the pictures were obtained, who took them or, for that matter, how they were smuggled out of Germany. However,' he told Willi Schröder, his *SS-Hauptsturmführer* assistant, 'the photographs of our soldiers enjoying the services of women prisoners might just prove more useful. It was either inside the camp or somewhere else indoors where they were working for the Reich. I need to speak to *Kommandant* Piorkowski. We fly to *München* tomorrow.'

SS-Hauptsturmführer Alexander Piorkowski was not looking forward to briefing his visitors from Berlin. Apparently, the Führer himself had been made aware of the Dachau document. Raging curses, he had ordered severe punishment for anyone whose negligence had, in any way, so undermined the German diplomatic effort in Washington to oppose the Lend-Lease bill. *Oberführer* Winkler, several ranks Piorkowski's senior, had warned in his initial telephone call that he intended to follow his orders to the letter.

Having welcomed them to his office, Piorkowski offered coffee and schnapps, which were declined. It was not reassuring. 'Well, *Hauptsturmführer* Piorkowski,' opened Winkler, 'you had better tell me what you have discovered thus far. How did this disaster take place within your command?' Neither, thought Piorkowski, was the formal use of his rank and name a good start. Berlin wanted a scapegoat.

'This camp has been turned over, *Herr Oberführer*,' he began nervously. 'There are no cameras here now.'

'But someone took a picture of one of your Jews in his striped uniform hanging from a gallows,' observed Winkler. 'So, obviously, your security system allowed a camera to be imported under the very noses of your guards.'

A native of Bremen, Alexander Piorkowski had initially trained as a mechanic before working as a travelling salesman. Having made his way through the ranks of the Party, like many of the grossly over-promoted Nazi hierarchy, he was neither well educated nor particularly intelligent. But he was cunning.

'I have given the matter much thought,' he replied, 'and I believe it may be possible to discover what – or how – this has happened. Of course, the more difficult way would be to demand that the person responsible for the in-camp pictures steps forward. But there are many different categories of prisoners here: for example, Jews, intellectuals, clergy opposed to the state, not to mention ethnic groups such as Poles or Slavs. So we could demand that our man identifies himself, with the threat that if not, other prisoners will be shot. However, there is no guarantee that such a method would ever force a confession or a betrayal.

'But that is only one of several possibilities.' He paused for effect, hoping to indicate that he had the ruthless ability to retain an iron control over his command.

'Which tells me you have a better solution,' replied Winkler, in what seemed a slightly less truculent tone. Obviously, thought Piorkowski, the *Oberführer's* head was just as much on the block as his own.

'Apparently, there are also pictures of women having sex with a small group of their guards,' he replied. 'My view is that this is less likely to have taken place in the camp, where my men are housed in large barrack huts. For a start, collecting up and marching the women would have been obvious.' He paused. 'No, I think this took place outside the camp, where women labourers and a small number of guards would be housed in close proximity. And there is only one place where we permanently house a labour force and guard detachment: there are two factories not too far away that make rifles and radios for the *Wehrmacht*. The men march daily to the radio factory. But all the women are assigned to – and billeted at – the rifle facility.'

Berndt Hoffmann was surprised when a telephone call from the *Kommandant* of Dachau informed him that an *SS-Oberführer* and his *SS-Hauptsturmführer* assistant would be visiting that afternoon. Winkler introduced himself and Schröder pleasantly enough. But his heart missed a beat when the *Oberführer* informed him that they were investigating the origin of photographs that had come to their attention.

'They show women engaged in sexual practices with German guards,' he went on. 'There are also photographs from within the Dachau *Konzentrationslager*,' he added, 'so it is reasonable to assume that the guards with the women also came from there. And this is the only facility outside the camp where both guards and women are located together. How many women do you employ here?' he asked, although he already knew the answer. He just wanted to gauge Hoffmann's reaction to his implied accusation.

'At the moment, forty,' Berndt Hoffmann replied smoothly, with no outward indication of alarm. 'They are used as assembly workers, alongside our skilled male machine operators, men who are not suitable for military service. Although we are training up some of the women so that they can also be used as machinists.'

'And this is a twenty-four-hour operation?' confirmed Winkler.

'*Ja*, two twelve-hour shifts. Except for Sunday, when the day and night shifts change over.'

'And where are the women situated when they are off-duty?'

'The women's dormitory is above the factory,' came the response. 'All production takes place on the ground floor. As well as the dormitory overhead, there are also some spare rooms that we use for storage. Oh, and two small barrack rooms for the guard contingent,' he added.

It was, thought Winkler, increasingly likely that this had been where the photographs had been taken. The off-duty guards would have had access to the women unseen by the supervisory staff on shift below.

The *Oberführer* turned to his assistant. 'Schröder, take the off-duty factory shift. You know what to do.'

Once they were alone, he said, 'So, Herr Hoffmann, we must wait for a while. Perhaps now some form of refreshment would be appreciated.'

Berndt opened the door to his office and asked his secretary to organise coffee. 'It is still available in Switzerland,' he informed Winkler once they were seated again. 'So, Herr *Oberführer*, how do you intend to proceed from here?'

'Schröder will talk to both shifts,' came the reply. 'We will give them twenty minutes to produce the person who took the photographs. After that, I am afraid your workforce will be depleted by one person every five minutes until we have our answer. Of course, you may indicate which of your trainee machinists you would prefer to save, if at all possible.'

Berndt Hoffmann could see no way out of this situation. But both men were a little surprised when Willi Schröder knocked on the door, opened it and pushed Eva Bergman into the room. 'This Jewish bitch stepped forward,' he said by way of explanation. 'She claims to know about the photographs.'

'Speak!' said Winkler harshly.

'I took them,' she said in a quiet but dignified voice. 'It is common knowledge that the guards abuse us. They boast about it in the beer halls when they are off duty. It happens almost every night. I was approached whilst I was on shift by a man dressed in a brown foreman's jacket, except I did not recognise him. He was not employed here. He wanted to discredit the Party by exposing the Dachau regime.'

'So you took the pictures,' said Winkler softly. 'What happened then?'

'Afterwards, he collected the camera. I have not seen him since.'

'We will take her back to the *Konzentrationslager*, Herr Hoffmann,' said Winkler. 'I believe further and more expert interrogation to be necessary.'

Berndt had little doubt that Eva would break under torture, and the true story would eventually be revealed.

'Sir,' she began, facing the still-seated *Oberführer*, 'I do not know your rank or who you are, but some of us here are living in hell. We have committed no crime, yet we are taken from our loved ones. We work long hours, the rations are barely adequate and the guards here use us as they wish. I, and others, am penetrated in every orifice, night after night.'

'Jews exist only to serve the state,' came the harsh reply.

'Then I will serve no more,' she replied, and bit down hard on something in her mouth. She smiled at Winkler, but it was a look of triumph. 'He did not give me only a camera,' were her last words. She collapsed onto her knees, hands clutching at her stomach, then rolled sideways, convulsed and finally lay still. Berndt detected a faint waft of almonds.

Winkler turned on him in a fury. 'All this happened in your factory,' he hissed accusingly.

'My responsibility,' Berndt Hoffmann replied evenly, 'is to make rifles for the *Wehrmacht*, which I do – thousands of them. But some of the workers are provided by the Party: your Party. And their security, whilst they are here, is the responsibility of guards provided by the Commandant of Dachau, who is also a member of your Party. I do not know what is at the bottom of all this, but I have lost a good worker. No doubt you will say that she can be replaced. But at the same time, you might wish to review your security. He laid heavy emphasis on his penultimate word.

The two visitors left, silent and angry. But they had been informed in no uncertain terms that the factory could not legally be held responsible. He partly closed the door to shield Eva's body from his secretary. 'Please have someone fetch me a blanket,' he asked quietly. 'Then we must make dignified arrangements for a very brave young lady.'

CHAPTER 29

'Yes,' repeated Jean Renaud quietly, 'now we really do have a problem. It's inconceivable that *Hauptmann* Brandt did not tell anyone where he was going tonight. There will definitely be an investigation. To be cleared, to survive, we have to prove that he left here to return to the hotel.'

'But then there is the problem of the body,' put in Johnny, 'not to mention the fact that it has two .38-inch rounds in it from a British Enfield No2 service revolver.'

'So,' Marie summarised, 'the vehicle has to be found, away from here, without Brandt's body but somehow suggesting that he had driven it there. I think I have the answer.'

Johnny and Jean carried the body from the cottage back to the house. First, they removed Brandt's greatcoat, hat and sidearm then placed it in Jean's Citroën traction. Fortunately, it was the convertible model which made the task easier. They drove for about a kilometre along cart tracks that did not leave the estate's land before stopping in a good-sized wood. Even with two of them digging, it was well past midnight before they returned to the cottage. But they were content that *Hauptmann* Horst Brandt's body would never be found.

There was some argument over who would drive the *Kübelwagen*. But Johnny won in the end, pointing out that in case they were seen, it had to be driven by a man, and he was rather younger than Jean and looked more like Brandt. He would drive the *Kübelwagen* wearing Brandt's greatcoat and hat. Johnny knew the area was peaceful, and Marie told him that no one had seen a roadblock at night for quite some time. Even so, he replaced the two rounds fired from his revolver. Lucky for them, it was only a few kilometres along a quiet country lane. He stopped well short of his destination and went forward on foot.

It was as Jean had assured him. The old bridge over the River Huisne, which ran through Nogent, was deserted. Moreover, it was on one of two routes the German could have chosen to return to the hotel. He studied the ancient stone sides. It would be too dangerous to try driving off the bridge – he could not risk finishing up jammed half on and half off. There were trees along his side of the road but just a hedge opposite. Beyond that, the grass bank sloped down to the water at a fairly good angle. He would have to take a run at the hedge then brake as best he could – he did not want the vehicle to sink below the surface or float off downstream.

First, he snagged Brandt's greatcoat firmly inside the vehicle. His uniform cap he pushed under the driver's seat. It might be found, or it might not. Finally, he placed his own weapon and ammunition by the roadside. After a good look round, he restarted the engine. There was more than enough room to accelerate.

The *Kübelwagen* needed momentum, but *too fast* was his immediate thought as they crashed through the hedge. He braked but they were still going to launch into the water. In desperation, he tried a sharp handbrake turn. The vehicle slewed sideways, and the driver's side began to lift. It was going over, and he could be trapped underneath. The passenger side hit the water. It slowed the rollover for a fraction, then almost gracefully, the *Kübelwagen* inverted itself into the river. Johnny scrambled desperately and managed to push off his seat and into the river even as his own side hit the water. He had to swim away for a few frantic strokes before his head broke the surface.

The current was quite strong after the winter rains, and he staggered out of the water several yards downstream. He studied his handiwork. It could not have gone better. Long skid marks in the turf led to an upside-down *Kübelwagen* with just its floor pan, wheels and exhaust sticking out from the water, but it had settled firmly into the riverbed. Hastily he waded back in. Ducking down, he felt that the windscreen was bent and the glass shattered, but the top of the driver's door was partly clear; just a few inches at the back had sunk into the mud. As a final touch, he managed to pull it open.

Johnny was cold now. He squeezed water off his clothes as best he could, collected his firearm and ammunition, and set off at a squelching jog to where he knew Jean would be waiting.

Back at the farmhouse, Jean lent him a robe whilst Monique gave him a large cup of coffee heavily laced with brandy. He slowly warmed up as they rehearsed their story. But on one thing, they were agreed. Somehow Johnny now had to get away from the estate as soon as possible.

It was no surprise when another *Kübelwagen* drove up to the farmhouse just before midday. Two soldiers remained seated in the back.

'Herr Renaud, Frau Renaud,' he said politely. '*Oberleutnant* Kurt Köhler – we met briefly when you were our guest at the *Oktoberfest* party last year.' His French was workmanlike if a little hesitant.

'I remember you,' Jean replied. 'It is good to see you again, but what brings you so far out of town this morning?'

'I believe *Hauptmann* Brandt was your guest for dinner last evening,' he asked them, not answering Jean's question.

'He was *a* guest,' said Monique. 'Mademoiselle Laval also joined us. That's Marie, my husband's assistant. *Hauptmann* Brandt recently hinted that he would like to meet her again. We were only too happy to help, and it was an enjoyable evening. If you allow for women's intuition, *Herr Oberleutnant*, I think he is rather taken with her.' They had discussed this in the early hours of the morning. Her use of the present tense had been deliberate.

'Then I am sorry to tell you,' replied Köhler, 'that we fear something has happened to him.'

'Happened to him,' she repeated, 'what do you mean?'

'His vehicle was found upside down in the river. Locals reported it to us. There was no one inside it. Even now, we are searching for a body.'

Monique allowed herself to collapse into an armchair as if shocked by the news. 'Shall we all be seated?' suggested Jean. He had no idea that his wife was such a good actress.

'I shall have to break the news to Marie,' said Jean gravely. 'She will be upset.' The two men were still standing. 'Can I offer you refreshment? Perhaps a coffee and a glass of cognac? I think we could all do with it after such news.'

'But there is one more thing,' Köhler persisted. 'Your dinner party, at what time did it finish? At what time did your guests leave?'

'It was quite late. Well, late for us country people,' Jean told him. 'I couldn't give you an exact time, but somewhere between ten and eleven. Half-ten would not be too far out.'

'But we know,' said Köhler slowly, 'that the accident, which we assume it was, happened quite some time afterwards. Locals say they heard a crash in the early hours of this morning. In fact, not all that long before first light. But, of course, they did not investigate immediately because of the curfew. So that begs the question of what happened in the hours between leaving your dinner party and the accident.

'If, as you say, the *Hauptmann* was attracted to her, then I think I must also speak with Fraulein Laval,' he told them. 'Perhaps you would be so kind as to tell me where I might find her?'

'She has a cottage on the estate,' Monique informed him. 'It's not far.' She turned to her husband. 'Why don't you ask her to join us, darling, whilst I make the coffee?'

'I will not have time for coffee,' Köhler informed them. 'I must get back to the search. Also, there are reports I must make. But thank you anyway, Frau Renaud.' He clicked his heels and bowed formally to her, Jean noticed, rather than making the Nazi salute.

He turned to Jean. 'Herr Renaud, please show me the way to the cottage. It may be that a brief word with your assistant will clear everything up. Then I can be on my way.'

Jean managed to conceal his alarm. But there was no way he could reasonably refuse the German's request. The trouble was, Johnny would also be there. If they were caught outside, or the *Oberleutnant* even saw the English pilot, there was a risk of last night's history repeating itself. Not to mention the problem of the two soldiers still seated in the *Kübelwagen*.

As they approached the cottage, Jean thought about calling out an advance greeting then promptly dismissed the idea. First, it might well make the German suspicious, and second, they would both recognise his voice. There was every possibility that it might be Johnny who came to the door.

Getting closer, Jean stepped forward quickly from the *Oberleutnant*, knocked on the door and called out, 'Marie, you have a visitor.' To his intense relief, it was she who answered his call, half opening the door. Looking over her shoulder, Jean could not see Johnny, but Marie could see the German officer.

'This is *Oberleutnant* Köhler,' he told her quickly. 'Apparently, *Hauptmann* Brandt has gone missing.'

Köhler had no intention of allowing the Frenchman to control the meeting. 'May we come inside, Fraulein Laval?' he asked firmly, stepping forward.

She stepped back and opened the door more widely. 'Good morning, Jean, *Herr Oberleutnant*,' she said. 'You had better step this way.'

The room served as a living and dining area with a small kitchen off to one side. Jean was relieved to see that the door to the bedroom was closed. Marie indicated that they should sit round the kitchen table. 'Now, how can I help you?' she asked.

Köhler repeated the story of the accident he had given to the Renauds. 'But there is a time discrepancy,' he went on. 'Herr Renaud tells me that the dinner party broke up between ten and eleven. However, we also know that you and *Hauptmann* Brandt left together, but the accident did not occur until some considerable time later.' He sat back, seemingly awaiting an explanation.

Marie rested her hands together on the table and sat for a few moments as if collecting her thoughts. Finally, she glanced up at the officer before looking down again, as if embarrassed.

'I can help you there,' she began, deliberately speaking softly. 'Horst and I, that is to say, *Hauptmann* Brandt,' she added quickly as if deliberately correcting herself, 'left at the same time. He did not know I lived here, so he asked if he could offer me a lift home. However, when he discovered that I lived in this estate cottage, he insisted on escorting me to the door.' She deliberately looked fleetingly at the German before casting her eyes down again.

'He was very gallant,' she went on, 'and it had been a most enjoyable evening, but we had not had much opportunity to talk. I mean, just the two of us,' she added. 'I invited him in, made coffee, and we talked and talked about anything and everything. He was proud to serve his country, but I could tell that he was also missing his homeland.' She paused as if trying to decide what to say next. Finally, she looked up at the *Oberleutnant* and, this time, held his gaze.

'We do not have a relationship,' she told him, 'but he is an interesting man, and I enjoyed his company. He asked if he might call upon me again, and I told him that he could, that I would look forward to it. It was getting very late, and he had to work the next day, so he kissed my hand and took his leave.'

'And what time would that have been?' asked Köhler, quite gently.

'It would have been some time after two in the morning,' she replied. 'I can't be sure, but you may know how it is, when you are getting to know somebody new, you are enjoying their company and neither of you wants the evening to end. Does that help you?' she concluded.

The German turned to Jean. 'Herr Renaud,' he said evenly, '*Hauptmann* Brandt walked the lady home. But his vehicle was parked outside your house. How is it that even at that time in the morning, you did not hear him leave?'

Marie did not give him time to answer. 'You may have noticed that the drive slopes gently away from the house,' she informed him. 'I did not want Jean and Monique to think that I might have been indiscreet, even though absolutely nothing improper had taken place. I asked Horst to let his vehicle roll back down to the lane before starting the engine. He promised me that he would. I am not surprised that he was true to his word and protected my reputation. Please let me know what happens… the result of your search…' Her voice trailed off sadly.

'Thank you for confiding in me, Fraulein Laval,' said Köhler gently. 'You have been most helpful. And please rest assured that my report will continue to respect your reputation.'

She waited for several minutes, watching them walk along the path back to the estate house, before opening the bedroom door. Johnny was replacing his revolver in a bedside cabinet. Marie left the cottage door open so that they could hear the departure of the *Kübelwagen*. Half an hour later, over a glass of Crémant to soothe frayed nerves, Jean raised a toast.

'You were both magnificent,' he told them, 'but remind me never to play poker with you ladies.'

After a light lunch, all four of them retired for a couple of hours to catch up on sleep after an exhausting and terrifying might.

*

It was Jean Renaud who solved Johnny's problem. They were together again at the main house for a late dinner. 'I used to have contacts at the British Embassy in Paris before the war,' he told the young airman. 'I served in Intelligence during the last one, so I made it clear that I had facilities that would be useful in any future conflict. Hence the presence of Marie on this estate. But before they pulled out, I was introduced to the "cousins", which is just unsubtle spy-speak for our American counterparts. As it happens, I also have the contract to supply their embassy with wine, which gives me every excuse to visit. So I'll go and see them. The Germans are particularly sensitive about not wanting to upset America, for obvious reasons, so with an American passport, you should have no difficulty crossing the border into Switzerland.'

'Do you think they will play ball, sir?' asked Johnny. 'That must be breaking just about every diplomatic rule and regulation in the book. There could be a hell of a stink if...' He broke off, not wanting to suggest that anything might go wrong.

'I'm not sure they would do it for anyone else,' Jean replied. 'But I am already a known asset, and they need me, probably as much for the wine as the information I can give them. If they demure, I'll just tell them that they'll have to buy wine from the Germans for the rest of the war,' he said with a wry smile. 'I think somehow that will persuade them! I have an appropriate camera. We'll take Johnny's photo first thing in the morning.'

He was as good as his word. Jean was away for two days. When he returned, they reassembled at the main house for dinner, after which he handed Johnny an envelope. 'American passport,' he said bluntly, 'suitably scuffed up and with a few neutral stamps. Also, accreditation papers – you're a junior political researcher employed by the embassy. I couldn't get you diplomatic immunity, but your identity will be confirmed if anyone phones the number on that business card. I also have some clothes for you, plus shoes, with New York labels. Luckily the ambassador's driver is about the same size as you. His boss had to promise to replace them before he was persuaded to hand them over.

'From Switzerland,' he went on, 'our people will fly you home either via Ireland or Gibraltar. All the Americans ask in return is that once you are safely on British soil, you destroy the documents. And that although the Royal Air Force will want to debrief you, please tell them you have given your word to say no more than that you made it out of France with some local assistance. Other than that, no more details. But I'm going to give you a name and a telephone number. He was my contact before we pulled out of France. If you come under too much pressure, ask that he be consulted. By the time you get back to England, we will have made him aware of the situation. And he has a lot of influence. If you do need to phone him, I think you will find that the uniformed end of the establishment will back off pretty quickly.

'Now,' he said, placing his palm down on the table, 'anyone for a cognac? And we'll drink to Johnny's safe return!'

'Just one,' said Monique, looking at Marie with a sympathetic smile. 'Then these two young people can escape for their last night in France together. But as we say, it must be *au revoir*.'

*

'Where the hell have you been?' demanded Squadron Leader Miles Beckett, although the hint of a smile played around his lips. 'I send you off on a simple mission, and you don't turn up till half a year later. Stradishall not good enough for you? I hear you've been swanning around in the South of France.'

Johnny decided to play it with a straight bat – almost. 'Actually, sir, it's only been a few weeks, and it was *central* France; before you ask, the weather was lovely.'

'But you arrived in Dublin days ago. Had a phone call from some woman in the Supply Ministry, of all places.'

Johnny knew that. Seated in Doreen Jackman's office, she had been happy for him to listen in. From Dublin, he had been flown to London for an intensive debrief. His American wardrobe had been exchanged gratefully for a good English one, courtesy of Messrs Gieves, which, to his delight, had cost him absolutely nothing.

'All I'm allowed to tell you, sir, is that I was hit by flak on the way over, sort of crash-landed, although my passenger and I were all right, and that the resistance got me back though Switzerland. Took a while. The wine and food were pretty good, though...'

The squadron leader was too old a hand to be wound up by a flight lieutenant. 'And another thing,' he went on, 'we had a signal from the Air Ministry. Apparently, you have broken your duck. You have been credited with a Heinkel He 111, and no questions to be asked. Who told them to do that, I have no idea – it seems you have friends in high places. But what you were doing taking on a Heinkel with one of my Lysanders, God only knows, because I'm damned if I do.'

Johnny said nothing.

After a couple of seconds of slightly awkward silence, the squadron leader looked out of the window at thick low cloud and steady drizzle. 'Bloody Irish weather,' he cursed. 'There'll be no flying tonight, which is just as well. When they heard you were coming back, your fellow officers decided to lay on a bit of a bash. I'll give you a lift over to the mess. I have a feeling it will be a long lunchtime.'

CHAPTER 30

Not long after their return from Le Touquet, Liliane asked Serge and Nicole to lunch. She served rabbit, snared on the farm and casseroled with red wine and a few of their own vegetables. By mutual agreement, discussion was shelved until the last of the *jus* had been mopped from their plates with crusty bread, and Serge had set a bottle of Yves' calvados on the table. They had been together only a couple of times since the raid, preferring to keep a low profile, and only on one occasion had the retrieval of their weaponry been mentioned.

'I'm against it,' said Liliane, opening the discussion. 'We still have what we need from the first drop, and if necessary, the RAF could always make another. After all, it's not as though we have anything immediate planned.'

'Maybe not,' conceded Serge, 'but we now have a small unit that could be re-formed at any time, and we only have just enough weapons as it is. Sooner or later, we are going to need more.'

'Two points,' put in Tadzio. 'First, collecting what's already here, assuming it's still where we left it, is probably no more dangerous than organising an airdrop. And it certainly saves a precious RAF mission, not to mention the risk of losing an aircraft and possibly a pilot.

'And second,' he continued, 'those weapons will deteriorate if we just leave them. Don't forget you deliberately didn't waste time stripping and cleaning them. We were too keen to clear the area. So they haven't been oiled and wrapped for storage. I can't help feeling it's a sin just to let them go to waste.'

No one spoke for several seconds. It was Nicole who broke the silence. 'There's another thing to consider,' she said quietly. 'Whilst it's long enough now for any search to have been called off, it will soon be spring. I can't imagine there will be much – if any – sailing whilst there's a war on, but as the weather warms up, club members will want to check on their dinghies to see if they need any maintenance after the winter. If the owner of the one we used to hide the weapons is amongst them, I can't imagine what might happen.'

'Perhaps we should vote on it,' Serge offered, only to be rewarded with a glare from Liliane. 'I say we do it,' he finished bluntly.

'I'm the only one here acting under orders,' Tadzio told them, 'and I feel it's my duty to try to retrieve them.'

Liliane turned questioningly to Nicole, who shook her head. 'I'm not going to vote,' she said. Her decision would have been to go ahead, but the motion was already carried, so her abstention would be less likely to hurt Liliane's feelings.

'How do you think you are going to transport a load of weapons from Étaples under the noses of the Germans?' asked Liliane. 'It's in a controlled zone. There's every chance you will be stopped and searched. You don't even have the right documents to be there.'

Serge shook his head. 'Don't forget. We'll be in German uniforms, armed and driving a *Kübelwagen*. I doubt the *Boche* will worry about one of their own vehicles being on the road.'

'The only issue remaining is who goes,' said Nicole. 'I know Serge is against it, but you have a far better chance of sneaking in and out using the back roads and country lanes with my local knowledge. A combination of our disguise plus me as a guide offers the best chance of success.'

Her announcement came as no surprise. 'Agreed,' said Tadzio eventually. 'Serge, your job is to put the *Kübelwagen* back together. I'll train Nicole up on the Schmeisser. It's about eighty kilometres each way. We'll try to go there and back in one day. But if for any reason we need to hole up overnight, we can use the barn or even Nicole's house. Be back the next day at the latest.'

For different reasons, both Liliane and Serge were less than delighted, but they accepted Tadzio's decision with good grace.

Serge watched with dismay as Nicole snipped off almost all of her hair. Lustrous dark blonde curls that had fallen to her shoulders now lay on the kitchen floor. Next, she styled it into a military short back and sides. She then tailored the smaller of the two uniforms to fit as well as possible. It lay between them on the kitchen table. She stood to take off her skirt and slip. Serge wondered if he was expected to look away. Nicole deliberately suppressed a smile as he stared, fixated, at the sight of her legs and knickers. They had lived very amicably together since Étaples. But he had not made any form of advance or gesture of intimacy, although she had caught him looking at her from time to time. He was definitely interested. Nicole had concluded that he was nervous and, perhaps surprisingly for a former legionnaire, almost certainly not very experienced with women.

'My breasts would be too obvious if I wore a *brassière*,' she said matter-of-factly, unbuttoning her blouse and undressing till she was naked from the waist up. Calmly, she put on the dead German's uniform shirt, now washed and with the bullet hole patched. She pulled on the trousers and jacket, slipped into the greatcoat, put on the hat, and lifted the collar as she would against the cold wind in an open *Kübelwagen*. The weight of the uniform flattened her shape. She announced that she would dirty her face on the day to disguise her feminine complexion. 'So what do you think?' she asked.

He had to admit that she looked the part even from where he sat. Slowly, she took off the entire uniform and walked forward until she stood right in front of his chair. 'If you wish, I will get dressed again,' she said softly, 'but I don't have to.' He stood, moving her back just a little, and began to unbutton his shirt. Nicole pushed down and kicked off her knickers, then perched on the edge of the kitchen table, her feet just touching the floor. She leant back, hands behind her, as he undressed. Her legs wrapped around him as he pushed gently. When he lifted her effortlessly, her arms were over his shoulders. It had been such a long time. She climaxed almost instantly as he burst forth inside her. Afterwards, he took her hand and led her to his bed. They made love again, slowly this time, and with infinite pleasure.

She was thinking of this a few days later as, with Tadzio driving, they were on their way to Étaples. An MP38 lay between her knees, its stock folded and the muzzle resting on the floor. He had given her an afternoon of instruction. Nicole had proved a good shot. The weapon was not designed to fire single rounds, but she could put the required short three- or four-round bursts into a target at twenty metres, with a grouping that almost always fell under one hand.

She was equally adept at changing the forward box magazine, which also served as a handgrip and held thirty-two nine-millimetre Parabellum cartridges. Even so, Nicole was slightly unnerved by Tadzio's warning never to bang the stock or the butt against anything. There was no safety, he told her, and this could jar back the bolt far enough to discharge a round from a cocked weapon. 'And don't put your hand on the barrel during or after firing,' he added. 'It'll be as hot as hell!' But as he had pointed out, she would be using it only as an absolute last resort.

Her thoughts went back to Serge and the conversation after their lovemaking. He had admitted to having very little association with women in his past life – in Paris because he was still young and in the Legion, because they were warned that it was an offence to incapacitate themselves with venereal disease. However, some of his comrades were quite prepared to take their chances. He also told her that he had taken a great liking to her way back in Étaples but had been somewhat in awe from the outset. She was an upper-class, highly educated young woman. He was just an old soldier, with no schooling past the age of fourteen and now just a garage hand. Not so upper-class after all, she smiled to herself, when she was leaning on a kitchen table with a bare backside and her legs wide open.

Tadzio saw her half-smile. He guessed whom and potentially what she was thinking about. When he had turned up next morning to help Serge put the *Kübelwagen* back together, the big, usually morose Frenchman was, for the first time since they had met, not sporting at least two days of stubble. His light-olive skin was clean and smooth. With his slightly hooked Arab nose, he looked positively dashing, even more so when a frequent grin showed perfect teeth. Tadzio had never seen him so clean, smart and happy. He was sure the reason for this was now seated beside him.

They had a map. Serge's father had left behind a collection of them, taking only those that would guide him to Paris and further south. The roads were almost empty, the occasional wood or charcoal-powered vehicle or horse and cart holding them up from time to time. But Nicole's local knowledge of twisting country lanes proved invaluable in that they met no other military vehicles or roadblocks, but this also made for slow progress. It was lunchtime before they were in the nearest lane to the barn. Nicole opened a gate, and Tadzio parked behind a thick hedge. They would walk over two fields and approach the barn on foot, fetching up the *Kübelwagen* only when ready to load.

Tadzio had Nicole wait a short distance away while he checked the building. It was deserted. He waved her over, and they entered together.

'It all looks the same,' Nicole whispered, then laughed. There was probably no one within half a kilometre of the place.

'Everything looks untouched. Even Klaus's Peugeot Légère is still here,' she said, setting off towards the dinghy at the rear where they had stashed everything.'

'Wait,' he called out anxiously. She froze. 'What would you do,' he asked, 'if you were German and you had discovered the weapons?' He did not wait for an answer. 'You would probably remove them, leave the car where it was and booby-trap either the building or the dinghy,' he told her. 'Come and stand back here, Nicole, and I'll make the approach. At least I know what to look for.'

It was shaded in the barn, even with the big double doors open, and there were no lights. Tadzio went outside and returned with a long, very thin branch broken off from the hedgerow. Holding it loosely in front of him between his thumb and index finger, he walked slowly forwards. The floor was concrete, so he had no fear of personnel mines, and the loosely held branch would bump back against a tripwire without setting off the attached explosive. After a few minutes, he had reached and circled the dinghy. The cover appeared to be exactly as Serge had left it, but that had been a few weeks ago. He couldn't be sure.

There was a long painter dangling from the dinghy's bow. He untied it, joined it to one of the tie-downs hanging loose from the cover and retreated as far as it would allow. Lying on the floor, he pulled gently. The canvas came almost completely off before it snagged. No matter. He inspected the contents. They had not been disturbed. 'Come over,' he called to Nicole, 'but just to be sure, walk exactly the same way through the barn.' He lifted out one of the Thompsons. 'Been fired,' he said, 'and it needs a pull-through, but barely any sign of rust.'

He looked at his watch. 'Took longer to get here than I thought,' he said. 'I'm not sure we have enough time to fetch the *Kübelwagen*, load this lot and get home before dark. And even if we are in uniform, I wouldn't want to get stopped by a curfew patrol, particularly as we get closer to the village. I vote we stay the night and start early in the morning.'

Nicole agreed. 'We can use my house,' she offered. 'I've brought the keys. I would love to be able to collect a few more clothes – even with Serge carrying my pack, I couldn't take all that much last time.' She sensed that he was happy with the idea. 'We could leave the *Kübelwagen* in the barn,' she added, 'and then it's just a short walk home.'

They took their weapons and a backpack containing a few essentials. Approaching from the rear of the property, Tadzio left her on the edge of the smallholding and approached the building. It seemed to be unoccupied. He worked his way slowly round to the front, looking through the windows.

'Someone's been inside,' he told her, 'looks like a forced entry, but the door has been nailed shut again. I'm pretty sure the house has been empty for quite some time. We can go in through the kitchen.'

Nicole was dismayed. Her house had indeed been occupied, at least for a while. There were empty wine bottles on the now-stained kitchen table. Dirty plates and cutlery had been thrown into the sink. Several cupboard doors had been left open. The whole house was a mess, drawers open, contents thrown to the floor, picture frames pulled apart and precious photographs tossed aside, some of them damaged.

'The bastards!' exclaimed Nicole.

'The house has been thoroughly searched,' replied Tadzio. 'But it could have been a whole lot worse. It looks as if a few men stayed here for a while, hoping you would return. I suspect that one of your neighbours fixed the front door after they had gone.'

'We can tidy up the worst of it,' she suggested.

'I wouldn't,' Tadzio countered. 'They probably check on the house from time to time. They would then see through the windows that things had been put back to normal. If it looks as if they have let you slip through their fingers, they might put a match to the place just for the hell of it.' He thought for a couple of seconds, then, 'I reckon we make ourselves comfortable for the night but leave everything just as we found it. You can still take a few things, if you wish – I doubt anyone's taken any sort of inventory, so that won't be noticed.'

'At least I can change into my own clothes for the evening,' she replied.

Back in the kitchen, they ate some of the rations they had brought with them. Nicole's drinks cupboard was empty, but she retrieved two bottles of wine from her garden shed, where she had stored a case of red underneath an upturned wheelbarrow. It had been one of many offerings from Klaus Huber, and there hadn't been room at the time in her kitchen cupboard. If the outhouses had been searched at all, it was done hastily. They were into their second glass when there was an urgent knocking on the door. They both picked up their weapon and took cover behind the kitchen table.

More urgent knocking. '*C'est qui?*' called out Nicole.

'*C'est moi, Adrienne,*' came the reply.

'It's Madame Toussaint, from next door,' she whispered.

Tadzio moved alongside the door and signalled that Nicole should let her in. He closed it behind them as the two women moved into the room. She turned quickly for an elderly lady. '*Mon Dieu,*' she exclaimed, seeing an armed Tadzio in German uniform.

'It's all right, Madame Toussaint,' Nicole hastened to explain, 'he's with me, and he's from England. But how did you know we were here?'

'It was pure chance,' she replied. 'I couldn't find *Minette* – my kitty.' She translated for Tadzio's benefit.'

'Thank you, Madame, but we can speak French,' he replied in her own language.

'Very well,' she continued, 'normally I would not go out after dark, but she had not come home for her supper. So I took a torch to the bottom of the garden, and I saw just the faintest gleam of light from behind your curtains. There had been no vehicles, so I did not think it was the *Boche*. It had to be you.'

'Did you find your cat?' asked Tadzio politely.

Madame Toussaint shook her head. 'No, but she will probably be on my doorstep in the morning. And in any case, I wanted to see Nicole.

'After you left,' she told her, 'I heard about the attack on the airfield. It was all round the village. Then the Germans turned up. They questioned me, but I told them I had not seen you for days. They went away but left some men in your house. I think there were three of them. Obviously, they were waiting to see if you returned. Finally, after two or three days, they left.

'I managed to nail up your door,' she went on. 'There are some in this village I do not trust. After that, the Germans came back now and then, but only in daylight. When they first saw the door nailed up, I told them I had done it and suggested they could look through the windows. I was told that if you came back, and I did not report it, I would be shot as a traitor.'

'Don't worry,' said Nicole, reassuring the elderly woman, 'we will leave in the morning, and I shall not return. Well, not unless the Germans are long gone,' she added.

'I would never have told them anyway,' Madame Toussaint said proudly, with a hint of bravado. 'Is there anything you need, just for tonight? You can stay with me if you wish.'

'Thank you,' said Tadzio, 'but we have everything here. It is better that you do not place yourself at risk.'

'Then I shall go back next door,' came the reply. 'God bless you, Nicole, and all the men say that it was very good, what happened at the airfield. The officer in charge and quite a few of his men were killed. I'll bid you good night.'

She rose to leave, missing the look on Nicole's face. 'I didn't know Klaus had been killed,' she said, closing the door.

'Must have happened in the firefight,' Tadzio replied, choosing his words carefully. The German had been alive when most of them had left. Serge was the last man out. He knew instantly what the legionnaire had done and why. Klaus Huber's off-duty association with Nicole would not have been a secret. His fellow officers probably just assumed they were having an affair. So he had shot Huber to protect her. But obviously, Serge had not told Nicole that Huber was dead. Tomorrow Tadzio would tell his friend that he was off the hook.

They did not make up the beds but just slept on the mattresses where they lay on the floor, dividing the night so that one of them kept watch whilst the other grabbed a few hours' sleep. Even so, they both felt fairly well rested when she locked up soon after first light. Everything at the barn was as they had left it. They loaded the *Kübelwagen* using the floor-well behind the front seats and concealed everything with the dinghy's canvas cover.

The drive through the coastal zone was uneventful. But on a country lane leading to the central square of a village west of Arras, they faced a German lorry and several soldiers – not manning a roadblock but standing around in the shade. There was room to pass, but it might prove awkward if they were flagged down. Failing to stop could attract a lot of firepower. Nicole reached down for her weapon.

Tadzio slowed almost to a crawl, but placed a restraining hand on her arm. To her surprise, he sounded the horn several times and waved. '*Morgen,*' he shouted – 'Morning.' To her surprise, the men waved back, also shouting a greeting. Nicole returned their waves. Once they had passed the lorry, Tadzio gradually accelerated, and they were soon out of sight. No attempt had been made to mount up and follow them.

'That was close,' exclaimed Nicole with relief.

'Not really,' Tadzio reasoned. 'I don't know what they were doing, maybe just having a smoke break. But when you are politely loathed by the entire population, it must get to you after a while. They just reacted naturally to a shout and a wave from a couple of friendly faces.' He grinned at her. 'Human nature!'

Tadzio slowed as they approached Serge's garage and checked that there was no traffic in sight, vehicles or pedestrians, before turning in and parking behind the house. Serge came out immediately, and Nicole ran into an embrace. Tadzio just stood by the *Kübelwagen* and smiled. He had been right. 'Do I have to unload this lot myself?' he asked eventually.

'We'll put the wagon in the barn,' Serge said. 'Then have a drink to celebrate. After that, Nicole, perhaps you would take a walk and let Liliane know that you are both back safe. Tadzio and I will hide the loot and start taking the vehicle to pieces. We should have everything stashed away before nightfall. Then we'll join you at the farm and really celebrate!'

By the time they reached the farm, there was a smell from something delicious pot roasting slowly in the range. '*Coq au vin*,' Liliane told them, and then, for Tadzio's benefit, 'chicken, homemade blackberry wine, vegetables. It wants another hour yet, so there's time for an apéritif.' They stayed the night to avoid breaking the curfew, with Nicole and Serge in the spare room. But it was just as well, she reflected. Serge might have had just a little difficulty walking home.

CHAPTER 31

Hedda resumed her embassy routine, but there had been nothing significant to report since she had sent evidence of the Dachau atrocities back to London. Although she and Werner were lovers, they had retained separate apartments in the Gestapo building. Paris in 1941 was an exceptionally enjoyable posting for a middle-ranking Nazi officer, and as much as Hedda was acutely aware of her real purpose in life, she could not help enjoying all that the city had to offer. As Head of Chancery Herr Richter was a pleasant and considerate superior, although she was aware that his relationship with Ambassador Abetz was, to say the least, difficult.

Gerhard Richter was an old-school, professional diplomat, educated and cultured. He spoke French efficiently and, she had discovered, excellent English. Ambassador Otto Abetz, by contrast, was a Party man with the rank of *SS-Brigadeführer* who owed his appointment to a close friendship with Minister of Foreign Affairs, Joachim von Ribbentrop. It grated with the ambassador that he had not been given the rank of *SS-Gruppenführer*, which meant that although senior by appointment, he did not outrank the other senior officer in Paris, *SS-Brigadeführer* Kurt von Scheuen.

Von Scheuen's responsibilities included security and finding labour for the Fatherland. The ambassador's brief, however, centred more on looting the country for works of art and wealth in general, particularly that belonging to Jews. Abetz was also quite sure that his Head of Chancery, with his *Hochdeutsch*, Savile Row elegance and diplomatic affectations, deliberately gave the impression of looking down at him. Although his assistant, the girl Anneliese, seemed pleasant enough. But high German accent or not, these days, the Party had the power. A fact of which he enjoyed reminding Richter from time to time.

Werner put on a jazz record at his apartment, as always played quietly because the Party disapproved of them. Hedda was finishing her glass of wine whilst he did the washing-up. It was a miserable evening, windy and raining, so they had decided to stay in and enjoy a quiet supper. She was wondering if later he would take her to bed.

'I meant to tell you,' he said as he came through from the small kitchen, 'I have to stay in Paris for the next week or so. The *Brigadeführer's* been recalled to Berlin, and I have to stand in for him. Hasn't happened before, but I suppose there's a first time for everything.'

'Interesting,' she remarked, 'because Head of Chancery told me the other day that the ambassador had also been recalled, although that's not unusual. I wonder if they are going for the same reason?' She thought nothing more of it.

Both the ambassador and the *Brigadeführer* were away for most of the week. The day following their return, Herr Richter asked her to stay on for a few minutes after the ambassador and Frau Becker had left for the day. She noticed a file on his desk that she knew from its cover markings to be highly classified.

'There will need to be a small addition to your next report,' he told her. 'The Führer requires additional military resources. France is quiet. There is no danger of any attack from the British, and the resistance is more or less under control. I am not in favour of shooting civilians for every German killed or injured, but nevertheless, it is effective.'

'Does this have anything to do with the ambassador's recall?' she asked. It was a perfectly reasonable question and aroused no suspicion.

'*Ja*,' he replied. 'In February, the Führer had to send massive reinforcements to North Africa to support the Italians after their 10th Army was virtually wiped out. But assembling Erwin Rommel's *Afrika Korps* has denuded our reserves. They must be reconstituted. At the conference, all occupied countries were instructed to determine the minimum force levels required to retain control and security. This information will enable the High Command to assemble a new formation in Germany.

That evening, Werner reported that he, too, had been given the same explanation. 'I might even be redeployed myself,' he added. It was not good news.

'The *Brigadeführer* was not best pleased,' he went on. 'He hoped to see his twin brother, who apparently does a similar job in Warsaw. But, there was nobody from Poland at the conference.'

Werner opened another bottle of wine, and they sat listening to a concert on the wireless. It was only the following day, his almost throwaway remark struck her as unusual. If the new formation was to be assembled in Germany, why had all other senior military officers and ambassadors been summoned, but not Poland's? After all, the country was relatively well subdued, with German forces occupying the western half up to the Bug River and the Russians on the eastern side. It would have been only natural to withdraw at least some units from the heavy *Wehrmacht* presence there.

So why leave all their forces in Poland? Russia, she knew, was not considered a threat. Moreover, the Molotov-Ribbentrop Pact, signed in August 1939, agreed that there would be no military conflict between the two states for ten years. Thus, Germany was able to invade western Poland in September 1939 without fear of Russian reprisal. Stalin had simply ordered an invasion of eastern Poland sixteen days later, citing the 'Spheres of Influence' accord also determined within the Pact.

The more she thought about it, the more Head of Chancery's explanation, whilst plausible, did not ring true. She was no military expert, but common sense suggested that the only reason for the full force level to be retained in Poland would be if that were the country from which they were to be deployed. Could that be why the troops were not returning to Germany? She suspected the true answer lay inside the folder that she had seen on Herr Richter's desk.

Her desk and Head of Chancery's faced inwards from the outside wall. They had no outer view when seated, but the light flooding in from windows behind them helped when reading. The desks were set well forward, leaving more than enough room behind them for two captains' chairs. Between them sat a steel filing cabinet against the wall. Access to both chairs meant passing in front of the cabinet, as there was insufficient room on the other side of each desk. Routinely Herr Richter unlocked it first thing in the morning, and whilst he was in the office, it was left open. But if he went out for any reason, it was always locked. Usually, she handed over any classified material she was working on so that he could secure it before they left for the day. Wednesdays, his 'Sports Afternoon', and Thursdays, when she usually worked late on the report, she would place classified documents in a large envelope, seal it, sign across the flap and hand it to the embassy's duty officer to put in his own safe till morning.

The security cabinet was protected by a lock mechanism opened by dialling a sequence of four pairs of numbers known only to her superior. At least, that was the theory. But Herr Richter had a habit of sometimes muttering one of the combination pairs under his breath to help remember them. She had not attempted to access the cabinet previously. It was too great a risk when she did not even know if it contained particularly useful material. But she did know three of the four pairs of numbers: eighty-eight, eleven and sixteen. That made sense, almost certainly his date of birth. But he had never revealed the final number, presumably because once entered, all he had to do was swing open the door.

She needed to look over his shoulder when next he dialled the combination. It would be too obvious to stand there whilst he went through the entire sequence. The next morning, she arrived for work a little earlier. As soon as he had taken off his hat and overcoat, she picked up a file from her desk and stood in the office doorway, as if looking for Frau Becker, who had yet to arrive. As usual, he stood before the cabinet. She watched him dial the first two numbers, then walked up behind him whilst he dialled the third.

Unable to reach her chair as he was blocking the way, Hedda turned to her right, placed the file on the side of her desk and opened it, leaning forward slightly as she did so. Herr Richter was now slightly behind and to her left as he rotated the dial. She turned her head so that she could just see his hand in her peripheral vision. The last number appeared to be fifteen. Perhaps that might have been the year he married. Either way, when he opened the door, she was still standing facing the side of her desk, document in hand, innocently reading something from the file.

Now that she had the combination, there was the problem of access. A Wednesday was out of the question. Herr Richter might be out, but there was always the chance that Frau Becker might walk into the office. Or even the ambassador, who had his own office entrance but sometimes used the connecting door. He was also aware that only Head of Chancery knew the combination. So it would have to be a Thursday evening.

Hedda remained at her desk well into early evening on Wednesday, hours after Richter had departed for his afternoon off. If asked, she would simply say that she had wanted to work on the extra input required for this next report. In reality, she did not know what the top-secret file would reveal, but she wanted to create time to study it on Thursday evening. Consequently, when Herr Richter bid her a courteous 'goodnight' on Thursday afternoon, telling her as he always did that she should try not to work too late, the report was almost finished. She had only another hour's work to do, and in any case, she did not want to open the cabinet before everyone working nearby had left the building. The ambassador had left his office a good hour ago. Finally, she set aside her finished report, checked that the outer office and typing section was empty, closed their office door and faced the security cabinet.

She rotated the dial this way and that to the first three numbers, then finally changed direction to align the mark onto fifteen. But when she tried the handle, the door would not budge. She forced down a rising sense of panic. Perhaps she had not seen fifteen after all. She gave the dial a random spin, as she had seen Herr Richter do every time he locked it, then repeated the sequence, ending with fourteen. Again, the same result. She would try sixteen, then thirteen and seventeen, but she would have to give up if that did not work. Then... success – and the door swung open. Perhaps an about-to-be Frau Richter had walked down the aisle in nineteen sixteen.

She extracted the file, almost closed the door then settled at her desk. The first paragraphs headed *Unternehmen Barbarossa* took her breath away. Less than two years after signing a non-aggression pact, Germany was planning to invade the Soviet Union!

It was worse than that. Preparation had even begun towards the end of 1940, under the codename 'Operation Otto', but Hitler had not approved the plan and demanded another, this time to be named 'Operation Barbarossa', after the twelfth-century Holy Roman Emperor Frederick Barbarossa.

She read that the strategic aim was to occupy western Russia. The country itself was dismissed, with typical German arrogance, as backward and primitive. Operation Barbarossa would provide a considerable resource of agricultural produce to feed Germany, not least from the grain baskets of Ukraine. Some of the population would be used as slave labour, either in situ or to relieve the shortage in Germany's industries. A huge bonus would be the acquisition of oil reserves in the Caucasus. Any existing urban populations no longer deemed necessary would simply be starved to death. The conquered territory would eventually be repopulated: *Lebensraum* for future German generations.

In the file, the military input took the view that whilst soldiers of the Red Army fought well, their officer class had all but disappeared in the 1930s purges, and their replacements were poorly trained and incompetent. The German generals believed that the Russian forces would not retreat into the interior. Ukraine, the Baltic States, and the Moscow and Leningrad regions were vital to the Red Army for supply reasons, thus offering the Axis troops a quick victory similar to the blitzkrieg so successful in France and the Low Countries.

With victory in Russia, Hitler's view was that Britain, eventually facing not only Germany's existing forces in western Europe but also massive reinforcements withdrawn from the east, would have no choice but to sue for peace. Even so, whilst German units were already deploying in Poland, a deception plan in the English Channel and Norway, involving training exercises with naval and air assets, was intended to support German claims that Britain was the real target.

The operation was scheduled to begin on 15th May, with the proviso that it might be postponed to 22nd June, due to continuing activity in the Balkans and an unusually wet spring that had left many rivers at full flood. This latter date, opined the generals, who had studied Napoleon's defeat, was the latest that would allow then to reach Moscow before the onset of the Russian winter. In all, plus of 153 divisions would advance into Russia, the largest and most powerful invasion force in history.

Her thoughts reeling from what she had just read, Hedda knew that she had to send the information back to London immediately. Photographs would have been ideal, but she could not afford to delay even for a week so that she could use a camera. It would have to be a précis. She began to type...

An hour later, she returned the file to the cabinet, taking care to place it exactly as found. Such were the thoughts swirling in her head that she almost made the mistake of adding her report before remembering that it had to go to the duty officer. With a sigh of relief, she spun the dial and checked that the door was now locked. Shortly after nine, she left the building, two folded sheets of paper in her underwear. Tomorrow, after lunch, she would mark the bench. If the chalk lines sloped one way, they signified a brush-pass. If the other, it meant a dead letter drop.

Hedda was exhausted when she let herself into her apartment. They had arranged that she would go to Werner's once she was finished at the embassy. He had promised to make a cold supper and would listen to his gramophone records or the wireless whilst awaiting her return. But first, she folded two sheets of paper and placed them inside a cheap powder compact, the contents of which had been removed. Uncertain where to leave it, she changed into more comfortable clothes and just stuffed the compact into a cardigan pocket. Taking a deep breath, she closed the door behind her and walked along the corridor.

Werner sensed that she was preoccupied with something but did not ask any questions. Hedda was rarely her usual cheerful self after working late on a Thursday evening. So he was not at all surprised when she drank rather more than her customary two or three glasses of wine, announced that she had a headache, kissed him goodnight rather absent-mindedly, and retired to her own flat and bed. His consolation prize was a Bach Brandenburg Concerto – number five, his favourite – and a couple of glasses of a decent Armagnac.

She arrived the next morning nursing a slight hangover, but again before Herr Richter. She wanted to see him open the cabinet, which he did perfectly smoothly, before removing a now-familiar file. There was absolutely nothing to suggest that he had noticed anything unusual. She had retrieved her weekly report and placed it on his desk. 'The Army is submitting their information through their own channels,' she informed him, 'but I have included a copy as an Annex to ours. I'm no expert on the *Wehrmacht*,' she added, 'but I have a feeling that they are going to be asked to think again. They don't seem to be offering up very much.'

'I know how many divisions the Führer requires,' came the reply, 'so your observation is very astute. But at least the Gestapo have come up with the required numbers. Speaking of which, how are you and that boyfriend of yours getting on? If he gets posted back to Germany, I hope you will not be thinking about joining him. The ambassador has a very good opinion of your work, as do I. He'll go through your report this morning, but it will be up to your usual high standard, and these days, both of us have the luxury of being able to just sign it off. So well done.'

'Thank you,' she said simply. 'And I hope Werner does not have to return to Germany. But even if he does, I don't think I want to apply for a transfer.'

'I'm glad to hear it,' came the response, and he began to work through her latest offering. Ten minutes later, he took it through the connecting door. 'He'll just skim it,' he said on his return. 'I bet you it's back within ten minutes.' In fact, it took six.

By lunchtime, she had waded through a small mountain of files in her 'in' tray. Hedda no longer waited to be invited to take the afternoon off; it had become part of her routine. She wished Head of Chancery a pleasant weekend and departed shortly after one o'clock.

On the way to the park, she purchased a magazine and, seated on her usual bench, pretended to read it. Several people walked past – two nannies pushing prams side by side and chattering, an elderly couple with a dog, one or two individuals, but they all disappeared from sight. After a quarter of an hour, she was confident that she was not being observed. She turned and, using the magazine as a shield, placed three sloping chalk marks on the top wooden slat of the bench. Urgent. Too bulky for radio transmission. A dead letter box. And tomorrow.

The compact, mercifully, was still in her cardigan pocket inside her wardrobe. Werner would be out that evening and most of Saturday, running some operation, but they would go out for lunch on Sunday. Hedda left after breakfast wearing her one pair of slacks, a warm cardigan and – unusually – a pair of tennis pumps. If anything went wrong, as a last resort, at least she could run.

She decided to walk and window-shop, slowly, so that she would arrive just before lunchtime. It also allowed her to practise her tradecraft. She was not being followed. It was a reasonably modest hotel, used but not entirely commandeered by the Germans for middle-ranking staff. The bar and restaurant, at least, were also open to civilians. Hedda ordered a glass of wine at the bar and took it to a window table.

After a while, she ordered another and left it on the table whilst she went to the ladies' room, which she knew to be empty as she had been watching. She entered the middle of five cubicles, locked the door behind her, stood on the toilet lid and placed her compact on the flat top of the cistern, in the centre and back against the wall. Finally, she used the facility, pulled the chain, made sure the compact had not moved, washed her hands and returned to her table. A few minutes later, she was back on the street.

It was late evening, and Werner was still not back. She had made supper and was listening to the wireless when there came an urgent knock on the door. She let him in but could see from his expression something was wrong.

'We mounted an operation today,' he began immediately, at the same time moving to a side table and pouring himself a large brandy. He turned to face her. 'We have been watching a particular individual for some time. We think he's no more than a courier, but we were hoping he would lead us to someone further up the resistance chain: he's a chemist by the name of Lucien Corbet.'

For a couple of seconds Hedda tried to remember where she had heard the name. 'I met him once,' she said quickly. 'He was at Simone Faucher's place when I went home early one afternoon.'

'Then he could well have been the other shooter when we were attacked,' said Werner. 'But either way, we now think he knew he was being watched. He was very clever – went out earlier this morning, and we were following. There were some countermeasures, which made us think we were on to something. But all he did was lead us around the streets for quite a while, take a few glasses of wine over a long lunch, then return home. Meanwhile, according to the one man left behind with orders to watch the house, his wife went out and eventually returned, carrying a string bag full of vegetables.'

'So why is there a problem?' asked Hedda.

'He went out again later this afternoon, carrying a small suitcase,' Werner replied. 'This time, his tradecraft was of a very high order. We almost lost him. But then our luck changed. He was recognised at the Gare de l'Est, where he bought a ticket for Switzerland. Our man delayed the train. When we eventually picked him up, he was carrying an Italian passport in the name of Giuliano Esposito. Sewn into the lining of his jacket were two typed pages detailing the plans for an Operation Barbarossa, the invasion of Russia.'

Hedda's hand flew to her mouth. 'We do not have a suspect,' he quickly reassured her. 'Madame Corbet has admitted picking up the document, but it was a dead letter drop. And the leak could have come from more than one source, military or political, although only a handful of personnel had access to the plan. But one of them could be in the embassy. *Brigadeführer* von Scheuen has ordered a sample of typing to be taken from all offices where someone did have access. Most likely, it was someone's personal assistant.'

'I didn't tell you because the less you knew, the better,' she said quietly. 'But it was me.'

CHAPTER 32

They talked for quite some time. 'It's an idea, swapping the typewriter,' Hedda conceded, 'but I would have to do it first thing tomorrow. The duty clerk's log would show that I had been in and out of the building, which I have never done on a Sunday. And besides, wherever we put the machine, someone with access to it will be interrogated. After seeing what happened to Simone Faucher, I don't think I want that on my conscience.'

'Then your cover is going to be blown,' said Werner flatly. 'You will have to leave immediately. We both know you would probably not survive interrogation. Even if you lived through it, they would put you on a train to one of our death camps.'

'I know we have avoided the subject,' she replied, 'but I do have an exit plan, somewhere to go before they get me back to England. What about you?'

'I can't stay here,' he said immediately. 'First, everyone knows that we are a couple. They would not believe that I did not know, and I, too, would be interrogated. And it would be harsh. I do not intend to finish up without finger- or toenails and probably minus a lot else besides. I vote we run, and we run together.'

'Then we both pack a small case and travel by train, first thing in the morning?' she suggested.

He nodded. 'Nothing is going to happen tonight. I shall travel in civilian clothes, French ones bought here, but I'll have my ID and service pistol. They might just come in handy.'

The following day, Hedda and Werner left his apartment for the last time. They had not expected to be challenged overnight, but any such activity would have been directed first to Hedda's front door, which might have allowed them to escape from the building. The streets were empty as they walked to the station.

Hedda bought the tickets – her hardly accented French was much the more fluent. 'We are on an early train,' she told him as they sat in a cold waiting room, 'and it's a slow one, stopping at most of the stations on the way, including Nogent-le-Retrou. But I have tickets to Nantes, so in the unlikely event that anyone checks, we could have got off just about anywhere. The whole journey is a distance of some four hundred kilometres.'

They travelled separately, so no one would recall seeing a couple. The train picked up and dropped any number of local travellers, none of whom attempted to engage them in more than just the occasional pleasantry. Hedda was content to reply. Werner just smiled and nodded. He was very relieved that no identity or document inspections were made, just one cursory ticket check when, unspoken, he handed his over and received a muttered '*merci*' as it was returned. They alighted separately, and he followed, some fifty metres behind, as Hedda left the station and walked from the town.

Fortunately, Marie was at home on Sunday afternoon when the woman she had met only once, and whom she knew only by her codename of Chaffinch, arrived at her door accompanied by a stranger. He introduced himself as Werner Scholtz and added that he was German.

'You had better come inside and tell me what's going on,' Marie told them.

'We have just come from Paris,' Hedda began once they were seated round the kitchen table. 'It's a long story…

'So you see,' she concluded, 'we have two pressing needs. First, to get the information on Operation Barbarossa back to London. Clearly, it's very urgent. And second, we, too, need to reach England. By tomorrow, we will be right at the top of the Gestapo's wanted list, so any help or suggestions you have to offer would be very much appreciated.'

'How much of the information you saw can you remember?' asked Marie. 'Could you put the salient facts into a statement that I can encode? It has to be short, though. Too long and I'm risking their detector vans.'

Half an hour later as she examined the draft, she said, 'It's more than I would like. But I should be able to get away with it. I have never seen a detector van in Nogent, so even if there is one in the area, which is unlikely, with any luck all it will get is a position line. I could be anywhere along just a single one of those, but it'll go through the estate, which can't be helped,' she observed. 'Fortunately, it's a huge area. And I'm confident that even if they searched, the radio is so well hidden it would never be found. Now, I'm going to have to talk to Jean and Monique.'

'Jean and Monique?' queried Werner.

'The Renauds,' Marie replied. 'They own this estate. They also help the resistance. And Jean hides my radio.'

Marie asked Jean to walk with her back to the cottage. She did not want to risk Hedda and Werner being seen on the estate. After introductions and a round of coffee and cake, they agreed that Marie would take up her schedule the following night. Meanwhile, Hedda would work on her draft to make it as tight as possible.

'Which brings us,' said Jean, 'to the subject of what we are going to do with the two of you,' his hand encompassed Hedda and Werner, 'until we get further instructions from London. There are more cottages like this one on the estate. You could stay in the most isolated one. It's secluded, like Marie's, and furnished. I can bring you some bedding and provisions from the main house. How does that sound?'

'We would be most grateful,' Werner replied for both of them.

By early evening they were well settled. The cottage had once been occupied by a family who worked on the estate's forestry, an activity that had long been discontinued. So, like Marie's, it was surrounded by trees and overgrown vegetation. It was basic, with just one bedroom and a living and kitchen area. There was an old stone sink and a small, wood-fired cooking range. Jean had lent them a wireless powered by a lead-acid battery, as there was no mains electricity, and they had two kerosene lamps. He had also been generous with provisions, particularly wine. Hedda set to heating water so that she could wash a few of the dusty but otherwise serviceable eating, drinking and cooking utensils found in the ancient wooden cupboards. After a simple meal of casseroled chicken and vegetables, and two bottles of wine, they curled up together in bed after an exhausting and nerve-wracking day. But the bedroom window was slightly ajar, open to the sounds of the forest, the door was wedged shut and Werner's pistol lay on his bedside table.

Hedda spent the next day trying to retype – on a machine borrowed from the Renaud's estate office – as much detail as she could remember on Operation Barbarossa. She recalled it surprisingly well, so it was considerably longer and more detailed than the transmitted version.

Towards dusk, Marie retrieved her radio and carried it to her cottage. She threw a long length of twine, one end weighted with an old spanner, high into the nearest tree. At the second attempt it fell across a branch and she jiggled the twine till the heavy metal tool fell within reach. Attaching the aerial, Marie hoisted it aloft. Back indoors, she selected a frequency crystal and tapped out her call sign. It was answered immediately. She was fast – every day, she religiously spent time practising her Morse. Three minutes was the standard limit to reduce the chance of detection. Despite Marie's skill, Hedda's message took an extra few seconds. She found that she was sweating slightly as she signed off. She would have to listen on her sked time from now on. Marie was relieved that all she had to do next time was listen out for her call sign. It would be London mostly on 'send'.

Jean, Hedda and Werner joined her once she had decoded the reply. 'They want you back as soon as possible,' she told Hedda and Werner. 'A Lysander will fly you out tomorrow or on the first night with suitable weather. We'll use a couple of our local people to have the field ready. It'll be a squash, but two of you will have to cram into the rear cockpit.' She turned to Jean. 'After they have gone, I need to go away for a couple of days. London has sent instructions. Apparently, they have lost contact with Tadzio – they think his radio is on the blink because it was playing up the last time he transmitted, which wasn't all that long ago. They want me to tell him when and where they will drop him another one.'

'Tadzio?' said Hedda quickly. 'Who's Tadzio?'

'He runs a resistance group up north,' said Marie, surprised by the urgency in Hedda's voice. 'I gather he's a Pole who got left behind after Dunkirk. He set himself up as a local, then escaped back to England. Now he's got a small private army, all ex-legionnaires, and they're well armed. We did a raid on a German radio unit a few months back – loaded their kit onto an aeroplane and flew it back to UK. It was quite a night!'

'Does he have a second name?' Hedda pressed her just as quickly.

'He did tell me, but I would have to think. It's unusual because he doesn't have a codename. Apparently, he was already using his own with the locals before he got back to England. But I gather he has French papers now.' She paused, obviously trying to remember. 'It's Jan… something…'

'Janicki!' exclaimed Hedda, pronouncing it as *Ya-niss-kee*, with the accent on the second syllable.

'How did you know?' asked Marie, surprised.

Something, perhaps more than anything the presence of Werner, told Hedda that she had to be very circumspect until she could gather more information. 'I knew him in the resistance, back in Poland,' she said simply, and left it at that.

But her mind was in turmoil as she and Werner lay in bed that night. Fortunately, he had not initiated any move to make love to her. She hoped that somehow she had managed not to give anything away during the rest of the evening after they had opened a bottle of cognac.

She was incredibly fond of Werner, and they had enjoyed a good life together in Paris. But, of course, being conspirators added an extra spice to the relationship. Still, she suspected that deep down, it was more a case of a mutual arrangement – two people each with a healthy sexual appetite fuelled by the uncertainty of surviving the war.

She thought back to the first time she and Tadzio had made love on his farm in Poland. She had been longing to see him again whilst at Bletchley, when they were back in England. They would have married but for his deployment to France. And it infuriated her that London had made no effort to tell her that he had survived the defeat at Dunkirk.

The next day dawned bright and clear and promised a good moon. Towards last light, Marius and Edouard turned up with the landing lights to help prepare the field, which was some distance from the cottage and right on the edge of the estate. All three had a Thompson, and Werner had his pistol, but the walk to the field was uneventful. Hearing the distant 'buzz' of a light aircraft engine, they switched on the battery-powered lights. A strip of white cloth tied to a branch served as a makeshift windsock.

The pilot cleared the hedge and dropped his Lysander into the field. Marie wondered whether Johnny Mertherwell was at the controls, but there was no way they could meet. The pilot turned back to the edge of the field and gunned the engine to bring the aeroplane back into the wind. They had agreed that Werner would enter first, in case she had to sit on his lap. He scrambled up the ladder on the port side and dropped into the aft seat. Hedda followed him halfway up the ladder till she was leaning over the side. The chirping blip-blip of the engine at tick-over made speech almost impossible. But she bent down.

'I'm not coming,' she shouted at him. 'Give them that.' She thrust an envelope containing the report she had prepared from memory into his lap, pulled down the cockpit canopy and jumped back to the ground. She ran from the aircraft sideways and forward so that the pilot could see her. He had no way of knowing what was happening, but fearing some sort of emergency, he didn't hesitate. The engine roared. The Lysander bounced across the grass, and inside three hundred yards was airborne and climbing.

'What the hell happened?' asked Marie as Marius and Edouard doused and recovered the lights. She was surprised to see tears coursing down Hedda's face.

'We're done here,' she told the two men. 'I'm taking this young lady back to my cottage.'

Astounded by the turn of events, Werner put on the headset provided in the back of the Lysander and considered his options. He still had his pistol. Perhaps the pilot could be ordered to divert, but where? France was out of the question. He would still be a hunted man. His thoughts were interrupted by the pilot.

'What the hell happened back there?' he asked. 'I thought there were supposed to be two pax, but she made a run for it, away from the aircraft. It looked like the enemy might have turned up – I was expecting a burst of machine-gun fire at any second. The only thing to do was take off, sharpish.'

'I do not know,' he replied, struggling with the switch to English. 'Perhaps we speak when in England.' The thought occurred to him that he could threaten the pilot with his pistol, maybe even divert to Ireland, but he dismissed the idea. As things stood, he would land as a volunteer. If the pilot refused, he could hardly carry out any threat he might make, and he would not be treated so well afterwards. Reluctantly he lapsed into silence. With the moon shining on the water, they crossed the French coast.

Marie opened a bottle of brandy – the poor girl looked as though she could do with a drink. 'Want to tell me about it?' she asked quietly, pushing a tumbler containing a good two fingers across the kitchen table.

'It's Tadzio Janicki,' Hedda said quietly after a first sip. 'I didn't tell you the full story. We weren't just together in the resistance in Poland. I was living with him. We escaped to England together and were engaged to be married. But he didn't come back from Dunkirk. The people who sent me here could have told me he was still alive, but they didn't. For the best part of a year, I had to assume he was dead. Had I known, I would never have started a relationship with Werner.' She paused, then added softly, 'Tadzio was the only man I have ever really loved.'

She wiped away a tear with the back of her hand. 'I suppose I should be overjoyed to learn that he's still alive. But everything is so messed up. It's hard to come to terms…'

'I thought you rather over-reacted when I mentioned his name,' Marie confided. 'I suspect they didn't tell you for security reasons.'

'So he probably doesn't know about me, either,' she said sadly.

'Are you going to contact him?' Marie asked gently. 'I presume that's why you didn't get on the plane.'

Hedda just nodded. 'Well, I have to go north tomorrow,' Marie told her. 'You heard me say they need another radio. I have to give them details of the drop. If you have French papers and want to come too, that's fine by me.' Hedda confirmed that she would.

'We'll go and see Monique first thing in the morning,' Marie told her, studying the French identity document. 'I'll cut and dye your hair, and between us, we have enough stuff to change your appearance so that it's approximate enough for your French photograph but not quite like the ones the Germans have of you already. And we can lend you some clothes – from smart business lady to country peasant!'

*

They were met at Tangmere by two armed military policemen. Presumably, the pilot had radioed ahead on another frequency. But he took comfort from the fact that they had not drawn their weapons. 'Are you carrying a firearm, sir?' one asked politely as he stepped away from the ladder.

He understood the question but did not know the English for where it was concealed.

'*Ja, eine Pistole*,' he replied, pointing to under his raincoat. One of them stepped forward and gently raised his arms before undoing the belt and letting the garment fall open. He removed the pistol, asked Werner to take off his raincoat, then walked behind him and carried out a very thorough pat-down.

'Come with us, please.' The other one beckoned. They walked a short distance to a large saloon parked on the grass.

He was driven to a cottage not far from the entrance to the airfield. To his surprise, a man and a woman were waiting for him in what seemed to be a small sitting room furnished with a sofa, two easy chairs and a low table.

'Won't you please be seated?' the woman asked in perfect German. 'Would you like a hot drink, or perhaps something stronger?'

'I have a document for you,' he said, taking the large folded manila envelope from his raincoat pocket. 'And thank you, a strong black coffee would be good.' She handed the envelope to her companion, who quickly withdrew the document and scanned through it. 'A lot more detail,' he said to nobody in particular, 'but we already have the gist of it. We have had our suspicions for some time, plus some other evidence, but this really confirms it. So tell me,' he looked at Werner directly, 'what is your role in all this, *Herr Sturmbannführer*? How is it that an *SS* officer appears to be working with one of our people?' His German was accented but functional, not as mellifluous as the woman's.

'It's a long story...' he began. He told them how he and Anneliese had met. Then the ambush. How they had gradually formed a relationship. After that, the Christmas in Germany, and how he had confronted her with his suspicion. He broke off when an orderly entered with a tray of coffee.

The drinks poured, he spoke of his own family and their small group opposing Hitler. Hence his actual role as a member of the SS. Finally, he described how Anneliese's suspicions had been aroused to the point where she had opened the safe and read the Barbarossa document. It was sheer bad luck, he concluded, that the courier had been arrested and they had been forced to run.

There was a moment of silence when he had finished speaking. 'So what will happen to me now?' he asked eventually.

'That is not up to us to decide,' the woman replied. 'I suspect you will be held somewhere whilst we work out what to do with you. But don't worry,' she added quickly, seeing the look of concern on his face. 'It won't be anything unpleasant. After what you have done for Anneliese, as you know her, you can hardly be considered an enemy. And there is no reason for you to try to escape back to Germany. For now, my companion here will drive you to a country house not too far from here. Of course, you will not be free to leave, but you will be well treated, and we will be in contact again in the not-too-distant future.'

'Thank you,' he responded, relieved that he was not to be incarcerated in some prisoner of war facility. 'But I am concerned for Anneliese...' He broke off.

'As are we,' the woman replied. 'If and when we have news, we will tell you. But finally, I have to ask, do you have any idea why, at the last moment, she chose not to be brought back to England?'

He thought for several moments. 'I might be wrong,' he said eventually, 'but perhaps I detected something last evening. It was after Marie had decoded her message. She mentioned that she had to contact someone because their radio was not working. The name was Tadzio, or something like that. Anneliese seized on the word. Marie had difficulty remembering his surname, but then Anneliese shouted it out.

'Apparently, they had been in the resistance together, back in Poland. She tried not to show it, but I could see she was affected by the news. Later, we returned to our cottage and opened a bottle of cognac. Anneliese seemed very withdrawn and preoccupied. She hardly said a word. Just put back a couple of stiff drinks and went to bed. Usually, we enjoy our evenings,' he opened his hands as if searching for an explanation, 'but last night, she was not at all her cheerful self. It's the only thing I can think of...' he finished lamely.

'You were not to know, but I am sure you are absolutely right,' the woman informed him kindly. 'This might be unfortunate news, after what you have just told us, but Anneliese was engaged to be married to Tadzio. Unfortunately, he went missing just before Dunkirk, although he eventually made it back to England sometime later. But by then, Anneliese had deployed to France.'

'I think you could use something stronger.' Her companion had not spoken for quite some time, suggesting that she might be the senior of the two. Although he did not usually drink it, Werner accepted gratefully a very large measure of whisky.

'Time to get going,' the man said when Werner set down his empty glass. He bid the woman a courteous 'goodnight' and followed the Englishman out to a waiting Humber. 'I'll drive,' he said, 'take the front seat.'

'Do you have a name I can use?' asked Werner as they set off.

'Just call me Bill,' came the reply.

But they lapsed into silence.

About an hour later, they drove through unguarded, open gates, up a long drive and parked in front of what Werner supposed the English would call a small manse. It was a modest but solid-looking brick building with three floors. A uniformed soldier with a rifle saluted with a, 'Good evening, sir.' There was a light on in the hall, and they entered through unlocked front double doors. A middle-aged woman dressed in a plain beige skirt and matching cardigan emerged from a kitchen.

'Mrs Jenks, a pot of coffee if you please. We'll take it in Mr Scholtz's room if you would be so kind.' Werner followed Bill to a simple bedroom on the first floor overlooking the front and side of the house, although the blackout curtains were drawn.

'Let me explain the rules,' said Bill as Werner looked around the room. 'This is a low-security establishment, where we accommodate guests we wish to detain but who have no reason to try to escape. Nevertheless, the house is surrounded at all times by a small number of armed reservists. You are free to walk in the grounds immediately alongside the house, but if you stray more than twenty-five yards away, they will, if necessary, open fire. For your own safety, I would confine your walks to daylight hours.'

Werner nodded to confirm that he understood.

'Either Mrs Jenks or another lady will look after your needs – meals, laundry and so forth – until we have decided what to do with you. There's also a library you can use and a wireless. Feel free to listen. Oh, and I'm sorry we had to give you what was probably not very good news this evening.' He inclined his head. 'There's a bottle of decent whisky in that cupboard if you feel like drowning your sorrows.'

'Thank you,' responded Werner. 'That is most considerate.'

'Then I'll bid you goodnight,' said Bill, offering his hand. 'You won't be here long. I expect I'll be back within a day or two.'

It was quite cold in the room. Werner switched on an electric fire, poured himself another large whisky and slumped into an armchair, keeping his coat on for now. Although she had hidden it well, Anneliese must have been overjoyed to learn that her fiancé was still alive. He felt deeply disappointed. They might even have married and raised a family, if they survived the war. Now, he couldn't help wondering whether, whilst they were together in Paris, she had meant more to him than the other way round. Either way, Anneliese had made her choice, so he would just have to accept it. Werner took a large pull at the single malt, something to which he could easily become accustomed.

He was also, he knew only too well, extremely fortunate. They could have treated him as a prisoner of war and thrown him into an internment camp. That would have been the end – word would, eventually, have got back to Germany. Orders would have been given to have him eliminated by his own countrymen. He would not have survived captivity. For now, the future was uncertain, but it could have been much, much worse.

CHAPTER 33

Doreen Jackman wriggled comfortably into the rear seat of Sir Manners' Bentley for the drive back to London. 'This is much nicer than a staff car, real luxury,' she said contentedly to her superior. 'But how on earth do you find the petrol?'

'Corporal Soames,' his hand indicated their uniformed lady driver, 'calculated how much fuel we would have used if she had driven the Humber. Then she worked out how much extra it would take to drive the Bentley. We divert His Majesty's fuel from the former, and I top it up using my own coupons. Been saving them,' he added. 'We are almost entirely horse-drawn on the estate. Madeleine even shops with a pony and trap. And by the way, I thought you handled that Scholtz interview rather well.

'Anyway,' he continued before she could respond, 'at least this way we can enjoy a snifter.' His hand moved to a cocktail cabinet. They shared a taste for Laphroaig.

She swirled and savoured the peaty single malt. 'Sir, have you thought yet what we are going to do with him?'

'Don't think I told you,' he replied, setting down his glass on top of the cabinet between them, 'but I know his people. Good, traditional German stock. His father's a retired general. Met him a couple of times before the war. We go to the same man in Savile

Row. Wife's a lovely lady, a former von-something or other. Not surprised to learn they are against Hitler. There might be an opportunity for us there, but it's early days.

'Think I'll let him stew in the house for a couple of days,' he went on, 'but I'm inclined to get to know him better before deciding. It might surprise you, but I've more than half a mind to take him to Stonebrook for the weekend as a house guest. At least it will take his mind off the Hedda issue.'

'We should have told them,' she replied, 'then Hedda would have returned as planned. My fault,' she admitted quietly.

'Nonsense,' he countered. 'You did what you thought was right. Both operations were safer if neither could be forced to betray the other. You acted correctly, and I agreed with you.'

'Thank you,' she said simply, 'but what are we going to do now? Hedda has always had a set of French papers, so by now, she's probably thinking about how to join Tadzio.'

'And to make matters worse, he's living with another woman,' added Sir Manners. 'How they will work that one out, God only knows. But come what may, we have to try to do something to frustrate the reinforcements for Barbarossa. We need something big to keep the Germans in France, and we have damn few resources on the ground. At the moment, Tadzio and his group of ex-legionnaires are the only formed unit we can task. And even then, it's no more than a section against the entire German occupation force.'

'What about that airfield?' she suggested, thinking out loud. 'When they blew that fuel train, it put them out of action for the best part of a week. It's a fighter and bomber station, and they are notoriously difficult to defend. Maybe even just a handful of trained men could do something spectacular. That would make quite a statement to the decision-makers in Paris and Berlin.'

Sir Manners noted that for security reasons, even though his driver had been thoroughly vetted, Doreen Jackman had voiced neither the name of Juvincourt nor its location, north and west of Reims.

'Dear lady,' he replied, raising his glass in salutation, 'I think you may have just come up with a jewel of an idea.'

*

Papers were being inspected at the station in Paris. Hedda's heart was racing because two plainclothes men stood next to the French policeman, but neither gave the two women a second glance. Monique and Marie's efforts, plus some somewhat ill-fitting, poor-quality clothes and a country headscarf, had the desired effect. They changed twice more before a local train dropped them in the village early that evening.

'The farm is a bit of a hike, and it'll be dark soon, but Serge lives in the village, so we'll go there first,' Marie announced. The door was opened by a tall, rather handsome young woman with dark blonde curls that framed her face. It looked like they were growing back from a not very expert cut.

'Hello, Nicole, we would like to speak with Serge if he is at home,' said Marie politely.

'And you are…?' came the reply. A hand flew to her mouth. 'My God, Marie,' she exclaimed. 'I'm sorry, I did not recognise you for a moment. Come in.' They followed her along the hall into a large kitchen. Serge stood from behind a table.

'*Marie, c'est vraiment toi,*' he exclaimed, walking quickly towards her and planting kisses on both cheeks. 'And who is this?'

'Her name is Hedda,' she replied. 'And I have a message for you and Tadzio.'

Introductions completed, Serge produced a jug of homemade blackberry and apple wine. 'First things first,' he told his visitors, 'so welcome.' She sipped. Even to Marie's well-educated palate, it tasted surprisingly good. She raised her glass, smiled and nodded approvingly.

'A friend makes it,' Serge responded. 'He does a fine calvados as well – we'll have some later, after supper.

'Can we speak freely?' he asked Marie, his head tilting slightly towards Hedda.

'Hedda is one of us,' she told him. 'And now the Germans are looking for her. That's probably all you need to know. But first, I'm here because I have to give Tadzio details of a drop. Then I suspect Hedda might want to ask you a few questions.'

'I think it would be better if you did not go to the farm in the morning,' Nicole responded softly to Hedda's query. 'It might be best if Serge asks Tadzio to come here.'

A suspicion formed in Hedda's mind. 'Is there someone else involved?' she asked, trying hard to keep the anxiety from her voice but not quite succeeding.

Wanting to offer support, Marie placed a hand over one of Hedda's. 'They were engaged to be married,' she said to Serge and Nicole, to save her friend from another painful explanation. 'But Hedda thought Tadzio had not returned from Dunkirk. She has only just discovered that he is still alive.'

Serge was about to say something, but Nicole raised a hand to cut him off. 'Let me,' she said, knowing that tact and sympathy were not his forte.

'I'm so sorry to have to tell you,' she began quietly, turning to Hedda. 'Tadzio is living with a young woman called Liliane. It's her farm. And she is about to have their first child – any day now.'

Hedda felt as if the blood had drained from her face. No one spoke. 'Then I am too late,' she said quietly after several seconds. 'Too late... by a long time.'

Serge topped up their glasses. Nicole announced that she would make some supper. Afterwards, Serge produced a bottle of Yves' calvados. But it was a sombre evening.

'I've decided,' she told them at breakfast. 'You go, Marie, and I'll stay here. Tell Tadzio that I'm all right, give him my love and say I wish him all the best.'

'I'll go with you, show you the way,' volunteered Serge. They were gone for most of the morning. Hedda was in the kitchen helping Nicole when they got back.

'There's someone in the front parlour,' Serge announced to Hedda. 'Says he would like to talk, but he'll understand if you don't want to see him, in which case he'll leave after a few minutes.'

Hedda's mind raced. At first, she was totally uncertain how to react, but then she came to a decision. 'I've come all this way…' she said. 'Excuse me.'

He stood when she opened the door. Then, for a few seconds, they just looked at each other. Afterwards, she was not sure who moved first, but they were in each others' arms, kissing frantically, lips, face, ears… Finally, by mutual consent, they parted. She sat on a sofa, Tadzio alongside her. It was easier to say things when you could just look down at the carpet, elbows on knees, hands together.

'I thought you were dead,' she said simply.

'My tank got blasted,' he replied. 'I met Liliane when I was on the run. She was on her own, a refugee, trying to get back to the family farm after her parents were killed – machine-gunned by the Luftwaffe. Took me ages to get back to England. All they would tell me was that you were *deployed*. Until this morning, I had no idea where, or even if you were still alive.'

'Didn't stop you getting her pregnant, did it?' Hedda pointed out, then instantly regretted the bitterness in her voice. 'What shall we do?' she said eventually.

'I have to stay here,' he said quietly. 'I'm still operational.'

'And now there's a child to consider,' she added.

Tadzio did not add to their misery by telling her that he knew he had been seduced and why. 'My cover has been blown,' she said at length. 'I'll try to get back to England. It looks like it will be a long war, and anything could happen. But, for now, go back to your woman and try to stay alive. The French have it just right. I'll say *au revoir*, Tadzio,' she whispered.

Tears were welling up, but Hedda shifted away before he could see them. Then, instead of returning to the kitchen, she took the stairs. Only later, when the sobbing had subsided, did she go down to rejoin the others.

'What now?' she asked Marie after Serge had handed her a glass of wine. From a bottle this time, she noticed, not the home-brew stuff. By implication, Hedda would not be seeing Tadzio again.

'There's a drop scheduled for tomorrow night,' came the reply, 'but we're not needed here. It's too late to go now, we could get to Paris but no further, so we'll catch a train home first thing in the morning. If that's all right with you?' she asked Nicole.

*

'We'll give him the target tonight,' Sir Manners said to Doreen Jackman and Bill Ives. 'He can have a look at it and then tell us what he thinks he can do. Then, if he needs more equipment, we can do another drop.' He opened his hands, palms uppermost. 'I accept that it's not much, but we have to do something to try to persuade Jerry that it would not be a good idea to send too much back to beef up Barbarossa.'

'What are our French colleagues doing, if anything?' asked Doreen.

'Spoke to my opposite number this afternoon,' came the reply. 'Trouble is, it's early days. Like ours, their resistance groups are really only embryo cells. This is a job for formed units, and Tadzio and his bunch of legionnaires comprise the only one we have.'

'Couldn't we help them out, drop in a few more men?' asked Bill Ives.

'Thought about it,' admitted Sir Manners. 'There wouldn't be any shortage of volunteers. But afterwards, Tadzio's lot can blend back into the community. Reinforcements could not. The chances of getting back even a small number of men are pretty much zero. They'll either finish up as POWs or, more likely, face a firing squad.' He steepled his fingers. 'But to answer your point, Doreen, the French say they will do what they can, but it will be small beer.

As many isolated pin-pricks as they can manage. That's why I want to ask Tadzio to take a look at Juvincourt.'

'Christ on a fucking bicycle,' Serge exploded when Tadzio gave him the news, then followed with an immediate *'sorry'* when Nicole slapped the table with her hand and glared at him. 'But they want us to attack a German airfield. And a big one at that. This is a hell of a lot more than just blowing a railway line and setting a few wagons on fire.'

'To be accurate, they want us to take a look at it first, and then go back to them,' Tadzio pointed out, 'and they want an answer as soon as possible.

'I'll go,' he said. 'You never know, my German might come in useful. I'll start with Hector in Reims. He's the nearest man we have to the airfield.'

It was not far from the station to Hector's bar in a rather run-down quarter of the city. When Tadzio arrived late morning, wearing a workman's boiler suit and a worn, stained jacket, the bar was half full with lunchtime drinkers. Hector, a fairly short, barrel-chested man with dank, dark hair, a swarthy round face bearing at least two days of stubble and wearing a greasy apron, recognised him immediately.

'*Mon Dieu, Monsieur Tadzio,*' his face broke into a broad grin, 'but it's good to see you again.' He took off his apron, threw it onto the zinc-topped bar and steered Tadzio by the elbow towards a table in an unoccupied corner of the room while shouting to the woman behind the bar to bring them two beers. 'But what a time we had,' he said quietly as they settled into their chairs. 'So how are the others, and what brings you to Reims on this miserable day?'

After a quick update on Serge and Nicole, Tadzio asked what he knew about the airfield at Juvincourt.

'Before the war, it was just a grass strip,' Hector began, 'but I hear the Germans are developing it into a huge airbase – lots of building: maintenance sheds, accommodation blocks, that sort of thing. Already there are two concrete runways, and I hear they are laying a third. My sources say they have even put in a spur so that fuel can be shunted up by rail.' He waited whilst their drinks were set down, and the waitress retreated. 'Altogether, a different kettle of fish from Le Touquet. Surely you're not thinking of taking that on? It's way out of our league.'

'Look, I can't tell you everything,' Tadzio replied, 'but both we and the French need to mount as many raids as possible and as soon as we can. The aim is to persuade Jerry that he can't strip France of troops that can be deployed elsewhere. Our contribution is to be Juvincourt.'

'We can take a look at it tomorrow if you wish,' said Hector. 'But it's about twenty-six kilometres from here.' About sixteen miles, thought Tadzio, converting to the English units he was now more accustomed to working with. 'We'll need a vehicle. It's too far to cycle,' Hector pressed on. 'I can borrow a small delivery truck that's been converted to charcoal. We can say that we are going to the farms around Juvincourt village to try to buy vegetables because there's a shortage here. That last bit's true enough,' he added bitterly. 'I struggle to put food on the table for my customers.'

Hector sent a boy out with messages, and that evening there was something of a reunion, with two more former legionnaires from the Le Touquet raid turning up for a simple supper of pottage. But there did not appear to be any shortage of beer, then wine and finally calvados. Tadzio slept very well in one of Hector's small, simply furnished guest rooms.

It was delivered as they were taking breakfast, a 1933 Renault OSB, a small flatbed that had seen better days. A horizontally slatted wooden fence had been constructed around the load space behind the cab. It was slow but ideal for their purpose. The morning was grey and overcast. They set off at nine and arrived over an hour later. The area around the airfield was well wooded, densely at times. 'This road goes along one side,' Hector announced. 'There's also a lane on the other side.' Tadzio could see that the trees and undergrowth had been felled between the fence and the road, and then back for another twenty metres or so into the woods on their right.

'Let's drive past slowly, then find somewhere to park and walk back through the woods,' suggested Tadzio. Hector grunted his agreement.

They left the Renault on the edge of the village, where it would not look out of place to an aircraft passing overhead. It took nearly an hour of pushing through woodland till they crossed a railway line and, soon afterwards, came to a forestry track that ran parallel with the airfield perimeter. They turned off just once to walk about half a kilometre to the edge of the wood, from where they could see the airfield. Then they had to walk back to Juvincourt, by which time they were starving. But an *estaminet*, unusually substantial for such a small village, provided a bowl of soup and a thick slice of bread. Neither, apparently, met the standard set by Hector in his own establishment. Several women were drinking and smoking at one end of the bar.

'No doubt to service the airmen,' commented Hector quietly, nodding towards a flight of stairs. 'The officers will have their own brothel somewhere else, but whoever owns this place must be making a fortune. If you wish, I could try talking to him, seeing as we are both in the same trade. I might learn something useful.'

Tadzio thought for a minute, then rejected the idea. 'Rather not,' he replied. 'If he's making a fortune, he's not going to be anti-German. More likely, he'll report anyone asking too many questions. So let's not risk showing our hand at this stage.'

Hector nodded his agreement. 'I'll pay for lunch,' he offered. 'Your French is good, but it'll stand out from a local accent. Can you pay me back later?' Tadzio confirmed that he would – he was, after all, very well provided with funds.

After lunch, they drove slowly along the lane that ran past the other side of the airfield. 'That's enough for today,' said Tadzio. 'But I need to take a more detailed look at that track. Let's head back to Reims.'

Tadzio begged paper and pencil and retired to his room to make a sketch and write a few notes whilst everything was fresh in his memory. He took supper with just Hector at the same corner table.

'You worry me,' Hector complained when Tadzio had not made any further comment on their day. '*Mes camerades* are not cowards. They will have a go at anything. And they have all seen action – which means that they are experienced enough to know that once we get inside that wire, very few of us, if any, are going to come back out again. I'm not sure we can ask that of them.'

Tadzio noted the 'we', the hint that Hector might not be prepared to reach out to his contacts for what he thought would be, in effect, a suicide mission.

He placed a placatory hand on the Frenchman's arm. 'And I'm not in the game of wasting any lives, either.' He placed heavy emphasis on the 'any'. 'I need to talk to London. In the meantime, can you arrange for someone to gather as much information on the base as possible? It should be easy enough to observe from the woods opposite the main gate. I want to know what local deliveries go in, any routine movements, details of any guards, that sort of thing.'

Hector replied that he could. 'I know what you need. We have just the man – used to be a sniper. The *Boche* will never see him.'

'Excellent,' Tadzio replied. 'I'll come back in a few days' time. Just bear with me for now. But I have a plan to hit Juvincourt where it really hurts, and I think you will like it.'

CHAPTER 34

Werner heard the telephone ringing in the hall. It was answered quickly by Mrs Jenks. His attention returned to a bowl of porridge and Saturday's *Times* newspaper. Food had been unlimited for Germans in Paris. Now he was beginning to realise the effects of the U-boat offensive on the British supply. He felt ridiculous, seated alone at a dining table with fourteen chairs. He could not bring himself to sit at either end, and besides, choosing a place at the side made it easier to spread out his newspaper.

Mrs Jenks appeared at the double doors, one of which had been left slightly ajar. 'That was London,' she informed him. 'Mr Bill asked me to tell you that he'll pick you up somewhere around eleven. And please to take all your things with you, as you will be away for the weekend.' He smiled to himself. Packing would take less than a minute. He had little more than the clothes he had been wearing on arrival, although the British had supplied him with a small suitcase, another shirt, a second pair of socks, some underwear and a small bag containing toiletries.

He enjoyed the drive. It allowed him to study the countryside, as well as England's towns and villages, different from those of France and his homeland. Bill, as he had been asked to call him, was content to drive without making conversation until, on the outskirts of London, they passed houses and shops that had been razed to the ground. 'Bomb damage,' he said without evident malice. 'Your Luftwaffe, every bloody night.'

He parked the car in a road that he said was called Baker Street, and Werner was shown to an office on the first floor, where he was greeted pleasantly by the woman who had initially interrogated him. This time she introduced herself as Doreen Jackman. 'Sit down,' she invited. 'I expect you would like some coffee?'

'What is to happen to me?' he asked when Bill had returned with a small tray bearing a coffee pot and three cups and saucers.

'You're going away for the weekend. Your transport will be along in a minute. Perhaps I shouldn't say any more, just leave it at that,' she told him.

Bill had taken station by one of the windows. 'He's here,' he told her, then to Werner, 'drink up, old chap, and I'll take you downstairs.'

At the kerb sat an extremely expensive-looking motor car. It did not, he thought, quite match his Mercedes roadster for looks because it was a four-door saloon. But, long and relatively low, it was undoubtedly a fine vehicle. The wings, boot and upper bodywork were all a polished black, as were the wire wheels. By contrast, the lower doors were a glossy, rich plum colour. Two enormous headlights sat on either side of its radiator, with a third set low, front centre, on a narrow apron behind the bumper. Above, on top of the long bonnet, stood the letter 'B'. Someone Werner had not met sat in the nearside rear seat, and there was a uniformed female driver at the wheel. A sign from Bill directed him to walk round the rear to take the seat behind the driver. He stepped onto the running board that ran back from the clamshell front wings and ducked through the open door.

'Good morning, Herr Scholtz,' said the stranger quietly, turning to offer his hand, which Werner accepted. 'My name is Fitzgibbon – Sir Manners Fitzgibbon. Bill Ives and Doreen

Jackman work for me. May I call you Werner?' His German was excellent.

'Please do, Sir Manners,' he replied politely in the same language, not least to show the stranger that he was aware of the correct form of address. Bill closed his door, and the car pulled away almost silently into the traffic.

'You must be wondering what is happening,' said Sir Manners after a short pause. 'I hope it is not presumptuous, but I believe you might welcome an invitation to be a house guest for the weekend. Not a party, though,' he added, 'just my immediate family and one other person.'

Werner replied that whilst he was not in any position to refuse, he accepted gratefully. However, he was curious to know why.

'Well, we need to discuss your future for a start,' Sir Manners informed him. 'And by the way, how are the general and your mother? Surviving the war, I hope?'

'You know them?' asked Werner, surprised.

'I first met your parents when your father was the defence attaché here in London. There was a reception at your embassy. Later I discovered that he and I both went to the same tailor in Savile Row. We met there by chance and had lunch together afterwards, at my club. Hitler was in power by then. I believe your father was more or less aware of my line of work. Either way, he confided his views. But enough of that.' He inclined his head forward towards their driver. 'We'll talk later. Why don't you try to improve your English?' He changed languages. 'Corporal Soames here has volunteered to give you some practice whilst she's driving. It makes a change from having to talk to me. So go ahead – I have a feeling you're going to need it for the rest of the war.' He opened his newspaper.

They eventually lapsed into a companionable silence, but Werner was surprised by the beautiful parkland as they approached the imposing country house of Stonebrook Hall. A young woman, a maidservant from her uniform, descended the steps quickly to open Sir Manners' door. A distinguished-looking older man in morning dress, clearly too old for military service, came down more cautiously and waited at the bottom to greet them.

'Good morning, Sir Manners. Mr Scholtz.' He made just the faintest bow.

'Thank you, Brook, and also to you.' Sir Manners turned and gestured for Werner to precede him up the steps and through double doors, then led across a hall and into a drawing room. A woman who did not look old enough to be Sir Manners' wife remained seated on a chaise longue. 'Darling, this is Herr Werner Scholtz. Werner, Lady Manners.'

He was too far away to take her hand, so he clicked his heels and bowed in the German fashion. She extended an arm, palm down. He stepped forward and just touched her hand with his lips. 'Please call me Madeleine,' Lady Manners invited, 'and I shall call you Werner.' Then, upright again, he was aware of a rather beautiful younger woman rising from an armchair nearer the windows. There was a small bassinet alongside it. She rose to her feet. 'Come on, Manny.' Lady Manners took her husband's arm. 'We will leave these young people to become acquainted.'

Werner watched as Sir Manners closed the door behind them. He turned to the young woman and glanced at her left hand. 'Fraulein,' he began in German, again a slight bow, then turning to English, 'I think you heard my name.'

To his surprise, she gave a small laugh. 'And I think you know of mine,' she said in perfect German. 'Although we have not been introduced. My name is Anneliese Hoffmann.'

Werner looked at her, astounded, until she said, 'Why don't you sit down? I'll tell you very briefly what has happened.' She indicated the bassinet. 'But Charles Dieter will wake up soon. He's named after his father and mine. If he does, you will have to excuse me whilst I feed him. Then it will probably be time for lunch.'

She thought for a moment. 'We don't have much time now, but let's take a turn round the park this afternoon. I'm fortunate.

Madeleine is spoiling me – one of the young girls in the household also acts as a part-time nanny.' Then, almost on cue, Charles Dieter began to stir. A gentle mewling quickly grew more impatient.

Alone in the drawing room, Werner sat, thinking about the past week's events. He was relieved when Brook knocked and entered to tell him that luncheon was served in the dining room. Obviously, that was what the British called *Mitagessen*. It was a long table, easily able to seat a dozen people or more. Sir Manners sat at its head, his wife on his right. 'We don't do the "either end" thing when it's just family,' he explained. 'Please sit here.' He indicated the chair to his left. 'Anneliese will join us in a few minutes.'

Brook was standing alongside a long sideboard, on which was arranged a selection of cold meats and salad. 'If you would kindly pour us all a glass of wine,' Sir Manners requested, 'we will look after ourselves from then on. Red or white, Werner?'

They sipped their drinks till Anneliese joined them, apologising for holding up lunch. Charles had settled, she told Madeleine. 'I'm sorry, I do not speak German,' Madeleine addressed Werner. 'Manny says you need to brush up your English. But if there's something you can't manage, please use your own language, and my husband or Anneliese can translate.'

'I try,' he said simply. Thereafter, the conversation was somewhat slow and basic, and the subject of war was avoided by mutual consent. Werner did manage to tell them of his home and his parents, although when he stumbled, it was Anneliese who translated. After a slice of apple tart and then coffee, it was she who excused them. Sir Manners and Madeleine watched from the dining-room window as, heads together, they walked down the drive.

'Monday, he's given a fairly brutal "dear John",' he said, a reference to letters given to soldiers from a girlfriend who had decided to end their relationship. 'Saturday, he meets a lovely young woman from his home country and his own class. Right now, he probably doesn't know his arse from his elbow. Sorry, dear,' he added, patting Madeleine's hand, which had threaded under his elbow as they stood, watching the young couple. 'Wonder if anything will come of it?' he mused.

'Manny, you are an incurable romantic,' she replied. 'But are you still of the same mind? For what it's worth, I rather like him.'

They walked for a long time. Sir Manners had told Anneliese that she was free to tell Werner her story, including the switch to put Hedda in the Paris embassy. He told her of their time in France together. He did not gloss over their relationship or the detail of how and why she had ended it.

'But what of you, Anneliese? I addressed you as Fraulein because I could not see a ring. I hope you have not lost your husband?'

'Please do not think too badly of me,' she replied in a small voice. 'He was a British officer, an assistant defence attaché in Switzerland, where my parents and I lived and worked. We were to be married. And he knew he was to become a father, but he was killed in an air raid whilst with Sir Manners in London. I don't wear a ring because I am not married.' The last sentence came as a statement of fact, flat and unemotional.

'The war has not been kind to either of us,' he said gently. 'But you are fortunate to have a fine son.'

'Thank you,' she said, 'for not being judgemental. That was a nice thing to say.'

They had been walking for over an hour. Finally, it was time to return. The talk turned to families, where they had lived, what they had done before the war. She wanted the conversation to last forever, and she had a feeling he felt the same. But once more, it was time for her to feed Charles.

Dinner was more relaxed, as Werner's English, which he had studied to a fairly advanced level at school but hardly used since, began to come back. Afterwards, Madeleine rose to take coffee in the drawing room. Automatically Anneliese stood to join her.

The table cleared, Brook set a decanter of Port in front of Sir Manners, who thanked him and said that he could stand down for the night. They would look after themselves. He then poured and, using his right hand, passed the decanter to the left so that Werner could do the same. He stood, glass in hand. 'The King,' he said.

Werner repeated the toast without hesitation. 'I will not honour Hitler,' he said, 'but may we drink to my homeland?' They did.

'So, what do you see as your future?' Sir Manners asked once they were seated again. He had switched back to German. Werner confessed that he had no idea. However, he mentioned that he was surprised by how pleasant all the staff had been, despite England being at war with Germany.

'Ah, I confess to having a hand in that,' replied Sir Manners. 'I told Brook that you sounded German because that's where your mother lived before the war. But now, you were fighting for England. A bit of a deception, I grant you, but not a word of a lie. He will have passed this on to the other members of staff.'

'Thank you, Sir Manners,' said Werner, 'but what will happen to me now?'

'Well, normally, it would be some form of internment,' he began. 'But in view of what you have done for Hedda already, I would like to suggest an alternative. First, I want you to take a week's leave, here, as a house guest, to work on your English. Madeleine will find you some books, and both she and Anneliese have agreed to spend as much time as they can giving you conversation lessons.'

'And then?' Werner queried.

'We know Hitler has agents in this country,' Sir Manners admitted. 'Just as we have ours over there. Your military intelligence put a lot of people into England when Hitler was contemplating invasion – Operation Sea Lion. Mostly they are not very good quality. We have already caught quite a few of them. They were not that difficult to spot – they are badly trained and poorly motivated. Letters were initially the main means of communication. Radios, though, are becoming more frequent. Either way, we have already cracked their *Abwehr* codes.'

'And where do I come in?' asked Werner when Sir Manners paused to marshal his thoughts.

'When they are caught, some agents just plead guilty and are executed,' Sir Manners resumed. 'But others are prepared to be turned to save their lives. We are developing a separate department to run this operation. It's headed up by a lieutenant colonel, name of Quentin Frobisher. The turned agents have two remits. First, we give them some not very important but genuine information that their masters can verify. But also we include disinformation to mislead and misdirect the enemy.'

'And the second task?' queried Werner, who was surprised to know that the *Abwehr's* operation had to be virtually an open book to the British.

'They ask for reinforcements: other agents, radios, money, that sort of thing, to be delivered by parachute drop. Of course, we are there to meet them. The whole *Abwehr* operation in England is virtually cut off at the knees.

'Frobisher is a brilliant chap. His organisation is set up in a facility we have established in Richmond, a suburb west and a bit south of Baker Street, where I picked you up this morning. But he's short of manpower and really needs a strong number two. So we had a chat the other day, and I told him a bit about you.

'I would never ask you to take up arms against your own countrymen,' Sir Manners continued, 'but would you be prepared to work in a counter-espionage role? You could be invaluable in talking to recently captured agents. Frobisher had the idea of putting you in with them as a fellow captive. After all, you are genuinely a fellow German officer. He thinks that could be a fast way of gaining information, just by talking with them.

'And when you are not doing that, he says you would be invaluable in other ways, not least in staff work and planning sting operations. For a start, you could check all messages sent out by our turned agents. With your experience, you would spot any attempt to use words or wording that might indicate that the message was being sent under duress. And when composing messages, you would never communicate or let slip anything that might suggest to the other side that you are not the genuine article. As Frobisher pointed out, it is a rare opportunity to have a genuine *Sturmbannführer* as an adviser.' He paused to let his words sink in. 'So,' he said eventually, 'how would you feel about that?'

Werner had been thinking about it throughout Sir Manners' presentation. 'As you say, I would not wish to take up arms against my fellow countrymen,' he admitted. 'Most of them have been conscripted into this war. But I was against Hitler from within the SS. So I see no conflict of interest in trying to thwart his intelligence service. Before, I had a mission from within. Now, it seems, I have a different role, and from the outside.'

'Excellent,' said Sir Manners, draining his glass. 'Now pass the Port; there's a good fellow.'

Sunday was to be a day of rest. The language training would begin in earnest tomorrow after Sir Manners had returned to London. Even so, only English was spoken. Few translations were necessary. Sir Manners and Madeleine went to church. Anneliese took Werner for a drive in her MG – which, she explained, had belonged to her fiancé and had subsequently been gifted to her by his parents. Afterwards, Werner was introduced to the tradition of a British Sunday lunch. All four of them walked it off around the estate. The rest of the afternoon was spent reading and listening to the wireless until they took a cold collation in the dining room. Afterwards, they played a few hands of bridge, which Madeleine had taught Anneliese and which, fortunately, Werner had played at home. After a large nightcap proffered by Sir Manners, Werner was quite content when Madeleine, pointing out that her husband usually made an early start on Mondays, proposed an early night. It had, after all, been quite a week.

Next morning, apart from when she was attending to Charles Dieter, his time was spent in conversation with Anneliese. This time it was a rule was that only English would be spoken – no translations allowed. She seemed an adept teacher. He wondered whether she had been tipped off, for she set about a series of seemingly structured lessons that could have been prepared in advance. Either way, after a couple of hours, his head was spinning.

Madeleine had taken the pony and trap to the village. She returned in triumph with two books. 'I knew the village store wouldn't have anything, but I went to see one of the teachers at the school. She's a good friend, so I was able to beg a dictionary and a fairly basic grammar book. You can keep them. If you read adult material as well – there's loads to choose from in the library, so help yourself – you should come on in leaps and bounds. How did the conversation class go?'

'I think we are both a bit exhausted,' Anneliese replied. 'I was going to suggest taking a walk down to the village pub so that Werner could sample the local atmosphere, but why don't we all go?'

Madeleine checked her watch. 'It's a nice idea, but I think I'll stay here and organise a cold lunch. You two go.' She could have gone with them – just a few words to the staff would have taken care of their midday meal, but Madeleine had a certain feeling, and she trusted her instincts. Anneliese felt only the slightest twinge of guilt when she realised how pleased she was that they were to walk out together, just the two of them.

She was not to know that Werner felt precisely the same way. He was, however, keenly aware that people sometimes rebounded into a new relationship because an old one had just ended. So he did think carefully about his growing attraction to this lovely German girl. It was, after all, barely a week since Anneliese had, effectively, left him. Physically the two women were vaguely similar. The genuine Anneliese was also tall and blonde with blue eyes – a classic Bavarian beauty. Wavy shoulder-length hair had been gathered to fall loosely onto her back, and her figure gave no hint that she had not long since given birth. But not only was this Anneliese also highly intelligent, she also exuded a lively but empathetic and caring personality. Werner told himself to be sensible and to presume nothing further. But he had to admit that he enjoyed her company beyond the remit of improving his English.

The saloon at The Green Man was empty, except for a middle-aged man polishing glasses. 'Good afternoon,' he greeted them both.

Anneliese smiled at him. 'We'll have a pint and a half of bitter, please?' she ordered. She also paid, which was unusual. But the landlord knew who she was. Brook had told him a long time ago that there was a guest at the hall, and he had seen her in the trap with Lady Manners. They took their drinks to a corner table. He watched as the stranger took his first sip and grimaced. He hadn't ordered, he hadn't paid and the landlord would have put a pound on the fact that he had just tasted English bitter for the first time. But he and Brook had been in the last lot together. If Tommy Brook was content, it was no business of his.

They walked slowly back to Stonebrook Hall, as if by unspoken agreement they wanted to prolong their time together. Madeleine watched as, side by side, they approached the front steps. *I was right*, she thought.

CHAPTER 35

Sir Manners studied the transcript of Tadzio's latest message. It was a good plan. And taking out an airfield by ground personnel based in France, plus whatever else the French could manage, would certainly send the right signal to Paris and Berlin. Tadzio had listed two requirements: weapons and, if possible, more manpower. The former, they could drop. But he had already thought about and dismissed the idea of additional personnel from the UK. The trouble was, as things stood, there were only nine former legionnaires, including Serge, plus Tadzio. Lack of manpower would limit the amount of damage they could inflict before having to cut and run.

'Get a message off to Marie, please.' He turned to Doreen Jackman. 'She and Hedda should be available; perhaps they could assist. And Marie has a couple of locals who might also be persuaded to join in. I believe they help her with drops in exchange for the weapons we provide for their cell, so that's another avenue she could explore.'

Hedda had moved in with Marie, and both women welcomed the company. But when Marie invited Marius and Edouard to the cottage and asked them to assist with an operation designed to help prevent the redeployment of German units, they were not enthusiastic. 'We are supposed to encourage the *Boche* to leave France,' Marius observed, 'not persuade them to keep more of their troops here.'

'Please,' Marie countered, exasperated. She knew the resistance was notoriously unwilling to cooperate with the British. 'Try to see the bigger picture. If units are transferred, they will eventually be used against us. Whatever happens, the British have to be able to fight on until they can persuade the Americans to enter the war. If England falls, the Germans will never leave France. Our country will be a vassal state for generations. Do you want this for your children and grandchildren?' She could not resist inserting a hint of scorn into her voice. The two Frenchmen had the good grace to look embarrassed. They did not meet her stare.

'And besides,' she pressed home, 'British airmen are risking their lives to support you with arms and ammunition. What do you expect their reaction will be if the resistance cannot even help with one small operation?' Her fingers tapped the table gently to signal her impatience. The two men looked at each other. Then Marius did turn his head to look at her directly.

'Let's try again,' said Hedda in her warmest voice. 'We will, of course, be with you. There will be no hand-to-hand fighting. We will not ask anything of you that would be unreasonable for your years. And there is no need to compromise your security – you don't have to use your real names or tell anyone where you are from. All they need to know is that you are resistance volunteers, and they will be only too glad to have you. But I can't give you any more detail at this stage because I don't have it myself. So let's assume you will at least think it over. How many men are we talking about?'

'We are a small cell,' Edouard replied reluctantly. 'Ages range from two in their thirties to ours. But we have all been in the military. The trouble is, there are only six of us.'

He took a last sip of his wine. 'All right,' he said eventually to Marie, 'I will talk to the others and recommend that we agree to help you.'

She transmitted one short message to London. *We can bring eight to the party, including us. Weapons needed on arrival.*

*

Tadzio caught the last train back from Reims, and it was dusk when he reached the farmhouse. Liliane greeted him without much enthusiasm. On the contrary, she disapproved of his absence, even for a few days. As she pointed out, quite fairly, he thought, in her final days of pregnancy, she could not be expected to do much on the farm. But she did offer to make him some supper and smiled weakly when he volunteered to make do with bread and cheese, which he fetched for himself. 'But I'll have a glass of wine with you,' she said, 'although just the one.'

Serge and Nicole arrived the next morning for a briefing. They all sat round the kitchen table. First, Tadzio drew a rough sketch of the airfield perimeter then filled in the two runways, accommodation area, hangars, workshop facilities and defensive positions. 'It's a big set-up,' he told them. 'We're talking at least two squadrons, one of fighters, Messerschmitt Bf 109s, and another of Heinkel bombers. Must be nearly thirty aircraft all together.'

'How did you find that out?' asked Serge.

'Hector knew someone who knew someone who worked at the base,' he replied. 'He also managed to lay his hands on a small motorcycle, ideal for my second visit. We had already looked at the two roads above and below the airfield. So, this time round, I spent a lot longer on the forestry track and the woods opposite the airfield perimeter. That's also where the railway spur is. It's not difficult to make progress through the undergrowth. I spent a good couple of hours plotting firing positions and escape routes. We don't have to use the airfield roads at all: the northern end of the track is off a country lane that's quite some distance away.

'We'll ask for a drop on Monday night, all being well,' he went

on, 'but we'll need some extra manpower and the pack mules.'
Serge undertook to organise this.

In the process of exchanging messages, Tadzio learned of
the extra people from Nogent who would be available. So, he
thought, a total of eighteen. And they had to get themselves plus
eight people and all their weapons into Reims, link up with the
rest of the legionnaires and, finally, move on to the airfield. Before
signing off, he did a rapid 'troops to task' calculation and increased
his original weapons order. As Serge and Nicole took their leave,
his thoughts were not so much on the operation. Instead, he was
thinking, how would he feel working again with Hedda?

*

The drop was from a Mk IV Bristol Blenheim fighter/light bomber.
Tadzio recognised it because the same aircraft had been used to
supply them in Poland after the Germans had invaded. Serge
had managed to borrow five animals, three mules and a couple
of farm ponies. He had also recruited Yves, who had brought his
brother Maurice, the railway conductor Claude Boulier who had
taken Tadzio by train to Boulogne, and Jean-Claude, the village
policeman. All were well armed.

They turned on the DZ lights and flashed the single Morse
letter 'T'. In response to their 'dash', the pilot flicked his lights
before turning to make a run over the field. The load had been
packed into well-padded cylindrical canvas containers. They
landed safely, and all six of them, with the lights now off, rushed
to tie them in pairs and hang them, one on each side, over the
animals. The Blenheim droned off towards Arras to make a leaflet
drop, which would explain the sound of two Bristol Mercury
925-horsepower radial engines to anyone who could recognise
it.

They all took a few glasses of Yves' calvados back at the
farmhouse before the men from the village departed, taking the

393

horses and mules with them. 'But we will need a lorry for the next stage,' said Tadzio. 'How's that coming on?'

'One of the advantages of running a café,' Serge replied, looking rather self-satisfied, 'is that the owner always knows someone with access to something or other. After you first mentioned it, I phoned Hector. He has found an Opel lorry, the one the Germans call the "Blitz". The *Wehrmacht* has any number of them in France, and they are not above commandeering them from French hauliers from time to time. They're ideal. Not too big, and with a canvas-covered frame above the sides of the load area, you can't see who or what's being transported. The owner is sympathetic and can always report it stolen. Unfortunately, it's dark blue, but with a *Kübelwagen* escort, we should be all right. I said I would bring it over tomorrow.

'It will take a couple of days to put the *Kübelwagen* back together,' he went on, 'but we should be ready by the end of the week. We can mount the assault any time from next weekend.'

'How are you planning to use it – the *Kübelwagen*, I mean?' asked Nicole, who had kept Liliane company whilst the men were at the drop.

'In front of the lorry,' Tadzio replied. 'It will look like a standard escort. It also adds extra firepower, in case we hit trouble.'

'Then I'll have to come,' said Nicole. 'You can't be on your own. It will look too suspicious. There has to be a driver and passenger in uniform up front, and we only have two sets. One of them has been tailored to fit me. I can't tailor it up again to fit any of your legionnaires. Besides, you said yourself that I'm good with a Schmeisser. And you're short of manpower. Surely you won't turn down an extra person?'

Serge muttered, 'Oh no, not again…' but said no more when Tadzio looked at him.

It was Liliane who protested. 'Someone's got to stay with me,' she complained.

Serge felt sorry for her, and in any case, she was right. 'Claude Boulier's wife would do it,' he offered. 'She's not a trained nurse, but she has been assisting at local births for years. And she's completely reliable.'

Nicole placed her hand over Liliane's. 'She would be a lot more use than me,' she offered gently. 'I have absolutely no experience.' The matter was settled. Including Nicole, and if Marie brought another seven from Nogent, he had a total of nineteen, including three women. It was not a lot to take on an entire German airfield.

*

Sir Manners was not due back from London until Saturday lunchtime, and Werner and Anneliese had worked together for a couple of hours that morning. Madeleine was off somewhere supervising activity on the estate. Anneliese announced that she had done all she could in the short time available, but he had made fantastic progress. Only during supper last evening Madeleine had remarked that conversation was now much easier. When he used short sentences with which he was very familiar, there was hardly any accent at all.

'Would you like to go to the pub for a drink?' he asked her. 'But I am embarrassed to say that I have yet to obtain any English money.'

'Doesn't matter,' she replied. 'Sir Manners has already said that I can take funds from the estate's petty cash, and he'll replace them. But I've got a better idea. Let's take the car, not too far because I don't have that much petrol, but it's a lovely day. What about a picnic?' she enthused. 'I know just the right place. Cook will help me pack a few things into a hamper, and no one will mind if we help ourselves to a couple of bottles of wine.'

They set off with the hamper on the rear luggage rack and a couple of blankets stuffed into the car. 'Just the right place' turned out to be a copse on the estate surrounding a good-sized pond. 'Sir Manners likes to come here and shoot duck,' she told him, 'but I would rather just sit and watch the moorhens.' They spread the blankets on the grass, and Werner opened a bottle of wine. 'It's just some sandwiches and cold apple pie,' Anneliese announced, 'but we can have a drink first.' Taken from the kitchen refrigerator, the Hock, part of Sir Manners' pre-war stock, was just the right temperature.

Werner was quiet for a couple of minutes. Then, finally, he said, 'Thank you for giving up so much time to improve my English. I have enjoyed my lessons…' he hesitated, then went on, 'but I would not have enjoyed them so much if I had not also enjoyed your company.'

It was Anneliese's turn to pause. 'If you are asking whether I have also enjoyed being with you,' she said eventually, 'then the answer is *yes*. I, too, have enjoyed our time together.'

They were lying back on one elbow, facing each other. '*Darf ich dich küssen?*' he asked quietly.

Anneliese had not expected this. She was sure she was blushing and that her heart rate had accelerated. 'Only English,' she said to give herself a couple of seconds. 'That's still the rule.'

'Then it is good that you have taught me well,' he said, conscious that she held his gaze. 'May I kiss you?'

Without waiting for an answer, he leaned towards her. They were almost touching when she reached behind his head and pulled him to her lips. They parted, as did his. The kiss was intense, two tongues exploring. Till, suddenly, she made an anxious murmuring noise and pulled away.

'I'm sorry,' he said uncertainly. 'Perhaps that was not right.'

'Idiot,' she said with a smile. 'My wine was between us. It was about to spill all over my blouse.' She moved her glass. Before Werner had time to do the same, she pushed him onto his back and was above him, kissing him again, just as before, then his face, neck and lips again. Finally, she broke away and moved off him, back onto one elbow.

He sat up. His wine glass was on its side, empty. 'Good job I had drunk most of it,' he said with an embarrassed grin, 'and we brought another bottle.'

'Don't be trivial,' she scolded, but she was smiling as she said it. 'You might have started it, but I have wanted to do that all week. Although our physical pleasure aside, do you think it was really such a good idea?'

'I don't know where I will be on Monday,' he replied. 'But I will ask Sir Manners if I may call on you again as soon as my duties permit.'

'That's very sweet of you,' she said, then, after a pause, 'but you don't have to.

'Think about it,' she went on, 'is there really much of a future for us? And I don't just mean the war. I am unmarried and have an illegitimate child... that does matter in society, you know. So perhaps I'm not the sort of person to whom a young man of your class should be directing his attentions. And I'm not sure your parents would welcome any sort of relationship. Just consider for a minute...' she finished quietly, 'what they might say.'

'You have forgotten to add that we have only known each other for a week,' he added gently.

'Perhaps I should have,' she replied with a sad smile, 'mentioned it, that is.'

'I have told you about your namesake,' he said gently, 'so we have had previous partners, making us equal. And although it has only been a week, we have probably spent more time together than most couples manage in a couple of months.'

'But it has been the best part of a year since Charles died,' she pointed out, 'whereas you and Hedda were together until not long ago.'

'I have thought about that a lot this past week,' he admitted. 'We were together because it suited both of us at the time. I admit I was upset when she made her choice, but with hindsight, I think that was more a case of hurt feelings. She found the person she had always loved, so I can but wish them both well. However, I have come to think and feel rather differently towards you. And that is why there is nothing I want more than to ask Sir Manners...' He tailed off.

'And Charles Dieter?' she asked gently.

'If things work out the way I hope we both wish,' he said quietly, 'then we would be a family.'

'Thank you,' she said. 'Now pour some more wine, please, then let's enjoy our picnic. But there's no need to speak to Sir Manners.'

'Why ever not?' he asked anxiously.

'Because Madeleine and I had a long talk last evening. She said you would always be welcome!'

*

Hedda, Marie and the six resistance men had arrived on Friday. Tadzio had arranged for the men to be accommodated on the farm, but Hedda insisted on staying with Serge and Nicole. She could not bring herself to share a house with Tadzio and Liliane. However, she and Marie were welcomed, whilst Serge walked on with the others. On Saturday morning, Tadzio held a training session in Liliane's barn to ensure that the Nogent contingent, all of whom had military experience, were proficient with the weapons they would be using. Serge had already confirmed that his legionnaires had the skills and experience they would need.

Madam Boulier had promised to arrive that evening. After the training session, they loaded the lorry and set off around midday; Tadzio and Nicole in the lead vehicle, Serge, accompanied by Marie, driving the truck. It was a risk, having someone in civilian clothes driving the second vehicle, but Tadzio's hoped that what looked like a small military convoy would not be flagged down even if they came across a roadblock. If they were, Tadzio would rely on his German to explain that they were moving weapons captured from the resistance, which was why some were not in uniform. If that failed, they would just have to shoot their way out.

They used country roads that avoided small towns, and their luck held. They did not encounter any roadblocks or German patrols. Eventually, approaching Reims from the west, they came to a lay-by specified by Hector and pulled off the road. Minutes later, another vehicle drew up. Hector stepped out from the passenger side, and the vehicle drove off. He took a rear seat in the *Kübelwagen*. 'Legionnaire,' he grunted in response to Tadzio's compliment on his timing. 'Go,' he instructed, indicating with a nod that they should carry straight on. After several turnings, they found themselves on a narrow lane, from which Hector told them to turn onto a rough and rutted track which led, eventually, to a good-sized farm complex, well back and out of sight from the road. A large barn stood with its double doors wide open, and a light was switched on inside. Both vehicles drove straight in, the Opel alongside the *Kübelwagen*.

Tadzio immediately recognised Guillaume, the farmer who had been on the Le Touquet raid, as had four more legionnaires, standing in the shadows behind him. 'We have two sentries out,' said Hector. If you hear a duck quacking, it's an artificial noise – a warning. But unfortunately, that's it. Jean-Paul couldn't make it – he got gored by a heifer and has a fair-sized hole in his thigh, so we are just seven.' Tadzio thanked his lucky stars that Nicole had also volunteered. 'There is some good news, though,' he concluded. 'I had someone check this morning. As we expected, the fuel train arrived overnight, and they have left the unloading till Monday morning.'

Guillaume's wife, Josette, had made a huge dish of potage with equipment borrowed from Hector's establishment, as were the bowls and glasses. The couple had no children, so nineteen of them stood around in the large farmhouse kitchen, eating and then drinking wine, till it was time for the visitors to retire to the barn. In front of the parked vehicles, Guillaume had provided a large area spread generously with clean straw.

After a breakfast of bread and cheese, they set off, late morning, for the airfield. Tadzio had reasoned that weekends, when traffic was almost non-existent, would be the best time to move. After all, the Germans would be less likely to set out standing patrols when little or nothing was on the road. But, as it had on the day before, their luck held.

Arriving at Juvincourt, they turned off the country lane and onto the northern end of the forestry track. The main gate to the airfield was opposite the far end. Hard standing had been constructed across the road from the entrance to run alongside the railway lines so that the fuel bowsers could unload from tanker wagons. The accommodation buildings, offices, workshops and hangars were sited north-west of the entrance and its guard room, parallel with the forestry track. The aircraft were parked deeper into the field. Some – but not all – of the fighters were inside sandbag emplacements, but not the much larger bombers.

Tadzio dismounted and walked in front of the lorry. It was quite dark under the overhead canopy, but he could see well enough to find the small strips of cloth he had tied to bushes and branches during his reconnaissance. Serge took the first group through the woodland to a position on the edge of the tree line across the road from the airfield. It took more than one trip to move the ammunition. Once he was satisfied that the group was set up and knew its targets, he gradually worked along the track until all six groups were deployed. They had to stop using the lorry: there were guards at the railway spur, and the final position was only about two hundred metres away. They reversed the vehicles to where an area alongside the track had been cleared, probably to store cut logs before they were collected. The lorry was able to turn around and park on the cleared area to face the way they had come, ready for an instant departure. The *Kübelwagen* they parked well behind it.

Each group retreated into the woodland to wait for first light. Everyone had a waterproof and something to eat and drink. It would be a long night, and there could be no smoking. Fortunately, the weather was benign, and eventually, just enough moonlight filtered through the trees. They made themselves comfortable as best they could.

It had taken time for the positions to be established, after which Serge and Tadzio walked the course, chatting in whispers with each group, offering encouragement. It was more of a morale exercise than for any tactical reason. The legionnaires were all cheerful, the Nogent men less so, but Tadzio knew they would all do their duty. Hedda's men would be determined not to be outshone by their Legion-trained companions. Eventually Serge, Tadzio and the three girls settled down in a small clearing between the two three-man teams. Yet again, they went through how Marie, Hedda and Nicole would destroy the fuel train.

CHAPTER 36

At the faintest hint of first light, Nicole asked Tadzio and Serge to turn their backs whilst two of them changed. It was damp and quite misty, but at least it was not raining. Hedda and Nicole opened their bags and dressed in skirts, blouses and warm jackets, which they left open to show slightly more cleavage than decency would suggest. They combed their hair and applied fresh make-up. Warm boots were discarded for shoes with solid medium heels. Nicole produced a bottle of cognac, and they both took a liberal mouthful before splashing a little more on their jackets. Marie had not changed. She looped a strap over her head to carry a satchel under her left arm. A Schmeisser rested on her back, and she tucked a 9mm Walther into the front of her trousers.

They had discussed the operation at length. Apparently, the Germans usually guarded their fuel trains with two men at the front, where the engine was set back a little, across the road from and just past the entrance and guard room. There would be two more either side halfway along the train, and the fifth and sixth were at the far end, as was the now-unmanned anti-aircraft wagon. Marie and Hedda had drawn lots to see who would place the charges, but it had to be one of them as Nicole was not trained with explosives. Marie had drawn the short straw, but secretly, she was quite pleased. Hedda and Nicole would have to distract the two front guards and submit to keeping them occupied whilst she crawled under the first four wagons before scuttling away afterwards.

Emerging from the undergrowth and onto the road, Hedda and Nicole walked the few steps towards the narrow strip of hard standing. They could just make out a sentry standing under the loom of an arc light on the other side of the entrance barrier. His vision would barely extend into the deep shadow across the road. They turned towards the train from the road as if they were about to walk alongside the railway line. Arm in arm, and not quite in a straight line, they approached the front of the locomotive. They were perhaps fifteen metres away when they were challenged by two young airmen, each armed with a standard Karabiner 98k 'Mauser' on a shoulder sling. Seeing two young women, apparently slightly the worse for wear, they did not bring the rifles into the aim.

Hedda used her German. 'Hello, boys,' she said with a smile. 'Cold morning to be standing out here!' Behind them, she could just make out the vague shape of two more guards who had to be at the middle of the train.

'Who are you, and what are you doing here?' the older one asked. He was probably in his mid-twenties. His companion looked to be still in his teens. Both moved to stand together in front of the locomotive.

They took their time and sauntered forwards. 'We're just two village girls,' Hedda told him. 'Been to a party on the base. This railway line is the shortest way home.'

'You are not allowed on the base,' came the reply. Suspicious now, or perhaps just cautious, he thumbed his weapon off his shoulder and held it horizontally at waist level, but it was not quite pointing in their direction.

'No, but there are ways and means, if you get my meaning,' she responded with a wink. 'And you don't even have to go through the main gate. Depends on who you know. And we know the right people, don't we?' she answered, looking towards Nicole, who said nothing.

'She don't speak no German, well, not much, anyway,' Hedda explained, deliberately disguising her usual *Hochdeutsch*.

'But you sound German,' her interrogator observed. 'How come?'

'French father, German mother,' she said by way of explanation. 'But my friend here—*elle est Française*,' she added as if to prove her bilingual dual nationality.

Nicole, who had studied languages at the Sorbonne, had followed the exchange perfectly. As they had rehearsed, she pulled the bottle of cognac from the depth of her jacket pocket and appeared to take a good swig – in reality, it was the merest sip.

She handed the bottle to Hedda, who did the same. 'Want some, warm your stomachs?' she asked from not much more than two metres away, tilting the neck of the bottle slightly towards them. The younger one, whose rifle was still at the shoulder, moved forward. But Hedda held up a hand. She withdrew her offer, bringing the bottle back to her chest.

'*Cigarette?*' said Nicole, using the French pronunciation, a rising inflection emphasising the request.

'*Zigarette, ja,*' the younger one replied. Watched by his companion, his hand moved to a breast pocket of the overalls he was wearing over his uniform, an extra layer against the cold. He and Nicole both stepped forward as he extracted a packet of twenty Luftwaffe Fliegers in their dun-yellow packet, a fighter aircraft depicted in black on the front. She took one, and they were close together as she accepted a light from his match. '*Merci,*' she said, looking up at him with a smile. Nicole did smoke very occasionally, but she did not risk inhaling. It would give the game away if she fell into a paroxysm of coughing.

Hedda had never smoked. She declined his offer but instead offered him the cognac, as if in fair exchange. He took a step back and took a generous mouthful, then passed the bottle to the older man. 'Karl,' the younger one said with a grin, pointing at his own chest. '*Und du…?*' His finger turned towards Nicole.

'*Je m'appelle Nicole*,' she answered, then repeated, pointing to herself, '*Nicole*.'

They passed casual information between them, Hedda purporting to act as interpreter… two more names… his was Rudi… where the Germans came from… what it was like being stationed in France… how the French people were finding the war… inconsequential stuff but understood mutually to be some sort of essential prelude. With their small group of four gathered in front of the locomotive, the sides were unguarded.

Looking to her left, Marie checked that she was far enough into the wood to be invisible from across the road. She could just make out one guard further along the train to her right through the mist. Presumably moving to keep warm, he took a few paces one way, then the other, stamping his feet at each turn. She waited until he was facing the other way, then ran in a crouch across the hard standing and slipped between the first two wagons. She had made up four devices using items included in their latest drop: trinitrotoluene, or TNT, detonators and timing devices, all packed into cases inset with a broad magnetic strip.

Hedda was standing close to the older man. Deliberately she gave an exaggerated shiver. 'It's cold,' she said, pulling her jacket around her and moving even closer to lean the side of her face against his chest. He handed the bottle back to Karl and put one arm around her, but encumbered by the rifle, that was all he could do. She put her arms around his waist and pulled their bodies together. He had probably not had a woman for weeks. He leant his rifle against the locomotive. After a few moments, as she expected, he decided to try his luck. His hand moved under her lapel. She let him fondle her breast, then pushed away a little. Her fingers were cold, but she managed to undo a couple of buttons on her blouse. Immediately his hand returned.

He kissed her. It left her unmoved, but it was not unpleasant. He must have smelt the cognac, although it was on his own breath as well. She placed her right hand on his crotch and squeezed gently. They broke apart. 'Money or cigarettes, but not here,' she said quietly, holding one of his hands and looking at the wood on the other side of the locomotive, where it almost reached the railway line. She took half a step towards it and gave a gentle tug. The temptation was overwhelming... a beautiful young woman who had been drinking – and was obviously quite happy to go with a German airman.

With his free hand, he shouldered his rifle. 'Karl, you stay here,' he ordered as he allowed her to lead him away.

In a small clearing, they stood, embracing, his rifle leaning against a tree. Her coat and blouse were wide open, and this Rudi person had pushed up her brasier to expose her breasts. He was beginning to explore them a little too uncomfortably. Trying to ignore his hands, she undid his fly buttons. Those on the overall were easy, but not the ones on his trousers underneath. She had to free the waistband and push down his undershorts so that she could take out his penis. She started stroking it. 'You like?' she asked softly. She would make him come – that was as far as she was prepared to go. But at least she would ensure that Marie had time to complete her task.

Marie crawled under the leading wagon, attached her device and set the timer. She had been taught that when it went off, the explosive also produced a strong, exothermic reaction. When she had not understood, they had explained that this was just a technical term for a lot of heat. More than enough, she knew, to ignite the contents above. Crawling under the wagons as fast as she could, she placed her final device then looked out to her left from under a coupling. She had to wait for a stamp, stamp, turn, forcing herself to accept that the devices could not possibly go off just yet. Finally, she was able to sprint for the wood.

His hand moved across Hedda's back, pinning both arms. The other pulled up her skirt, and his thumb hooked into her knickers.

She felt an ankle behind her. Obviously, he had no intention of being satisfied with a hand job. He was about to trip her to the ground and force full intercourse. She cupped him completely, as if to caress, then closed her thumb, hard, and squeezed, twisted and pulled as viciously as she could. He released her. At the same time, she stiffened her fingers into an arrowhead and punched them into his throat, cutting short his gasping roar of anguish. Hedda stepped back. He was bent over, both hands clutching his crotch. She stepped sideways and carefully aligned the instep of her shoe to strike with all her force against the inside of his right knee. There was a sharp crack. He fell on his side to the forest floor, moaning pitifully. One hand stayed where it was, and the other moved to the ruined knee.

'Look on it as a favour,' she said, adjusting her clothing. 'You will be invalided out of the war.' She turned, picked up his rifle and set off back to the locomotive.

To her surprise, Nicole and Karl were leaning, side by side, against the front of the engine. His arm was round her shoulders, and they were both smoking. The empty bottle was on the ground. 'Where's Rudi?' he asked as she emerged from between the trees. 'And why are you pointing his rifle at me?' His arm was no longer around Nicole, who had edged away. She stood between Karl and his own weapon. Quickly she picked it up and took a few steps to stand beside Hedda.

'Don't hurt him,' Nicole said, in German so that he would understand. 'He's a decent enough young lad.'

'Your friend Rudi needed behaviour lessons. He's in there,' Hedda's head flicked left towards the trees, 'but you had better go and help him. He might not get back here on his own.' She waved the barrel of her rifle sideways to reinforce her order. 'Go on, move. Then I won't have to shoot you.'

He walked, slowly at first, as if he were expecting to be shot in the back. As soon as he disappeared from view, they heard him call out Rudi's name. There was a faint answering shout. It was fully daylight by now but still misty. Without bothering to check on the guards further along the train, they turned and ran across the hard standing and into the trees on the other side. After a couple of metres, they found Marie waiting for them. They set off to find the track they had used to emerge almost opposite the main gate. It would lead to the forest track where the others were waiting.

They had almost reached the others when a ripple of explosions came from behind. After a few seconds, a huge black cloud emerged above the trees behind them. Then more blasts… 'Sounds like it's spreading along the train,' said Marie. The sound of the explosions had been the agreed signal. A distant ripple of hollow-sounding *thumps* was drowned out by the deeper, more resounding salvo of two heavier mortars. A relieved-looking Tadzio emerged and beckoned them to follow quickly along the track towards the nearest fire position.

Serge had allocated two men to each of the two-inch mortars, an experienced legionnaire and one of Hedda's party to act as loader and spotter. Aiming was by eye. The HE – or high-explosive – bomb would not launch when dropped down the short tube, so a firing pin was fitted into the breach. Although they had not practised live firing, they had talked it through, and Hedda's men were competent as a number two. Tadzio smiled to himself. It sounded like they were pretty much up to the maximum firing rate of eight rounds a minute. However, the range of the light mortar was only about four hundred and sixty metres, so as targets, Tadzio had first allocated the aircraft within range, and then the buildings. Two of the mortars had a lucky first-round hit. A pair of *Messerschmitt Bf 109*s burst into flames. Hopefully, more would be damaged by blast and shrapnel as high-explosive bombs, each weighing almost a kilogram, rained into the area. An air-raid siren rose in pitch to crescendo into its shrieking wail. People began to rush from buildings.

One of the two three-inch mortars was being crewed by two of Serge's legionnaires with a resistance man correcting their aim.

The other was being handled by Serge, who was grinning like a demon, whilst his fellow legionnaire acted as loader. They, too, were using a resistance man as spotter. The three-inch mortars could fire a high-explosive shell weighing four and a half kilograms out to a range of almost a mile. The furthest bombers were well within range. Some crumpled from a direct hit and burst into flame. Others were damaged and disabled. Then, parked too close together, a fire began to spread from one to another. Suddenly there was a massive explosion. One of the machines must have returned overnight with its bomb load intact. Smoke and flames were now so thick that the target was all but invisible. They gave it a few more shells, just for luck, but the bomber force had been all but obliterated.

The two three-inch crews adjusted on to the fighters. Seeing this, two of the four smaller mortars switched to the accommodation area. Scores of half-dressed airmen were milling around, wondering if they were under an air raid. Once they realised that the buildings themselves were being targeted, they ran for the shelters, which were little more than trenches surrounded by a wall of sandbags. The mortars took a terrible toll, killing and maiming many of the airmen still in the open. On the other side of the road, Tadzio realised that the two three-inch crews had stopped firing – they were out of ammunition. The other teams could not have much left. The carnage on the airfield looked complete, but rounds from the direction of the main entrance and guard room were beginning to slap through the trees above their heads. Tadzio waited until there was a second of silence then blew one long blast on his whistle.

They had done enough. They left the two three-inch mortars. Even disassembled, each was a three-man carry. They had taken long enough to set in place and assemble. Besides, leaving them would suggest to the Germans that the British had mounted this attack. But Serge had argued vehemently for the two-inch. They could come in really handy again. So the crews grabbed what they could, their light mortars and what little there was left of the ammunition, and ran for the lorry. It had been agreed that Hedda would drive with Marie alongside her in the cab. The men threw their weapons and themselves into the back.

Serge and Tadzio grabbed two cans of petrol from the back of the lorry and ran to the *Kübelwagen*. Lifting the bonnet, they removed the filler cap from the tank before standing back and sloshing the contents of the cans all over the vehicle. Hedda drove the lorry a short distance away, along the track. Much as they were reluctant to lose the vehicle, it had served its purpose. Tadzio was concerned that the commandant of the airfield might launch an aircraft. A blue civilian lorry on its own would be one thing. A convoy fleeing from the scene would immediately be suspect. They used the last of the petrol to lay a short trail, onto which Serge threw a match. The fuel-soaked *Kübelwagen* ignited with a satisfying 'whoompf'.

Safely inside the back of the lorry, they pulled down the canvas flap and tied it in place. They were quite some distance from the airfield when a solitary fighter flew overhead and then turned to circle them. Marie wound down the window and waved. To their intense relief, the pilot flew off, presumably satisfied, to investigate something else. The lorry stopped twice on the outskirts of Reims. At each halt, a group of grinning legionnaires insisted on hugging and kissing Serge and, somewhat to his discomfort, a reluctant Tadzio, before jumping off. A third, final halt near the railway station allowed Marie and her men to debus. They would be on a train back to Paris well before any additional checks could be set up. Hedda, however, had announced that she would stay. She accepted that this was an emotional decision. But she had made up her mind that morning after she had crippled the airman. Guillaume took Marie's place in the cab to guide Hedda along the last and more complicated part of the route back to his farm. There was a collective feeling of adrenalin and exhaustion when finally she switched off the engine inside the barn.

Nevertheless, the five of them immediately unloaded the lorry into one corner then covered everything with a huge mound of hay. 'We're going to wait a few days till things die down and the Germans have stopped crawling all over the place, then divide the weapons and ammunition between two or three more secure hides,' Guillaume confirmed. 'We will have more than one cache in the area – the *Boche* will never find them,' he added confidently.

This, they had all agreed, was – after the attack itself – the most dangerous part of the entire operation. Tadzio expected the Germans to flood the area with patrols. Guillaume thought it unlikely that they would visit the farm. There had to be several hundred farms and smallholdings within a thirty-six-kilometre circle around the airport. But for the next few days, they could expect movement around the area to be watched closely, with particular attention paid to all forms of transport. Any passenger – road or rail – had to be prepared to show papers and answer questions. If a small patrol chanced to visit, then five of them, heavily armed, ought to be able to survive a firefight. But otherwise, they would have to stay put until Hector turned up to report that things were more or less back to normal.

Monday evening was hardly a celebration. Josette produced an excellent chicken casserole, and they all enjoyed a few glasses of wine. However, they were still on edge after the operation, as evidenced by four Schmeissers and a Thompson leaning against a kitchen wall. Tiredness eventually kicked in, and after a nightcap of Yves's calvados, which Tadzio had not known Serge had brought with him, the four retired to the barn. Serge and Nicole made a small space around their heaped-up straw 'mattress' and surrounded it with a low wall of bales. Hedda just thickened her own straw bedding and lay fully dressed upon it, a rolled-up jumper for a pillow and outer clothing as blankets. Tadzio settled himself a respectable distance away.

Try as she might, Hedda could not sleep. Working with Tadzio again had reminded her of times past. She thought about their life together, on his family farm in Poland... the operations the partisans had mounted... the fact that he had slept in the barn so that women or children could spend nights in a warm bedroom to recover from living in the forest... the day he had fallen in the pigpen, and she had returned from the village to find him naked, washing off the foul-smelling slurry at the pump in the yard... the hot bath they had shared in the kitchen afterwards before they made love for the first time.

She stood, picked up her improvised bedding and walked over to where he lay. She placed her pillow next to his, lay down behind him, settled her clothing over both of them and curled her arm over his waist. After the day's events and food and drinks that evening, he barely stirred. She was asleep within minutes. At some time in the night, only half awake, she turned over. Then, she realised, so had he. A smile played over her lips when his arm went around her, pulling them together.

CHAPTER 37

Oberstleutnant Jürgen Bahrenburg considered himself fortunate not to have been relieved of his appointment. It could still happen. Of the two *Staffeln* under his command, he had lost well over half of his bomber force and several fighters, the latter being protected to some extent by their improvised shelters.

This morning the mess dining room was unusually empty. Most of the pilots had volunteered to help their ground crew, working non-stop for twenty-four hours after the attack to make as many 'survivors' as airworthy as possible. This frequently meant cannibalising parts from other machines that would not fly again. The medical centre was full to overflowing, and the burial parties had yet to complete their task.

Opposite, *Leutnant* Carl Weis was buttering a slice of dark brown rye bread. He had time for breakfast as his machine wasn't damaged in the attack. A waiter handed the *Oberstleutnant* a hand-written message. He had asked his intelligence officer to check whether any blue lorries had been reported missing in the general area. On Monday, a local wholesale vegetable merchant had apparently reported the theft of a blue Blitz over the weekend.

'Carl,' he addressed the young officer opposite, who was now attacking a plate of ham and eggs, 'are you sure about the vehicle you reported after you took off yesterday morning?'

'*Ja ja, Herr Oberstleutnant*,' came the reply. 'There was only one lorry. It was a blue Blitz, same as the ones we use, but the driver and passenger were both women, and it was already over halfway to Reims. It looked innocent enough, so I flew off to check some other traffic on the opposite side of the airfield. Afterwards, I flew back for another look but couldn't find it. The lorry was probably somewhere in the city, so easy to miss in narrow streets between tall buildings.'

Bahrenburg finished his coffee and sent for his staff car. An hour later, he was speaking to *SS-Sturmbannführer* Werner Krause, head of the SS detachment in Reims. They were driven in the *Oberstleutnant's* car, an interpreter in the front seat beside the driver, although both officers had a good if not advanced facility with French. A squad of six uniformed men followed in a second military vehicle.

Their destination was a vegetable warehouse owned by Lucien Dubois, who supplied Hector's café amongst other establishments in the locality. He and Hector had been school friends together, although he had chosen to be a merchant whilst Hector had run off to join the Legion. He was a regular customer at the café, and his views of – and hatred for – Germans were well known. Lucien's father had been killed in the Great War, and his mother had struggled to bring up their three boys. Despite being told he might have to report it stolen, he had readily agreed to lend one of his lorries. Hector, remembering the over-flight, told him it might have been compromised. Hence his visit to the police the previous afternoon.

Lucien had a large apartment above the warehouse, where he lived with his wife Micheline and their daughter Colette. They had wanted more children, but Colette remained an only child. Lucien Dubois was short and stout, with brown hair, green eyes and an ever more jowly face. The general food shortage did not overly inconvenience a vegetable merchant. Micheline was taller with black hair and a good figure. Friends often remarked how surprising it was that, with her willowy, classic good looks, she had married the dumpy Dubois. But she, too, had endured an impoverished upbringing, and the ambitious young merchant had won her over. They had built a successful business together. Fortunately for her, Colette Dubois had inherited her mother's build and looks. At thirteen years, she promised to become a beauty.

With *Sturmbannführer* Krause in the lead, they entered the warehouse through double doors left standing open. Both Krause and Bahrenburg noted that neither door showed any sign of damage. Inside the vast warehouse, two men were loading a small lorry. They stopped what they were doing and turned to face the Germans.

'Dubois?' asked Krause bluntly. One of them pointed to an office area partitioned off at the other end of the building. 'One of you stay here, keep an eye on these two,' he ordered, indicating the men by the lorry. 'They don't leave the building.' Followed by the rest of his entourage, he walked the length of the warehouse and faced Dubois, who had opened the office door. 'Who else is here?' he demanded through the interpreter.

Dubois pointed to a staircase. 'Only my family, upstairs in the apartment,' he replied, trying hard not to appear flustered, although he felt the exact opposite. Krause pointed his finger at the Frenchman then flicked it. 'Upstairs,' he indicated, 'the rest of you, with me.' *Oberstleutnant* Bahrenburg followed the SS man, content, for now, to let the more junior officer take the lead. Their boots rumbled on the wooden steps. At the top, Dubois hesitated. Krause leaned past him, opened a door and pushed him inside. The others followed.

They entered a large living room that was expensively furnished, in stark contrast with the emptiness of the floor below. It was pleasantly warmed by an open coal fire. Micheline Dubois had been seated with her daughter at a table by the window, apparently engaged in a lesson. They stood as her husband was pushed again towards the centre of the room.

'What is the meaning of this?' she asked evenly, careful not to raise her voice.

'Speak only when you are spoken to,' commanded Krause brusquely. He looked around, then at Dubois. 'Very comfortable,' he remarked casually. 'You are living well, no doubt on profit at the expense of the Reich.'

'I… I do supply the garrison, sir,' stammered Dubois, 'but most of my customers are French.'

The *Oberstleutnant* moved to stand directly in front of the Frenchman, almost nose to nose, as Krause moved to stand in front of Madame Dubois. Colette was standing partly behind her mother. 'What is your name, girl?' he asked, not unkindly.

'Please, she is only…' began Micheline, but she stopped short when Krause raised his hand, although he did not actually strike her.

'I will not tell you again,' he warned. He turned back to the daughter. 'Your name?' He was not interested in the answer. His purpose was simply to encourage the obviously frightened young girl to start talking. It worked.

'Colette, sir,' she replied, very softly, then more confidently, 'Colette Dubois.'

'I am not going to hurt you,' he told her gently, knowing it was a lie. He would if he thought it would serve their purpose. 'But please just tell me something. I want to know how observant, how clever you are. So, two simple questions: first, how many lorries do you have?'

She was puzzled by the question, but nevertheless, knowing the answer, she gave it. 'Two, sir,' she offered quietly.

'And before you all have your dinner together, each evening, where are they parked, when they are not being used?'

'Why, in the warehouse, sir,' she replied automatically.

'Thank you, Colette,' he said, then returned to stand next to the *Oberstleutnant*, who now addressed Dubois.

'Yesterday morning,' he began, his voice cold and unemotional, 'my airfield was attacked. Heavy weapons were used, which could only have been transported in a vehicle. Valuable aircraft were destroyed. Many of my men were killed. An entire fuel train was blown up. Are you with me so far?'

'Yes, sir,' he responded, although he seemed less confident now. 'But if it's about my lorry, it was stolen. I reported it. You can check—'

The *Oberstleutnant* stood aside, and Krause took over. First, his hand gripped the Frenchman's jaw firmly, and he turned his head slightly, so they were facing each other. 'In the chaos after the attack,' he began, 'the *Oberstleutnant* had the presence of mind to order a flight by an undamaged aircraft. The pilot, who has exceptionally good eyesight, reported a blue Blitz travelling away from the airfield and towards Reims. I repeat, exceptionally good eyesight.' The implication that the pilot had read the number plate was not lost on Dubois, even though Krause was bluffing. The Frenchman was starting to sweat.

'You reported that your lorry had been stolen. Even though it was parked inside your warehouse. Even though there is no sign of forced entry.' He gripped the Frenchman harder now, his fingers pushing vice-like into his cheeks. 'I believe that report was to cover yourself. You were part of that raid.'

He released Dubois, whose lower lip was now trembling. He turned to his five men and indicated two of them. 'Bring the girl over here.' Then, to a third, 'Keep the woman over there!'

Held firmly by her upper arms, the girl was brought to the centre of the room. 'Please cover Dubois,' he said to Bahrenburg, who calmly drew his automatic. 'If he moves, *Herr Oberstleutnant*, kindly put a bullet into his leg.'

Colette wore a white blouse, elastic-ruched at the top, peasant fashion. It was not quite off the shoulder. Krause pulled it down on both sides, exposing the top of the slip covering her budding breasts. Colette's eyes filled with tears.

'She's nice, isn't she?' he asked his two soldiers holding her. Micheline Dubois gave a strangled cry and tried to rush to her daughter, only to earn a sharp tap to her stomach from the muzzle of the soldier's rifle. She folded over. Krause turned back to Dubois.

'I will have the truth, you worthless piece of French shit,' he said, his voice rising with anger. 'Otherwise, these two men will have my full permission to do what they wish with your daughter. Their only problem will be deciding who has her first, on that rug in front of your fireplace.' He flicked his fingers towards the translator so that the family would be in absolutely no doubt.

Dubois hesitated. At a nod from Krause, the two men began to move her towards the rug...

'Tell him, you fool,' his wife screamed. 'He lent it out,' she shouted. 'Please, let her go. I'll tell you.' She had to control a sob before shouting again. 'That Hector who runs the café where he goes drinking. He collected it last week but never said what they would do with it.'

'It is true. I was not on the raid,' said a visibly trembling and sweating Dubois.

'Let the girl go,' Krause commanded. Colette ran to her mother, and they embraced, both still weeping. 'Take him away,' he ordered the two soldiers. Dubois left the room at rifle-point. Krause turned to Micheline and her daughter. 'You will remain here for the rest of the day. I shall leave two men behind. If I have to return, you know what will happen...'

A little shaken by the turn of events, he admitted to himself, *Oberstleutnant* Bahrenburg holstered his automatic and followed the others from the room.

*

Hector, too, had realised that he would be at risk in the period after the raid. A life of crime in his youth and then years in the Legion had taught him to take precautions. The yard behind his café backed on to a narrow alleyway, just wide enough for a delivery van and accessed via a solid door set into a wall. A shed in the yard usually provided storage for tinned and dry goods for the kitchen, but now it also contained the motorcycle borrowed for Tadzio's second visit. Each morning, as a precaution, he started and warmed the engine. And in exchange for a few coins and a warming meal at lunchtime, a young lad kept watch outside the front of his establishment.

Had he been better trained in counter-terrorist operations, the *Oberleutnant* leading the squad despatched to arrest Hector would have made a thorough reconnaissance. But, instead, he made the mistake of thinking that it would be sufficient to halt outside the café, disgorge his men from the lorry and rush in to arrest its proprietor.

The lorry made the final turn into the street, perhaps eighty metres from its destination. The lad dashed inside and shouted, '*Allemands.*' Hector did not even pause to remove his apron. He ran to open the gate, glanced outside and then hurried into the shed. The bike's engine fired up with his first kick. He was out in the alley and accelerating away even as the first soldiers ran through the front door. Safely a few streets away, he stopped and removed a warm coat, gauntlets, goggles and a soft leather helmet from the pannier. He then stuffed his apron inside and made himself ready for the journey. He was on his way again in less than two minutes. A dazed waitress explained that Monsieur Hector was at work in the kitchen. Two doors left wide open, first to the yard and then into the alley, told their story.

Traffic was light in the city and non-existent in the countryside. Hector arrived, untroubled, at Guillaume's farm. Once they had all gathered in the kitchen, Tadzio asked him if he had come to confirm that the situation in Reims had returned to normal. But even as he spoke, the look on Hector's face told him that it was not good news.

'The goons came for me,' he said bluntly. 'As you can see, I got clear. But that means they somehow got to Dubois. It might have been the lorry – maybe they got suspicious when he reported it stolen. Either way, we are safe for now. Fortunately, he can only report that I drove it away. I didn't tell him that Serge would collect it from me.'

'Thank Christ you put in a cut-out,' Serge confirmed. 'Does he know any of the others, those of us on the raid?'

Hector shook his head.

'So what will you do now?' Serge asked.

'My wife and the girl can run the café,' he replied. 'I can't go back.'

'You can stay here,' said Guillaume. 'We have plenty of room, and I could do with some help on the farm. Then, later, I can let your wife know that you are all right.'

'Just for a short while, thanks,' he replied. 'But if they eventually find me here,' his head inclined towards Guillaume and Josette, 'you will both be shot. I can't risk that, so I'll go south into Vichy France. I have some good Legion friends in Marseille. The resistance is growing in strength down there under de Gaulle's people in exile. We'll let things die down up here, and then in a few months, the wife can sell up and join me. After that, it shouldn't be too difficult to start over.'

'What shall we do with the lorry?' asked Nicole. 'Now that they know about it, we can't risk driving it back to the village.'

'But there are enough of them on the road,' said Tadzio. He turned to Hector and Guillaume. 'Let's change the colour and plates,' he suggested. 'Anything but blue – black would be ideal. There isn't a lot of metalwork to cover. If you know someone who could let us have new plates and a couple of tins of paint, we could give it a quick once-over.'

'I know someone who would provide both,' offered Hector. 'He's a customer, but I happen to know he's also a car thief. We were friends before I joined the Legion. Guillaume could take the bike, and if he mentions my name, I'm sure he'll help.'

They had stayed with Guillaume and Josette longer than intended, but by the following evening, the Blitz had been roughly hand-painted. Finally, on Thursday morning, Tadzio announced that they had reduced the risk as much as possible. They would attempt to return to the farm the following day.

That evening they held an extended discussion round the kitchen table. Tadzio pointed out that he had fulfilled his remit. He *had* set up and armed a cell, an extremely good one. The probability was that they could continue to be a thorn in the side of the *Boche*. Perhaps Guillaume could replace him as leader. The fact that the cell was based in the countryside around Reims rather than in an isolated village was, if anything, a bonus.

'We will need a radio eventually,' offered Guillaume. 'Otherwise, how can we communicate with London?'

'I can leave you mine,' Tadzio replied. 'It's in an empty house in the village. But would you know how to use it?'

'Not me,' Guillaume told him, 'but one of the men on the raid was a trained operator in the Legion. He'll have no trouble coping with it, and he'll know how to avoid being caught by the detection vans.'

'Fine, I'll give you details of my schedule times, frequencies and call sign,' Tadzio confirmed. 'It's Tango Juliet, my initials.'

Hedda had been listening intently. They had not slept together intimately since that first night back from the raid, but she had not given up hope entirely.

'From what you are saying,' she said, choosing her words very carefully, 'you rather imply that your mission here is over. What are your plans?'

'I'm still under command,' he replied, 'although I'm no longer a serving soldier. If I have done what I was sent here to do, I have a duty to consult London and make myself available for redeployment. Who knows how long the war will last,' he went on, 'so much as it might seem a nice idea, in all conscience, I can't see myself farming in France for the duration.'

'Which means...' She trailed off, hardly daring to wait for the answer.

'Almost certainly back to England,' he confirmed. 'Liliane is not going to like it. I'm prepared to wait a while till she feels able to travel with the baby, but then I'll offer her the chance to try to escape all together, as a family.'

Hedda's heart sank. Sadly, she had to accept that Tadzio had made the only honourable decision. She hesitated, but then said, 'Marie could probably help there. She hasn't given me any details, but I gather she has contacts that would help you on your way. I suggest you travel first to Nogent. I'll let her know that you might be arriving as soon as I get back there. I think she has already sent more than one young pilot on his way.'

Tadzio sensed her feelings. 'Thank you,' he said quietly.

*

Tadzio said he would ride the motorcycle a good hundred metres ahead of the lorry. They would travel slowly, and he would not be carrying a weapon. If, on rounding a bend, he came across a roadblock, he would stop very briefly, still in sight of the lorry. This was the signal for them to reverse away. Then to avoid suspicion, he would ride up to the Germans. He had genuine papers and spoke their language, so he was confident he could talk his way through. They would endeavour to meet up again just outside the next but one village beyond the checkpoint. Without his motorcycle, for a while, those following in the lorry would be more at risk, but there were three of them, heavily armed.

It was a slow journey, but they were not stopped. Eventually, they were so far from Juvincourt and Reims that Tadzio had no reason to fear additional German patrols. Serge, Nicole and Hedda remained in the village. Tadzio left the motorcycle in Serge's workshop and drove the lorry to the farm. The door opened, but it was Madame Boulier who stood there as he closed the barn door.

'Where have you been?' she asked him. 'You should have been back days ago.' Clearly, she was annoyed.

'I'm sorry,' he told her, 'but it could not be avoided.'

'Liliane is resting,' she said a little more gently. 'You had better make your peace when she wakes up. And don't make a noise. She won't thank you if you disturb your daughter.'

He took off his boots, padded into the kitchen and set two glasses on the table. 'Will you join me, Madame,' he asked her politely, taking the last bottle of Yves' calvados from a cupboard, 'in a toast to the health of mother and daughter?'

She tossed back the full measure then reached for her coat. 'Congratulations, and now I'm off home,' she said, 'before we lose the daylight. There's a casserole in the meat safe. And good luck,' she smiled at him as she turned for the door, 'I think you might need it.'

Liliane entered the kitchen a few minutes later, carrying a tiny baby heavily wrapped in a shawl.

'I heard voices and then the door,' she said, 'so I knew you had arrived. Madame Boulier would not have left, otherwise. So where have you been? You should have been back two or three days ago.' The question, he thought, had been asked in a perfectly calm voice. But he knew she would have been worried.

Before saying anything, Tadzio placed his arm around her shoulders and pushed the edge of the shawl aside. A tiny version of a familiar face smiled at him. For just a second, he was puzzled, then it flashed back to him. 'She's beautiful,' he said softly, 'and just like my late sister, Aniela. And how are you, Liliane? Did everything go all right? I'll tell you my news in a few minutes,' he added.

She nodded. 'I'm fine,' she replied. 'She was born on Monday. It hurt like hell, although Madame Boulier couldn't have been better. But I had forgotten you had a sister.'

'She was the youngest of the three of us,' he explained. 'Me, then Jan and finally Aniela. Sadly, she died in Poland just as the war was starting.' He did not tell her that they had found their sister after the Germans had passed through the family farm. She had been violated and brutally murdered. But looking at the newly born child… there was just a little hair, black, like Aniela's, with her green eyes – and that adorable, determined little face… it was almost as if she had returned to life. He felt a lump forming in his throat. 'Can we call her that?' he asked gently.

'It's not a French name,' Liliane replied. 'It might be better not to register her with a Polish first name. But it could be the middle one. Would that be all right?'

'You choose the first one, then,' he said gratefully. 'I don't mind.'

'My mother was an Alice,' she said sadly. 'What about Alice Aniela? It has a lovely ring to it?'

'Alice Aniela it is,' he said firmly.

CHAPTER 38

It was not until the following day that Tadzio broached the subject of his future, explaining that now his task had been accomplished, he would probably be ordered to return to England.

'If it was just me,' he told her, 'I could probably arrange to be collected by an RAF Lysander. But Serge and Nicole want to go as well, plus a fourth agent you haven't met. They all feel vulnerable. Hector is going south, to Marseille, but he's not there yet. If he's caught, there's a chance he might be forced to name others, Serge included. And if anything goes wrong with the new cell in Reims, that could also be a problem. Serge wants to join the Free French forces in England,' he concluded.

'And when are you leaving?' she replied.

'We,' he corrected. 'I suggest we wait for a few days until you feel confident about travelling with Alice Aniela, then we go as a family. I know the people I work for will smooth everything out for you at the other end.'

Liliane was silent for a full minute. 'No,' she said eventually, 'I don't think so.'

'Why not?' he exclaimed, both in surprise and exasperation. 'What on earth's the matter? Don't you want us to be together, as a family?'

'Yes,' she said quietly, 'but not in England.

'I was born in this house,' she went on, 'and this farm is all I have left. First, I'm damned if I'm going to abandon it and just leave it for someone else, probably some stinking collaborator. And besides, what would I do in England? I don't speak the language well enough, so what work could I do? You will be sent somewhere else, whilst I would just be stuck with a young baby to look after. And supposing something happens to you, or you get killed. What then? What do I live on? At least here I have the farm. I can survive and look after Alice. And with you three gone, whatever happens to Hector or in Reims, there is nothing left to link the *Boche* back to me.'

Uncertain how to respond, Tadzio said nothing.

'The war has to end sometime,' she continued. 'If England wins, I'll still be here. If not, peacetime in France will have to get better, even under the Germans. That day at the pool, I thought – I tried – to keep you here. But I failed, and you went back anyway.' She smiled sadly. 'I do have some feelings for you, but I have always known that sooner or later, you would have to make the same choice again...'

'I'll wait for a few days until you are fully recovered,' he told her. 'You won't be able to farm much for a while, but I'll leave you enough money to employ someone, at least part-time. I was given a very substantial amount of cash for this mission, and I have used hardly any of it. So I'll take some money for the journey, but the rest I'll leave with you. It should last for a long time. And I'm so sorry,' he added. 'I wish I *could* just stay, but I can't.'

'I have to feed Alice,' she said quietly, standing to leave the room. Sadly, he couldn't help noticing that Liliane had not used her Polish name again. Now she was just Alice.

Liliane recovered well from giving birth. Tadzio decided to contact London. However, if they ordered his return, he would prefer that they all moved to Nogent sooner rather than later, breaking any link to the farm.

'These results are outstanding,' enthused Sir Manners, tapping the photographs on his desk.

'They had to wait a while because of low cloud cover,' said Doreen Jackman with a barely concealed grin, 'but the RAF managed a Spitfire photo recce sortie over the weekend. Probably whilst you were enjoying your Sunday lunch. No doubt some of the planes will have been repaired. But the photographic interpreters have counted the number of carcasses that have been shoved out of the way. We know there were two of their *Staffeln* originally, so it looks as though about six fighters have been destroyed or damaged beyond repair, and at least a half of the bomber fleet, probably more.'

'I wish we still had Hedda in post at the embassy,' he mused, 'then we'd know for sure. But I bet after this, plus whatever the French have managed to achieve, they will think twice before pulling too many units out of France to support Barbarossa. Have we heard from Tadzio?' he queried.

'Not yet,' she replied, 'but we will soon, I expect.'

It was the following day, Tuesday, when she reported a message. 'Came through on his schedule last night,' she told him. 'Tadzio has set up a complete new cell, and their operator will make contact in a week or so using his old sked and call sign. He's asking if he should return to the UK, in which case he would like to bring out Chaffinch, plus a French couple. No more details.'

'What do you think?' queried Sir Manners.

'I'm inclined to agree. He's had long enough in the field. So has Hedda. But four of them create a problem. If we fly them out, it would have to be a Lysander at Nugent, two sorties at least. We have already used that field quite a few times. I'm not sure we should take the risk.'

'Tadzio and Hedda are pretty resourceful,' observed Sir Manners. 'Don't know about the French couple, but if he wants to bring them out, there's a good reason. I would trust his judgement. Could they all come out through Spain?'

'Quite a few of our airmen have made it through France successfully,' she mused. 'And they haven't had the advantage of civilian ID, not to mention speaking the language. It's not guaranteed, but it's certainly feasible. I would say the odds are favourable.'

'Then that's what we'll do,' Sir Manners decided. 'Can you let him know?'

*

She gave him only a light kiss on the lips and a squeeze on his upper arm when he left to walk to the village. 'The radio's gone,' Serge told him. 'Claude Boulier put it on a train, to be collected at the other end. But, as he said, nobody looks twice at a man in a railway uniform pushing a hand barrow towards the guards' van.'

They took the train to Paris, two couples travelling apart from each other, each of them carrying only a small case. They had a story prepared – going south to seek work on the wine estates – but the entire journey proved uneventful. It was early evening when they walked from the station at Nogent. Marie was delighted to welcome Hedda and the others warmly. She settled Serge and Nicole into the accommodation used previously by Hedda and Werner. Hedda would share with Marie, and Tadzio would bed down in the living room. Afterwards, they gathered in Marie's cottage for supper.

'I wasn't with you to celebrate the raid,' she told them. 'So we'll do it now – and we are going to open more than a couple of bottles!'

The next morning she consulted Marius and Edouard. 'Four people,' she told them over coffee in a small café on the edge of town. 'Two French, Serge and Nicole, and Hedda and Tadzio, who both work for the British. You met them all on the raid, so you can be sure they are genuine. I know the resistance has set up escape lines into Spain. Can you help us, or at least put me in touch with someone who can?'

The two men looked at each other. Because of the extreme risks involved, they had not shared this side of their resistance operations with Marie or Jean and Monique Renaud. It was Marius who replied. 'We have fought alongside these people,' he said eventually, 'so yes, we can help you. I will have to talk with my cell. We will let you know the arrangements.'

*

A few days later, they left not as a group of four but again as two couples. This time they travelled on separate days, and they would not meet up again until they were almost at the border with Spain. Marius insisted that Tadzio went with Nicole and Serge with Hedda, so that each pair had a fluent French speaker, useful if they were engaged in conversation during a document inspection. They were passed from address to address, using country railway routes and avoiding the main express lines. The people who housed them along the way were taking an enormous risk. Discovery would have meant a firing squad or one of the German death camps.

They were asked for their papers on two occasions, but cover stories had been planned for various stages of the route, and the inspections passed without incident. Ten days later, they were together again at a safe house, a farm building fifteen kilometres south of Perpignan. Their final move was by bicycle, following a hand-drawn map provided by their host. Some twenty kilometres took them to another isolated house near the small town of Céret, at the foot of the Pyrenees. The door was opened by a young woman probably in her mid-twenties. She was tall, slim, dark-haired, olive-skinned and had brown eyes – perhaps, thought Tadzio, a mixture of French and Spanish ancestry. A rather long, slightly hooked nose and thin lips meant that she was no beauty, but her face suggested barely suppressed humour and a lively intelligence. She smiled, stepped back from the door and beckoned them into her kitchen.

'I am Jacqueline,' she introduced herself. 'You will rest here for a day, and then if the weather is all right, we will make the crossing tomorrow night.'

'Who will be our guide, Mademoiselle?' asked Tadzio.

'I will,' she replied. 'But it is Madame – I am a widow.'

'I am sorry,' said Nicole quietly. 'So, too, am I.'

'The war,' she said sadly, 'it touches so many of us.' But she recovered quickly. 'Let me show you where you will sleep,' she offered, 'then you will take a drink after your long ride. I knew you would come today, so there is a casserole that we can heat up later. I am provided with funds,' she did not explain further, 'so there is beer and wine, and even some whisky if you prefer.' She did not offer the source of her financial support, but Tadzio suspected that it originated from London.

Established round the kitchen table, each with a drink to hand, Jacqueline began to tell them about the next stage of their journey. She began by stating her approval of their stout footwear and sensible outdoor clothes. 'I have taken refugees across in thin clothing and shoes with holes in them, all they had left in the world. Some have almost died from bad weather and exhaustion,' she explained. 'But you are all young, and you look fit.'

Jacqueline went on to tell them that in a straight line, it was about fourteen kilometres to the Spanish town of La Jonquera, but they would be crossing the Pyrenees, so the massive gradients would significantly increase this distance. Also, there might be French guards loyal to the Vichy government on this side of the border, Spanish on the other. 'But we usually hear them talking or smell their cigarette smoke,' she explained, 'then we have to find another way around.' Tadzio decided not to ask what would happen if they didn't hear them first.

'I am told,' she continued, 'that you are all experienced with firearms. I always carry an automatic pistol,' she explained, 'a standard French Army issue MAB Model D.'

'Nine round magazine,' Serge put in.

She ignored the interruption. 'It gives me an option,' she explained, 'if it ever looks like I am about to be caught. Usually, I am the only one who is armed. But for tomorrow night, I can provide one for each of you, if you wish. I can take a small rucksack and bring them back with me, in case the Spanish police stop you once you are clear of the border.' Tadzio would have liked a Schmeisser, although in the dark, it would be close range only. A pistol would have to do. They all approved.

'Do any of you have any French money?' she asked.

Tadzio wondered whether they were being asked for a bribe. They all had some, he more than the others. 'You must leave it with me,' she instructed. 'If the Spanish police catch you, they will charge you with money-laundering. Once you are in a Spanish jail, it will be harder for the British consulate to get you out.'

They also decided to leave behind all the spare shoes and clothing they had used for the journey south. Although not ideal, they would probably be better than what some future refugees might have. Hedda and Nicole had brought trousers for the crossing. They all had boots, warm pullovers and a thick cloth jacket that stopped short above the knee.

They set off as darkness fell. It was a waning moon, there was very little light and Jacqueline warned them to stay close, one behind the other. At first, the trek was through farmland, although they followed paths and tracks, reasonably easy-going. But soon, they were into the foothills. At first, Jacqueline had set quite a fast pace, but now she slowed. She had been climbing these hills and mountains all her adult life. But she knew that no matter how fit her charges might be, they would not have trained for terrain like this. At this early stage, they were able to walk without too much laboured breathing. They stopped after the first hour.

'Five minutes,' she told them. She was barely out of breath, but she noticed that by now, the other four were breathing more heavily. 'That was the easy part,' she said. 'From now on, we are out of the farmland and trees and onto the mountain.' They seemed to be heading for where it dipped into a pass, high in the distance. Their path narrowed till it was little more than a goat track strewn with boulders. It would be all too easy to turn an ankle. Patchy snow gave way to a light covering. The temperature had been dropping steadily for the past hour. It was a clear night, which helped them see where they were treading. For the time of year, Jacqueline told them at the next stop, conditions were good.

Tadzio thought they had been walking for between three and four hours. There wasn't enough light to see his watch. There was more snow now. He and Hedda were coping well, but Serge was holding Nicole's hand, pulling her along, although he, too, was in some discomfort. He was stumbling occasionally and weaving slightly from side to side. Tadzio realised he was probably at least ten years older than the rest of them. But finally, the track levelled out, then they began to descend, and best of all, mercifully, they dropped below the snow line. They came to a small clearing, from where the path continued on the other side.

Jacqueline turned to face them. 'Congratulations,' she said, with a broad grin, 'you are now in Spain!' Serge hugged Nicole; Tadzio hugged Hedda. Jacqueline stood by patiently. 'This is as far as I go,' she said eventually. 'Follow this track,' she instructed, 'and eventually, it will widen out. A couple of kilometres further on, it will become a rough forestry road. If you meet anyone, there is plenty of cover. Another kilometre, and you will be in farmland again. There will be a barn and farmhouse to your left, but keep going until you find a much larger barn to your right. It's set back in a field about one hundred metres along a track. You will be met at the barn. Now please give me back your pistols. And good luck!'

432

With the weapons stowed in her small haversack, she kissed each of them on both cheeks and turned back towards France. She did not look back.

'Quite a girl,' said Hedda in admiration. 'And we have the easy part. From now on, it's all downhill. She's got to do what we have just done all over again.'

'Let me take point,' Serge offered. 'If you stay a few metres behind, I can warn you if we meet anyone.' He set off down the track and they followed. There was a faint lightening of pre-dawn in the east.

It was sunrise by the time they found the barn. As they approached, a door opened just wide enough for a man to emerge. They stopped, five metres away. The young man who walked towards them wore grey flannels and a warm, blue Guernsey crew-neck pullover.

'You're early,' he said with a boyish grin. 'Must have made jolly good time, what?' He offered his hand first to Hedda. 'Sanz-Sutton's my name. Please call me James.'

'Is that English or Spanish?' she asked.

'Dual nationality,' he replied. 'Mater's from Barcelona. Pa's British Army. I'm the most junior lifeform at our embassy in Madrid. My first posting.'

'And if I believe that, I'll believe anything,' said Hedda sweetly.

The introductions accomplished, Sanz-Sutton pulled open first one barn door and then the other. Inside stood a Humber Super Snipe bearing CD plates. 'I gather you are an important set of people,' he told them, 'so the embassy sent me to collect you.'

'Where are we going?' asked Nicole.

'Madrid, Miss,' he told her. 'We'll set you up with passports, then it's on to Gibraltar. You take the train to the village of La Linea and just walk across the border. From Gib, you fly home to Blighty. If one of you gentlemen will sit in the front, there's room for three in the back. There's a bag of sandwiches and some orange juice to keep you going – I expect you will be hungry after crossing the Pyrenees.'

*

They were airlifted to Plymouth in a Royal Air Force Catalina seaplane returning from Malta. A uniformed ATS driver apologised for her vehicle, a ten-horsepower Austin. It was quite a squash for three of them in the back, but, she explained, it would be more reliable than the train. And it was not as though they had much luggage – just a few essentials provided by the Madrid embassy. It was late in the evening when they were delivered to the same safe house Tadzio and Hedda had used previously. It had been stocked with food and drink, and a note from Doreen Jackman asked them to report for debriefing at ten the following morning.

'Knew you were coming,' answered Doreen Jackman when Tadzio asked how they had known when to arrange their reception in Spain. 'Marie told us when you left, and the French told her when you set off from Perpignan. So unless the weather turned foul, we knew when you would be crossing, and we were also told exactly where to meet you.'

They spent Thursday morning recounting every detail of their activities together in France. Bill Ives and Doreen took copious notes. Then, in the afternoon, they drafted a full report. 'We'll have all the detail,' he told them, 'but Sir Manners will pass a précis on to Winston – he likes everything on one side of one piece of paper.'

'Not your Prime Minister, surely?' queried Nicole, surprised.

'Yes, Madam,' Bill replied. 'A lot of, shall I say, the establishment, rather look down on our organisation. But the PM's a great enthusiast of special operations. Look at this. We deployed only two people, three if you include Marie, yet you blew up two fuel trains, lifted a radar set and destroyed a good number of enemy aircraft. Not to mention almost certainly influencing the availability of troops for Russia and setting up an entirely new resistance cell that has already been in contact. He'll love it, and it's all the ammunition he'll ever need to encourage the training of more and more personnel for future operations.'

434

Serge asked what would happen to himself and Nicole. 'We'll sort something out next week,' he was told by Bill Ives. 'But if you want to join the Free French, that's easily arranged. And we can certainly use Nicole's language skills – we can discuss the options.'

'Hedda, you and Tadzio must take some leave,' said Doreen Jackman. 'But congratulations to both of you. It's been an outstanding operation. Sir Manners wants to thank you all in person, so he's hoping that you will be his house guests this weekend. I have taken the liberty of arranging for a staff car to take you to Stonebrook Hall tomorrow afternoon.

'If there are other guests,' she cautioned, 'be prepared to keep the details of your time in France to yourselves.' That evening they dined informally at a local restaurant. The bill would go to what the proprietor believed to be a Miss Jackman's personal account.

Hedda had seen it before, although it seemed a very long time ago. The other three gasped as they took in the long, sweeping drive through parkland on the approach to the imposing elegance of Stonebrook Hall. They were even more surprised to be greeted by Brook in wing collar and tails, who opened Hedda's door with a huge smile and, 'Welcome back, Miss Sommerfeld, or would you prefer Miss Szymborska?' Serge and Nicole had not even known that she was half Polish.

Hedda made the introductions, and Madeleine welcomed them in the drawing room. 'Sir Manners should be here any time soon,' she told them, 'then we'll take tea.'

Four other people joined them. Hedda gasped when Werner Scholz entered the room, but he nodded to acknowledge her presence and gave her a good-natured smile as he introduced himself to the others. 'We can talk later,' he said amiably to Hedda. She was relieved that he appeared to harbour no ill feelings. His English had certainly improved.

He was accompanied by a young woman who settled a baby into a carrycot. She turned to Hedda and stared openly for several seconds. 'So this is the young lady who took my name and impersonated me at the embassy in Paris,' she said with a smile. 'I am the genuine Anneliese Hoffmann.' She offered her hand. Serge and Nicole just looked at each other. They had no idea that Hedda had been a spy for the British in addition to fighting with the resistance.

'And I'm Peregrine,' said a young lad who looked to be ten or eleven years old.

'Perry, be a dear,' said his mother. 'Show Monsieur Moreau and Madame Nicole to their room. Monsieur Moreau does not speak English, but Madame Nicole will translate for you.' Tadzio noted how tactfully Madeleine had not given Nicole's different surname to her son.

'Sir, were you really in the Foreign Legion?' he blurted. Nicole translated.

'*Oui*,' said Serge with a nod.

Clearly, Peregrine was totally in awe of the burly, dark-skinned Frenchman. '*Suivez-moi, s'il vous plaît*,' Peregrine announced proudly.

'He's been practising that all morning,' said Madeleine to Hedda as they left the room. 'But I wanted to have a private word. I hope I'm not being indelicate, but Doreen gave me a ring. I know you and Tadzio were living together in Poland, and you were engaged to be married before the war. So I have put you two together, but there is another room available if I am speaking out of turn.'

Tadzio had the good grace to look embarrassed. Hedda thought for a moment. There had been that night in the barn, after the raid on the airfield. But they had not been intimate since then. She took her time, looking at Tadzio. Regardless of what had happened to both of them in France, she still loved him. And she had absolutely no doubt that his feelings for her were the same. 'That will be perfectly all right,' she said very slowly and clearly, her mind made up, 'because when all is said and done, I found him first.'